Herbert George Wells was born in Bromley, Kent in 1866. In 1884, after working as a draper's apprentice and pupil-teacher, he won a scholarship to the Normal School of Science, South Kensington, studying under T.H. Huxley. He was awarded a first-class honours degree in biology and resumed teaching, but was forced to retire after suffering an injury. He worked in poverty in London while experimenting in journalism and stories, and published textbooks on biology and pathophysiology, but it was publication of *The Time Machine* in 1895 that launched his literary career.

Wells' early works saw him write many scientific romances (such as *The Time Machine*, *The Island of Doctor Moreau* and *The Invisible Man*) and short stories. These 'scientific romances' employed themes which are now seen as classic tropes of SF (time travel, alien invasion, the ethics of mankind playing God). In the first decade of the twentieth century, he began to write a number of non-SF novels (such as *Ann Veronica* and *The History of Mr Polly*), as well as numerous sociological and political books and tracts. As his career progressed, Wells increasingly used fiction as a platform for the ideas and visions of a world-state which preoccupied him, culminating in *The Shape of Things to Come* in 1933. However, the Second World War and the cataclysm of Hiroshima confirmed the pessimism which had accompanied his exuberant hopes and visions. He worked almost to his death, in 1946, and in his final two decades produced nearly forty books.

Wells is now renowned as one of the greatest SF writers of all time, and has been labelled 'the father of science fiction'. This collection contains four of his works, which are still powerful, terrifying and resonant over a hundred years after some of them were first written. This is in part due to scientific advances, which have brought many of Wells' ideas about space travel and genetic engineering closer to reality.

'Wells occupies an honoured place in science fiction. Without him, indeed, I can't see how any of it could have happened'   Kingsley Amis

Also by H.G. Wells:

NOVELS:

The Time Machine (1895)
The Island of Doctor Moreau (1896)
The Invisible Man (1897)
The War of the Worlds (1898)
The Sleeper Awakes (1899)
Love and Mr Lewisham (1900)
The First Men in the Moon (1901)
The Food of the Gods (1904)
Kipps (1905)
In the Days of the Comet (1906)
The War in the Air (1908)
Ann Veronica (1909)
The History of Mr Polly (1910)
Tono Bungay (1909)
Men Like Gods (1923)
The Shape of Things to Come (1933)

SHORT STORIES:

The Flying Man (1893)
Aepyornis Island (1894)
A Deal in Ostriches (1894)
The Diamond Maker (1894)
The Flowering of the Strange Orchid (1894)
The Hammerpond Park Burglary (1894)
In the Modern Vein: An Unsympathetic Love Story (1894)
The Jilting of Jane (1894)
The Lord of the Dynamos (1894)
The Stolen Bacillus (1894)
Through a Window (1894)
The Treasure in the Forest (1894)
The Triumphs of a Taxidermist (1894)
Argonauts of the Air (1895)
A Catastrophe (1895)
The Cone (1895)
The Moth (1895)
Pollock and the Porroh Man (1895)
The Reconciliation (1895)
The Remarkable Case of Davidson's Eyes (1895)
The Temptation of Harringay (1895)
The Apple (1896)
In the Abyss (1896)

The Plattner Story (1896)
The Purple Pileus (1896)
The Red Room (1896)
The Sea Raiders (1896)
A Slip Under the Microscope (1896)
The Story of the Late Mr Elvesham (1896)
Under the Knife (1896)
The Crystal Egg (1897)
The Lost Inheritance (1897)
The Star (1897)
A Story of the Days to Come (1897)
A Story of the Stone Age (1897)
Jimmy Goggles the God (1898)
The Man who Could Work Miracles (1898)
Miss Winchelsea's Heart (1898)
Mr Ledbetter's Vacation (1898)
The Stolen Body (1898)
Mr Brisher's Treasure (1899)
A Vision of Judgement (1899)
A Dream of Armageddon (1901)
Filmer (1901)
Mr Skelmersdale in Fairyland (1901)
The New Accelerator (1901)
The Inexperienced Ghost (1902)
The Land Ironclads (1903)
The Magic Shop (1903)
The Truth About Pyecraft (1903)
The Valley of Spiders (1903)
The Country of the Blind (1904)
The Empire of the Ants (1905)
The Door in the Wall (1906)
The Beautiful Suit (1909)
Little Mother up the Morderberg (1910)
My First Aeroplane (1910)
The Sad Story of a Dramatic Critic (1915)
The Story of the Last Trump (1915)
The Grisly Folk (1921)
The Pearl of Love (1924)
The Queer Story of Brownlow's Newspaper (1932)
Answer to Prayer (1937)

H.G. WELLS

CLASSIC COLLECTION II

In the Days of the Comet, Men Like Gods,
The Sleeper Awakes, The War in the Air

GOLLANCZ
LONDON

This edition copyright © Literary Executors of the Estate of
H.G. Wells 2011
Interior illustrations copyright © Les Edwards 2011
All rights reserved

In the Days of the Comet © 1906, Men Like Gods © 1923,
The Sleeper Awakes © 1899, The War in the Air © 1908

The right of H.G. Wells to be identified as the author of this
work has been asserted by him in accordance with the
Copyright, Designs and Patents Act 1988.

First published in Great Britain in 2011
by Gollancz
an imprint of the Orion Publishing Group
Orion House, 5 Upper St Martin's Lane,
London WC2H 9EA
An Hachette UK Company

A CIP catalogue record for this book
is available from the British Library

ISBN 978 0 575 09522 9

1 3 5 7 9 10 8 6 4 2

Typeset by Input Data Services Ltd, Bridgwater, Somerset

Printed and bound by CPI Group (UK) Ltd, Croydon, CR0 4YY

The Orion Publishing Group's policy is to use papers
that are natural, renewable and recyclable products and
made from wood grown in sustainable forests. The logging
and manufacturing processes are expected to conform to
the environmental regulations of the country of origin.

www.orionbooks.co.uk

Contents

IN THE DAYS OF THE COMET

The Man Who Wrote in the Tower

I saw a grey-haired man, a figure of hale age, sitting at a desk and writing.

He seemed to be in a room in a tower, very high, so that through the tall window on his left one perceived only distances, a remote horizon of sea, a headland and that vague haze and glitter in the sunset that many miles away marks a city. All the appointments of this room were orderly and beautiful, and in some subtle quality, in this small difference and that, new to me and strange. They were in no fashion I could name, and the simple costume the man wore suggested neither period nor country. It might, I thought, be the Happy Future, or Utopia, or the Land of Simple Dreams; an errant mote of memory, Henry James's phrase and story of 'The Great Good Place', twinkled across my mind, and passed and left no light.

The man I saw wrote with a thing like a fountain pen, a modern touch that prohibited any historical retrospection, and as he finished each sheet, writing in an easy flowing hand, he added it to a growing pile upon a graceful little table under the window. His last done sheets lay loose, partly covering others that were clipped together into fascicles.

Clearly he was unaware of my presence, and I stood waiting until his pen should come to a pause. Old as he certainly was he wrote with a steady hand. . . .

I discovered that a concave speculum hung slantingly high over his head; a movement in this caught my attention sharply, and I looked up to see, distorted and made fantastic but bright and beautifully coloured, the magnified, reflected, evasive rendering of a palace, of a

3

terrace, of the vista of a great roadway with many people, people exaggerated, impossible-looking because of the curvature of the mirror, going to and fro. I turned my head quickly that I might see more clearly through the window behind me, but it was too high for me to survey this nearer scene directly, and after a momentary pause I came back to that distorting mirror again.

But now the writer was leaning back in his chair. He put down his pen and sighed the half resentful sigh – 'ah! you, work, you! How you gratify and tire me!' – of a man who has been writing to his satisfaction.

'What is this place,' I asked, 'and who are you?'

He looked around with the quick movement of surprise.

'What is this place?' I repeated, 'and where am I?'

He regarded me steadfastly for a moment under his wrinkled brows, and then his expression softened to a smile. He pointed to a chair beside the table. 'I am writing,' he said.

'About this?'

'About the change.'

I sat down. It was a very comfortable chair, and well placed under the light.

'If you would like to read—' he said.

I indicated the manuscript. 'This explains?' I asked.

'That explains,' he answered.

He drew a fresh sheet of paper toward him as he looked at me.

I glanced from him about his apartment and back to the little table. A fascicle marked very distinctly 'I' caught my attention, and I took it up. I smiled in his friendly eyes. 'Very well,' said I, suddenly at my ease, and he nodded and went on writing. And in a mood between confidence and curiosity, I began to read.

This is the story that happy, active-looking old man in that pleasant place had written.

BOOK THE FIRST
The Comet

Dust in the Shadows

Section 1

I have set myself to write the story of the Great Change, so far as it has affected my own life and the lives of one or two people closely connected with me, primarily to please myself.

Long ago in my crude unhappy youth, I conceived the desire of writing a book. To scribble secretly and dream of authorship was one of my chief alleviations, and I read with a sympathetic envy every scrap I could get about the world of literature and the lives of literary people. It is something, even amidst this present happiness, to find leisure and opportunity to take up and partially realize these old and hopeless dreams. But that alone, in a world where so much of vivid and increasing interest presents itself to be done, even by an old man, would not, I think, suffice to set me at this desk. I find some such recapitulation of my past as this will involve, is becoming necessary to my own secure mental continuity. The passage of years brings a man at last to retrospection; at seventy-two one's youth is far more important than it was at forty. And I am out of touch with my youth. The old life seems so cut off from the new, so alien and so unreasonable, that at times I find it bordering upon the incredible. The data have gone, the buildings and places. I stopped dead the other afternoon in my walk across the moor, where once the dismal outskirts of Swathinglea straggled toward Leet, and asked, 'Was it here indeed that I crouched among the weeds and refuse and broken crockery and loaded my revolver ready for murder? Did ever such a thing happen in my life? Was such a mood and thought and intention ever possible to me? Rather, has not some queer nightmare spirit out of dreamland slipped a pseudo-memory into the records of my vanished life?'

There must be many alive still who have the same perplexities. And I think too that those who are now growing up to take our places in the great enterprise of mankind, will need many such narratives as mine for even the most partial conception of the old world of shadows that came before our day. It chances too that my case is fairly typical of the Change; I was caught midway in a gust of passion; and a curious accident put me for a time in the very nucleus of the new order.

My memory takes me back across the interval of fifty years to a little room with a sash window open to a starry sky, and instantly there returns to me the characteristic smell of that room, the penetrating odour of an ill-trimmed lamp, burning cheap paraffin. Lighting by electricity had then been perfected for fifteen years, but still the larger portion of the world used these lamps. All this first scene will go, in my mind at least, to that olfactory accompaniment. That was the evening smell of the room. By day it had a more subtle aroma, a closeness, a peculiar sort of faint pungency that I associate – I know not why – with dust.

Let me describe this room to you in detail. It was perhaps eight feet by seven in area and rather higher than either of these dimensions; the ceiling was of plaster, cracked and bulging in places, grey with the soot of the lamp, and in one place discoloured by a system of yellow and olive-green stains caused by the percolation of damp from above. The walls were covered with dun-coloured paper, upon which had been printed in oblique reiteration a crimson shape, something of the nature of a curly ostrich feather, or an acanthus flower, that had in its less faded moments a sort of dingy gaiety. There were several big plaster-rimmed wounds in this, caused by Parload's ineffectual attempts to get nails into the wall, whereby there might hang pictures. One nail had hit between two bricks and got home, and from this depended, sustained a little insecurely by frayed and knotted blind-cord, Parload's hanging bookshelves, planks painted over with a treacly blue enamel and further decorated by a fringe of pinked American cloth insecurely fixed by tacks. Below this was a little table that behaved with a mulish vindictiveness to any knee that was thrust beneath it suddenly; it was covered with a cloth whose pattern of red and black had been rendered less monotonous by the accidents of Parload's versatile ink bottle, and on it, leitmotif of the whole, stood and stank the lamp. This lamp, you must understand, was of some whitish translucent substance that was neither china nor glass, it had a shade of the same substance, a shade that did not protect the eyes of a reader in any measure, and it seemed admirably adapted to bring into pitiless prominence the fact that, after the lamp's trimming, dust and paraffin had been smeared over its exterior with a reckless generosity. The uneven floor boards of this apartment were covered with scratched enamel of chocolate hue, on which a small island of frayed carpet dimly blossomed in the dust and shadows.

There was a very small grate, made of cast-iron in one piece and painted buff, and a still smaller misfit of a cast-iron fender that confessed the grey stone of the hearth. No fire was laid, only a few scraps of torn paper and the bowl of a broken corncob pipe were visible behind the bars, and in the corner and rather thrust away was an angular japanned coal-box with a damaged hinge. It was the custom in those days to warm every room separately from a separate fireplace, more prolific of dirt than heat, and the rickety sash window, the small chimney, and the loose-fitting door were expected to organize the ventilation of the room among themselves without any further direction.

Parload's truckle bed hid its grey sheets beneath an old patchwork counterpane on one side of the room, and veiled his boxes and suchlike oddments, and invading the two corners of the window were an old whatnot and the washhandstand, on which were distributed the simple appliances of his toilet.

This washhandstand had been made of deal by some one with an excess of turnery appliances in a hurry, who had tried to distract attention from the rough economies of his workmanship by an arresting ornamentation of blobs and bulbs upon the joints and legs. Apparently the piece had then been placed in the hands of some person of infinite leisure equipped with a pot of ocherous paint, varnish, and a set of flexible combs. This person had first painted the article, then, I fancy, smeared it with varnish, and then sat down to work with the combs to streak and comb the varnish into a weird imitation of the grain of some nightmare timber. The washhandstand so made had evidently had a prolonged career of violent use, had been chipped, kicked, splintered, punched, stained, scorched, hammered, desiccated, damped, and defiled, had met indeed with almost every possible adventure except a conflagration or a scrubbing, until at last it had come to this high refuge of Parload's attic to sustain the simple requirements of Parload's personal cleanliness. There were, in chief, a basin and a jug of water and a slop-pail of tin, and, further, a piece of yellow soap in a tray, a tooth-brush, a rat-tailed shaving brush, one huckaback towel, and one or two other minor articles. In those days only very prosperous people had more than such an equipage, and it is to be remarked that every drop of water Parload used had to be carried by an unfortunate servant girl, – the 'slavey', Parload called her – up from the basement to the top of the house and subsequently down again. Already we begin to forget how modern an invention is personal cleanliness. It is a fact that Parload had never stripped for a swim in his life; never had a simultaneous bath all over his body since his childhood. Not one in fifty of us did in the days of which I am telling you.

A chest, also singularly grained and streaked, of two large and two small drawers, held Parload's reserve of garments, and pegs on the door carried his two hats and completed this inventory of a 'bed-sitting-room' as I knew it before the Change. But I had forgotten – there was also a chair with a 'squab' that apologized inadequately for the defects of its cane seat. I forgot that for the moment because I was sitting on the chair on the occasion that best begins this story.

I have described Parload's room with such particularity because it will help you to understand the key in which my earlier chapters are written, but you must not imagine that this singular equipment or the smell of the lamp engaged my attention at that time to the slightest degree. I took all this grimy unpleasantness as if it were the most natural and proper setting for existence imaginable. It was the world as I knew it. My mind was entirely occupied then by graver and intenser matters, and it is only now in the distant retrospect that I see these details of environment as being remarkable, as significant, as indeed obviously the outward visible manifestations of the old world disorder in our hearts.

Section 2

Parload stood at the open window, opera-glass in hand, and sought and found and was uncertain about and lost again, the new comet.

I thought the comet no more than a nuisance then because I wanted to talk of other matters. But Parload was full of it. My head was hot, I was feverish with interlacing annoyances and bitterness, I wanted to open my heart to him – at least I wanted to relieve my heart by some romantic rendering of my troubles – and I gave but little heed to the things he told me. It was the first time I had heard of this new speck among the countless specks of heaven, and I did not care if I never heard of the thing again.

We were two youths much of an age together, Parload was two and twenty, and eight months older than I. He was – I think his proper definition was 'engrossing clerk' to a little solicitor in Overcastle, while

I was third in the office staff of Rawdon's pot-bank in Clayton. We had met first in the 'Parliament' of the Young Men's Christian Association of Swathinglea; we had found we attended simultaneous classes in Overcastle, he in science and I in shorthand, and had started a practice of walking home together, and so our friendship came into being. (Swathinglea, Clayton, and Overcastle were contiguous towns, I should mention, in the great industrial area of the Midlands.) We had shared each other's secret of religious doubt, we had confided to one another a common interest in Socialism, he had come twice to supper at my mother's on a Sunday night, and I was free of his apartment. He was then a tall, flaxen-haired, gawky youth, with a disproportionate development of neck and wrist, and capable of vast enthusiasm; he gave two evenings a week to the evening classes of the organized science school in Overcastle, physiography was his favourite 'subject,' and through this insidious opening of his mind the wonder of outer space had come to take possession of his soul. He had commandeered an old opera-glass from his uncle who farmed at Leet over the moors, he had bought a cheap paper planisphere and *Whitaker's Almanac*, and for a time day and moonlight were mere blank interruptions to the one satisfactory reality in his life – stargazing. It was the deeps that had seized him, the immensities, and the mysterious possibilities that might float unlit in that unplumbed abyss. With infinite labour and the help of a very precise article in *The Heavens*, a little monthly magazine that catered for those who were under this obsession, he had at last got his opera-glass upon the new visitor to our system from outer space. He gazed in a sort of rapture upon that quivering little smudge of light among the shining pinpoints – and gazed. My troubles had to wait for him.

'Wonderful,' he sighed, and then as though his first emphasis did not satisfy him, 'wonderful!'

He turned to me. 'Wouldn't you like to see?'

I had to look, and then I had to listen, how that this scarce-visible intruder was to be, was presently to be, one of the largest comets this world has ever seen, how that its course must bring it within at most – so many score of millions of miles from the earth, a mere step, Parload seemed to think that; how that the spectroscope was already sounding its chemical secrets, perplexed by the unprecedented band in the green, how it was even now being photographed in the very act of unwinding – in an unusual direction – a sunward tail (which presently it wound up again), and all the while in a sort of undertow I was thinking first of Nettie Stuart and the letter she had just written me, and then of old Rawdon's detestable face as I had seen it that afternoon.

Now I planned answers to Nettie and now belated repartees to my employer, and then again 'Nettie' was blazing all across the background of my thoughts. . . .

Nettie Stuart was daughter of the head gardener of the rich Mr Verrall's widow, and she and I had kissed and become sweethearts before we were eighteen years old. My mother and hers were second cousins and old schoolfellows, and though my mother had been widowed untimely by a train accident, and had been reduced to letting lodgings (she was the Clayton curate's landlady), a position esteemed much lower than that of Mrs Stuart, a kindly custom of occasional visits to the gardener's cottage at Checkshill Towers still kept the friends in touch. Commonly I went with her. And I remember it was in the dusk of one bright evening in July, one of those long golden evenings that do not so much give way to night as admit at last, upon courtesy, the moon and a choice retinue of stars, that Nettie and I, at the pond of goldfish where the yew-bordered walks converged, made our shy beginners' vow. I remember still – something will always stir in me at that memory – the tremulous emotion of that adventure. Nettie was dressed in white, her hair went off in waves of soft darkness from above her dark shining eyes; there was a little necklace of pearls about her sweetly modelled neck, and a little coin of gold that nestled in her throat. I kissed her half-reluctant lips, and for three years of my life thereafter – nay! I almost think for all the rest of her life and mine – I could have died for her sake.

You must understand – and every year it becomes increasingly difficult to understand – how entirely different the world was then from what it is now. It was a dark world; it was full of preventable disorder, preventable diseases, and preventable pain, of harshness and stupid unpremeditated cruelties; but yet, it may be even by virtue of the general darkness, there were moments of a rare and evanescent beauty that seem no longer possible in my experience. The great Change has come for ever more, happiness and beauty are our atmosphere, there is peace on earth and good will to all men. None would dare to dream of returning to the sorrows of the former time, and yet that misery was pierced, ever and again its grey curtain was stabbed through and through by joys of an intensity, by perceptions of a keenness that it seems to me are now altogether gone out of life. Is it the Change, I wonder, that has robbed life of its extremes, or is it perhaps only this, that youth has left me – even the strength of middle years leaves me now – and taken its despairs and raptures, leaving me judgment, perhaps, sympathy, memories?

I cannot tell. One would need to be young now and to have been young then as well, to decide that impossible problem.

Perhaps a cool observer even in the old days would have found little beauty in our grouping. I have our two photographs at hand in this bureau as I write, and they show me a gawky youth in ill-fitting ready-made clothing, and Nettie – Indeed Nettie is badly dressed, and her attitude is more than a little stiff; but I can see her through the picture, and her living brightness and something of that mystery of charm she had for me, comes back again to my mind. Her face has triumphed over the photographer – or I would long ago have cast this picture away.

The reality of beauty yields itself to no words. I wish that I had the sister art and could draw in my margin something that escapes description. There was a sort of gravity in her eyes. There was something, a matter of the minutest difference, about her upper lip so that her mouth closed sweetly and broke very sweetly to a smile. That grave, sweet smile!

After we had kissed and decided not to tell our parents for awhile of the irrevocable choice we had made, the time came for us to part, shyly and before others, and I and my mother went off back across the moonlit park – the bracken thickets rustling with startled deer – to the railway station at Checkshill and so to our dingy basement in Clayton, and I saw no more of Nettie – except that I saw her in my thoughts – for nearly a year. But at our next meeting it was decided that we must correspond, and this we did with much elaboration of secrecy, for Nettie would have no one at home, not even her only sister, know of her attachment. So I had to send my precious documents sealed and under cover by way of a confidential schoolfellow of hers who lived near London. . . . I could write that address down now, though house and street and suburb have gone beyond any man's tracing.

Our correspondence began our estrangement, because for the first time we came into more than sensuous contact and our minds sought expression.

Now you must understand that the world of thought in those days was in the strangest condition, it was choked with obsolete inadequate formulae, it was tortuous to a maze-like degree with secondary contrivances and adaptations, suppressions, conventions, and subterfuges. Base immediacies fouled the truth on every man's lips. I was brought up by my mother in a quaint old-fashioned narrow faith in certain religious formulae, certain rules of conduct, certain conceptions of social and political order, that had no more relevance to the realities and needs of everyday contemporary life than if they were clean linen that had been put away with lavender in a drawer. Indeed, her religion did actually smell of lavender; on Sundays she put away all the things of reality, the garments and even the furnishings of everyday, hid her hands, that were gnarled and sometimes chapped with scrubbing, in black, carefully mended gloves, assumed her old black silk dress and bonnet and took me, unnaturally clean and sweet also, to church. There we sang and bowed and heard sonorous prayers and joined in sonorous responses, and rose with a congregational sigh refreshed and relieved when the doxology, with its opening 'Now to God the Father, God the Son,' lowed out the tame, brief sermon. There was a hell in that religion of my mother's, a red-haired hell of curly flames that had once been very terrible; there was a devil, who was also ex officio the British King's enemy, and much denunciation of the wicked lusts of the flesh; we were expected to believe that most of our poor unhappy world was to atone for its muddle and trouble here by suffering exquisite torments for ever after, world without end, Amen. But indeed those curly flames looked rather jolly. The whole thing had been mellowed and faded into a gentle unreality long before my time; if it had much terror even in my childhood I have forgotten it, it was not so terrible as the giant who was killed by the Beanstalk, and I see it all now as a setting for my poor old mother's worn and grimy face, and almost lovingly as a part of her. And Mr Gabbitas, our plump little lodger, strangely transformed in his vestments and lifting his voice manfully to the quality of those Elizabethan prayers, seemed, I think, to give her a special and peculiar interest with God. She radiated her own tremulous gentleness upon Him, and redeemed Him from all the implications of vindictive theologians; she was in truth, had I but perceived it, the effectual answer to all she would have taught me.

So I see it now, but there is something harsh in the earnest intensity of youth, and having at first taken all these things quite seriously, the fiery hell and God's vindictiveness at any neglect, as though they were as much a matter of fact as Bladden's iron-works and Rawdon's pot-bank, I presently with an equal seriousness flung them out of my mind again.

Mr Gabbitas, you see, did sometimes, as the phrase went, 'take notice' of me, he had induced me to go on reading after I left school, and with the best intentions in the world and to anticipate the poison of the times, he had lent me Burble's 'Scepticism Answered', and drawn my attention to the library of the Institute in Clayton.

The excellent Burble was a great shock to me. It seemed clear from his answers to the sceptic that the case for doctrinal orthodoxy and all that faded and by no means awful hereafter, which I had hitherto

14

accepted as I accepted the sun, was an extremely poor one, and to hammer home that idea the first book I got from the Institute happened to be an American edition of the collected works of Shelley, his gassy prose as well as his atmospheric verse. I was soon ripe for blatant unbelief. And at the Young Men's Christian Association I presently made the acquaintance of Parload, who told me, under promises of the most sinister secrecy, that he was 'a Socialist out and out.' He lent me several copies of a periodical with the clamant title of *The Clarion*, which was just taking up a crusade against the accepted religion. The adolescent years of any fairly intelligent youth lie open, and will always lie healthily open, to the contagion of philosophical doubts, of scorns and new ideas, and I will confess I had the fever of that phase badly. Doubt, I say, but it was not so much doubt – which is a complex thing – as startled emphatic denial. 'Have I believed THIS!' And I was also, you must remember, just beginning love-letters to Nettie.

We live now in these days, when the Great Change has been in most things accomplished, in a time when every one is being educated to a sort of intellectual gentleness, a gentleness that abates nothing from our vigour, and it is hard to understand the stifled and struggling manner in which my generation of common young men did its thinking. To think at all about certain questions was an act of rebellion that set one oscillating between the furtive and the defiant. People begin to find Shelley – for all his melody – noisy and ill conditioned now because his Anarchs have vanished, yet there was a time when novel thought HAD to go to that tune of breaking glass. It becomes a little difficult to imagine the yeasty state of mind, the disposition to shout and say, 'Yah!' at constituted authority, to sustain a persistent note of provocation such as we raw youngsters displayed. I began to read with avidity such writing as Carlyle, Browning and Heine have left for the perplexity of posterity, and not only to read and admire but to imitate. My letters to Nettie, after one or two genuinely intended displays of perfervid tenderness, broke out toward theology, sociology and the cosmos in turgid and startling expressions. No doubt they puzzled her extremely.

I retain the keenest sympathy and something inexplicably near to envy for my own departed youth, but I should find it difficult to maintain my case against any one who would condemn me altogether as having been a very silly, posturing, emotional hobbledehoy indeed and quite like my faded photograph. And when I try to recall what exactly must have been the quality and tenor of my more sustained efforts to write memorably to my sweetheart, I confess I shiver ... Yet I wish they were not all destroyed.

Her letters to me were simple enough, written in a roundish, unformed hand and badly phrased. Her first two or three showed a shy pleasure in the use of the word 'dear,' and I remember being first puzzled and then, when I understood, delighted, because she had written 'Willie ASTHORE' under my name. 'Asthore,' I gathered, meant 'darling'. But when the evidences of my fermentation began, her answers were less happy.

I will not weary you with the story of how we quarrelled in our silly youthful way, and how I went the next Sunday, all uninvited, to Checkshill, and made it worse, and how afterward I wrote a letter that she thought was 'lovely', and mended the matter. Nor will I tell of all our subsequent fluctuations of misunderstanding. Always I was the offender and the final penitent until this last trouble that was now beginning; and in between we had some tender near moments, and I loved her very greatly. There was this misfortune in the business, that in the darkness, and alone, I thought with great intensity of her, of her eyes, of her touch, of her sweet and delightful presence, but when I sat down to write I thought of Shelley and Burns and myself, and other such irrelevant matters. When one is in love, in this fermenting way, it is harder to make love than it is when one does not love at all. And as for Nettie, she loved, I know, not me but those gentle mysteries. It was not my voice should rouse her dreams to passion . . . So our letters continued to jar. Then suddenly she wrote me one doubting whether she could ever care for any one who was a Socialist and did not believe in Church, and then hard upon it came another note with unexpected novelties of phrasing. She thought we were not suited to each other, we differed so in tastes and ideas, she had long thought of releasing me from our engagement. In fact, though I really did not apprehend it fully at the first shock, I was dismissed. Her letter had reached me when I came home after old Rawdon's none too civil refusal to raise my wages. On this particular evening of which I write, therefore, I was in a state of feverish adjustment to two new and amazing, two nearly overwhelming facts, that I was neither indispensable to Nettie nor at Rawdon's. And to talk of comets!

Where did I stand?

I had grown so accustomed to think of Nettie as inseparably mine – the whole tradition of 'true love' pointed me to that – that for her to face about with these precise small phrases toward abandonment, after we had kissed and whispered and come so close in the little adventurous familiarities of the young, shocked me profoundly. I! I! And Rawdon didn't find me indispensable either. I felt I was suddenly repudiated by the universe and threatened with effacement, that in some positive and emphatic way I must at once assert myself. There was no balm in the religion I had learnt, or in the irreligion I had adopted, for wounded self-love.

Should I fling up Rawdon's place at once and then in some extraordinary, swift manner make the fortune of Frobisher's adjacent and closely competitive pot-bank?

The first part of that programme, at any rate, would be easy of accomplishment, to go to Rawdon and say, 'You will hear from me again,' but for the rest, Frobisher might fail me. That, however, was a secondary issue. The predominant affair was with Nettie. I found my mind thick-shot with flying fragments of rhetoric that might be of service in the letter I would write her. Scorn, irony, tenderness – what was it to be?

'Bother!' said Parload, suddenly.

'What?' said I.

'They're firing up at Bladden's iron-works, and the smoke comes right across my bit of sky.'

The interruption came just as I was ripe to discharge my thoughts upon him.

'Parload,' said I, 'very likely I shall have to leave all this. Old Rawdon won't give me a rise in my wages, and after having asked I don't think I can stand going on upon the old terms anymore. See? So I may have to clear out of Clayton for good and all.'

Section 3

That made Parload put down the opera-glass and look at me. 'It's a bad time to change just now,' he said after a little pause.

Rawdon had said as much, in a less agreeable tone.

But with Parload I felt always a disposition to the heroic note. 'I'm tired,' I said, 'of humdrum drudgery for other men. One may as well starve one's body out of a place as to starve one's soul in one.'

'I don't know about that altogether,' began Parload, slowly ...

And with that we began one of our interminable conversations, one of those long, wandering, intensely generalizing, diffusely personal talks that will be dear to the hearts of intelligent youths until the world comes to an end. The Change has not abolished that, anyhow.

It would be an incredible feat of memory for me now to recall all that meandering haze of words, indeed I recall scarcely any of it, though its circumstances and atmosphere stand out, a sharp, clear picture in my mind. I posed after my manner and behaved very foolishly no doubt, a wounded, smarting egotist, and Parload played his part of the philosopher preoccupied with the deeps.

We were presently abroad, walking through the warm summer's night and talking all the more freely for that. But one thing that I said I can remember. 'I wish at times,' said I, with a gesture at the heavens, 'that comet of yours or some such thing would indeed strike this world – and wipe us all away, strikes, wars, tumults, loves, jealousies, and all the wretchedness of life!'

'Ah!' said Parload, and the thought seemed to hang about him.

'It could only add to the miseries of life,' he said irrelevantly, when presently I was discoursing of other things.

'What would?'

'Collision with a comet. It would only throw things back. It would only make what was left of life more savage than it is at present.'

'But why should ANYTHING be left of life?' said I. . . .

That was our style, you know, and meanwhile we walked together up the narrow street outside his lodging, up the stepway and the lanes toward Clayton Crest and the high road.

But my memories carry me back so effectually to those days before the Change that I forget that now all these places have been altered beyond recognition, that the narrow street and the stepway and the view from Clayton Crest, and indeed all the world in which I was born and bred and made, has vanished clean away, out of space and out of time, and wellnigh out of the imagination of all those who are younger by a generation than I. You cannot see, as I can see, the dark empty way between the mean houses, the dark empty way lit by a bleary gas-lamp at the corner, you cannot feel the hard checkered pavement under your boots, you cannot mark the dimly lit windows here and there, and the shadows upon the ugly and often patched and crooked blinds of the people cooped within. Nor can you presently pass the beerhouse with its brighter gas and its queer, screening windows, nor get a whiff of foul air and foul language from its door, nor see the crumpled furtive figure – some rascal child – that slinks past us down the steps.

We crossed the longer street, up which a clumsy steam tram, vomiting smoke and sparks, made its clangorous way, and adown which one saw the greasy brilliance of shop fronts and the naphtha flares of hawkers' barrows dripping fire into the night. A hazy movement of people swayed along that road, and we heard the voice of an itinerant preacher from a waste place between the houses. You cannot see these things as I can see them, nor can you figure – unless you know the pictures that great artist Hyde has left the world – the effect of the great hoarding by which we passed, lit below by a gas-lamp and towering up to a sudden sharp black edge against the pallid sky.

Those hoardings! They were the brightest coloured things in all that vanished world. Upon them, in successive layers of paste and paper, all the rough enterprises of that time joined in chromatic discord; pill vendors and preachers, theatres and charities, marvellous soaps and astonishing pickles, typewriting machines and sewing machines, mingled in a sort of visualized clamour. And passing that there was a muddy lane of cinders, a lane without a light, that used its many puddles to borrow a star or so from the sky. We splashed along unheeding as we talked.

Then across the allotments, a wilderness of cabbages and evil-looking sheds, past a gaunt abandoned factory, and so to the high road. The high road ascended in a curve past a few houses and a beerhouse or so, and round until all the valley in which four industrial towns lay crowded and confluent was overlooked.

I will admit that with the twilight there came a spell of weird magnificence over all that land and brooded on it until dawn. The horrible meanness of its details was veiled, the hutches that were homes, the bristling multitudes of chimneys, the ugly patches of unwilling vegetation amidst the makeshift fences of barrel-stave and wire. The rusty scars that framed the opposite ridges where the iron ore was taken and the barren mountains of slag from the blast furnaces were veiled; the reek and boiling smoke and dust from foundry, pot-bank, and furnace, transfigured and assimilated by the night. The dust-laden atmosphere that was grey oppression through the day became at sundown a mystery of deep translucent colours, of blues and purples, of sombre and vivid reds, of strange bright clearnesses of green and yellow athwart the darkling sky. Each upstart furnace, when its monarch sun had gone, crowned itself with flames, the dark cinder heaps began to glow with quivering fires, and each pot-bank squatted rebellious in a volcanic coronet of light. The empire of the day broke into a thousand feudal baronies of burning coal. The minor streets across the valley picked themselves out with gas-lamps of faint yellow, that brightened and mingled at all the principal squares and crossings with the greenish pallor of incandescent mantles and the high cold glare of the electric arc. The interlacing railways lifted bright signal-boxes over their intersections, and signal stars of red and green in rectangular constellations. The trains became articulated black serpents breathing fire.

Moreover, high overhead, like a thing put out of reach and near forgotten, Parload had rediscovered a realm that was ruled by neither sun nor furnace, the universe of stars.

This was the scene of many a talk we two had held together. And if in the daytime we went right over the crest and looked westward there was farmland, there were parks and great mansions, the spire of a distant cathedral, and sometimes when the weather was near raining, the crests of remote mountains hung clearly in the sky. Beyond the range of sight indeed, out beyond, there was Checkshill; I felt it there always, and in the darkness more than I did by day. Checkshill, and Nettie!

And to us two youngsters as we walked along the cinder path beside the rutted road and argued out our perplexities, it seemed that this ridge gave us compendiously a view of our whole world.

There on the one hand in a crowded darkness, about the ugly factories and work-places, the workers herded together, ill clothed, ill nourished, ill taught, badly and expensively served at every occasion in life, uncertain even of their insufficient livelihood from day to day, the chapels and churches and public-houses swelling up amidst their wretched homes like saprophytes amidst a general corruption, and on the other, in space, freedom, and dignity, scarce heeding the few cottages, as overcrowded as they were picturesque, in which the labourers festered, lived the landlords and masters who owned pot-banks and forge and farm and mine. Far away, distant, beautiful, irrelevant, from out of a little cluster of secondhand bookshops, ecclesiastical residences, and the inns and incidentals of a decaying market town, the cathedral of Lowchester pointed a beautiful, unemphatic spire to vague incredible skies. So it seemed to us that the whole world was planned in those youthful first impressions.

We saw everything simple, as young men will. We had our angry, confident solutions, and whosoever would criticize them was a friend of the robbers. It was a clear case of robbery, we held, visibly so; there in those great houses lurked the Landlord and the Capitalist, with his scoundrel the Lawyer, with his cheat the Priest, and we others were all the victims of their deliberate villainies. No doubt they winked and chuckled over their rare wines, amidst their dazzling, wickedly dressed women, and plotted further grinding for the faces of the poor. And amidst all the squalor on the other hand, amidst brutalities, ignorance, and drunkenness, suffered multitudinously their blameless victim, the Working Man. And we, almost at the first glance, had found all this out, it had merely to be asserted now with sufficient rhetoric and vehemence to change the face of the whole world. The Working Man would arise – in the form of a Labour Party, and with young men like Parload and myself to represent him – and come to his own, and then—?

Then the robbers would get it hot, and everything would be extremely satisfactory.

Unless my memory plays me strange tricks that does no injustice to the creed of thought and action that Parload and I held as the final result of human wisdom. We believed it with heat, and rejected with heat the most obvious qualification of its harshness. At times in our great talks we were full of heady hopes for the near triumph of our doctrine, more often our mood was hot resentment at the wickedness and stupidity that delayed so plain and simple a reconstruction of the order of the world. Then we grew malignant, and thought of barricades and significant violence. I was very bitter, I know, upon this night of which I am now particularly telling, and the only face upon the hydra of Capitalism and Monopoly that I could see at all clearly, smiled exactly as old Rawdon had smiled when he refused to give me more than a paltry twenty shillings a week.

I wanted intensely to salve my self-respect by some revenge upon him, and I felt that if that could be done by slaying the hydra, I might drag its carcass to the feet of Nettie, and settle my other trouble as well. 'What do you think of me NOW, Nettie?'

That at any rate comes near enough to the quality of my thinking, then, for you to imagine how I gesticulated and spouted to Parload that night. You figure us as little black figures, unprepossessing in the outline, set in the midst of that desolating night of flaming industrialism, and my little voice with a rhetorical twang protesting, denouncing. . . .

You will consider those notions of my youth poor silly violent stuff; particularly if you are of the younger generation born since the Change you will be of that opinion. Nowadays the whole world thinks clearly, thinks with deliberation, pellucid certainties, you find it impossible to imagine how any other thinking could have been possible. Let me tell you then how you can bring yourself to something like the condition of our former state. In the first place you must get yourself out of health by unwise drinking and eating, and out of condition by neglecting your exercise, then you must contrive to be worried very much and made very anxious and uncomfortable, and then you must work very hard for four or five days and for long hours every day at something too petty to be interesting, too complex to be mechanical, and without any personal significance to you whatever. This done, get straightway into a room that is not ventilated at all, and that is already full of foul air, and there set yourself to think out some very complicated problem. In a very little while you will find yourself in a state of intellectual muddle, annoyed, impatient, snatching at the obvious presently in choosing and rejecting conclusions haphazard. Try to play chess under such conditions and you will play stupidly and lose your temper. Try to do anything that taxes the brain or temper and you will fail.

Now, the whole world before the Change was as sick and feverish as that, it was worried and overworked and perplexed by problems that would not get stated simply, that changed and evaded solution, it was in an atmosphere that had corrupted and thickened past breathing; there was no thorough cool thinking in the world at all. There was nothing in the mind of the world anywhere but half-truths, hasty assumptions, hallucinations, and emotions. Nothing. . . .

I know it seems incredible, that already some of the younger men are beginning to doubt the greatness of the Change our world has undergone, but read – read the newspapers of that time. Every age becomes mitigated and a little ennobled in our minds as it recedes into the past. It is the part of those who like myself have stories of that time to tell, to supply, by a scrupulous spiritual realism, some antidote to that glamour.

Section 4

Always with Parload I was chief talker.

I can look back upon myself with, I believe, an almost perfect detachment, things have so changed that indeed now I am another being, with scarce anything in common with that boastful foolish youngster whose troubles I recall. I see him vulgarly theatrical, egotistical, insincere, indeed I do not like him save with that instinctive material sympathy that is the fruit of incessant intimacy. Because he was myself I may be able to feel and write understandingly about motives that will put him out of sympathy with nearly every reader, but why should I palliate or defend his quality?

Always, I say, I did the talking, and it would have amazed me beyond measure if any one had told me that mine was not the greater intelligence in these wordy encounters. Parload was a quiet youth, and stiff and restrained in all things, while I had that supreme gift for young men and democracies, the gift of copious expression. Parload I diagnosed in my secret heart as a trifle dull; he posed as pregnant quiet, I thought, and was obsessed by the congenial notion of 'scientific caution.' I did not remark that while my hands were chiefly useful for gesticulation or holding a pen Parload's hands could do all sorts of things, and I did not think therefore that fibres must run from those fingers to something in his brain. Nor, though I bragged perpetually of my shorthand, of my literature, of my indispensable share in Rawdon's business, did Parload lay stress on the conics and calculus he 'mugged' in the organized science school. Parload is a famous man now, a great figure in a great time, his work upon intersecting radiations has broadened the intellectual horizon of mankind for ever, and I, who am at best a hewer of intellectual wood, a drawer of living water, can smile, and he can smile, to think how I patronized and posed and jabbered over him in the darkness of those early days.

That night I was shrill and eloquent beyond measure. Rawdon was, of course, the hub upon which I went round – Rawdon and the Rawdonesque employer and the injustice of 'wages slavery' and all the immediate conditions of that industrial blind alley up which it seemed our lives were thrust. But ever and again I glanced at other things. Nettie was always there in the background of my mind, regarding me enigmatically. It was part of my pose to Parload that I had a romantic love-affair somewhere away beyond the sphere of our intercourse, and that note gave a Byronic resonance to many of the nonsensical things I produced for his astonishment.

I will not weary you with too detailed an account of the talk of a foolish youth who was also distressed and unhappy, and whose voice was balm for the humiliations that smarted in his eyes. Indeed, now in many particulars I cannot disentangle this harangue of which I tell from many of the things I may have said in other talks to Parload. For example, I forget if it was then or before or afterwards that, as it were by accident, I let out what might be taken as an admission that I was addicted to drugs.

'You shouldn't do that,' said Parload, suddenly. 'It won't do to poison your brains with that.'

My brains, my eloquence, were to be very important assets to our party in the coming revolution. . . .

But one thing does clearly belong to this particular conversation I am recalling. When I started out it was quite settled in the back of my mind that I must not leave Rawdon's. I simply wanted to abuse my employer to Parload. But I talked myself quite out of touch with all the cogent reasons there were for sticking to my place, and I got home that night irrevocably committed to a spirited – not to say a defiant – policy with my employer.

'I can't stand Rawdon's much longer,' I said to Parload by way of a flourish.

'There's hard times coming,' said Parload.

'Next winter.'

'Sooner. The Americans have been overproducing, and they mean to dump. The iron trade is going to have convulsions.'

'I don't care. Pot-banks are steady.'

'With a corner in borax? No. I've heard—'

'What have you heard?'

'Office secrets. But it's no secret there's trouble coming to potters. There's been borrowing and speculation. The masters don't stick to one business as they used to do. I can tell that much. Half the valley may be "playing" before two months are out.' Parload delivered himself of this unusually long speech in his most pithy and weighty manner.

'Playing' was our local euphemism for a time when there was no work and no money for a man, a time of stagnation and dreary hungry loafing day after day. Such interludes seemed in those days a necessary consequence of industrial organization.

'You'd better stick to Rawdon's,' said Parload.

'Ugh,' said I, affecting a noble disgust.

'There'll be trouble,' said Parload.

'Who cares?' said I. 'Let there be trouble – the more the better. This system has got to end, sooner or later. These capitalists with their speculation and corners and trusts make things go from bad to worse. Why should I cower in Rawdon's office, like a frightened dog, while hunger walks the streets? Hunger is the master revolutionary. When he comes we ought to turn out and salute him. Anyway, I'M going to do so now.'

'That's all very well,' began Parload.

'I'm tired of it,' I said. 'I want to come to grips with all these Rawdons. I think perhaps if I was hungry and savage I could talk to hungry men—'

'There's your mother,' said Parload, in his slow judicial way.

That WAS a difficulty.

I got over it by a rhetorical turn. 'Why should one sacrifice the future of the world – why should one even sacrifice one's own future – because one's mother is totally destitute of imagination?'

Section 5

It was late when I parted from Parload and came back to my own home.

Our house stood in a highly respectable little square near the Clayton parish church. Mr Gabbitas, the curate of all work, lodged on our ground floor, and upstairs there was an old lady, Miss Holroyd, who painted flowers on china and maintained her blind sister in an adjacent room; my mother and I lived in the basement and slept in the attics. The front of the house was veiled by a Virginian creeper that defied the Clayton air and clustered in untidy dependent masses over the wooden porch.

As I came up the steps I had a glimpse of Mr Gabbitas printing photographs by candle light in his room. It was the chief delight of his little life to spend his holiday abroad in the company of a queer little snap-shot camera, and to return with a great multitude of foggy and sinister negatives that he had made in beautiful and interesting places. These the camera company would develop for him on advantageous terms, and he would spend his evenings the year through in printing from them in order to inflict copies upon his undeserving friends. There was a long frameful of his work in the Clayton National School, for example, inscribed in old English lettering, 'Italian Travel Pictures, by the Rev. E. B. Gabbitas'. For this it seemed he lived and travelled and had his being. It was his only real joy. By his shaded light I could see his sharp little nose, his little pale eyes behind his glasses, his mouth pursed up with the endeavour of his employment.

'Hireling Liar,' I muttered, for was not he also part of the system, part of the scheme of robbery that made wages serfs of Parload and me? – though his share in the proceedings was certainly small.

'Hireling Liar,' said I, standing in the darkness, outside even his faint glow of travelled culture . . .

My mother let me in.

She looked at me, mutely, because she knew there was something wrong and that it was no use for her to ask what.

'Good night, mummy,' said I, and kissed her a little roughly, and lit and took my candle and went off at once up the staircase to bed, not looking back at her.

'I've kept some supper for you, dear.'

'Don't want any supper.'

'But, dearie—'

'Good night, mother,' and I went up and slammed my door upon her, blew out my candle, and lay down at once upon my bed, lay there a long time before I got up to undress.

There were times when that dumb beseeching of my mother's face irritated me unspeakably. It did so that night. I felt I had to struggle against it, that I could not exist if I gave way to its pleadings, and it hurt me and divided me to resist it, almost beyond endurance. It was clear to me that I had to think out for myself religious problems, social problems, questions of conduct, questions of expediency, that her poor dear simple beliefs could not help me at all – and she did not understand! Hers was the accepted religion, her only social ideas were blind submissions to the accepted order – to laws, to doctors, to clergymen, lawyers, masters, and all respectable persons in authority over us, and with her to believe was to fear. She knew from a thousand little signs – though still at times I went to church with her – that I was passing out of touch of all these things that ruled her life, into some terrible unknown. From things I said she could infer such clumsy concealments as I made. She felt my socialism, felt my spirit in revolt against the accepted order, felt the impotent resentments that filled me with bitterness against all she held sacred. Yet, you know, it was not her dear gods she sought to defend so much as me! She seemed always to be wanting to say to me, 'Dear, I know it's hard – but revolt is harder. Don't make war on it, dear – don't! Don't do anything to offend it. I'm sure it will hurt you if you do – it will hurt you if you do.'

She had been cowed into submission, as so many women of that time had been, by the sheer brutality of the accepted thing. The existing order dominated her into a worship of abject observances. It had bent her, aged her, robbed her of eyesight so that at fifty-five she peered through cheap spectacles at my face, and saw it only dimly, filled her with a habit of anxiety, made her hands–Her poor dear hands! Not in the whole world now could you find a woman with hands so grimy, so needle-worn, so misshapen by toil, so chapped and coarsened, so evilly entreated. . . . At any rate, there is this I can say for myself, that my bitterness against the world and fortune was for her sake as well as for my own.

Yet that night I pushed by her harshly. I answered her curtly, left her concerned and perplexed in the passage, and slammed my door upon her.

And for a long time I lay raging at the hardship and evil of life, at the contempt of Rawdon, and the loveless coolness of Nettie's letter, at my weakness and insignificance, at the things I found intolerable, and the things I could not mend. Over and over went my poor little brain, tired out and unable to stop on my treadmill of troubles. Nettie. Rawdon. My mother. Gabbitas. Nettie . . .

Suddenly I came upon emotional exhaustion. Some clock was striking midnight. After all, I was young; I had these quick transitions. I remember quite distinctly, I stood up abruptly, undressed very quickly in the dark, and had hardly touched my pillow again before I was asleep.

But how my mother slept that night I do not know.

Oddly enough, I do not blame myself for behaving like this to my mother, though my conscience blames me acutely for my arrogance to Parload. I regret my behaviour to my mother before the days of the Change, it is a scar among my memories that will always be a little painful to the end of my days, but I do not see how something of the sort was to be escaped under those former conditions. In that time of muddle and obscurity people were overtaken by needs and toil and hot passions before they had the chance of even a year or so of clear thinking; they settled down to an intense and strenuous application to some partial but immediate duty, and the growth of thought ceased in them. They set and hardened into narrow ways. Few women remained capable of a new idea after five and twenty, few men after thirty-one or two. Discontent with the thing that existed was regarded as immoral, it was certainly an annoyance, and the only protest against it, the only effort against that universal tendency in all human institutions to thicken and clog, to work loosely and badly, to rust and weaken towards catastrophes, came from the young – the crude unmerciful young. It seemed in those days to thoughtful men the harsh law of being – that either we must submit to our elders and be stifled, or disregard them, disobey them, thrust them aside, and make our little step of progress before we too ossified and became obstructive in our turn.

My pushing past my mother, my irresponsive departure to my own silent meditations, was, I now perceive, a figure of the whole hard relationship between parents and son in those days. There appeared no other way; that perpetually recurring tragedy was, it seemed, part of the very nature of the progress of the world. We did not think then that minds might grow ripe without growing rigid, or children honour their parents and still think for themselves. We were angry and hasty because we stifled in the darkness, in a poisoned and vitiated air. That deliberate animation of the intelligence which is now the universal quality, that vigour with consideration, that judgment with confident enterprise which shine through all our world, were things disintegrated and unknown in the corrupting atmosphere of our former state.

(So the first fascicle ended. I put it aside and looked for the second.
'Well?' said the man who wrote.
'This is fiction?'
'It's my story.'
'But you – Amidst this beauty – You are not this ill-conditioned, squalidly bred lad of whom I have been reading?'
He smiled. 'There intervenes a certain Change,' he said. 'Have I not hinted at that?'
I hesitated upon a question, then saw the second fascicle at hand, and picked it up.)

CHAPTER THE SECOND

Nettie

Section 1

I cannot now remember (the story resumed), what interval separated that evening on which Parload first showed me the comet – I think I only pretended to see it then – and the Sunday afternoon I spent at Checkshill.

Between the two there was time enough for me to give notice and leave Rawdon's, to seek for some other situation very strenuously in vain, to think and say many hard and violent things to my mother and to Parload, and to pass through some phases of very profound wretchedness. There must have been a passionate correspondence with Nettie, but all the froth and fury of that has faded now out of my memory. All I have clear now is that I wrote one magnificent farewell to her, casting her off forever, and that I got in reply a prim little note to say, that even if there was to be an end to everything, that was no excuse for writing such things as I had done, and then I think I wrote again in a vein I considered satirical. To that she did not reply. That interval was at least three weeks, and probably four, because the comet which had been on the first occasion only a dubious speck in the sky, certainly visible only when it was magnified, was now a great white presence, brighter than Jupiter, and casting a shadow on its own account. It was now actively present in the world of human thought, every one was talking about it, every one was looking for its waxing splendour as the sun went down – the papers, the music-halls, the hoardings, echoed it.

Yes; the comet was already dominant before I went over to make everything clear to Nettie. And Parload had spent two hoarded pounds in buying himself a spectroscope, so that he could see for himself, night after night, that mysterious, that stimulating line – the unknown line in the green. How many times I wonder did I look at the smudgy, quivering symbol of the unknown things that were rushing upon us out of the inhuman void, before I rebelled? But at last I could stand it no longer, and I reproached Parload very bitterly for wasting his time in 'astronomical dilettantism'.

'Here,' said I. 'We're on the verge of the biggest lockout in the history of this countryside; here's distress and hunger coming, here's all the capitalistic competitive system like a wound inflamed, and you spend your time gaping at that damned silly streak of nothing in the sky!'

Parload stared at me. 'Yes, I do,' he said slowly, as though it was a new idea. 'Don't I? . . . I wonder why.'

'*I* want to start meetings of an evening on Howden's Waste.'

'You think they'd listen?'

'They'd listen fast enough now.'

'They didn't before,' said Parload, looking at his pet instrument.

'There was a demonstration of unemployed at Swathinglea on Sunday. They got to stone throwing.'

Parload said nothing for a little while and I said several things. He seemed to be considering something.

'But, after all,' he said at last, with an awkward movement towards his spectroscope, 'that does signify something.'

'The comet?'

'Yes.'

'What can it signify? You don't want me to believe in astrology. What does it matter what flames in the heavens – when men are starving on earth?'

'It's – it's science.'

'Science! What we want now is socialism – not science.'

He still seemed reluctant to give up his comet.

'Socialism's all right,' he said, 'but if that thing up there WAS to hit the earth it might matter.'

'Nothing matters but human beings.'

'Suppose it killed them all.'

'Oh,' said I, 'that's Rot.'

'I wonder,' said Parload, dreadfully divided in his allegiance.

He looked at the comet. He seemed on the verge of repeating his growing information about the nearness of the paths of the earth and comet, and all that might ensue from that. So I cut in with something

29

I had got out of a now forgotten writer called Ruskin, a volcano of beautiful language and nonsensical suggestions, who prevailed very greatly with eloquent excitable young men in those days. Something it was about the insignificance of science and the supreme importance of Life. Parload stood listening, half turned towards the sky with the tips of his fingers on his spectroscope. He seemed to come to a sudden decision.

'No. I don't agree with you, Leadford,' he said. 'You don't understand about science.'

Parload rarely argued with that bluntness of opposition. I was so used to entire possession of our talk that his brief contradiction struck me like a blow. 'Don't agree with me!' I repeated.

'No,' said Parload.

'But how?'

'I believe science is of more importance than socialism,' he said. 'Socialism's a theory. Science – science is something more.'

And that was really all he seemed to be able to say.

We embarked upon one of those queer arguments illiterate young men used always to find so heating. Science or Socialism? It was, of course, like arguing which is right, left handedness or a taste for onions, it was an altogether impossible opposition. But the range of my rhetoric enabled me at last to exasperate Parload, and his mere repudiation of my conclusions sufficed to exasperate me, and we ended in the key of a positive quarrel. 'Oh, very well!' said I. 'So long as I know where we are!'

I slammed his door as though I dynamited his house, and went raging down the street, but I felt that he was already back at the window worshipping his blessed line in the green, before I got round the corner.

I had to walk for an hour or so, before I was cool enough to go home.

And it was Parload who had first introduced me to socialism!

Recreant!

The most extraordinary things used to run through my head in those days. I will confess that my mind ran persistently that evening upon revolutions after the best French pattern, and I sat on a Committee of Safety and tried backsliders. Parload was there, among the prisoners, backsliderissimus, aware too late of the error of his ways. His hands were tied behind his back ready for the shambles; through the open door one heard the voice of justice, the rude justice of the people. I was sorry, but I had to do my duty.

'If we punish those who would betray us to Kings,' said I, with a

30

sorrowful deliberation, 'how much the more must we punish those who would give over the State to the pursuit of useless knowledge'; and so with a gloomy satisfaction sent him off to the guillotine.

'Ah, Parload! Parload! If only you'd listened to me earlier, Parload. . . .'

None the less that quarrel made me extremely unhappy. Parload was my only gossip, and it cost me much to keep away from him and think evil of him with no one to listen to me, evening after evening.

That was a very miserable time for me, even before my last visit to Checkshill. My long unemployed hours hung heavily on my hands. I kept away from home all day, partly to support a fiction that I was sedulously seeking another situation, and partly to escape the persistent question in my mother's eyes. 'Why did you quarrel with Mr Rawdon? Why DID you? Why do you keep on going about with a sullen face and risk offending IT more?' I spent most of the morning in the newspaper-room of the public library, writing impossible applications for impossible posts – I remember that among other things of the sort I offered my services to a firm of private detectives, a sinister breed of traders upon base jealousies now happily vanished from the world, and wrote apropos of an advertisement for 'stevedores' that I did not know what the duties of a stevedore might be, but that I was apt and willing to learn – and in the afternoons and evenings I wandered through the strange lights and shadows of my native valley and hated all created things. Until my wanderings were checked by the discovery that I was wearing out my boots.

The stagnant inconclusive malaria of that time!

I perceive that I was an evil-tempered, ill-disposed youth with a great capacity for hatred, BUT —

There was an excuse for hate.

It was wrong of me to hate individuals, to be rude, harsh, and vindictive to this person or that, but indeed it would have been equally wrong to have taken the manifest offer life made me, without resentment. I see now clearly and calmly, what I then felt obscurely and with an unbalanced intensity, that my conditions were intolerable. My work was tedious and labourious and it took up an unreasonable proportion of my time, I was ill clothed, ill fed, ill housed, ill educated and ill trained, my will was suppressed and cramped to the pitch of torture, I had no reasonable pride in myself and no reasonable chance of putting anything right. It was a life hardly worth living. That a large proportion of the people about me had no better a lot, that many had a worse, does not affect these facts. It was a life in which contentment would have been disgraceful. If some of them were contented or resigned, so much the worse for every one. No doubt it was hasty and foolish of me to throw up my situation, but everything was so obviously aimless and foolish in our social organization that I do not feel disposed to blame myself even for that, except in so far as it pained my mother and caused her anxiety.

Think of the one comprehensive fact of the lockout!

That year was a bad year, a year of world-wide economic disorganization. Through their want of intelligent direction the great 'Trust' of American ironmasters, a gang of energetic, narrow-minded furnace owners, had smelted far more iron than the whole world had any demand for. (In those days there existed no means of estimating any need of that sort beforehand.) They had done this without even consulting the ironmasters of any other country. During their period of activity they had drawn into their employment a great number of workers, and had erected a huge productive plant. It is manifestly just that people who do headlong stupid things of this sort should suffer, but in the old days it was quite possible, it was customary for the real blunderers in such disasters, to shift nearly all the consequences of their incapacity. No one thought it wrong for a light-witted 'captain of industry' who had led his workpeople into overproduction, into the disproportionate manufacture, that is to say, of some particular article, to abandon and dismiss them, nor was there anything to prevent the sudden frantic underselling of some trade rival in order to surprise and destroy his trade, secure his customers for one's own destined needs, and shift a portion of one's punishment upon him. This operation of spasmodic underselling was known as 'dumping'. The American ironmasters were now dumping on the British market. The British employers were, of course, taking their loss out of their workpeople as much as possible, but in addition they were agitating for some legislation that would prevent – not stupid relative excess in production, but 'dumping' – not the disease, but the consequences of the disease. The necessary knowledge to prevent either dumping or its causes, the uncorrelated production of commodities, did not exist, but this hardly weighed with them at all, and in answer to their demands there had arisen a curious party of retaliatory-protectionists who combined vague proposals for spasmodic responses to these convulsive attacks from foreign manufacturers, with the very evident intention of achieving financial adventures. The dishonest and reckless elements were indeed so evident in this movement as to add very greatly to the general atmosphere of distrust and insecurity, and in the recoil from the prospect of fiscal power in the hands of the class of men known as the 'New Financiers', one heard frightened old-fashioned statesmen asserting with passion that 'dumping' didn't occur, or that it was a very charming sort of thing to happen. Nobody would face and handle the rather intricate truth of the business. The whole effect upon the mind of a cool observer was of a covey of unsubstantial jabbering minds drifting over a series of irrational economic cataclysms, prices and employment tumbled about like towers in an earthquake, and amidst the shifting masses were the common work-people going on with their lives as well as they could, suffering, perplexed, unorganized, and for anything but violent, fruitless protests, impotent. You cannot hope now to understand the infinite want of adjustment in the old order of things. At one time there were people dying of actual starvation in India, while men were burning unsalable wheat in America. It sounds like the account of a particularly mad dream, does it not? It was a dream, a dream from which no one on earth expected an awakening.

To us youngsters with the positiveness, the rationalism of youth, it seemed that the strikes and lockouts, the overproduction and misery could not possibly result simply from ignorance and want of thought and feeling. We needed more dramatic factors than these mental fogs, these mere atmospheric devils. We fled therefore to that common refuge of the unhappy ignorant, a belief in callous insensate plots – we called them 'plots' – against the poor.

You can still see how we figured it in any museum by looking up the caricatures of capital and labour that adorned the German and American socialistic papers of the old time.

Section 2

I had cast Nettie off in an eloquent epistle, had really imagined the affair was over forever – 'I've done with women,' I said to Parload – and then there was silence for more than a week.

Before that week was over I was wondering with a growing emotion what next would happen between us.

I found myself thinking constantly of Nettie, picturing her – sometimes with stern satisfaction, sometimes with sympathetic remorse – mourning, regretting, realizing the absolute end that had come between us. At the bottom of my heart I no more believed that there was an end between us, than that an end would come to the world. Had we not kissed one another, had we not achieved an atmosphere of whispering nearness, breached our virgin shyness with one another? Of course she was mine, of course I was hers, and separations and final quarrels and harshness and distance were no more than flourishes upon that eternal fact. So at least I felt the thing, however I shaped my thoughts.

Whenever my imagination got to work as that week drew to its close, she came in as a matter of course, I thought of her recurrently all day and dreamt of her at night. On Saturday night I dreamt of her very vividly. Her face was flushed and wet with tears, her hair a little disordered, and when I spoke to her she turned away. In some manner this dream left in my mind a feeling of distress and anxiety. In the morning I had a raging thirst to see her.

That Sunday my mother wanted me to go to church very particularly. She had a double reason for that; she thought that it would certainly exercise a favourable influence upon my search for a situation throughout the next week, and in addition Mr Gabbitas, with a certain mystery behind his glasses, had promised to see what he could do for me, and she wanted to keep him up to that promise. I half consented, and then my desire for Nettie took hold of me. I told my mother I wasn't going to church, and set off about eleven to walk the seventeen miles to Checkshill.

It greatly intensified the fatigue of that long tramp that the sole of my boot presently split at the toe, and after I had cut the flapping portion off, a nail worked through and began to torment me. However, the boot looked all right after that operation and gave no audible hint of my discomfort. I got some bread and cheese at a little inn on the way, and was in Checkshill park about four. I did not go by the road past the house and so round to the gardens, but cut over the crest beyond the second keeper's cottage, along a path Nettie used to call her own. It was a mere deer track. It led up a miniature valley and through a pretty dell in which we had been accustomed to meet, and so through the hollies and along a narrow path close by the wall of the shrubbery to the gardens. In my memory that walk through the park before I came upon Nettie stands out very vividly. The long tramp before it is foreshortened to a mere effect of dusty road and painful boot, but the bracken valley and sudden tumult of doubts and unwonted expectations that came to me, stands out now as something significant, as something unforgettable, something essential to the meaning of all that followed. Where should I meet her? What would she say? I had asked these questions before and found an answer. Now they came again with a trail of fresh implications and I had no answer for them at all. As I approached Nettie she ceased to be the mere butt of my egotistical self-projection, the custodian of my sexual pride, and drew together and became over and above this a personality of her own, a personality and a mystery, a sphinx I had evaded only to meet again.

I find a little difficulty in describing the quality of the old-world love-making so that it may be understandable now.

We young people had practically no preparation at all for the stir and emotions of adolescence. Towards the young the world maintained a conspiracy of stimulating silences. There came no initiation. There were books, stories of a curiously conventional kind that insisted on certain qualities in every love affair and greatly intensified one's natural desire for them, perfect trust, perfect loyalty, lifelong devotion. Much of the complex essentials of love were altogether hidden. One read these things, got accidental glimpses of this and that, wondered and forgot, and so one grew. Then strange emotions, novel alarming desires, dreams strangely charged with feeling; an inexplicable impulse of self-abandonment began to tickle queerly amongst the familiar purely egotistical and materialistic things of boyhood and girlhood. We were like misguided travellers who had camped in the dry bed of a tropical river. Presently we were knee deep and neck deep in the flood. Our beings were suddenly going out from ourselves seeking other beings – we knew not why. This novel craving for abandonment to some one of the other sex, bore us away. We were ashamed and full of desire. We kept the thing a guilty secret, and were resolved to satisfy it against all the world. In this state it was we drifted in the most accidental way against some other blindly seeking creature, and linked like nascent atoms.

We were obsessed by the books we read, by all the talk about us that once we had linked ourselves we were linked for life. Then afterwards we discovered that other was also an egotism, a thing of ideas and impulses, that failed to correspond with ours.

So it was, I say, with the young of my class and most of the young people in our world. So it came about that I sought Nettie on the Sunday afternoon and suddenly came upon her, light bodied, slenderly feminine, hazel eyed, with her soft sweet young face under the shady brim of her hat of straw, the pretty Venus I had resolved should be wholly and exclusively mine.

There, all unaware of me still, she stood, my essential feminine, the embodiment of the inner thing in life for me – and moreover an unknown other, a person like myself.

She held a little book in her hand, open as if she were walking along and reading it. That chanced to be her pose, but indeed she was standing quite still, looking away towards the grey and lichenous shrubbery wall and, as I think now, listening. Her lips were a little apart, curved to that faint, sweet shadow of a smile.

Section 3

I recall with a vivid precision her queer start when she heard the rustle of my approaching feet, her surprise, her eyes almost of dismay for me. I could recollect, I believe, every significant word she spoke during our meeting, and most of what I said to her. At least, it seems I could, though indeed I may deceive myself. But I will not make the attempt. We were both too ill-educated to speak our full meanings, we stamped out our feelings with clumsy stereotyped phrases; you who are better taught would fail to catch our intention. The effect would be inanity. But our first words I may give you, because though they conveyed nothing to me at the time, afterwards they meant much.

'YOU, Willie!' she said.

'I have come,' I said – forgetting in the instant all the elaborate things I had intended to say. 'I thought I would surprise you—'

'Surprise me?'

'Yes.'

She stared at me for a moment. I can see her pretty face now as it looked at me – her impenetrable dear face. She laughed a queer little laugh and her colour went for a moment, and then so soon as she had spoken, came back again.

'Surprise me at what?' she said with a rising note.

I was too intent to explain myself to think of what might lie in that.

'I wanted to tell you,' I said, 'that I didn't mean quite ... the things I put in my letter.'

Section 4

When I and Nettie had been sixteen we had been just of an age and contemporaries altogether. Now we were a year and three-quarters older, and she – her metamorphosis was almost complete, and I was still only at the beginning of a man's long adolescence.

In an instant she grasped the situation. The hidden motives of her quick ripened little mind flashed out their intuitive scheme of action. She treated me with that neat perfection of understanding a young woman has for a boy.

'But how did you come?' she asked.

I told her I had walked.

'Walked!' In an instant she was leading me towards the gardens.

I MUST be tired. I must come home with her at once and sit down. Indeed it was near tea-time (the Stuarts had tea at the old-fashioned hour of five). Every one would be SO surprised to see me. Fancy walking! Fancy! But she supposed a man thought nothing of seventeen miles. When COULD I have started!

All the while, keeping me at a distance, without even the touch of her hand.

'But, Nettie! I came over to talk to you?'

'My dear boy! Tea first, if you please! And besides – aren't we talking?'

The 'dear boy' was a new note, that sounded oddly to me.

She quickened her pace a little.

'I wanted to explain—' I began.

Whatever I wanted to explain I had no chance to do so. I said a few discrepant things that she answered rather by her intonation than her words.

When we were well past the shrubbery, she slackened a little in her urgency, and so we came along the slope under the beeches to the garden. She kept her bright, straightforward-looking girlish eyes on me as we went; it seemed she did so all the time, but now I know, better than I did then, that every now and then she glanced over me and behind me towards the shrubbery. And all the while, behind her quick breathless inconsecutive talk she was thinking.

Her dress marked the end of her transition.

Can I recall it?

Not, I am afraid, in the terms a woman would use. But her bright brown hair, which had once flowed down her back in a jolly pig-tail tied with a bit of scarlet ribbon, was now caught up into an intricacy of pretty curves above her little ear and cheek, and the soft long lines of her neck; her white dress had descended to her feet; her slender waist, which had once been a mere geographical expression, an imaginary line like the equator, was now a thing of flexible beauty. A year ago she had been a pretty girl's face sticking out from a little unimportant frock that was carried upon an extremely active and efficient pair of brown-stockinged legs. Now there was coming a strange new body that flowed beneath her clothes with a sinuous insistence. Every movement, and particularly the novel droop of her hand and arm to the unaccustomed skirts she gathered about her, and a graceful forward inclination that had come to her, called softly to my eyes. A very fine scarf – I suppose you would call it a scarf – of green gossamer, that some new wakened instinct had told her to fling about her shoulders, clung now closely to the young undulations of her body, and now streamed fluttering

37

out for a moment in a breath of wind, and like some shy independent tentacle with a secret to impart, came into momentary contact with my arm.

She caught it back and reproved it.

We went through the green gate in the high garden wall. I held it open for her to pass through, for this was one of my restricted stock of stiff politenesses, and then for a second she was near touching me. So we came to the trim array of flower-beds near the head gardener's cottage and the vistas of 'glass' on our left. We walked between the box edgings and beds of begonias and into the shadow of a yew hedge within twenty yards of that very pond with the gold-fish, at whose brim we had plighted our vows, and so we came to the wistaria-smothered porch.

The door was wide open, and she walked in before me. 'Guess who has come to see us!' she cried.

Her father answered indistinctly from the parlour, and a chair creaked. I judged he was disturbed in his nap.

'Mother!' she called in her clear young voice. 'Puss!'

Puss was her sister.

She told them in a marvelling key that I had walked all the way from Clayton, and they gathered about me and echoed her notes of surprise.

'You'd better sit down, Willie,' said her father; 'now you have got here. How's your mother?'

He looked at me curiously as he spoke.

He was dressed in his Sunday clothes, a sort of brownish tweeds, but the waistcoat was unbuttoned for greater comfort in his slumbers. He was a brown-eyed ruddy man, and I still have now in my mind the bright effect of the red-golden hairs that started out from his cheek to flow down into his beard. He was short but strongly built, and his beard and moustache were the biggest things about him. She had taken all the possibility of beauty he possessed, his clear skin, his bright hazel-brown eyes, and wedded them to a certain quickness she got from her mother. Her mother I remember as a sharp-eyed woman of great activity; she seems to me now to have been perpetually bringing in or taking out meals or doing some such service, and to me – for my mother's sake and my own – she was always welcoming and kind. Puss was a youngster of fourteen perhaps, of whom a hard bright stare, and a pale skin like her mother's, are the chief traces on my memory. All these people were very kind to me, and among them there was a common recognition, sometimes very agreeably finding expression, that I was – 'clever'. They all stood about me as if they were a little at a loss.

'Sit down!' said her father. 'Give him a chair, Puss.'

We talked a little stiffly – they were evidently surprised by my sudden apparition, dusty, fatigued and white faced; but Nettie did not remain to keep the conversation going.

'There!' she cried suddenly, as if she were vexed. 'I declare!' and she darted out of the room.

'Lord! what a girl it is!' said Mrs Stuart. 'I don't know what's come to her.'

It was half an hour before Nettie came back. It seemed a long time to me, and yet she had been running, for when she came in again she was out of breath. In the meantime, I had thrown out casually that I had given up my place at Rawdon's. 'I can do better than that,' I said.

'I left my book in the dell,' she said, panting. 'Is tea ready?' and that was her apology ...

We didn't shake down into comfort even with the coming of the tea-things. Tea at the gardener's cottage was a serious meal, with a big cake and little cakes, and preserves and fruit, a fine spread upon a table. You must imagine me, sullen, awkward, and preoccupied, perplexed by the something that was inexplicably unexpected in Nettie, saying little, and glowering across the cake at her, and all the eloquence I had been concentrating for the previous twenty-four hours, miserably lost somewhere in the back of my mind. Nettie's father tried to set me talking; he had a liking for my gift of ready speech, for his own ideas came with difficulty, and it pleased and astonished him to hear me pouring out my views. Indeed, over there I was, I think, even more talkative than with Parload, though to the world at large I was a shy young lout. 'You ought to write it out for the newspapers,' he used to say. 'That's what you ought to do. I never heard such nonsense.'

Or, 'You've got the gift of the gab, young man. We ought to ha' made a lawyer of you.'

But that afternoon, even in his eyes, I didn't shine. Failing any other stimulus, he reverted to my search for a situation, but even that did not engage me.

Section 5

For a long time I feared I should have to go back to Clayton without another word to Nettie, she seemed insensible to the need I felt for a talk with her, and I was thinking even of a sudden demand for that before them all. It was a transparent manoeuvre of her mother's who had been watching my face, that sent us out at last together to do something – I forget now what – in one of the greenhouses. Whatever that little mission may have been it was the merest, most barefaced excuse, a door to shut, or a window to close, and I don't think it got done.

Nettie hesitated and obeyed. She led the way through one of the hot-houses. It was a low, steamy, brick-floored alley between staging that bore a close crowd of pots and ferns, and behind big branching plants that were spread and nailed overhead so as to make an impervious cover of leaves, and in that close green privacy she stopped and turned on me suddenly like a creature at bay. 'Isn't the maidenhair fern lovely?' she said, and looked at me with eyes that said, 'NOW.'

'Nettie,' I began, 'I was a fool to write to you as I did.'

She startled me by the assent that flashed out upon her face. But she said nothing, and stood waiting.

'Nettie,' I plunged, 'I can't do without you. I – I love you.'

'If you loved me,' she said trimly, watching the white fingers she plunged among the green branches of a selaginella, 'could you write the things you do to me?'

'I don't mean them,' I said. 'At least not always.'

I thought really they were very good letters, and that Nettie was stupid to think otherwise, but I was for the moment clearly aware of the impossibility of conveying that to her.

'You wrote them.'

'But then I tramp seventeen miles to say I don't mean them.'

'Yes. But perhaps you do.'

I think I was at a loss; then I said, not very clearly, 'I don't.'

'You think you – you love me, Willie. But you don't.'

'I do. Nettie! You know I do.'

For answer she shook her head.

I made what I thought was a most heroic plunge. 'Nettie,' I said, 'I'd rather have you than – than my own opinions.'

The selaginella still engaged her. 'You think so now,' she said.

I broke out into protestations.

'No,' she said shortly. 'It's different now.'

'But why should two letters make so much difference?' I said.

'It isn't only the letters. But it is different. It's different for good.'

She halted a little with that sentence, seeking her expression. She looked up abruptly into my eyes and moved, indeed slightly, but with the intimation that she thought our talk might end.

But I did not mean it to end like that.

'For good?' said I. 'No! . . . Nettie! Nettie! You don't mean that!'

'I do,' she said deliberately, still looking at me, and with all her pose conveying her finality. She seemed to brace herself for the outbreak that must follow.

Of course I became wordy. But I did not submerge her. She stood entrenched, firing her contradictions like guns into my scattered discursive attack. I remember that our talk took the absurd form of disputing whether I could be in love with her or not. And there was I, present in evidence, in a deepening and widening distress of soul because she could stand there, defensive, brighter and prettier than ever, and in some inexplicable way cut off from me and inaccessible.

You know, we had never been together before without little enterprises of endearment, without a faintly guilty, quite delightful excitement.

I pleaded, I argued. I tried to show that even my harsh and difficult letters came from my desire to come wholly into contact with her. I made exaggerated fine statements of the longing I felt for her when I was away, of the shock and misery of finding her estranged and cool. She looked at me, feeling the emotion of my speech and impervious to its ideas. I had no doubt – whatever poverty in my words, coolly written down now – that I was eloquent then. I meant most intensely what I said, indeed I was wholly concentrated upon it. I was set upon conveying to her with absolute sincerity my sense of distance, and the greatness of my desire. I toiled toward her painfully and obstinately through a jungle of words.

Her face changed very slowly – by such imperceptible degrees as when at dawn light comes into a clear sky. I could feel that I touched her, that her hardness was in some manner melting, her determination softening toward hesitations. The habit of an old familiarity lurked somewhere within her. But she would not let me reach her.

'No,' she cried abruptly, starting into motion.

She laid a hand on my arm. A wonderful new friendliness came into her voice. 'It's impossible, Willie. Everything is different now – everything. We made a mistake. We two young sillies made a mistake and everything is different for ever. Yes, yes.'

She turned about.

'Nettie!' cried I, and still protesting, pursued her along the narrow alley between the staging toward the hot-house door. I pursued her like an accusation, and she went before me like one who is guilty and ashamed. So I recall it now.

She would not let me talk to her again.

Yet I could see that my talk to her had altogether abolished the clear-cut distance of our meeting in the park. Ever and again I found her hazel eyes upon me. They expressed something novel – a surprise, as though she realized an unwonted relationship, and a sympathetic pity. And still – something defensive.

When we got back to the cottage, I fell talking rather more freely with her father about the nationalization of railways, and my spirits and temper had so far mended at the realization that I could still produce an effect upon Nettie, that I was even playful with Puss. Mrs Stuart judged from that that things were better with me than they were, and began to beam mightily.

But Nettie remained thoughtful and said very little. She was lost in perplexities I could not fathom, and presently she slipped away from us and went upstairs.

Section 6

I was, of course, too footsore to walk back to Clayton, but I had a shilling and a penny in my pocket for the train between Checkshill and Two-Mile Stone, and that much of the distance I proposed to do in the train. And when I got ready to go, Nettie amazed me by waking up to the most remarkable solicitude for me. I must, she said, go by the road. It was altogether too dark for the short way to the lodge gates.

I pointed out that it was moonlight. 'With the comet thrown in,' said old Stuart.

'No,' she insisted, 'you MUST go by the road.'

I still disputed.

She was standing near me. 'To please ME,' she urged, in a quick undertone, and with a persuasive look that puzzled me. Even in the moment I asked myself why should this please her?

I might have agreed had she not followed that up with, 'The hollies by the shrubbery are as dark as pitch. And there's the deer-hounds.'

'I'm not afraid of the dark,' said I. 'Nor of the deer-hounds, either.'

'But those dogs! Supposing one was loose!'

That was a girl's argument, a girl who still had to understand that fear is an overt argument only for her own sex. I thought too of those grisly lank brutes straining at their chains and the chorus they could make of a night when they heard belated footsteps along the edge of the Killing Wood, and the thought banished my wish to please her. Like most imaginative natures I was acutely capable of dreads and retreats, and constantly occupied with their suppression and concealment, and to refuse the short cut when it might appear that I did it on account of half a dozen almost certainly chained dogs was impossible.

So I set off in spite of her, feeling valiant and glad to be so easily brave, but a little sorry that she should think herself crossed by me.

A thin cloud veiled the moon, and the way under the beeches was dark and indistinct. I was not so preoccupied with my love-affairs as to neglect what I will confess was always my custom at night across that wild and lonely park. I made myself a club by fastening a big flint to one end of my twisted handkerchief and tying the other about my wrist, and with this in my pocket, went on comforted.

And it chanced that as I emerged from the hollies by the corner of the shrubbery I was startled to come unexpectedly upon a young man in evening dress smoking a cigar.

I was walking on turf, so that the sound I made was slight. He stood clear in the moonlight, his cigar glowed like a blood-red star, and it did not occur to me at the time that I advanced towards him almost invisibly in an impenetrable shadow.

'Hullo,' he cried, with a sort of amiable challenge. 'I'm here first!'

I came out into the light. 'Who cares if you are?' said I.

I had jumped at once to an interpretation of his words. I knew that there was an intermittent dispute between the House people and the villager public about the use of this track, and it is needless to say where my sympathies fell in that dispute.

'Eh?' he cried in surprise.

'Thought I would run away, I suppose,' said I, and came close up to him.

All my enormous hatred of his class had flared up at the sight of his costume, at the fancied challenge of his words. I knew him. He was Edward Verrall, son of the man who owned not only this great estate but more than half of Rawdon's pot-bank, and who had interests and possessions, collieries and rents, all over the district of the Four Towns. He was a gallant youngster, people said, and very clever. Young as he was there was talk of parliament for him; he had been a great success at the university, and he was being sedulously popularized among us. He took with a light confidence, as a matter of course, advantages that I would have faced the rack to get, and I firmly believed myself a better man than he. He was, as he stood there, a concentrated figure of all that filled me with bitterness. One day he had stopped in a motor outside our house, and I remember the thrill of rage with which I had noted the dutiful admiration in my mother's eyes as she peered through her blind at him. 'That's young Mr Verrall,' she said. 'They say he's very clever.'

'They would,' I answered. 'Damn them and him!'

But that is by the way.

He was clearly astonished to find himself face to face with a man. His note changed.

'Who the devil are YOU?' he asked.

My retort was the cheap expedient of re-echoing, 'Who the devil are you?'

'WELL,' he said.

'I'm coming along this path if I like,' I said. 'See? It's a public path – just as this used to be public land. You've stolen the land – you and yours, and now you want to steal the right of way. You'll ask us to get off the face of the earth next. I sha'n't oblige. See?'

I was shorter and I suppose a couple of years younger than he, but I had the improvised club in my pocket gripped ready, and I would have fought with him very cheerfully. But he fell a step backward as I came toward him.

'Socialist, I presume?' he said, alert and quiet and with the faintest note of badinage.

'One of many.'

'We're all socialists nowadays,' he remarked philosophically, 'and I haven't the faintest intention of disputing your right of way.'

'You'd better not,' I said.

'No!'

'No.'

He replaced his cigar, and there was a brief pause. 'Catching a train?' he threw out.

It seemed absurd not to answer. 'Yes,' I said shortly.

He said it was a pleasant evening for a walk.

I hovered for a moment and there was my path before me, and he stood aside. There seemed nothing to do but go on. 'Good night,' said he, as that intention took effect.

I growled a surly good-night.

I felt like a bombshell of swearing that must presently burst with some violence as I went on my silent way. He had so completely got the best of our encounter.

Section 7

There comes a memory, an odd intermixture of two entirely divergent things, that stands out with the intensest vividness.

As I went across the last open meadow, following the short cut to Checkshill station, I perceived I had two shadows.

The thing jumped into my mind and stopped its tumid flow for a moment. I remember the intelligent detachment of my sudden interest. I turned sharply, and stood looking at the moon and the great white comet, that the drift of the clouds had now rather suddenly unveiled.

The comet was perhaps twenty degrees from the moon. What a wonderful thing it looked floating there, a greenish-white apparition in the dark blue deeps! It looked brighter than the moon because it was smaller, but the shadow it cast, though clearer cut, was much fainter than the moon's shadow ... I went on noting these facts, watching my two shadows precede me.

I am totally unable to account for the sequence of my thoughts on this occasion. But suddenly, as if I had come on this new fact round a corner, the comet was out of my mind again, and I was face to face with an absolutely new idea. I wonder sometimes if the two shadows I cast, one with a sort of feminine faintness with regard to the other and not quite so tall, may not have suggested the word or the thought of an assignation to my mind. All that I have clear is that with the certitude of intuition I knew what it was that had brought the youth in evening dress outside the shrubbery. Of course! He had come to meet Nettie!

Once the mental process was started it took no time at all. The day which had been full of perplexities for me, the mysterious invisible thing that had held Nettie and myself apart, the unaccountable strange something in her manner, was revealed and explained.

I knew now why she had looked guilty at my appearance, what had brought her out that afternoon, why she had hurried me in, the nature of the 'book' she had run back to fetch, the reason why she had wanted me to go back by the high-road, and why she had pitied me. It was all in the instant clear to me.

You must imagine me a black little creature, suddenly stricken still – for a moment standing rigid – and then again suddenly becoming active with an impotent gesture, becoming audible with an inarticulate cry, with two little shadows mocking my dismay, and about this figure you must conceive a great wide space of moonlit grass, rimmed by the looming suggestion of distant trees – trees very low and faint and dim, and over it all the domed serenity of that wonderful luminous night.

For a little while this realization stunned my mind. My thoughts came to a pause, staring at my discovery. Meanwhile my feet and my previous direction carried me through the warm darkness to Checkshill station with its little lights, to the ticket-office window, and so to the train.

I remember myself as it were waking up to the thing – I was alone in one of the dingy 'third-class' compartments of that time – and the sudden nearly frantic insurgence of my rage. I stood up with the cry of an angry animal, and smote my fist with all my strength against the panel of wood before me. . . .

Curiously enough I have completely forgotten my mood after that for a little while, but I know that later, for a minute perhaps, I hung for a time out of the carriage with the door open, contemplating a leap from the train. It was to be a dramatic leap, and then I would go storming back to her, denounce her, overwhelm her; and I hung, urging myself to do it. I don't remember how it was I decided not to do this, at last, but in the end I didn't.

When the train stopped at the next station I had given up all thoughts of going back. I was sitting in the corner of the carriage with my bruised and wounded hand pressed under my arm, and still insensible to its pain, trying to think out clearly a scheme of action – action that should express the monstrous indignation that possessed me.

CHAPTER THE THIRD

The Revolver

Section 1

'That comet is going to hit the earth!'

So said one of the two men who got into the train and settled down.

'Ah!' said the other man.

'They do say that it is made of gas, that comet. We sha'n't blow up, shall us?' . . .

What did it matter to me?

I was thinking of revenge – revenge against the primary conditions of my being. I was thinking of Nettie and her lover. I was firmly resolved he should not have her – though I had to kill them both to prevent it. I did not care what else might happen, if only that end was ensured. All my thwarted passions had turned to rage. I would have accepted eternal torment that night without a second thought, to be certain of revenge. A hundred possibilities of action, a hundred stormy situations, a whirl of violent schemes, chased one another through my shamed, exasperated mind. The sole prospect I could endure was of some gigantic, inexorably cruel vindication of my humiliated self.

And Nettie? I loved Nettie still, but now with the intensest jealousy, with the keen, unmeasuring hatred of wounded pride, and baffled, passionate desire.

Section 2

As I came down the hill from Clayton Crest – for my shilling and a penny only permitted my travelling by train as far as Two-Mile Stone,

47

and thence I had to walk over the hill – I remember very vividly a little man with a shrill voice who was preaching under a gas-lamp against a hoarding to a thin crowd of Sunday evening loafers. He was a short man, bald, with a little fair curly beard and hair and watery blue eyes, and he was preaching that the end of the world drew near.

I think that is the first time I heard any one link the comet with the end of the world. He had got that jumbled up with international politics and prophecies from the Book of Daniel.

I stopped to hear him only for a moment or so. I do not think I should have halted at all but his crowd blocked my path, and the sight of his queer wild expression, the gesture of his upward-pointing finger, held me.

'There is the end of all your Sins and Follies,' he bawled. 'There! There is the Star of Judgments, the Judgments of the most High God! It is appointed unto all men to die – unto all men to die' – his voice changed to a curious flat chant – 'and after death, the Judgment! The Judgment!'

I pushed and threaded my way through the bystanders and went on, and his curious harsh flat voice pursued me. I went on with the thoughts that had occupied me before – where I could buy a revolver, and how I might master its use – and probably I should have forgotten all about him had he not taken a part in the hideous dream that ended the little sleep I had that night. For the most part I lay awake thinking of Nettie and her lover.

Then came three strange days – three days that seem now to have been wholly concentrated upon one business.

This dominant business was the purchase of my revolver. I held myself resolutely to the idea that I must either restore myself by some extraordinary act of vigour and violence in Nettie's eyes or I must kill her. I would not let myself fall away from that. I felt that if I let this matter pass, my last shred of pride and honour would pass with it, that for the rest of my life I should never deserve the slightest respect or any woman's love. Pride kept me to my purpose between my gusts of passion.

Yet it was not easy to buy that revolver.

I had a kind of shyness of the moment when I should have to face the shopman, and I was particularly anxious to have a story ready if he should see fit to ask questions why I bought such a thing. I determined to say I was going to Texas, and I thought it might prove useful there. Texas in those days had the reputation of a wild lawless land. As I knew nothing of calibre or impact, I wanted also to be able to ask with a steady face at what distance a man or woman could be killed by the weapon that might be offered me. I was pretty cool-headed in relation to such practical aspects of my affair. I had some little difficulty in finding a gunsmith. In Clayton there were some rook-rifles and so forth in a cycle shop, but the only revolvers these people had impressed me as being too small and toylike for my purpose. It was in a pawnshop window in the narrow High Street of Swathinglea that I found my choice, a reasonably clumsy and serious-looking implement ticketed 'As used in the American army'.

I had drawn out my balance from the savings bank, matter of two pounds and more, to make this purchase, and I found it at last a very easy transaction. The pawnbroker told me where I could get ammunition, and I went home that night with bulging pockets, an armed man.

The purchase of my revolver was, I say, the chief business of those days, but you must not think I was so intent upon it as to be insensible to the stirring things that were happening in the streets through which I went seeking the means to effect my purpose. They were full of murmurings: the whole region of the Four Towns scowled lowering from its narrow doors. The ordinary healthy flow of people going to work, people going about their business, was chilled and checked. Numbers of men stood about the streets in knots and groups, as corpuscles gather and catch in the blood-vessels in the opening stages of inflammation. The women looked haggard and worried. The iron-workers had refused the proposed reduction of their wages, and the lockout had begun. They were already at 'play'. The Conciliation Board was doing its best to keep the coal-miners and masters from a breach, but young Lord Redcar, the greatest of our coal owners and landlord of all Swathinglea and half Clayton, was taking a fine upstanding attitude that made the breach inevitable. He was a handsome young man, a gallant young man; his pride revolted at the idea of being dictated to by a 'lot of bally miners', and he meant, he said, to make a fight for it. The world had treated him sumptuously from his earliest years; the shares in the common stock of five thousand people had gone to pay for his handsome upbringing, and large, romantic, expensive ambitions filled his generously nurtured mind. He had early distinguished himself at Oxford by his scornful attitude towards democracy. There was something that appealed to the imagination in his fine antagonism to the crowd – on the one hand, was the brilliant young nobleman, picturesquely alone; on the other, the ugly, inexpressive multitude, dressed inelegantly in shop-clothes, under-educated, under-fed, envious, base, and with a wicked disinclination for work and a wicked appetite for the good things it could so rarely

49

get. For common imaginative purposes one left out the policeman from the design, the stalwart policeman protecting his lordship, and ignored the fact that while Lord Redcar had his hands immediately and legally on the workman's shelter and bread, they could touch him to the skin only by some violent breach of the law.

He lived at Lowchester House, five miles or so beyond Checkshill; but partly to show how little he cared for his antagonists, and partly no doubt to keep himself in touch with the negotiations that were still going on, he was visible almost every day in and about the Four Towns, driving that big motor car of his that could take him sixty miles an hour. The English passion for fair play one might have thought sufficient to rob this bold procedure of any dangerous possibilities, but he did not go altogether free from insult, and on one occasion at least an intoxi- cated Irish woman shook her fist at him. . . .

A dark, quiet crowd, that was greater each day, a crowd more than half women, brooded as a cloud will sometimes brood permanently upon a mountain crest, in the market-place outside the Clayton Town Hall, where the conference was held. . . .

I consider myself justified in regarding Lord Redcar's passing auto- mobile with a special animosity because of the leaks in our roof.

We held our little house on lease; the owner was a mean, saving old man named Pettigrew, who lived in a villa adorned with plaster images of dogs and goats, at Overcastle, and in spite of our specific agreement, he would do no repairs for us at all. He rested secure in my mother's timidity. Once, long ago, she had been behind-hand with her rent, with half of her quarter's rent, and he had extended the days of grace a month; her sense that some day she might need the same mercy again made her his abject slave. She was afraid even to ask that he should cause the roof to be mended for fear he might take offence. But one night the rain poured in on her bed and gave her a cold, and stained and soaked her poor old patchwork counterpane. Then she got me to compose an excessively polite letter to old Pettigrew, begging him as a favour to perform his legal obligations. It is part of the general imbecility of those days that such one-sided law as existed was a profound mystery to the common people, its provisions impossible to ascertain, its machinery impossible to set in motion. Instead of the clearly written code, the lucid statements of rules and principles that are now at the service of every one, the law was the muddle secret of the legal profession. Poor people, overworked people, had constantly to submit to petty wrongs because of the intolerable uncertainty not only of law but of cost, and of the demands upon time and energy, proceedings might make. There was indeed no justice for any one too poor to command a good solicitor's deference and loyalty; there was nothing but rough police protection and the magistrate's grudging or eccentric advice for the mass of the population. The civil law, in particular, was a mysterious upper-class weapon, and I can imagine no injustice that would have been sufficient to induce my poor old mother to appeal to it.

All this begins to sound incredible. I can only assure you that it was so.

But I, when I learned that old Pettigrew had been down to tell my mother all about his rheumatism, to inspect the roof, and to allege that nothing was needed, gave way to my most frequent emotion in those days, a burning indignation, and took the matter into my own hands. I wrote and asked him, with a withering air of technicality, to have the roof repaired 'as per agreement', and added, 'if not done in one week from now we shall be obliged to take proceedings.' I had not mentioned this high line of conduct to my mother at first, and so when old Pettigrew came down in a state of great agitation with my letter in his hand, she was almost equally agitated.

'How could you write to old Mr Pettigrew like that?' she asked me.

I said that old Pettigrew was a shameful old rascal, or words to that effect, and I am afraid I behaved in a very undutiful way to her when she said that she had settled everything with him – she wouldn't say how, but I could guess well enough – and that I was to promise her, promise her faithfully, to do nothing more in the matter. I wouldn't promise her.

And – having nothing better to employ me then – I presently went raging to old Pettigrew in order to put the whole thing before him in what I considered the proper light. Old Pettigrew evaded my illumination; he saw me coming up his front steps – I can still see his queer old nose and the crinkled brow over his eye and the little wisp of grey hair that showed over the corner of his window-blind – and he instructed his servant to put up the chain when she answered the door, and to tell me that he would not see me. So I had to fall back upon my pen.

Then it was, as I had no idea what were the proper 'proceedings' to take, the brilliant idea occurred to me of appealing to Lord Redcar as the ground landlord, and, as it were, our feudal chief, and pointing out to him that his security for his rent was depreciating in old Pettigrew's hands. I added some general observations on leaseholds, the taxation of ground rents, and the private ownership of the soil. And Lord Redcar, whose spirit revolted at democracy, and who cultivated a pert humiliating manner with his inferiors to show as much, earned my distinguished hatred for ever by causing his secretary to present his compliments to me, and his request that I would mind my own business and leave him to manage his. At which I was so greatly enraged that I first tore this note into minute innumerable pieces, and then dashed it dramatically all over the floor of my room – from which, to keep my mother from the job, I afterward had to pick it up labouriously on all-fours.

I was still meditating a tremendous retort, an indictment of all Lord Redcar's class, their manners, morals, economic and political crimes, when my trouble with Nettie arose to swamp all minor troubles. Yet, not so completely but that I snarled aloud when his lordship's motor-car whizzed by me, as I went about upon my long meandering quest for a weapon. And I discovered after a time that my mother had bruised her knee and was lame. Fearing to irritate me by bringing the thing before me again, she had set herself to move her bed out of the way of the drip without my help, and she had knocked her knee. All her poor furnishings, I discovered, were cowering now close to the peeling bedroom walls; there had come a vast discoloration of the ceiling, and a washing-tub was in occupation of the middle of her chamber. . . .

It is necessary that I should set these things before you, should give the key of inconvenience and uneasiness in which all things were arranged, should suggest the breath of trouble that stirred along the hot summer streets, the anxiety about the strike, the rumours and indignations, the gatherings and meetings, the increasing gravity of the policemen's faces, the combative headlines of the local papers, the knots of picketers who scrutinized any one who passed near the silent, smokeless forges, but in my mind, you must understand, such impressions came and went irregularly; they made a moving back-ground, changing undertones, to my preoccupation by that darkly shaping purpose to which a revolver was so imperative an essential.

Along the darkling streets, amidst the sullen crowds, the thought of Nettie, my Nettie, and her gentleman lover made ever a vivid inflammatory spot of purpose in my brain.

Section 3

It was three days after this – on Wednesday, that is to say – that the first of those sinister outbreaks occurred that ended in the bloody affair of Peacock Grove and the flooding out of the entire line of the Swathinglea collieries. It was the only one of these disturbances I was destined to see, and at most a mere trivial preliminary of that struggle.

The accounts that have been written of this affair vary very widely. To read them is to realize the extraordinary carelessness of truth that dishonoured the press of those latter days. In my bureau I have several files of the daily papers of the old time – I collected them, as a matter of fact – and three or four of about that date I have just this moment taken out and looked through to refresh my impression of what I saw. They lie before me – queer, shrivelled, incredible things; the cheap paper has already become brittle and brown and split along the creases, the ink faded or smeared, and I have to handle them with the utmost care when I glance among their raging headlines. As I sit here in this serene place, their quality throughout, their arrangement, their tone, their arguments and exhortations, read as though they came from drugged and drunken men. They give one the effect of faded bawling, of screams and shouts heard faintly in a little gramophone. .... It is only on Monday I find, and buried deep below the war news, that these publications contain any intimation that unusual happenings were forward in Clayton and Swathinglea.

What I saw was towards evening. I had been learning to shoot with my new possession. I had walked out with it four or five miles across a patch of moorland and down to a secluded little coppice full of blue-bells, halfway along the high-road between Leet and Stafford. Here I had spent the afternoon, experimenting and practising with careful deliberation and grim persistence. I had brought an old kite-frame of cane with me, that folded and unfolded, and each shot-hole I made I marked and numbered to compare with my other endeavours. At last I was satisfied that I could hit a playing-card at thirty paces nine times out of ten; the light was getting too bad for me to see my pencilled bull's-eye, and in that state of quiet moodiness that sometimes comes with hunger to passionate men, I returned by the way of Swathinglea towards my home.

The road I followed came down between banks of wretched-looking working-men's houses, in close-packed rows on either side, and took upon itself the role of Swathinglea High Street, where, at a lamp and a pillar-box, the steam-trams began. So far that dirty hot way had been unusually quiet and empty, but beyond the corner, where the first group of beershops clustered, it became populous. It was very quiet still, even the children were a little inactive, but there were a lot of people standing dispersedly in little groups, and with a general direction towards the gates of the Bantock Burden coalpit.

The place was being picketed, although at that time the miners were still nominally at work, and the conferences between masters and men still in session at Clayton Town Hall. But one of the men employed at the Bantock Burden pit, Jack Briscoe, was a socialist, and he had distinguished himself by a violent letter upon the crisis to the leading socialistic paper in England, *The Clarion*, in which he had adventured among the motives of Lord Redcar. The publication of this had been followed by instant dismissal. As Lord Redcar wrote a day or so later to the *Times* – I have that *Times*, I have all the London papers of the last month before the Change —

'The man was paid off and kicked out. Any self-respecting employer would do the same.' The thing had happened overnight, and the men did not at once take a clear line upon what was, after all, a very intricate and debatable occasion. But they came out in a sort of semiofficial strike from all Lord Redcar's collieries beyond the canal that besets Swathinglea. They did so without formal notice, committing a breach of contract by this sudden cessation. But in the long labour struggles of the old days the workers were constantly putting themselves in the wrong and committing illegalities through that overpowering craving for dramatic promptness natural to uneducated minds.

All the men had not come out of the Bantock Burden pit. Something was wrong there, an indecision if nothing else; the mine was still working, and there was a rumour that men from Durham had been held in readiness by Lord Redcar, and were already in the mine. Now, it is absolutely impossible to ascertain certainly how things stood at that time. The newspapers say this and that, but nothing trustworthy remains.

I believe I should have gone striding athwart the dark stage of that stagnant industrial drama without asking a question, if Lord Redcar had not chanced to come upon the scene about the same time as myself and incontinently end its stagnation.

He had promised that if the men wanted a struggle he would put up the best fight they had ever had, and he had been active all that afternoon in meeting the quarrel half way, and preparing as conspicuously as possible for the scratch force of 'blacklegs' – as we called them – who were, he said and we believed, to replace the strikers in his pits.

I was an eye-witness of the whole of the affair outside the Bantock Burden pit, and – I do not know what happened.

Picture to yourself how the thing came to me.

I was descending a steep, cobbled, excavated road between banked-up footways, perhaps six feet high, upon which, in a monotonous series, opened the living room doors of rows of dark, low cottages. The perspective of squat blue slate roofs and clustering chimneys drifted downward towards the irregular open space before the colliery –

a space covered with coaly, wheel-scarred mud, with a patch of weedy dump to the left and the colliery gates to the right. Beyond, the High Street with shops resumed again in good earnest and went on, and the lines of the steam-tramway that started out from before my feet, and were here shining and acutely visible with reflected skylight and here lost in a shadow, took up for one acute moment the greasy yellow irradiation of a newly lit gaslamp as they vanished round the bend. Beyond, spread a darkling marsh of homes, an infinitude of little smoking hovels, and emergent, meagre churches, public-houses, board schools, and other buildings amidst the prevailing chimneys of Swath-inglea. To the right, very clear and relatively high, the Bantock Burden pit-mouth was marked by a gaunt lattice bearing a great black wheel, very sharp and distinct in the twilight, and beyond, in an irregular perspective, were others following the lie of the seams. The general effect, as one came down the hill, was of a dark compressed life beneath a very high and wide and luminous evening sky, against which these pit-wheels rose. And ruling the calm spaciousness of that heaven was the great comet, now green-white, and wonderful for all who had eyes to see.

The fading afterglow of the sunset threw up all the contours and skyline to the west, and the comet rose eastward out of the pouring tumult of smoke from Bladden's forges. The moon had still to rise.

By this time the comet had begun to assume the cloudlike form still familiar through the medium of a thousand photographs and sketches. At first it had been an almost telescopic speck; it had brightened to the dimensions of the greatest star in the heavens; it had still grown, hour by hour, in its incredibly swift, its noiseless and inevitable rush upon our earth, until it had equalled and surpassed the moon. Now it was the most splendid thing this sky of earth has ever held. I have never seen a photograph that gave a proper idea of it. Never at any time did it assume the conventional tailed outline, comets are supposed to have. Astronomers talked of its double tail, one preceding it and one trailing behind it, but these were foreshortened to nothing, so that it had rather the form of a bellying puff of luminous smoke with an intenser, brighter heart. It rose a hot yellow colour, and only began to show its distinctive greenness when it was clear of the mists of the evening.

It compelled attention for a space. For all my earthly concentration of mind, I could but stare at it for a moment with a vague anticipation that, after all, in some way so strange and glorious an object must have significance, could not possibly be a matter of absolute indifference to the scheme and values of my life.

But how?

I thought of Parload. I thought of the panic and uneasiness that was spreading in this very matter, and the assurances of scientific men that the thing weighed so little – at the utmost a few hundred tons of thinly diffused gas and dust – that even were it to smite this earth fully, nothing could possibly ensue. And, after all, said I, what earthly significance has any one found in the stars?

Then, as one still descended, the houses and buildings rose up, the presence of those watching groups of people, the tension of the situation; and one forgot the sky.

Preoccupied with myself and with my dark dream about Nettie and my honour, I threaded my course through the stagnating threat of this gathering, and was caught unawares, when suddenly the whole scene flashed into drama. . . .

The attention of every one swung round with an irresistible magnetism towards the High Street, and caught me as a rush of waters might catch a wisp of hay. Abruptly the whole crowd was sounding one note. It was not a word, it was a sound that mingled threat and protest, something between a prolonged 'Ah!' and 'Ugh!' Then with a hoarse intensity of anger came a low heavy booing, 'Boo! boo – oo!' a note stupidly expressive of animal savagery. 'Toot, toot!' said Lord Redcar's automobile in ridiculous repartee. 'Toot, toot!' One heard it whizzing and throbbing as the crowd obliged it to slow down.

Everybody seemed in motion towards the colliery gates, I, too, with the others.

I heard a shout. Through the dark figures about me I saw the motor-car stop and move forward again, and had a glimpse of something writhing on the ground.

It was alleged afterwards that Lord Redcar was driving, and that he quite deliberately knocked down a little boy who would not get out of his way. It is asserted with equal confidence that the boy was a man who tried to pass across the front of the motor-car as it came slowly through the crowd, who escaped by a hair's breadth, and then slipped on the tram-rail and fell down. I have both accounts set forth, under screaming headlines, in two of these sere newspapers upon my desk. No one could ever ascertain the truth. Indeed, in such a blind tumult of passion, could there be any truth?

There was a rush forward, the horn of the car sounded, everything swayed violently to the right for perhaps ten yards or so, and there was a report like a pistol-shot.

For a moment every one seemed running away. A woman, carrying a shawl-wrapped child, blundered into me, and sent me reeling back.

Every one thought of firearms, but, as a matter of fact, something had gone wrong with the motor, what in those old-fashioned contrivances was called a backfire. A thin puff of bluish smoke hung in the air behind the thing. The majority of the people scattered back in a disorderly fashion, and left a clear space about the struggle that centred upon the motor-car.

The man or boy who had fallen was lying on the ground with no one near him, a black lump, an extended arm and two sprawling feet. The motor-car had stopped, and its three occupants were standing up. Six or seven black figures surrounded the car, and appeared to be holding on to it as if to prevent it from starting again; one – it was Mitchell, a well-known labour leader – argued in fierce low tones with Lord Redcar. I could not hear anything they said, I was not near enough. Behind me the colliery gates were open, and there was a sense of help coming to the motor-car from that direction.

There was an unoccupied muddy space for fifty yards, perhaps, between car and gate, and then the wheels and head of the pit rose black against the sky. I was one of a rude semicircle of people that hung as yet indeterminate in action about this dispute.

It was natural, I suppose, that my fingers should close upon the revolver in my pocket.

I advanced with the vaguest intentions in the world, and not so quickly but that several men hurried past me to join the little knot holding up the car.

Lord Redcar, in his big furry overcoat, towered up over the group about him; his gestures were free and threatening, and his voice loud. He made a fine figure there, I must admit; he was a big, fair, handsome young man with a fine tenor voice and an instinct for gallant effect. My eyes were drawn to him at first wholly. He seemed a symbol, a triumphant symbol, of all that the theory of aristocracy claims, of all that filled my soul with resentment. His chauffeur sat crouched together, peering at the crowd under his lordship's arm. But Mitchell showed as a sturdy figure also, and his voice was firm and loud.

'You've hurt that lad,' said Mitchell, over and over again. 'You'll wait here till you see if he's hurt.'

'I'll wait here or not as I please,' said Redcar; and to the chauffeur, 'Here! get down and look at it!'

'You'd better not get down,' said Mitchell; and the chauffeur stood bent and hesitating on the step.

The man on the back seat stood up, leant forward, and spoke to Lord Redcar, and for the first time my attention was drawn to him. It was young Verrall! His handsome face shone clear and fine in the green pallor of the comet.

I ceased to hear the quarrel that was raising the voice of Mitchell and Lord Redcar. This new fact sent them spinning into the background. Young Verrall!

It was my own purpose coming to meet me half way.

There was to be a fight here, it seemed certain to come to a scuffle, and here we were —

What was I to do? I thought very swiftly. Unless my memory cheats me, I acted with swift decision. My hand tightened on my revolver, and then I remembered it was unloaded. I had thought my course out in an instant. I turned round and pushed my way out of the angry crowd that was now surging back towards the motor-car.

It would be quiet and out of sight, I thought, among the dump heaps across the road, and there I might load unobserved . . .

A big young man striding forward with his fists clenched, halted for one second at the sight of me.

'What!' said he. 'Ain't afraid of them, are you?'

I glanced over my shoulder and back at him, was near showing him my pistol, and the expression changed in his eyes. He hung perplexed at me. Then with a grunt he went on.

I heard the voices growing loud and sharp behind me.

I hesitated, half turned towards the dispute, then set off running towards the heaps. Some instinct told me not to be detected loading. I was cool enough therefore to think of the aftermath of the thing I meant to do.

I looked back once again towards the swaying discussion – or was it a fight now? and then I dropped into the hollow, knelt among the weeds, and loaded with eager trembling fingers. I loaded one chamber, got up and went back a dozen paces, thought of possibilities, vacillated, returned and loaded all the others. I did it slowly because I felt a little clumsy, and at the end came a moment of inspection – had I forgotten any thing? And then for a few seconds I crouched before I rose, resisting the first gust of reaction against my impulse. I took thought, and for a moment that great green-white meteor overhead swam back into my conscious mind. For the first time then I linked it clearly with all the fierce violence that had crept into human life. I joined up that with what I meant to do. I was going to shoot young Verrall as it were under the benediction of that green glare. ·

But about Nettie?

I found it impossible to think out that obvious complication.

I came up over the heap again, and walked slowly back towards the wrangle.

Of course I had to kill him. . . .

Now I would have you believe I did not want to murder young Verrall at all at that particular time. I had not pictured such circumstances as these, I had never thought of him in connection with Lord Redcar and our black industrial world. He was in that distant other world of Checkshill, the world of parks and gardens, the world of sunlit emotions and Nettie. His appearance here was disconcerting. I was taken by surprise. I was too tired and hungry to think clearly, and the hard implication of our antagonism prevailed with me. In the tumult of my passed emotions I had thought constantly of conflicts, confrontations, deeds of violence, and now the memory of these things took possession of me as though they were irrevocable resolutions.

There was a sharp exclamation, the shriek of a woman, and the crowd came surging back. The fight had begun.

Lord Redcar, I believe, had jumped down from his car and felled Mitchell, and men were already running out to his assistance from the colliery gates.

I had some difficulty in shoving through the crowd; I can still remember very vividly being jammed at one time between two big men so that my arms were pinned to my sides, but all the other details are gone out of my mind until I found myself almost violently projected forward into the 'scrap'.

I blundered against the corner of the motor-car, and came round it face to face with young Verrall, who was descending from the back compartment. His face was touched with orange from the automobile's big lamps, which conflicted with the shadows of the comet light, and distorted him oddly. That effect lasted but an instant, but it put me out. Then he came a step forward, and the ruddy lights and queerness vanished.

I don't think he recognized me, but he perceived immediately I meant attacking. He struck out at once at me a haphazard blow, and touched me on the cheek.

Instinctively I let go of the pistol, snatched my right hand out of my pocket and brought it up in a belated parry, and then let out with my left full in his chest.

It sent him staggering, and as he went back I saw recognition mingle with astonishment in his face.

'You know me, you swine,' I cried and hit again.

Then I was spinning sideways, half-stunned, with a huge lump of a fist under my jaw. I had an impression of Lord Redcar as a great furry bulk, towering like some Homeric hero above the fray. I went down before him – it made him seem to rush up – and he ignored me further. His big flat voice counselled young Verrall—

'Cut, Teddy! It won't do. The picketa's got i'on bahs. . . .'

Feet swayed about me, and some hobnailed miner kicked my ankle and went stumbling. There were shouts and curses, and then everything had swept past me. I rolled over on my face and beheld the chauffeur, young Verrall and Lord Redcar – the latter holding up his long skirts of fur, and making a grotesque figure – one behind the other, in full bolt across a coldly comet-lit interval, towards the open gates of the colliery.

I raised myself up on my hands.

Young Verrall!

I had not even drawn my revolver – I had forgotten it. I was covered with coaly mud – knees, elbows, shoulders, back. I had not even drawn my revolver! . . .

A feeling of ridiculous impotence overwhelmed me. I struggled painfully to my feet.

I hesitated for a moment towards the gates of the colliery, and then went limping homeward, thwarted, painful, confused, and ashamed. I had not the heart nor desire to help in the wrecking and burning of Lord Redcar's motor.

Section 4

In the night, fever, pain, fatigue – it may be the indigestion of my supper of bread and cheese – roused me at last out of a hag-rid sleep to face despair. I was a soul lost amidst desolations and shame, dishonoured, evilly treated, hopeless. I raged against the God I denied, and cursed him as I lay.

And it was in the nature of my fever, which was indeed only half fatigue and illness, and the rest the disorder of passionate youth, that Nettie, a strangely distorted Nettie, should come through the brief dreams that marked the exhaustions of that vigil, to dominate my misery. I was sensible, with an exaggerated distinctness, of the intensity of her physical charm for me, of her every grace and beauty; she took to herself the whole gamut of desire in me and the whole gamut of pride. She, bodily, was my lost honour. It was not only loss but disgrace to lose her. She stood for life and all that was denied; she mocked me as a creature of failure and defeat. My spirit raised itself towards her, and then the bruise upon my jaw glowed with a dull heat, and I rolled in the mud again before my rivals.

There were times when something near madness took me, and I gnashed my teeth and dug my nails into my hands and ceased to curse and cry out only by reason of the insufficiency of words. And once towards dawn I got out of bed, and sat by my looking-glass with my revolver loaded in my hand. I stood up at last and put it carefully in my drawer and locked it – out of reach of any gusty impulse. After that I slept for a little while.

Such nights were nothing rare and strange in that old order of the world. Never a city, never a night the whole year round, but amidst those who slept were those who waked, plumbing the deeps of wrath and misery. Countless thousands there were so ill, so troubled, they agonized near to the very border-line of madness, each one the centre of a universe darkened and lost.

The next day I spent in gloomy lethargy.

I had intended to go to Checkshill that day, but my bruised ankle was too swollen for that to be possible. I sat indoors in the downstairs kitchen, with my foot bandaged, and mused darkly and read. My dear old mother waited on me, and her brown eyes watched me and wondered at my black silences, my frowning preoccupations. I had not told her how it was my ankle came to be bruised and my clothes muddy. She had brushed my clothes in the morning before I got up.

Ah well! Mothers are not treated in that way now. That I suppose must console me. I wonder how far you will be able to picture that dark, grimy, untidy room, with its bare deal table, its tattered wall paper, the saucepans and kettle on the narrow, cheap, but by no means economical range, the ashes under the fireplace, the rust-spotted steel fender on which my bandaged feet rested; I wonder how near you can come to seeing the scowling pale-faced hobbledehoy I was, unshaven and collarless, in the Windsor chair, and the little timid, dirty, devoted old woman who hovered about me with love peering out from her puckered eyelids ...

When she went out to buy some vegetables in the middle of the morning she got me a half-penny journal. It was just such a one as these upon my desk, only that the copy I read was damp from the press, and these are so dry and brittle, they crack if I touch them. I have a copy of the actual issue I read that morning; it was a paper called emphatically the *New Paper*, but everybody bought it and everybody called it the 'yell'. It was full that morning of stupendous news and still more stupendous headlines, so stupendous that for a little while I was roused from my egotistical broodings to wider interests. For it seemed that Germany and England were on the brink of war.

Of all the monstrous irrational phenomena of the former time, war was certainly the most strikingly insane. In reality it was probably far less mischievous than such quieter evil as, for example, the general acquiescence in the private ownership of land, but its evil consequences showed so plainly that even in those days of stifling confusion one marvelled at it. On no conceivable grounds was there any sense in modern war. Save for the slaughter and mangling of a multitude of people, the destruction of vast quantities of material, and the waste of innumerable units of energy, it effected nothing. The old war of savage and barbaric nations did at least change humanity, you assumed yourselves to be a superior tribe in physique and discipline, you demonstrated this upon your neighbours, and if successful you took their land and their women and perpetuated and enlarged your super-iority. The new war changed nothing but the colour of maps, the design of postage stamps, and the relationship of a few accidentally conspicuous individuals. In one of the last of these international epileptic fits, for example, the English, with much dysentery and bad poetry, and a few hundred deaths in battle, conquered the South African Boers at a gross cost of about three thousand pounds per head – they could have bought the whole of that preposterous imitation of a nation for a tenth of that sum – and except for a few substitutions of personalities, this group of partially corrupt officials in the place of that, and so forth, the permanent change was altogether insignificant. (But an excitable young man in Austria committed suicide when at length the Transvaal ceased to be a 'nation'.) Men went through the seat of that war after it was all over, and found humanity unchanged, except for a general impoverishment, and the convenience of an un-limited supply of empty ration tins and barbed wire and cartridge cases – unchanged and resuming with a slight perplexity all its old habits and misunderstandings, the nigger still in his slum-like kraal, the white in his ugly ill-managed shanty ...

But we in England saw all these things, or did not see them, through the mirage of the *New Paper*, in a light of mania. All my adolescence from fourteen to seventeen went to the music of that monstrous resonating futility, the cheering, the anxieties, the songs and the waving of flags, the wrongs of generous Buller and the glorious heroism of De Wet – who ALWAYS got away; that was the great point about the heroic De Wet – and it never occurred to us that the total population we fought against was less than half the number of those who lived cramped ignoble lives within the compass of the Four Towns.

But before and after that stupid conflict of stupidities, a greater antagonism was coming into being, was slowly and quietly defining itself as a thing inevitable, sinking now a little out of attention only to resume more emphatically, now flashing into some acute definitive expression and now percolating and pervading some new region of thought, and that was the antagonism of Germany and Great Britain.

When I think of that growing proportion of readers who belong entirely to the new order, who are growing up with only the vaguest early memories of the old world, I find the greatest difficulty in writing down the unintelligible confusions that were matter of fact to their fathers.

Here were we British, forty-one millions of people, in a state of almost indescribably aimless, economic and moral muddle that we had neither the courage, the energy, nor the intelligence to improve, that most of us had hardly the courage to think about, and with our affairs hopelessly entangled with the entirely different confusions of three hundred and fifty million other persons scattered about the globe, and here were the Germans over against us, fifty-six millions, in a state of confusion no whit better than our own, and the noisy little creatures who directed papers and wrote books and gave lectures, and generally in that time of world-dementia pretended to be the national mind, were busy in both countries, with a sort of infernal unanimity, exhorting – and not only exhorting but successfully per-suading – the two peoples to divert such small common store of material, moral and intellectual energy as either possessed, into the purely destructive and wasteful business of war. And – I have to tell you these things even if you do not believe them, because they are vital to my story – there was not a man alive who could have told you of any real permanent benefit, of anything whatever to counterbalance the obvious waste and evil, that would result from a war between England and Germany, whether England shattered Germany or was smashed and overwhelmed, or whatever the end might be.

The thing was, in fact, an enormous irrational obsession, it was, in the microcosm of our nation, curiously parallel to the egotistical wrath and jealousy that swayed my individual microcosm. It measured the excess of common emotion over the common intelligence, the legacy of inordinate passion we have received from the brute from which we came. Just as I had become the slave of my own surprise and anger and went hither and thither with a loaded revolver, seeking and intending vague fluctuating crimes, so these two nations went about the earth, hot eared and muddle headed, with loaded navies and armies terribly ready at hand. Only there was not even a Nettie to justify their stupidity. There was nothing but quiet imaginary thwarting on either side.

And the press was the chief instrument that kept these two huge multitudes of people directed against one another.

The press – those newspapers that are now so strange to us – like the 'Empires', the 'Nations', the Trusts, and all the other great monstrous shapes of that extraordinary time – was in the nature of an unanticipated accident. It had happened, as weeds happen in abandoned gardens, just as all our world has happened, – because there was no clear Will in the world to bring about anything better. Towards the end this 'press' was almost entirely under the direction of youngish men of that eager, rather unintelligent type, that is never able to detect itself aimless, that pursues nothing with incredible pride and zeal, and if you would really understand this mad era the comet brought to an end, you must keep in mind that every phase in the production of these queer old things was pervaded by a strong aimless energy and happened in a concentrated rush.

Let me describe to you, very briefly, a newspaper day.

Figure first, then, a hastily erected and still more hastily designed building in a dirty, paper-littered back street of old London, and a number of shabbily dressed men coming and going in this with projectile swiftness, and within this factory companies of printers, tensely active with nimble fingers – they were always speeding up the printers – ply their type-setting machines, and cast and arrange masses of metal in a sort of kitchen inferno, above which, in a beehive of little brightly lit rooms, dishevelled men sit and scribble. There is a throbbing of telephones and a clicking of telegraph needles, a rushing of messengers, a running to and fro of heated men, clutching proofs and copy. Then begins a clatter roar of machinery catching the infection, going faster and faster, and whizzing and banging – engineers, who have never had time to wash since their birth, flying about with oil-cans, while paper runs off its rolls with a shudder of haste. The proprietor you must suppose arriving explosively on a swift motor-car, leaping out before the thing is at a standstill, with letters and documents clutched in his hand, rushing in, resolute to 'hustle', getting wonderfully in everybody's way. At the sight of him even the messenger boys who are waiting, get up and scamper to and fro. Sprinkle your vision with collisions, curses, incoherencies. You imagine all the parts of this complex lunatic machine working hysterically toward a crescendo of haste and excitement as the night wears on. At last the only things that seem to travel slowly in all those tearing vibrating premises are the hands of the clock.

Slowly things draw on toward publication, the consummation of all those stresses. Then in the small hours, into the now dark and deserted streets comes a wild whirl of carts and men, the place spurts paper at every door, bales, heaps, torrents of papers, that are snatched and flung about in what looks like a free fight, and off with a rush and clatter east, west, north and south. The interest passes outwardly; the men from the little rooms are going homeward, the printers disperse yawning, the roaring presses slacken. The paper exists. Distribution follows manufacture, and we follow the bundles.

Our vision becomes a vision of dispersal. You see those bundles hurling into stations, catching trains by a hair's breadth, speeding on their way, breaking up, smaller bundles of them hurled with a fierce accuracy out upon the platforms that rush by, and then everywhere a division of these smaller bundles into still smaller bundles, into dispersing parcels, into separate papers, and the dawn happens unnoticed amidst a great running and shouting of boys, a shoving through letter slots, openings of windows, spreading out upon book-stalls. For the space of a few hours you must figure the whole country dotted white with rustling papers – placards everywhere vociferating the hurried lie for the day; men and women in trains, men and women eating and reading, men by study-fenders, people sitting up in bed, mothers and sons and daughters waiting for father to finish – a million scattered people reading – reading headlong – or feverishly ready to read. It is just as if some vehement jet had sprayed that white foam of papers over the surface of the land . . .

And then you know, wonderfully gone – gone utterly, vanished as foam might vanish upon the sand.

Nonsense! The whole affair a noisy paroxysm of nonsense, unreasonable excitement, witless mischief, and waste of strength – signifying nothing. . . .

And one of those white parcels was the paper I held in my hands, as I sat with a bandaged foot on the steel fender in that dark underground kitchen of my mother's, clean roused from my personal troubles by the yelp of the headlines. She sat, sleeves tucked up from her ropy arms, peeling potatoes as I read.

It was like one of a flood of disease germs that have invaded a body, that paper. There I was, one corpuscle in the big amorphous body of the English community, one of forty-one million such corpuscles and, for all my preoccupations, these potent headlines, this paper ferment, caught me and swung me about. And all over the country that day, millions read as I read, and came round into line with me, under the same magnetic spell, came round – how did we say it? – Ah! – 'to face the foe'.

The comet had been driven into obscurity overleaf. The column headed 'Distinguished Scientist says Comet will Strike our Earth. Does it Matter?' went unread. 'Germany' – I usually figured this mythical malignant creature as a corseted stiff-moustached Emperor enhanced by heraldic black wings and a large sword – had insulted our flag. That was the message of the *New Paper*, and the monster towered over me, threatening fresh outrages, visibly spitting upon my faultless country's colours. Somebody had hoisted a British flag on the right bank of some tropical river I had never heard of before, and a drunken German officer under ambiguous instructions had torn it down. Then one of the convenient abundant natives of the country, a British subject indisputably, had been shot in the leg. But the facts were by no means clear. Nothing was clear except that we were not going to stand any nonsense from Germany. Whatever had or had not happened we meant to have an apology for, and apparently they did not mean apologizing.

'HAS WAR COME AT LAST?'

That was the headline. One's heart leapt to assent. ...

There were hours that day when I clean forgot Nettie, in dreaming of battles and victories by land and sea, of shell fire, and entrenchments, and the heaped slaughter of many thousands of men.

But the next morning I started for Checkshill, started, I remember, in a curiously hopeful state of mind, oblivious of comets, strikes, and wars.

Section 5

You must understand that I had no set plan of murder when I walked over to Checkshill. I had no set plan of any sort. There was a great confusion of dramatically conceived intentions in my head, scenes of threatening and denunciation and terror, but I did not mean to kill. The revolver was to turn upon my rival my disadvantage in age and physique. ...

But that was not it really! The revolver! – I took the revolver because I had the revolver and was a foolish young lout. It was a dramatic sort of thing to take. I had, I say, no plan at all.

Ever and again during that second trudge to Checkshill I was irradiated with a novel unreasonable hope. I had awakened in the morning with the hope, it may have been the last unfaded trail of some obliterated dream, that after all Nettie might relent towards me, that her heart was kind towards me in spite of all that I imagined had happened. I even thought it possible that I might have misinterpreted

66

what I had seen. Perhaps she would explain everything. My revolver was in my pocket for all that.

I limped at the outset, but after the second mile my ankle warmed to forgetfulness, and the rest of the way I walked well. Suppose, after all, I was wrong?

I was still debating that, as I came through the park. By the corner of the paddock near the keeper's cottage, I was reminded by some belated blue hyacinths of a time when I and Nettie had gathered them together. It seemed impossible that we could really have parted ourselves for good and all. A wave of tenderness flowed over me, and still flooded me as I came through the little dell and drew towards the hollies. But there the sweet Nettie of my boy's love faded, and I thought of the new Nettie of desire and the man I had come upon in the moonlight, I thought of the narrow, hot purpose that had grown so strongly out of my springtime freshness, and my mood darkened to night.

I crossed the beech wood and came towards the gardens with a resolute and sorrowful heart. When I reached the green door in the garden wall I was seized for a space with so violent a trembling that I could not grip the latch to lift it, for I no longer had any doubt how this would end. That trembling was succeeded by a feeling of cold, and whiteness, and self-pity. I was astonished to find myself grimacing, to feel my cheeks wet, and thereupon I gave way completely to a wild passion of weeping. I must take just a little time before the thing was done. ... I turned away from the door and stumbled for a little distance, sobbing loudly, and lay down out of sight among the bracken, and so presently became calm again. I lay there some time. I had half a mind to desist, and then my emotion passed like the shadow of a cloud, and I walked very coolly into the gardens.

Through the open door of one of the glass houses I saw old Stuart. He was leaning against the staging, his hands in his pockets, and so deep in thought he gave no heed to me.

I hesitated and went on towards the cottage, slowly.

Something struck me as unusual about the place, but I could not tell at first what it was. One of the bedroom windows was open, and the customary short blind, with its brass upper rail partly unfastened, drooped obliquely across the vacant space. It looked negligent and odd, for usually everything about the cottage was conspicuously trim.

The door was standing wide open, and everything was still. But giving that usually orderly hall an odd look – it was about half-past two in the afternoon – was a pile of three dirty plates, with used knives and forks upon them, on one of the hall chairs.

I went into the hall, looked into either room, and hesitated.

Then I fell to upon the door-knocker and gave a loud rat-tattoo, and followed this up with an amiable 'Hel-lo!'

For a time no one answered me, and I stood listening and expectant, with my fingers about my weapon. Some one moved about upstairs presently, and was still again. The tension of waiting seemed to brace my nerves.

I had my hand on the knocker for the second time, when Puss appeared in the doorway.

For a moment we remained staring at one another without speaking. Her hair was dishevelled, her face dirty, tear-stained, and irregularly red. Her expression at the sight of me was pure astonishment. I thought she was about to say something, and then she had darted away out of the house again.

'I say, Puss!' I said. 'Puss!'

I followed her out of the door. 'Puss! What's the matter? Where's Nettie?'

She vanished round the corner of the house.

I hesitated, perplexed whether I should pursue her. What did it all mean? Then I heard some one upstairs.

'Willie!' cried the voice of Mrs Stuart. 'Is that you?'

'Yes,' I answered. 'Where's every one? Where's Nettie? I want to have a talk with her.'

She did not answer, but I heard her dress rustle as she moved. I judged she was upon the landing overhead.

I paused at the foot of the stairs, expecting her to appear and come down.

Suddenly came a strange sound, a rush of sounds, words jumbled and hurrying, confused and shapeless, borne along upon a note of throaty distress that at last submerged the words altogether and ended in a wail. Except that it came from a woman's throat it was exactly the babbling sound of a weeping child with a grievance. 'I can't,' she said, 'I can't,' and that was all I could distinguish. It was to my young ears the strangest sound conceivable from a kindly motherly little woman, whom I had always thought of chiefly as an unparalleled maker of cakes. It frightened me. I went upstairs at once in a state of infinite alarm, and there she was upon the landing, leaning forward over the top of the chest of drawers beside her open bedroom door, and weeping. I never saw such weeping. One thick strand of black hair had escaped, and hung with a spiral twist down her back; never before had I noticed that she had grey hairs.

As I came up upon the landing her voice rose again. 'Oh that

I should have to tell you, Willie! Oh that I should have to tell you!' She dropped her head again, and a fresh gust of tears swept all further words away.

I said nothing, I was too astonished; but I drew nearer to her, and waited. . . .

I never saw such weeping; the extraordinary wetness of her dripping handkerchief abides with me to this day.

'That I should have lived to see this day!' she wailed. 'I had rather a thousand times she was struck dead at my feet.'

I began to understand.

'Mrs Stuart,' I said, clearing my throat; 'what has become of Nettie?'

'That I should have lived to see this day!' she said by way of reply.

I waited till her passion abated.

There came a lull. I forgot the weapon in my pocket. I said nothing, and suddenly she stood erect before me, wiping her swollen eyes. 'Willie,' she gulped, 'she's gone!'

'Nettie?'

'Gone! . . . Run away. . . . Run away from her home. Oh, Willie, Willie! The shame of it! The sin and shame of it!'

She flung herself upon my shoulder, and clung to me, and began again to wish her daughter lying dead at our feet.

'There, there,' said I, and all my being was a-tremble. 'Where has she gone?' I said as softly as I could.

But for the time she was preoccupied with her own sorrow, and I had to hold her there, and comfort her with the blackness of finality spreading over my soul.

'Where has she gone?' I asked for the fourth time.

'I don't know – we don't know. And oh, Willie, she went out yesterday morning! I said to her, "Nettie," I said to her, "you're mighty fine for a morning call." "Fine clo's for a fine day," she said, and that was her last words to me! – Willie! – the child I suckled at my breast!'

'Yes, yes. But where has she gone?' I said.

She went on with sobs, and now telling her story with a sort of fragmentary hurry: 'She went out bright and shining, out of this house for ever. She was smiling, Willie – as if she was glad to be going. ('Glad to be going,' I echoed with soundless lips.) "You're mighty fine for the morning," I says; "mighty fine." "Let the girl be pretty," says her father, "while she's young!" And somewhere she'd got a parcel of her things hidden to pick up, and she was going off – out of this house for ever!'

She became quiet.

'Let the girl be pretty,' she repeated; 'let the girl be pretty while she's young. . . . Oh! how can we go on LIVING, Willie? He doesn't show it, but he's like a stricken beast. He's wounded to the heart. She was always his favourite. He never seemed to care for Puss like he did for her. And she's wounded him—'

'Where has she gone?' I reverted at last to that.

'We don't know. She leaves her own blood, she trusts herself – Oh, Willie, it'll kill me! I wish she and me together were lying in our graves.'

'But' – I moistened my lips and spoke slowly – 'she may have gone to marry.'

'If that was so! I've prayed to God it might be so, Willie. I've prayed that he'd take pity on her – him, I mean, she's with.'

I jerked out: 'Who's that?'

'In her letter, she said he was a gentleman. She did say he was a gentleman.'

'In her letter. Has she written? Can I see her letter?'

'Her father took it.'

'But if she writes – When did she write?'

'It came this morning.'

'But where did it come from? You can tell—'

'She didn't say. She said she was happy. She said love took one like a storm—'

'Curse that! Where is her letter? Let me see it. And as for this gentleman—'

She stared at me.

'You know who it is.'

'Willie!' she protested.

'You know who it is, whether she said or not?' Her eyes made a mute unconfident denial.

'Young Verrall?'

She made no answer. 'All I could do for you, Willie,' she began presently.

'Was it young Verrall?' I insisted.

For a second, perhaps, we faced one another in stark understanding. ... Then she plumped back to the chest of drawers, and her wet pocket-handkerchief, and I knew she sought refuge from my relentless eyes.

My pity for her vanished. She knew it was her mistress's son as well as I! And for some time she had known, she had felt.

I hovered over her for a moment, sick with amazed disgust. I suddenly bethought me of old Stuart, out in the greenhouse, and turned and went downstairs. As I did so, I looked up to see Mrs Stuart moving droopingly and lamely back into her own room.

Section 6

Old Stuart was pitiful.

I found him still inert in the greenhouse where I had first seen him. He did not move as I drew near him; he glanced at me, and then stared hard again at the flowerpots before him.

'Eh, Willie,' he said, 'this is a black day for all of us.'

'What are you going to do?' I asked.

'The missus takes on so,' he said. 'I came out here.'

'What do you mean to do?'

'What IS a man to do in such a case?'

'Do!' I cried, 'why – Do!'

'He ought to marry her,' he said.

'By God, yes!' I cried. 'He must do that anyhow.'

'He ought to. It's – it's cruel. But what am I to do? Suppose he won't? Likely he won't. What then?'

He drooped with an intensified despair.

'Here's this cottage,' he said, pursuing some contracted argument. 'We've lived here all our lives, you might say. . . . Clear out. At my age. . . . One can't die in a slum.'

I stood before him for a space, speculating what thoughts might fill the gaps between these broken words. I found his lethargy, and the dimly shaped mental attitudes his words indicated, abominable. I said abruptly, 'You have her letter?'

He dived into his breast-pocket, became motionless for ten seconds, then woke up again and produced her letter. He drew it clumsily from its envelope, and handed it to me silently.

'Why!' he cried, looking at me for the first time. 'What's come to your chin, Willie?'

'It's nothing,' I said. 'It's a bruise'; and I opened the letter.

It was written on greenish tinted fancy note-paper, and with all and more than Nettie's usual triteness and inadequacy of expression. Her handwriting bore no traces of emotion; it was round and upright and clear as though it had been done in a writing lesson. Always her letters were like masks upon her image; they fell like curtains before the changing charm of her face; one altogether forgot the sound of her light clear voice, confronted by a perplexing stereotyped thing that had mysteriously got a hold upon one's heart and pride. How did that letter run? —

'MY DEAR MOTHER,

'Do not be distressed at my going away. I have gone somewhere safe, and with some one who cares for me very much. I am sorry for

71

your sakes, but it seems that it had to be. Love is a very difficult thing, and takes hold of one in ways one does not expect. Do not think I am ashamed about this, I glory in my love, and you must not trouble too much about me. I am very, very happy (deeply underlined).

'Fondest love to Father and Puss.

'Your loving

'Nettie.'

That queer little document! I can *see* it now for the childish simple thing it was, but at the time I read it in a suppressed anguish of rage. It plunged me into a pit of hopeless shame; there seemed to remain no pride for me in life until I had revenge. I stood staring at those rounded upstanding letters, not trusting myself to speak or move. At last I stole a glance at Stuart.

He held the envelope in his hand, and stared down at the postmark between his horny thumbnails.

'You can't even tell where she is,' he said, turning the thing round in a hopeless manner, and then desisting. 'It's hard on us, Willie. Here she is; she hadn't anything to complain of; a sort of pet for all of us. Not even made to do her share of the 'ousework. And she goes off and leaves us like a bird that's learnt to fly. Can't TRUST us, that's what takes me. Puts 'erself – But there! What's to happen to her?'

'What's to happen to him?'

He shook his head to show that problem was beyond him.

'You'll go after her,' I said in an even voice; 'you'll make him marry her?'

'Where am I to go?' he asked helplessly, and held out the envelope with a gesture; 'and what could I do? Even if I knew – How could I leave the gardens?'

'Great God!' I cried, 'not leave these gardens! It's your Honour, man! If she was my daughter – if she was my daughter – I'd tear the world to pieces!' . . . I choked. 'You mean to stand it?'

'What can I do?'

'Make him marry her! Horsewhip him! Horsewhip him, I say! – I'd strangle him!'

He scratched slowly at his hairy cheek, opened his mouth, and shook his head. Then, with an intolerable note of sluggish gentle wisdom, he said, 'People of our sort, Willie, can't do things like that.'

I came near to raving. I had a wild impulse to strike him in the face. Once in my boyhood I happened upon a bird terribly mangled by some cat, and killed it in a frenzy of horror and pity. I had a gust of that same emotion now, as this shameful mutilated soul fluttered in the dust, before me. Then, you know, I dismissed him from the case.

72

'May I look?' I asked.

He held out the envelope reluctantly.

'There it is,' he said, and pointing with his garden-rough forefinger. 'I.A.P.A.M.P. What can you make of that?'

I took the thing in my hands. The adhesive stamp customary in those days was defaced by a circular postmark, which bore the name of the office of departure and the date. The impact in this particular case had been light or made without sufficient ink, and half the letters of the name had left no impression. I could distinguish——

IAPAMP

and very faintly below D.S.O.

I guessed the name in an instant flash of intuition. It was Shapham-bury. The very gaps shaped that to my mind. Perhaps in a sort of semi-visibility other letters were there, at least hinting themselves. It was a place somewhere on the east coast, I knew, either in Norfolk or Suffolk.

'Why!' cried I – and stopped.

What was the good of telling him?

Old Stuart had glanced up sharply, I am inclined to think almost fearfully, into my face. 'You – you haven't got it?' he said.

Shaphambury – I should remember that.

'You don't think you got it?' he said.

I handed the envelope back to him.

'For a moment I thought it might be Hampton,' I said.

'Hampton,' he repeated. 'Hampton. How could you make Hamp-ton?' He turned the envelope about. 'H.A.M. – why, Willie, you're a worse hand at the job than me!'

He replaced the letter in the envelope and stood erect to put this back in his breast pocket.

I did not mean to take any risks in this affair. I drew a stump of pencil from my waistcoat pocket, turned a little away from him and wrote 'Shaphambury' very quickly on my frayed and rather grimy shirt cuff.

'Well,' said I, with an air of having done nothing remarkable.

I turned to him with some unimportant observation – I have forgotten what.

I never finished whatever vague remark I commenced.

I looked up to see a third person waiting at the greenhouse door.

It was old Mrs Verrall.

I wonder if I can convey the effect of her to you. She was a little old lady with extraordinarily flaxen hair, her weak aquiline features were pursed up into an assumption of dignity, and she was richly dressed. I would like to underline that 'richly dressed', or have the words printed in florid old English or Gothic lettering. No one on earth is now quite so richly dressed as she was, no one old or young indulges in so quiet and yet so profound a sumptuosity. But you must not imagine any extravagance of outline or any beauty or richness of colour. The predominant colours were black and fur browns, and the effect of richness was due entirely to the extreme costliness of the materials employed. She affected silk brocades with rich and elaborate patterns, priceless black lace over creamy or purple satin, intricate trimmings through which threads and bands of velvet wriggled, and in the winter rare furs. Her gloves fitted exquisitely, and ostentatiously simple chains of fine gold and pearls, and a great number of bracelets, laced about her little person. One was forced to feel that the slightest article she wore cost more than all the wardrobe of a dozen girls like Nettie; her bonnet affected the simplicity that is beyond rubies. Richness, that is the first quality about this old lady that I would like to convey to you, and the second was cleanliness. You felt that old Mrs Verrall was exquisitely clean. If you had boiled my poor dear old mother in soda for a month you couldn't have got her so clean as Mrs Verrall constantly and manifestly was. And pervading all her presence shone her third great quality, her manifest confidence in the respectful subordination of the world.

She was pale and a little out of breath that day, but without any loss of her ultimate confidence, and it was clear to me that she had come to interview Stuart upon the outbreak of passion that had bridged the gulf between their families.

And here again I find myself writing in an unknown language, so far as my younger readers are concerned. You who know only the world that followed the Great Change will find much that I am telling inconceivable. Upon these points I cannot appeal, as I have appealed for other confirmations, to the old newspapers; these were the things that no one wrote about because every one understood and every one had taken up an attitude. There were in England and America, and indeed throughout the world, two great informal divisions of human beings – the Secure and the Insecure. There was not and never had been in either country a nobility – it was and remains a common error that the British peers were noble – neither in law nor custom were there noble families, and we altogether lacked the edification one found in Russia, for example, of a poor nobility. A peerage was an hereditary possession that, like the family land, concerned only the eldest sons of the house; it radiated no lustre of noblesse oblige. The rest of the world were in law and practice common – and all America was common. But through the private ownership of land that had resulted from the neglect of feudal obligations in Britain and the utter want of political foresight in the Americas, large masses of property had become artificially stable in the hands of a small minority, to whom it was necessary to mortgage all new public and private enterprises, and who were held together not by any tradition of service and nobility but by the natural sympathy of common interests and a common large scale of living. It was a class without any very definite boundaries; vigourous individualities, by methods for the most part violent and questionable, were constantly thrusting themselves from insecurity to security, and the sons and daughters of secure people, by marrying insecurity or by wild extravagance or flagrant vice, would sink into the life of anxiety and insufficiency which was the ordinary life of man. The rest of the population was landless and, except by working directly or indirectly for the Secure, had no legal right to exist. And such was the shallowness and insufficiency of our thought, such the stifled egotism of all our feelings before the Last Days, that very few indeed of the Secure could be found to doubt that this was the natural and only conceivable order of the world.

It is the life of the Insecure under the old order that I am displaying, and I hope that I am conveying something of its hopeless bitterness to you, but you must not imagine that the Secure lived lives of paradisiacal happiness. The pit of insecurity below them made itself felt, even though it was not comprehended. Life about them was ugly; the sight of ugly and mean houses, of ill-dressed people, the vulgar appeals of the dealers in popular commodities, were not to be escaped. There was below the threshold of their minds an uneasiness; they not only did not think clearly about social economy but they displayed an instinctive disinclination to think. Their security was not so perfect that they had not a dread of falling towards the pit, they were always lashing themselves by new ropes, their cultivation of 'connexions', of interests, their desire to confirm and improve their positions, was a constant ignoble preoccupation. You must read Thackeray to get the full flavour of their lives. Then the bacterium was apt to disregard class distinctions, and they were never really happy in their servants. Read their surviving books. Each generation bewails the decay of that 'fidelity' of servants, no generation ever saw. A world that is squalid in one corner is squalid altogether, but that they never understood. They believed there was not enough of anything to go round, they believed that this was the intention of God and an incurable condition of life, and they held passionately and with a sense of right to their disproportionate share. They maintained a common intercourse as 'Society' of all who were practically secure, and their choice of that word is exhaustively eloquent of the quality of their philosophy. But, if you can master these alien ideas upon which the old system rested, just in the same measure will you understand the horror these people had for marriages with the Insecure. In the case of their girls and women it was extraordinarily rare, and in the case of either sex it was regarded as a disastrous social crime. Anything was better than that.

You are probably aware of the hideous fate that was only too probably the lot, during those last dark days, of every girl of the insecure classes who loved and gave way to the impulse of self-abandonment without marriage, and so you will understand the peculiar situation of Nettie with young Verrall. One or other had to suffer. And as they were both in a state of great emotional exaltation and capable of strange generosities toward each other, it was an open question and naturally a source of great anxiety to a mother in Mrs Verrall's position, whether the sufferer might not be her son – whether as the outcome of that glowing irresponsible commerce Nettie might not return prospective mistress of Checkshill Towers. The chances were greatly against that conclusion, but such things did occur.

These laws and customs sound, I know, like a record of some nasty-minded lunatic's inventions. They were invincible facts in that vanished world into which, by some accident, I had been born, and it was the dream of any better state of things that was scouted as lunacy. Just think of it! This girl I loved with all my soul, for whom I was ready to sacrifice my life, was not good enough to marry young Verrall. And I had only to look at his even, handsome, characterless face to perceive a creature weaker and no better than myself. She was to be his pleasure until he chose to cast her aside, and the poison of our social system had so saturated her nature – his evening dress, his freedom and his money had seemed so fine to her and I so clothed in squalor – that to that prospect she had consented. And to resent the social conventions that created their situation, was called 'class envy', and gently born preachers reproached us for the mildest resentment against an injustice no living man would now either endure or consent to profit by.

What was the sense of saying 'peace' when there was no peace? If there was one hope in the disorders of that old world it lay in revolt and conflict to the death.

But if you can really grasp the shameful grotesqueness of the old life, you will begin to appreciate the interpretation of old Mrs Verrall's appearance that leapt up at once in my mind.

She had come to compromise the disaster!

And the Stuarts WOULD compromise! I saw that only too well.

An enormous disgust at the prospect of the imminent encounter between Stuart and his mistress made me behave in a violent and irrational way. I wanted to escape seeing that, seeing even Stuart's first gesture in that, at any cost.

'I'm off,' said I, and turned my back on him without any further farewell.

My line of retreat lay by the old lady, and so I advanced toward her.

I saw her expression change, her mouth fell a little way open, her forehead wrinkled, and her eyes grew round. She found me a queer customer even at the first sight, and there was something in the manner of my advance that took away her breath.

She stood at the top of the three or four steps that descended to the level of the hothouse floor. She receded a pace or two, with a certain offended dignity at the determination of my rush.

I gave her no sort of salutation.

Well, as a matter of fact, I did give her a sort of salutation. There is no occasion for me to begin apologizing now for the thing I said to her – I strip these things before you – if only I can get them stark enough you will understand and forgive. I was filled with a brutal and overpowering desire to insult her.

And so I addressed this poor little expensive old woman in the following terms, converting her by a violent metonymy into a comprehensive plural. 'You infernal land thieves!' I said point-blank into her face. 'HAVE YOU COME TO OFFER THEM MONEY?'

And without waiting to test her powers of repartee I passed rudely beyond her and vanished, striding with my fists clenched, out of her world again ...

I have tried since to imagine how the thing must have looked to her. So far as her particular universe went I had not existed at all, or I had existed only as a dim black thing, an insignificant speck, far away across her park in irrelevant, unimportant transit, until this moment when she came, sedately troubled, into her own secure gardens and sought for Stuart among the greenhouses. Then abruptly I flashed into being down that green-walled, brick-floored vista as a black-avised, ill-clad young man, who first stared and then advanced scowling towards

77

her. Once in existence I developed rapidly. I grew larger in perspective and became more and more important and sinister every moment. I came up the steps with inconceivable hostility and disrespect in my bearing, towered over her, becoming for an instant at least a sort of second French Revolution, and delivered myself with the intensest concentration of those wicked and incomprehensible words. Just for a second I threatened annihilation. Happily that was my climax.

And then I had gone by, and the Universe was very much as it had always been except for the wild swirl in it, and the faint sense of insecurity my episode left in its wake.

The thing that never entered my head in those days was that a large proportion of the rich were rich in absolute good faith. I thought they saw things exactly as I saw them, and wickedly denied. But indeed old Mrs Verrall was no more capable of doubting the perfection of her family's right to dominate a wide country side, than she was of examining the Thirty-nine Articles or dealing with any other of the adamantine pillars upon which her universe rested in security.

No doubt I startled and frightened her tremendously. But she could not understand.

None of her sort of people ever did seem to understand such livid flashes of hate, as ever and again lit the crowded darkness below their feet. The thing leapt out of the black for a moment and vanished, like a threatening figure by a desolate roadside lit for a moment by one's belated carriage-lamp and then swallowed up by the night. They counted it with nightmares, and did their best to forget what was evidently as insignificant as it was disturbing.

CHAPTER THE FOURTH

War

Section 1

From that moment when I insulted old Mrs Verrall I became representative, I was a man who stood for all the disinherited of the world. I had no hope of pride or pleasure left in me, I was raging rebellion against God and mankind. There were no more vague intentions swaying me this way and that; I was perfectly clear now upon what I meant to do. I would make my protest and die.

I would make my protest and die. I was going to kill Nettie – Nettie who had smiled and promised and given herself to another, and who stood now for all the conceivable delightfulnesses, the lost imaginations of the youthful heart, the unattainable joys in life; and Verrall who stood for all who profited by the incurable injustice of our social order. I would kill them both. And that being done I would blow my brains out and see what vengeance followed my blank refusal to live.

So indeed I was resolved. I raged monstrously. And above me, abolishing the stars, triumphant over the yellow waning moon that followed it below, the giant meteor towered up towards the zenith.

'Let me only kill!' I cried. 'Let me only kill!'

So I shouted in my frenzy. I was in a fever that defied hunger and fatigue; for a long time I had prowled over the heath towards Lowchester talking to myself, and now that night had fully come I was tramping homeward, walking the long seventeen miles without a thought of rest. And I had eaten nothing since the morning.

I suppose I must count myself mad, but I can recall my ravings.

There were times when I walked weeping through that brightness

79

that was neither night nor day. There were times when I reasoned in a topsy-turvy fashion with what I called the Spirit of All Things. But always I spoke to that white glory in the sky.

'Why am I here only to suffer ignominies?' I asked. 'Why have you made me with pride that cannot be satisfied, with desires that turn and rend me? Is it a jest, this world – a joke you play on your guests? I – even I – have a better humour than that!'

'Why not learn from me a certain decency of mercy? Why not undo? Have I ever tormented – day by day, some wretched worm – making filth for it to trail through, filth that disgusts it, starving it, bruising it, mocking it? Why should you? Your jokes are clumsy. Try – try some milder fun up there; do you hear? Something that doesn't hurt so infernally.'

'You say this is your purpose – your purpose with me. You are making something with me – birth pangs of a soul. Ah! How can I believe you? You forget I have eyes for other things. Let my own case go, but what of that frog beneath the cart-wheel, God? – and the bird the cat had torn?'

And after such blasphemies I would fling out a ridiculous little debating society hand. 'Answer me that!'

A week ago it had been moonlight, white and black and hard across the spaces of the park, but now the light was livid and full of the quality of haze. An extraordinarily low white mist, not three feet above the ground, drifted broodingly across the grass, and the trees rose ghostly out of that phantom sea. Great and shadowy and strange was the world that night, no one seemed abroad; I and my little cracked voice drifted solitary through the silent mysteries. Sometimes I argued as I have told, sometimes I tumbled along in moody vacuity, sometimes my torment was vivid and acute.

Abruptly out of apathy would come a boiling paroxysm of fury, when I thought of Nettie mocking me and laughing, and of her and Verrall clasped in one another's arms.

'I will not have it so!' I screamed. 'I will not have it so!'

And in one of these raving fits I drew my revolver from my pocket and fired into the quiet night. Three times I fired it.

The bullets tore through the air, the startled trees told one another in diminishing echoes the thing I had done, and then, with a slow finality, the vast and patient night healed again to calm. My shots, my curses and blasphemies, my prayers – for anon I prayed – that Silence took them all.

It was – how can I express it? – a stifled outcry tranquillized, lost, amid the serene assumptions, the overwhelming empire of that brightness. The noise of my shots, the impact upon things, had for the instant been enormous, then it had passed away. I found myself standing with the revolver held up, astonished, my emotions penetrated by something I could not understand. Then I looked up over my shoulder at the great star, and remained staring at it.

'Who are YOU?' I said at last.

I was like a man in a solitary desert who has suddenly heard a voice. . . .

That, too, passed.

As I came over Clayton Crest I recalled that I missed the multitude that now night after night walked out to stare at the comet, and the little preacher in the waste beyond the hoardings, who warned sinners to repent before the Judgment, was not in his usual place.

It was long past midnight, and every one had gone home. But I did not think of this at first, and the solitude perplexed me and left a memory behind. The gas-lamps were all extinguished because of the brightness of the comet, and that too was unfamiliar. The little newsagent in the still High Street had shut up and gone to bed, but one belated board had been put out late and forgotten, and it still bore its placard.

The word upon it – there was but one word upon it in staring letters – was: 'WAR.'

You figure that empty mean street, emptily echoing to my footsteps – no soul awake and audible but me. Then my halt at the placard. And amidst that sleeping stillness, smeared hastily upon the board, a little askew and crumpled, but quite distinct beneath that cool meteoric glare, preposterous and appalling, the measureless evil of that word —

'WAR!'

Section 2

I awoke in that state of equanimity that so often follows an emotional drenching.

It was late, and my mother was beside my bed. She had some breakfast for me on a battered tray.

'Don't get up yet, dear,' she said. 'You've been sleeping. It was three o'clock when you got home last night. You must have been tired out.'

'Your poor face,' she went on, 'was as white as a sheet and your eyes shining. . . . It frightened me to let you in. And you stumbled on the stairs.'

My eyes went quietly to my coat pocket, where something still

81

bulged. She probably had not noticed. 'I went to Checkshill,' I said. 'You know – perhaps—?'

'I got a letter last evening, dear,' and as she bent near me to put the tray upon my knees, she kissed my hair softly. For a moment we both remained still, resting on that, her cheek just touching my head.

I took the tray from her to end the pause.

'Don't touch my clothes, mummy,' I said sharply, as she moved towards them. 'I'm still equal to a clothes-brush.'

And then, as she turned away, I astonished her by saying, 'You dear mother, you! A little – I understand. Only – now – dear mother; oh! let me be! Let me be!'

And, with the docility of a good servant, she went from me. Dear heart of submission that the world and I had used so ill!

It seemed to me that morning that I could never give way to a gust of passion again. A sorrowful firmness of the mind possessed me. My purpose seemed now as inflexible as iron; there was neither love nor hate nor fear left in me – only I pitied my mother greatly for all that was still to come. I ate my breakfast slowly, and thought where I could find out about Shaphambury, and how I might hope to get there. I had not five shillings in the world.

I dressed methodically, choosing the least frayed of my collars, and shaving much more carefully than was my wont; then I went down to the Public Library to consult a map.

Shaphambury was on the coast of Essex, a long and complicated journey from Clayton. I went to the railway-station and made some memoranda from the time-tables. The porters I asked were not very clear about Shaphambury, but the booking-office clerk was helpful, and we puzzled out all I wanted to know. Then I came out into the coaly street again. At the least I ought to have two pounds.

I went back to the Public Library and into the newspaper room to think over this problem.

A fact intruded itself upon me. People seemed in an altogether exceptional stir about the morning journals, there was something unusual in the air of the room, more people and more talking than usual, and for a moment I was puzzled. Then I bethought me: 'This war with Germany, of course!' A naval battle was supposed to be in progress in the North Sea. Let them! I returned to the consideration of my own affairs.

Parload?

Could I go and make it up with him, and then borrow? I weighed the chances of that. Then I thought of selling or pawning something, but that seemed difficult. My winter overcoat had not cost a pound

82

when it was new, my watch was not likely to fetch many shillings. Still, both these things might be factors. I thought with a certain repugnance of the little store my mother was probably making for the rent. She was very secretive about that, and it was locked in an old tea-caddy in her bedroom. I knew it would be almost impossible to get any of that money from her willingly, and though I told myself that in this issue of passion and death no detail mattered, I could not get rid of tormenting scruples whenever I thought of that tea-caddy. Was there no other course? Perhaps after every other source had been tapped I might supplement with a few shillings frankly begged from her. 'These others,' I said to myself, thinking without passion for once of the sons of the Secure, 'would find it difficult to run their romances on a pawnshop basis. However, we must manage it.'

I felt the day was passing on, but I did not get excited about that. 'Slow is swiftest,' Parload used to say, and I meant to get everything thought out completely, to take a long aim and then to act as a bullet flies.

I hesitated at a pawnshop on my way home to my midday meal, but I determined not to pledge my watch until I could bring my overcoat also.

I ate silently, revolving plans.

Section 3

After our midday dinner – it was a potato-pie, mostly potato with some scraps of cabbage and bacon – I put on my overcoat and got it out of the house while my mother was in the scullery at the back.

A scullery in the old world was, in the case of such houses as ours, a damp, unsavoury, mainly subterranean region behind the dark living-room kitchen, that was rendered more than typically dirty in our case by the fact that into it the coal-cellar, a yawning pit of black unclean-ness, opened, and diffused small crunchable particles about the uneven brick floor. It was the region of 'washing-up', that greasy, damp func-tion that followed every meal; its atmosphere had ever a cooling steaminess and the memory of boiled cabbage, and the sooty black stains where saucepan or kettle had been put down for a minute, scraps of potato-peel caught by the strainer of the escape-pipe, and rags of a quite indescribable horribleness of acquisition, called 'dish-clouts', rise in my memory at the name. The altar of this place was the 'sink', a tank of stone, revolting to a refined touch, grease-filmed and unpleasant to see, and above this was a tap for cold water, so arranged that when the water descended it splashed and wetted whoever had turned it on.

This tap was our water supply. And in such a place you must fancy a little old woman, rather incompetent and very gentle, a soul of unselfishness and sacrifice, in dirty clothes, all come from their original colours to a common dusty dark grey, in worn, ill-fitting boots, with hands distorted by ill use, and untidy greying hair – my mother. In the winter her hands would be 'chapped', and she would have a cough. And while she washes up I go out, to sell my overcoat and watch in order that I may desert her.

I gave way to queer hesitations in pawning my two negotiable articles. A weakly indisposition to pawn in Clayton, where the pawn-broker knew me, carried me to the door of the place in Lynch Street, Swathinglea, where I had bought my revolver.

Then came an idea that I was giving too many facts about myself to one man, and I came back to Clayton after all. I forget how much money I got, but I remember that it was rather less than the sum I had made out to be the single fare to Shaphambury. Still deliberate, I went back to the Public Library to find out whether it was possible, by walking for ten or twelve miles anywhere, to shorten the journey. My boots were in a dreadful state, the sole of the left one also was now peeling off, and I could not help perceiving that all my plans might be wrecked if at this crisis I went on shoe leather in which I could only shuffle. So long as I went softly they would serve, but not for hard walking. I went to the shoemaker in Hacker Street, but he would not promise any repairs for me under forty-eight hours.

I got back home about five minutes to three, resolved to start by the five train for Birmingham in any case, but still dissatisfied about my money. I thought of pawning a book or something of that sort, but I could think of nothing of obvious value in the house. My mother's silver – two gravy-spoons and a salt-cellar – had been pawned for some weeks, since, in fact, the June quarter day. But my mind was full of hypothetical opportunities.

As I came up the steps to our door, I remarked that Mr Gabbitas looked at me suddenly round his dull red curtains with a sort of alarmed resolution in his eye and vanished, and as I walked along the passage he opened his door upon me suddenly and intercepted me.

You are figuring me, I hope, as a dark and sullen lout in shabby, cheap, old-world clothes that are shiny at all the wearing surfaces, and with a discoloured red tie and frayed linen. My left hand keeps in my pocket as though there is something it prefers to keep a grip upon there. Mr Gabbitas was shorter than I, and the first note he struck in the impression he made upon any one was of something bright and birdlike. I think he wanted to be birdlike, he possessed the possibility of an avian charm, but, as a matter of fact, there was nothing of the glowing vitality of the bird in his being. And a bird is never out of breath and with an open mouth. He was in the clerical dress of that time, that costume that seems now almost the strangest of all our old-world clothing, and he presented it in its cheapest form – black of a poor texture, ill-fitting, strangely cut. Its long skirts accentuated the tubbiness of his body, the shortness of his legs. The white tie below his all-round collar, beneath his innocent large-spectacled face, was a little grubby, and between his not very clean teeth he held a briar pipe. His complexion was whitish, and although he was only thirty-three or four perhaps, his sandy hair was already thinning from the top of his head.

To your eye, now, he would seem the strangest figure, in the utter disregard of all physical beauty or dignity about him. You would find him extraordinarily odd, but in the old days he met not only with acceptance but respect. He was alive until within a year or so ago, but his later appearance changed. As I saw him that afternoon he was a very slovenly, ungainly little human being indeed, not only was his clothing altogether ugly and queer, but had you stripped the man stark, you would certainly have seen in the bulging paunch that comes from flabby muscles and flabbily controlled appetites, and in the rounded shoulders and flawed and yellowish skin, the same failure of any effort towards clean beauty. You had an instinctive sense that so he had been from the beginning. You felt he was not only drifting through life, eating what came in his way, believing what came in his way, doing without any vigour what came in his way, but that into life also he had drifted. You could not believe him the child of pride and high resolve, or of any splendid passion of love. He had just HAPPENED ... But we all happened then. Why am I taking this tone over this poor little curate in particular?

'Hello!' he said, with an assumption of friendly ease. 'Haven't seen you for weeks! Come in and have a gossip.'

An invitation from the drawing-room lodger was in the nature of a command. I would have liked very greatly to have refused it, never was invitation more inopportune, but I had not the wit to think of an excuse. 'All right,' I said awkwardly, and he held the door open for me.

'I'd be very glad if you would,' he amplified. 'One doesn't get much opportunity of intelligent talk in this parish.'

What the devil was he up to, was my secret preoccupation. He fussed about me with a nervous hospitality, talking in jumpy fragments, rubbing his hands together, and taking peeps at me over and round his glasses. As I sat down in his leather-covered armchair, I had an odd memory of the one in the Clayton dentist's operating-room – I know not why.

'They're going to give us trouble in the North Sea, it seems,' he remarked with a sort of innocent zest. 'I'm glad they mean fighting.'

There was an air of culture about his room that always cowed me, and that made me constrained even on this occasion. The table under the window was littered with photographic material and the later albums of his continental souvenirs, and on the American cloth trimmed shelves that filled the recesses on either side of the fireplace were what I used to think in those days a quite incredible number of books – perhaps eight hundred altogether, including the reverend gentleman's photograph albums and college and school text-books. This suggestion of learning was enforced by the little wooden shield bearing a college coat-of-arms that hung over the looking-glass, and by a photograph of Mr Gabbitas in cap and gown in an Oxford frame that adorned the opposite wall. And in the middle of that wall stood his writing-desk, which I knew to have pigeon-holes when it was open, and which made him seem not merely cultured but literary. At that he wrote sermons, composing them himself!

'Yes,' he said, taking possession of the hearthrug, 'the war had to come sooner or later. If we smash their fleet for them now; well, there's an end to the matter!'

He stood on his toes and then bumped down on his heels, and looked blandly through his spectacles at a water-colour by his sister – the subject was a bunch of violets – above the sideboard which was his pantry and tea-chest and cellar. 'Yes,' he said as he did so.

I coughed, and wondered how I might presently get away.

He invited me to smoke – that queer old practice! – and then when I declined, began talking in a confidential tone of this 'dreadful business' of the strikes. 'The war won't improve THAT outlook,' he said, and was very grave for a moment.

He spoke of the want of thought for their wives and children shown by the colliers in striking merely for the sake of the union, and this stirred me to controversy, and distracted me a little from my resolution to escape.

'I don't quite agree with that,' I said, clearing my throat. 'If the men didn't strike for the union now, if they let that be broken up, where would they be when the pinch of reductions did come?'

To which he replied that they couldn't expect to get top-price wages when the masters were selling bottom-price coal. I replied, 'That isn't it. The masters don't treat them fairly. They have to protect themselves.'

To which Mr Gabbitas answered, 'Well, I don't know. I've been in the Four Towns some time, and I must say I don't think the balance of injustice falls on the masters' side.'

'It falls on the men,' I agreed, wilfully misunderstanding him.

And so we worked our way toward an argument. 'Confound this argument!' I thought; but I had no skill in self-extraction, and my irritation crept into my voice. Three little spots of colour came into the cheeks and nose of Mr Gabbitas, but his voice showed nothing of his ruffled temper.

'You see,' I said, 'I'm a socialist. I don't think this world was made for a small minority to dance on the faces of every one else.'

'My dear fellow,' said the Rev. Gabbitas, 'I'M a socialist too. Who isn't. But that doesn't lead me to class hatred.'

'You haven't felt the heel of this confounded system. I have.'

'Ah!' said he; and catching him on that note came a rap at the front door, and, as he hung suspended, the sound of my mother letting some one in and a timid rap.

'NOW,' thought I, and stood up, resolutely, but he would not let me. 'No, no, no!' said he. 'It's only for the Dorcas money.'

He put his hand against my chest with an effect of physical compulsion, and cried, 'Come in!'

'Our talk's just getting interesting,' he protested; and there entered Miss Ramell, an elderly little young lady who was mighty in Church help in Clayton.

He greeted her – she took no notice of me – and went to his bureau, and I remained standing by my chair but unable to get out of the room. 'I'm not interrupting?' asked Miss Ramell.

'Not in the least,' he said; drew out the carriers and opened his desk. I could not help seeing what he did.

I was so fretted by my impotence to leave him that at the moment it did not connect at all with the research of the morning that he was taking out money. I listened sullenly to his talk with Miss Ramell, and saw only, as they say in Wales, with the front of my eyes, the small flat drawer that had, it seemed, quite a number of sovereigns scattered over its floor. 'They're so unreasonable,' complained Miss Ramell. Who could be otherwise in a social organization that bordered on insanity?

I turned away from them, put my foot on the fender, stuck my elbow on the plush-fringed mantelboard, and studied the photographs, pipes and ash-trays that adorned it. What was it I had to think out before I went to the station?

Of course! My mind made a queer little reluctant leap – it felt like being forced to leap over a bottomless chasm – and alighted upon the sovereigns that were just disappearing again as Mr Gabbitas shut his drawer.

'I won't interrupt your talk further,' said Miss Ramell, receding doorward.

Mr Gabbitas played round her politely, and opened the door for her and conducted her into the passage, and for a moment or so I had the fullest sense of proximity to those – it seemed to me there must be ten or twelve – sovereigns. . . .

The front door closed and he returned. My chance of escape had gone.

Section 4

'I MUST be going,' I said, with a curiously reinforced desire to get away out of that room.

'My dear chap!' he insisted, 'I can't think of it. Surely – there's nothing to call you away.' Then with an evident desire to shift the venue of our talk, he asked, 'You never told me what you thought of Burble's little book.'

I was now, beneath my dull display of submission, furiously angry with him. It occurred to me to ask myself why I should defer and qualify my opinions to him. Why should I pretend a feeling of intellectual and social inferiority toward him. He asked what I thought of Burble. I resolved to tell him – if necessary with arrogance. Then perhaps he would release me. I did not sit down again, but stood by the corner of the fireplace.

'That was the little book you lent me last summer?' I said.

'He reasons closely, eh?' he said, and indicated the armchair with a flat hand, and beamed persuasively.

I remained standing. 'I didn't think much of his reasoning powers,' I said.

'He was one of the cleverest bishops London ever had.'

'That may be. But he was dodging about in a jolly feeble case,' said I.

'You mean?'

'That he's wrong. I don't think he proves his case. I don't think Christianity is true. He knows himself for the pretender he is. His reasoning's – Rot.'

Mr Gabbitas went, I think, a shade paler than his wont, and propitiation vanished from his manner. His eyes and mouth were round, his face seemed to get round, his eyebrows curved at my remarks.

'I'm sorry you think that,' he said at last, with a catch in his breath.

He did not repeat his suggestion that I should sit. He made a step or two toward the window and turned. 'I suppose you will admit—' he began, with a faintly irritating note of intellectual condescension.

I will not tell you of his arguments or mine. You will find if you care to look for them, in out-of-the-way corners of our book museums, the shrivelled cheap publications – the publications of the Rationalist Press Association, for example – on which my arguments were based. Lying in that curious limbo with them, mixed up with them and indistinguishable, are the endless 'Replies' of orthodoxy, like the mixed dead in some hard-fought trench. All those disputes of our fathers, and they were sometimes furious disputes, have gone now beyond the range of comprehension. You younger people, I know, read them with impatient perplexity. You cannot understand how sane creatures could imagine they had joined issue at all in most of these controversies. All the old methods of systematic thinking, the queer absurdities of the Aristotelian logic, have followed magic numbers and mystical numbers, and the Rumpelstiltskin magic of names now into the blackness of the unthinkable. You can no more understand our theological passions than you can understand the fancies that made all ancient peoples speak of their gods only by circumlocutions, that made savages pine away and die because they had been photographed, or an Elizabethan farmer turn back from a day's expedition because he had met three crows. Even I, who have been through it all, recall our controversies now with something near incredulity.

Faith we can understand to-day, all men live by faith, but in the old time every one confused quite hopelessly Faith and a forced, incredible Belief in certain pseudo-concrete statements. I am inclined to say that neither believers nor unbelievers had faith as we understand it – they had insufficient intellectual power. They could not trust unless they had something to see and touch and say, like their barbarous ancestors who could not make a bargain without exchange of tokens. If they no longer worshipped stocks and stones, or eked out their needs with pilgrimages and images, they still held fiercely to audible images, to printed words and formulae.

But why revive the echoes of the ancient logomachies?

Suffice it that we lost our tempers very readily in pursuit of God and Truth, and said exquisitely foolish things on either side. And on the whole – from the impartial perspective of my three and seventy years – I adjudicate that if my dialectic was bad, that of the Rev. Gabbitas was altogether worse.

Little pink spots came into his cheeks, a squealing note into his voice. We interrupted each other more and more rudely. We invented facts and appealed to authorities whose names I mispronounced; and, finding Gabbitas shy of the higher criticism and the Germans, I used the names of Karl Marx and Engels as Bible exegetes with no little effect. A silly wrangle! a preposterous wrangle! – you must imagine our talk becoming louder, with a developing quarrelsome note – my mother no doubt hovering on the staircase and listening in alarm as who should say, 'My dear, don't offend it! Oh, don't offend it! Mr Gabbitas enjoys its friendship. Try to think whatever Mr Gabbitas says' – though we still kept in touch with a pretence of mutual deference. The ethical superiority of Christianity to all other religions came to the fore – I know not how. We dealt with the matter in bold, imaginative generalizations, because of the insufficiency of our historical knowledge. I was moved to denounce Christianity as the ethic of slaves, and declare myself a disciple of a German writer of no little vogue in those days, named Nietzsche. For a disciple I must confess I was particularly ill acquainted with the works of the master. Indeed, all I knew of him had come to me through a two-column article in *The Clarion* for the previous week. . . . But the Rev. Gabbitas did not read *The Clarion*.

I am, I know, putting a strain upon your credulity when I tell you that I now have little doubt that the Rev. Gabbitas was absolutely ignorant even of the name of Nietzsche, although that writer presented a separate and distinct attitude of attack upon the faith that was in the reverend gentleman's keeping.

'I'm a disciple of Nietzsche,' said I, with an air of extensive explanation.

He shied away so awkwardly at the name that I repeated it at once.

'But do you know what Nietzsche says?' I pressed him viciously.

'He has certainly been adequately answered,' said he, still trying to carry it off.

'Who by?' I rapped out hotly. 'Tell me that!' and became mercilessly expectant.

Section 5

A happy accident relieved Mr Gabbitas from the embarrassment of that challenge, and carried me another step along my course of personal disaster.

It came on the heels of my question in the form of a clatter of horses without, and the gride and cessation of wheels. I glimpsed a straw-hatted coachman and a pair of greys. It seemed an incredibly magnificent carriage for Clayton.

'Eh!' said the Rev. Gabbitas, going to the window. 'Why, it's old Mrs Verrall! It's old Mrs Verrall. Really! What CAN she want with me?'

He turned to me, and the flush of controversy had passed and his face shone like the sun. It was not every day, I perceived, that Mrs Verrall came to see him.

'I get so many interruptions,' he said, almost grinning. 'You must excuse me a minute! Then – then I'll tell you about that fellow. But don't go. I pray you don't go. I can assure you. . . . MOST interesting.'

He went out of the room waving vague prohibitory gestures.

'I MUST go,' I cried after him.

'No, no, no!' in the passage. 'I've got your answer,' I think it was he added, and 'quite mistaken'; and I saw him running down the steps to talk to the old lady.

I swore. I made three steps to the window, and this brought me within a yard of that accursed drawer.

I glanced at it, and then at that old woman who was so absolutely powerful, and instantly her son and Nettie's face were flaming in my brain. The Stuarts had, no doubt, already accepted accomplished facts. And I too —

What was I doing here? What was I doing here while judgment escaped me?

I woke up. I was injected with energy. I took one reassuring look at the curate's obsequious back, at the old lady's projected nose and quivering hand, and then with swift, clean movements I had the little drawer open, four sovereigns in my pocket, and the drawer shut again. Then again at the window – they were still talking.

That was all right. He might not look in that drawer for hours. I glanced at his clock. Twenty minutes still before the Birmingham train. Time to buy a pair of boots and get away. But how was I to get to the station?

I went out boldly into the passage, and took my hat and stick. . . . Walk past him?

Yes. That was all right! He could not argue with me while so important a person engaged him. . . . I came boldly down the steps.

'I want a list made, Mr Gabbitas, of all the really DESERVING cases,' old Mrs Verrall was saying.

It is curious, but it did not occur to me that here was a mother whose son I was going to kill. I did not see her in that aspect at all. Instead, I was possessed by a realization of the blazing imbecility of a social system that gave this palsied old woman the power to give or withhold the urgent necessities of life from hundreds of her fellow-creatures just according to her poor, foolish old fancies of desert.

'We could make a PROVISIONAL list of that sort,' he was saying, and glanced round with a preoccupied expression at me.

'I MUST go,' I said at his flash of inquiry, and added, 'I'll be back in twenty minutes,' and went on my way. He turned again to his patroness as though he forgot me on the instant. Perhaps after all he was not sorry.

I felt extraordinarily cool and capable, exhilarated, if anything, by this prompt, effectual theft. After all, my great determination would achieve itself. I was no longer oppressed by a sense of obstacles, I felt I could grasp accidents and turn them to my advantage. I would go now down Hacker Street to the little shoemaker's – get a sound, good pair of boots – ten minutes – and then to the railway-station – five minutes more – and off? I felt as efficient and non-moral as if I was Nietzsche's Over-man already come. It did not occur to me that the curate's clock might have a considerable margin of error.

Section 6

I missed the train.

Partly that was because the curate's clock was slow, and partly it was due to the commercial obstinacy of the shoemaker, who would try on another pair after I had declared my time was up. I bought the final pair however, gave him a wrong address for the return of the old ones, and only ceased to feel like the Nietzschean Over-man, when I saw the train running out of the station.

Even then I did not lose my head. It occurred to me almost at once that, in the event of a prompt pursuit, there would be a great advantage in not taking a train from Clayton; that, indeed, to have done so would have been an error from which only luck had saved me. As it was, I had already been very indiscreet in my inquiries about Shaphambury; for once on the scent the clerk could not fail to remember me. Now the chances were against his coming into the case. I did not go into the station therefore at all, I made no demonstration of having missed the train, but walked quietly past, down the road, crossed the iron footbridge, and took the way back circuitously by White's brickfields and the allotments to the way over Clayton Crest to Two-Mile Stone, where I calculated I should have an ample margin for the 6.13 train.

I was not very greatly excited or alarmed then. Suppose, I reasoned, that by some accident the curate goes to that drawer at once: will he be certain to miss four out of ten or eleven sovereigns? If he does, will

92

he at once think I have taken them? If he does, will he act at once or wait for my return? If he acts at once, will he talk to my mother or call in the police? Then there are a dozen roads and even railways out of the Clayton region, how is he to know which I have taken? Suppose he goes straight at once to the right station, they will not remember my departure for the simple reason that I didn't depart. But they may remember about Shaphambury? It was unlikely.

I resolved not to go directly to Shaphambury from Birmingham, but to go thence to Monkshampton, thence to Wyvern, and then come down on Shaphambury from the north. That might involve a night at some intermediate stopping-place but it would effectually conceal me from any but the most persistent pursuit. And this was not a case of murder yet, but only the theft of four sovereigns.

I had argued away all anxiety before I reached Clayton Crest.

At the Crest I looked back. What a world it was! And suddenly it came to me that I was looking at this world for the last time. If I overtook the fugitives and succeeded, I should die with them – or hang. I stopped and looked back more attentively at that wide ugly valley.

It was my native valley, and I was going out of it, I thought never to return, and yet in that last prospect, the group of towns that had borne me and dwarfed and crippled and made me, seemed, in some indefinable manner, strange. I was, perhaps, more used to seeing it from this comprehensive viewpoint when it was veiled and softened by night; now it came out in all its weekday reek, under a clear afternoon sun. That may account a little for its unfamiliarity. And perhaps, too, there was something in the emotions through which I had been passing for a week and more, to intensify my insight, to enable me to pierce the unusual, to question the accepted. But it came to me then, I am sure, for the first time, how promiscuous, how higgledy-piggledy was the whole of that jumble of mines and homes, collieries and potbanks, railway yards, canals, schools, forges and blast furnaces, churches, chapels, allotment hovels, a vast irregular agglomeration of ugly smoking accidents in which men lived as happy as frogs in a dustbin. Each thing jostled and damaged the other things about it, each thing ignored the other things about it; the smoke of the furnace defiled the potbank clay, the clatter of the railway deafened the worshippers in church, the public-house thrust corruption at the school doors, the dismal homes squeezed miserably amidst the monstrosities of industrialism, with an effect of groping imbecility. Humanity choked amidst its products, and all its energy went in increasing its disorder, like a blind stricken thing that struggles and sinks in a morass.

I did not think these things clearly that afternoon. Much less did I ask how I, with my murderous purpose, stood to them all. I write down that realization of disorder and suffocation here and now as though I had thought it, but indeed then I only felt it, felt it transitorily as I looked back, and then stood with the thing escaping from my mind.

I should never see that country-side again.

I came back to that. At any rate I wasn't sorry. The chances were I should die in sweet air, under a clean sky.

From distant Swathinglea came a little sound, the minute undulation of a remote crowd, and then rapidly three shots.

That held me perplexed for a space. . . . Well, anyhow I was leaving it all! Thank God I was leaving it all! Then, as I turned to go on, I thought of my mother.

It seemed an evil world in which to leave one's mother. My thoughts focused upon her very vividly for a moment. Down there, under that afternoon light, she was going to and fro, unaware as yet that she had lost me, bent and poking about in the darkling underground kitchen, perhaps carrying a lamp into the scullery to trim, or sitting patiently, staring into the fire, waiting tea for me. A great pity for her, a great remorse at the blacker troubles that lowered over her innocent head, came to me. Why, after all, was I doing this thing?

Why?

I stopped again dead, with the hill crest rising between me and home. I had more than half a mind to return to her.

Then I thought of the curate's sovereigns. If he has missed them already, what should I return to? And, even if I returned, how could I put them back?

And what of the night after I renounced my revenge? What of the time when young Verrall came back? And Nettie?

No! The thing had to be done.

But at least I might have kissed my mother before I came away, left her some message, reassured her at least for a little while. All night she would listen and wait for me. . . .

Should I send her a telegram from Two-Mile Stone?

It was no good now; too late, too late. To do that would be to tell the course I had taken, to bring pursuit upon me, swift and sure, if pursuit there was to be. No. My mother must suffer!

I went on grimly towards Two-Mile Stone, but now as if some greater will than mine directed my footsteps thither.

I reached Birmingham before darkness came, and just caught the last train for Monkshampton, where I had planned to pass the night.

The Pursuit of the Two Lovers

Section 1

As the train carried me on from Birmingham to Monkshampton, it carried me not only into a country where I had never been before, but out of the commonplace daylight and the touch and quality of ordinary things, into the strange unprecedented night that was ruled by the giant meteor of the last days.

There was at that time a curious accentuation of the common alternation of night and day. They became separated with a widening difference of value in regard to all mundane affairs. During the day, the comet was an item in the newspapers, it was jostled by a thousand more living interests, it was as nothing in the skirts of the war storm that was now upon us. It was an astronomical phenomenon, somewhere away over China, millions of miles away in the deeps. We forgot it. But directly the sun sank one turned ever and again towards the east, and the meteor resumed its sway over us.

One waited for its rising, and yet each night it came as a surprise. Always it rose brighter than one had dared to think, always larger and with some wonderful change in its outline, and now with a strange, less luminous, greener disc upon it that grew with its growth, the umbra of the earth. It shone also with its own light, so that this shadow was not hard or black, but it shone phosphorescently and with a diminishing intensity where the stimulus of the sun's rays was withdrawn. As it ascended toward the zenith, as the last trailing daylight went after the abdicating sun, its greenish white illumination banished the realities of day, diffused a bright ghostliness over all things. It changed the starless sky about it to an extraordinary deep blue, the profoundest colour in the world, such as I have never seen before or since. I remember, too, that as I peered from the train that was rattling me along to Monkshampton, I perceived and was puzzled by a coppery red light that mingled with all the shadows that were cast by it.

It turned our ugly English industrial towns to phantom cities. Everywhere the local authorities discontinued street lighting – one could read small print in the glare, – and so at Monkshampton I went about through pale, white, unfamiliar streets, whose electric globes had shadows on the path. Lit windows here and there burnt ruddy orange, like holes cut in some dream curtain that hung before a furnace. A policeman with noiseless feet showed me an inn woven of moonshine, a green-faced man opened to us, and there I abode the night. And the next morning it opened with a mighty clatter, and was a dirty little beerhouse that stank of beer, and there was a fat and grimy landlord with red spots upon his neck, and much noisy traffic going by on the cobbles outside.

I came out, after I had paid my bill, into a street that echoed to the bawlings of two newsvendors and to the noisy yappings of a dog they had raised to emulation. They were shouting: 'Great British disaster in the North Sea. A battleship lost with all hands!'

I bought a paper, went on to the railway station reading such details as were given of this triumph of the old civilization, of the blowing up of this great iron ship, full of guns and explosives and the most costly and beautiful machinery of which that time was capable, together with nine hundred able-bodied men, all of them above the average, by a contact mine towed by a German submarine. I read myself into a fever of warlike emotions. Not only did I forget the meteor, but for a time I forgot even the purpose that took me on to the railway station, bought my ticket, and was now carrying me onward to Shaphambury.

So the hot day came to its own again, and people forgot the night.

Each night, there shone upon us more and more insistently, beauty, wonder, the promise of the deeps, and we were hushed, and marvelled for a space. And at the first grey sounds of dawn again, at the shooting of bolts and the noise of milk-carts, we forgot, and the dusty habitual day came yawning and stretching back again. The stains of coal smoke crept across the heavens, and we rose to the soiled disorderly routine of life.

'Thus life has always been,' we said; 'thus it will always be.'

The glory of those nights was almost universally regarded as spectacular merely. It signified nothing to us. So far as western Europe went, it was only a small and ignorant section of the lower classes who regarded the comet as a portent of the end of the world. Abroad, where there were peasantries, it was different, but in England the peasantry had already disappeared. Every one read. The newspaper, in the quiet days before our swift quarrel with Germany rushed to its climax, had absolutely dispelled all possibilities of a panic in this matter. The very tramps upon the high-roads, the children in the nursery, had learnt that at the utmost the whole of that shining cloud could weigh but a few score tons. This fact had been shown quite conclusively by the enormous deflections that had at last swung it round squarely at our world. It had passed near three of the smallest asteroids without producing the minutest perceptible deflection in their course; while, on its own part, it had described a course through nearly three degrees. When it struck our earth there was to be a magnificent spectacle, no doubt, for those who were on the right side of our planet to see, but beyond that nothing. It was doubtful whether we were on the right side. The meteor would loom larger and larger in the sky, but with the umbra of our earth eating its heart of brightness out, and at last it would be the whole sky, a sky of luminous green clouds, with a white brightness about the horizon, west and east. Then a pause – a pause of not very exactly definite duration – and then, no doubt, a great blaze of shooting stars. They might be of some unwonted colour because of the unknown element that line in the green revealed. For a little while the zenith would spout shooting stars. Some, it was hoped, would reach the earth and be available for analysis.

That, science said, would be all. The green clouds would whirl and vanish, and there might be thunderstorms. But through the attenuated wisps of comet shine, the old sky, the old stars, would reappear, and all would be as it had been before. And since this was to happen between one and eleven in the morning of the approaching Tuesday – I slept at Monkshampton on Saturday night, – it would be only partially visible, if visible at all, on our side of the earth. Perhaps, if it came late, one would see no more than a shooting star low down in the sky. All this we had with the utmost assurances of science. Still it did not prevent the last nights being the most beautiful and memorable of human experiences.

The nights had become very warm, and when next day I had ranged Shaphambury in vain, I was greatly tormented, as that unparalleled glory of the night returned, to think that under its splendid benediction young Verrall and Nettie made love to one another.

I walked backwards and forwards, backwards and forwards, along the sea front, peering into the faces of the young couples who promenaded, with my hand in my pocket ready, and a curious ache in my heart that had no kindred ~~with~~ rage. Until at last all the promenaders had gone home to bed, and I was alone with the star.

My train from Wyvern to Shaphambury that morning was a whole hour late; they said it was on account of the movement of troops to meet a possible raid from the Elbe.

Section 2

Shaphambury seemed an odd place to me even then. But something was quickening in me at that time to feel the oddness of many accepted things. Now in the retrospect I see it as intensely queer. The whole place was strange to my untravelled eyes; the sea even was strange. Only twice in my life had I been at the seaside before, and then I had gone by excursion to places on the Welsh coast whose great cliffs of rock and mountain backgrounds made the effect of the horizon very different from what it is upon the East Anglian seaboard. Here what they call a cliff was a crumbling bank of whitey-brown earth not fifty feet high.

So soon as I arrived I made a systematic exploration of Shaphambury. To this day I retain the clearest memories of the plan I shaped out then, and how my inquiries were incommoded by the overpowering desire of every one to talk of the chances of a German raid, before the Channel Fleet got round to us. I slept at a small public-house in a Shaphambury back street on Sunday night. I did not get on to Shaphambury from Wyvern until two in the afternoon, because of the infrequency of Sunday trains, and I got no clue whatever until late in the afternoon of Monday. As the little local train bumped into sight of the place round the curve of a swelling hill, one saw a series of undulating grassy spaces, amidst which a number of conspicuous notice-boards appealed to the eye and cut up the distant sea horizon. Most of these referred to comestibles or to remedies to follow the comestibles; and they were coloured with a view to be memorable rather than beautiful, to 'stand out' amidst the gentle greyish tones of the east coast scenery. The greater number, I may remark, of the advertisements that were so conspicuous a factor in the life of those days, and which rendered our vast tree-pulp newspapers possible, referred to foods, drinks, tobacco, and the drugs that promised a restoration of the equanimity these other articles had destroyed. Wherever one went one was reminded in glaring letters that, after all, man was little better than a worm, that eyeless, earless thing that burrows and lives uncomplainingly amidst nutritious dirt, 'an alimentary canal with the subservient appendages thereto'. But in addition to such

98

boards there were also the big black and white boards of various grandiloquently named 'estates'. The individualistic enterprise of that time had led to the plotting out of nearly all the country round the seaside towns into roads and building-plots – all but a small portion of the south and east coast was in this condition, and had the promises of those schemes been realized the entire population of the island might have been accommodated upon the sea frontiers. Nothing of the sort happened, of course; the whole of this uglification of the coastline was done to stimulate a little foolish gambling in plots, and one saw everywhere agents' boards in every state of freshness and decay, ill-made exploitation roads overgrown with grass, and here and there, at a corner, a label, 'Trafalgar Avenue', or 'Sea View Road'. Here and there, too, some small investor, some shopman with 'savings', had delivered his soul to the local builders and built himself a house, and there it stood, ill-designed, mean-looking, isolated, ill-placed on a cheaply fenced plot, athwart which his domestic washing fluttered in the breeze amidst a bleak desolation of enterprise. Then presently our railway crossed a high road, and a row of mean yellow brick houses – workmen's cottages, and the filthy black sheds that made the 'allotments' of that time a universal eyesore, marked our approach to the more central areas of – I quote the local guidebook – 'one of the most delightful resorts in the East Anglian poppy-land'. Then more mean houses, the gaunt ungainliness of the electric force station – it had a huge chimney, because no one understood how to make combustion of coal complete – and then we were in the railway station, and barely three-quarters of a mile from the centre of this haunt of health and pleasure.

I inspected the town thoroughly before I made my inquiries. The road began badly with a row of cheap, pretentious, insolvent-looking shops, a public-house and a cab-stand, but, after an interval of little red villas that were partly hidden amidst shrubbery gardens, broke into a confusedly bright but not unpleasing High Street, shuttered that afternoon and sabbatically still. Somewhere in the background a church bell jangled, and children in bright, new-looking clothes were going to Sunday-school. Thence through a square of stuccoed lodging-houses, that seemed a finer and cleaner version of my native square, I came to a garden of asphalt and euonymus – the Sea Front. I sat down on a cast-iron seat, and surveyed first of all the broad stretches of muddy, sandy beach, with its queer wheeled bathing machines, painted with the advertisements of somebody's pills – and then at the house fronts that stared out upon these visceral counsels. Boarding-houses, private hotels and lodging-houses in terraces clustered closely right and left of me, and then came to an end; in one direction scaffolding marked a building enterprise in progress, in the other, after a waste interval, rose a monstrous bulging red shape, a huge hotel, that dwarfed all other things. Northward were low pale cliffs with white denticulations of tents, where the local volunteers, all under arms, lay encamped, and southward, a spreading waste of sandy dunes, with occasional bushes and clumps of stunted pine and an advertisement board or so. A hard blue sky hung over all this prospect, the sunshine cast inky shadows, and eastward was a whitish sea. It was Sunday, and the midday meal still held people indoors.

A queer world! thought I even then – to you now it must seem impossibly queer, – and after an interval I forced myself back to my own affair.

How was I to ask? What was I to ask for? I puzzled for a long time over that – at first I was a little tired and indolent – and then presently I had a flow of ideas.

My solution was fairly ingenious. I invented the following story. I happened to be taking a holiday in Shaphambury, and I was making use of the opportunity to seek the owner of a valuable feather boa, which had been left behind in the hotel of my uncle at Wyvern by a young lady, travelling with a young gentleman – no doubt a youthful married couple. They had reached Shaphambury somewhen on Thursday. I went over the story many times, and gave my imaginary uncle and his hotel plausible names. At any rate this yarn would serve as a complete justification for all the questions I might wish to ask.

I settled that, but I still sat for a time, wanting the energy to begin. Then I turned toward the big hotel. Its gorgeous magnificence seemed to my inexpert judgment to indicate the very place a rich young man of good family would select.

Huge draught-proof doors were swung round for me by an ironically polite under-porter in a magnificent green uniform, who looked at my clothes as he listened to my question and then with a German accent referred me to a gorgeous head porter, who directed me to a princely young man behind a counter of brass and polish, like a bank – like several banks. This young man, while he answered me, kept his eye on my collar and tie – and I knew that they were abominable.

'I want to find a lady and gentleman who came to Shaphambury on Tuesday,' I said.

'Friends of yours?' he asked with a terrible fineness of irony.

I made out at last that here at any rate the young people had not been. They might have lunched there, but they had had no room. But

I went out – door opened again for me obsequiously – in a state of social discomfiture, and did not attack any other establishment that afternoon.

My resolution had come to a sort of ebb. More people were promenading, and their Sunday smartness abashed me. I forgot my purpose in an acute sense of myself. I felt that the bulge of my pocket caused by the revolver was conspicuous, and I was ashamed. I went along the sea front away from the town, and presently lay down among pebbles and sea poppies. This mood of reaction prevailed with me all that afternoon. In the evening, about sundown, I went to the station and asked questions of the outporters there. But outporters, I found, were a class of men who remembered luggage rather than people, and I had no sort of idea what luggage young Verrall and Nettie were likely to have with them.

Then I fell into conversation with a salacious wooden-legged old man with a silver ring, who swept the steps that went down to the beach from the parade. He knew much about young couples, but only in general terms, and nothing of the particular young couple I sought. He reminded me in the most disagreeable way of the sensuous aspects of life, and I was not sorry when presently a gunboat appeared in the offing signalling the coastguard and the camp, and cut short his observations upon holidays, beaches and morals.

I went, and now I was past my ebb, and sat in a seat upon the parade, and watched the brightening of those rising clouds of chilly fire that made the ruddy west seem tame. My midday lassitude was going, my blood was running warmer again. And as the twilight and that filmy brightness replaced the dusty sunlight and robbed this unfamiliar place of all its matter-of-fact queerness, its sense of aimless materialism, romance returned to me, and passion, and my thoughts of honour and revenge. I remember that change of mood as occurring very vividly on this occasion, but I fancy that less distinctly I had felt this before many times. In the old times, night and the starlight had an effect of intimate reality the daytime did not possess. The daytime – as one saw it in towns and populous places – had hold of one, no doubt, but only as an uproar might, it was distracting, conflicting, insistent. Darkness veiled the more salient aspects of those agglomerations of human absurdity, and one could exist – one could imagine.

I had a queer illusion that night, that Nettie and her lover were close at hand, that suddenly I should come on them. I have already told how I went through the dusk seeking them in every couple that drew near. And I dropped asleep at last in an unfamiliar bedroom hung with gaudily decorated texts, cursing myself for having wasted a day.

Section 3

I sought them in vain the next morning, but after midday I came in quick succession on a perplexing multitude of clues. After failing to find any young couple that corresponded to young Verrall and Nettie, I presently discovered an unsatisfactory quartet of couples.

Any of these four couples might have been the one I sought; with regard to none of them was there conviction. They had all arrived either on Wednesday or Thursday. Two couples were still in occupation of their rooms, but neither of these were at home. Late in the afternoon I reduced my list by eliminating a young man in drab, with side whiskers and long cuffs, accompanied by a lady, of thirty or more, of consciously ladylike type. I was disgusted at the sight of them; the other two young people had gone for a long walk, and though I watched their boarding-house until the fiery cloud shone out above, sharing and mingling in an unusually splendid sunset, I missed them. Then I discovered them dining at a separate table in the bow window, with red-shaded candles between them, peering out ever and again at this splendour that was neither night nor day. The girl in her pink evening dress looked very light and pretty to me – pretty enough to enrage me, – she had well shaped arms and white, well-modelled shoulders, and the turn of her cheek and the fair hair about her ears was full of subtle delights; but she was not Nettie, and the happy man with her was that odd degenerate type our old aristocracy produced with such odd frequency, chinless, large bony nose, small fair head, languid expression, and a neck that had demanded and received a veritable sleeve of collar. I stood outside in the meteor's livid light, hating them and cursing them for having delayed me so long. I stood until it was evident they remarked me, a black shape of envy, silhouetted against the glare.

That finished Shaphambury. The question I now had to debate was which of the remaining couples I had to pursue.

I walked back to the parade trying to reason my next step out, and muttering to myself, because there was something in that luminous wonderfulness that touched one's brain, and made one feel a little light-headed.

One couple had gone to London; the other had gone to the Bungalow village at Bone Cliff. Where, I wondered, was Bone Cliff?

I came upon my wooden-legged man at the top of his steps.

'Hullo,' said I.

He pointed seaward with his pipe, his silver ring shone in the sky light.

'Rum,' he said.

'What is?' I asked.

'Search-lights! Smoke! Ships going north! If it wasn't for this blasted Milky Way gone green up there, we might see.'

He was too intent to heed my questions for a time. Then he vouchsafed over his shoulder —

'Know Bungalow village? – rather. Artis' and such. Nice goings on! Mixed bathing – something scandalous. Yes.'

'But where is it?' I said, suddenly exasperated.

'There!' he said. 'What's that flicker? A gunflash – or I'm a lost soul!'

'You'd hear,' I said, 'long before it was near enough to see a flash.'

He didn't answer. Only by making it clear I would distract him until he told me what I wanted to know could I get him to turn from his absorbed contemplation of that phantom dance between the sea rim and the shine. Indeed I gripped his arm and shook him. Then he turned upon me cursing.

'Seven miles,' he said, 'along this road. And now go to 'ell with yer!'

I answered with some foul insult by way of thanks, and so we parted, and I set off towards the bungalow village.

I found a policeman, standing star-gazing, a little way beyond the end of the parade, and verified the wooden-legged man's directions.

'It's a lonely road, you know,' he called after me. . . .

I had an odd intuition that now at last I was on the right track. I left the dark masses of Shaphambury behind me, and pushed out into the dim pallor of that night, with the quiet assurance of a traveller who nears his end.

The incidents of that long tramp I do not recall in any orderly succession, the one progressive thing is my memory of a growing fatigue. The sea was for the most part smooth and shining like a mirror, a great expanse of reflecting silver, barred by slow broad undulations, but at one time a little breeze breathed like a faint sigh and ruffled their long bodies into faint scaly ripples that never completely died out again. The way was sometimes sandy, thick with silvery colourless sand, and sometimes chalky and lumpy, with lumps that had shining facets; a black scrub was scattered, sometimes in thickets, sometimes in single bunches, among the somnolent hummocks of sand. At one place came grass, and ghostly great sheep looming up among the grey. After a time black pinewoods intervened, and made sustained darknesses along the road, woods that frayed out at the edges to weirdly warped and stunted trees. Then isolated pine witches would appear, and make their rigid gestures at me as I passed. Grotesquely incongruous amidst these forms, I presently came on estate boards, appealing, 'Houses can be built to suit purchaser,' to the silence, to the shadows, and the glare.

Once I remember the persistent barking of a dog from somewhere inland of me, and several times I took out and examined my revolver very carefully. I must, of course, have been full of my intention when I did that, I must have been thinking of Nettie and revenge, but I cannot now recall those emotions at all. Only I see again very distinctly the greenish gleams that ran over lock and barrel as I turned the weapon in my hand.

Then there was the sky, the wonderful, luminous, starless, moonless sky, and the empty blue deeps of the edge of it, between the meteor and the sea. And once – strange phantoms! – I saw far out upon the shine, and very small and distant, three long black warships, without masts, or sails, or smoke, or any lights, dark, deadly, furtive things, travelling very swiftly and keeping an equal distance. And when I looked again they were very small, and then the shine had swallowed them up.

Then once a flash and what I thought was a gun, until I looked up and saw a fading trail of greenish light still hanging in the sky. And after that there was a shiver and whispering in the air, a stronger throbbing in one's arteries, a sense of refreshment, a renewal of purpose. . . .

Somewhere upon my way the road forked, but I do not remember whether that was near Shaphambury or near the end of my walk. The hesitation between two rutted unmade roads alone remains clear in my mind.

At last I grew weary. I came to piled heaps of decaying seaweed and cart tracks running this way and that, and then I had missed the road and was stumbling among sand hummocks quite close to the sea. I came out on the edge of the dimly glittering sandy beach, and something phosphorescent drew me to the water's edge. I bent down and peered at the little luminous specks that floated in the ripples.

Presently with a sigh I stood erect, and contemplated the lonely peace of that last wonderful night. The meteor had now trailed its shining nets across the whole space of the sky and was beginning to set; in the east the blue was coming to its own again; the sea was an intense edge of blackness, and now, escaped from that great shine, and faint and still tremulously valiant, one weak elusive star could just be seen, hovering on the verge of the invisible.

How beautiful it was! how still and beautiful! Peace! peace! – the peace that passeth understanding, robed in light descending! . . .

My heart swelled, and suddenly I was weeping.

There was something new and strange in my blood. It came to me that indeed I did not want to kill.

I did not want to kill. I did not want to be the servant of my passions any more. A great desire had come to me to escape from life, from the daylight which is heat and conflict and desire, into that cool night of eternity – and rest. I had played – I had done.

I stood upon the edge of the great ocean, and I was filled with an inarticulate spirit of prayer, and I desired greatly – peace from myself.

And presently, there in the east, would come again the red dis-colouring curtain over these mysteries, the finite world again, the grey and growing harsh certainties of dawn. My resolve I knew would take up with me again. This was a rest for me, an interlude, but to-morrow I should be William Leadford once more, ill-nourished, ill-dressed, ill-equipped and clumsy, a thief and shamed, a wound upon the face of life, a source of trouble and sorrow even to the mother I loved; no hope in life left for me now but revenge before my death.

Why this paltry thing, revenge? It entered into my thoughts that I might end the matter now and let these others go.

To wade out into the sea, into this warm lapping that mingled the natures of water and light, to stand there breast-high, to thrust my revolver barrel into my mouth—?

Why not?

I swung about with an effort. I walked slowly up the beach thinking. . . .

I turned and looked back at the sea. No! Something within me said, 'No!'

I must think.

It was troublesome to go further because the hummocks and the tangled bushes began. I sat down amidst a black cluster of shrubs, and rested, chin on hand. I drew my revolver from my pocket and looked at it, and held it in my hand. Life? Or Death? . . .

I seemed to be probing the very deeps of being, but indeed imper-ceptibly I fell asleep, and sat dreaming.

Section 4

Two people were bathing in the sea.

I had awakened. It was still that white and wonderful night, and the blue band of clear sky was no wider than before. These people must have come into sight as I fell asleep, and awakened me almost at once. They waded breast-deep in the water, emerging, coming shoreward, a woman, with her hair coiled about her head, and in pursuit of her a man, graceful figures of black and silver, with a bright green surge flowing off from them, a pattering of flashing wavelets about them. He smote the water and splashed it towards her, she retaliated, and then they were knee-deep, and then for an instant their feet broke the long silver margin of the sea.

Each wore a tightly fitting bathing dress that hid nothing of the shining, dripping beauty of their youthful forms.

She glanced over her shoulder and found him nearer than she thought, started, gesticulated, gave a little cry that pierced me to the heart, and fled up the beach obliquely towards me, running like the wind, and passed me, vanished amidst the black distorted bushes, and was gone – she and her pursuer, in a moment, over the ridge of sand.

I heard him shout between exhaustion and laughter. . . .

And suddenly I was a thing of bestial fury, standing up with hands held up and clenched, rigid in gesture of impotent threatening, against the sky. . . .

For this striving, swift thing of light and beauty was Nettie – and this was the man for whom I had been betrayed!

And, it blazed upon me, I might have died there by the sheer ebbing of my will – unavenged!

In another moment I was running and stumbling, revolver in hand, in quiet unsuspected pursuit of them, through the soft and noiseless sand.

Section 5

I came up over the little ridge and discovered the bungalow village I had been seeking, nestling in a crescent lap of dunes. A door slammed, the two runners had vanished, and I halted staring.

There was a group of three bungalows nearer to me than the others. Into one of these three they had gone, and I was too late to see which. All had doors and windows carelessly open, and none showed a light.

This place, upon which I had at last happened, was a fruit of the reaction of artistic-minded and carelessly living people against the costly and uncomfortable social stiffness of the more formal seaside resorts of that time. It was, you must understand, the custom of the steam-railway companies to sell their carriages after they had been obsolete for a sufficient length of years, and some genius had hit upon the possibility of turning these into little habitable cabins for the summer holiday. The thing had become a fashion with a certain Bohemian-spirited class; they added cabin to cabin, and these little

106

improvised homes, gaily painted and with broad verandas and sup-
plementary leantos added to their accommodation, made the brightest
contrast conceivable to the dull rigidities of the decorous resorts. Of
course there were many discomforts in such camping that had to be
faced cheerfully, and so this broad sandy beach was sacred to high
spirits and the young. Art muslin and banjoes, Chinese lanterns and
frying, are leading 'notes', I find, in the impression of those who once
knew such places well. But so far as I was concerned this odd settlement
of pleasure-squatters was a mystery as well as a surprise, enhanced
rather than mitigated by an imaginative suggestion or so I had received
from the wooden-legged man at Shaphambury. I saw the thing as no
gathering of light hearts and gay idleness, but grimly – after the manner
of poor men poisoned by the suppression of all their cravings after joy.
To the poor man, to the grimy workers, beauty and cleanness were
absolutely denied; out of a life of greasy dirt, of muddied desires, they
watched their happier fellows with a bitter envy and foul, tormenting
suspicions. Fancy a world in which the common people held love to
be a sort of beastliness, own sister to being drunk! . . .

There was in the old time always something cruel at the bottom of
this business of sexual love. At least that is the impression I have
brought with me across the gulf of the great Change. To succeed in
love seemed such triumph as no other success could give, but to fail
was as if one was tainted. . . .

I felt no sense of singularity that this thread of savagery should
run through these emotions of mine and become now the whole
strand of these emotions. I believed, and I think I was right in
believing, that the love of all true lovers was a sort of defiance then,
that they closed a system in each other's arms and mocked the
world without. You loved against the world, and these two loved
AT me. They had their business with one another, under the threat
of a watchful fierceness. A sword, a sharp sword, the keenest edge
in life, lay among their roses.

Whatever may be true of this for others, for me and my imagination,
at any rate, it was altogether true. I was never for dalliance, I was never
a jesting lover. I wanted fiercely; I made love impatiently. Perhaps I had
written irrelevant love-letters for that very reason; because with this
stark theme I could not play . . .

The thought of Nettie's shining form, of her shrinking bold abandon
to her easy conqueror, gave me now a body of rage that was nearly too
strong for my heart and nerves and the tense powers of my merely
physical being. I came down among the pale sand-heaps slowly towards
that queer village of careless sensuality, and now within my puny body

I was coldly sharpset for pain and death, a darkly gleaming hate, a sword of evil, drawn.

Section 6

I halted, and stood planning what I had to do.

Should I go to bungalow after bungalow until one of the two I sought answered to my rap? But suppose some servant intervened!

Should I wait where I was – perhaps until morning – watching? And meanwhile—

All the nearer bungalows were very still now. If I walked softly to them, from open windows, from something seen or overheard, I might get a clue to guide me. Should I advance circuitously, creeping upon them, or should I walk straight to the door? It was bright enough for her to recognize me clearly at a distance of many paces.

The difficulty to my mind lay in this, that if I involved other people by questions, I might at last confront my betrayers with these others close about me, ready to snatch my weapon and seize my hands. Besides, what names might they bear here?

'Boom!' the sound crept upon my senses, and then again it came.

I turned impatiently as one turns upon an impertinence, and beheld a great ironclad not four miles out, steaming fast across the dappled silver, and from its funnels sparks, intensely red, poured out into the night. As I turned, came the hot flash of its guns, firing seaward, and answering this, red flashes and a streaming smoke in the line between sea and sky. So I remembered it, and I remember myself staring at it – in a state of stupid arrest. It was an irrelevance. What had these things to do with me?

With a shuddering hiss, a rocket from a headland beyond the village leapt up and burst hot gold against the glare, and the sound of the third and fourth guns reached me.

The windows of the dark bungalows, one after another, leapt out, squares of ruddy brightness that flared and flickered and became steadily bright. Dark heads appeared looking seaward, a door opened, and sent out a brief lane of yellow to mingle and be lost in the comet's brightness. That brought me back to the business in hand.

'Boom! boom!' and when I looked again at the great ironclad, a little torchlike spurt of flame wavered behind her funnels. I could hear the throb and clangor of her straining engines. . . .

I became aware of the voices of people calling to one another in the village. A white-robed, hooded figure, some man in a bathing wrap, absurdly suggestive of an Arab in his burnous, came out from one of the nearer bungalows, and stood clear and still and shadowless in the glare.

He put his hands to shade his seaward eyes, and shouted to people within.

The people within – MY people! My fingers tightened on my revolver. What was this war nonsense to me? I would go round among the hummocks with the idea of approaching the three bungalows inconspicuously from the flank. This fight at sea might serve my purpose – except for that, it had no interest for me at all. Boom! boom! The huge voluminous concussions rushed past me, beat at my heart and passed. In a moment Nettie would come out to see.

First one and then two other wrappered figures came out of the bungalows to join the first. His arm pointed seaward, and his voice, a full tenor, rose in explanation. I could hear some of the words. 'It's a German!' he said. 'She's caught.'

Some one disputed that, and there followed a little indistinct babble of argument. I went on slowly in the circuit I had marked out, watching these people as I went.

They shouted together with such a common intensity of direction that I halted and looked seaward. I saw the tall fountain flung by a shot that had just missed the great warship. A second rose still nearer us, a third, and a fourth, and then a great uprush of dust, a whirling cloud, leapt out of the headland whence the rocket had come, and spread with a slow deliberation right and left. Hard on that an enormous crash, and the man with the full voice leapt and cried, 'Hit!'

Let me see! Of course, I had to go round beyond the bungalows, and then come up towards the group from behind.

A high-pitched woman's voice called, 'Honeymooners! honeymooners! Come out and see!'

Something gleamed in the shadow of the nearer bungalow, and a man's voice answered from within. What he said I did not catch, but suddenly I heard Nettie calling very distinctly, 'We've been bathing.'

The man who had first come out shouted, 'Don't you hear the guns? They're fighting – not five miles from shore.'

'Eh?' answered the bungalow, and a window opened.

'Out there!'

I did not hear the reply, because of the faint rustle of my own movements. Clearly these people were all too much occupied by the battle to look in my direction, and so I walked now straight towards the darkness that held Nettie and the black desire of my heart.

'Look!' cried some one, and pointed skyward.

I glanced up, and behold! The sky was streaked with bright green trails. They radiated from a point halfway between the western horizon and the zenith, and within the shining clouds of the meteor a streaming movement had begun, so that it seemed to be pouring both westwardly and back toward the east, with a crackling sound, as though the whole heaven was stippled over with phantom pistol-shots. It seemed to me then as if the meteor was coming to help me, descending with those thousand pistols like a curtain to fend off this unmeaning foolishness of the sea.

'Boom!' went a gun on the big ironclad, and 'boom!' and the guns of the pursuing cruisers flashed in reply.

To glance up at that streaky, stirring light scum of the sky made one's head swim. I stood for a moment dazed, and more than a little giddy. I had a curious instant of purely speculative thought. Suppose, after all, the fanatics were right, and the world WAS coming to an end! What a score that would be for Parload!

Then it came into my head that all these things were happening to consecrate my revenge! The war below, the heavens above, were the thunderous garment of my deed. I heard Nettie's voice cry out not fifty yards away, and my passion surged again. I was to return to her amid these terrors bearing unanticipated death. I was to possess her, with a bullet, amidst thunderings and fear. At the thought I lifted up my voice to a shout that went unheard, and advanced now recklessly, revolver displayed in my hand.

It was fifty yards, forty yards, thirty yards – the little group of people, still heedless of me, was larger and more important now, the green-shot sky and the fighting ships remoter. Some one darted out from the bungalow, with an interrupted question, and stopped, suddenly aware of me. It was Nettie, with some coquettish dark wrap about her, and the green glare shining on her sweet face and white throat. I could see her expression, stricken with dismay and terror, at my advance, as though something had seized her by the heart and held her still – a target for my shots.

'Boom!' came the ironclad's gunshot like a command. 'Bang!' the bullet leapt from my hand. Do you know, I did not want to shoot her then. Indeed I did not want to shoot her then! Bang! and I had fired again, still striding on, and – each time it seemed I had missed.

She moved a step or so toward me, still staring, and then someone intervened, and near beside her I saw young Verrall.

A heavy stranger, the man in the hooded bath-gown, a fat, foreign-looking man, came out of nowhere like a shield before them. He seemed a preposterous interruption. His face was full of astonishment and terror. He rushed across my path with arms extended and open hands, as one might try to stop a runaway horse. He shouted some nonsense. He seemed to want to dissuade me, as though dissuasion had anything to do with it now.

'Not you, you fool!' I said hoarsely. 'Not you!' But he hid Nettie nevertheless.

By an enormous effort I resisted a mechanical impulse to shoot through his fat body. Anyhow, I knew I mustn't shoot him. For a moment I was in doubt, then I became very active, turned aside abruptly and dodged his pawing arm to the left, and so found two others irresolutely in my way. I fired a third shot in the air, just over their heads, and ran at them. They hastened left and right; I pulled up and faced about within a yard of a foxy-faced young man coming sideways, who seemed about to grapple me. At my resolute halt he fell back a pace, ducked, and threw up a defensive arm, and then I perceived the course was clear, and ahead of me, young Verrall and Nettie – he was holding her arm to help her – running away. 'Of course!' said I. .

I fired a fourth ineffectual shot, and then in an access of fury at my misses, started out to run them down and shoot them barrel to backbone. 'These people!' I said, dismissing all these interferences. . . . 'A yard,' I panted, speaking aloud to myself, 'a yard! Till then, take care, you mustn't – mustn't shoot again.'

Some one pursued me, perhaps several people – I do not know, we left them all behind. . . .

We ran. For a space I was altogether intent upon the swift monotony of flight and pursuit. The sands were changed to a whirl of green moonshine, the air was thunder. A luminous green haze rolled about us. What did such things matter? We ran. Did I gain or lose? that was the question. They ran through a gap in a broken fence that sprang up abruptly out of nothingness and turned to the right. I noted we were in a road. But this green mist! One seemed to plough through it. They were fading into it, and at that thought I made a spurt that won a dozen feet or more.

She staggered. He gripped her arm, and dragged her forward. They doubled to the left. We were off the road again and on turf. It felt like turf. I tripped and fell at a ditch that was somehow full of smoke, and was up again, but now they were phantoms half gone into the livid swirls about me. . . .

Still I ran.

On, on! I groaned with the violence of my effort. I staggered again and swore. I felt the concussions of great guns tear past me through the murk.

They were gone! Everything was going, but I kept on running. Once more I stumbled. There was something about my feet that impeded me, tall grass or heather, but I could not see what it was, only this smoke that eddied about my knees. There was a noise and spinning in my brain, a vain resistance to a dark green curtain that was falling, falling, falling, fold upon fold. Everything grew darker and darker.

I made one last frantic effort, and raised my revolver, fired my penultimate shot at a venture, and fell headlong to the ground.

And behold! the green curtain was a black one, and the earth and I and all things ceased to be.

BOOK THE SECOND
The Green Vapours

CHAPTER THE FIRST

The Change

Section 1

I seemed to awaken out of a refreshing sleep.

I did not awaken with a start, but opened my eyes, and lay very comfortably looking at a line of extraordinarily scarlet poppies that glowed against a glowing sky. It was the sky of a magnificent sunrise, and an archipelago of gold-beached purple islands floated in a sea of golden green. The poppies too, swan-necked buds, blazing corollas, translucent stout seed-vessels, stoutly upheld, had a luminous quality, seemed wrought only from some more solid kind of light.

I stared unwonderingly at these things for a time, and then there rose upon my consciousness, intermingling with these, the bristling golden green heads of growing barley.

A remote faint question, where I might be, drifted and vanished again in my mind. Everything was very still.

Everything was as still as death.

I felt very light, full of the sense of physical well-being. I perceived I was lying on my side in a little trampled space in a weedy, flowering barley field, that was in some inexplicable way saturated with light and beauty. I sat up, and remained for a long time filled with the delight and charm of the delicate little convolvulus that twined among the barley stems, the pimpernel that laced the ground below.

Then that question returned. What was this place? How had I come to be sleeping here?

I could not remember.

It perplexed me that somehow my body felt strange to me. It was unfamiliar – I could not tell how – and the barley, and the beautiful weeds, and the slowly developing glory of the dawn behind; all those things partook of the same unfamiliarity. I felt as though I was a thing in some very luminous painted window, as though this dawn broke through me. I felt I was part of some exquisite picture painted in light and joy.

A faint breeze bent and rustled the barley-heads, and jogged my mind forward.

Who was I? That was a good way of beginning.

I held up my left hand and arm before me, a grubby hand, a frayed cuff; but with a quality of painted unreality, transfigured as a beggar might have been by Botticelli. I looked for a time steadfastly at a beautiful pearl sleeve-link.

I remembered Willie Leadford, who had owned that arm and hand, as though he had been some one else.

Of course! My history – its rough outline rather than the immediate past – began to shape itself in my memory, very small, very bright and inaccessible, like a thing watched through a microscope. Clayton and Swathinglea returned to my mind; the slums and darkness, Dürer-esque, minute and in their rich dark colours pleasing, and through them I went towards my destiny. I sat hands on knees recalling that queer passionate career that had ended with my futile shot into the growing darkness of the End. The thought of that shot awoke my emotions again.

There was something in it now, something absurd, that made me smile pityingly.

Poor little angry, miserable creature! Poor little angry, miserable world!

I sighed for pity, not only pity for myself, but for all the hot hearts, the tormented brains, the straining, striving things of hope and pain, who had found their peace at last beneath the pouring mist and suffocation of the comet. Because certainly that world was over and done. They were all so weak and unhappy, and I was now so strong and so serene. For I felt sure I was dead; no one living could have this perfect assurance of good, this strong and confident peace. I had made an end of the fever called living. I was dead, and it was all right, and these—?

I felt an inconsistency.

These, then, must be the barley fields of God! – the still and silent barley fields of God, full of unfading poppy flowers whose seeds bear peace.

Section 2

It was queer to find barley fields in heaven, but no doubt there were many surprises in store for me.

How still everything was! Peace! The peace that passeth understanding. After all it had come to me! But, indeed, everything was very still! No bird sang. Surely I was alone in the world! No birds sang. Yes, and all the distant sounds of life had ceased, the lowing of cattle, the barking of dogs. . . .

Something that was like fear beatified came into my heart. It was all right, I knew; but to be alone! I stood up and met the hot summons of the rising sun, hurrying towards me, as it were, with glad tidings, over the spikes of the barley. . . .

Blinded, I made a step. My foot struck something hard, and I looked down to discover my revolver, a blue-black thing, like a dead snake at my feet.

For a moment that puzzled me.

Then I clean forgot about it. The wonder of the quiet took possession of my soul. Dawn, and no birds singing!

How beautiful was the world! How beautiful, but how still! I walked slowly through the barley towards a line of elder bushes, wayfaring tree and bramble that made the hedge of the field. I noted as I passed along a dead shrew mouse, as it seemed to me, among the halms; then a still toad. I was surprised that this did not leap aside from my footfalls, and I stooped and picked it up. Its body was limp like life, but it made no struggle, the brightness of its eye was veiled, it did not move in my hand.

It seems to me now that I stood holding that lifeless little creature for some time. Then very softly I stooped down and replaced it. I was trembling – trembling with a nameless emotion. I looked with quickened eyes closely among the barley stems, and behold, now everywhere I saw beetles, flies, and little creatures that did not move, lying as they fell when the vapours overcame them; they seemed no more than painted things. Some were novel creatures to me. I was very unfamiliar with natural things. 'My God!' I cried; 'but is it only I—?'

And then at my next movement something squealed sharply. I turned about, but I could not see it, only I saw a little stir in a rut and heard the diminishing rustle of the unseen creature's flight. And at that I turned to my toad again, and its eye moved and it stirred. And presently, with infirm and hesitating gestures, it stretched its limbs and began to crawl away from me.

But wonder, that gentle sister of fear, had me now. I saw a little way ahead a brown and crimson butterfly perched upon a cornflower. I thought at first it was the breeze that stirred it, and then I saw its wings were quivering. And even as I watched it, it started into life, and spread itself, and fluttered into the air.

I watched it fly, a turn this way, a turn that, until suddenly it seemed to vanish. And now, life was returning to this thing and that on every side of me, with slow stretchings and bendings, with twitterings, with a little start and stir. . . .

I came slowly, stepping very carefully because of these drugged, feebly awakening things, through the barley to the hedge. It was a very glorious hedge, so that it held my eyes. It flowed along and interlaced like splendid music. It was rich with lupin, honeysuckle, campions and ragged robin; bed straw, hops and wild clematis twined and hung among its branches, and all along its ditch border the starry stitchwort lifted its childish faces, and chorused in lines and masses. Never had I seen such a symphony of note-like flowers and tendrils and leaves. And suddenly in its depths, I heard a chirrup and the whirr of startled wings.

Nothing was dead, but everything had changed to beauty! And I stood for a time with clean and happy eyes looking at the intricate delicacy before me and marvelling how richly God has made his worlds. . . .

'Tweedle-Tweezle,' a lark had shot the stillness with his shining thread of song; one lark, and then presently another, invisibly in the air, making out of that blue quiet a woven cloth of gold. . . .

The earth recreated – only by the reiteration of such phrases may I hope to give the intense freshness of that dawn. For a time I was altogether taken up with the beautiful details of being, as regardless of my old life of jealous passion and impatient sorrow as though I was Adam new made. I could tell you now with infinite particularity of the shut flowers that opened as I looked, of tendrils and grass blades, of a blue-tit I picked up very tenderly – never before had I remarked the great delicacy of feathers – that presently disclosed its bright black eye and judged me, and perched, swaying fearlessly, upon my finger, and spread unhurried wings and flew away, and of a great ebullition of tadpoles in the ditch; like all the things that lived beneath the water, they had passed unaltered through the Change. Amid such incidents, I lived those first great moments, losing for a time in the wonder of each little part the mighty wonder of the whole.

A little path ran between hedge and barley, and along this, leisurely and content and glad, looking at this beautiful thing and that, moving a step and stopping, then moving on again, I came presently to a stile, and deep below it, and overgrown, was a lane.

And on the worn oak of the stile was a round label, and on the label these words, 'Swindells' G 90 Pills.'

I sat myself astraddle on the stile, not fully grasping all the implications of these words. But they perplexed me even more than the revolver and my dirty cuff.

About me now the birds lifted up their little hearts and sang, ever more birds and more.

I read the label over and over again, and joined it to the fact that I still wore my former clothes, and that my revolver had been lying at my feet. One conclusion stared out at me. This was no new planet, no glorious hereafter such as I had supposed. This beautiful wonderland was the world, the same old world of my rage and death! But at least it was like meeting a familiar house-slut, washed and dignified, dressed in a queen's robes, worshipful and fine. . . .

It might be the old world indeed, but something new lay upon all things, a glowing certitude of health and happiness. It might be the old world, but the dust and fury of the old life was certainly done. At least I had no doubt of that.

I recalled the last phases of my former life, that darkling climax of pursuit and anger and universal darkness and the whirling green vapours of extinction. The comet had struck the earth and made an end to all things; of that too I was assured.

But afterwards? . . .

And now?

The imaginations of my boyhood came back as speculative possibilities. In those days I had believed firmly in the necessary advent of a last day, a great coming out of the sky, trumpetings and fear, the Resurrection, and the Judgment. My roving fancy now suggested to me that this Judgment must have come and passed. That it had passed and in some manner missed me. I was left alone here, in a swept and garnished world (except, of course, for this label of Swindells') to begin again perhaps. . . .

No doubt Swindells has got his deserts.

My mind ran for a time on Swindells, on the imbecile pushfulness of that extinct creature, dealing in rubbish, covering the country-side with lies in order to get – what had he sought? – a silly, ugly, great house, a temper-destroying motor-car, a number of disrespectful, abject servants; thwarted intrigues for a party-fund baronetcy as the crest of his life, perhaps. You cannot imagine the littleness of those former times; their naive, queer absurdities! And for the first time in my existence I thought of these things without bitterness. In the former days I had seen wickedness, I had seen tragedy, but now I saw only the extraordinary foolishness of the old life. The ludicrous side of human wealth and importance turned itself upon me, a shining novelty, poured down upon me like the sunrise, and engulfed me in laughter. Swindells! Swindells, damned! My vision of Judgment became a delightful burlesque. I saw the chuckling Angel sayer with his face veiled, and the corporeal presence of Swindells upheld amidst the laughter of the spheres. 'Here's a thing, and a very pretty thing, and what's to be done with this very pretty thing?' I saw a soul being drawn from a rotund, substantial-looking body like a whelk from its shell. . . .

I laughed loudly and long. And behold! even as I laughed the keen point of things accomplished stabbed my mirth, and I was weeping, weeping aloud, convulsed with weeping, and the tears were pouring down my face.

Section 3

Everywhere the awakening came with the sunrise. We awakened to the gladness of the morning; we walked dazzled in a light that was joy. Everywhere that was so. It was always morning. It was morning because, until the direct rays of the sun touched it, the changing nitrogen of our atmosphere did not pass into its permanent phase, and the sleepers lay as they had fallen. In its intermediate state the air hung inert, incapable of producing either revival or stupefaction, no longer green, but not yet changed to the gas that now lives in us. . . .

To every one, I think, came some parallel to the mental states I have already sought to describe – a wonder, an impression of joyful novelty. There was also very commonly a certain confusion of the intelligence, a difficulty in self-recognition. I remember clearly as I sat on my stile that presently I had the clearest doubts of my own identity and fell into the oddest metaphysical questionings. 'If this be I,' I said, 'then how is it I am no longer madly seeking Nettie? Nettie is now the remotest thing – and all my wrongs. Why have I suddenly passed out of all that passion? Why does not the thought of Verrall quicken my pulses?' . . .

I was only one of many millions who that morning had the same doubts. I suppose one knows one's self for one's self when one returns from sleep or insensibility by the familiarity of one's bodily sensations, and that morning all our most intimate bodily sensations were changed. The intimate chemical processes of life were changed, its nervous metaboly. For the fluctuating, uncertain, passion-darkened thought and feeling of the old time came steady, full-bodied, whole-some processes. Touch was different, sight was different, sound and all the senses were subtler; had it not been that our thought was steadier and fuller, I believe great multitudes of men would have gone mad. But, as it was, we understood. The dominant impression I would convey in this account of the Change is one of enormous release, of a vast substantial exaltation. There was an effect, as it were, of light-headedness that was also clear-headedness, and the alteration in one's bodily sensations, instead of producing the mental obfuscation, the loss of identity that was a common mental trouble under former conditions, gave simply a new detachment from the tumid passions and entanglements of the personal life.

In this story of my bitter, restricted youth that I have been telling you, I have sought constantly to convey the narrowness, the intensity, the confusion, muddle, and dusty heat of the old world. It was quite clear to me, within an hour of my awakening, that all that was, in some mysterious way, over and done. That, too, was the common experience. Men stood up; they took the new air into their lungs – a deep long breath, and the past fell from them; they could forgive, they could disregard, they could attempt. . . . And it was no new thing, no miracle that sets aside the former order of the world. It was a change in material conditions, a change in the atmosphere, that at one bound had released them. Some of them it had released to death. . . . Indeed, man himself had changed not at all. We knew before the Change, the meanest knew, by glowing moments in ourselves and others, by his-tories and music and beautiful things, by heroic instances and splendid stories, how fine mankind could be, how fine almost any human being could upon occasion be; but the poison in the air, its poverty in all the nobler elements which made such moments rare and remarkable – all that has changed. The air was changed, and the Spirit of Man that had drowsed and slumbered and dreamt dull and evil things, awakened, and stood with wonder-clean eyes, refreshed, looking again on life.

Section 4

The miracle of the awakening came to me in solitude, the laughter, and then the tears. Only after some time did I come upon another man. Until I heard his voice calling I did not seem to feel there were any other people in the world. All that seemed past, with all the stresses that were past. I had come out of the individual pit in which my shy egotism had lurked, I had overflowed to all humanity, I had seemed to be all humanity; I had laughed at Swindells as I could have laughed

123

at myself, and this shout that came to me seemed like the coming of an unexpected thought in my own mind. But when it was repeated I answered.

'I am hurt,' said the voice, and I descended into the lane forthwith, and so came upon Melmount sitting near the ditch with his back to me.

Some of the incidental sensory impressions of that morning bit so deeply into my mind that I verily believe, when at last I face the greater mysteries that lie beyond this life, when the things of this life fade from me as the mists of the morning fade before the sun, these irrelevant petty details will be the last to leave me, will be the last wisps visible of that attenuating veil. I believe, for instance, I could match the fur upon the collar of his great motoring coat now, could paint the dull red tinge of his big cheek with his fair eyelashes just catching the light and showing beyond. His hat was off, his dome-shaped head, with its smooth hair between red and extreme fairness, was bent forward in scrutiny of his twisted foot. His back seemed enormous. And there was something about the mere massive sight of him that filled me with liking.

'What's wrong?' said I.

'I say,' he said, in his full deliberate tones, straining round to see me and showing a profile, a well-modelled nose, a sensitive, clumsy, big lip, known to every caricaturist in the world, 'I'm in a fix. I fell and wrenched my ankle. Where are you?'

I walked round him and stood looking at his face. I perceived he had his gaiter and sock and boot off, the motor gauntlets had been cast aside, and he was kneading the injured part in an exploratory manner with his thick thumbs.

'By Jove!' I said, 'you're Melmount!'

'Melmount!' He thought. 'That's my name,' he said, without looking up. . . . 'But it doesn't affect my ankle.'

We remained silent for few moments except for a grunt of pain from him.

'Do you know?' I asked, 'what has happened to things?'

He seemed to complete his diagnosis. 'It's not broken,' he said.

'Do you know,' I repeated, 'what has happened to everything?'

'No,' he said, looking up at me incuriously for the first time.

'There's some difference—'

'There's a difference.' He smiled, a smile of unexpected pleasantness, and an interest was coming into his eyes. 'I've been a little preoccupied with my own internal sensations. I remark an extraordinary brightness about things. Is that it?'

'That's part of it. And a queer feeling, a clear-headedness—'

He surveyed me and meditated gravely. 'I woke up,' he said, feeling his way in his memory.

'And I.'

'I lost my way – I forget quite how. There was a curious green fog.' He stared at his foot, remembering. 'Something to do with a comet. I was by a hedge in the darkness. Tried to run. ... Then I must have pitched into this lane. Look!' He pointed with his head. 'There's a wooden rail new broken there. I must have stumbled over that out of the field above.' He scrutinized this and concluded. 'Yes. ...'

'It was dark,' I said, 'and a sort of green gas came out of nothing everywhere. That is the last I remember.'

'And then you woke up? So did I. . . . In a state of great bewilderment. Certainly there's something odd in the air. I was – I was rushing along a road in a motor-car, very much excited and preoccupied. I got down—' He held out a triumphant finger. 'Ironclads! NOW I've got it! We'd strung our fleet from here to Texel. We'd got right across them and the Elbe mined. We'd lost the *Lord Warden*. By Jove, yes. The *Lord Warden*! A battleship that cost two million pounds – and that fool Rigby said it didn't matter! Eleven hundred men went down. ... I remember now. We were sweeping up the North Sea like a net, with the North Atlantic fleet waiting at the Faroes for 'em – and not one of 'em had three days' coal! Now, was that a dream? No! I told a lot of people as much – a meeting was it? – to reassure them. They were warlike but extremely frightened. Queer people – paunchy and bald like gnomes, most of them. Where? Of course! We had it all over – a big dinner – oysters! – Colchester. I'd been there, just to show all this raid scare was nonsense. And I was coming back here. . . . But it doesn't seem as though that was – recent. I suppose it was. Yes, of course! – it was. I got out of my car at the bottom of the rise with the idea of walking along the cliff path, because every one said one of their battleships was being chased along the shore. That's clear! I heard their guns—'

He reflected. 'Queer I should have forgotten! Did YOU hear any guns?'

I said I had heard them.

'Was it last night?'

'Late last night. One or two in the morning.'

He leant back on his hand and looked at me, smiling frankly. 'Even now,' he said, 'it's odd, but the whole of that seems like a silly dream. Do you think there WAS a *Lord Warden*? Do you really believe we

125

sank all that machinery – for fun? It was a dream. And yet – it happened.'

By all the standards of the former time it would have been remarkable that I talked quite easily and freely with so great a man. 'Yes,' I said; 'that's it. One feels one has awakened – from something more than that green gas. As though the other things also – weren't quite real.'

He knitted his brows and felt the calf of his leg thoughtfully. 'I made a speech at Colchester,' he said.

I thought he was going to add something more about that, but there lingered a habit of reticence in the man that held him for the moment. 'It is a very curious thing,' he broke away; 'that this pain should be, on the whole, more interesting than disagreeable.'

'You are in pain?'

'My ankle is! It's either broken or badly sprained – I think sprained; it's very painful to move, but personally I'm not in pain. That sort of general sickness that comes with local injury – not a trace of it! ...' He mused and remarked, 'I was speaking at Colchester, and saying things about the war. I begin to see it better. The reporters – scribble, scribble. Max Sutaine, 1885. Hubbub. Compliments about the oysters. Mm – mm. ... What was it? About the war? A war that must needs be long and bloody, taking toll from castle and cottage, taking toll! ... Rhetorical gusto! Was I drunk last night?'

His eyebrows puckered. He had drawn up his right knee, his elbow rested thereon and his chin on his fist. The deep-set grey eyes beneath his thatch of eyebrow stared at unknown things. 'My God!' he murmured, 'My God!' with a note of disgust. He made a big brooding figure in the sunlight, he had an effect of more than physical largeness; he made me feel that it became me to wait upon his thinking. I had never met a man of this sort before; I did not know such men existed. ...

It is a curious thing, that I cannot now recall any ideas whatever that I had before the Change about the personalities of statesmen, but I doubt if ever in those days I thought of them at all as tangible individual human beings, conceivably of some intellectual complexity. I believe that my impression was a straightforward blend of caricature and newspaper leader. I certainly had no respect for them. And now without servility or any insincerity whatever, as if it were a first-fruit of the Change, I found myself in the presence of a human being towards whom I perceived myself inferior and subordinate, before whom I stood without servility or any insincerity whatever, in an attitude of respect and attention. My inflamed, my rancid egotism –

126

or was it after all only the chances of life? – had never once permitted that before the Change.

He emerged from his thoughts, still with a faint perplexity in his manner. 'That speech I made last night,' he said, 'was damned mischievous nonsense, you know. Nothing can alter that. Nothing. . . . No! . . . Little fat gnomes in evening dress – gobbling oysters. Gulp!'

It was a most natural part of the wonder of that morning that he should adopt this incredible note of frankness, and that it should abate nothing from my respect for him.

'Yes,' he said, 'you are right. It's all indisputable fact, and I can't believe it was anything but a dream.'

Section 5

That memory stands out against the dark past of the world with extraordinary clearness and brightness. The air, I remember, was full of the calling and piping and singing of birds. I have a curious persuasion too that there was a distant happy clamour of pealing bells, but that I am half convinced is a mistake. Nevertheless, there was something in the fresh bite of things, in the dewy newness of sensation that set bells rejoicing in one's brain. And that big, fair, pensive man sitting on the ground had beauty even in his clumsy pose, as though indeed some Great Master of strength and humour had made him.

And – it is so hard now to convey these things – he spoke to me, a stranger, without reservations, carelessly, as men now speak to men. Before those days, not only did we think badly, but what we thought, a thousand short-sighted considerations, dignity, objective discipline, discretion, a hundred kindred aspects of shabbiness of soul, made us muffle before we told it to our fellow-men.

'It's all returning now,' he said, and told me half soliloquizingly what was in his mind.

I wish I could give every word he said to me; he struck out image after image to my nascent intelligence, with swift broken fragments of speech. If I had a precise full memory of that morning I should give it you, verbatim, minutely. But here, save for the little sharp things that stand out, I find only blurred general impressions. Throughout I have to make up again his half-forgotten sentences and speeches, and be content with giving you the general effect. But I can see and hear him now as he said, 'The dream got worst at the end. The war – a perfectly horrible business! Horrible! And it was just like a nightmare, you couldn't do anything to escape from it – every one was driven!'

His sense of indiscretion was gone.

127

He opened the war out to me – as every one sees it now. Only that morning it was astonishing. He sat there on the ground, absurdly forgetful of his bare and swollen foot, treating me as the humblest accessory and as altogether an equal, talking out to himself the great obsessions of his mind. 'We could have prevented it! Any of us who chose to speak out could have prevented it. A little decent frankness. What was there to prevent us being frank with one another? Their emperor – his position was a pile of ridiculous assumptions, no doubt, but at bottom – he was a sane man.' He touched off the emperor in a few pithy words, the German press, the German people, and our own. He put it as we should put it all now, but with a certain heat as of a man half guilty and wholly resentful. 'Their damned little buttoned-up professors!' he cried, incidentally. 'Were there ever such men? And ours! Some of us might have taken a firmer line. . . . If a lot of us had taken a firmer line and squashed that nonsense early. . . .'

He lapsed into inaudible whisperings, into silence. . . .

I stood regarding him, understanding him, learning marvellously from him. It is a fact that for the best part of the morning of the Change I forgot Nettie and Verrall as completely as though they were no more than characters in some novel that I had put aside to finish at my leisure, in order that I might talk to this man.

'Eh, well,' he said, waking startlingly from his thoughts. 'Here we are awakened! The thing can't go on now; all this must end. How it ever began—! My dear boy, how did all those things ever begin? I feel like a new Adam. . . . Do you think this has happened – generally? Or shall we find all these gnomes and things? . . . Who cares?'

He made as if to rise, and remembered his ankle. He suggested I should help him as far as his bungalow. There seemed nothing strange to either of us that he should requisition my services or that I should cheerfully obey. I helped him bandage his ankle, and we set out, I his crutch, the two of us making up a sort of limping quadruped, along the winding lane toward the cliffs and the sea.

Section 6

His bungalow beyond the golf links was, perhaps, a mile and a quarter from the lane. We went down to the beach margin and along the pallid wave-smoothed sands, and we got along by making a swaying, hopping, tripod dance forward until I began to give under him, and then, as soon as we could, sitting down. His ankle was, in fact, broken, and he could not put it to the ground without exquisite pain. So that it took us nearly two hours to get to the house, and it would have taken longer if his butler-valet had not come out to assist me. They had found motor-car and chauffeur smashed and still at the bend of the road near the house, and had been on that side looking for Melmount, or they would have seen us before.

For most of that time we were sitting now on turf, now on a chalk boulder, now on a timber groin, and talking one to the other, with the frankness proper to the intercourse of men of good intent, without reservations or aggressions, in the common, open fashion of contemporary intercourse to-day, but which then, nevertheless, was the rarest and strangest thing in the world. He for the most part talked, but at some shape of a question I told him – as plainly as I could tell of passions that had for a time become incomprehensible to me – of my murderous pursuit of Nettie and her lover, and how the green vapours overcame me. He watched me with grave eyes and nodded understandingly, and afterwards he asked me brief penetrating questions about my education, my upbringing, my work. There was a deliberation in his manner, brief full pauses, that had in them no element of delay.

'Yes,' he said, 'yes – of course. What a fool I have been!' and said no more until we had made another of our tripod struggles along the beach. At first I did not see the connection of my story with that self-accusation.

'Suppose,' he said, panting on the groin, 'there had been such a thing as a statesman! ...'

He turned to me. 'If one had decided all this muddle shall end! If one had taken it, as an artist takes his clay, as a man who builds takes site and stone, and made—' He flung out his big broad hand at the glories of sky and sea, and drew a deep breath, 'something to fit that setting.'

He added in explanation, 'Then there wouldn't have been such stories as yours at all, you know. ...'

'Tell me more about it,' he said, 'tell me all about yourself. I feel all these things have passed away, all these things are to be changed for ever. ... You won't be what you have been from this time forth. All the things you have done – don't matter now. To us, at any rate, they don't matter at all. We have met, who were separated in that darkness behind us. Tell me.

'Yes,' he said; and I told my story straight and as frankly as I have told it to you. 'And there, where those little skerries of weed rock run out to the ebb, beyond the headland, is Bungalow village. What did you do with your pistol?'

'I left it lying there – among the barley.'

He glanced at me from under his light eyelashes. 'If others feel like you and I,' he said, 'there'll be a lot of pistols left among the barley to-day. . . .'

So we talked, I and that great, strong man, with the love of brothers so plain between us it needed not a word. Our souls went out to one another in stark good faith; never before had I had anything but a guarded watchfulness for any fellow-man. Still I see him, upon that wild desolate beach of the ebb tide, I see him leaning against the shelly buttress of a groin, looking down at the poor drowned sailor whose body we presently found. For we found a newly drowned man who had just chanced to miss this great dawn in which we rejoiced. We found him lying in a pool of water, among brown weeds in the dark shadow of the timberings. You must not overrate the horrors of the former days; in those days it was scarcely more common to see death in England than it would be to-day. This dead man was a sailor from the *Rother Adler*, the great German battleship that – had we but known it – lay not four miles away along the coast amidst ploughed-up mountains of chalk ooze, a torn and battered mass of machinery, wholly submerged at high water, and holding in its interstices nine hundred drowned brave men, all strong and skilful, all once capable of doing fine things. . . .

I remember that poor boy very vividly. He had been drowned during the anaesthesia of the green gas, his fair young face was quiet and calm, but the skin of his chest had been crinkled by scalding water and his right arm was bent queerly back. Even to this needless death and all its tale of cruelty, beauty and dignity had come. Everything flowed together to significance as we stood there, I, the ill-clad, cheaply equipped proletarian, and Melmount in his great fur-trimmed coat – he was hot with walking but he had not thought to remove it – leaning upon the clumsy groins and pitying this poor victim of the war he had helped to make. 'Poor lad!' he said, 'poor lad! A child we blunderers sent to death! Do look at the quiet beauty of that face, that body – to be flung aside like this!'

(I remember that near this dead man's hand a stranded starfish writhed its slowly feeling limbs, struggling back towards the sea. It left grooved traces in the sand.)

'There must be no more of this,' panted Melmount, leaning on my shoulder, 'no more of this. . . .'

But most I recall Melmount as he talked a little later, sitting upon a great chalk boulder with the sunlight on his big, perspiration-dewed face. He made his resolves. 'We must end war,' he said, in that full whisper of his; 'it is stupidity. With so many people able to read and think – even as it is – there is no need of anything of the sort. Gods! What have we rulers been at? ... Drowsing like people in a stifling room, too dull and sleepy and too base towards each other for any one to get up and open the window. What haven't we been at?'

A great powerful figure he sits there still in my memory, perplexed and astonished at himself and all things. 'We must change all this,' he repeated, and threw out his broad hands in a powerful gesture against the sea and sky. 'We have done so weakly – Heaven alone knows why!' I can see him now, queer giant that he looked on that dawnlit beach of splendour, the sea birds flying about us and that crumpled death hard by, no bad symbol in his clumsiness and needless heat of the unawakened powers of the former time. I remember it as an integral part of that picture that far away across the sandy stretches one of those white estate boards I have described, stuck up a little askew amidst the yellow-green turf upon the crest of the low cliffs.

He talked with a sort of wonder of the former things. 'Has it ever dawned upon you to imagine the pettiness – the pettiness! – of every soul concerned in a declaration of war?' he asked. He went on, as though speech was necessary to make it credible, to describe Laycock, who first gave the horror words at the cabinet council, 'an undersized Oxford prig with a tenoring voice and a garbage of Greek – the sort of little fool who is brought up on the admiration of his elder sisters. ...

'All the time almost,' he said, 'I was watching him – thinking what an ass he was to be trusted with men's lives. ... I might have done better to have thought that of myself. I was doing nothing to prevent it all! The damned little imbecile was up to his neck in the drama of the thing, he liked to trumpet it out, he goggled round at us. "Then it is war!"' he said. Richover shrugged his shoulders. I made some slight protest and gave in. ... Afterward I dreamt of him.

'What a lot we were! All a little scared at ourselves – all, as it were, instrumental. ...

'And it's fools like that lead to things like this!' He jerked his head at that dead man near by us.

'It will be interesting to know what has happened to the world. ... This green vapour – queer stuff. But I know what has happened to me. It's Conversion. I've always known. ... But this is being a fool. Talk! I'm going to stop it.'

He motioned to rise with his clumsy outstretched hands.

'Stop what?' said I, stepping forward instinctively to help him.

'War,' he said in his great whisper, putting his big hand on my shoulder but making no further attempt to arise, 'I'm going to put an end to war – to any sort of war! And all these things that must end.

The world is beautiful, life is great and splendid, we had only to lift up our eyes and see. Think of the glories through which we have been driving, like a herd of swine in a garden place. The colour in life – the sounds – the shapes! We have had our jealousies, our quarrels, our ticklish rights, our invincible prejudices, our vulgar enterprise and sluggish timidities, we have chattered and pecked one another and fouled the world – like daws in the temple, like unclean birds in the holy place of God. All my life has been foolishness and pettiness, gross pleasures and mean discretions – all. I am a meagre dark thing in this morning's glow, a penitence, a shame! And, but for God's mercy, I might have died this night – like that poor lad there – amidst the squalor of my sins! No more of this! No more of this! – whether the whole world has changed or no, matters nothing. WE TWO HAVE SEEN THIS DAWN! ...'

He paused.

'I will arise and go unto my Father,' he began presently, 'and will say unto Him—'

His voice died away in an inaudible whisper. His hand tightened painfully on my shoulder and he rose. ...

The Awakening

Section 1

So the great Day came to me.

And even as I had awakened so in that same dawn the whole world awoke.

For the whole world of living things had been overtaken by the same tide of insensibility; in an hour, at the touch of this new gas in the comet, the shiver of catalytic change had passed about the globe. They say it was the nitrogen of the air, the old AZOTE, that in the twinkling of an eye was changed out of itself, and in an hour or so became a respirable gas, differing indeed from oxygen, but helping and sustaining its action, a bath of strength and healing for nerve and brain. I do not know the precise changes that occurred, nor the names our chemists give them, my work has carried me away from such things, only this I know – I and all men were renewed.

I picture to myself this thing happening in space, a planetary moment, the faint smudge, the slender whirl of meteor, drawing nearer to this planet, – this planet like a ball, like a shaded rounded ball, floating in the void, with its little, nearly impalpable coat of cloud and air, with its dark pools of ocean, its gleaming ridges of land. And as that midge from the void touches it, the transparent gaseous outer shell clouds in an instant green and then slowly clears again. . . .

Thereafter, for three hours or more, – we know the minimum time for the Change was almost exactly three hours because all the clocks and watches kept going – everywhere, no man nor beast nor bird nor any living thing that breathes the air stirred at all but lay still. . . .

Everywhere on earth that day, in the ears of every one who breathed, there had been the same humming in the air, the same rush of green vapours, the crepitation, the streaming down of shooting stars. The Hindoo had stayed his morning's work in the fields to stare and marvel and fall, the blue-clothed Chinaman fell head foremost athwart his midday bowl of rice, the Japanese merchant came out from some chaffering in his office amazed and presently lay there before his door, the evening gazers by the Golden Gates were overtaken as they waited for the rising of the great star. This had happened in every city of the world, in every lonely valley, in every home and house and shelter and every open place. On the high seas, the crowding steamship passengers, eager for any wonder, gaped and marvelled, and were suddenly terror-stricken, and struggled for the gangways and were overcome, the captain staggered on the bridge and fell, the stoker fell headlong among his coals, the engines throbbed upon their way untended, the fishing craft drove by without a hail, with swaying rudder, heeling and dipping. . . .

The great voice of material Fate cried Halt! And in the midst of the play the actors staggered, dropped, and were still. The figure runs from my pen. In New York that very thing occurred. Most of the theatrical audiences dispersed, but in two crowded houses the company, fearing a panic, went on playing amidst the gloom, and the people, trained by many a previous disaster, stuck to their seats. There they sat, the back rows only moving a little, and there, in disciplined lines, they drooped and failed, nodded, and fell forward or slid down upon the floor. I am told by Parload – though indeed I know nothing of the reasoning on which his confidence rests – that within an hour of the great moment of impact the first green modification of nitrogen had dissolved and passed away, leaving the air as translucent as ever. The rest of that wonderful interlude was clear, had any had eyes to see its clearness. In London it was night, but in New York, for example, people were in the full bustle of the evening's enjoyment, in Chicago they were sitting down to dinner, the whole world was abroad. The moonlight must have illuminated streets and squares littered with crumpled figures, through which such electric cars as had no automatic brakes had ploughed on their way until they were stopped by the fallen bodies. People lay in their dress clothes, in dining-rooms, restaurants, on staircases, in halls, everywhere just as they had been overcome. Men gambling, men drinking, thieves lurking in hidden places, sinful couples, were caught, to arise with awakened mind and conscience amidst the disorder of their sin. America the comet reached in the full tide of evening life, but Britain lay asleep. But as I have told, Britain did not slumber so deeply but that she was in the full tide of what may have been battle and a great victory. Up and down the North Sea her warships swept together like a net about their foes. On land, too, that night was to have decided great issues. The German camps were under arms from Redingen to Markirch, their infantry columns were lying in swathes like mown hay, in arrested night march on every track between Longuyon and Thiancourt, and between Avricourt and Donen. The hills beyond Spincourt were dusted thick with hidden French riflemen; the thin lash of the French skirmishers sprawled out amidst spades and unfinished rifle-pits in coils that wrapped about the heads of the German columns, thence along the Vosges watershed and out across the frontier near Belfort nearly to the Rhine. . . .

The Hungarian, the Italian peasant, yawned and thought the morning dark, and turned over to fall into a dreamless sleep; the Mahometan world spread its carpet and was taken in prayer. And in Sydney, in Melbourne, in New Zealand, the thing was a fog in the afternoon, that scattered the crowd on race-courses and cricket-fields, and stopped the unloading of shipping and brought men out from their afternoon rest to stagger and litter the streets. . . .

Section 2

My thoughts go into the woods and wildernesses and jungles of the world, to the wild life that shared man's suspension, and I think of a thousand feral acts interrupted and truncated – as it were frozen, like the frozen words Pantagruel met at sea. Not only men it was that were quieted, all living creatures that breathe the air became insensible, impassive things. Motionless brutes and birds lay amidst the drooping trees and herbage in the universal twilight, the tiger sprawled beside his fresh-struck victim, who bled to death in a dreamless sleep. The very flies came sailing down the air with wings outspread; the spider hung crumpled in his loaded net; like some gaily painted snowflake the butterfly drifted to earth and grounded, and was still. And as a queer contrast one gathers that the fishes in the sea suffered not at all. . . .

Speaking of the fishes reminds me of a queer little inset upon that great world-dreaming. The odd fate of the crew of the submarine vessel B 94 has always seemed memorable to me. So far as I know, they were the only men alive who never saw that veil of green drawn across the world. All the while that the stillness held above, they were working into the mouth of the Elbe, past the booms and the mines, very slowly and carefully, a sinister crustacean of steel, explosive crammed, along the muddy bottom. They trailed a long clue that was to guide their fellows from the mother ship floating awash outside. Then in the long channel beyond the forts they came up at last to mark down their victims and get air. That must have been before the twilight of dawn, for they tell of the brightness of the stars. They were amazed to find themselves not three hundred yards from an ironclad that had run ashore in the mud, and heeled over with the falling tide. It was afire amidships, but no one heeded that – no one in all that strange clear silence heeded that – and not only this wrecked vessel, but all the dark ships lying about them, it seemed to their perplexed and startled minds must be full of dead men!

Theirs I think must have been one of the strangest of all experiences; they were never insensible; at once, and, I am told, with a sudden catch of laughter, they began to breathe the new air. None of them has proved a writer; we have no picture of their wonder, no description of what was said. But we know these men were active and awake for an hour and a half at least before the general awakening came, and when at last the Germans stirred and sat up they found these strangers in possession of their battleship, the submarine carelessly adrift, and the Englishmen, begrimed and weary, but with a sort of furious exultation, still busy, in the bright dawn, rescuing insensible enemies from the sinking conflagration. . . .

But the thought of certain stokers the sailors of the submarine failed altogether to save brings me back to the thread of grotesque horror that runs through all this event, the thread I cannot overlook for all the splendours of human well-being that have come from it. I cannot forget the unguided ships that drove ashore, that went down in disaster with all their sleeping hands, nor how, inland, motor-cars rushed to destruction upon the roads, and trains upon the railways kept on in spite of signals, to be found at last by their amazed, reviving drivers standing on unfamiliar lines, their fires exhausted, or, less lucky, to be discovered by astonished peasants or awakening porters smashed and crumpled up into heaps of smoking, crackling ruin. The foundry fires of the Four Towns still blazed, the smoke of our burning still denied the sky. Fires burnt indeed the brighter for the Change – and spread. . . .

Section 3

Picture to yourself what happened between the printing and composing of the copy of the *New Paper* that lies before me now. It was the first newspaper that was printed upon earth after the Great Change. It was pocket-worn and browned, made of a paper no man ever intended for preservation. I found it on the arbour table in the inn garden while I was waiting for Nettie and Verrall, before that last conversation of which I have presently to tell. As I look at it all that scene comes back to me, and Nettie stands in her white raiment against a blue-green background of sunlit garden, scrutinizing my face as I read. . . .

It is so frayed that the sheet cracks along the folds and comes to pieces in my hands. It lies upon my desk, a dead souvenir of the dead ages of the world, of the ancient passions of my heart. I know we discussed its news, but for the life of me I cannot recall what we said, only I remember that Nettie said very little, and that Verrall for a time read it over my shoulder. And I did not like him to read over my shoulder. . . .

The document before me must have helped us through the first awkwardness of that meeting.

But of all that we said and did then I must tell in a later chapter. . . .

It is easy to see the *New Paper* had been set up overnight, and then large pieces of the stereo plates replaced subsequently. I do not know enough of the old methods of printing to know precisely what happened. The thing gives one an impression of large pieces of type having been cut away and replaced by fresh blocks. There is something very rough and ready about it all, and the new portions print darker and more smudgily than the old, except towards the left, where they have missed ink and indented. A friend of mine, who knows something of the old typography, has suggested to me that the machinery actually in use for the *New Paper* was damaged that night, and that on the morning of the Change Banghurst borrowed a neighbouring office – perhaps in financial dependence upon him – to print in.

The outer pages belong entirely to the old period, the only parts of the paper that had undergone alteration are the two middle leaves. Here we found set forth in a curious little four-column oblong of print, WHAT HAS HAPPENED. This cut across a column with scare headings beginning, 'Great Naval Battle Now in Progress. The Fate of Two Empires in the Balance. Reported Loss of Two More—'

These things, one gathered, were beneath notice now. Probably it was guesswork, and fabricated news in the first instance.

It is curious to piece together the worn and frayed fragments, and reread this discoloured first intelligence of the new epoch.

The simple clear statements in the replaced portion of the paper impressed me at the time, I remember, as bald and strange, in that framework of shouting bad English. Now they seem like the voice of a sane man amidst a vast faded violence. But they witness to the prompt recovery of London from the gas; the new, swift energy of rebound in that huge population. I am surprised now, as I reread, to note how much research, experiment and induction must have been accomplished in the day that elapsed before the paper was printed. . . . But that is by the way. As I sit and muse over this partly carbonized sheet, that same curious remote vision comes again to me that quickened in my mind that morning, a vision of those newspaper offices I have already described to you going through the crisis.

The catalytic wave must have caught the place in full swing, in its nocturnal high fever, indeed in a quite exceptional state of fever, what with the comet and the war, and more particularly with the war. Very probably the Change crept into the office imperceptibly, amidst the noise and shouting, and the glare of electric light that made the night atmosphere in that place; even the green flashes may have passed unobserved there, the preliminary descending trails of green vapour seemed no more than unseasonable drifting wisps of London fog. (In those days London even in summer was not safe against dark fogs.) And then at the last the Change poured in and overtook them.

If there was any warning at all for them, it must have been a sudden universal tumult in the street, and then a much more universal quiet. They could have had no other intimation.

There was no time to stop the presses before the main development of green vapour had overwhelmed every one. It must have folded about them, tumbled them to the earth, masked and stilled them. My imagination is always curiously stirred by the thought of that, because I suppose it is the first picture I succeeded in making for myself of what had happened in the towns. It has never quite lost its strangeness for me that when the Change came, machinery went on working. I don't precisely know why that should have seemed so strange to me, but it did, and still to a certain extent does. One is so accustomed, I suppose, to regard machinery as an extension of human personality that the extent of its autonomy the Change displayed came as a shock to me. The electric lights, for example, hazy green-haloed nebulas, must have gone on burning at least for a time; amidst the thickening darkness the huge presses must have roared on, printing, folding, throwing aside copy after copy of that fabricated battle report with its quarter column of scare headlines, and all the place must have still quivered and throbbed with the familiar roar of the engines. And this though no men ruled here at all any more! Here and there beneath that thickening fog the crumpled or outstretched forms of men lay still.

A wonderful thing that must have seemed, had any man had by chance the power of resistance to the vapour, and could he have walked amidst it.

And soon the machines must have exhausted their feed of ink and paper, and thumped and banged and rattled emptily amidst the general quiet. Then I suppose the furnaces failed for want of stoking, the steam pressure fell in the pistons, the machinery slackened, the lights burnt dim, and came and went with the ebb of energy from the power-station. Who can tell precisely the sequence of these things now?

And then, you know, amidst the weakening and terminating noises of men, the green vapour cleared and vanished, in an hour indeed it had gone, and it may be a breeze stirred and blew and went about the earth.

The noises of life were all dying away, but some there were that abated nothing, that sounded triumphantly amidst the universal ebb. To a heedless world the church towers tolled out two and then three. Clocks ticked and chimed everywhere about the earth to deafened ears. . . .

And then came the first flush of morning, the first rustlings of the revival. Perhaps in that office the filaments of the lamps were still glowing, the machinery was still pulsing weakly, when the crumpled, booted heaps of cloth became men again and began to stir and stare. The chapel of the printers was, no doubt, shocked to find itself asleep. Amidst that dazzling dawn the *New Paper* woke to wonder, stood up and blinked at its amazing self. . . .

The clocks of the city churches, one pursuing another, struck four. The staffs, crumpled and dishevelled, but with a strange refreshment in their veins, stood about the damaged machinery, marvelling and questioning; the editor read his overnight headlines with incredulous laughter. There was much involuntary laughter that morning. Outside, the mail men patted the necks and rubbed the knees of their awakening horses. . . .

Then, you know, slowly and with much conversation and doubt, they set about to produce the paper.

Imagine those bemused, perplexed people, carried on by the inertia of their old occupations and doing their best with an enterprise that had suddenly become altogether extraordinary and irrational. They worked amidst questionings, and yet light-heartedly. At every stage there must have been interruptions for discussion. The paper only got down to Menton five days late.

Then let me give you a vivid little impression I received of a certain prosaic person, a grocer, named Wiggins, and how he passed through the Change. I heard this man's story in the post-office at Menton, when, in the afternoon of the First Day, I bethought me to telegraph to my mother. The place was also a grocer's shop, and I found him and the proprietor talking as I went in. They were trade competitors, and Wiggins had just come across the street to break the hostile silence of a score of years. The sparkle of the Change was in their eyes, their slightly flushed cheeks, their more elastic gestures, spoke of new physical influences that had invaded their beings.

'It did us no good, all our hatred,' Mr Wiggins said to me, explaining the emotion of their encounter; 'it did our customers no good. I've come to tell him that. You bear that in mind, young man, if ever you come to have a shop of your own. It was a sort of stupid bitterness possessed us, and I can't make out we didn't see it before in that light. Not so much downright wickedness it wasn't as stupidity. A stupid jealousy! Think of it! – two human beings within a stone's throw, who have not spoken for twenty years, hardening our hearts against each other!'

'I can't think how we came to such a state, Mr Wiggins,' said the other, packing tea into pound packets out of mere habit as he spoke. 'It was wicked pride and obstinacy. We KNEW it was foolish all the time.'

I stood affixing the adhesive stamp to my telegram.

'Only the other morning,' he went on to me, 'I was cutting French eggs. Selling at a loss to do it. He'd marked down with a great staring ticket to ninepence a dozen – I saw it as I went past. Here's my answer!' He indicated a ticket. 'Eightpence a dozen – same as sold elsewhere for ninepence.' A whole penny down, bang off! Just a touch above cost – if that – and even then—' He leant over the counter to say impressively, 'NOT THE SAME EGGS!'

'Now, what people in their senses would do things like that?' said Mr Wiggins.

I sent my telegram – the proprietor dispatched it for me, and while he did so I fell exchanging experiences with Mr Wiggins. He knew no more than I did then the nature of the change that had come over things. He had been alarmed by the green flashes, he said, so much so that after watching for a time from behind his bedroom window blind, he had got up and hastily dressed and made his family get up also, so that they might be ready for the end. He made them put on their

Sunday clothes. They all went out into the garden together, their minds divided between admiration at the gloriousness of the spectacle and a great and growing awe. They were Dissenters, and very religious people out of business hours, and it seemed to them in those last magnificent moments that, after all, science must be wrong and the fanatics right. With the green vapours came conviction, and they prepared to meet their God. . . .

This man, you must understand, was a common-looking man, in his shirt-sleeves and with an apron about his paunch, and he told his story in an Anglian accent that sounded mean and clipped to my Staffordshire ears; he told his story without a thought of pride, and as it were incidentally, and yet he gave me a vision of something heroic.

These people did not run hither and thither as many people did. These four simple, common people stood beyond their back door in their garden pathway between the gooseberry bushes, with the terrors of their God and His Judgments closing in upon them, swiftly and wonderfully – and there they began to sing. There they stood, father and mother and two daughters, chanting out stoutly, but no doubt a little flatly after the manner of their kind—

'In Zion's Hope abiding,
My soul in Triumph sings—'

until one by one they fell, and lay still.

The postmaster had heard them in the gathering darkness, 'In Zion's Hope abiding.' . . .

It was the most extraordinary thing in the world to hear this flushed and happy-eyed man telling that story of his recent death. It did not seem at all possible to have happened in the last twelve hours. It was minute and remote, these people who went singing through the darkling to their God. It was like a scene shown to me, very small and very distinctly painted, in a locket.

But that effect was not confined to this particular thing. A vast number of things that had happened before the coming of the comet had undergone the same transfiguring reduction. Other people, too, I have learnt since, had the same illusion, a sense of enlargement. It seems to me even now that the little dark creature who had stormed across England in pursuit of Nettie and her lover must have been about an inch high, that all that previous life of ours had been an ill-lit marionette show, acted in the twilight. . . .

141

Section 5

The figure of my mother comes always into my conception of the Change.

I remember how one day she confessed herself.

She had been very sleepless that night, she said, and took the reports of the falling stars for shooting; there had been rioting in Clayton and all through Swathinglea all day, and so she got out of bed to look. She had a dim sense that I was in all such troubles.

But she was not looking when the Change came.

'When I saw the stars a-raining down, dear,' she said, 'and thought of you out in it, I thought there'd be no harm in saying a prayer for you, dear? I thought you wouldn't mind that.'

And so I got another of my pictures – the green vapours come and go, and there by her patched coverlet that dear old woman kneels and droops, still clasping her poor gnarled hands in the attitude of prayer – prayer to IT – for me!

Through the meagre curtains and blinds of the flawed refracting window I see the stars above the chimneys fade, the pale light of dawn creeps into the sky, and her candle flares and dies. . . .

That also went with me through the stillness – that silent kneeling figure, that frozen prayer to God to shield me, silent in a silent world, rushing through the emptiness of space. . . .

Section 6

With the dawn that awakening went about the earth. I have told how it came to me, and how I walked in wonder through the transfigured cornfields of Shaphambury. It came to every one. Near me, and for the time, clear forgotten by me, Verrall and Nettie woke – woke near one another, each heard before all other sounds the other's voice amidst the stillness, and the light. And the scattered people who had run to and fro, and fallen on the beach of Bungalow village, awoke; the sleeping villagers of Menton started, and sat up in that unwonted freshness and newness; the contorted figures in the garden, with the hymn still upon their lips, stirred amidst the flowers, and touched each other timidly, and thought of Paradise. My mother found herself crouched against the bed, and rose – rose with a glad invincible conviction of accepted prayer. . . .

Already, when it came to us, the soldiers, crowded between the lines of dusty poplars along the road to Allarmont, were chatting and sharing coffee with the French riflemen, who had hailed them from their carefully hidden pits among the vineyards up the slopes of Beauville. A certain perplexity had come to these marksmen, who had dropped asleep tensely ready for the rocket that should wake the whirr and rattle of their magazines. At the sight and sound of the stir and human confusion in the roadway below, it had come to each man individually that he could not shoot. One conscript, at least, has told his story of his awakening, and how curious he thought the rifle there beside him in his pit, how he took it on his knees to examine. Then, as his memory of its purpose grew clearer, he dropped the thing, and stood up with a kind of joyful horror at the crime escaped, to look more closely at the men he was to have assassinated. 'Brave types,' he thought, they looked for such a fate. The summoning rocket never flew. Below, the men did not fall into ranks again, but sat by the roadside, or stood in groups talking, discussing with a novel incredulity the ostensible causes of the war. 'The Emperor!' said they; and 'Oh, nonsense! We're civilized men. Get some one else for this job! ... Where's the coffee?'

The officers held their own horses, and talked to the men frankly, regardless of discipline. Some Frenchmen out of the rifle-pits came sauntering down the hill. Others stood doubtfully, rifles still in hand. Curious faces scanned these latter. Little arguments sprang as: 'Shoot at us! Nonsense! They're respectable French citizens.' There is a picture of it all, very bright and detailed in the morning light, in the battle gallery amidst the ruins at old Nancy, and one sees the old-world uniform of the 'soldier', the odd caps and belts and boots, the ammunition-belt, the water-bottle, the sort of tourist's pack the men carried, a queer elaborate equipment. The soldiers had awakened one by one, first one and then another. I wonder sometimes whether, perhaps, if the two armies had come awake in an instant, the battle, by mere habit and inertia, might not have begun. But the men who waked first, sat up, looked about them in astonishment, had time to think a little.

Section 7

Everywhere there was laughter, everywhere tears.

· Men and women in the common life, finding themselves suddenly lit and exalted, capable of doing what had hitherto been impossible, incapable of doing what had hitherto been irresistible, happy, hopeful, unselfishly energetic, rejected altogether the supposition that this was merely a change in the blood and material texture of life. They denied the bodies God had given them, as once the Upper Nile savages struck out their canine teeth, because these made them like the beasts. They declared that this was the coming of a spirit, and nothing else would satisfy their need for explanations. And in a sense the Spirit came. The Great Revival sprang directly from the Change – the last, the deepest, widest, and most enduring of all the vast inundations of religious emotion that go by that name.

But indeed it differed essentially from its innumerable predecessors. The former revivals were a phase of fever, this was the first movement of health, it was altogether quieter, more intellectual, more private, more religious than any of those others. In the old time, and more especially in the Protestant countries where the things of religion were outspoken, and the absence of confession and well-trained priests made religious states of emotion explosive and contagious, revivalism upon various scales was a normal phase in the religious life, revivals were always going on – now a little disturbance of consciences in a village, now an evening of emotion in a Mission Room, now a great storm that swept a continent, and now an organized effort that came to town with bands and banners and handbills and motor-cars for the saving of souls. Never at any time did I take part in nor was I attracted by any of these movements. My nature, although passionate, was too critical (or sceptical if you like, for it amounts to the same thing) and shy to be drawn into these whirls; but on several occasions Parload and I sat, scoffing, but nevertheless disturbed, in the back seats of revivalist meetings.

I saw enough of them to understand their nature, and I am not surprised to learn now that before the comet came, all about the world, even among savages, even among cannibals, these same, or at any rate closely similar, periodic upheavals went on. The world was stifling; it was in a fever, and these phenomena were neither more nor less than the instinctive struggle of the organism against the ebb of its powers, the clogging of its veins, the limitation of its life. Invariably these revivals followed periods of sordid and restricted living. Men obeyed their base immediate motives until the world grew unendurably bitter. Some disappointment, some thwarting, lit up for them – darkly indeed, but yet enough for indistinct vision – the crowded squalor, the dark inclosure of life. A sudden disgust with the insensate smallness of the old-world way of living, a realization of sin, a sense of the unworthiness of all individual things, a desire for something comprehensive, sustaining, something greater, for wider communions and less habitual things, filled them. Their souls, which were shaped for wider issues, cried out suddenly amidst the petty interests, the narrow prohibitions, of life, 'Not this! not this!' A great passion to escape from the jealous prison of themselves, an inarticulate, stammering, weeping passion shook them. . . .

I have seen – I remember how once in Clayton Calvinistic Methodist chapel I saw – his spotty fat face strangely distorted under the flickering gas-flares – old Pallet the ironmonger repent. He went to the form of repentance, a bench reserved for such exhibitions, and slobbered out his sorrow and disgust for some sexual indelicacy – he was a widower – and I can see now how his loose fat body quivered and swayed with his grief. He poured it out to five hundred people, from whom in common times he hid his every thought and purpose. And it is a fact, it shows where reality lay, that we two youngsters laughed not at all at that blubbering grotesque, we did not even think the distant shadow of a smile. We two sat grave and intent – perhaps wondering.

Only afterwards and with an effort did we scoff. . . .

Those old-time revivals were, I say, the convulsive movements of a body that suffocates. They are the clearest manifestations from before the Change of a sense in all men that things were not right. But they were too often but momentary illuminations. Their force spent itself in inco-ordinated shouting, gesticulations, tears. They were but flashes of outlook. Disgust of the narrow life, of all baseness, took shape in narrowness and baseness. The quickened soul ended the night a hypocrite; prophets disputed for precedence; seductions, it is altogether indisputable, were frequent among penitents! and Ananias went home converted and returned with a falsified gift. And it was almost universal that the converted should be impatient and immoderate, scornful of reason and a choice of expedients, opposed to balance, skill and knowledge. Incontinently full of grace, like thin old wine-skins over-filled, they felt they must burst if once they came into contact with hard fact and sane direction.

So the former revivals spent themselves, but the Great Revival did not spend itself, but grew to be, for the majority of Christendom at least, the permanent expression of the Change. For many it has taken the shape of an outright declaration that this was the Second Advent – it is not for me to discuss the validity of that suggestion, for nearly all it has amounted to an enduring broadening of all the issues of life. . . .

Section 8

One irrelevant memory comes back to me, irrelevant, and yet by some subtle trick of quality it summarizes the Change for me. It is the memory of a woman's very beautiful face, a woman with a flushed face and tear-bright eyes who went by me without speaking, rapt in some secret purpose. I passed her when in the afternoon of the first day, struck by a sudden remorse, I went down to Menton to send a telegram to my mother telling her all was well with me. Whither this woman went I do not know, nor whence she came; I never saw her again, and only her face, glowing with that new and luminous resolve, stands out for me. . . .

But that expression was the world's.

CHAPTER THE THIRD
The Cabinet Council

Section 1

And what a strange unprecedented thing was that cabinet council at which I was present, the council that was held two days later in Melmount's bungalow, and which convened the conference to frame the constitution of the World State. I was there because it was convenient for me to stay with Melmount. I had nowhere to go particularly, and there was no one at his bungalow, to which his broken ankle confined him, but a secretary and a valet to help him to begin his share of the enormous labours that evidently lay before the rulers of the world. I wrote shorthand, and as there was not even a phonograph available, I went in so soon as his ankle had been dressed, and sat at his desk to write at his dictation. It is characteristic of the odd slackness that went with the spasmodic violence of the old epoch, that the secretary could not use shorthand and that there was no telephone whatever in the place. Every message had to be taken to the village post-office in that grocer's shop at Menton, half a mile away. ... So I sat in the back of Melmount's room, his desk had been thrust aside, and made such memoranda as were needed. At that time his room seemed to me the most beautifully furnished in the world, and I could identify now the vivid cheerfulness of the chintz of the sofa on which the great statesman lay just in front of me, the fine rich paper, the red sealing-wax, the silver equipage of the desk I used. I know now that my presence in that room was a strange and remarkable thing, the open door, even the coming and going of Parker the secretary, innovations. In the old days a cabinet council was a secret conclave, secrecy and furtiveness were in the texture of all public life. In the old days everybody was always keeping something back from somebody, being wary and cunning, prevaricating, misleading – for the most part for no reason at all. Almost unnoticed, that secrecy had dropped out of life.

I close my eyes and see those men again, hear their deliberating voices. First I see them a little diffusely in the cold explicitness of daylight, and then concentrated and drawn together amidst the shadow and mystery about shaded lamps. Integral to this and very clear is the memory of biscuit crumbs and a drop of spilt water, that at first stood shining upon and then sank into the green table-cloth. . . .

I remember particularly the figure of Lord Adisham. He came to the bungalow a day before the others, because he was Melmount's personal friend. Let me describe this statesman to you, this one of the fifteen men who made the last war. He was the youngest member of the Government, and an altogether pleasant and sunny man of forty. He had a clear profile to his clean grey face, a smiling eye, a friendly, careful voice upon his thin, clean-shaven lips, an easy disabusing manner. He had the perfect quality of a man who had fallen easily into a place prepared for him. He had the temperament of what we used to call a philosopher – an indifferent, that is to say. The Change had caught him at his week-end recreation, fly-fishing; and, indeed, he said, I remember, that he recovered to find himself with his head within a yard of the water's brim. In times of crisis Lord Adisham invariably went fly-fishing at the week-end to keep his mind in tone, and when there was no crisis then there was nothing he liked so much to do as fly-fishing, and so, of course, as there was nothing to prevent it, he fished. He came resolved, among other things, to give up fly-fishing altogether. I was present when he came to Melmount, and heard him say as much; and by a more naive route it was evident that he had arrived at the same scheme of intention as my master. I left them to talk, but afterwards I came back to take down their long telegrams to their coming colleagues. He was, no doubt, as profoundly affected as Melmount by the Change, but his tricks of civility and irony and acceptable humour had survived the Change, and he expressed his altered attitude, his expanded emotions, in a quaint modification of the old-time man-of-the-world style, with excessive moderation, with a trained horror of the enthusiasm that swayed him.

These fifteen men who ruled the British Empire were curiously unlike anything I had expected, and I watched them intently whenever my services were not in request. They made a peculiar class at that time, these English politicians and statesmen, a class that has now completely passed away. In some respects they were unlike the statesmen of any other region of the world, and I do not find that any really adequate account remains of them. .... Perhaps you are a reader of the old books. If so, you will find them rendered with a note of hostile exaggeration by Dickens in *Bleak House*, with a mingling of gross flattery and keen ridicule by Disraeli, who ruled among them accidentally by misunderstanding them and pleasing the court, and all their assumptions are set forth, portentously, perhaps, but truthfully, so far as people of the 'permanent official' class saw them, in the novels of Mrs Humphry Ward. All these books are still in this world and at the disposal of the curious, and in addition the philosopher Bagehot and the picturesque historian Macaulay give something of their method of thinking, the novelist Thackeray skirts the seamy side of their social life, and there are some good passages of irony, personal descriptions, and reminiscence to be found in the *Twentieth Century Garner* from the pens of such writers, for example, as Sidney Low. But a picture of them as a whole is wanting. Then they were too near and too great; now, very rapidly, they have become incomprehensible.

We common people of the old time based our conception of our statesmen almost entirely on the caricatures that formed the most powerful weapon in political controversy. Like almost every main feature of the old condition of things these caricatures were an unanticipated development, they were a sort of parasitic outgrowth from, which had finally altogether replaced, the thin and vague aspirations of the original democratic ideals. They presented not only the personalities who led our public life, but the most sacred structural conceptions of that life, in ludicrous, vulgar and dishonourable aspects that in the end came near to destroying entirely all grave and honourable emotion or motive towards the State. The state of Britain was represented nearly always by a red-faced, purse-proud farmer with an enormous belly, that fine dream of freedom, the United States, by a cunning, lean-faced rascal in striped trousers and a blue coat. The chief ministers of state were pickpockets, washerwomen, clowns, whales, asses, elephants, and what not, and issues that affected the welfare of millions of men were dressed and judged like a rally in some idiotic pantomime. A tragic war in South Africa, that wrecked many thousand homes, impoverished two whole lands, and brought death and disablement to fifty thousand men, was presented as a quite comical quarrel between a violent queer being named Chamberlain, with an eyeglass, an orchid, and a short temper, and 'old Kroojer', an obstinate and very cunning old man in a shocking bad hat. The conflict was carried through in a mood sometimes of brutish irritability and sometimes of lax slovenliness, the merry peculator plied his trade congenially in that asinine squabble, and behind these fooleries and masked by them, marched Fate – until at last the clowning of the booth opened and revealed – hunger and suffering, brands burning and swords and shame. .... These men had come to fame and power in that atmosphere, and to me that day there was the oddest suggestion in them of actors who have suddenly laid aside grotesque and foolish parts; the paint was washed from their faces, the posing put aside.

Even when the presentation was not frankly grotesque and degrading it was entirely misleading. When I read of Laycock, for example, there arises a picture of a large, active, if a little wrong-headed, intelligence in a compact heroic body, emitting that 'Goliath' speech of his that did so much to precipitate hostilities, it tallies not at all with the stammering, high-pitched, slightly bald, and very conscience-stricken personage I saw, nor with Melmount's contemptuous first description of him. I doubt if the world at large will ever get a proper vision of those men as they were before the Change. Each year they pass more and more incredibly beyond our intellectual sympathy. Our estrangement cannot, indeed, rob them of their portion in the past, but it will rob them of any effect of reality. The whole of their history becomes more and more foreign, more and more like some queer barbaric drama played in a forgotten tongue. There they strut through their weird metamorphoses of caricature, those premiers and presidents, their height preposterously exaggerated by political buskins, their faces covered by great resonant inhuman masks, their voices couched in the foolish idiom of public utterance, disguised beyond any semblance to sane humanity, roaring and squeaking through the public press. There it stands, this incomprehensible faded show, a thing left on one side, and now still and deserted by any interest, its many emptinesses as inexplicable now as the cruelties of medieval Venice, the theology of old Byzantium. And they ruled and influenced the lives of nearly a quarter of mankind, these politicians, their clownish conflicts swayed the world, made mirth perhaps, made excitement, and permitted – infinite misery.

I saw these men quickened indeed by the Change, but still wearing the queer clothing of the old time, the manners and conventions of the old time; if they had disengaged themselves from the outlook of the old time they still had to refer back to it constantly as a common starting-point. My refreshed intelligence was equal to that, so that I think I did indeed see them. There was Gorrell-Browning, the Chancellor of the Duchy; I remember him as a big round-faced man, the essential vanity and foolishness of whose expression, whose habit of voluminous platitudinous speech, triumphed absurdly once or twice over the roused spirit within. He struggled with it, he burlesqued himself, and laughed. Suddenly he said simply, intensely – it was a moment for every one of clean, clear pain, 'I have been a vain and self-indulgent and presumptuous old man. I am of little use here. I have given myself to politics and intrigues, and life is gone from me.' Then for a long time he sat still. There was Carton, the Lord Chancellor, a white-faced man with understanding, he had a heavy, shaven face that might have stood among the busts of the Caesars, a slow, elaborating voice, with self-indulgent, slightly oblique and triumphant lips, and a momentary, voluntary, humourous twinkle. 'We have to forgive,' he said. 'We have to forgive – even ourselves.'

These two were at the top corner of the table, so that I saw their faces well. Madgett, the Home Secretary, a smaller man with wrinkled eyebrows and a frozen smile on his thin wry mouth, came next to Carton; he contributed little to the discussion save intelligent comments, and when the electric lights above glowed out, the shadows deepened queerly in his eye-sockets and gave him the quizzical expression of an ironical goblin. Next him was that great peer, the Earl of Richover, whose self-indulgent indolence had accepted the role of a twentieth-century British Roman patrician of culture, who had divided his time almost equally between his jockeys, politics, and the composition of literary studies in the key of his role. 'We have done nothing worth doing,' he said. 'As for me, I have cut a figure!' He reflected – no doubt on his ample patrician years, on the fine great houses that had been his setting, the teeming race-courses that had roared his name, the enthusiastic meetings he had fed with fine hopes, the futile Olympian beginnings. . . . 'I have been a fool,' he said compactly. They heard him in a sympathetic and respectful silence.

Gurker, the Chancellor of the Exchequer, was partially occulted, so far as I was concerned, by the back of Lord Adisham. Ever and again Gurker protruded into the discussion, swaying forward, a deep throaty voice, a big nose, a coarse mouth with a drooping everted lower lip, eyes peering amidst folds and wrinkles. He made his confession for his race. 'We Jews,' he said, 'have gone through the system of this world, creating nothing, consolidating many things, destroying much. Our racial self-conceit has been monstrous. We seem to have used our ample coarse intellectuality for no other purpose than to develop and master and maintain the convention of property, to turn life into a sort of mercantile chess and spend our winnings grossly. . . . We have had no sense of service to mankind. Beauty which is godhead – we made it a possession.'

These men and these sayings particularly remain in my memory. Perhaps, indeed, I wrote them down at the time, but that I do not now remember. How Sir Digby Privet, Revel, Markheimer, and the others sat I do not now recall; they came in as voices, interruptions, imperfectly assigned comments. . . .

One got a queer impression that except perhaps for Gurker or Revel these men had not particularly wanted the power they held; had desired to do nothing very much in the positions they had secured. They had found themselves in the cabinet, and until this moment of illumination they had not been ashamed; but they had made no ungentlemanly fuss about the matter. Eight of that fifteen came from the same school, had gone through an entirely parallel education; some Greek linguistics, some elementary mathematics, some emasculated 'science', a little history, a little reading in the silent or timidly orthodox English literature of the seventeenth, eighteenth and nineteenth centuries, all eight had imbibed the same dull gentlemanly tradition of behaviour; essentially boyish, unimaginative – with neither keen swords nor art in it, a tradition apt to slobber into sentiment at a crisis and make a great virtue of a simple duty rather clumsily done. None of these eight had made any real experiments with life, they had lived in blinkers, they had been passed from nurse to governess, from governess to preparatory school, from Eton to Oxford, from Oxford to the politico-social routine. Even their vices and lapses had been according to certain conceptions of good form. They had all gone to the races surreptitiously from Eton, had all cut up to town from Oxford to see life – music-hall life – had all come to heel again. Now suddenly they discovered their limitations.

'What are we to do?' asked Melmount. 'We have awakened; this empire in our hands. . . .' I know this will seem the most fabulous of all the things I have to tell of the old order, but, indeed, I saw it with my eyes, I heard it with my ears. It is a fact that this group of men who constituted the Government of one-fifth of the habitable land of the earth, who ruled over a million of armed men, who had such navies as mankind had never seen before, whose empire of nations, tongues, peoples still dazzles in these greater days, had no common idea whatever of what they meant to do with the world. They had been a Government for three long years, and before the Change came to them it had never even occurred to them that it was necessary to have a common idea. There was no common idea at all. That great empire was no more than a thing adrift, an aimless thing that ate and drank and slept and bore arms, and was inordinately proud of itself because it had chanced to happen. It had no plan, no intention; it meant nothing at all. And the other great empires adrift, perilously adrift like marine mines, were in the self-same case. Absurd as a British cabinet council must seem to you now, it was no whit more absurd than the controlling ganglion, autocratic council, president's committee, or what not, of each of its blind rivals..

Section 2

I remember as one thing that struck me very forcibly at the time, the absence of any discussion, any difference of opinion, about the broad principles of our present state. These men had lived hitherto in a system of conventions and acquired motives, loyalty to a party, loyalty to various secret agreements and understandings, loyalty to the Crown; they had all been capable of the keenest attention to precedence, all capable of the most complete suppression of subversive doubts and inquiries, all had their religious emotions under perfect control. They had seemed protected by invisible but impenetrable barriers from all the heady and destructive speculations, the socialistic, republican and communistic theories that one may still trace through the literature of the last days of the comet. But now it was as if the very moment of the awakening those barriers and defences had vanished, as if the green vapours had washed through their minds and dissolved and swept away a hundred once rigid boundaries and obstacles. They had admitted and assimilated at once all that was good in the ill-dressed propagandas that had clamoured so vehemently and vainly at the doors of their minds in the former days. It was exactly like the awakening from an absurd and limiting dream. They had come out together naturally and inevitably upon the broad daylight platform of obvious and reasonable agreement upon which we and all the order of our world now stand.

Let me try to give the chief things that had vanished from their minds. There was, first, the ancient system of 'ownership' that made such an extraordinary tangle of our administration of the land upon which we lived. In the old time no one believed in that as either just or ideally convenient, but every one accepted it. The community which lived upon the land was supposed to have waived its necessary connection with the land, except in certain limited instances of highway and common. All the rest of the land was cut up in the maddest way into patches and oblongs and triangles of various sizes between a hundred square miles and a few acres, and placed under the nearly absolute government of a series of administrators called landowners. They owned the land almost as a man now owns his hat; they bought it and sold it, and cut it up like cheese or ham; they were free to ruin it, or leave it waste, or erect upon it horrible and devastating eyesores. If the community needed a road or a tramway, if it wanted a town or a village in any position, nay, even if it wanted to go to and fro, it had to do so by exorbitant treaties with each of the monarchs whose territory was involved. No man could find foothold on the face of the earth until he had paid toll and homage to one of them. They had practically no relations and no duties to the nominal, municipal, or national Government amidst whose larger areas their own dominions lay. ... This sounds, I know, like a lunatic's dream, but mankind was that lunatic; and not only in the old countries of Europe and Asia, where this system had arisen out of the rational delegation of local control to territorial magnates, who had in the universal baseness of those times at last altogether evaded and escaped their duties, did it obtain, but the 'new countries', as we called them then – the United States of America, the Cape Colony, Australia and New Zealand – spent much of the nineteenth century in the frantic giving away of land for ever to any casual person who would take it. Was there coal, was there petroleum or gold, was there rich soil or harbourage, or the site for a fine city, these obsessed and witless Governments cried out for scramblers, and a stream of shabby, tricky and violent adventurers set out to found a new section of the landed aristocracy of the world. After a brief century of hope and pride, the great republic of the United States of America, the hope as it was deemed of mankind, became for the most part a drifting crowd of landless men; landlords and railway lords, food lords (for the land is food) and mineral lords ruled its life, gave it Universities as one gave coins to a mendicant, and spent its resources upon such vain, tawdry and foolish luxuries as the world had never seen before. Here was a thing none of these statesmen before the Change would have regarded as anything but the natural order of the world, which not one of them now regarded as anything but the mad and vanished illusion of a period of dementia.

And as it was with the question of the land, so was it also with a hundred other systems and institutions and complicated and disingenuous factors in the life of man. They spoke of trade, and I realized for the first time there could be buying and selling that was no loss to any man; they spoke of industrial organization, and one saw it under captains who sought no base advantages. The haze of old associations, of personal entanglements and habitual recognitions had been dispelled from every stage and process of the social training of men. Things long hidden appeared discovered with an amazing clearness and nakedness. These men who had awakened, laughed dissolvent laughs, and the old muddle of schools and colleges, books and traditions, the old fumbling, half-figurative, half-formal teaching of the Churches, the complex of weakening and confusing suggestions and hints, amidst which the pride and honour of adolescence doubted and stumbled and fell, became nothing but a curious and pleasantly faded memory. 'There must be a common training of the young,' said Richover; 'a frank initiation. We have not so much educated them as hidden things from them, and set traps. And it might have been so easy – it can all be done so easily.'

That hangs in my memory as the refrain of that council, 'It can all be done so easily,' but when they said it then, it came to my ears with a quality of enormous refreshment and power. It can all be done so easily, given frankness, given courage. Time was when these platitudes had the freshness and wonder of a gospel.

In this enlarged outlook the war with the Germans – that mythical, heroic, armed female, Germany, had vanished from men's imaginations – was a mere exhausted episode. A truce had already been arranged by Melmount, and these ministers, after some marvelling reminiscences, set aside the matter of peace as a mere question of particular arrangements. ... The whole scheme of the world's government had become fluid and provisional in their minds, in small details as in great, the unanalysable tangle of wards and vestries, districts and municipalities, counties, states, boards and nations, the interlacing, overlapping and conflicting authorities, the felt of little interests and claims, in which an innumerable and insatiable multitude of lawyers, agents, managers, bosses, organizers lived like fleas in a dirty old coat, the web of the conflicts, jealousies, heated patchings up and jobbings apart, of the old order – they flung it all on one side.

'What are the new needs?' said Melmount. 'This muddle is too rotten to handle. We're beginning again. Well, let us begin afresh.'

Section 3

'Let us begin afresh!' This piece of obvious common sense seemed then to me instinct with courage, the noblest of words. My heart went out to him as he spoke. It was, indeed, that day as vague as it was valiant; we did not at all see the forms of what we were thus beginning. All that we saw was the clear inevitableness that the old order should end. ...

And then in a little space of time mankind in halting but effectual brotherhood was moving out to make its world anew. Those early years, those first and second decades of the new epoch, were in their daily detail a time of rejoicing toil; one saw chiefly one's own share in that, and little of the whole. It is only now that I look back at it all from these ripe years, from this high tower, that I see the dramatic sequence of its changes, see the cruel old confusions of the ancient time become clarified, simplified, and dissolve and vanish away. Where is that old world now? Where is London, that sombre city of smoke and drifting darkness, full of the deep roar and haunting music of disorder, with its oily, shining, mud-rimmed, barge-crowded river, its black pinnacles and blackened dome, its sad wildernesses of smut-greyed houses, its myriads of draggled prostitutes, its millions of hurrying clerks? The very leaves upon its trees were foul with greasy black defilements. Where is lime-white Paris, with its green and disciplined foliage, its hard unflinching tastefulness, its smartly organized viciousness, and the myriads of workers, noisily shod, streaming over the bridges in the grey cold light of dawn. Where is New York, the high city of clanger and infuriated energy, wind swept and competition swept, its huge buildings jostling one another and straining ever upward for a place in the sky, the fallen pitilessly overshadowed. Where are its lurking corners of heavy and costly luxury, the shameful bludgeoning bribing vice of its ill ruled underways, and all the gaunt extravagant ugliness of its strenuous life? And where now is Philadelphia, with its innumerable small and isolated homes, and Chicago with its interminable blood-stained stockyards, its polyglot underworld of furious discontent.

All these vast cities have given way and gone, even as my native Potteries and the Black Country have gone, and the lives that were caught, crippled, starved and maimed amidst their labyrinths, their forgotten and neglected maladjustments, and their vast, inhuman, ill-conceived industrial machinery have escaped – to life. Those cities of growth and accident are altogether gone, never a chimney smokes about our world today, and the sound of the weeping of children who toiled and hungered, the dull despair of overburdened women, the noise of brute quarrels in alleys, all shameful pleasures and all the ugly grossness of wealthy pride have gone with them, with the utter change in our lives. As I look back into the past I see a vast exultant dust of house-breaking and removal rise up into the clear air that followed the hour of the green vapours, I live again the Year of Tents, the Year of Scaffolding, and like the triumph of a new theme in a piece of music – the great cities of our new days arise. Come Caerlyon and Armedon, the twin cities of lower England, with the winding summer city of the Thames between, and I see the gaunt dirt of old Edinburgh die to rise again white and tall beneath the shadow of her ancient hill; and Dublin too, reshaped, returning enriched, fair, spacious, the city of rich laughter and warm hearts, gleaming gaily in a shaft of sunlight through the soft warm rain. I see the great cities America has planned and made; the Golden City, with ever-ripening fruit along its broad warm ways, and the bell-glad City of a Thousand Spires. I see again as I have seen, the city of theatres and meeting-places, the City of the Sunlight Bight, and the new city that is still called Utah; and dominated by its observatory dome and the plain and dignified lines of the university facade upon the cliff, Martenabar the great white winter city of the upland snows. And the lesser places, too, the townships, the quiet resting-places, villages half forest with a brawl of streams down their streets, villages laced with avenues of cedar, villages of garden, of roses and wonderful flowers and the perpetual humming of bees. And through all the world go our children, our sons the old world would have made into servile clerks and shopmen, plough drudges and servants; our daughters who were erst anaemic drudges, prostitutes, sluts, anxiety-racked mothers or sere, repining failures; they go about this world glad and brave, learning, living, doing, happy and rejoicing, brave and free. I think of them wandering in the clear quiet of the ruins of Rome, among the tombs of Egypt or the temples of Athens, of their coming to Mainington and its strange happiness, to Orba and the wonder of its white and slender tower. . . . But who can tell of the fullness and pleasure of life, who can number all our new cities in the world? – cities made by the loving hands of men for living men, cities men weep to enter, so fair they are, so gracious and so kind. . . .

Some vision surely of these things must have been vouchsafed me as I sat there behind Melmount's couch, but now my knowledge of accomplished things has mingled with and effaced my expectations. Something indeed I must have foreseen – or else why was my heart so glad?

BOOK THE THIRD
The New World

CHAPTER THE FIRST

Love after the Change

Section 1

So far I have said nothing of Nettie. I have departed widely from my individual story. I have tried to give you the effect of the change in relation to the general framework of human life, its effect of swift, magnificent dawn, of an overpowering letting in and inundation of light, and the spirit of living. In my memory all my life before the Change has the quality of a dark passage, with the dimmest side gleams of beauty that come and go. The rest is dull pain and darkness. Then suddenly the walls, the bitter confines, are smitten and vanish, and I walk, blinded, perplexed, and yet rejoicing, in this sweet, beautiful world, in its fair incessant variety, its satisfaction, its opportunities, exultant in this glorious gift of life. Had I the power of music I would make a world-wide motif swell and amplify, gather to itself this theme and that, and rise at last to sheer ecstasy of triumph and rejoicing. It should be all sound, all pride, all the hope of outsetting in the morning brightness, all the glee of unexpected happenings, all the gladness of painful effort suddenly come to its reward; it should be like blossoms new opened and the happy play of children, like tearful, happy mothers holding their first-born, like cities building to the sound of music, and great ships, all hung with flags and wine bespattered, gliding down through cheering multitudes to their first meeting with the sea. Through it all should march Hope, confident Hope, radiant and invincible, until at last it would be the triumph march of Hope the conqueror, coming with trumpetings and banners through the wide-flung gates of the world.

And then out of that luminous haze of gladness comes Nettie, transfigured.

So she came again to me – amazing, a thing incredibly forgotten.

She comes back, and Verrall is in her company. She comes back into my memories now, just as she came back then, rather quaintly at first – at first not seen very clearly, a little distorted by intervening things, seen with a doubt, as I saw her through the slightly discoloured panes of crinkled glass in the window of the Menton post-office and grocer's shop. It was on the second day after the Change, and I had been sending telegrams for Melmount, who was making arrangements for his departure for Downing Street. I saw the two of them at first as small, flawed figures. The glass made them seem curved, and it enhanced and altered their gestures and paces. I felt it became me to say 'Peace' to them, and I went out, to the jangling of the door-bell. At the sight of me they stopped short, and Verrall cried with the note of one who has sought, 'Here he is!' And Nettie cried, 'Willie!'

I went towards them, and all the perspectives of my reconstructed universe altered as I did so.

I seemed to see these two for the first time; how fine they were, how graceful and human. It was as though I had never really looked at them before, and, indeed, always before I had beheld them through a mist of selfish passion. They had shared the universal darkness and dwarfing of the former time; they shared the universal exaltation of the new. Now suddenly Nettie, and the love of Nettie, a great passion for Nettie, lived again in me. This change which had enlarged men's hearts had made no end to love. Indeed, it had enormously enlarged and glorified love. She stepped into the centre of that dream of world reconstruction that filled my mind and took possession of it all. A little wisp of hair had blown across her cheek, her lips fell apart in that sweet smile of hers; her eyes were full of wonder, of a welcoming scrutiny, of an infinitely courageous friendliness.

I took her outstretched hand, and wonder overwhelmed me. 'I wanted to kill you,' I said simply, trying to grasp that idea. It seemed now like stabbing the stars, or murdering the sunlight.

'Afterwards we looked for you,' said Verrall; 'and we could not find you. . . . We heard another shot.'

I turned my eyes to him, and Nettie's hand fell from me. It was then I thought of how they had fallen together, and what it must have been to have awakened in that dawn with Nettie by one's side. I had a vision of them as I had glimpsed them last amidst the thickening vapours, close together, hand in hand. The green hawks of the Change spread their darkling wings above their last stumbling paces. So they fell. And awoke – lovers together in a morning of Paradise. Who can tell how bright the sunshine was to them, how fair the flowers, how sweet the singing of the birds? . . .

This was the thought of my heart. But my lips were saying, 'When I awoke I threw my pistol away.' Sheer blankness kept my thoughts silent for a little while; I said empty things. 'I am very glad I did not kill you – that you are here, so fair and well. . . .'

'I am going away back to Clayton on the day after tomorrow,' I said, breaking away to explanations. 'I have been writing shorthand here for Melmount, but that is almost over now. . . .'

Neither of them said a word, and though all facts had suddenly ceased to matter anything, I went on informatively, 'He is to be taken to Downing Street where there is a proper staff, so that there will be no need of me. . . . Of course, you're a little perplexed at my being with Melmount. You see I met him – by accident – directly I recovered. I found him with a broken ankle – in that lane. . . . I am to go now to the Four Towns to help prepare a report. So that I am glad to see you both again' – I found a catch in my voice – 'to say good-bye to you, and wish you well.'

This was after the quality of what had come into my mind when first I saw them through the grocer's window, but it was not what I felt and thought as I said it. I went on saying it because otherwise there would have been a gap. It had come to me that it was going to be hard to part from Nettie. My words sounded with an effect of unreality. I stopped, and we stood for a moment in silence looking at one another.

It was I, I think, who was discovering most. I was realizing for the first time how little the Change had altered in my essential nature. I had forgotten this business of love for a time in a world of wonder. That was all. Nothing was lost from my nature, nothing had gone, only the power of thought and restraint had been wonderfully increased and new interests had been forced upon me. The Green Vapours had passed, our minds were swept and garnished, but we were ourselves still, though living in a new and finer air. My affinities were unchanged; Nettie's personal charm for me was only quickened by the enhancement of my perceptions. In her presence, meeting her eyes, instantly my desire, no longer frantic but sane, was awake again.

It was just like going to Checkshill in the old time, after writing about socialism. . . .

I relinquished her hand. It was absurd to part in these terms.

So we all felt it. We hung awkwardly over our sense of that. It was Verrall, I think, who shaped the thought for me, and said that to-morrow then we must meet and say good-bye, and so turned our encounter into a transitory making of arrangements. We settled we would come to the inn at Menton, all three of us, and take our midday meal together . . .

Yes, it was clear that was all we had to say now. . . .

We parted a little awkwardly. I went on down the village street, not looking back, surprised at myself, and infinitely perplexed. It was as if I had discovered something overlooked that disarranged all my plans, something entirely disconcerting. For the first time I went back pre-occupied and without eagerness to Melmount's work. I wanted to go on thinking about Nettie; my mind had suddenly become voluminously productive concerning her and Verrall.

Section 2

The talk we three had together in the dawn of the new time is very strongly impressed upon my memory. There was something fresh and simple about it, something young and flushed and exalted. We took up, we handled with a certain naive timidity, the most difficult questions the Change had raised for men to solve. I recall we made little of them. All the old scheme of human life had dissolved and passed away, the narrow competitiveness, the greed and base aggression, the jealous aloofness of soul from soul. Where had it left us? That was what we and a thousand million others were discussing . . .

It chances that this last meeting with Nettie is inseparably asso-ciated – I don't know why – with the landlady of the Menton inn.

The Menton inn was one of the rare pleasant corners of the old order; it was an inn of an unusual prosperity, much frequented by visitors from Shaphambury, and given to the serving of lunches and teas. It had a broad mossy bowling-green, and round about it were creeper-covered arbours amidst beds of snap-dragon, and hollyhock, and blue delphinium, and many such tall familiar summer flowers. These stood out against a background of laurels and holly, and above these again rose the gables of the inn and its signpost – a white-horsed George slaying the dragon – against copper beeches under the sky.

While I waited for Nettie and Verrall in this agreeable trysting place, I talked to the landlady – a broad-shouldered, smiling, freckled woman – about the morning of the Change. That motherly, abundant, red-haired figure of health was buoyantly sure that everything in the world was now to be changed for the better. That confidence, and something in her voice, made me love her as I talked to her. 'Now we're awake,' she said, 'all sorts of things will be put right that hadn't any sense in them. Why? Oh! I'm sure of it.'

Her kind blue eyes met mine in an infinitude of friendliness. Her lips in her pauses shaped in a pretty faint smile.

Old tradition was strong in us; all English inns in those days charged the unexpected, and I asked what our lunch was to cost.

'Pay or not,' she said, 'and what you like. It's holiday these days. I suppose we'll still have paying and charging, however we manage it, but it won't be the worry it has been – that I feel sure. It's the part I never had no fancy for. Many a time I peeped through the bushes worrying to think what was just and right to me and mine, and what would send 'em away satisfied. It isn't the money I care for. There'll be mighty changes, be sure of that; but here I'll stay, and make people happy – them that go by on the roads. It's a pleasant place here when people are merry; it's only when they're jealous, or mean, or tired, or eat up beyond any stomach's digesting, or when they got the drink in 'em that Satan comes into this garden. Many's the happy face I've seen here, and many that come again like friends, but nothing to equal what's going to be, now things are being set right.'

She smiled, that bounteous woman, with the joy of life and hope. 'You shall have an omelet,' she said, 'you and your friends; such an omelet – like they'll have 'em in heaven! I feel there's cooking in me these days like I've never cooked before. I'm rejoiced to have it to do. . . .'

It was just then that Nettie and Verrall appeared under a rustic archway of crimson roses that led out from the inn. Nettie wore white and a sun-hat, and Verrall was a figure of grey. 'Here are my friends,' I said; but for all the magic of the Change, something passed athwart the sunlight in my soul like the passing of the shadow of a cloud. 'A pretty couple,' said the landlady, as they crossed the velvet green toward us. . . .

They were indeed a pretty couple, but that did not greatly gladden me. No – I winced a little at that.

Section 3

This old newspaper, this first reissue of the *New Paper*, desiccated last relic of a vanished age, is like the little piece of identification the superstitious of the old days – those queer religionists who brought a certain black-clad Mrs Piper to the help of Christ – used to put into the hand of a clairvoyant. At the crisp touch of it I look across a gulf of fifty years and see again the three of us sitting about that table in the arbour, and I smell again the smell of the sweet-briar that filled the air about us, and hear in our long pauses the abundant murmuring of bees among the heliotrope of the borders.

It is the dawn of the new time, but we bear, all three of us, the marks and liveries of the old.

I see myself, a dark, ill-dressed youth, with the bruise Lord Redcar gave me still blue and yellow beneath my jaw; and young Verrall sits cornerwise to me, better grown, better dressed, fair and quiet, two years my senior indeed, but looking no older than I because of his light complexion; and opposite me is Nettie, with dark eyes upon my face, graver and more beautiful than I had ever seen her in the former time. Her dress is still that white one she had worn when I came upon her in the park, and still about her dainty neck she wears her string of pearls and that little coin of gold. She is so much the same, she is so changed; a girl then and now a woman – and all my agony and all the marvel of the Change between! Over the end of the green table about which we sit, a spotless cloth is spread, it bears a pleasant lunch spread out with a simple equipage. Behind me is the liberal sunshine of the green and various garden. I see it all. Again I sit there, eating awkwardly, this paper lies upon the table and Verrall talks of the Change.

'You can't imagine,' he says in his sure, fine accents, 'how much the Change has destroyed of me. I still don't feel awake. Men of my sort are so tremendously MADE; I never suspected it before.'

He leans over the table towards me with an evident desire to make himself perfectly understood. 'I find myself like some creature that is taken out of its shell – soft and new. I was trained to dress in a certain way, to behave in a certain way, to think in a certain way; I see now it's all wrong and narrow – most of it anyhow – a system of class shibboleths. We were decent to each other in order to be a gang to the rest of the world. Gentlemen indeed! But it's perplexing—'

I can hear his voice saying that now, and see the lift of his eyebrows and his pleasant smile.

He paused. He had wanted to say that, but it was not the thing we had to say.

I leant forward a little and took hold of my glass very tightly. 'You two,' I said, 'will marry?'

They looked at one another.

Nettie spoke very softly. 'I did not mean to marry when I came away,' she said.

'I know,' I answered. I looked up with a sense of effort and met Verrall's eyes.

He answered me. 'I think we two have joined our lives. . . . But the thing that took us was a sort of madness.'

I nodded. 'All passion,' I said, 'is madness.' Then I fell into a doubting of those words.

'Why did we do these things?' he said, turning to her suddenly.

Her hands were clasped under her chin, her eyes downcast.

'We HAD to,' she said, with her old trick of inadequate expression. Then she seemed to open out suddenly.

'Willie,' she cried with a sudden directness, with her eyes appealing to me, 'I didn't mean to treat you badly – indeed I didn't. I kept thinking of you – and of father and mother, all the time. Only it didn't seem to move me. It didn't move me not one bit from the way I had chosen.'

'Chosen!' I said.

'Something seemed to have hold of me,' she admitted. 'It's all so unaccountable. . . .'

She gave a little gesture of despair.

Verrall's fingers played on the cloth for a space. Then he turned his face to me again.

'Something said "Take her." Everything. It was a raging desire – for her. I don't know. Everything contributed to that – or counted for nothing. You—'

'Go on,' said I.

'When I knew of you—'

I looked at Nettie. 'You never told him about me?' I said, feeling, as it were, a sting out of the old time.

Verrall answered for her. 'No. But things dropped; I saw you that night, my instincts were all awake. I knew it was you.'

'You triumphed over me? . . . If I could I would have triumphed over you,' I said. 'But go on!'

'Everything conspired to make it the finest thing in life. It had an air of generous recklessness. It meant mischief, it might mean failure in that life of politics and affairs, for which I was trained, which it was my honour to follow. That made it all the finer. It meant ruin or misery for Nettie. That made it all the finer. No sane or decent man would have approved of what we did. That made it more splendid than ever. I had all the advantages of position and used them basely. That mattered not at all.'

'Yes,' I said; 'it is true. And the same dark wave that lifted you, swept me on to follow. With that revolver – and blubbering with hate. And the word to you, Nettie, what was it? "Give?" Hurl yourself down the steep?'

Nettie's hands fell upon the table. 'I can't tell what it was,' she said, speaking bare-hearted straight to me. 'Girls aren't trained as men are trained to look into their minds. I can't see it yet. All sorts of mean little motives were there – over and above the "must". Mean motives. I kept thinking of his clothes.' She smiled – a flash of brightness at Verrall. 'I kept thinking of being like a lady and sitting in an hotel – with men like butlers waiting. It's the dreadful truth, Willie. Things as mean as that! Things meaner than that!'

I can see her now pleading with me, speaking with a frankness as bright and amazing as the dawn of the first great morning.

'It wasn't all mean,' I said slowly, after a pause.

'No!' They spoke together.

'But a woman chooses more than a man does,' Nettie added. 'I saw it all in little bright pictures. Do you know – that jacket – there's something – You won't mind my telling you? But you won't now!'

I nodded, 'No.'

She spoke as if she spoke to my soul, very quietly and very earnestly, seeking to give the truth. 'Something cottony in that cloth of yours,' she said. 'I know there's something horrible in being swung round by things like that, but they did swing me round. In the old time – to have confessed that! And I hated Clayton – and the grime of it. That kitchen! Your mother's dreadful kitchen! And besides, Willie, I was afraid of you. I didn't understand you and I did him. It's different now – but then I knew what he meant. And there was his voice.'

'Yes,' I said to Verrall, making these discoveries quietly, 'yes, Verrall, you have a good voice. Queer I never thought of that before!'

We sat silently for a time before our vivisected passions.

'Gods!' I cried, 'and there was our poor little top-hamper of intelligence on all these waves of instinct and wordless desire, these foaming things of touch and sight and feeling, like – like a coop of hens washed overboard and clucking amidst the seas.'

Verrall laughed approval of the image I had struck out. 'A week ago,' he said, trying it further, 'we were clinging to our chicken coops and going with the heave and pour. That was true enough a week ago. But to-day—?'

'To-day,' I said, 'the wind has fallen. The world storm is over. And each chicken coop has changed by a miracle to a vessel that makes head against the sea.'

Section 4

'What are we to do?' asked Verrall.

Nettie drew a deep crimson carnation from the bowl before us, and began very neatly and deliberately to turn down the sepals of its calyx and remove, one by one, its petals. I remember that went on through all our talk. She put those ragged crimson shreds in a long row and adjusted them and readjusted them. When at last I was alone with these vestiges the pattern was still incomplete.

'Well,' said I, 'the matter seems fairly simple. You two' – I swallowed it – 'love one another.'

I paused. They answered me by silence, by a thoughtful silence.

'You belong to each other. I have thought it over and looked at it from many points of view. I happened to want – impossible things. . . . I behaved badly. I had no right to pursue you.' I turned to Verrall. 'You hold yourself bound to her?'

He nodded assent.

'No social influence, no fading out of all this generous clearness in the air – for that might happen – will change you back . . .?'

He answered me with honest eyes meeting mine, 'No, Leadford, no!'

'I did not know you,' I said. 'I thought of you as something very different from this.'

'I was,' he interpolated.

'Now,' I said, 'it is all changed.'

Then I halted – for my thread had slipped away from me.

'As for me,' I went on, and glanced at Nettie's downcast face, and then sat forward with my eyes upon the flowers between us, 'since I am swayed and shall be swayed by an affection for Nettie, since that affection is rich with the seeds of desire, since to see her yours and wholly yours is not to be endured by me – I must turn about and go from you; you must avoid me and I you. . . . We must divide the world like Jacob and Esau. . . . I must direct myself with all the will I have to other things. After all – this passion is not life! It is perhaps for brutes and savages, but for men. No! We must part and I must forget. What else is there but that?'

I did not look up, I sat very tense with the red petals printing an indelible memory in my brain, but I felt the assent of Verrall's pose. There were some moments of silence. Then Nettie spoke. 'But—' she said, and ceased.

I waited for a little while. I sighed and leant back in my chair. 'It is perfectly simple,' I smiled, 'now that we have cool heads.'

'But IS it simple?' asked Nettie, and slashed my discourse out of being.

I looked up and found her with her eyes on Verrall. 'You see,' she

171

said, 'I like Willie. It's hard to say what one feels – but I don't want him to go away like that.'

'But then,' objected Verrall, 'how—?'

'No,' said Nettie, and swept her half-arranged carnation petals back into a heap of confusion. She began to arrange them very quickly into one long straight line.

'It's so difficult— I've never before in all my life tried to get to the bottom of my mind. For one thing, I've not treated Willie properly. He – he counted on me. I know he did. I was his hope. I was a promised delight – something, something to crown life – better than anything he had ever had. And a secret pride. . . . He lived upon me. I knew – when we two began to meet together, you and I – It was a sort of treachery to him—'

'Treachery!' I said. 'You were only feeling your way through all these perplexities.'

'You thought it treachery.'

'I don't now.'

'I did. In a sense I think so still. For you had need of me.'

I made a slight protest at this doctrine and fell thinking.

'And even when he was trying to kill us,' she said to her lover, 'I felt for him down in the bottom of my mind. I can understand all the horrible things, the humiliation – the humiliation! he went through.'

'Yes,' I said, 'but I don't see—'

'I don't see. I'm only trying to see. But you know, Willie, you are a part of my life. I have known you longer than I have known Edward. I know you better. Indeed I know you with all my heart. You think all your talk was thrown away upon me, that I never understood that side of you, or your ambitions or anything. I did. More than I thought at the time. Now – now it is all clear to me. What I had to understand in you was something deeper than Edward brought me. I have it now. . . . You are a part of my life, and I don't want to cut all that off from me now I have comprehended it, and throw it away.'

'But you love Verrall.'

'Love is such a queer thing! . . . Is there one love? I mean, only one love?' She turned to Verrall. 'I know I love you. I can speak out about that now. Before this morning I couldn't have done. It's just as though my mind had got out of a scented prison. But what is it, this love for you? It's a mass of fancies – things about you – ways you look, ways you have. It's the senses – and the senses of certain beauties. Flattery too, things you said, hopes and deceptions for myself. And all that had rolled up together and taken to itself the wild help of those deep emotions that slumbered in my body; it seemed everything. But it wasn't. How can I describe it? It was like having a very bright lamp with a thick shade – everything else in the room was hidden. But you take the shade off and there they are – it is the same light – still there! Only it lights every one!'

Her voice ceased. For awhile no one spoke, and Nettie, with a quick movement, swept the petals into the shape of a pyramid.

Figures of speech always distract me, and it ran through my mind like some puzzling refrain, 'It is still the same light. . . .'

'No woman believes these things,' she asserted abruptly.

'What things?'

'No woman ever has believed them.'

'You have to choose a man,' said Verrall, apprehending her before I did.

'We're brought up to that. We're told – it's in books, in stories, in the way people look, in the way they behave – one day there will come a man. He will be everything, no one else will be anything. Leave everything else; live in him.'

'And a man, too, is taught that of some woman,' said Verrall.

'Only men don't believe it! They have more obstinate minds. . . . Men have never behaved as though they believed it. One need not be old to know that. By nature they don't believe it. But a woman believes nothing by nature. She goes into a mould hiding her secret thoughts almost from herself.'

'She used to,' I said.

'You haven't,' said Verrall, 'anyhow.'

'I've come out. It's this comet. And Willie. And because I never really believed in the mould at all – even if I thought I did. It's stupid to send Willie off – shamed, cast out, never to see him again – when I like him as much as I do. It is cruel, it is wicked and ugly, to prance over him as if he was a defeated enemy, and pretend I'm going to be happy just the same. There's no sense in a rule of life that prescribes that. It's selfish. It's brutish. It's like something that has no sense. I—' there was a sob in her voice: 'Willie! I WON'T.'

I sat lowering, I mused with my eyes upon her quick fingers.

'It IS brutish,' I said at last, with a careful unemotional deliberation. 'Nevertheless – it is in the nature of things. . . . No! . . . You see, after all, we are still half brutes, Nettie. And men, as you say, are more obstinate than women. The comet hasn't altered that; it's only made it clearer. We have come into being through a tumult of blind forces. . . . I come back to what I said just now; we have found our poor reasonable minds, our wills to live well, ourselves, adrift on a wash of instincts, passions, instinctive prejudices, half animal stupidities. . . .

Here we are like people clinging to something – like people awakening – upon a raft.'

'We come back at last to my question,' said Verrall, softly; 'what are we to do?'

'Part,' I said. 'You see, Nettie, these bodies of ours are not the bodies of angels. They are the same bodies – I have read somewhere that in our bodies you can find evidence of the lowliest ancestry; that about our inward ears – I think it is – and about our teeth, there remains still something of the fish, that there are bones that recall little – what is it? – marsupial forebears – and a hundred traces of the ape. Even your beautiful body, Nettie, carries this taint. No! Hear me out.' I leant forward earnestly. 'Our emotions, our passions, our desires, the substance of them, like the substance of our bodies, is an animal, a competing thing, as well as a desiring thing. You speak to us now a mind to minds – one can do that when one has had exercise and when one has eaten, when one is not doing anything – but when one turns to live, one turns again to matter.'

'Yes,' said Nettie, slowly following me, 'but you control it.'

'Only through a measure of obedience. There is no magic in the business – to conquer matter, we must divide the enemy, and take matter as an ally. Nowadays it is indeed true, by faith a man can remove mountains; he can say to a mountain, Be thou removed and be thou cast into the sea; but he does it because he helps and trusts his brother men, because he has the wit and patience and courage to win over to his side iron, steel, obedience, dynamite, cranes, trucks, the money of other people. . . . To conquer my desire for you, I must not perpetually thwart it by your presence; I must go away so that I may not see you, I must take up other interests, thrust myself into struggles and discussions—'

'And forget?' said Nettie.

'Not forget,' I said; 'but anyhow – cease to brood upon you.'

She hung on that for some moments.

'No,' she said, demolished her last pattern and looked up at Verrall as he stirred.

Verrall leant forward on the table, elbows upon it, and the fingers of his two hands intertwined.

'You know,' he said, 'I haven't thought much of these things. At school and the university, one doesn't. . . . It was part of the system to prevent it. They'll alter all that, no doubt. We seem' – he thought – 'to be skating about over questions that one came to at last in Greek – with variorum readings – in Plato, but which it never occurred to any one to translate out of a dead language into living realities. . . .' He halted and answered some unspoken question from his own mind with, 'No. I think with Leadford, Nettie, that, as he put it, it is in the nature of things for men to be exclusive. . . . Minds are free things and go about the world, but only one man can possess a woman. You must dismiss rivals. We are made for the struggle for existence – we ARE the struggle for existence; the things that live are the struggle for existence incarnate – and that works out that the men struggle for their mates; for each woman one prevails. The others go away.'

'Like animals,' said Nettie.

'Yes. . . .'

'There are many things in life,' I said, 'but that is the rough universal truth.'

'But,' said Nettie, 'you don't struggle. That has been altered because men have minds.'

'You choose,' I said.

'If I don't choose to choose?'

'You have chosen.'

She gave a little impatient 'Oh! Why are women always the slaves of sex? Is this great age of Reason and Light that has come to alter nothing of that? And men too! I think it is all – stupid. I do not believe this is the right solution of the thing, or anything but the bad habits of the time that was . . . Instinct! You don't let your instincts rule you in a lot of other things. Here am I between you. Here is Edward. I – love him because he is gay and pleasant, and because – because I LIKE him! Here is Willie – a part of me – my first secret, my oldest friend! Why must I not have both? Am I not a mind that you must think of me as nothing but a woman? imagine me always as a thing to struggle for?' She paused; then she made her distressful proposition to me. 'Let us three keep together,' she said. 'Let us not part. To part is hate, Willie. Why should we not anyhow keep friends? Meet and talk?'

'Talk?' I said. 'About this sort of thing?'

I looked across at Verrall and met his eyes, and we studied one another. It was the clean, straight scrutiny of honest antagonism. 'No,' I decided. 'Between us, nothing of that sort can be.'

'Ever?' said Nettie.

'Never,' I said, convinced.

I made an effort within myself. 'We cannot tamper with the law and customs of these things,' I said; 'these passions are too close to one's essential self. Better surgery than a lingering disease! From Nettie my love – asks all. A man's love is not devotion – it is a demand, a challenge. And besides' – and here I forced my theme – 'I have given myself now to a new mistress – and it is I, Nettie, who am unfaithful.

175

Behind you and above you rises the coming City of the World, and I am in that building. Dear heart! you are only happiness – and that – Indeed that calls! If it is only that my life blood shall christen the foundation stones – I could almost hope that should be my part, Nettie – I will join myself in that.' I threw all the conviction I could into these words. .... 'No conflict of passion,' I added a little lamely, 'must distract me.'

There was a pause.

'Then we must part,' said Nettie, with the eyes of a woman one strikes in the face. I nodded assent. ....

There was a little pause, and then I stood up. We stood up, all three. We parted almost sullenly, with no more memorable words, and I was left presently in the arbour alone.

I do not think I watched them go. I only remember myself left there somehow – horribly empty and alone. I sat down again and fell into a deep shapeless musing.

Section 5

Suddenly I looked up. Nettie had come back and stood looking down at me.

'Since we talked I have been thinking,' she said. 'Edward has let me come to you alone. And I feel perhaps I can talk better to you alone.'

I said nothing and that embarrassed her.

'I don't think we ought to part,' she said.

'No – I don't think we ought to part,' she repeated.

'One lives,' she said, 'in different ways. I wonder if you will understand what I am saying, Willie. It is hard to say what I feel. But I want it said. If we are to part for ever I want it said – very plainly. Always before I have had the woman's instinct and the woman's training which makes one hide. But – Edward is not all of me. Think of what I am saying – Edward is not all of me. .... I wish I could tell you better how I see it. I am not all of myself. You, at any rate, are a part of me and I cannot bear to leave you. And I cannot see why I should leave you. There is a sort of blood link between us, Willie. We grew together. We are in one another's bones. I understand you. Now indeed I understand. In some way I have come to an understanding at a stride. Indeed I understand you and your dream. I want to help you. Edward – Edward has no dreams. .... It is dreadful to me, Willie, to think we two are to part.'

'But we have settled that – part we must.'

'But WHY?'

176

'I love you.'

'Well, and why should I hide it Willie? – I love you. . . .' Our eyes met. She flushed, she went on resolutely: 'You are stupid. The whole thing is stupid. I love you both.'

I said, 'You do not understand what you say. No!'

'You mean that I must go.'

'Yes, yes. Go!'

For a moment we looked at one another, mute, as though deep down in the unfathomable darkness below the surface and present reality of things dumb meanings strove to be. She made to speak and desisted.

'But MUST I go?' she said at last, with quivering lips, and the tears in her eyes were stars. Then she began, 'Willie—'

'Go!' I interrupted her. . . . 'Yes.'

Then again we were still.

She stood there, a tearful figure of pity, longing for me, pitying me. Something of that wider love, that will carry our descendants at last out of all the limits, the hard, clear obligations of our personal life, moved us, like the first breath of a coming wind out of heaven that stirs and passes away. I had an impulse to take her hand and kiss it, and then a trembling came to me, and I knew that if I touched her, my strength would all pass from me. . . .

And so, standing at a distance one from the other, we parted, and Nettie went, reluctant and looking back, with the man she had chosen, to the lot she had chosen, out of my life – like the sunlight out of my life. . . .

Then, you know, I suppose I folded up this newspaper and put it in my pocket. But my memory of that meeting ends with the face of Nettie turning to go.

Section 6

I remember all that very distinctly to this day. I could almost vouch for the words I have put into our several mouths. Then comes a blank. I have a dim memory of being back in the house near the Links and the bustle of Melmount's departure, of finding Parker's energy distasteful, and of going away down the road with a strong desire to say good-bye to Melmount alone.

Perhaps I was already doubting my decision to part for ever from Nettie, for I think I had it in mind to tell him all that had been said and done. . . .

I don't think I had a word with him or anything but a hurried hand

177

clasp. I am not sure. It has gone out of my mind. But I have a very clear and certain memory of my phase of bleak desolation as I watched his car recede and climb and vanish over Mapleborough Hill, and that I got there my first full and definite intimation that, after all, this great Change and my new wide aims in life, were not to mean indiscriminate happiness for me. I had a sense of protest, as against extreme unfairness, as I saw him go. 'It is too soon,' I said to myself, 'to leave me alone.'

I felt I had sacrificed too much, that after I had said good-bye to the hot immediate life of passion, to Nettie and desire, to physical and personal rivalry, to all that was most intensely myself, it was wrong to leave me alone and sore hearted, to go on at once with these steely cold duties of the wider life. I felt new born, and naked, and at a loss.

'Work!' I said with an effort at the heroic, and turned about with a sigh, and I was glad that the way I had to go would at least take me to my mother. . . .

But, curiously enough, I remember myself as being fairly cheerful in the town of Birmingham that night, I recall an active and interested mood. I spent the night in Birmingham because the train service on was disarranged, and I could not get on. I went to listen to a band that was playing its brassy old-world music in the public park, and I fell into conversation with a man who said he had been a reporter upon one of their minor local papers. He was full and keen upon all the plans of reconstruction that were now shaping over the lives of humanity, and I know that something of that noble dream came back to me with his words and phrases. We walked up to a place called Bourneville by moonlight, and talked of the new social groupings that must replace the old isolated homes, and how the people would be housed.

This Bourneville was germane to that matter. It had been an attempt on the part of a private firm of manufacturers to improve the housing of their workers. To our ideas to-day it would seem the feeblest of benevolent efforts, but at the time it was extraordinary and famous, and people came long journeys to see its trim cottages with baths sunk under the kitchen floors (of all conceivable places), and other brilliant inventions. No one seemed to see the danger to liberty in that aggressive age, that might arise through making workpeople tenants and debtors of their employer, though an Act called the Truck Act had long ago intervened to prevent minor developments in the same direction. . . . But I and my chance acquaintance seemed that night always to have been aware of that possibility, and we had no doubt in our minds of the public nature of the housing duty. Our interest lay rather in the possibility of common nurseries and kitchens and public rooms that should economize toil and give people space and freedom.

It was very interesting, but still a little cheerless, and when I lay in bed that night I thought of Nettie and the queer modifications of preference she had made, and among other things and in a way, I prayed. I prayed that night, let me confess it, to an image I had set up in my heart, an image that still serves with me as a symbol for things inconceivable, to a Master Artificer, the unseen captain of all who go about the building of the world, the making of mankind.

But before and after I prayed I imagined I was talking and reasoning and meeting again with Nettie. . . . She never came into the temple of that worshipping with me.

CHAPTER THE SECOND

My Mother's Last Days

Section 1

Next day I came home to Clayton.

The new strange brightness of the world was all the brighter there, for the host of dark distressful memories, of darkened childhood, toilsome youth, embittered adolescence that wove about the place for me. It seemed to me that I saw morning there for the first time. No chimneys smoked that day, no furnaces were burning, the people were busy with other things. The clear strong sun, the sparkle in the dustless air, made a strange gaiety in the narrow streets. I passed a number of smiling people coming home from the public breakfasts that were given in the Town Hall until better things could be arranged, and happened on Parload among them. 'You were right about that comet,' I sang out at the sight of him; and he came towards me and clasped my hand.

'What are people doing here?' said I.

'They're sending us food from outside,' he said, 'and we're going to level all these slums – and shift into tents on to the moors'; and he began to tell me of many things that were being arranged, the Midland land committees had got to work with remarkable celerity and direct-ness of purpose, and the redistribution of population was already in its broad outlines planned. He was working at an improvised college of engineering. Until schemes of work were made out, almost every one was going to school again to get as much technical training as they could against the demands of the huge enterprise of reconstruction that was now beginning.

He walked with me to my door, and there I met old Pettigrew coming down the steps. He looked dusty and tired, but his eye was brighter than it used to be, and he carried in a rather unaccustomed manner, a workman's tool basket.

'How's the rheumatism, Mr Pettigrew?' I asked.

'Dietary,' said old Pettigrew, 'can work wonders. . . .' He looked me in the eye. 'These houses,' he said, 'will have to come down, I suppose, and our notions of property must undergo very considerable revision – in the light of reason; but meanwhile I've been doing something to patch that disgraceful roof of mine! To think that I could have dodged and evaded—'

He raised a deprecatory hand, drew down the loose corners of his ample mouth, and shook his old head.

'The past is past, Mr Pettigrew.'

'Your poor dear mother! So good and honest a woman! So simple and kind and forgiving! To think of it! My dear young man!' – he said it manfully – 'I'm ashamed.'

'The whole world blushed at dawn the other day, Mr Pettigrew,' I said, 'and did it very prettily. That's over now. God knows, who is NOT ashamed of all that came before last Tuesday.'

I held out a forgiving hand, naively forgetful that in this place I was a thief, and he took it and went his way, shaking his head and repeating he was ashamed, but I think a little comforted.

The door opened and my poor old mother's face, marvellously cleaned, appeared. 'Ah, Willie, boy! YOU. You!'

I ran up the steps to her, for I feared she might fall.

How she clung to me in the passage, the dear woman! . . .

But first she shut the front door. The old habit of respect for my unaccountable temper still swayed her. 'Ah deary!' she said, 'ah deary! But you were sorely tried,' and kept her face close to my shoulder, lest she should offend me by the sight of the tears that welled within her.

She made a sort of gulping noise and was quiet for a while, holding me very tightly to her heart with her worn, long hands

She thanked me presently for my telegram, and I put my arm about her and drew her into the living room.

'It's all well with me, mother dear,' I said, 'and the dark times are over – are done with for ever, mother.'

Whereupon she had courage and gave way and sobbed aloud, none chiding her.

She had not let me know she could still weep for five grimy years. . . .

Section 2

Dear heart! There remained for her but a very brief while in this world that had been renewed. I did not know how short that time would be, but the little I could do – perhaps after all it was not little to her – to atone for the harshness of my days of wrath and rebellion, I did. I took care to be constantly with her, for I perceived now her curious need of me. It was not that we had ideas to exchange or pleasures to share, but she liked to see me at table, to watch me working, to have me go to and fro. There was no toil for her any more in the world, but only such light services as are easy and pleasant for a worn and weary old woman to do, and I think she was happy even at her end.

She kept to her queer old eighteenth-century version of religion, too, without a change. She had worn this particular amulet so long it was a part of her. Yet the Change was evident even in that persistence. I said to her one day, 'But do you still believe in that hell of flame, dear mother? You – with your tender heart!'

She vowed she did.

Some theological intricacy made it necessary to her, but still—

She looked thoughtfully at a bank of primulas before her for a time, and then laid her tremulous hand impressively on my arm. 'You know, Willie, dear,' she said, as though she was clearing up a childish misunderstanding of mine, 'I don't think any one will GO there. I never DID think that. ...'

Section 3

That talk stands out in my memory because of that agreeable theological decision of hers, but it was only one of a great number of talks. It used to be pleasant in the afternoon, after the day's work was done and before one went on with the evening's study – how odd it would have seemed in the old time for a young man of the industrial class to be doing postgraduate work in sociology, and how much a matter of course it seems now! – to walk out into the gardens of Lowchester House, and smoke a cigarette or so and let her talk ramblingly of the things that interested her. ... Physically the Great Change did not do so very much to reinvigorate her – she had lived in that dismal underground kitchen in Clayton too long for any material rejuvenescence – she glowed out indeed as a dying spark among the ashes might glow under a draught of fresh air – and assuredly it hastened her end. But those closing days were very tranquil, full of an effortless contentment. With her, life was like a rainy, windy day that clears only to show the sunset afterglow. The light has passed. She acquired no new habits amid the comforts of the new life, did no new things, but only found a happier light upon the old.

She lived with a number of other old ladies belonging to our commune in the upper rooms of Lowchester House. Those upper apartments were simple and ample, fine and well done in the Georgian style, and they had been organized to give the maximum of comfort and conveniences and to economize the need of skilled attendance. We had taken over the various 'great houses', as they used to be called, to make communal dining-rooms and so forth – their kitchens were conveniently large – and pleasant places for the old people of over sixty whose time of ease had come, and for suchlike public uses. We had done this not only with Lord Redcar's house, but also with Checkshill House – where old Mrs Verrall made a dignified and capable hostess, – and indeed with most of the fine residences in the beautiful wide country between the Four Towns district and the Welsh mountains. About these great houses there had usually been good outbuildings, laundries, married servants' quarters, stabling, dairies, and the like, suitably masked by trees, we turned these into homes, and to them we added first tents and wood chalets and afterwards quadrangular residential buildings. In order to be near my mother I had two small rooms in the new collegiate buildings which our commune was almost the first to possess, and they were very convenient for the station of the high-speed electric railway that took me down to our daily conferences and my secretarial and statistical work in Clayton.

Ours had been one of the first modern communes to get in order; we were greatly helped by the energy of Lord Redcar, who had a fine feeling for the picturesque associations of his ancestral home – the detour that took our line through the beeches and bracken and blue-bells of the West Wood and saved the pleasant open wildness of the park was one of his suggestions; and we had many reasons to be proud of our surroundings. Nearly all the other communes that sprang up all over the pleasant parkland round the industrial valley of the Four Towns, as the workers moved out, came to us to study the architecture of the residential squares and quadrangles with which we had replaced the back streets between the great houses and the ecclesiastical residences about the cathedral, and the way in which we had adapted all these buildings to our new social needs. Some claimed to have improved on us. But they could not emulate the rhododendron garden out beyond our shrubberies; that was a thing altogether our own in our part of England, because of its ripeness and of the rarity of good peat free from lime.

These gardens had been planned under the third Lord Redcar, fifty years ago and more; they abounded in rhododendra and azaleas, and were in places so well sheltered and sunny that great magnolias flourished and flowered. There were tall trees smothered in crimson and yellow climbing roses, and an endless variety of flowering shrubs and fine conifers, and such pampas grass as no other garden can show. And barred by the broad shadows of these, were glades and broad spaces of emerald turf, and here and there banks of pegged roses, and flower-beds, and banks given over some to spring bulbs, and some to primroses and primulas and polyanthuses. My mother loved these latter banks and the little round staring eyes of their innumerable yellow, ruddy brown, and purple corollas, more than anything else the gardens could show, and in the spring of the Year of Scaffolding she would go with me day after day to the seat that showed them in the greatest multitude.

It gave her, I think, among other agreeable impressions, a sense of gentle opulence. In the old time she had never known what it was to have more than enough of anything agreeable in the world at all.

We would sit and think, or talk – there was a curious effect of complete understanding between us whether we talked or were still.

'Heaven,' she said to me one day, 'Heaven is a garden.'

I was moved to tease her a little. 'There's jewels, you know, walls and gates of jewels – and singing.'

'For such as like them,' said my mother firmly, and thought for a while. 'There'll be things for all of us, o' course. But for me it couldn't be Heaven, dear, unless it was a garden – a nice sunny garden. . . . And feeling such as we're fond of, are close and handy by'

You of your happier generation cannot realize the wonderfulness of those early days in the new epoch, the sense of security, the extra-ordinary effects of contrast. In the morning, except in high summer, I was up before dawn, and breakfasted upon the swift, smooth train, and perhaps saw the sunrise as I rushed out of the little tunnel that pierced Clayton Crest, and so to work like a man. Now that we had got all the homes and schools and all the softness of life away from our coal and iron ore and clay, now that a thousand obstructive 'rights' and timidities had been swept aside, we could let ourselves go, we merged this enterprise with that, cut across this or that anciently obstructive piece of private land, joined and separated, effected gigantic consolidations and gigantic economies, and the valley, no longer a pit of squalid human tragedies and meanly conflicting industries, grew into a sort of beauty of its own, a savage inhuman beauty of force and machinery and flames. One was a Titan in that Etna. Then back one came at midday to bath and change in the train, and so to the leisurely gossiping lunch in the club dining-room in Lowchester House, and the refreshment of these green and sunlit afternoon tranquillities.

Sometimes in her profounder moments my mother doubted whether all this last phase of her life was not a dream.

'A dream,' I used to say, 'a dream indeed – but a dream that is one step nearer awakening than that nightmare of the former days.'

She found great comfort and assurance in my altered clothes – she liked the new fashions of dress, she alleged. It was not simply altered clothes. I did grow two inches, broaden some inches round my chest, and increase in weight three stones before I was twenty-three. I wore a soft brown cloth and she would caress my sleeve and admire it greatly – she had the woman's sense of texture very strong in her.

Sometimes she would muse upon the past, rubbing together her poor rough hands – they never got softened – one over the other. She told me much I had not heard before about my father, and her own early life. It was like finding flat and faded flowers in a book still faintly sweet, to realize that once my mother had been loved with passion; that my remote father had once shed hot tears of tenderness in her arms. And she would sometimes even speak tentatively in those narrow, old-world phrases that her lips could rob of all their bitter narrowness, of Nettie.

'She wasn't worthy of you, dear,' she would say abruptly, leaving me to guess the person she intended.

'No man is worthy of a woman's love,' I answered. 'No woman is worthy of a man's. I love her, dear mother, and that you cannot alter.'

'There's others,' she would muse.

'Not for me,' I said. 'No! I didn't fire a shot that time; I burnt my magazine. I can't begin again, mother, not from the beginning.'

She sighed and said no more then.

At another time she said – I think her words were: 'You'll be lonely when I'm gone dear.'

'You'll not think of going, then,' I said.

'Eh, dear! but man and maid should come together.'

I said nothing to that.

'You brood overmuch on Nettie, dear. If I could see you married to some sweet girl of a woman, some good, KIND girl—'

'Dear mother, I'm married enough. Perhaps some day— Who knows? I can wait.'

'But to have nothing to do with women!'

'I have my friends. Don't you trouble, mother. There's plentiful work for a man in this world though the heart of love is cast out from him. Nettie was life and beauty for me – is – will be. Don't think I've lost too much, mother.'

(Because in my heart I told myself the end had still to come.)

And once she sprang a question on me suddenly that surprised me. 'Where are they now?' she asked.

'Who?'

'Nettie and – him.'

She had pierced to the marrow of my thoughts. 'I don't know,' I said shortly.

Her shrivelled hand just fluttered into touch of mine.

'It's better so,' she said, as if pleading. 'Indeed . . . it is better so.'

There was something in her quivering old voice that for a moment took me back across an epoch, to the protests of the former time, to those counsels of submission, those appeals not to offend It, that had always stirred an angry spirit of rebellion within me.

'That is the thing I doubt,' I said, and abruptly I felt I could talk no more to her of Nettie. I got up and walked away from her, and came back after a while, to speak of other things, with a bunch of daffodils for her in my hand.

But I did not always spend my afternoons with her. There were days when my crushed hunger for Nettie rose again, and then I had to be alone; I walked, or bicycled, and presently I found a new interest and relief in learning to ride. For the horse was already very swiftly reaping the benefit to the Change. Hardly anywhere was the inhumanity of horse traction to be found after the first year of the new epoch, everywhere lugging and dragging and straining was done by machines, and the horse had become a beautiful instrument for the pleasure and carriage of youth. I rode both in the saddle and, what is finer, naked and barebacked. I found violent exercises were good for the states of enormous melancholy that came upon me, and when at last horse riding palled, I went and joined the aviators who practised soaring upon aeroplanes beyond Horsemarden Hill. . . . But at least every alternate day I spent with my mother, and altogether I think I gave her two-thirds of my afternoons.

Section 4

When presently that illness, that fading weakness that made an eu-thanasia for so many of the older people in the beginning of the new time, took hold upon my mother, there came Anna Reeves to daughter her – after our new custom. She chose to come. She was already known to us a little from chance meetings and chance services she had done my mother in the garden; she sought to give her help. She seemed then just one of those plainly good girls the world at its worst has never failed to produce, who were indeed in the dark old times the hidden antiseptic of all our hustling, hating, faithless lives. They made their secret voiceless worship, they did their steadfast, uninspired, unthanked, unselfish work as helpful daughters, as nurses, as faithful servants, as the humble providences of homes. She was almost exactly three years older than I. At first I found no beauty in her, she was short but rather sturdy and ruddy, with red-tinged hair, and fair hairy brows and red-brown eyes. But her freckled hands I found, were full of apt help, her voice carried good cheer. . . .

At first she was no more than a blue-clad, white-aproned bene-volence, that moved in the shadows behind the bed on which my old mother lay and sank restfully to death. She would come forward to anticipate some little need, to proffer some simple comfort, and always then my mother smiled on her. In a little while I discovered the beauty of that helpful poise of her woman's body, I discovered the grace of untiring goodness, the sweetness of a tender pity, and the great riches of her voice, of her few reassuring words and phrases. I noted and remembered very clearly how once my mother's lean old hand patted the firm gold-flecked strength of hers, as it went by upon its duties with the coverlet.

'She is a good girl to me,' said my mother one day. 'A good girl. Like a daughter should be. . . . I never had a daughter – really.' She mused peacefully for a space. 'Your little sister died,' she said.

I had never heard of that little sister.

'November the tenth,' said my mother. 'Twenty-nine months and three days. . . . I cried. I cried. That was before you came, dear. So long ago – and I can see it now. I was a young wife then, and your father was very kind. But I can see its hands, its dear little quiet hands. . . . Dear, they say that now – now they will not let the little children die.'

'No, dear mother,' I said. 'We shall do better now.'

'The club doctor could not come. Your father went twice. There was some one else, some one who paid. So your father went on into Swathinglea, and that man wouldn't come unless he had his fee. And your father had changed his clothes to look more respectable and he hadn't any money, not even his tram fare home. It seemed cruel to be waiting there with my baby thing in pain. . . . And I can't help thinking perhaps we might have saved her. . . . But it was like that with the poor

187

always in the bad old times – always. When the doctor came at last he was angry. "Why wasn't I called before?" he said, and he took no pains. He was angry because some one hadn't explained. I begged him – but it was too late.'

She said these things very quietly with drooping eyelids, like one who describes a dream. 'We are going to manage all these things better now,' I said, feeling a strange resentment at this pitiful little story her faded, matter-of-fact voice was telling me.

'She talked,' my mother went on. 'She talked for her age wonderfully. . . . Hippopotamus.'

'Eh?' I said.

'Hippopotamus, dear – quite plainly one day, when her father was showing her pictures . . . And her little prayers. "Now I lay me. . . . down to sleep." . . . I made her little socks. Knitted they was, dear, and the heel most difficult.'

Her eyes were closed now. She spoke no longer to me but to herself. She whispered other vague things, little sentences, ghosts of long dead moments. . . . Her words grew less distinct.

Presently she was asleep and I got up and went out of the room, but my mind was queerly obsessed by the thought of that little life that had been glad and hopeful only to pass so inexplicably out of hope again into nonentity, this sister of whom I had never heard before. . . .

And presently I was in a black rage at all the irrecoverable sorrows of the past, of that great ocean of avoidable suffering of which this was but one luminous and quivering red drop. I walked in the garden and the garden was too small for me; I went out to wander on the moors. 'The past is past,' I cried, and all the while across the gulf of five and twenty years I could hear my poor mother's heart-wrung weeping for that daughter baby who had suffered and died. Indeed that old spirit of rebellion has not altogether died in me, for all the transformation of the new time. . . . I quieted down at last to a thin and austere comfort in thinking that the whole is not told to us, that it cannot perhaps be told to such minds as ours; and anyhow, and what was far more sustaining, that now we have strength and courage and this new gift of wise love, whatever cruel and sad things marred the past, none of these sorrowful things that made the very warp and woof of the old life, need now go on happening. We could foresee, we could prevent and save. 'The past is past,' I said, between sighing and resolve, as I came into view again on my homeward way of the hundred sunset-lit windows of old Lowchester House. 'Those sorrows are sorrows no more.'

But I could not altogether cheat that common sadness of the new time, that memory, and insoluble riddle of the countless lives that had stumbled and failed in pain and darkness before our air grew clear.

Beltane and New Year's Eve

Section 1

In the end my mother died rather suddenly, and her death came as a shock to me. Diagnosis was still very inadequate at that time. The doctors were, of course, fully alive to the incredible defects of their common training and were doing all they could to supply its deficiencies, but they were still extraordinarily ignorant. Some unintelligently observed factor of her illness came into play with her, and she became feverish and sank and died very quickly. I do not know what remedial measures were attempted. I hardly knew what was happening until the whole thing was over.

At that time my attention was much engaged by the stir of the great Beltane festival that was held on May-day in the Year of Scaffolding. It was the first of the ten great rubbish burnings that opened the new age. Young people nowadays can scarcely hope to imagine the enormous quantities of pure litter and useless accumulation with which we had to deal; had we not set aside a special day and season, the whole world would have been an incessant reek of small fires; and it was, I think, a happy idea to revive this ancient festival of the May and November burnings. It was inevitable that the old idea of purification should revive with the name, it was felt to be a burning of other than material encumbrances, innumerable quasi-spiritual things, deeds, documents, debts, vindictive records, went up on those great flares. People passed praying between the fires, and it was a fine symbol of the new and wiser tolerance that had come to men, that those who still found their comfort in the orthodox faiths came hither unpersuaded, to pray that all hate might be burnt out of their professions. For even in the fires of Baal, now that men have done with base hatred, one may find the living God.

Endless were the things we had to destroy in those great purgings. First, there were nearly all the houses and buildings of the old time. In the end we did not save in England one building in five thousand that was standing when the comet came. Year by year, as we made our homes afresh in accordance with the saner needs of our new social families, we swept away more and more of those horrible structures, the ancient residential houses, hastily built, without imagination, without beauty, without common honesty, without even comfort or convenience, in which the early twentieth century had sheltered until scarcely one remained; we saved nothing but what was beautiful or interesting out of all their gaunt and melancholy abundance. The actual houses, of course, we could not drag to our fires, but we brought all their ill-fitting deal doors, their dreadful window sashes, their servant-tormenting staircases, their dank, dark cupboards, the verminous papers from their scaly walls, their dust and dirt-sodden carpets, their ill-designed and yet pretentious tables and chairs, sideboards and chests of drawers, the old dirt-saturated books, their ornaments – their dirty, decayed, and altogether painful ornaments – amidst which I remember there were sometimes even STUFFED DEAD BIRDS! – we burnt them all. The paint-plastered woodwork, with coat above coat of nasty paint, that in particular blazed finely. I have already tried to give you an impression of old-world furniture, of Parload's bedroom, my mother's room, Mr Gabbitas's sitting-room, but, thank Heaven! there is nothing in life now to convey the peculiar dinginess of it all. For one thing, there is no more imperfect combustion of coal going on everywhere, and no roadways like grassless open scars along the earth from which dust pours out perpetually. We burnt and destroyed most of our private buildings and all the woodwork, all our furniture, except a few score thousand pieces of distinct and intentional beauty, from which our present forms have developed, nearly all our hangings and carpets, and also we destroyed almost every scrap of old-world clothing. Only a few carefully disinfected types and vestiges of that remain now in our museums.

One writes now with a peculiar horror of the dress of the old world. The men's clothes were worn without any cleansing process at all, except an occasional superficial brushing, for periods of a year or so; they were made of dark obscurely mixed patterns to conceal the stage of defilement they had reached, and they were of a felted and porous texture admirably calculated to accumulate drifting matter. Many

women wore skirts of similar substances, and of so long and inconvenient a form that they inevitably trailed among all the abomination
of our horse-frequented roads. It was our boast in England that the
whole of our population was booted – their feet were for the most part
ugly enough to need it, – but it becomes now inconceivable how they
could have imprisoned their feet in the amazing cases of leather and
imitations of leather they used. I have heard it said that a large part of
the physical decline that was apparent in our people during the closing
years of the nineteenth century, though no doubt due in part to the
miscellaneous badness of the food they ate, was in the main attributable
to the vileness of the common footwear. They shirked open-air exercise
altogether because their boots wore out ruinously and pinched and
hurt them if they took it. I have mentioned, I think, the part my own
boots played in the squalid drama of my adolescence. I had a sense of
unholy triumph over a fallen enemy when at last I found myself
steering truck after truck of cheap boots and shoes (unsold stock from
Swathinglea) to the run-off by the top of the Glanville blast furnaces.

'Plup!' they would drop into the cone when Beltane came, and the
roar of their burning would fill the air. Never a cold would come from
the saturation of their brown paper soles, never a corn from their
foolish shapes, never a nail in them get home at last in suffering
flesh. . . .

Most of our public buildings we destroyed and burnt as we reshaped
our plan of habitation, our theatre sheds, our banks, and inconvenient
business warrens, our factories (these in the first year of all), and all
the 'unmeaning repetition' of silly little sham Gothic churches and
meeting-houses, mean looking shells of stone and mortar without love,
invention, or any beauty at all in them, that men had thrust into the
face of their sweated God, even as they thrust cheap food into
the mouths of their sweated workers; all these we also swept away in
the course of that first decade. Then we had the whole of the superseded
steam-railway system to scrap and get rid of, stations, signals, fences,
rolling stock; a plant of ill-planned, smoke-distributing nuisance
apparatus, that would, under former conditions, have maintained an
offensive dwindling obstructive life for perhaps half a century. Then
also there was a great harvest of fences, notice boards, hoardings, ugly
sheds, all the corrugated iron in the world, and everything that was
smeared with tar, all our gas works and petroleum stores, all our horse
vehicles and vans and lorries had to be erased. . . . But I have said
enough now perhaps to give some idea of the bulk and quality of our
great bonfires, our burnings up, our meltings down, our toil of sheer
wreckage, over and above the constructive effort, in those early years.

But these were the coarse material bases of the Phoenix fires of the world. These were but the outward and visible signs of the innumerable claims, rights, adhesions, debts, bills, deeds and charters that were cast upon the fires; a vast accumulation of insignia and uniforms neither curious enough nor beautiful enough to preserve, went to swell the blaze, and all (saving a few truly glorious trophies and memories) of our symbols, our apparatus and material of war. Then innumerable triumphs of our old, bastard, half-commercial, fine-art were presently condemned, great oil paintings, done to please the half-educated middle-class, glared for a moment and were gone, Academy marbles crumbled to useful lime, a gross multitude of silly statuettes and decorative crockery, and hangings, and embroideries, and bad music, and musical instruments shared this fate. And books, countless books, too, and bales of newspapers went also to these pyres. From the private houses in Swathinglea alone – which I had deemed, perhaps not unjustly, altogether illiterate – we gathered a whole dust-cart full of cheap ill-printed editions of the minor English classics – for the most part very dull stuff indeed and still clean – and about a truckload of thumbed and dog-eared penny fiction, watery base stuff, the dropsy of our nation's mind. . . . And it seemed to me that when we gathered those books and papers together, we gathered together something more than print and paper, we gathered warped and crippled ideas and contagious base suggestions, the formulae of dull tolerances and stupid impatiences, the mean defensive ingenuities of sluggish habits of think-ing and timid and indolent evasions. There was more than a touch of malignant satisfaction for me in helping gather it all together.

I was so busy, I say, with my share in this dustman's work that I did not notice, as I should otherwise have done, the little indications of change in my mother's state. Indeed, I thought her a little stronger; she was slightly flushed, slightly more talkative. . . .

On Beltane Eve, and our Lowchester rummage being finished, I went along the valley to the far end of Swathinglea to help sort the stock of the detached group of potbanks there – their chief output had been mantel ornaments in imitation of marble, and there was very little sorting, I found, to be done – and there it was nurse Anna found me at last by telephone, and told me my mother had died in the morning suddenly and very shortly after my departure.

For a while I did not seem to believe it; this obviously imminent event stunned me when it came, as though I had never had an anticipatory moment. For a while I went on working, and then almost apathetically, in a mood of half-reluctant curiosity, I started for Lowchester.

When I got there the last offices were over, and I was shown my old mother's peaceful white face, very still, but a little cold and stern to me, a little unfamiliar, lying among white flowers.

I went in alone to her, into that quiet room, and stood for a long time by her bedside. I sat down then and thought. . . .

Then at last, strangely hushed, and with the deeps of my loneliness opening beneath me, I came out of that room and down into the world again, a bright-eyed, active world, very noisy, happy, and busy with its last preparations for the mighty cremation of past and super-seded things.

Section 2

I remember that first Beltane festival as the most terribly lonely night in my life. It stands in my mind in fragments, fragments of intense feeling with forgotten gaps between.

I recall very distinctly being upon the great staircase of Lowchester House (though I don't remember getting there from the room in which my mother lay), and how upon the landing I met Anna ascending as I came down. She had but just heard of my return, and she was hurrying upstairs to me. She stopped and so did I, and we stood and clasped hands, and she scrutinized my face in the way women sometimes do. So we remained for a second or so. I could say nothing to her at all, but I could feel the wave of her emotion. I halted, answered the earnest pressure of her hand, relinquished it, and after a queer second of hesitation went on down, returning to my own preoccupations. It did not occur to me at all then to ask myself what she might be thinking or feeling.

I remember the corridor full of mellow evening light, and how I went mechanically some paces toward the dining-room. Then at the sight of the little tables, and a gusty outburst of talking voices as some one in front of me swung the door open and to, I remembered that I did not want to eat. . . . After that comes an impression of myself walking across the open grass in front of the house, and the purpose I had of getting alone upon the moors, and how somebody passing me said something about a hat. I had come out without my hat.

A fragment of thought has linked itself with an effect of long shadows upon turf golden with the light of the sinking sun. The world was singularly empty, I thought, without either Nettie or my mother. There wasn't any sense in it any more. Nettie was already back in my mind then. . . .

Then I am out on the moors. I avoided the crests where the bonfires were being piled, and sought the lonely places. . . .

I remember very clearly sitting on a gate beyond the park, in a fold just below the crest, that hid the Beacon Hill bonfire and its crowd, and I was looking at and admiring the sunset. The golden earth and sky seemed like a little bubble that floated in the globe of human futility. . . . Then in the twilight I walked along an unknown, bat-haunted road between high hedges.

I did not sleep under a roof that night. But I hungered and ate. I ate near midnight at a little inn over toward Birmingham, and miles away from my home. Instinctively I had avoided the crests where the bonfire crowds gathered, but here there were many people, and I had to share a table with a man who had some useless mortgage deeds to burn. I talked to him about them – but my soul stood at a great distance behind my lips . . .

Soon each hilltop bore a little tulip-shaped flame flower. Little black figures clustered round and dotted the base of its petals, and as for the rest of the multitude abroad, the kindly night swallowed them up. By leaving the roads and clear paths and wandering in the fields I contrived to keep alone, though the confused noise of voices and the roaring and crackling of great fires was always near me.

I wandered into a lonely meadow, and presently in a hollow of deep shadows I lay down to stare at the stars. I lay hidden in the darkness, and ever and again the sough and uproar of the Beltane fires that were burning up the sere follies of a vanished age, and the shouting of the people passing through the fires and praying to be delivered from the prison of themselves, reached my ears. . . .

And I thought of my mother, and then of my new loneliness and the hunger of my heart for Nettie.

I thought of many things that night, but chiefly of the overflowing personal love and tenderness that had come to me in the wake of the Change, of the greater need, the unsatisfied need in which I stood, for this one person who could fulfil all my desires. So long as my mother had lived, she had in a measure held my heart, given me a food these emotions could live upon, and mitigated that emptiness of spirit, but now suddenly that one possible comfort had left me. There had been many at the season of the Change who had thought that this great enlargement of mankind would abolish personal love; but indeed it had only made it finer, fuller, more vitally necessary. They had thought that, seeing men now were all full of the joyful passion to make and do, and glad and loving and of willing service to all their fellows, there would be no need of the one intimate trusting communion that had been the finest thing of the former life. And indeed, so far as this was a matter of advantage and the struggle for existence, they were right. But so far as it was a matter of the spirit and the fine perceptions of life, it was altogether wrong.

We had indeed not eliminated personal love, we had but stripped it of its base wrappings, of its pride, its suspicions, its mercenary and competitive elements, until at last it stood up in our minds stark, shining and invincible. Through all the fine, divaricating ways of the new life, it grew ever more evident, there were for every one certain persons, mysteriously and indescribably in the key of one's self, whose mere presence gave pleasure, whose mere existence was interest, whose idiosyncrasy blended with accident to make a completing and predominant harmony for their predestined lovers. They were the essential thing in life. Without them the fine brave show of the rejuvenated world was a caparisoned steed without a rider, a bowl without a flower, a theatre without a play. . . . And to me that night of Beltane, it was as clear as white flames that Nettie, and Nettie alone, roused those harmonies in me. And she had gone! I had sent her from me; I knew not whither she had gone. I had in my first virtuous foolishness cut her out of my life for ever!

So I saw it then, and I lay unseen in the darkness and called upon Nettie, and wept for her, lay upon my face and wept for her, while the glad people went to and fro, and the smoke streamed thick across the distant stars, and the red reflections, the shadows and the fluctuating glares, danced over the face of the world.

No! the Change had freed us from our baser passions indeed, from habitual and mechanical concupiscence and mean issues and coarse imaginings, but from the passions of love it had not freed us. It had but brought the lord of life, Eros, to his own. All through the long sorrow of that night I, who had rejected him, confessed his sway with tears and inappeasable regrets . . .

I cannot give the remotest guess of when I rose up, nor of my tortuous wanderings in the valleys between the midnight fires, nor how I evaded the laughing and rejoicing multitudes who went streaming home between three and four, to resume their lives, swept and garnished, stripped and clean. But at dawn, when the ashes of the world's gladness were ceasing to glow – it was a bleak dawn that made me shiver in my thin summer clothes – I came across a field to a little copse full of dim blue hyacinths. A queer sense of familiarity arrested my steps, and I stood puzzled. Then I was moved to go a dozen paces from the path, and at once a singularly misshapen tree hitched itself into a notch in my memory. This was the place! Here I had stood, there I had placed my old kite, and shot with my revolver, learning to use it, against the day when I should encounter Verrall.

Kite and revolver had gone now, and all my hot and narrow past, its last vestiges had shrivelled and vanished in the whirling gusts of the Beltane fires. So I walked through a world of grey ashes at last, back to the great house in which the dead, deserted image of my dear lost mother lay.

Section 3

I came back to Lowchester House very tired, very wretched; exhausted by my fruitless longing for Nettie. I had no thought of what lay before me.

A miserable attraction drew me into the great house to look again on the stillness that had been my mother's face, and as I came into that room, Anna, who had been sitting by the open window, rose to meet me. She had the air of one who waits. She, too, was pale with watching; all night she had watched between the dead within and the Beltane fires abroad, and longed for my coming. I stood mute between her and the bedside. . . .

'Willie,' she whispered, and eyes and body seemed incarnate pity.

An unseen presence drew us together. My mother's face became resolute, commanding. I turned to Anna as a child may turn to its nurse. I put my hands about her strong shoulders, she folded me to her, and my heart gave way. I buried my face in her breast and clung to her weakly, and burst into a passion of weeping. . . .

She held me with hungry arms. She whispered to me, 'There, there!' as one whispers comfort to a child. . . . Suddenly she was kissing me. She kissed me with a hungry intensity of passion, on my cheeks, on my lips. She kissed me on my lips with lips that were salt with tears. And I returned her kisses . . .

Then abruptly we desisted and stood apart – looking at one another.

Section 4

It seems to me as if the intense memory of Nettie vanished utterly out of my mind at the touch of Anna's lips. I loved Anna.

We went to the council of our group – commune it was then called – and she was given me in marriage, and within a year she had borne me a son. We saw much of one another, and talked ourselves very close together. My faithful friend she became and has been always, and for a time we were passionate lovers. Always she has loved me and kept my soul full of tender gratitude and love for her; always when we met our hands and eyes clasped in friendly greeting, all through our lives from that hour we have been each other's secure help and refuge, each other's ungrudging fastness of help and sweetly frank and open speech. . . . And after a little while my love and desire for Nettie returned as though it had never faded away.

No one will have a difficulty now in understanding how that could be, but in the evil days of the world malaria, that would have been held to be the most impossible thing. I should have had to crush that second love out of my thoughts, to have kept it secret from Anna, to have lied about it to all the world. The old-world theory was there was only one love – we who float upon a sea of love find that hard to understand. The whole nature of a man was supposed to go out to the one girl or woman who possessed him, her whole nature to go out to him. Nothing was left over – it was a discreditable thing to have any overplus at all. They formed a secret secluded system of two, two and such children as she bore him. All other women he was held bound to find no beauty in, no sweetness, no interest; and she likewise, in no other man. The old-time men and women went apart in couples, into defensive little houses, like beasts into little pits, and in these 'homes' they sat down purposing to love, but really coming very soon to jealous watching of this extravagant mutual proprietorship. All freshness passed very speedily out of their love, out of their conversation, all pride out of their common life. To permit each other freedom was blank dishonour. That I and Anna should love, and after our love-journey together, go about our separate lives and dine at the public tables, until the advent of her motherhood, would have seemed a terrible strain upon our unmitigable loyalty. And that I should have it in me to go on loving Nettie – who loved in different manner both Verrall and me – would have outraged the very quintessence of the old convention.

In the old days love was a cruel proprietary thing. But now Anna could let Nettie live in the world of my mind, as freely as a rose will suffer the presence of white lilies. If I could hear notes that were not in her compass, she was glad, because she loved me, that I should listen to other music than hers. And she, too, could see the beauty of Nettie. Life is so rich and generous now, giving friendship, and a thousand tender interests and helps and comforts, that no one stints another of the full realization of all possibilities of beauty. For me from the beginning Nettie was the figure of beauty, the shape and colour of the divine principle that lights the world. For every one there are certain types, certain faces and forms, gestures, voices and intonations that have that inexplicable unanalysable quality. These come through the crowd of kindly friendly fellow-men and women – one's own. These touch one mysteriously, stir deeps that must otherwise slumber, pierce and interpret the world. To refuse this interpretation is to refuse the sun, to darken and deaden all life. . . . I loved Nettie, I loved all who were like her, in the measure that they were like her, in voice, or eyes, or form, or smile. And between my wife and me there was no bitterness that the great goddess, the life-giver, Aphrodite, Queen of the living Seas, came to my imagination so. It qualified our mutual love not at all, since now in our changed world love is unstinted; it is a golden net about our globe that nets all humanity together.

I thought of Nettie much, and always movingly beautiful things restored me to her, all fine music, all pure deep colour, all tender and solemn things. The stars were hers, and the mystery of moonlight; the sun she wore in her hair, powdered finely, beaten into gleams and threads of sunlight in the wisps and strands of her hair. . . . Then suddenly one day a letter came to me from her, in her unaltered clear handwriting, but in a new language of expression, telling me many things. She had learnt of my mother's death, and the thought of me had grown so strong as to pierce the silence I had imposed on her. We wrote to one another – like common friends with a certain restraint between us at first, and with a great longing to see her once more arising in my heart. For a time I left that hunger unexpressed, and then I was moved to tell it to her. And so on New Year's Day in the Year Four, she came to Lowchester and me. How I remember that coming, across the gulf of fifty years! I went out across the park to meet her, so that we should meet alone. The windless morning was clear and cold, the ground new carpeted with snow, and all the trees motionless lace and glitter of frosty crystals. The rising sun had touched the white with a spirit of gold, and my heart beat and sang within me. I remember now the snowy shoulder of the down, sunlit against the bright blue sky. And presently I saw the woman I loved coming through the white still trees. . . .

I had made a goddess of Nettie, and behold she was a fellow-creature! She came, warm-wrapped and tremulous, to me, with the tender promise of tears in her eyes, with her hands outstretched and that dear smile quivering upon her lips. She stepped out of the dream I had made of her, a thing of needs and regrets and human kindliness. Her hands as I took them were a little cold. The goddess shone through her indeed, glowed in all her body, she was a worshipful temple of love for me – yes. But I could feel, like a thing new discovered, the texture and sinews of her living, her dear personal and mortal hands. . . .

The Window of the Tower

This was as much as this pleasant-looking, grey-haired man had written. I had been lost in his story throughout the earlier portions of it, forgetful of the writer and his gracious room, and the high tower in which he was sitting. But gradually, as I drew near the end, the sense of strangeness returned to me. It was more and more evident to me that this was a different humanity from any I had known, unreal, having different customs, different beliefs, different interpretations, different emotions. It was no mere change in conditions and institutions the comet had wrought. It had made a change of heart and mind. In a manner it had dehumanized the world, robbed it of its spites, its little intense jealousies, its inconsistencies, its humour. At the end, and particularly after the death of his mother, I felt his story had slipped away from my sympathies altogether. Those Beltane fires had burnt something in him that worked living still and unsubdued in me, that rebelled in particular at that return of Nettie. I became a little inattentive. I no longer felt with him, nor gathered a sense of complete understanding from his phrases. His Lord Eros indeed! He and these transfigured people – they were beautiful and noble people, like the people one sees in great pictures, like the gods of noble sculpture, but they had no nearer fellowship than these to men. As the change was realized, with every stage of realization the gulf widened and it was harder to follow his words.

I put down the last fascicle of all, and met his friendly eyes. It was hard to dislike him.

I felt a subtle embarrassment in putting the question that perplexed me. And yet it seemed so material to me I had to put it. 'And did you—?' I asked. 'Were you – lovers?'

His eyebrows rose. 'Of course.'

'But your wife—?'

It was manifest he did not understand me.

I hesitated still more. I was perplexed by a conviction of baseness. 'But—' I began. 'You remained lovers?'

'Yes.' I had grave doubts if I understood him. Or he me.

I made a still more courageous attempt. 'And had Nettie no other lovers?'

'A beautiful woman like that! I know not how many loved beauty in her, nor what she found in others. But we four from that time were very close, you understand, we were friends, helpers, personal lovers in a world of lovers.'

'Four?'

'There was Verrall.'

Then suddenly it came to me that the thoughts that stirred in my mind were sinister and base, that the queer suspicions, the coarseness and coarse jealousies of my old world were over and done for these more finely living souls. 'You made,' I said, trying to be liberal minded, 'a home together.'

'A home!' He looked at me, and, I know not why, I glanced down at my feet. What a clumsy, ill-made thing a boot is, and how hard and colourless seemed my clothing! How harshly I stood out amidst these fine, perfected things. I had a moment of rebellious detestation. I wanted to get out of all this. After all, it wasn't my style. I wanted intensely to say something that would bring him down a peg, make sure, as it were, of my suspicions by launching an offensive accusation. I looked up and he was standing.

'I forgot,' he said. 'You are pretending the old world is still going on. A home!'

He put out his hand, and quite noiselessly the great window widened down to us, and the splendid nearer prospect of that dreamland city was before me. There for one clear moment I saw it; its galleries and open spaces, its trees of golden fruit and crystal waters, its music and rejoicing, love and beauty without ceasing flowing through its varied and intricate streets. And the nearer people I saw now directly and plainly, and no longer in the distorted mirror that hung overhead. They really did not justify my suspicions, and yet—! They were such people as one sees on earth – save that they were changed. How can I express that change? As a woman is changed in the eyes of her lover, as a woman is changed by the love of a lover. They were exalted.

I stood up beside him and looked out. I was a little flushed, my ears a little reddened, by the inconvenience of my curiosities, and by my uneasy sense of profound moral differences. He was taller than I. . . .

'This is our home,' he said smiling, and with thoughtful eyes on me.

MEN LIKE GODS

BOOK THE FIRST
The Irruption of the Earthlings

CHAPTER THE FIRST

Mr Barnstaple Takes a Holiday

I

Mr Barnstaple found himself in urgent need of a holiday, and he had no one to go with and nowhere to go. He was overworked. And he was tired of home.

He was a man of strong natural affections; he loved his family extremely so that he knew it by heart, and when he was in these jaded moods it bored him acutely. His three sons, who were all growing up, seemed to get leggier and larger every clay; they sat down in the chairs he was just going to sit down in; they played him off his own pianola; they filled the house with hoarse, vast laughter at jokes that one couldn't demand to be told; they cut in on the elderly harmless flirtations that had hitherto been one of his chief consolations in this vale; they beat him at tennis; they fought playfully on the landings, and fell downstairs by twos and threes with an enormous racket. Their hats were everywhere. They were late for breakfast. They went to bed every night in a storm of uproar: 'Haw, Haw, Haw – *bump!*' and their mother seemed to like it. They all cost money, with a cheerful disregard of the fact that everything had gone up except Mr Barnstaple's earning power. And when he said a few plain truths about Mr Lloyd George at meal-times, or made the slightest attempt to raise the tone of the table-talk above the level of the silliest persiflage, their attention wandered ostentatiously. ... At any rate it *seemed* ostentatiously.

He wanted badly to get away from his family to some place where he could think of its various members with quiet pride and affection, and otherwise not be disturbed by them. ...

And also he wanted to get away for a time from Mr Peeve. The very streets were becoming a torment to him, he wanted never to see a newspaper or a newspaper placard again. He was obsessed by apprehensions of some sort of financial and economic smash that would make the great war seem a mere incidental catastrophe. This was because he was sub-editor and general factotum of the *Liberal,* that well-known organ of the more depressing aspects of advanced thought, and the unvarying pessimism of Mr Peeve, his chief, was infecting him more and more. Formerly it had been possible to put up a sort of resistance to Mr Peeve by joking furtively about his gloom with the other members of the staff, but now there were no other members of the staff: they had all been retrenched by Mr Peeve in a mood of financial despondency. Practically, now, nobody wrote regularly for the *Liberal* except Mr Barnstaple and Mr Peeve. So Mr Peeve had it all his own way with Mr Barnstaple. He would sit hunched up in the editorial chair, with his hands deep in his trouser pockets, taking a gloomy view of everything, sometimes for two hours together. Mr Barnstaple's natural tendency was towards a modest hopefulness and a belief in progress, but Mr Peeve held very strongly that a belief in progress was at least six years out of date, and that the brightest hope that remained to Liberalism was for a good Day of Judgment soon. And having finished the copy of what the staff, when there was a staff, used to call his weekly indigest, Mr Peeve would depart and leave Mr Barnstaple to get the rest of the paper together for the next week.

Even in ordinary times Mr Peeve would have been hard enough to live with; but the times were not ordinary, they were full of disagreeable occurrences that made his melancholy anticipations all too plausible. The great coal lock-out had been going on for a month and seemed to foreshadow the commercial ruin of England; every morning brought intelligence of fresh outrages from Ireland, unforgivable and unforgettable outrages; a prolonged drought threatened the harvests of the world; the League of Nations, of which Mr Barnstaple had hoped enormous things in the great days of President Wilson, was a melancholy and self-satisfied futility; everywhere there was conflict, everywhere unreason; seven-eighths of the world seemed to be sinking down towards chronic disorder and social dissolution. Even without Mr Peeve it would have been difficult enough to have made headway against the facts.

Mr Barnstaple was, indeed, ceasing to secrete hope, and for such types as he, hope is the essential solvent without which there is no digesting life. His hope had always been in liberalism and generous liberal effort, but he was beginning to think that liberalism would never do anything more for ever than sit hunched up with its hands in its pockets grumbling and peeving at the activities of baser but more energetic men. Whose scrambling activities would inevitably wreck the world.

Night and day now, Mr Barnstaple was worrying about the world at large. By night even more than by day, for sleep was leaving him. And he was haunted by a dreadful craving to bring out a number of the *Liberal* of his very own – to alter it all after Mr Peeve had gone away, to cut out all the dyspeptic stuff, the miserable, empty girding at this wrong and that, the gloating on cruel and unhappy things, the exaggeration of the simple, natural, human misdeeds of Mr Lloyd George, the appeals to Lord Grey, Lord Robert Cecil, Lord Lansdowne, the Pope, Queen Anne, or the Emperor Frederick Barbarossa (it varied from week to week), to arise and give voice and form to the young aspirations of a world reborn, and, instead, to fill the number with – Utopia! to say to the amazed readers of the *Liberal:* Here are things that have to be done! Here are the things we are going to do! What a blow it would be for Mr Peeve at his Sunday breakfast! For once, too astonished to secrete abnormally, he might even digest that meal!

But this was the most foolish of dreaming. There were the three young Barnstaples at home and their need for a decent start in life to consider. And beautiful as the thing was as a dream, Mr Barnstaple had a very unpleasant conviction that he was not really clever enough to pull such a thing off. He would make a mess of it somehow. . . .

One might jump from the frying-pan into the fire. The *Liberal* was a dreary, discouraging, ungenerous paper, but anyhow it was not a base and wicked paper.

Still, if there was to be no such disastrous outbreak it was imperative that Mr Barnstaple should rest from Mr Peeve for a time. Once or twice already he had contradicted him. A row might occur anywhen. And the first step towards resting from Mr Peeve was evidently to see a doctor. So Mr Barnstaple went to a doctor.

'My nerves are getting out of control,' said Mr Barnstaple. 'I feel horribly neurasthenic.'

'You are suffering from neurasthenia,' said the doctor.

'I dread my daily work.'

'You want a holiday.'

'You think I need a change?'

'As complete a change as you can manage.'

'Can you recommend any place where I could go?'

'Where do you want to go?'

'Nowhere definite. I thought you could recommend—'

'Let some place attract you – and go there. Do nothing to force your inclinations at the present time.'

Mr Barnstaple paid the doctor the sum of one guinea, and armed with these instructions prepared to break the news of his illness and his necessary absence to Mr Peeve whenever the occasion seemed ripe for doing so.

2

For a time this prospective holiday was merely a fresh addition to Mr Barnstaple's already excessive burthen of worries. To decide to get away was to find oneself face to face at once with three apparently insurmountable problems: How to get away? Whither? And since Mr Barnstaple was one of those people who tire very quickly of their own company: With whom? A sharp gleam of furtive scheming crept into the candid misery that had recently become Mr Barnstaple's habitual expression. But then, no one took much notice of Mr Barnstaple's expressions.

One thing was very clear in his mind. Not a word of this holiday must be breathed at home. If once Mrs Barnstaple got wind of it, he knew exactly what would happen. She would, with an air of competent devotion, take charge of the entire business. 'You must have a *good* holiday,' she would say. She would select some rather distant and expensive resort in Cornwall or Scotland or Brittany, she would buy a lot of outfit, she would have afterthoughts to swell the luggage with inconvenient parcels at the last moment, and she would bring the boys. Probably she would arrange for one or two groups of acquaintances to come to the same place to 'liven things up'. If they did they were certain to bring the worst sides of their natures with them and to develop into the most indefatigable of bores. There would be no conversation. There would be much unreal laughter. There would be endless games. . . . *No!*

But how is a man to go away for a holiday without his wife getting wind of it? Somehow a bag must be packed and smuggled out of the house. . . .

The most hopeful thing about Mr Barnstaple's position from Mr Barnstaple's point of view was that he owned a small automobile of his very own. It was natural that this car should play a large part in his secret plannings. It seemed to offer the easiest means of getting away; it converted the possible answer to Whither? from a fixed and definite place into what mathematicians call, I believe, a locus; and there was something so companionable about the little beast that it did to a slight but quite perceptible extent answer the question, With whom? It was a two-seater. It was known in the family as the Foot Bath, Colman's Mustard, and the Yellow Peril. As these names suggest, it was a low, open car of a clear yellow colour. Mr Barnstaple used it to come up to the office from Sydenham because it did thirty-three miles to the gallon and was ever so much cheaper than a season ticket. It stood up in the court under the office window during the day. At Sydenham it lived in a shed of which Mr Barnstaple carried the only key. So far he had managed to prevent the boys from either driving it or taking it to pieces. At times Mrs Barnstaple made him drive her about Sydenham for her shopping, but she did not really like the little car because it exposed her to the elements too much and made her dusty and dishevelled. Both by reason of all that it made possible and by reason of all that it debarred, the little car was clearly indicated as the medium for the needed holiday. And Mr Barnstaple really liked driving it. He drove very badly, but he drove very carefully; and though it sometimes stopped and refused to proceed, it did not do, or at any rate it had not so far done, as most other things did in Mr Barnstaple's life, which was to go due east when he turned the steering wheel west. So that it gave him an agreeable sense of mastery.

In the end Mr Barnstaple made his decisions with great rapidity. Opportunity suddenly opened in front of him. Thursday was his day at the printer's, and he came home on Thursday evening feeling horribly jaded. The weather kept obstinately hot and dry. It made it none the less distressing that this drought presaged famine and misery for half the world. And London was in full season, smart and grinning: if anything it was a sillier year than 1913, the great tango year, which, in the light of subsequent events, Mr Barnstaple had hitherto regarded as the silliest year in the world's history. The *Star* had the usual batch of bad news along the margin of the sporting and fashionable intelligence that got the displayed space. Fighting was going on between the Russians and Poles, and also in Ireland, Asia Minor, the India frontier, and Eastern Siberia. There had been three new horrible murders. The miners were still out, and a big engineering strike was threatened. There had been only standing room in the down train and it had started twenty minutes late.

He found a note from his wife explaining that her cousins at Wimbledon had telegraphed that there was an unexpected chance of seeing the tennis there with Mademoiselle Lenglen and all the rest of the champions, and that she had gone over with the boys and would not be back until late. It would do their game no end of good, she said, to see some really first-class tennis. Also it was the servants' social that night. Would he mind being left alone in the house for once? The servants would put him out some cold supper before they went.

Mr Barnstaple read this note with resignation. While he ate his supper he ran his eye over a pamphlet a Chinese friend had sent him to show how the Japanese were deliberately breaking up what was left of the civilization and education of China.

It was only as he was sitting and smoking a pipe in his little back garden after supper that he realized all that being left alone in the house meant for him.

Then suddenly he became very active. He rang up Mr Peeve, told him of the doctor's verdict, explained that the affairs of the *Liberal* were just then in a particularly leavable state, and got his holiday. Then he went to his bedroom and packed up a hasty selection of things to take with him in an old Gladstone bag that was not likely to be immediately missed, and put this in the dickey of his car. After which he spent some time upon a letter which he addressed to his wife and put away very carefully in his breast pocket.

Then he locked up the car-shed and composed himself in a deck-chair in the garden with his pipe and a nice thoughtful book on the Bankruptcy of Europe, so as to look and feel as innocent as possible before his family came home.

When his wife returned he told her casually that he believed he was suffering from neurasthenia, and that he had arranged to run up to London on the morrow and consult a doctor in the matter.

Mrs Barnstaple wanted to choose him a doctor, but he got out of that by saying that he had to consider Peeve in the matter and that Peeve was very strongly set on the man he had already in fact consulted. And when Mrs Barnstaple said that she believed they *all* wanted a good holiday, he just grunted in a non-committal manner.

In this way Mr Barnstaple was able to get right away from his house with all the necessary luggage for some weeks' holiday, without arousing any insurmountable opposition. He started next morning Londonward. The traffic on the way was gay and plentiful, but by no means troublesome, and the Yellow Peril was running so sweetly that she might almost have been named the Golden Hope. In Camberwell he turned into the Camberwell New Road and made his way to the post-office at the top of Vauxhall Bridge Road. There he drew up. He was scared but elated by what he was doing. He went into the post-office and sent his wife a telegram. 'Dr Pagan,' he wrote, 'says solitude and rest urgently needed so am going off Lake District recuperate have got bag and things expecting this letter follows.'

Then he came outside and fumbled in his pocket and produced

and posted the letter he had written so carefully overnight. It was deliberately scrawled to suggest neurasthenia at an acute phase. Dr Pagan, it explained, had ordered an immediate holiday and suggested that Mr Barnstaple should 'wander north'. It would be better to cut off all letters for a few days, or even a week or so. He would not trouble to write unless something went wrong. No news would be good news. Rest assured all would be well. As soon as he had a certain address for letters he would wire it, but only very urgent things were to be sent on.

After this he resumed his seat in his car with such a sense of freedom as he had never felt since his first holidays from his first school. He made for the Great North Road, but at the traffic jam at Hyde Park Corner he allowed the policeman to turn him down towards Knightsbridge, and afterwards at the corner where the Bath Road forks away from the Oxford Road an obstructive van put him into the former. But it did not matter very much. Any way led to Elsewhere and he could work northward later.

3

The day was one of those days of gay sunshine that were characteristic of the great drought of 1921. It was not in the least sultry. Indeed there was a freshness about it that blended with Mr Barnstaple's mood to convince him that there were quite agreeable adventures before him. Hope had already returned to him. He knew he was on the way out of things, though as yet he had not the slightest suspicion how completely out of things the way was going to take him. It would be quite a little adventure presently to stop at an inn and get some lunch, and if he felt lonely as he went on he would give somebody a lift and talk. It would be quite easy to give people lifts because so long as his back was generally towards Sydenham and the *Liberal* office, it did not matter at all now in which direction he went.

A little way out of Slough he was passed by an enormous grey touring car. It made him start and swerve. It came up alongside him without a sound, and though according to his only very slightly inaccurate speedometer, he was doing a good twenty-seven miles an hour, it had passed him in a moment. Its occupants, he noted, were three gentlemen and a lady. They were all sitting up and looking backward as though they were interested in something that was following them. They went by too quickly for him to note more than that the lady was radiantly lovely in an immediate and indisputable

213

way, and that the gentleman nearest to him had a peculiarly elfin yet elderly face.

Before he could recover from the *éclat* of this passage a car with the voice of a prehistoric saurian warned him that he was again being overtaken. This was how Mr Barnstaple liked being passed. By negotiation. He slowed down, abandoned any claim to the crown of the road and made encouraging gestures with his hand. A large, smooth, swift Limousine availed itself of his permission to use the thirty odd feet or so of road to the right of him. It was carrying a fair load of luggage, but except for a young gentleman with an eye-glass who was sitting beside the driver, he saw nothing of its passengers. It swept round a corner ahead in the wake of the touring car.

Now even a mechanical foot-bath does not like being passed in this lordly fashion on a bright morning on the open road. Mr Barnstaple's accelerator went down and he came round that corner a good ten miles per hour faster than his usual cautious practice. He found the road quite clear ahead of him.

Indeed he found the road much too clear ahead of him. It stretched straight in front of him for perhaps a third of a mile. On the left were a low, well-trimmed hedge, scattered trees, level fields, some small cottages lying back, remote poplars, and a distant view of Windsor Castle. On the right were level fields, a small inn, and a background of low, wooded hills. A conspicuous feature in this tranquil landscape was the board advertisement of a riverside hotel at Maidenhead. Before him was a sort of heat flicker in the air and two or three little dust whirls spinning along the road. And there was not a sign of the grey touring car and not a sign of the Limousine.

It took Mr Barnstaple the better part of two seconds to realize the full astonishment of this fact. Neither to right nor left was there any possible side road down which either car could have vanished. And if they had already got round the further bend, then they must be travelling at the rate of two or three hundred miles per hour!

It was Mr Barnstaple's excellent custom whenever he was in doubt to slow down. He slowed down now. He went on at a pace of perhaps fifteen miles an hour, staring open-mouthed about the empty landscape for some clue to this mysterious disappearance. Curiously enough he had no feeling that he himself was in any sort of danger.

Then his car seemed to strike something and skidded. It skidded round so violently that for a moment or so Mr Barnstaple lost his head. He could not remember what ought to be done when a car skids. He recalled something vaguely about steering in the direction in which the car is skidding, but he could not make out in the excitement of the moment in what direction the car was skidding.

Afterwards he remembered that at this point he heard a sound. It was exactly the same sound, coming as the climax of an accumulating pressure, sharp like the snapping of a lute string, which one hears at the end – or beginning – of insensibility under anaesthetics.

He had seemed to twist round towards the hedge on the right, but now he found the road ahead of him again. He touched his accelerator and then slowed down and stopped. He stopped in the profoundest astonishment.

This was an entirely different road from the one he had been upon half a minute before. The hedges had changed, the trees had altered, Windsor Castle had vanished, and – a small compensation – the big Limousine was in sight again. It was standing by the roadside about two hundred yards away.

CHAPTER THE SECOND

The Wonderful Road

I

For a time Mr Barnstaple's attention was very unequally divided between the Limousine, whose passengers were now descending, and the scenery about him. This latter was indeed so strange and beautiful that it was only as people who must be sharing his admiration and amazement and who therefore might conceivably help to elucidate and relieve his growing and quite overwhelming perplexity, that the little group ahead presently arose to any importance in his consciousness.

The road itself, instead of being the packed together pebbles and dirt smeared with tar with a surface of grit, dust, and animal excrement, of a normal English high road, was apparently made of glass, clear in places as still water and in places milky or opalescent, shot with streaks of soft colour or glittering richly with clouds of embedded golden flakes. It was perhaps twelve or fifteen yards wide. On either side was a band of greensward, of a finer grass than Mr Barnstaple had ever seen before – and he was an expert and observant mower of lawns – and beyond this a wide border of flowers. Where Mr Barnstaple sat agape in his car and perhaps for thirty yards in either direction this border was a mass of some unfamiliar blossom of forget-me-not blue. Then the colour was broken by an increasing number of tall, pure white spikes that finally ousted the blue altogether from the bed. On the opposite side of the way these same spikes were mingled with masses of plants bearing seed-pods equally strange to Mr Barnstaple, which varied through a series of blues and mauves and purples to an intense crimson. Beyond this gloriously coloured foam of flowers spread flat meadows on which creamy cattle were grazing. Three close at hand, a little startled perhaps by Mr Barnstaple's sudden apparition, chewed the cud and regarded him with benevolently speculative eyes. They had long horns and dewlaps like the cattle of South Europe and India. From these benign creatures Mr Barnstaple's eyes went to a long line of flame-shaped trees, to a colonnade of white and gold, and to a background of snow-clad mountains. A few tall, white clouds were sailing across a sky of dazzling blue. The air impressed Mr Barnstaple as being astonishingly clear and sweet.

Except for the cows and the little group of people standing by the Limousine, Mr Barnstaple could see no other living creature. The motorists were standing still and staring about them. A sound of querulous voices came to him.

A sharp crepitation at his back turned Mr Barnstaple's attention round. By the side of the road in the direction from which conceivably he had come were the ruins of what appeared to be a very recently demolished stone house. Beside it were two large apple trees freshly twisted and riven, as if by some explosion, and out of the centre of it came a column of smoke and this sound of things catching fire. And the contorted lines of these shattered apple trees helped Mr Barnstaple to realize that some of the flowers by the wayside near at hand were also bent down to one side as if by the passage of a recent violent gust of wind. Yet he had heard no explosion nor felt any wind.

He stared for a time and then turned as if for an explanation to the Limousine. Three of these people were now coming along the road towards him, led by a tall, slender, grey-headed gentleman in a felt hat and a long motoring dust-coat. He had a small upturned face with a little nose that scarce sufficed for the springs of his gilt glasses. Mr Barnstaple restarted his engine and drove slowly to meet them.

As soon as he judged himself within hearing distance he stopped and put his head over the side of the Yellow Peril with a question. At the same moment the tall, grey-headed gentleman asked practically the same question:

'Can you tell me at all, sir, where we *are?*

2

'Five minutes ago,' said Mr Barnstaple, 'I should have said we were on the Maidenhead Road. Near Slough.'

'Exactly!' said the tall gentleman in earnest, argumentative tones.

217

'Exactly! And I maintain that there is not the slightest reason for supposing that we are not still on the Maidenhead Road.'

The challenge of the dialectician rang in his voice.

'It doesn't *look* like the Maidenhead Road,' said Mr Barnstaple.

'Agreed! But are we to judge by appearances or are we to judge by the direct continuity of our experience? The Maidenhead Road led to this, was in continuity with this, and therefore I hold that this is the Maidenhead Road.'

'Those mountains?' considered Mr Barnstaple.

'Windsor Castle ought to be there,' said the tall gentleman brightly as if he gave a point in a gambit.

'*Was* there five minutes ago,' said Mr Barnstaple.

'Then obviously those mountains are some sort of a camouflage,' said the tall gentleman triumphantly, 'and the whole of this business is, as they say nowadays, a put-up thing.'

'It seems to be remarkably well put up,' said Mr Barnstaple.

Came a pause during which Mr Barnstaple surveyed the tall gentleman's companions. The tall gentleman he knew perfectly well. He had seen him a score of times at public meetings and public dinners. He was Mr Cecil Burleigh, the great conservative leader. He was not only distinguished as a politician; he was eminent as a private gentleman, a philosopher and a man of universal intelligence. Behind him stood a short, thick-set, middle-aged young man, unknown to Mr Barnstaple, the natural hostility of whose appearance was greatly enhanced by an eye-glass. The third member of the little group was also a familiar form, but for a time Mr Barnstaple could not place him. He had a clean-shaven, round, plump face and a well-nourished person and his costume suggested either a high church clergyman or a prosperous Roman Catholic priest.

The young man with the eye-glass now spoke in a kind of impotent falsetto. 'I came down to Taplow Court by road not a month ago and there was certainly nothing of this sort on the way then.'

'I admit there are difficulties,' said Mr Burleigh with gusto. 'I admit there are considerable difficulties. Still, I venture to think my main proposition holds.'

'*You* don't think this is the Maidenhead Road?' said the gentleman with the eye-glass flatly to Mr Barnstaple.

'It seems too perfect for a put-up thing,' said Mr Barnstaple with a mild obstinacy.

'But, my dear Sir!' protested Mr Burleigh, 'this road is *notorious* for nursery seedsmen and sometimes they arrange the most astonishing displays. As an advertisement.'

'Then why don't we go straight on to Taplow Court now?' asked the gentleman with the eyeglass.

'Because,' said Mr Burleigh, with the touch of asperity natural when one has to insist on a fact already clearly known, and obstinately overlooked, 'Rupert insists that we are in some other world. And won't go on. That is why. He has always had too much imagination. He thinks that things that don't exist *can* exist. And now he imagines himself in some sort of scientific romance and out of our world altogether. In another dimension. I sometimes think it would have been better for all of us if Rupert had taken to writing romances – instead of living them. If you, as his secretary, think that you will be able to get him on to Taplow in time for lunch with the Windsor people—'

Mr Burleigh indicated by a gesture ideas for which he found words inadequate.

Mr Barnstaple had already noted a slow-moving, intent, sandy-complexioned figure in a grey top hat with a black band that the caricaturists had made familiar, exploring the flowery tangle beside the Limousine. This then must be no less well-known a person than Rupert Catskill, the Secretary of State for War. For once, Mr Barnstaple found himself in entire agreement with this all too adventurous politician. This was another world. Mr Barnstaple got out of his car and addressed himself to Mr Burleigh. 'I think we may get a lot of light upon just where we are, Sir, if we explore this building which is burning here close at hand. I thought just now that I saw a figure lying on the slope close behind it. If we could catch one of the hoaxers—'

He left his sentence unfinished because he did not believe for a moment that they were being hoaxed. Mr Burleigh had fallen very much in his opinion in the last five minutes.

All four men turned their faces to the smoking ruin.

'It's a very extraordinary thing that there isn't a soul in sight,' remarked the eye-glass gentleman, searching the horizon.

'Well, I see no harm whatever in finding out what is burning,' said Mr Burleigh and led the way, upholding an intelligent, anticipatory face, towards the wrecked house between the broken trees.

But before he had gone a dozen paces the attention of the little group was recalled to the Limousine by a loud scream of terror from the lady who had remained seated therein.

3

'Really this is too much!' cried Mr Burleigh with a note of genuine

219

exasperation. 'There must surely be police regulations to prevent this kind of thing.'

'It's out of some travelling menagerie,' said the gentleman with the eye-glass. 'What ought we to do?'

'It looks tame,' said Mr Barnstaple, but without any impulse to put his theory to the test.

'It might easily frighten people very seriously,' said Mr Burleigh. And lifting up a bland voice he shouted: 'Don't be alarmed, Stella! It's probably quite tame and harmless. Don't *irritate* it with that sunshade. It might fly at you. Stel-*la!*'

'It' was a big and beautifully marked leopard which had come very softly out of the flowers and sat down like a great cat in the middle of the glass road at the side of the big car. It was blinking and moving its head from side to side rhythmically, with an expression of puzzled interest, as the lady, in accordance with the best traditions of such cases, opened and shut her parasol at it as rapidly as she could. The chauffeur had taken cover behind the car. Mr Rupert Catskill stood staring, knee-deep in flowers, apparently only made aware of the creature's existence by the same scream that had attracted the attention of Mr Burleigh and his companions.

Mr Catskill was the first to act, and his act showed his mettle. It was at once discreet and bold. 'Stop flopping that sunshade, Lady Stella,' he said. 'Let me – I will – catch its eye.'

He made a detour round the car so as to come face to face with the animal. Then for a moment he stood, as it were displaying himself, a resolute little figure in a grey frock coat and a black-banded top hat. He held out a cautious hand, not too suddenly for fear of startling the creature. '*Poossy!*' he said.

The leopard, relieved by the cessation of Lady Stella's sunshade, regarded him with interest and curiosity. He drew closer. The leopard extended its muzzle and sniffed.

'If it will only let me stroke it,' said Mr Catskill, and came within arm's length.

The beast sniffed the extended hand with an expression of incredulity. Then with a suddenness that sent Mr Catskill back several paces, it sneezed. It sneezed again much more violently, regarded Mr Catskill reproachfully for a moment and then leapt lightly over the flower-bed and made off in the direction of the white and golden colonnade. The grazing cattle in the field, Mr Barnstaple noted, watched its passage without the slightest sign of dismay.

Mr Catskill remained in a slightly expanded state in the middle of the road. 'No animal,' he remarked, 'can stand up to the steadfast gaze of the human eye. Not one. It is a riddle for your materialist. . . . Shall we join Mr Cecil, Lady Stella? He seems to have found something to look at down there. The man in the little yellow car may know where he is. Hm?'

He assisted the lady to get out of the car and the two came on after Mr Barnstaple's party, which was now again approaching the burning house. The chauffeur, evidently not wishing to be left alone with the Limousine in this world of incredible possibilities, followed as closely as respect permitted.

CHAPTER THE THIRD

The Beautiful People

I

The fire in the little house did not seem to be making headway. The smoke that came from it was much less now than when Mr Barnstaple had first observed it. As they came close they found a quantity of twisted bits of bright metal and fragments of broken glass among the shattered masonry. The suggestion of exploded scientific apparatus was very strong. Then almost simultaneously the entire party became aware of a body lying on the grassy slope behind the ruins. It was the body of a man in the prime of life, naked except for a couple of bracelets and a necklace and girdle, and blood was oozing from his mouth and nostrils. With a kind of awe Mr Barnstaple knelt down beside this prostrate figure and felt its still heart. He had never seen so beautiful a face and body before.

'*Dead*,' he whispered.

'Look!' cried the shrill voice of the man with the eye-glass. 'Another!'

He was pointing to something that was hidden from Mr Barnstaple by a piece of wall. Mr Barnstaple had to get up and climb over a heap of rubble before he could see this second find. It was a slender girl, clothed as little as the man. She had evidently been flung with enormous violence against the wall and killed instantaneously. Her face was quite undistorted although her skull had been crushed in from behind; her perfect mouth and green-grey eyes were a little open and her expression was that of one who is still thinking out some difficult but interesting problem. She did not seem in the least dead but merely disregardful. One hand still grasped a copper implement with a handle of glass. The other lay limp and prone.

For some seconds nobody spoke. It was as if they all feared to interrupt the current of her thoughts.

Then Mr Barnstaple heard the voice of the priestly gentleman speaking very softly behind him. 'What a *perfect* form!' he said.

'I admit I was wrong,' said Mr Burleigh with deliberation. 'I have been wrong. . . . These are no earthly people. Manifestly. And *ergo*, we are not on earth. I cannot imagine what has happened nor where we are. In the face of sufficient evidence I have never hesitated to retract an opinion. This world we are in is not our world. It is something—'

He paused. 'It is something very wonderful indeed.'

'And the Windsor party,' said Mr Catskill without any apparent regret, 'must have its lunch without us.'

'But then,' said the clerical gentleman, 'what world *are* we in, and how did we get here?'

'Ah! *there*,' said Mr Burleigh blandly, 'you go altogether beyond my poor powers of guessing. We are here in some world that is singularly like our world and singularly unlike it. It must be in some way related to our world or we could not be here. But how it can be related, is, I confess, a hopeless mystery to me. Maybe we are in some other dimension of space than those we wot of. But my poor head whirls at the thought of these dimensions. I am – I am *mazed – mazed.*'

'Einstein,' injected the gentleman with the eye-glass compactly and with evident self-satisfaction.

'Exactly!' said Mr Burleigh. 'Einstein might make it clear to us. Or dear old Haldane might undertake to explain it and fog us up with that adipose Hegelianism of his. But I am neither Haldane nor Einstein. Here we are in some world which is, for all practical purposes, including the purposes of our week-end engagements, Nowhere. Or if you prefer the Greek of it, we are in Utopia. And as I do not see that there is any manifest way out of it again, I suppose the thing we have to do as rational creatures is to make the best of it. And watch our opportunities. It is certainly a very lovely world. The loveliness is even greater than the wonder. And there are human beings here – with minds. I judge from all this material lying about, it is a world in which experimental chemistry is pursued – pursued indeed to the bitter end – under almost idyllic conditions. Chemistry – and nakedness. I feel bound to confess that whether we are to regard these two people who have apparently just blown themselves up here as Greek gods or as naked savages, seems to me to be altogether a question of individual taste. I admit a bias for the Greek god – and goddess.'

'Except that it is a little difficult to think of two dead immortals,' squeaked the gentleman of the eye-glass in the tone of one who scores a point.

Mr Burleigh was about to reply, and to judge from his ruffled expression his reply would have been of a disciplinary nature. But instead he exclaimed sharply and turned round to face two newcomers. The whole party had become aware of them at the same moment. Two stark Apollos stood over the ruin and were regarding our Earthlings with an astonishment at least as great as that they created.

One spoke, and Mr Barnstaple was astonished beyond measure to find understandable words reverberating in his mind.

'Red Gods!' cried the Utopian. 'What things are you? And how did you get into the world?'

(English! It would have been far less astounding if they had spoken Greek. But that they should speak any known language was a matter for incredulous amazement.)

2

Mr Cecil Burleigh was the least disconcerted of the party. 'Now,' he said, 'we may hope to learn something definite – face to face with rational and articulate creatures.'

He cleared his throat, grasped the lapels of his long dust-coat with two long nervous hands and assumed the duties of spokesman. 'We are quite unable, gentlemen, to account for our presence here,' he said. 'We are as puzzled as you are. We have discovered ourselves suddenly in your world instead of our own.'

'You come from another world?'

'Exactly. A quite different world. In which we have all our natural and proper places. We were travelling in that world of ours in – Ah! – certain vehicles, when suddenly we discovered ourselves here. Intruders, I admit, but, I can assure you, innocent and unpremeditated intruders.'

'You do not know how it is that Arden and Greenlake have failed in their experiment and how it is that they are dead?'

'If Arden and Greenlake are the names of these two beautiful young people here, we know nothing about them except that we found them lying as you see them when we came from the road hither to find out or, in fact, to inquire—'

He cleared his throat and left his sentence with a floating end.

The Utopian, if we may for convenience call him that, who had first spoken, looked now at his companion and seemed to question him mutely. Then he turned to the Earthlings again. He spoke and again those clear tones rang, not – so it seemed to Mr Barnstaple – in his ears but within his head.

'It will be well if you and your friends do not trample this wreckage. It will be well if you all return to the road. Come with me. My brother here will put an end to this burning and do what needs to be done to our brother and sister. And afterwards this place will be examined by those who understand the work that was going on here.'

'We must throw ourselves entirely upon your hospitality,' said Mr Burleigh. 'We are entirely at your disposal. This encounter, let me repeat, was not of our seeking.'

'Though we should certainly have sought it if we had known of its possibility,' said Mr Catskill, addressing the world at large and glancing at Mr Barnstaple as if for confirmation. 'We find this world of yours – *most* attractive.'

'At the first encounter,' the gentleman with the eye-glass endorsed, 'a *most* attractive world.'

As they returned through the thick-growing flowers to the road, in the wake of the Utopian and Mr Burleigh, Mr Barnstaple found Lady Stella rustling up beside him. Her words, in this setting of pure wonder, filled him with amazement at their serene and invincible ordinariness. 'Haven't we met before somewhere – at lunch or something – Mr – Mr—?'

Was all this no more than a show? He stared at her blankly for a moment before supplying her with:

'Barnstaple.'

'Mr Barnstaple?'

His mind came into line with hers.

'I've never had that pleasure, Lady Stella. Though, of course, I know you – I know you very well from your photographs in the weekly illustrated papers.'

'Did you hear what it was that Mr Cecil was saying just now? About this being Utopia?'

'He said we might *call* it Utopia.'

'So like Mr Cecil. But is it Utopia? – *really* Utopia?'

'I've always longed so to be in Utopia,' the lady went on without waiting for Mr Barnstaple's reply to her question. 'What splendid young men these two Utopians appear to be! They must, I am sure, belong to its aristocracy – in spite of their – informal – costume. Or even because of it.' ...

Mr Barnstaple had a happy thought. 'I have also recognized Mr Burleigh and Mr Rupert Catskill, Lady Stella, but I should be so glad if you would tell me who the young gentleman with the eye-glass is, and the clerical gentleman. They are close behind us.'

Lady Stella imparted her information in a charmingly confidential undertone. 'The eye-glass,' she murmured, 'is – I am going to spell it – F.R.E.D.D.Y. M.U.S.H. Taste. Good taste. He is awfully clever at finding out young poets and all that sort of literary thing. And he's Rupert's secretary. If there is a literary Academy, they say, he's certain to be in it. He's dreadfully critical and sarcastic. We were going to Taplow for a perfectly intellectual week-end, quite like the old times. So soon as the Windsor people had gone again, that is. . . . Mr Gosse was coming and Max Beerbohm – and everyone like that. But nowadays something always happens. Always. . . . The unexpected – almost excessively. . . . The clerical collar' – she glanced back to judge whether she was within earshot of the gentleman under discussion – 'is Father Amerton, who is so dreadfully outspoken about the sins of society and all *that* sort of thing. It's odd, but out of the pulpit he's inclined to be shy and quiet and a little awkward with the forks and spoons. Paradoxical, isn't it?'

'Of *course!*' cried Mr Barnstaple. 'I remember him now. I knew his face but I couldn't place it. Thank you so much, Lady Stella.'

3

There was something very reassuring to Mr Barnstaple in the company of these famous and conspicuous people and particularly in the company of Lady Stella. She was indeed heartening; she brought so much of the dear old world with her, and she was so manifestly prepared to subjugate this new world to its standards at the earliest possible opportunity. She fended off much of the wonder and beauty that had threatened to submerge Mr Barnstaple altogether. Meeting her and her company was in itself for a man in his position a minor but considerable adventure that helped to bridge the gulf of astonishment between the humdrum of his normal experiences and this all too bracing Utopian air. It solidified, it – if one may use the word in such a connexion – it *degraded* the luminous splendour about him towards complete credibility that it should also be seen and commented on by her and by Mr Burleigh, and viewed through the appraising monocle of Mr Freddy Mush. It brought it within range of the things that get into the newspapers. Mr Barnstaple alone in Utopia might have been so completely overawed as to have been mentally overthrown. This easy-mannered-brown-skinned divinity who was now exchanging questions with

226

Mr Burleigh was made mentally accessible by that great man's intervention.

Yet it was with something very like a catching of the breath that Mr Barnstaple's attention reverted from the Limousine people to this noble-seeming world into which he and they had fallen. What sort of beings really were these men and women of a world where ill-bred weeds, it seemed, had ceased to thrust and fight amidst the flowers, and where leopards void of feline malice looked out with friendly eyes upon the passer-by?

It was astounding that the first two inhabitants they had found in this world of subjugated nature should be lying dead, victims, it would seem, of some hazardous experiment. It was still more astonishing that this other pair who called themselves the brothers of the dead man and woman should betray so little grief or dismay at the tragedy. There had been no emotional scene at all, Mr Barnstaple realized, no consternation or weeping. They were evidently much more puzzled and interested than either horrified or distressed.

The Utopian who had remained in the ruin had carried out the body of the girl to lay it beside her companion's, and he had now, Mr Barnstaple saw, returned to a close scrutiny of the wreckage of the experiment.

But now more of these people were coming upon the scene. They had aeroplanes in this world, for two small ones, noiseless and swift in their flight as swallows, had landed in the fields near by. A man had come up along the road on a machine like a small two-wheeled two-seater with its wheels in series, bicycle fashion; lighter and neater it was than any earthly automobile and mysteriously able to stand up on its two wheels while standing still. A burst of laughter from down the road called Mr Barnstaple's attention to a group of these Utopians who had apparently found something exquisitely ridiculous in the engine of the Limousine. Most of these people were as scantily clothed and as beautifully built as the two dead experimentalists, but one or two were wearing big hats of straw, and one who seemed to be an older woman of thirty or more wore a robe of white bordered by an intense red line. She was speaking now to Mr Burleigh.

Although she was a score of yards away, her speech presented itself in Mr Barnstaple's mind with great distinctness.

'We do not even know as yet what connexion your coming into our world may have with the explosion that has just happened here or whether, indeed, it has any connexion. We want to inquire into both these things. It will be reasonable, we think, to take you and all the possessions you have brought with you to a convenient place for a conference not very far from here. We are arranging for machines to take you thither. There perhaps you will eat. I do not know when you are accustomed to eat?'

'Refreshment,' said Mr Burleigh, rather catching at the idea. 'Some refreshment would certainly be acceptable before very long. In fact, had we not fallen so sharply out of our own world into yours, by this time we should have been lunching – lunching in the best of company.'

'Wonder and lunch,' thought Mr Barnstaple. Man is a creature who must eat by necessity whether he wonder or no. Mr Barnstaple perceived indeed that he was already hungry and that the air he was breathing was a keen and appetizing air.

The Utopian seemed struck by a novel idea. 'Do you eat several times a day? What sort of things do you eat?'

'Oh! Surely! They're *not* vegetarians!' cried Mr Mush sharply in a protesting parenthesis, dropping his eye-glass from its socket.

They were all hungry. It showed upon their faces.

'We are all accustomed to eat several times a day,' said Mr Burleigh. 'Perhaps it would be well if I were to give you a brief résumé of our dietary. There may be differences. We begin, as a rule, with a simple cup of tea and the thinnest slice of bread-and-butter brought to the bedside. Then comes breakfast.' ... He proceeded to a masterly summary of his gastronomic day, giving clearly and attractively the particulars of an English breakfast, eggs to be boiled four and a half minutes, neither more nor less, lunch with any light wine, tea rather a social rally than a serious meal, dinner, in some detail, the occasional resort to supper. It was one of those clear statements which would have rejoiced the House of Commons, light, even gay, and yet with a trace of earnestness. The Utopian woman regarded him with deepening interest as he proceeded. 'Do you all eat in this fashion?' she asked.

Mr Burleigh ran his eye over his party. 'I cannot answer for Mr – Mr—?'

'Barnstaple. ... Yes, I eat in much the same fashion.'

For some reason the Utopian woman smiled at him. She had very pretty brown eyes, and though he liked her to smile he wished that she had not smiled in the way she did.

'And you sleep?' she asked.

'From six to ten hours, according to circumstances,' said Mr Burleigh.

'And you make love?'

The question perplexed and to a certain extent shocked our Earth-lings. What exactly did she mean? For some moments no one framed a reply. Mr Barnstaple's mind was filled with a hurrying rush of strange possibilities.

Then Mr Burleigh, with his fine intelligence and the quick evasiveness of a modern leader of men, stepped into the breach. 'Not habitually, I can is assure you,' he said. 'Not habitually.'

The woman with the red-bordered robe seemed to think this over for a swift moment. Then she smiled faintly.

'We must take you somewhere where we can talk of all these things,' she said. 'Manifestly you come from some strange other world. Our men of knowledge must get together with you and exchange ideas.'

4

At half-past ten that morning Mr Barnstaple had been motoring along the main road through Slough, and now at half-past one he was soaring through wonderland with his own world half forgotten. 'Marvellous,' he repeated. 'Marvellous. I knew that I should have a good holiday. But *this, this* —!'

He was extraordinarily happy with the bright, unclouded happiness of a perfect dream. Never before had he enjoyed the delights of an explorer in new lands, never before had he hoped to experience these delights. Only a few weeks before he had written an article for the *Liberal* lamenting the 'End of the Age of Exploration', an article so thoroughly and aimlessly depressing that it had pleased Mr Peeve extremely. He recalled that exploit now with but the faintest twinge of remorse.

The Earthling party had been distributed among four small aeroplanes, and as Mr Barnstaple and his companion, Father Amerton, rose in the air, he looked back to see the automobiles and luggage being lifted with astonishing ease into two lightly built lorries. Each lorry put out a pair of glittering arms and lifted up its automobile as a nurse might lift up a baby.

By contemporary earthly standards of safety Mr Barnstaple's aviator flew very low. There were times when he passed between trees rather than over them, and this, even if at first it was a little alarming, permitted a fairly close inspection of the landscape. For the earlier part of the journey it was garden pasture with grazing creamy cattle and patches of brilliantly coloured vegetation of a nature unknown to Mr Barnstaple. Amidst this cultivation narrow tracks, which may have been foot or cycle tracks, threaded their way. Here and there ran a road bordered with flowers and shaded by fruit trees.

There were few houses and no towns or villages at all. The houses varied very greatly in size, from little isolated buildings which Mr Barnstaple thought might be elegant summer-houses or little temples, to clusters of roofs and turrets which reminded him of country châteaux or suggested extensive farming or dairying establishments. Here and there people were working in the fields or going to and fro on foot or on machines, but the effect of the whole was of an extremely underpopulated land.

It became evident that they were going to cross the range of snowy mountains that had so suddenly blotted the distant view of Windsor Castle from the landscape.

As they approached these mountains, broad stretches of golden corn-land replaced the green of the pastures and then the cultivation became more diversified. He noted unmistakable vineyards on sunny slopes, and the number of workers visible and the habitations multiplied. The little squadron of aeroplanes flew up a broad valley towards a pass so that Mr Barnstaple was able to scrutinize the mountain scenery. Came chestnut woods and at last pines. There were Cyclopean turbines athwart the mountain torrents and long, low, many-windowed buildings that might serve some industrial purpose. A skilfully graded road with exceedingly bold, light and beautiful viaducts mounted towards the pass. There were more people, he thought, in the highland country than in the levels below, though still far fewer than he would have seen upon any comparable countryside on earth.

Ten minutes of craggy desolation with the snowfields of a great glacier on one side intervened before he descended into the upland valley on the Conference Place where presently he alighted. This was a sort of lap in the mountain, terraced by masonry so boldly designed that it seemed a part of the geological substance of the mountain itself. It faced towards a wide artificial lake retained by a stupendous dam from the lower reaches of the valley. At intervals along this dam there were great stone pillars dimly suggestive of seated figures. He glimpsed a wide plain beyond, which reminded him of the valley of the Po, and then as he descended the straight line of the dam came up to hide this further vision.

Upon these terraces, and particularly upon the lower ones, were groups and clusters of flowerlike buildings, and he distinguished paths and steps and pools of water as if the whole place were a garden.

The aeroplanes made an easy landing on a turfy expanse. Close at hand was a graceful chalet that ran out from the shores of the lake over the water, and afforded mooring to a flotilla of gaily coloured boats. . . .

It was Father Amerton who had drawn Mr Barnstaple's attention to the absence of villages. He now remarked that there was no church in sight and that nowhere had they seen any spires or belfries. But Mr Barnstaple thought that some of the smaller buildings might be temples or shrines. 'Religion may take different forms here,' he said.

'And how few babies or little children are visible!' Father Amerton remarked. 'Nowhere have I seen a mother with her child.'

'On the other side of the mountains there was a place like the playing field of a big school. There were children there and one or two older people dressed in white.'

'I saw that. But I was thinking of babes. Compare this with what one would see in Italy.

'The most beautiful and desirable young women,' added the reverend gentleman; '*most* desirable – and not a sign of maternity!'

Their aviator, a sun-tanned blond with very blue eyes, helped them out of his machine, and they stood watching the descent of the other members of their party. Mr Barnstaple was astonished to note how rapidly he was becoming familiarized with the colour and harmony of this new world; the strangest things in the whole spectacle now were the figures and clothing of his associates. Mr Rupert Catskill in his celebrated grey top hat, Mr Mush with his preposterous eye-glass, the peculiar long slenderness of Mr Burleigh, and the square leather-clad lines of Mr Burleigh's chauffeur, struck him as being far more incredible than the graceful Utopian forms about him.

The aviator's interest and amusement enhanced Mr Barnstaple's perception of his companions' oddity. And then came a wave of profound doubt.

'I suppose this is *really* real,' he said to Father Amerton.

'Really real! What else can it be?'

'I suppose we are not dreaming all this.'

'Are your dreams and my dreams likely to coincide?'

'Yes; but there are quite impossible things – absolutely impossible things.'

'As, for instance?'

'Well, how is it that these people are speaking to us in English – modern English?'

'I never thought of that. It is rather incredible. They don't talk in English to one another.'

Mr Barnstaple stared in round-eyed amazement at Father Amerton, struck for the first time by a still more incredible fact. 'They don't talk in *anything* to one another,' he said. 'And we haven't noticed it until this moment!'

The Shadow of Einstein Falls across the Story But Passes Lightly By

I

Except for that one perplexing fact that all these Utopians had apparently a complete command of idiomatic English, Mr Barnstaple found his vision of this new world developing with a congruity that no dream in his experience had ever possessed. It was so coherent, so orderly, that less and less was it like a strange world at all and more and more like an arrival in some foreign but very highly civilized country.

Under the direction of the brown-eyed woman in the scarlet-edged robe, the Earthlings were established in their quarters near the Conference Place in the most hospitable and comfortable fashion conceivable. Five or six youths and girls made it their business to initiate the strangers in the little details of Utopian domesticity. The separate buildings in which they were lodged had each an agreeable little dressing-room, and the bed, which had sheets of the finest linen and a very light puffy coverlet, stood in an open loggia – too open Lady Stella thought, but then as she said, 'One feels so safe here.' The luggage appeared and the valises were identified as if they were in some hospitable earthly mansion.

But Lady Stella had to turn two rather too friendly youths out of her apartment before she could open her dressing-bag and administer refreshment to her complexion.

A few minutes later some excitement was caused by an outbreak of wild laughter and the sounds of an amiable but hysterical struggle that came from Lady Stella's retreat. The girl who had remained with her had displayed a quite feminine interest in her equipment and had come upon a particularly charming and diaphanous sleeping suit. For some obscure reason this secret daintiness amused the young Utopian extremely, and it was with some difficulty that Lady Stella restrained her from putting the garment on and dancing out in it for a public display. 'Then *you* put it on,' the girl insisted.

'But you don't understand,' cried Lady Stella. 'It's almost – *sacred!* It's for nobody to see – *ever.*'

'But *why?*' the Utopian asked, puzzled beyond measure.

Lady Stella found an answer impossible.

The light meal that followed was by terrestrial standards an entirely satisfactory one. The anxiety of Mr Freddy Mush was completely allayed; there were cold chicken and ham and a very pleasant meat pâté. There were also rather coarse-grained but most palatable bread, pure butter, an exquisite salad, fruit, cheese of the Gruyère type, and a light white wine which won from Mr Burleigh the tribute that 'Moselle never did anything better.'

'You find our food very like your own?' asked the woman in the red-trimmed robe.

'Eckquithit quality,' said Mr Mush with his mouth rather full.

'Food has changed very little in the last three thousand years. People had found out all the best things to eat long before the last Age of Confusion.'

'It's too real to be real,' Mr Barnstaple repeated to himself. 'Too real to be real.'

He looked at his companions, elated, interested and eating with appreciation.

If it wasn't for the absurdity of these Utopians speaking English with a clearness that tapped like a hammer inside his head Mr Barnstaple would have had no doubt whatever of its reality.

No servants waited at the clothless stone table; the woman in the white and scarlet robe and the two aviators shared the meal and the guests attended to each other's requirements. Mr Burleigh's chauffeur was for modestly shrinking to another table until the great statesman reassured him with: 'Sit down there, Penk. Next to Mr Mush.' Other Utopians with friendly but keenly observant eyes upon the Earthlings came into the great pillared veranda in which the meal had been set, and smiled and stood about or sat down. There were no introductions and few social formalities.

'All this is most reassuring,' said Mr Burleigh. 'Most reassuring. I'm bound to say these beat the Chatsworth peaches. Is that cream, my dear Rupert, in the little brown jar in front of you? ... I guessed as much. If you are sure you can spare it, Rupert. . . . Thank you.'

233

Several of the Utopians made themselves known by name to the Earthlings. All their voices sounded singularly alike to Mr Barnstaple and the words were as clear as print. The brown-eyed woman's name was Lychnis. A man with a beard who might perhaps, Mr Barnstaple thought, have been as old as forty, was either Urthred or Adam or Edom, the name for all its sharpness of enunciation had been very difficult to catch. It was as if large print *hesitated*. Urthred conveyed that he was an ethnologist and historian and that he desired to learn all that he possibly could about the ways of our world. He impressed Mr Barnstaple as having the easy carriage of some earthly financier or great newspaper proprietor rather than the diffidence natural in our own everyday world to a merely learned man. Another of their hosts, Serpentine, was also, Mr Barnstaple learnt with surprise, for his bearing too was almost masterful, a scientific man. He called himself something that Mr Barnstaple could not catch. First it sounded like 'atomic mechanician', and then oddly enough it sounded like 'molecular chemist'. And then Mr Barnstaple heard Mr Burleigh say to Mr Mush, 'He said "physio-chemist", didn't he?'

'*I* thought he just called himself a materialist,' said Mr Mush.

'I thought he said he weighed things,' said Lady Stella.

'Their intonation is peculiar,' said Mr Burleigh. 'Sometimes they are almost too loud for comfort and then there is a kind of gap in the sounds.' ...

When the meal was at an end the whole party removed to another little building that was evidently planned for classes and discussions. It had a semicircular apse round which ran a series of white tablets which evidently functioned at times as a lecturer's blackboard, since there were black and coloured pencils and cloths for erasure lying on a marble ledge at a convenient height below the tablets. The lecturer could walk from point to point of this semicircle as he talked. Lychnis, Urthred, Serpentine and the Earthlings seated themselves on a semicircular bench below this lecturer's track, and there was accommodation for about eighty or a hundred people upon the seats before them. All these were occupied, and beyond stood a number of graceful groups against a background of rhododendron-like bushes, between which Mr Barnstaple caught glimpses of grassy vistas leading down to the shining waters of the lake.

They were going to talk over this extraordinary irruption into their world. Could anything be more reasonable than to talk it over? Could anything be more fantastically impossible?

'Odd that there are no swallows,' said Mr Mush suddenly in Mr Barnstaple's ear. 'I wonder why there are no swallows.'

Mr Barnstaple's attention went to the empty sky. 'No gnats nor flies perhaps,' he suggested. It was odd that he had not missed the swallows before.

'Sssh!' said Lady Stella. 'He's beginning.'

3

This incredible conference began. It was opened by the man named Serpentine, and he stood before his audience and seemed to make a speech. His lips moved, his hands assisted his statements; his expression followed his utterance. And yet Mr Barnstaple had the most subtle and indefensible doubt whether indeed Serpentine was speaking. There was something odd about the whole thing. Sometimes the thing said sounded with a peculiar resonance in his head; sometimes it was indistinct and elusive like an object seen through troubled waters; sometimes, though Serpentine still moved his fine hands and looked towards his hearers, there were gaps of absolute silence – as if for brief intervals Mr Barnstaple had gone deaf. ... Yet it was a discourse; it held together and it held Mr Barnstaple's attention.

Serpentine had the manner of one who is taking great pains to be as simple as possible with a rather intricate question. He spoke, as it were, in propositions with a pause between each. 'It had long been known,' he began, 'that the possible number of dimensions, like the possible number of anything else that could be enumerated, was unlimited!'

Yes, Mr Barnstaple had got that, but it proved too much for Mr Freddy Mush.

'Oh, Lord!' he said. 'Dimensions!' and dropped his eye-glass and became despondently inattentive.

'For most practical purposes,' Serpentine continued, 'the particular universe, the particular system of events, in which we found ourselves and of which we formed part, could be regarded as occurring in a space of three rectilinear dimensions and as undergoing translation, which translation was in fact duration, through a fourth dimension, *time*. Such a system of events was necessarily a gravitational system.'

'Er!' said Mr Burleigh sharply. 'Excuse me! I don't see that.'

So he, at any rate, was following it too.

'Any universe that endures must necessarily gravitate,' Serpentine repeated, as if he were asserting some self-evident fact.

'For the life of me I can't see that,' said Mr Burleigh after a moment's reflection.

Serpentine considered him for a moment. 'It *is* so,' he said, and went on with his discourse. Our minds, he continued, had been evolved in the form of this practical conception of things, they accepted it as true, and it was only by great efforts of sustained analysis that we were able to realize that this universe in which we lived not only extended but was, as it were, slightly bent and contorted, into a number of other long unsuspected spatial dimensions. It extended beyond its three chief spatial dimensions into these others just as a thin sheet of paper, which is practically two dimensional, extended not only by virtue of its thickness but also of its crinkles and curvature into a third dimension.

'Am I going deaf?' asked Lady Stella in a stage whisper. 'I can't catch a word of all this.'

'Nor I,' said Father Amerton.

Mr Burleigh made a pacifying gesture towards these unfortunates without taking his eyes off Serpentine's face. Mr Barnstaple knitted his brows, clasped his knees, knotted his fingers, held on desperately.

He *must* be hearing – of course he was hearing!

Serpentine proceeded to explain that just as it would be possible for any number of practically two-dimensional universes to lie side by side, like sheets of paper, in a three-dimensional space, so in the many-dimensional space about which the ill-equipped human mind is still slowly and painfully acquiring knowledge, it is possible for an innumerable quantity of practically three-dimensional universes to lie, as it were, side by side and to undergo a roughly parallel movement through time. The speculative work of Lonestone and Cephalus had long since given the soundest basis for the belief that there actually were a very great number of such space-and-time universes, parallel to one another and resembling each other, nearly but not exactly, much as the leaves of a book might resemble one another. All of them would have duration, all of them would be gravitating systems—

(Mr Burleigh shook his head to show that still he didn't see it.)

—And those lying closest together would most nearly resemble each other. How closely they now had an opportunity of learning. For the daring attempts of those two great geniuses, Arden and Greenlake, to use the – (*inaudible*) – thrust of the atom to rotate a portion of the Utopian material universe in that dimension, the F dimension, into which it had long been known to extend for perhaps the length of a man's arm, to rotate this fragment of Utopian matter, much as a gate is swung on its hinges, had manifestly been altogether successful. The

236

gate had swung back again bringing with it a breath of close air, a storm of dust and, to the immense amazement of Utopia, three sets of visitors from an unknown world.

'*Three?*' whispered Mr Barnstaple doubtfully. 'Did he say *three?*' [Serpentine disregarded him.]

'Our brother and sister have been killed by some unexpected release of force, but their experiment has opened a way that now need never be closed again, out of the present spatial limitations of Utopia into a whole vast folio of hitherto unimagined worlds. Close at hand to us, even as Lonestone guessed ages ago, nearer to us, as he put it, than the blood in our hearts—'

('Nearer to us than breathing and closer than hands and feet,' Father Amerton misquoted, waking up suddenly. 'But what is he talking about? I don't catch it.')

'— we discover another planet, much the same size as ours to judge by the scale of its inhabitants, circulating, we may certainly assume, round a sun like that in our skies, a planet bearing life and being slowly subjugated, even as our own is being subjugated, by intelligent life which has evidently evolved under almost exactly parallel conditions to those of our own evolution. This sister universe to ours is, so far as we may judge by appearances, a little retarded in time in relation to our own. Our visitors wear something very like the clothing and display physical characteristics resembling those of our ancestors during the last Age of Confusion. ...

'We are not yet justified in supposing that their history has been strictly parallel to ours. No two particles of matter are alike; no two vibrations. In all the dimensions of being, in all the universes of God, there has never been and there can never be an exact repetition. That we have come to realize is the one impossible thing. Nevertheless, this world you call Earth is manifestly very near and like to this universe of ours. ...

'We are eager to learn from you Earthlings, to check our history, which is still very imperfectly known, by your experiences, to show you what we know, to make out what may be possible and desirable in intercourse and help between the people of your planet and ours. We, here, are the merest beginners in knowledge; we have learnt as yet scarcely anything more than the immensity of the things that we have yet to learn and do. In a million kindred things our two worlds may perhaps teach each other and help each other. ...

'Possibly there are streaks of heredity in your planet that have failed to develop or that have died out in ours. Possibly there are elements or minerals in one world that are rare or wanting in the other. ... The structure of your atoms (?) ... our worlds may intermarry (?) ... to their common invigoration. ...'

He passed into the inaudible just when Mr Barnstaple was most moved and most eager to follow what he was saying. Yet a deaf man would have judged he was still speaking.

Mr Barnstaple met the eye of Mr Rupert Catskill, as distressed and puzzled as his own. Father Amerton's face was buried in his hands. Lady Stella and Mr Mush were whispering softly together; they had long since given up any pretence of listening.

'Such,' said Serpentine, abruptly becoming audible again, 'is our first rough interpretation of your apparition in our world and of the possibilities of our interaction. I have put our ideas before you as plainly as I can. I would suggest that now one of you tell us simply and plainly what *you* conceive to be the truth about your world in relation to ours.'

CHAPTER THE FIFTH

The Governance and History of Utopia

I

Came a pause. The Earthlings looked at one another and their gaze seemed to converge upon Mr Cecil Burleigh. That statesman feigned to be unaware of the general expectation. 'Rupert,' he said. 'Won't *you?*'

'I reserve my comments,' said Mr Catskill.

'Father Amerton, you are accustomed to treat of other worlds.'

'Not in your presence, Mr Cecil. No.'

'But what am I to tell them?'

'What you think of it,' said Mr Barnstaple.

'Exactly,' said Mr Catskill. 'Tell them what you think of it.'

No one else appeared to be worthy of consideration. Mr Burleigh rose slowly and walked thoughtfully to the centre of the semicircle. He grasped his coat lapels and remained for some moments with face downcast as if considering what he was about to say. 'Mr Serpentine,' he began at last, raising a candid countenance and regarding the blue sky above the distant lake through his glasses. 'Ladies and Gentlemen—'

He was going to make a speech! – as though he was at a Primrose League garden party – or Geneva. It was preposterous and yet, what else was there to be done?

'I must confess, Sir, that although I am by no means a novice at public speaking, I find myself on this occasion somewhat at a loss. Your admirable discourse, Sir, simple, direct, lucid, compact, and rising at times to passages of unaffected eloquence, has set me a pattern that

I would fain follow – and before which, in all modesty, I quail. You ask me to tell you as plainly and clearly as possible the outline facts as we conceive them about this kindred world out of which with so little premeditation we have come to you. So far as my poor powers of understanding or discussing such recondite matters go, I do not think I can better or indeed supplement in any way your marvellous exposition of the mathematical aspects of the case. What you have told us embodies the latest, finest thoughts of terrestrial science and goes, indeed, far beyond our current ideas. On certain matters, in, for example, the relationship of time and gravitation, I feel bound to admit that I do not go with you, but that is rather a failure to understand your position than any positive dissent. Upon the broader aspects of the case there need be no difficulties between us. We accept your main proposition unreservedly; namely, that we conceive ourselves to be living in a parallel universe to yours, on a planet the very brother of your own, indeed quite amazingly like yours, having regard to all the possible contrasts we might have found here. We are attracted by and strongly disposed to accept your view that our system is, in all probability, a little less seasoned and mellowed by the touch of time than yours, short perhaps by some hundreds or some thousands of years of your experiences. Assuming this, it is inevitable, Sir, that a certain humility should mingle in our attitude towards you. As your juniors it becomes us not to instruct but to learn. It is for us to ask: What have you done? To what have you reached? rather than to display to you with an artless arrogance all that still remains for us to learn and do. . . .'

'No!' said Mr Barnstaple to himself but half audibly. 'This is a dream. . . . If it were anyone else. . . .'

He rubbed his knuckles into his eyes and opened them again, and there he was still, sitting next to Mr Mush in the midst of these Olympian divinities. And Mr Burleigh, that polished sceptic, who never believed, who was never astonished, was leaning forward on his toes and speaking, speaking, with the assurance of a man who has made ten thousand speeches. He could not have been more sure of himself and his audience in the Guildhall in London. And they were understanding him! Which was absurd!

There was nothing to do but to fall in with this stupendous absurdity – and sit and listen. Sometimes Mr Barnstaple's mind wandered altogether from what Mr Burleigh was saying. Then it returned and hung desperately to his discourse. In his halting, parliamentary way, his hands trifling with his glasses or clinging to the lapels of his coat, Mr Burleigh was giving Utopia a brief account of the world of men, seeking to be elementary and lucid and reasonable, telling them of states and empires, of wars and the Great War, of economic organization and disorganization, of revolutions and Bolshevism, of the terrible Russian famine that was beginning, of the difficulties of finding honest statesmen and officials, and of the unhelpfulness of newspapers, of all the dark and troubled spectacle of human life. Serpentine had used the term 'the Last Age of Confusion', and Mr Burleigh had seized upon the phrase and was making much of it. . . .

It was a great oratorical impromptu. It must have gone on for an hour, and the Utopians listened with keen, attentive faces, now and then nodding their acceptance and recognition of this statement or that. 'Very like,' would come tapping into Mr Barnstaple's brain. 'With us also – in the Age of Confusion.'

At last Mr Burleigh, with the steady deliberation of an old parliamentary hand, drew to his end. Compliments.

He bowed. He had done. Mr Mush startled everyone by a vigourous hand-clapping in which no one else joined.

The tension in Mr Barnstaple's mind had become intolerable. He leapt to his feet.

2

He stood making those weak propitiatory gestures that come so naturally to the inexperienced speaker. 'Ladies and Gentlemen,' he said. 'Utopians, Mr Burleigh! I crave your pardon for a moment. There is a little matter. Urgent.'

For a brief interval he was speechless.

Then he found attention and encouragement in the eye of Urthred.

'Something I don't understand. Something incredible – I mean, incompatible. The little rift. Turns everything into a fantastic phantasmagoria.'

The intelligence in Urthred's eye was very encouraging. Mr Barnstaple abandoned any attempt to address the company as a whole, and spoke directly to Urthred.

'You live in Utopia, hundreds of thousands of years in advance of us. How is it that you are able to talk contemporary English – to use exactly the same language that we do? I ask you, how is that? It is incredible. It jars. It makes a dream of you. And yet you are not a dream? It makes me feel – almost – insane.'

Urthred smiled pleasantly. 'We *don't* speak English,' he said.

Mr Barnstaple felt the ground slipping from under his feet. 'But I *hear* you speaking English,' he said.

241

'Nevertheless we do not speak it,' said Urthred.

He smiled still more broadly. 'We don't – for ordinary purposes – speak anything.'

Mr Barnstaple, with his brain resigning its functions, maintained his pose of deferential attention.

'Ages ago,' Urthred continued, 'we certainly used to speak languages. We made sounds and we heard sounds. People used to think, and then chose and arranged words and uttered them. The hearer heard, noted, and retranslated the sounds into ideas. Then, in some manner which we still do not understand perfectly, people began to *get* the idea before it was clothed in words and uttered in sounds. They began to hear in their minds, as soon as the speaker had arranged his ideas and before he put them into word symbols even in his own mind. They knew what he was going to say before he said it. This direct transmission presently became common; it was found out that with a little effort most people could get over to each other in this fashion to some extent, and the new mode of communication was developed systematically.

'That is what we do now habitually in this world. We think directly *to* each other. We determine to convey the thought and it is conveyed at once – provided the distance is not too great. We use sounds in this world now only for poetry and pleasure and in moments of emotion or to shout at a distance, or with animals, not for the transmission of ideas from human mind to kindred human mind any more. When I think to you, the thought, *so far as it finds corresponding ideas and suitable words in your mind,* is reflected in your mind. My thought clothes itself in words in your mind, which words you seem to hear – and naturally enough in your own language and your own habitual phrases. Very probably the members of your party are hearing what I am saying to you, each with his own individual difference of vocabulary and phrasing.'

Mr Barnstaple had been punctuating this discourse with sharp, intelligent nods, coming now and then to the verge of interruption. Now he broke out with: 'And that is why occasionally – as for instance when Mr Serpentine made his wonderful explanation just now – when you soar into ideas of which we haven't even a shadow in our minds, we just hear nothing at all.'

'Are there such gaps?' asked Urthred.

'Many, I fear – for all of us,' said Mr Burleigh.

'It's like being deaf in spots,' said Lady Stella. 'Large spots.'

Father Amerton nodded agreement.

'And that is why we cannot be clear whether you are called Urthred or Adam, and why I have found myself confusing Arden and Green-trees and Forest in my mind.'

'I hope that now you are mentally more at your ease?' said Urthred.

'Oh, quite,' said Mr Barnstaple. 'Quite. And all things considered, it is really very convenient for us that there should be this method of transmission. For otherwise I do not see how we could have avoided weeks of linguistic bother, first principles of our respective grammars, logic, significs, and so forth, boring stuff for the most part, before we could have got to anything like our present understanding.'

'A very good point indeed,' said Mr Burleigh, turning round to Mr Barnstaple in a very friendly way. 'A very good point indeed. I should never have noted it if you had not called my attention to it. It is quite extraordinary; I had not noted anything of this – this difference. I was occupied, I am bound to confess, by my own thoughts. I supposed they were speaking English. Took it for granted.'

3

It seemed to Mr Barnstaple that this wonderful experience was now so complete that there remained nothing more to wonder at except its absolute credibility. He sat in this beautiful little building looking out upon dreamland flowers and the sunlit lake amidst this strange mingling of week-end English costumes and this more than Olympian nudity that had already ceased to startle him, he listened and occasionally participated in the long informal conversation that now ensued. It was a discussion that brought to light the most amazing and fundamental differences of moral and social outlook. Yet everything had now assumed a reality that made it altogether natural to suppose that he would presently go home to write about it in the *Liberal* and tell his wife, as much as might seem advisable at the time, about the manners and costumes of this hitherto undiscovered world. He had not even a sense of intervening distances. Sydenham might have been just round the corner.

Presently two pretty young girls made tea at an equipage among the rhododendra and brought it round to people. Tea! It was what we should call China tea, very delicate, and served in little cups without handles, Chinese fashion, but it was real and very refreshing tea.

The earlier curiosities of the Earthlings turned upon methods of government. This was perhaps natural in the presence of two such statesmen as Mr Burleigh and Mr Catskill.

'What form of government do you have?' asked Mr Burleigh. 'Is it a monarchy or an autocracy or a pure democracy? Do you separate the executive and the legislative? And is there one central government for all your planet, or are there several governing centres?'

It was conveyed to Mr Burleigh and his companions with some difficulty that there was no central government in Utopia at all.

'But surely,' said Mr Burleigh, 'there is someone or something, some council or bureau or what not, somewhere, with which the final decision rests in cases of collective action for the common welfare, Some ultimate seat and organ of sovereignty, it seems to me, there *must* be.' ...

No, the Utopians declared, there was no such concentration of authority in their world. In the past there had been, but it had long since diffused back into the general body of the community. Decisions in regard to any particular matter were made by the people who knew most about that matter.

'But suppose it is a decision that has to be generally observed? A rule affecting the public health, for example? Who would enforce it?'

'It would not need to be enforced. Why should it?'

'But suppose someone refused to obey your regulation?'

'We should inquire why he or she did not conform. There might be some exceptional reason.'

'But failing that?'

'We should make an inquiry into his mental and moral health.'

'The mind doctor takes the place of the policeman,' said Mr Burleigh.

'I should prefer the policeman,' said Mr Rupert Catskill.

'You *would*, Rupert,' said Mr Burleigh as who should say: '*Got* you that time.'

'Then do you mean to say,' he continued, addressing the Utopians with an expression of great intelligence, 'that your affairs are all managed by special bodies or organizations – one scarcely knows what to call them – without any co-ordination of their activities?'

'The activities of our world,' said Urthred, 'are all co-ordinated to secure the general freedom. We have a number of intelligences directed to the general psychology of the race and to the interaction of one collective function upon another.'

'Well, isn't that group of intelligences a governing class?' said Mr Burleigh.

'Not in the sense that they exercise any arbitrary will,' said Urthred. 'They deal with general relations, that is all. But they rank no higher, they have no more precedence on that account than a philosopher has over a scientific specialist.'

'This is a republic indeed!' said Mr Burleigh. 'But how it works and how it came about I cannot imagine. Your state is probably a highly socialistic one?'

'You still live in a world in which nearly everything except the air, the high roads, the high seas and the wilderness is privately owned?'

'We do,' said Mr Catskill. 'Owned – and competed for.'

'We have been through that stage. We found at last that private property in all but very personal things was an intolerable nuisance to mankind. We got rid of it. An artist or a scientific man has complete control of all the material he needs, we all own our tools and appliances and have rooms and places of our own, but there is no property for trade or speculation. All this militant property, this property of manoeuvre, has been quite got rid of. But how we got rid of it is a long story. It was not done in a few years. The exaggeration of private property was an entirely natural and necessary stage in the development of human nature. It led at last to monstrous results, but it was only through these monstrous and catastrophic results that men learnt the need and nature of the limitations of private property.'

Mr Burleigh had assumed an attitude which was obviously habitual to him. He sat very low in his chair with his long legs crossed in front of him and the thumb and fingers of one hand placed with meticulous exactness against those of the other.

'I must confess,' he said, 'that I am most interested in the peculiar form of Anarchism which seems to prevail here. Unless I misunderstand you completely every man attends to his own business as the servant of the state. I take it you have – you must correct me if I am wrong – a great number of people concerned in the production and distribution and preparation of food; they inquire, I assume, into the needs of the world, they satisfy them and they are a law unto themselves in their way of doing it. They conduct researches, they make experiments. Nobody compels, obliges, restrains or prevents them. ('People talk to them about it,' said Urthred with a faint smile.) And again others produce and manufacture and study metals for all mankind and are also a law unto themselves. Others again see to the habitability of your world, plan and arrange these delightful habitations, say who shall use them and how they shall be used. Others pursue pure science. Others experiment with sensory and imaginative possibilities and are artists. Others again teach.'

'They are very important,' said Lychnis.

'And they all do it in harmony – and due proportion. Without either a central legislature or executive. I will admit that all this seems admirable – but impossible. Nothing of the sort has ever been even suggested yet in the world from which we come.'

'Something of the sort was suggested long ago by the Guild Social-ists,' said Mr Barnstaple.

'Dear me!' said Mr Burleigh. 'I know very little about the Guild Socialists. Who were they? Tell me.'

Mr Barnstaple tacitly declined that task. 'The idea is quite familiar to our younger people,' he said. 'Laski calls it the pluralistic state, as distinguished from the monistic state in which sovereignty is con-centrated. Even the Chinese have it. A Pekin professor, Mr S. C. Chang, has written a pamphlet on what he calls "Professionalism". I read it only a few weeks ago. He sent it to the office of the *Liberal.* He points out how undesirable it is and how unnecessary for China to pass through a phase of democratic politics on the western model. He wants China to go right straight on to a collateral independence of functional classes, mandarins, industrials, agricultural workers and so forth, much as we seem to find it here. Though that of course involves an educational revolution. Decidedly the germ of what you call Anarchism here is also in the air we come from.'

'Dear me!' said Mr Burleigh, looking more intelligent and appre-ciative than ever. 'And is that so? I had *no* idea—!'

4

The conversation continued desultory in form and yet the exchange of ideas was rapid and effective. Quite soon, as it seemed to Mr Barnstaple, an outline of the history of Utopia from the Last Age of Confusion onward shaped itself in his mind.

The more he learnt of that Last Age of Confusion the more it seemed to resemble the present time on earth. In those days the Utopians had worn abundant clothing and lived in towns quite after the earthly fashion. A fortunate conspiracy of accidents rather than any set design had opened for them some centuries of opportunity and expansion. Climatic phases and political chances had smiled upon the race after a long period of recurrent shortage, pestilence and destructive warfare. For the first time the Utopians had been able to explore the whole planet on which they lived, and these explorations had brought great virgin areas under the axe, the spade and the plough. There had been an enormous increase in real wealth and in leisure and liberty. Many thousands of people were lifted out of the normal squalor of human life to positions in which they could, if they chose, think and act with unprecedented freedom. A few, a sufficient few, did. A vigourous development of scientific inquiry began and, trailing after it a multitude of ingenious inventions, produced a great enlargement of practical human power.

There had been previous outbreaks of the scientific intelligence in Utopia, but none before had ever occurred in such favourable circumstances or lasted long enough to come to abundant practical fruition. Now in a couple of brief centuries the Utopians, who had hitherto crawled about their planet like sluggish ants or travelled parasitically on larger and swifter animals, found themselves able to fly rapidly or speak instantaneously to any other point on the planet. They found themselves, too, in possession of mechanical power on a scale beyond all previous experience, and not simply of mechanical power; physiological and then psychological science followed in the wake of physics and chemistry, and extraordinary possibilities of control over his own body and over his social life dawned upon the Utopian. But these things came, when at last they did come, so rapidly and confusingly that it was only a small minority of people who realized the possibilities, as distinguished from the concrete achievements, of this tremendous expansion of knowledge. The rest took the novel inventions as they came, haphazard, with as little adjustment as possible of their thoughts and ways of living to the new necessities these novelties implied.

The first response of the general population of Utopia to the prospect of power, leisure and freedom thus opened out to it was proliferation. It behaved just as senselessly and mechanically as any other animal or vegetable species would have done. It bred until it had completely swamped the ampler opportunity that had opened before it. It spent the great gifts of science as rapidly as it got them in a mere insensate multiplication of the common life. At one time in the Last Age of Confusion the population of Utopia had mounted to over two thousand million. ...

'But what is it now?' asked Mr Burleigh.

About two hundred and fifty million, the Utopians told him. That had been the maximum population that could live a fully developed life upon the surface of Utopia. But now with increasing resources the population was being increased.

A gasp of horror came from Father Amerton. He had been dreading this realization for some time. It struck at his moral foundations. 'And you dare to *regulate* increase! You control it! Your women consent to bear children as they are needed – or refrain!'

'Of course,' said Urthred. 'Why not?'

'I feared as much,' said Father Amerton, and leaning forward he covered his face with his hands, murmuring, 'I felt this in the

247

atmosphere! The human stud farm! Refusing to create souls! The *wickedness* of it! Oh, my God!'

Mr Burleigh regarded the emotion of the reverend gentleman through his glasses with a slightly shocked expression. He detested catchwords. But Father Amerton stood for very valuable conservative elements in the community. Mr Burleigh turned to the Utopian again. 'That is extremely interesting,' he said. 'Even at present our earth contrives to carry a population of at least five times that amount.'

'But twenty millions or so will starve this winter, you told us a little while ago – in a place called Russia. And only a very small proportion of the rest are leading what even you would call full and spacious lives?'

'Nevertheless the contrast is very striking,' said Mr Burleigh.

'It is terrible!' said Father Amerton.

The overcrowding of the planet in the Last Age of Confusion was, these Utopians insisted, the fundamental evil out of which all the others that afflicted the race arose. An overwhelming flood of new-comers poured into the world and swamped every effort the intelligent minority could make to educate a sufficient proportion of them to meet the demands of the new and still rapidly changing conditions of life. And the intelligent minority was not itself in any position to control the racial destiny. These great masses of population that had been blundered into existence, swayed by damaged and decaying traditions and amenable to the crudest suggestions, were the natural prey and support of every adventurer with a mind blatant enough and a conception of success coarse enough to appeal to them. The economic system, clumsily and convulsively reconstructed to meet the new conditions of mechanical production and distribution, became more and more a cruel and impudent exploitation of the multitudinous congestion of the common man by the predatory and acquisitive few. That all too common common man was hustled through misery and subjection from his cradle to his grave; he was cajoled and lied to, he was bought, sold and dominated by an impudent minority, bolder and no doubt more energetic, but in all other respects no more intelligent than himself. It was difficult, Urthred said, for a Utopian nowadays to convey the monstrous stupidity, wastefulness and vulgarity to which these rich and powerful men of the Last Age of Confusion attained.

('We will not trouble you,' said Mr Burleigh. 'Unhappily – we know. . . . We know. Only too well do we know.')

Upon this festering, excessive mass of population disasters des-cended at last like wasps upon a heap of rotting fruit. It was its natural, inevitable destiny. A war that affected nearly the whole planet dislocated its flimsy financial system and most of its economic machinery beyond any possibility of repair. Civil wars and clumsily conceived attempts at social revolution continued the disorganization. A series of years of bad weather accentuated the general shortage. The exploiting adventurers, too stupid to realize what had happened, continued to cheat and hoodwink the commonalty and burke any rally of honest men, as wasps will continue to eat even after their bodies have been cut away. The effort to make passed out of Utopian life, triumphantly superseded by the effort to get. Production dwindled down towards the vanishing point. Accumulated wealth vanished. An overwhelming system of debt, a swarm of creditors, morally incapable of helpful renunciation, crushed out all fresh initiative.

The long diastole in Utopian affairs that had begun with the great discoveries, passed into a phase of rapid systole. What plenty and pleasure was still possible in the world was filched all the more greedily by the adventurers of finance and speculative business. Organized science had long since been commercialized, and was 'applied' now chiefly to a hunt for profitable patents and the forestalling of necessary supplies. The neglected lamp of pure science waned, flickered and seemed likely to go out again altogether, leaving Utopia in the beginning of a new series of Dark Ages like those before the age of discovery began. . . .

'It is really *very* like a gloomy diagnosis of our own outlook,' said Mr Burleigh. 'Extraordinarily like. How Dean Inge would have enjoyed all this!'

'To an infidel of his stamp, no doubt, it would seem most enjoyable,' said Father Amerton a little incoherently.

These comments annoyed Mr Barnstaple, who was urgent to hear more.

'And then,' he said to Urthred, 'what happened?'

5

What happened, Mr Barnstaple gathered, was a deliberate change in Utopian thought. A growing number of people were coming to understand that amidst the powerful and easily released forces that science and organization had brought within reach of man, the old conception of social life in the state, as a limited and legalized struggle of men and women to get the better of one another, was becoming too dangerous to endure, just as the increased dreadfulness of modern weapons was making the separate sovereignty of nations too dangerous to endure. There had to be new ideas and new conventions of human association if history was not to end in disaster and collapse.

All societies were based on the limitation by laws and taboos and treaties of the primordial fierce combativeness of the ancestral man – ape; that ancient spirit of self-assertion had now to undergo new restrictions commensurate with the new powers and dangers of the race. The idea of competition to possess, as the ruling idea of intercourse, was, like some ill-controlled furnace, threatening to consume the machine it had formerly driven. The idea of creative service had to replace it. To that idea the human mind and will had to be turned if social life was to be saved. Propositions that had seemed, in former ages, to be inspired and exalted idealism began now to be recognized not simply as sober psychological truth but as practical and urgently necessary truth. In explaining this Urthred expressed himself in a manner that recalled to Mr Barnstaple's mind certain very familiar phrases; he seemed to be saying that whosoever would save his life should lose it, and that whosoever would give his life should thereby gain the whole world.

Father Amerton's thoughts, it seemed, were also responding in the same manner. For he suddenly interrupted with: 'But what you are saying is a quotation!'

Urthred admitted that he had a quotation in mind, a passage from the teachings of a man of great poetic power who had lived long ago in the days of spoken words.

He would have proceeded, but Father Amerton was too excited to let him do so. 'But who was this teacher?' he asked. 'Where did he live? How was he born? How did he die?'

A picture was flashed upon Mr Barnstaple's consciousness of a solitary-looking, pale-faced figure, beaten and bleeding, surrounded by armoured guards, in the midst of a thrusting, jostling, sun-bit crowd which filled a narrow, high-walled street. Behind, some huge, ugly implement was borne along, dipping and swaying with the swaying of the multitude. . . .

'Did he die upon the Cross in *this* world also?' cried Father Amerton. 'Did he die upon the Cross?'

This prophet in Utopia they learnt had died very painfully, but not upon the Cross. He had been tortured in some way, but neither the Utopians nor these particular Earthlings had sufficient knowledge of the technicalities of torture to get any idea over about that, and then apparently he had been fastened upon a slowly turning wheel and exposed until he died. It was the abominable punishment of a cruel and conquering race, and it had been inflicted upon him because his doctrine of universal service had alarmed the rich and dominant who did not serve. Mr Barnstaple had a momentary vision of a twisted figure upon that wheel of torture in the blazing sun. And, marvellous triumph over death! out of a world that could do such a deed had come this great peace and universal beauty about him!

But Father Amerton was pressing his questions. 'But did you not realize who he was? Did not this world suspect?'

A great many people thought that this man was a God. But he had been accustomed to call himself merely a son of God or a son of Man.

Father Amerton stuck to his point. 'But you worship him now?'

'We follow his teaching because it was wonderful and true,' said Urthred.

'But worship?'

'No.'

'But does nobody worship? There *were* those who worshipped him?'

There were those who worshipped him. There were those who quailed before the stern magnificence of his teaching and yet who had a tormenting sense that he was right in some profound way. So they played a trick upon their own uneasy consciences by treating him as a magical god instead of as a light to their souls. They interwove with his execution ancient traditions of sacrificial kings. Instead of receiving him frankly and clearly and making him a part of their understandings and wills they pretended to eat him mystically and make him a part of their bodies. They turned his wheel into a miraculous symbol, and they confused it with the equator and the sun and the ecliptic and indeed with anything else that was round. In cases of ill-luck, ill-health or bad weather it was believed to be very helpful for the believer to describe a circle in the air with the forefinger.

And since this teacher's memory was very dear to the ignorant multitude because of his gentleness and charity, it was seized upon by cunning and aggressive types who constituted themselves champions and exponents of the wheel, who grew rich and powerful in its name, led people into great wars for its sake and used it as a cover and justification for envy, hatred, tyranny and dark desires. Until at last men said that had that ancient prophet come again to Utopia, his own triumphant wheel would have crushed and destroyed him afresh. . . .

Father Amerton seemed inattentive to this communication. He was seeing it from another angle. 'But surely,' he said, 'there is a remnant of believers still! Despised perhaps – but a remnant?'

There was no remnant. The whole world followed that Teacher of Teachers, but no one worshipped him. On some old treasured buildings the wheel was still to be seen carved, often with the most fantastic decorative elaborations. And in museums and collections there were multitudes of pictures, images, charms and the like.

'I don't understand this,' said Father Amerton. 'It is too terrible. I am at a loss. I do not understand.'

<h2 style="text-align:center">6</h2>

A fair and rather slender man with a delicately beautiful face whose name, Mr Barnstaple was to learn later, was Lion, presently took over from Urthred the burthen of explaining and answering the questions of the Earthlings.

He was one of the educational co-ordinators in Utopia. He made it clear that the change over in Utopian affairs had been no sudden revolution. No new system of laws and customs, no new method of economic co-operation based on the idea of universal service to the common good, had sprung abruptly into being complete and finished. Throughout a long period, before and during the Last Age of Confusion, the foundations of the new state were laid by a growing multitude of inquirers and workers, having no set plan or preconceived method, but brought into unconscious co-operation by a common impulse to service and a common lucidity and veracity of mind. It was only towards the climax of the Last Age of Confusion in Utopia that psychological science began to develop with any vigour, comparable to the vigour of the development of geographical and physical science during the preceding centuries. And the social and economic disorder which was checking experimental science and crippling the organized work of the universities was stimulating inquiry into the processes of human association and making it desperate and fearless.

The impression given Mr Barnstaple was not of one of those violent changes which our world has learnt to call revolutions, but of an increase of light, a dawn of new ideas, in which the things of the old order went on for a time with diminishing vigour until people began as a matter of common sense to do the new things in the place of the old.

The beginnings of the new order were in discussions, books and psychological labouratories; the soil in which it grew was found in schools and colleges. The old order gave small rewards to the schoolmaster, but its dominant types were too busy with the struggle for wealth and power to take much heed of teaching: it was left to any man or woman who would give thought and labour without much hope of tangible rewards, to shape the world anew in the minds of the young. And they did so shape it. In a world ruled ostensibly by adventurer politicians, in a world where men came to power through floundering business enterprises and financial cunning, it was presently being taught and understood that extensive private property was socially a nuisance, and that the state could not do its work properly nor education produce its proper results, side by side with a class of irresponsible rich people. For, by their very nature, they assailed, they corrupted, they undermined every state undertaking; their flaunting existences distorted and disguised all the values of life. They had to go, for the good of the race.

'Didn't they fight?' asked Mr Catskill pugnaciously.

They had fought irregularly but fiercely. The fight to delay or arrest the coming of the universal scientific state, the educational state, in Utopia, had gone on as a conscious struggle for nearly five centuries. The fight against it was the fight of greedy, passionate, prejudiced and self-seeking men against the crystallization into concrete realities of this new idea of association for service. It was fought wherever ideas were spread; it was fought with dismissals and threats and boycotts and storms of violence, with lies and false accusations, with prosecutions and imprisonments, with lynching-rope, tar and feathers, paraffin, bludgeon and rifle, bomb and gun.

But the service of the new idea that had been launched into the world never failed; it seized upon the men and women it needed with compelling power. Before the scientific state was established in Utopia more than a million martyrs had been killed for it, and those who had suffered lesser wrongs were beyond all reckoning. Point after point was won in education, in social laws, in economic method. No date could be fixed for the change. A time came when Utopia perceived that it was day and that a new order of things had replaced the old. . . .

'So it must be,' said Mr Barnstaple, as though Utopia were not already present about him. 'So it must be.'

A question was being answered. Every Utopian child is taught to the full measure of its possibilities and directed to the work that is indicated by its desires and capacity. It is born well. It is born of perfectly healthy parents; its mother has chosen to bear it after due thought and preparation. It grows up under perfectly healthy conditions; its natural impulses to play and learn are gratified by the subtlest educational methods; hands, eyes and limbs are given every opportunity of training and growth; it learns to draw, write, express itself, use a great variety of symbols to assist and extend its thought. Kindness and civility become ingrained habits, for all about it are kind and civil. And in particular the growth of its imagination is watched and encouraged. It learns the wonderful history of its world and its race, how man has struggled and still struggles out of his earlier animal narrowness and egotism towards an empire over being that is still but faintly apprehended through dense veils of ignorance. All its desires are made fine; it learns from poetry, from example and the love of those about it to lose its solicitude for itself in love; its sexual passions are turned against its selfishness, its curiosity flowers into scientific passion, its combativeness is set to fight disorder, its inherent pride and ambition are directed towards an honourable share in the common achievement. It goes to the work that attracts it and chooses what it will do.

If the individual is indolent there is no great loss, there is plenty for all in Utopia, but then it will find no lovers, nor will it ever bear children, because no one in Utopia loves those who have neither energy nor distinction. There is much pride of the mate in Utopian love. And there is no idle rich 'society' in Utopia, nor games and shows for the mere looker-on. There is nothing for the mere looker-on. It is a pleasant world indeed for holidays, but not for those who would continuously do nothing.

For centuries now Utopian science has been able to discriminate among births, and nearly every Utopian alive would have ranked as an energetic creative spirit in former days. There are few dull and no really defective people in Utopia; the idle strains, the people of lethargic dispositions or weak imaginations, have mostly died out; the melancholic type has taken its dismissal and gone; spiteful and malignant characters are disappearing. The vast majority of Utopians are active, sanguine, inventive, receptive and good-tempered.

'And you have not even a parliament?' asked Mr Burleigh, still incredulous.

Utopia has no parliament, no politics, no private wealth, no business competition, no police nor prisons, no lunatics, no defectives nor cripples, and it has none of these things because it has schools and teachers who are all that schools and teachers can be. Politics, trade and competition are the methods of adjustment of a crude society. Such methods of adjustment have been laid aside in Utopia for more than a thousand years. There is no rule nor government needed by adult Utopians because all the rule and government they need they have had in childhood and youth.

Said Lion: '*Our education is our government.*'

CHAPTER THE SIXTH

Some Earthly Criticisms

I

At times during that memorable afternoon and evening it seemed to Mr Barnstaple that he was involved in nothing more remarkable than an extraordinary dialogue about government and history, a dialogue that had in some inexplicable way become spectacular; it was as if all this was happening only in his mind; and then the absolute reality of his adventure would return to him with overwhelming power and his intellectual interest fade to inattention in the astounding strangeness of his position. In these latter phases he would find his gaze wandering from face to face of the Utopians who surrounded him, resting for a time on some exquisite detail of the architecture of the building and then coming back to these divinely graceful forms.

Then incredulously he would revert to his fellow Earthlings.

Not one of these Utopian faces but was as candid, earnest and beautiful as the angelic faces of an Italian painting. One woman was strangely like Michael Angelo's Delphic Sibyl. They sat in easy attitudes, men and women together, for the most part concentrated on the discussion, but every now and then Mr Barnstaple would meet the direct scrutiny of a pair of friendly eyes or find some Utopian face intent upon the costume of Lady Stella or the eye-glass of Mr Mush.

Mr Barnstaple's first impression of the Utopians had been that they were all young people; now he perceived that many of these faces had a quality of vigourous maturity. None showed any of the distinctive marks of age as this world notes them, but both Urthred and Lion had lines of experience about eyes and lips and brow.

The effect of these people upon Mr Barnstaple mingled stupefaction with familiarity in the strangest way. He had a feeling that he had always known that such a race could exist and that this knowledge had supplied the implicit standard of a thousand judgments upon human affairs, and at the same time he was astonished to the pitch of incredulity to find himself in the same world with them. They were at once normal and wonderful in comparison with himself and his companions who were, on their part, at the same time queer and perfectly matter of fact.

And together with a strong desire to become friendly and intimate with these fine and gracious persons, to give himself to them and to associate them with himself by service and reciprocal acts, there was an awe and fear of them that made him shrink from contact with them and quiver at their touch. He desired their personal recognition of himself as a fellow and companion so greatly that his sense of his own ungraciousness and unworthiness overwhelmed him. He wanted to bow down before them. Beneath all the light and loveliness of things about him lurked the intolerable premonition of his ultimate rejection from this new world.

So great was the impression made by the Utopians upon Mr Barnstaple, so entirely did he yield himself up to his joyful acceptance of their grace and physical splendour, that for a time he had no attention left over to note how different from his own were the reactions of several of his Earthling companions. The aloofness of the Utopians from the queerness, grotesqueness and cruelty of normal earthly life made him ready for the most uncritical approval of their institutions and ways of life.

It was the behaviour of Father Amerton which first awakened him to the fact that it was possible to disapprove of these wonderful people very highly and to display a very considerable hostility to them. At first Father Amerton had kept a round-faced, round-eyed wonder above his round collar; he had shown a disposition to give the lead to anyone who chose to take it, and he had said not a word until the naked beauty of dead Greenlake had surprised him into an expression of unclerical appreciation. But during the journey to the lakeside and the meal and the opening arrangements of the conference there was a reaction, and this first naive and deferential astonishment gave place to an attitude of resistance and hostility. It was as if this new world which had begun by being a spectacle had taken on the quality of a proposition which he felt he had either to accept or confute. Perhaps it was that the habit of mind of a public censor was too strong for him and that he could not feel normal again until he began to condemn.

Perhaps he was really shocked and distressed by the virtual nudity of these lovely bodies about him. But he began presently to make queer grunts and coughs, to mutter to himself, and to betray an increasing incapacity to keep still.

He broke out first into an interruption when the question of population was raised. For a little while his intelligence prevailed over this emotional stir when the prophet of the wheel was discussed, but then his gathering preoccupations resumed their sway.

'I must speak out,' Mr Barnstaple heard him mutter. 'I must speak out.'

Now suddenly he began to ask questions. 'There are some things I want to have clear,' he said. 'I want to know what moral state this so-called Utopia is in. Excuse me!'

He got up. He stood with wavering hands, unable for a moment to begin. Then he went to the end of the row of seats and placed himself so that his hands could rest on the back of a seat. He passed his fingers through his hair and he seemed to be inhaling deeply. An unwonted animation came into his face, which reddened and began to shine. A horrible suspicion crossed the mind of Mr Barnstaple that so it was he must stand when he began those weekly sermons of his, those fearless denunciations of almost everything, in the church of St Barnabas in the West. The suspicion deepened to a still more horrible certainty.

'Friends, Brothers of this new world – I have certain things to say to you that I cannot delay saying. I want to ask you some soul-searching questions. I want to deal plainly with you about some plain and simple but very fundamental matters. I want to put things to you frankly and as man to man, not being mealy-mouthed about urgent if delicate things. Let me come without parley to what I have to say. I want to ask you if, in this so-called state of Utopia, you still have and respect and honour the most sacred thing in social life. Do you still respect the marriage bond?'

He paused, and in the pause the Utopian reply came through to Mr Barnstaple: 'In Utopia there are no bonds.'

But Father Amerton was not asking questions with any desire for answers; he was asking questions pulpit-fashion.

'I want to know,' he was booming out, 'if that holy union revealed to our first parents in the Garden of Eden holds good here, if that sanctified lifelong association of one man and one woman, in good fortune and ill fortune, excluding every other sort of intimacy, is the rule of your lives. I want to know—'

'But he *doesn't* want to know,' came a Utopian intervention.

'– if that shielded and guarded dual purity—'

Mr Burleigh raised a long white hand. 'Father Amerton,' he protested, '*please.*'

The hand of Mr Burleigh was a potent hand that might still wave towards preferment. Few things under heaven could stop Father Amerton when he was once launched upon one of his soul storms, but the hand of Mr Burleigh was among such things.

'— has followed another still more precious gift and been cast aside here and utterly rejected of men? What is it, Mr Burleigh?'

'I wish you would not press this matter further just at present, Father Amerton. Until we have learnt a little more. Institutions are, manifestly, very different here. Even the institution of marriage may be different.'

The preacher's face lowered. 'Mr Burleigh,' he said, 'I *must.* If my suspicions are right, I want to strip this world forthwith of its hectic pretence to a sort of health and virtue.'

'Not much stripping required,' said Mr Burleigh's chauffeur, in a very audible aside.

A certain testiness became evident in Mr Burleigh's voice.

'Then ask questions,' he said. 'Ask questions. Don't orate, please. They don't want us to orate.'

'I've asked my question,' said Father Amerton sulkily with a rhetorical glare at Urthred, and remained standing.

The answer came clear and explicit. In Utopia there was no compulsion for men and women to go about in indissoluble pairs. For most Utopians that would be inconvenient. Very often men and women, whose work brought them closely together, were lovers and kept very much together, as Arden and Greenlake had done. But they were not obliged to do that.

There had not always been this freedom. In the old crowded days of conflict, and especially among the agricultural workers and employed people of Utopia, men and women who had been lovers were bound together under severe penalties for life. They lived together in a small home which the woman kept in order for the man, she was his servant and bore him as many children as possible, while he got food for them. The children were desired because they were soon helpful on the land or as wage earners. But the necessities that had subjugated women to that sort of pairing had passed away.

People paired indeed with their chosen mates, but they did so by an inner necessity and not by any outward compulsion.

Father Amerton had listened with ill-concealed impatience. Now he jumped with: 'Then I was right, and you have abolished the family?' His finger pointed at Urthred made it almost a personal accusation.

No. Utopia had not abolished the family. It had enlarged and glorified the family until it embraced the whole world. Long ago that prophet of the wheel, whom Father Amerton seemed to respect, had preached that very enlargement of the ancient narrowness of home. They had told him while he preached that his mother and his brethren stood without and claimed his attention. But he would not go to them. He had turned to the crowd that listened to his words: 'Behold my mother and my brethren!'

Father Amerton slapped the seat-back in front of him loudly and startlingly. 'A quibble,' he cried, 'a quibble! Satan too can quote the scriptures.'

It was clear to Mr Barnstaple that Father Amerton was not in complete control of himself. He was frightened by what he was doing and yet impelled to do it. He was too excited to think clearly or control his voice properly, so that he shouted and boomed in the wildest way. He was 'letting himself go' and trusting to the habits of the pulpit of St Barnabas to bring him through.

'I perceive now how you stand. Only too well do I perceive how you stand. From the outset I guessed how things were with you. I waited – I waited to be perfectly sure, before I bore my testimony. But it speaks for itself – the shamelessness of your costume, the licentious freedom of your manners! Young men and women, smiling, joining hands, near to caressing, when averted eyes, averted eyes, are the least tribute you could pay to modesty! And this vile talk – of lovers loving – without bonds or blessings, without rules or restraint. What does it mean? Whither does it lead? Do not imagine because I am a priest, a man pure and virginal in spite of great temptations, do not imagine that I do not understand! Have I no vision of the secret places of the heart? Do not the wounded sinners, the broken potsherds, creep to me with their pitiful confessions? And I will tell you plainly whither you go and how you stand? This so-called freedom of yours is nothing but licence. Your so-called Utopia, I see plainly, is nothing but a hell of unbridled indulgence! Unbridled indulgence!'

Mr Burleigh held up a protesting hand, but Father Amerton's eloquence soared over the obstruction.

He beat upon the back of the seat before him. 'I will bear my witness,' he shouted. 'I will bear my witness. I will make no bones about it. I refuse to mince matters, I tell you. You are all living – in promiscuity! That is the word for it. In animal promiscuity! In *bestial* promiscuity!'

Mr Burleigh had sprung to his feet. He was holding up his two hands and motioning the London Boanerges to sit down. 'No, no!' he cried. 'You must *stop*, Mr Amerton. Really, you must stop. You are being insulting. You do not understand. Sit *down*, please. I insist.'

'*Sit down and hold your peace*,' said a very clear voice. 'Or you will be taken away.'

Something made Father Amerton aware of a still figure at his elbow. He met the eyes of a lithe young man who was scrutinizing his build as a portrait painter might scrutinize a new sitter. There was no threat in his bearing, he stood quite still, and yet his appearance threw an extraordinary quality of evanescence about Father Amerton. The great preacher's voice died in his throat.

Mr Burleigh's bland voice was lifted to avert a conflict. 'Mr Serpentine, Sir, I appeal to you and apologize. He is not fully responsible. We others regret the interruption – the incident. I pray you, please do not take him away, whatever taking away may mean. I will answer personally for his good behaviour. ... *Do* sit down, Mr Amerton, *please; now;* or I shall wash my hands of the whole business.'

Father Amerton hesitated.

'My time will come,' he said and looked the young man in the eyes for a moment and then went back to his seat.

Urthred spoke quietly and clearly. 'You Earthlings are difficult guests to entertain. This is not all. ... Manifestly this man's mind is very unclean. His sexual imagination is evidently inflamed and diseased. He is angry and anxious to insult and wound. And his noises are terrific. Tomorrow he must be examined and dealt with.'

'How?' said Father Amerton, his round face suddenly grey. 'How do you mean – *dealt* with?'

'*Please* do not talk,' said Mr Burleigh. '*Please* do not talk any more. You have done quite enough mischief. ...'

For the time the incident seemed at an end, but it had left a queer little twinge of fear in Mr Barnstaple's heart. These Utopians were very gentle-mannered and gracious people indeed, but just for a moment the hand of power had seemed to hover over the Earthling party. Sunlight and beauty were all about the visitors, nevertheless they were strangers and quite helpless strangers in an unknown world. The Utopian faces were kindly and their eyes curious and in a manner friendly, but much more observant than friendly. It was as if they looked across some impassable gulf of difference.

And then Mr Barnstaple in the midst of his distress met the brown eyes of Lychnis, and they were kindlier than the eyes of the other Utopians. She, at least, understood the fear that had come to him, he felt, and she was willing to reassure him and be his friend. Mr Barnstaple looked at her, feeling for the moment much as a stray dog might do who approaches a doubtfully amiable group and gets a friendly glance and a greeting.

2

Another mind that was also in active resistance to Utopia was that of Mr Freddy Mush. He had no quarrel indeed with the religion or morals or social organization of Utopia. He had long since learnt that no gentleman of serious aesthetic pretensions betrays any interest whatever in such matters. His perceptions were by hypothesis too fine for them. But presently he made it clear that there had been something very ancient and beautiful called the 'Balance of Nature' which the scientific methods of Utopia had destroyed. What this Balance of Nature of his was, and how it worked on Earth, neither the Utopians nor Mr Barnstaple were able to understand very clearly. Under cross-examination Mr Mush grew pink and restive and his eye-glass flashed defensively. 'I hold by the swallows,' he repeated. 'If you can't see my point about that I don't know what else I can say.'

He began with the fact and reverted to the fact that there were no swallows to be seen in Utopia, and there were no swallows to be seen in Utopia because there were no gnats nor midges. There had been an enormous deliberate reduction of insect life in Utopia, and that had seriously affected every sort of creature that was directly or indirectly dependent upon insect life. So soon as the new state of affairs was securely established in Utopia and the educational state working, the attention of the Utopian community had been given to the long-cherished idea of a systematic extermination of tiresome and mis-chievous species. A careful inquiry was made into the harmfulness and the possibility of eliminating the house-fly for example, wasps and hornets, various species of mice and rats, rabbits, stinging nettles. Ten thousand species, from disease-germ to rhinoceros and hyena, were put upon their trial. Every species found was given an advocate. Of each it was asked: What good is it? What harm does it do? How can it be extirpated? What else may go with it if it goes? Is it worth while wiping it out of existence? Or can it be mitigated and retained? And even when the verdict was death final and complete, Utopia set about the business of extermination with great caution. A reserve would be kept and was in many cases still being kept, in some secure isolation, of every species condemned.

Most infectious and contagious fevers had been completely stamped out; some had gone very easily; some had only been driven out of human life by proclaiming a war and subjecting the whole population

261

to discipline. Many internal and external parasites of man and animals had also been got rid of completely. And further, there had been a great cleansing of the world from noxious insects, from weeds and vermin and hostile beasts. The mosquito had gone, the house-fly, the blow-fly, and indeed a great multitude of flies had gone; they had been driven out of life by campaigns involving an immense effort and extending over many generations. It had been infinitely more easy to get rid of such big annoyances as the hyena and the wolf than to abolish these smaller pests. The attack upon the flies had involved the virtual rebuilding of a large proportion of Utopian houses and a minute cleansing of them all throughout the planet.

The question of what else would go if a certain species went was one of the most subtle that Utopia had to face. Certain insects, for example, were destructive and offensive grubs in the opening stage of their lives, were evil as caterpillar or pupa and then became either beautiful in themselves or necessary to the fertilization of some useful or exquisite flowers. Others offensive in themselves were a necessary irreplaceable food to pleasant and desirable creatures. It was not true that swallows had gone from Utopia, but they had become extremely rare; and rare too were a number of little insectivorous birds, the fly-catcher for example, that harlequin of the air. But they had not died out altogether; the extermination of insects had not gone to that length; sufficient species had remained to make some districts still habitable for these delightful birds.

Many otherwise obnoxious plants were a convenient source of chemically complex substances that were still costly or tedious to make synthetically, and so had kept a restricted place in life. Plants and flowers, always simpler and more plastic in the hands of the breeder and hybridizer than animals, had been enormously changed in Utopia. Our Earthlings were to find a hundred sorts of foliage and of graceful and scented blossoms that were altogether strange to them. Plants, Mr Barnstaple learnt, had been trained and bred to make new and unprecedented secretions, waxes, gums, essential oils and the like, of the most desirable quality.

There had been much befriending and taming of big animals; the larger carnivora, combed and cleaned, reduced to a milk dietary, emasculated in spirit and altogether be-catted, were pets and orna-ments in Utopia. The almost extinct elephant had increased again and Utopia had saved her giraffes. The brown bear had always been dis-posed to sweets and vegetarianism and had greatly improved in intel-ligence. The dog had given up barking and was comparatively rare. Sporting dogs were not used nor small pet animals.

Horses Mr Barnstaple did not see, but as he was a very modern urban type he did not miss them very much and he did not ask any questions about them while he was actually in Utopia. He never found out whether they had or had not become extinct.

As he heard on his first afternoon in that world of this revision and editing, this weeding and cultivation of the kingdoms of nature by mankind, it seemed to him to be the most natural and necessary phase in human history. 'After all,' he said to himself, 'it was a good invention to say that man was created a gardener.'

And now man was weeding and cultivating his own strain. . . .

The Utopians told of eugenic beginnings, of a new and surer decision in the choice of parents, of an increasing certainty in the science of heredity; and as Mr Barnstaple contrasted the firm clear beauty of face and limb that every Utopian displayed with the carelessly assembled features and bodily disproportions of his earthly associates, he realized that already, with but three thousand years or so of advantage, these Utopians were passing beyond man towards a nobler humanity. They were becoming different in kind.

3

They were different in kind.

As the questions and explanations and exchanges of that afternoon went on, it became more and more evident to Mr Barnstaple that the difference of their bodies was as nothing to the differences of their minds. Innately better to begin with, the minds of these children of light had grown up uninjured by any such tremendous frictions, concealments, ambiguities and ignorances as cripple the growing mind of an Earthling. They were clear and frank and direct. They had never developed that defensive suspicion of the teacher, that resistance to instruction, which is the natural response to teaching that is half aggression. They were beautifully unwary in their communications. The ironies, concealments, insincerities, vanities and pretensions of earthly conversation seemed unknown to them. Mr Barnstaple found this mental nakedness of theirs as sweet and refreshing as the mountain air he was breathing. It amazed him that they could be so patient and lucid with beings so underbred.

Underbred was the word he used in his mind. Himself, he felt the most underbred of all; he was afraid of these Utopians; snobbish and abject before them, he was like a mannerless earthy lout in a drawing-room, and he was bitterly ashamed of his own abjection. All the other Earthlings except Mr Burleigh and Lady Stella betrayed the defensive spite of consciously inferior creatures struggling against that consciousness.

Like Father Amerton, Mr Burleigh's chauffeur was evidently greatly shocked and disturbed by the unclothed condition of the Utopians; his feelings expressed themselves by gestures, grimaces and an occasional sarcastic comment such as 'I *don't* think!' or 'What O!' These he addressed for the most part to Mr Barnstaple, for whom, as the owner of a very little old car, he evidently mingled feelings of profound contempt and social fellowship. He would also direct Mr Barnstaple's attention to anything that he considered remarkable in bearing or gesture, by means of a peculiar stare and grimace combined with raised eyebrows. He had a way of pointing with his mouth and nose that Mr Barnstaple under more normal circumstances might have found entertaining.

Lady Stella, who had impressed Mr Barnstaple at first as a very great lady of the modern type, he was now beginning to feel was on her defence and becoming rather too ladylike. Mr Burleigh however retained a certain aristocratic sublimity. He had been a great man on earth for all his life and it was evident that he saw no reason why he should not be accepted as a great man in Utopia. On earth he had done little and had been intelligently receptive with the happiest results. That alert, questioning mind of his, free of all persuasions, convictions or revolutionary desires, fell with the utmost ease into the pose of a distinguished person inspecting, in a sympathetic but entirely non-committal manner, the institutions of an alien state. 'Tell me,' that engaging phrase, laced his conversation.

The evening was drawing on; the clear Utopian sky was glowing with the gold of sunset and a towering mass of cloud above the lake was fading from pink to a dark purple, when Mr Rupert Catskill imposed himself upon Mr Barnstaple's attention. He was fretting in his place. 'I have something to say,' he said. 'I have something to say.'

Presently he jumped up and walked to the centre of the semicircle from which Mr Burleigh had spoken earlier in the afternoon. 'Mr Serpentine,' he said. 'Mr Burleigh. There are a few things I should be glad to say – if you can give me this opportunity of saying them.'

4

He took off his grey top hat, went back and placed it on his seat and returned to the centre of the apse. He put back his coat tails, rested his hands on his hips, thrust his head forward, regarded his audience for a moment with an expression half cunning, half defiant, muttered something inaudible and began.

His opening was not prepossessing. There was some slight impediment in his speech, the little brother of a lisp, against which his voice beat gutturally. His first few sentences had an effect of being jerked out by unsteady efforts. Then it became evident to Mr Barnstaple that Mr Catskill was expressing a very definite point of view, he was offering a reasoned and intelligible view of Utopia. Mr Barnstaple disagreed with that criticism, indeed he disagreed with it violently, but he had to recognize that it expressed an understandable attitude of mind.

Mr Catskill began with a sweeping admission of the beauty and order of Utopia. He praised the 'glowing health' he saw 'on every cheek', the wealth, tranquillity and comfort of Utopian life. They had 'tamed the forces of nature and subjugated them altogether to one sole end, to the material comfort of the race'.

'But Arden and Greenlake?' murmured Mr Barnstaple.

Mr Catskill did not hear or heed the interruption. 'The first effect, Mr Speaker – Mr Serpentine, I *should* say – the first effect upon an earthly mind is overwhelming. Is it any wonder' – he glanced at Mr Burleigh and Mr Barnstaple – 'is it any wonder that admiration has carried some of us off our feet? Is it any wonder that for a time your almost magic beauty has charmed us into forgetting much that is in our own natures – into forgetting deep and mysterious impulses, cravings, necessities, so that we have been ready to say, "Here at last is Lotus Land. Here let us abide, let us adapt ourselves to this planned and ordered splendour and live our lives out here and die." I, too, Mr – Mr Serpentine, succumbed to that magic for a time. But only for a time. Already, Sir, I find myself full of questionings.' ...

His bright, headlong mind had seized upon the fact that every phase in the weeding and cleansing of Utopia from pests and parasites and diseases had been accompanied by the possibility of collateral limitations and losses; or perhaps it would be juster to say that that fact had seized upon his mind. He ignored the deliberation and precautions that had accompanied every step in the process of making a world securely healthy and wholesome for human activity. He assumed there had been losses with every gain, he went on to exaggerate these losses and ran on glibly to the inevitable metaphor of throwing away the baby with its bath – inevitable, that is, for a British parliamentarian. The Utopians, he declared, were living lives of extraordinary ease, safety and 'may I say so – indulgence' ('They work,' said Mr Barnstaple), but with a thousand annoyances and disagreeables gone had not something else greater and more precious gone also? Life on earth was, he admitted, insecure, full of pains and anxieties, full indeed of miseries and distresses and anguish, but also, and indeed by reason of these very things, it had moments of intensity, hopes, joyful surprises, escapes, attainments, such as the ordered life of Utopia could not possibly afford. 'You have been getting away from conflicts and distresses. Have you not also been getting away from the living and quivering realities of life?'

He launched out upon a eulogy of earthly life. He extolled the vitality of life upon earth as though there were no signs of vitality in the high splendour about him. He spoke of the 'thunder of our crowded cities', of the 'urge of our teeming millions', of the 'broad tides of commerce and industrial effort and warfare', that 'swayed and came and went in the hives and harbours of our race'.

He had the knack of the plausible phrase and that imaginative touch which makes for eloquence. Mr Barnstaple forgot that slight impediment and the thickness of the voice that said these things. Mr Catskill boldly admitted all the earthly evils and dangers that Mr Burleigh had retailed. Everything that Mr Burleigh had said was true. All that he had said fell indeed far short of the truth. Famine we knew, and pestilence. We suffered from a thousand diseases that Utopia had eliminated. We were afflicted by a thousand afflictions that were known to Utopia now only by ancient tradition. 'The rats gnaw and the summer flies persecute and madden. At times life reeks and stinks. I admit it, Sir, I admit it. We go down far below your extremest experiences into discomforts and miseries, anxieties and anguish of soul and body, into bitterness, terror and despair. Yea. But do we not also go higher? I challenge you with that. What can you know in this immense safety of the intensity, the frantic, terror-driven intensity, of many of our efforts? What can you know of reprieves and interludes and escapes? Think of our many happinesses beyond your ken! What do you know here of the sweet early days of convalescence? Of going for a holiday out of disagreeable surroundings? Of taking some great risk to body or fortune and bringing it off? Of winning a bet against enormous odds? Of coming out of prison? And, Sir, it has been said that there are those in our world who have found a fascination even in pain itself. Because our life is dreadfuller, Sir, it has, and it must have, moments that are infinitely brighter than yours. It is titanic, Sir, where this is merely tidy. And we are inured to it and hardened by it. We are tempered to a finer edge. That is the point to which I am coming. Ask us to give up our earthly disorder, our miseries and distresses, our high death-rates and our hideous diseases, and at the first question every man and woman in the world would say, "Yes! Willingly, Yes!" At the first question, Sir!'

Mr Catskill held his audience for a moment on his extended finger.

'And then we should begin to take thought. We should ask, as you say your naturalists asked about your flies and suchlike offensive small game, we should ask, "What goes with it? What is the price?" And when we learnt that the price was to surrender that intensity of life, that tormented energy, that pickled and experienced toughness, that rat-like, wolf-like toughness our perpetual struggle engenders, we should hesitate. We should hesitate. In the end, Sir, I believe, I hope and believe, indeed I pray and believe, we should say, "No!" We should say, "No!"'

Mr Catskill was now in a state of great cerebral exaltation. He was making short thrusting gestures with his clenched fist. His voice rose and fell and boomed; he swayed and turned about, glanced for the approval of his fellow Earthlings, flung stray smiles at Mr Burleigh.

This idea that our poor wrangling, nerveless, chance-driven world was really a fierce and close-knit system of powerful reactions in contrast with the evening serenities of a made and finished Utopia, had taken complete possession of his mind. 'Never before, Sir, have I realized, as I realize now, the high, the terrible and adventurous destinies of our earthly race. I look upon this Golden Lotus Land of yours, this divine perfected land from which all conflict has been banished—'

Mr Barnstaple caught a faint smile on the face of the woman who had reminded him of the Delphic Sibyl.

'— and I admit and admire its order and beauty as some dusty and resolute pilgrim might pause, on his exalted and mysterious quest, and admit and admire the order and beauty of the pleasant gardens of some prosperous Sybarite. And like that pilgrim I may beg leave, Sir, to question the wisdom of your way of living. For I take it, Sir, that it is now a proven thing that life and all the energy and beauty of life are begotten by struggle and competition and conflict; we were moulded and wrought in hardship, and so, Sir, were you. And yet you dream here that you have eliminated conflict for ever. Your economic state, I gather, is some form of socialism; you have abolished competition in all the businesses of peace. Your political state is one universal unity; you have altogether cut out the bracing and ennobling threat and the purging and terrifying experience of war. Everything is ordered and provided for. Everything is secure. Everything is secure, Sir, except for one thing. . . .

'I grieve to trouble your tranquillity, Sir, but I must breathe the name of that one forgotten thing – *degeneration!* What is there here to prevent degeneration? Are you preventing degeneration?

'What penalties are there any longer for indolence? What rewards for exceptional energy and effort? What is there to keep men industrious, what watchful, when there is no personal danger and no personal loss but only some remote danger or injury to the community? For a time by a sort of inertia you may keep going. You may seem to be making a success of things. I admit it, you *do* seem to be making a success of things. Autumnal glory! Sunset splendour! *While about you in universes parallel to yours, parallel races still toil, still suffer, still compete and eliminate and gather strength and energy!*'

Mr Catskill flourished his hand at the Utopians in rhetorical triumph.

'I would not have you think, Sir, that these criticisms of your world are offered in a hostile spirit. They are offered in the most amiable and helpful spirit. I am the skeleton, but the most friendly and apologetic skeleton, at your feast. I ask my searching and disagreeable question because I must. Is it indeed the wise way that you have chosen? You have sweetness and light – and leisure. Granted. But if there is all this multitude of Universes, of which you have told us, Mr Serpentine, so clearly and illuminatingly, and if one may suddenly open into another as ours has done into yours, I would ask you most earnestly how safe is your sweetness, your light and your leisure? We talk here, separated by we know not how flimsy a partition from innumerable worlds. And at that thought, Sir, it seems to me that as I stand here in the great golden calm of this place I can almost hear the trampling of hungry myriads as fierce and persistent as rats or wolves, the snarling voices of races inured to every pain and cruelty, the threat of terrible heroisms and pitiless aggressions. . . .'

He brought his discourse to an abrupt end. He smiled faintly; it seemed to Mr Barnstaple that he triumphed over Utopia. He stood with hands on his hips and, as if he bent his body by that method, bowed stiffly. 'Sir,' he said with that ghost of a lisp of his, his eye on Mr Burleigh, 'I have said my say.'

He turned about and regarded Mr Barnstaple for a moment with his face screwed up almost to the appearance of a wink. He nodded his head, as if he tapped a nail with a hammer, jerked himself into activity, and returned to his proper place.

5

Urthred did not so much answer Mr Catskill as sit, elbow on knee and chin on hand, thinking audibly about him.

'The gnawing vigour of the rat,' he mused, 'the craving pursuit of the wolf, the mechanical persistence of wasp and fly and disease germ, have gone out of our world. That is true. We have obliterated that much of life's devouring forces. And lost nothing worth having. Pain, filth, indignity for ourselves – or any creatures; they have gone or they go. But it is not true that competition has gone from our world. Why does he say it has? Everyone here works to his or her utmost – for service and distinction. None may cheat himself out of toil or duty as men did in the age of confusion, when the mean and acquisitive lived and bred in luxury upon the heedlessness of more generous types. Why does he say we degenerate? He has been told better already. The indolent and inferior do not procreate here. And why should he threaten us with fancies of irruptions from other, fiercer, more barbaric worlds? It is we who can open the doors into such other universes or close them as we choose. Because we know. We can go to them – when we know enough we shall – but they cannot come to us. There is no way but knowledge out of the cages of life. . . . What is the matter with the mind of this man?

'These Earthlings are only in the beginnings of science. They are still for all practical ends in that phase of fear and taboos that came also in the development of Utopia before confidence and un- derstanding. Out of which phase our own world struggled during the Last Age of Confusion. The minds of these Earthlings are full of fears and prohibitions, and though it has dawned upon them that they may possibly control their universe, the thought is too terrible yet for them to face. They avert their minds from it. They still want to go on thinking, as their fathers did before them, that the universe is being managed for them better than they can control it for themselves. Because if that is so, they are free to obey their own violent little individual motives. Leave things to God, they cry, or leave them to Competition.'

'Evolution was our blessed word,' said Mr Barnstaple, deeply inter- ested.

'It is all the same thing – God, or Evolution, or what you will – so long as you mean a Power beyond your own which excuses you from your duty. Utopia says, "Do not leave things at all. Take hold." But these Earthlings still lack the habit of looking at reality – undraped. This man with the white linen fetter round his neck is afraid even to look upon men and women as they are. He is disgustingly excited by the common human body. This man with the glass lens before his left eye struggles to believe that there is a wise old Mother Nature behind the appearances of things, keeping a Balance. It was fantastic to hear about his Balance of Nature. Cannot he with two eyes and a lens see better than that? This last man who spoke so impressively, thinks that this old Beldame Nature is a limitless source of will and energy if only we submit to her freaks and cruelties and imitate her most savage moods, if only we sufficiently thrust and kill and rob and ravish one another. ... He too preaches the old fatalism and believes it is the teaching of science. ...

'These Earthlings do not yet dare to see what our Mother Nature is. At the back of their minds is still the desire to abandon themselves to her. They do not see that except for our eyes and wills, she is purposeless and blind. She is not awful, she is horrible. She takes no heed to our standards, nor to any standards of excellence. She made us by accident; all her children are bastards – undesired; she will cherish or expose them, pet or starve or torment without rhyme or reason. She does not heed, she does not care. She will lift us up to power and intelligence, or debase us to the mean feebleness of the rabbit or the slimy white filthiness of a thousand of her parasitic inventions. There must be good in her because she made all that is good in us – but also there is endless evil. Do not you Earthlings see the dirt of her, the cruelty, the insane indignity of much of her work?'

'Phew! Worse than "Nature red in tooth and claw,"' murmured Mr Freddy Mush.

'These things are plain,' mused Urthred. 'If they dared to see.

'Half the species of life in our planet also, half and more than half of all the things alive, were ugly or obnoxious, inane, miserable, wretched, with elaborate diseases, helplessly ill-adjusted to Nature's continually fluctuating conditions, when first we took this old Hag, our Mother, in hand. We have, after centuries of struggle, suppressed her nastier fancies, and washed her and combed her and taught her to respect and heed the last child of her wantonings – Man. With Man came Logos, the Word and the Will into our universe, to watch it and fear it, to learn it and cease to fear it, to know it and comprehend it and master it. So that we of Utopia are no longer the beaten and starved children of Nature, but her free and adolescent sons. We have taken over the Old Lady's Estate. Every day we learn a little better how to master this little planet. Every day our thoughts go out more surely to our inheritance, the stars. And the deeps beyond and beneath the stars.'

'You have reached the stars?' cried Mr Barnstaple.

'Not yet. Not even the other planets. But very plainly the time draws near when those great distances will cease to restrain us. ...'

He paused. 'Many of us will have to go out into the deeps of space. ... And never return ... Giving their lives. ...

'And into these new spaces – countless brave men. . . .'

Urthred turned towards Mr Catskill. 'We find your frankly expressed thoughts particularly interesting today. You help us to understand the past of our own world. You help us to deal with an urgent problem that we will presently explain to you. There are thoughts and ideas like yours in our ancient literature of two or three thousand years ago, the same preaching of selfish violence as though it was a virtue. Even then intelligent men knew better, and you yourself might know better if you were not wilfully set in wrong opinions. But it is plain to see from your manner and bearing that you are very wilful indeed in your opinions.

'You are not, you must realize, a very beautiful person, and probably you are not very beautiful in your pleasures and proceedings. But you have superabundant energy, and so it is natural for you to turn to the excitements of risk and escape, to think that the best thing in life is the sensation of conflict and winning. Also in the economic confusion of such a world as yours there is an intolerable amount of toil that must be done, toil so disagreeable that it makes everyone of spirit anxious to thrust away as much of it as possible and to claim exemption from it on account of nobility, gallantry or good fortune. People in your world no doubt persuade themselves very easily that they are justifiably exempted, and you are under that persuasion. You live in a world of classes. Your badly trained mind has been under no necessity to invent its own excuses; the class into which you were born had all its excuses ready for you. So it is you take the best of everything without scruple and you adventure with life, chiefly at the expense of other people, with a mind trained by all its circumstances to resist the idea that there is any possible way of human living that can be steadfast and disciplined and at the same time vigourous and happy. You have argued against that persuasion all your life as though it were your personal enemy. It is your personal enemy; it condemns your way of life altogether, it damns you utterly for your adventures.

'Confronted now with an ordered and achieved beauty of living you still resist; you resist to escape dismay; you argue that this world of ours is unromantic, wanting in intensity, decadent, feeble. Now – in the matter of physical strength, grip hands with that young man who sits beside you.'

Mr Catskill glanced at the extended hand and shook his head knowingly. 'You go on talking,' he said.

'Yet when I tell you that neither our wills nor our bodies are as feeble as yours, your mind resists obstinately. You will not believe it. If for a moment your mind admits it, afterwards it recoils to the system of persuasions that protect your self-esteem. Only one of you accepts our world at all, and he does so rather because he is weary of yours than willing for ours. So I suppose it has to be. Yours are Age of Confusion minds, trained to conflict, trained to insecurity and secret self-seeking. In that fashion Nature and your state have taught you to live and so you must needs live until you die. Such lessons are to be unlearnt only in ten thousand generations, by the slow education of three thousand years.

'And we are puzzled by the question, what are we to do with you? We will try our utmost to deal fairly and friendly with you if you will respect our laws and ways.

'But it will be very difficult, we know, for you. You do not realize yet how difficult your habits and preconceptions will make it for you. Your party so far has behaved very reasonably and properly, in act if not in thought. But we have had another experience of Earthling ways today of a much more tragic kind. Your talk of fiercer, barbaric worlds breaking in upon us has had its grotesque parallel in reality today. It is true; there is something fierce and ratlike and dangerous about Earthly men. You are not the only Earthlings who came into Utopia through this gate that swung open for a moment today. There are others—'

'Of course!' said Mr Barnstaple. 'I should have guessed it! That third lot!'

'There is yet another of these queer locomotive machines of yours in Utopia.'

'The grey car!' said Mr Barnstaple to Mr Burleigh. 'It wasn't a hundred yards ahead of you.'

'Raced us from Hounslow,' said Mr Burleigh's driver. 'Real hot stuff.'

Mr Burleigh turned to Mr Freddy Mush. 'I think you said you recognized someone?'

'Lord Barralonga, Sir, almost to a certainty, and I *think* Miss Greeta Grey.'

'There were two other men,' said Mr Barnstaple.

'They will complicate things,' said Mr Burleigh.

'They do complicate things,' said Urthred. 'They have killed a man.'

'A Utopian?'

'These other people – there are five of them – whose names you seem to know, came into Utopia just in front of your two vehicles. Instead of stopping as you did when they found themselves on a new, strange road, they seem to have quickened their pace very considerably. They passed some men and women and they made extraordinary gestures to them and abominable noises produced by an instrument specially designed for that purpose. Further on they encountered a silver cheetah and charged at it and ran right over it, breaking its back. They do not seem to have paused to see what became of it. A young man named Gold came out into the road to ask them to stop. But their machine is made in the most fantastic way, very complex and very foolish. It is quite unable to stop short suddenly. It is not driven by a single engine that is completely controlled. It has a complicated internal conflict. It has a sort of engine that drives it forward by a complex cogged gear on the axle of the hind wheels and it has various clumsy stopping contrivances by means of friction at certain points. You can apparently drive the engine at the utmost speed and at the same time jam the wheels to prevent them going round. When this young man stepped forward in front of them, they were quite unable to stop. They may have tried to do so. They say they did. Their machine swerved dangerously and struck him with its side.'

'And killed him?'

'And killed him instantly. His body was horribly injured. ... But they did not stop even for that. They slowed down and had a hasty consultation, and then seeing that people were coming they set their machine in motion again and made off. They seem to have been seized with a panic fear of restraint and punishment. Their motives are very difficult to understand. At any rate they went on. They rode on and on into our country for some hours. An aeroplane was presently set to follow them and another to clear the road in front of them. It was very difficult to clear the road because neither our people nor our animals understand such vehicles as theirs – nor such behaviour. In the after-noon they got among mountains and evidently found our roads much too smooth and difficult for their machine. It made extraordinary noises as though it was gritting its teeth, and emitted a blue vapour with an offensive smell. At one corner where it should have stopped short, it skated about and slid suddenly sideways and rolled over a cliff and fell for perhaps twice the height of a man into a torrent.'

'And they were killed?' asked Mr Burleigh, with, as it seemed to Mr Barnstaple, a touch of eagerness in his voice.

'Not one of them.'

'Oh!' said Mr Burleigh, 'then what happened?'

'One of them has a broken arm and another is badly cut about the face. The other two men and the woman are uninjured except for fright and shock. When our people came up to them the four men held their hands above their heads. Apparently they feared they would be killed at once and did this as an appeal for mercy.'

'And what are you doing with them?'

'We are bringing them here. It is better, we think, to keep all you Earthlings together. At present we cannot imagine what must be done to you. We want to learn from you and we want to be friendly with you if it is possible. It has been suggested that you should be returned to your world. In the end that may be the best thing to do. But at present we do not know enough to do this certainly. Arden and Greenlake, when they made the attempt to rotate a part of our matter through the F dimension, believed that they would rotate it in empty space in that dimension. The fact that you were there and were caught into our universe, is the most unexpected thing that has happened in Utopia for a thousand years.'

The Bringing in of Lord Barralonga's Party

I

The conference broke up upon this announcement, but Lord Barralonga and his party were not brought to the Conference Gardens until long after dark. No effort was made to restrain or control the movements of the Earthlings. Mr Burleigh walked down to the lake with Lady Stella and the psychologist whose name was Lion, asking and answering questions. Mr Burleigh's chauffeur wandered rather disconsolately, keeping within hail of his employer. Mr Rupert Catskill took Mr Mush off by the arm as if to give him instructions.

Mr Barnstaple wanted to walk about alone to recall and digest the astounding realizations of the afternoon and to accustom himself to the wonder of this beautiful world, so beautiful and now in the twilight so mysterious also, with its trees and flowers becoming dim and shapeless notes of pallor and blackness and with the clear forms and gracious proportions of its buildings melting into a twilight indistinctness.

The earthliness of his companions intervened between him and this world into which he felt he might otherwise have been accepted and absorbed. He was in it, but in it only as a strange and discordant intruder. Yet he loved it already and desired it and was passionately anxious to become a part of it. He had a vague but very powerful feeling that if only he could get away from his companions, if only in some way he could cast off his earthly clothing and everything upon him that marked him as earthly and linked him to earth, he would by the very act of casting that off become himself native to Utopia, and then that this tormenting sense, this bleak, distressing strangeness would vanish out of his mind. He would suddenly find himself a Utopian in nature and reality, and it was Earth that would become the incredible dream, a dream that would fade at last completely out of his mind.

For a time, however, Father Amerton's need of a hearer prevented any such detachment from earthly thoughts and things. He stuck close to Mr Barnstaple and maintained a stream of questions and comments that threw over this Utopian scene the quality of some Earl's Court exhibition that the two of them were visiting and criticizing together. It was evidently so provisional, so disputable and unreal to him, that at any moment Mr Barnstaple felt he would express no astonishment if a rift in the scenery suddenly let in the clatter of the Earl's Court railway station or gave a glimpse of the conventional Gothic spire of St Barnabas in the West.

At first Father Amerton's mind was busy chiefly with the fact that on the morrow he was to be 'dealt with' on account of the scene in the conference. 'How *can* they deal with me?' he said for the fourth time.

'I beg your pardon,' said Mr Barnstaple. Every time Mr Amerton began speaking Mr Barnstaple said, 'I beg your pardon,' in order to convey to him that he was interrupting a train of thought. But every time Mr Barnstaple said, 'I beg your pardon,' Mr Amerton would merely remark, 'You ought to consult someone about your hearing,' and then go on with what he had to say.

'How can I be *dealt with?*' he asked of Mr Barnstaple and the circumambient dusk. 'How can I be dealt with?'

'Oh! psycho-analysis or something of that sort,' said Mr Barnstaple.

'It takes two to play at that game,' said Father Amerton, but it seemed to Mr Barnstaple with a slight flavour of relief in his tone. 'Whatever they ask me, whatever they suggest to me, I will not fail – I will bear my witness.'

'I have no doubt they will find it hard to suppress you,' said Mr Barnstaple bitterly. . . .

For a time they walked among the tall sweet-smelling, white-flowered shrubs in silence. Now and then Mr Barnstaple would quicken or slacken his pace with the idea of increasing his distance from Father Amerton, but quite mechanically Father Amerton responded to these efforts. 'Promiscuity,' he began again presently. 'What other word could you use?'

'I really beg your pardon,' said Mr Barnstaple.

'What other word could I have used *but* "promiscuity"? What else could one expect, with people running about in this amazing want of costume, but the morals of the monkeys' cage? They admit that our institution of marriage is practically unknown to them!'

'It's a different world,' said Mr Barnstaple irritably. 'A different world.'

'The Laws of Morality hold good for every conceivable world.'

'But in a world in which people propagated by fission and there was no sex?'

'Morality would be simpler but it would be the same morality.' . . .

Presently Mr Barnstaple was begging his pardon again.

'I was saying that this is a lost world.'

'It doesn't *look* lost,' said Mr Barnstaple.

'It has rejected and forgotten Salvation.'

Mr Barnstaple put his hands in his pocket and began to whistle the barcarolle from 'The Tales of Hoffman', very softly to himself. Would Father Amerton never leave him? Could nothing be done with Father Amerton? At the old shows at Earl's Court there used to be wire baskets for waste paper and cigarette ends and bores generally. If one could only tip Father Amerton suddenly into some such receptacle!

'Salvation has been offered them, and they have rejected it and wellnigh forgotten it. And that is why we have been sent to them. We have been sent to them to recall them to the One Thing that Matters, to the One Forgotten Thing. Once more we have to raise the healing symbol as Moses raised it in the Wilderness. Ours is no light mission. We have been sent into this Hell of sensuous materialism—'

'Oh, *Lord!*' said Mr Barnstaple, and relapsed into the barcarolle. . . .

'I *beg* your pardon,' he exclaimed again presently.

'Where is the Pole Star? What has happened to the Wain?'

Mr Barnstaple looked up.

He had not thought of the stars before, and he looked up prepared in this fresh Universe to see the strangest constellations. But just as the life and size of the planet they were on ran closely parallel to the earth's, so he beheld above him a starry vault of familiar forms. And just as the Utopian world failed to be altogether parallel to its sister universe, so did these constellations seem to be a little out in their drawing. Orion, he thought, straddled wider and with a great unfamiliar nebula at one corner, and it was true – the Wain was flattened out and the pointers pointed to a great void in the heavens.

'Their Pole Star gone! The Pointers, the Wain askew! It is symbolical,' said Father Amerton.

It was only too obviously going to be symbolical. Mr Barnstaple realized that a fresh storm of eloquence was imminent from Father Amerton. At any cost he felt this nuisance must be abated.

On earth Mr Barnstaple had been a passive victim to bores of all sorts, delicately and painfully considerate of the mental limitations that made their insensitive pressure possible. But the free air of Utopia had already mounted to his head and released initiatives that his excessively deferential recognition of others had hitherto restrained. He had had enough of Father Amerton; it was necessary to turn off Father Amerton, and he now proceeded to do so with a simple directness that surprised himself.

'Father Amerton,' he said, 'I have a confession to make to you.'

'Ah!' cried Father Amerton. 'Please – anything?'

'You have been walking about with me and shouting at my ears until I am strongly impelled to murder you.'

'If what I have said has struck home—'

'It hasn't struck home. It has been a tiresome, silly, deafening jab-bering in my ears. It wearies me indescribably. It prevents my attending to the marvellous things about us. I see exactly what you mean when you say that there is no Pole Star here and that that is symbolical. Before you begin I appreciate the symbol, and a very obvious, weak and ultimately inaccurate symbol it is. But you are one of those obstinate spirits who believes in spite of all evidence that the eternal hills are still eternal and the fixed stars fixed for ever. I want you to understand that I am entirely out of sympathy with all this stuff of yours. You seem to embody all that is wrong and ugly and impossible in Catholic teaching. I agree with these Utopians that there is something wrong with your mind about sex, in all probability a nasty twist given to it in early life, and that what you keep saying and hinting about sexual life here is horrible and outrageous. And I am equally hostile to you and exasperated and repelled by you when you speak of religion proper. You make religion disgusting just as you make sex disgusting. You are a dirty priest. What you call Christianity is a black and ugly superstition, a mere excuse for malignity and persecution. It is an outrage upon Christ. If you are a Christian, then most passionately I declare myself *not* a Christian. But there are other meanings for Christianity than those you put upon it, and in another sense this Utopia here is Christian beyond all dreaming. Utterly beyond your understanding. We have come into this glorious world, which, com-pared to our world, is like a bowl of crystal compared to an old tin can, and you have the insufferable impudence to say that we have been sent hither as missionaries to teach them – God knows what!'

'God *does* know what,' said Father Amerton, a little taken aback, but coming up very pluckily.

'Oh!' cried Mr Barnstaple, and was for a moment speechless.

'Listen to me, my Friend,' said Father Amerton, catching at his sleeve.

'Not for my life!' cried Mr Barnstaple, recoiling. 'See! Down that vista, away there on the shore of the lake, those black figures are Mr Burleigh, Mr Mush and Lady Stella. They brought you here. They belong to your party and you belong to them. If they had not wanted your company you would not have been in their car. Go to them. I will not have you with me any longer. I refuse you and reject you. That is your way. This, by this little building, is mine. Don't follow me, or I will lay hands on you and bring in these Utopians to interfere between us. . . . Forgive my plainness, Mr Amerton. But get away from me! Get away from me!'

Mr Barnstaple turned, and seeing that Father Amerton stood hesitating at the parting of the ways, took to his heels and ran from him.

He fled along an alley behind tall hedges, turned sharply to the right and then to the left, passed over a high bridge that crossed in front of a cascade that flung a dash of spray in his face, blundered by two couples of lovers who whispered softly in the darkling, ran deviously across flower-studded turf, and at last threw himself down breathless upon the steps that led up to a terrace that looked towards lake and mountains, and was adorned, it seemed in the dim light, with squat stone figures of seated vigilant animals and men.

'Ye merciful stars!' cried Mr Barnstaple. 'At last I am alone.'

He sat on these steps for a long time with his eyes upon the scene about him, drinking in the satisfying realization that for a brief interval at any rate, with no earthly presence to intervene, he and Utopia were face to face.

3

He could not call this world the world of his dreams because he had never dared to dream of any world so closely shaped to the desires and imaginations of his heart. But surely this world it was, or a world the very fellow of it, that had lain deep beneath the thoughts and dreams of thousands of sane and troubled men and women in the world of disorder from which he had come. It was no world of empty peace, no such golden decadence of indulgence as Mr Catskill tried to imagine it; it was a world, Mr Barnstaple perceived, intensely militant, conquering and to conquer, prevailing over the obduracy of force and matter, over the lifeless separations of empty space and all the antagonistic mysteries of being.

In Utopia in the past, obscured by the superficial exploits of statesmen like Burleigh and Catskill and the competition of traders and exploiters every whit as vile and vulgar as their earthly compeers, the work of quiet and patient thinkers and teachers had gone on and the foundations which sustained this serene intensity of activity had been laid. How few of these pioneers had ever felt more than a transitory gleam of the righteous loveliness of the world their lives made possible!

And yet even in the hate and turmoil and distresses of the Days of Confusion there must have been earnest enough of the exquisite and glorious possibilities of life. Over the foulest slums the sunset called to the imaginations of men, and from mountain ridges, across great valleys, from cliffs and hillsides and by the uncertain and terrible splendours of the sea, men must have had glimpses of the conceivable and attainable magnificence of being. Every flower petal, every sunlit leaf, the vitality of young things, the happy moments of the human mind transcending itself in art, all these things must have been material for hope, incentive to effort. And now at last – this world!

Mr Barnstaple lifted up his hands like one who worships to the friendly multitude of the stars above him.

'I have seen,' he whispered. 'I have seen.'

Little lights and soft glows of illumination were coming out here and there over this great park of flowerlike buildings and garden spaces that sloped down towards the lake. A circling aeroplane, itself a star, hummed softly overhead.

A slender girl came past him down the steps and paused at the sight of him.

'Are you one of the Earthlings?' came the question, and a beam of soft light shone momentarily upon Mr Barnstaple from the bracelet on her arm.

'I came today,' said Mr Barnstaple, peering up at her.

'You are the man who came alone in a little machine of tin, with rubber air-bags round the wheels, very rusty underneath, and painted yellow. I have been looking at it.'

'It is not a bad little car,' said Mr Barnstaple.

'At first we thought the priest came in it with you.'

'He is no friend of mine.'

'There were priests like that in Utopia many years ago. They caused much mischief among the people.'

'He was with the other lot,' said Mr Barnstaple. 'For their weekend party I should think him – rather a mistake.'

She sat down a step or so above him.

'It is wonderful that you should come here out of your world to us. Do you find this world of ours very wonderful? I suppose many things that seem quite commonplace to me because I have been born among them seem wonderful to you.'

'You are not very old?'

'I am eleven. I am learning the history of the Ages of Confusion, and they say your world is still in an Age of Confusion. It is just as though you came to us out of the past – out of history. I was in the Conference and I was watching your face. You love this present world of ours – at least you love it much more than your other people do.'

'I want to live all the rest of my life in it.'

'I wonder if that is possible?'

'Why should it not be possible? It will be easier than sending me back. I should not be very much in the way. I should only be here for twenty or thirty years at the most, and I would learn everything I could and do everything I was told.'

'But isn't there work that you have to do in your own world?'

Mr Barnstaple made no answer to that. He did not seem to hear it. It was the girl who presently broke the silence.

'They say that when we Utopians are young, before our minds and characters are fully formed and matured, we are very like the men and women of the Age of Confusion. We are more egotistical then, they tell us; life about us is still so unknown, that we are adventurous and romantic. I suppose I am egotistical yet – and adventurous. And it does still seem to me that in spite of many terrible and dreadful things there was much that must have been wildly exciting and desirable in that past – which is still so like your present. What can it have been like to have been a general entering a conquered city? Or a prince being crowned? Or to be rich and able to astonish people by acts of power and benevolence? Or to be a martyr led out to die for some splendid misunderstood cause?'

'These things sound better in stories and histories than in reality,' said Mr Barnstaple after due consideration. 'Did you hear Mr Rupert Catskill, the last of the Earthlings to make a speech?'

'He thought romantically – but he did not look romantic.'

'He has lived most romantically. He has fought bravely in wars. He has been a prisoner and escaped wonderfully from prison. His violent imaginations have caused the deaths of thousands of people. And presently we shall see another romantic adventurer in this Lord Barralonga they are bringing hither. He is enormously rich and he tries to astonish people with his wealth – just as you have dreamt of astonishing people.'

'Are they not astonished?'

'Romance is not reality.' said Mr Barnstaple. 'He is one of a number of floundering, corrupting rich men who are a weariness to themselves and an intolerable nuisance to the rest of our world. They want to do vulgar, showy things. This man Barralonga was an assistant to a photographer and something of an actor when a certain invention called moving pictures came into our world. He became a great prospector in the business of showing these pictures, partly by accident, partly by the unscrupulous cheating of various inventors. Then he launched out into speculations in shipping and in a trade we carry on in our world in frozen meat brought from great distances. He made food costly for many people and impossible for some, and so he grew rich. For in our world men grow wealthy by intercepting rather than by serving. And having become ignobly rich, certain of our politicians, for whom he did some timely services, ennobled him by giving him the title of Lord. Do you understand the things I am saying? Was your Age of Confusion so like ours? *You did not know it was so ugly.* Forgive me if I disillusion you about the Age of Confusion and its romantic possibilities. But I have just stepped out of the dust and disorder and noise of its indiscipline, out of limitation, cruelties and distresses, out of a weariness in which hope dies. . . . Perhaps if my world attracts you you may yet have an opportunity of adventuring out of all this into its disorders. . . . That will be an adventure indeed. . . . Who knows what may happen between our worlds? . . . But you will not like it, I am afraid. You cannot imagine how dirty our world is. . . . Dirt and disease, these are in the trailing skirts of all romance.' . . .

A silence fell between them; he followed his own thoughts and the girl sat and wondered over him.

At length he spoke again.

'Shall I tell you what I was thinking of when you spoke to me?'

'Yes?'

'Your world is the consummation of a million ancient dreams. It is wonderful! It is wonder, high as heaven. But it is a great grief to me that two dear friends of mine cannot be here with me to see what I am seeing. It is queer how strong the thought of them is in my mind. One has passed now beyond all the universes, alas! – but the other is still in my world. You are a student, my dear; everyone of your world, I suppose, is a student here, but in our world students are a class apart. We three were happy together because we were students and not yet caught into the mills of senseless toil, and we were none the less happy perhaps because we were miserably poor and often hungry together. We used to talk and dispute together and in our students' debating society, discussing the disorders of our world and how some day they might be bettered. Was there, in your Age of Confusion, that sort of eager, hopeful, poverty-struck student life?'

'Go on,' said the girl with her eyes intent on his dim profile. 'In old novels I have read of just that hungry, dreaming student world.'

'We three agreed that the supreme need of our time was education. We agreed that was the highest service we could join. We all set about it in our various ways, I the least useful of the three. My friends and I drifted a little apart. They edited a great monthly periodical that helped to keep the world of science together, and my friend, serving a careful and grudging firm of publishers, edited school books for them, conducted an educational paper, and also inspected schools for our university. He was too heedless of pay and profit ever to become even passably well off though these publishers profited greatly by his work; his whole life was a continual service of toil for teaching; he did not take as much as a month's holiday in any year in his life. While he lived I thought little of the work he was doing, but since he died I have heard from teachers whose schools he inspected, and from book writers whom he advised, of the incessant high quality of his toil and the patience and sympathy of his work. On such lives as his this Utopia in which your sweet life is opening is founded; on such lives our world of earth will yet build its Utopia. But the life of this friend of mine ended abruptly in a way that tore my heart. He worked too hard and too long through a crisis in which it was inconvenient for him to take a holiday. His nervous system broke down with shocking suddenness, his mind gave way, he passed into a phase of acute melancholia and – died. For it is perfectly true, old Nature has neither righteousness nor pity. This happened a few weeks ago. That other old friend and I, with his wife, who had been his tireless helper, were chief among the mourners at his funeral. Tonight the memory of that comes back to me with extraordinary vividness. I do not know how you dispose of your dead here, but on earth the dead are mostly buried in the earth.'

'We are burnt,' said the girl.

'Those who are liberal-minded in our world burn also. Our friend was burnt, and we stood and took our part in a service according to the rites of our ancient religion in which we no longer believed, and presently we saw his coffin, covered with wreaths of flowers, slide from before us out of our sight through the gates that led to the furnaces of the crematorium, and as it went, taking with it so much of my youth, I saw that my other dear old friend was sobbing, and I too was wrung to the pitch of tears to think that so valiant and devoted and industrious a life should end, as it seemed, so miserably and thanklessly. The priest had been reading a long contentious discourse by a theological writer named Paul, full of bad arguments by analogy and weak assertions. I wished that instead of the ideas of this ingenious ancient we could have had some discourse upon the real nobility of our friend, on the pride and intensity of his work and on his scorn for mercenary things. All his life he had worked with unlimited devotion for such a world as this, and yet I doubt if he had ever had any realization of the clearer, nobler life for man that his life of toil and the toil of such lives as his were making sure and certain in the days to come. He lived by faith. He lived too much by faith. There was not enough sunlight in his life. If I could have him here now – and that other dear friend who grieved for him so bitterly; if I could have them both here; if I could give up my place here to them so that they could see, as I see, the real greatness of their lives reflected in these great consequences of such lives as theirs – then, then I could rejoice in Utopia indeed. . . . But I feel now as if I had taken my old friend's savings and was spending them on myself.' . . .

Mr Barnstaple suddenly remembered the youth of his hearer. 'Forgive me, my dear child, for running on in this fashion. But your voice was kind.'

The girl's answer was to bend down and brush his extended hand with her soft lips.

Then suddenly she sprang to her feet. 'Look at that light,' she said, 'among the stars!'

Mr Barnstaple stood up beside her.

'That is the aeroplane bringing Lord Barralonga and his party; Lord Barralonga who killed a man today! Is he a very big, strong man – ungovernable and wonderful?'

Mr Barnstaple, struck by a sudden doubt, looked sharply at the sweet upturned face beside him.

'I have never seen him. But I believe he is a youngish, baldish, undersized man, who suffers very gravely from a disordered liver and kidneys. This has prevented the dissipation of his energies upon youthful sports and pleasures and enabled him to concentrate upon the acquisition of property. And so he was able to buy the noble title that touches your imagination. Come with me and look at him.'

The girl stood still and met his eyes. She was eleven years old and she was as tall as he was.

'But was there no romance in the past?'

'Only in the hearts of the young. And it died.'

'But is there no romance?'

'Endless romance – and it has all to come. It comes for you.'

4

The bringing in of Lord Barralonga and his party was something of an anti-climax to Mr Barnstaple's wonderful day. He was tired and, quite unreasonably, he resented the invasion of Utopia by these people.

The two parties of Earthlings were brought together in a brightly lit hall near the lawn upon which the Barralonga aeroplane had come down. The newcomers came in in a group together, blinking, travel-worn and weary-looking. But it was evident they were greatly relieved to encounter other Earthlings in what was to them a still intensely puzzling experience. For they had had nothing to compare with the calm and lucid discussion of the Conference Place. Their lapse into this strange world was still an incomprehensible riddle for them.

Lord Barralonga was the owner of the gnome-like face that had looked out at Mr Barnstaple when the large grey car had passed him on the Maidenhead Road. His skull was very low and broad above his brows so that he reminded Mr Barnstaple of the flat stopper of a glass bottle. He looked hot and tired, he was considerably dishevelled as if from a struggle, and one arm was in a sling; his little brown eyes were as alert and wary as those of a wicked urchin in the hands of a policeman. Sticking close to him like a familiar spirit was a small, almost jockey-like chauffeur, whom he addressed as 'Ridley'. Ridley's face also was marked by the stern determination of a man in a difficult position not in any manner to give himself away. His left cheek and ear had been cut in the automobile smash and were liberally adorned with sticking-plaster. Miss Greeta Grey, the lady of the party, was a frankly blonde beauty in a white flannel tailor-made suit. She was extraordinarily unruffled by the circumstances in which she found herself; it was as if she had no sense whatever of their strangeness. She carried herself with the habitual hauteur of a beautiful girl almost professionally exposed to the risk of unworthy advances. Anywhere.

The other two people of the party were a grey-faced, grey-clad American, also very wary-eyed, who was, Mr Barnstaple learnt from Mr Mush, Hunker, the Cinema King, and a thoroughly ruffled-looking Frenchman, a dark, smartly dressed man, with an imperfect command of English, who seemed rather to have fallen into Lord Barralonga's party than to have belonged to it properly. Mr Barnstaple's mind leapt to the conclusion, and nothing occurred afterwards to change his opinion, that some interest in the cinematograph had brought this

287

gentleman within range of Lord Barralonga's hospitality and that he had been caught, as a foreigner may so easily be caught, into the embrace of a thoroughly uncongenial week-end expedition.

As Lord Barralonga and Mr Hunker came forward to greet Mr Burleigh and Mr Catskill, this Frenchman addressed himself to Mr Barnstaple with the inquiry whether he spoke French.

'I cannot understand,' he said. 'We were to have gone to Viltshire – Wiltshire, and then one 'orrible thing has happen after another. What is it we have come to and what sort of people are all these people who speak most excellent French? Is it a joke of Lord Barralonga, or a dream, or what has happen to us?'

Mr Barnstaple attempted some explanation.

'Another dimension,' said the Frenchman, 'another worl'. That is all very well. But I have my business to attend to in London. I have no need to be brought back in this way to France, some sort of France, some other France in some other worl'. It is too much of a joke altogether.'

Mr Barnstaple attempted some further exposition. It was clear from his interlocutor's puzzled face that the phrases he used were too difficult. He turned helplessly to Lady Stella and found her ready to undertake the task. 'This lady,' he said, 'will be able to make things plain to you. Lady Stella, this is Monsieur—'

'Emile Dupont,' the Frenchman bowed. 'I am what you call a journalist and publicist. I am interested in the cinematograph from the point of view of education and propaganda. It is why I am here with his Lordship Barralonga.'

French conversation was Lady Stella's chief accomplishment. She sailed into it now very readily. She took over the elucidation of M. Dupont, and only interrupted it to tell Miss Greeta Grey how pleasant it was to have another woman with her in this strange world.

Relieved of M. Dupont, Mr Barnstaple stood back and surveyed the little group of Earthlings in the centre of the hall and the circle of tall, watchful Utopians about them and rather aloof from them. Mr Burleigh was being distantly cordial to Lord Barralonga, and Mr Hunker was saying what a great pleasure it was to him to meet 'Britain's foremost statesman'. Mr Catskill stood in the most friendly manner beside Barralonga; they knew each other well; and Father Amerton exchanged comments with Mr Mush. Ridley and Penk, after some moments of austere regard, had gone apart to discuss the technicalities of the day's experience in undertones. Nobody paid any attention to Mr Barnstaple.

It was like a meeting at a railway station. It was like a reception. It was utterly incredible and altogether commonplace. He was weary. He was saturated and exhausted by wonder.

'Oh, I am going to my bed!' he yawned suddenly. 'I am going to my little bed.'

He made his way through the friendly-eyed Utopians out into the calm starlight. He nodded to the strange nebula at the corner of Orion as a weary parent might nod to importunate offspring. He would consider it again in the morning. He staggered drowsily through the gardens to his own particular retreat.

He disrobed and went to sleep as immediately and profoundly as a tired child.

CHAPTER THE EIGHTH

Early Morning in Utopia

I

Mr Barnstaple awakened slowly out of profound slumber.

He had a vague feeling that a very delightful and wonderful dream was slipping from him. He tried to keep on with the dream and not to open his eyes. It was about a great world of beautiful people who had freed themselves from a thousand earthly troubles. But it dissolved and faded from his mind. It was not often nowadays that dreams came to Mr Barnstaple. He lay very still with his eyes closed, reluctantly coming awake to the affairs of every day.

The cares and worries of the last fortnight resumed their sway. Would he ever be able to get away for a holiday by himself? Then he remembered that he had already got his valise stowed away in the Yellow Peril. But surely that was not last night; that was the night before last, and he had started – he remembered now starting and the little thrill of getting through the gate before Mrs Barnstaple suspected anything. He opened his eyes and fixed them on a white ceiling, trying to recall that journey. He remembered turning into the Camberwell New Road and the bright exhilaration of the morning, Vauxhall Bridge and that nasty tangle of traffic at Hyde Park Corner. He always maintained that the west of London was far more difficult for motoring than the east. Then – had he gone to Uxbridge? No. He recalled the road to Slough and then came a blank in his mind.

What a very good ceiling this was! Not a crack nor a stain!

But how had he spent the rest of the day? He must have got somewhere because here he was in a thoroughly comfortable bed – an excellent bed. With a thrush singing. He had always maintained that a good thrush could knock spots off a nightingale, but this thrush was a perfect Caruso. And another answering it! In July! Pangbourne and Caversham were wonderful places for nightingales. In June. But this was July – and thrushes. . . . Across these drowsy thought-phantoms came the figure of Mr Rupert Catskill, hands on hips, face and head thrust forward speaking, saying astonishing things. To a naked seated figure with a grave intent face. And other figures. One with a face like the Delphic Sibyl. Mr Barnstaple began to remember that in some way he had got himself mixed up with a week-end party at Taplow Court. Now had this speech been given at Taplow Court? At Taplow Court they wear clothes. But perhaps the aristocracy in retirement and privacy—?

Utopia? . . . But was it possible?

Mr Barnstaple sat up in his bed in a state of extreme amazement. 'Impossible!' he said. He was lying in a little loggia half open to the air. Between the slender pillars of fluted glass he saw a range of snow-topped mountains, and in the foreground a great cluster of tall spikes bearing deep red flowers. The bird was still singing – a glorified thrush, in a glorified world. Now he remembered everything. Now it was all clear. The sudden twisting of the car, the sound like the snapping of a fiddle string and – Utopia! Now he had it all, from the sight of sweet dead Greenlake to the bringing in of Lord Barralonga under the strange unfamiliar stars. It was no dream. He looked at his hand on the exquisitely fine coverlet. He felt his rough chin. It was a world real enough for shaving – and for a very definite readiness for breakfast. Very – for he had missed his supper. And as if in answer to his thought a smiling girl appeared ascending the steps to his sleeping-place and bearing a little tray. After all, there was much to be said for Mr Burleigh. To his swift statesmanship it was that Mr Barnstaple owed this morning cup of tea.

'Good morning,' said Mr Barnstaple.

'Why not?' said the young Utopian, and put down his tea and smiled at him in a motherly fashion and departed.

'Why not a good morning, I suppose,' said Mr Barnstaple and meditated for a moment, chin on knees, and then gave his attention to the bread-and-butter and tea.

2

The little dressing-room in which he found his clothes lying just as he had dumped them overnight, was at once extraordinarily simple and extraordinarily full of interest for Mr Barnstaple. He paddled about it humming as he examined it.

The bath was much shallower than an ordinary earthly bath; apparently the Utopians did not believe in lying down and stewing. And the forms of everything were different, simpler and more graceful. On earth he reflected art was largely wit. The artist had a certain limited selection of obdurate materials and certain needs, and his work was a clever reconciliation of the obduracy and the necessity and of the idiosyncrasy of the substance to the aesthetic preconceptions of the human mind. How delightful, for example, was the earthly carpenter dealing cleverly with the grain and character of this wood or that. But here the artist had a limitless control of material, and that element of witty adaptation had gone out of his work. His data were the human mind and body. Everything in this little room was unobtrusively but perfectly convenient – and difficult to misuse. If you splashed too much a thoughtful outer rim tidied things up for you.

In a tray by the bath was a very big fine sponge. So either Utopians still dived for sponges or they grew them or trained them (who could tell?) to come up of their own accord.

As he set out his toilet things a tumbler was pushed off a glass shelf on to the floor and did not break. Mr Barnstaple in an experimental mood dropped it again and still it did not break.

He could not find taps at first though there was a big washing basin as well as a bath. Then he perceived a number of studs on the walls with black marks that might be Utopian writing. He experimented. He found very hot water and then very cold water filling his bath, a fountain of probably soapy warm water, and other fluids – one with an odour of pine and one with a subdued odour of chlorine. The Utopian characters on these studs set him musing for a time; they were the first writing he had seen; they appeared to be word characters, but whether they represented sounds or were greatly simplified hieroglyphics he could not imagine. Then his mind went off at a tangent in another direction because the only metal apparent in this dressing-room was gold. There was, he noted, an extraordinary lot of gold in the room. It was set and inlaid in gold. The soft yellow lines gleamed and glittered. Gold evidently was cheap in Utopia. Perhaps they knew how to make it.

He roused himself to the business of his toilet. There was no looking-glass in the room, but when he tried what he thought was the handle of a cupboard door, he found himself opening a triple full-length mirror. Afterwards he was to discover that there were no displayed mirrors in Utopia; Utopians, he was to learn, thought it

292

indecent to be reminded of themselves in that way. The Utopian method was to scrutinize oneself, see that one was all right and then forget oneself for the rest of the day. He stood now surveying his pyjamad and unshaven self with extreme disfavour. Why do respectable citizens favour such ugly pink-striped pyjamas? When he unpacked his nail brush and tooth brush, shaving brush and washing glove, they seemed to him to have the coarseness of a popular burlesque His tooth brush was a particularly ignoble instrument. He wished now he had bought a new one at the chemist's shop near Victoria Station.

And what nasty queer things his clothes were!

He had a fantastic idea of adopting Utopian ideas of costume, but a reflective moment before his mirror restrained him. Then he remembered that he had packed a silk tennis shirt and flannels. Suppose he wore those, without a collar stud or tie – and went bare-footed?

He surveyed his feet. As feet went on earth they were not unsightly feet. But on earth they had been just wasted.

3

A particularly clean and radiant Mr Barnstaple, white-clad, bare-necked and bare-footed, presently emerged into the Utopian sunrise. He smiled. stretched his arms and took a deep breath of the sweet air. Then suddenly his face became hard and resolute.

From another little sleeping house not two hundred yards away Father Amerton was emerging. Intuitively Mr Barnstaple knew he meant either to forgive or be forgiven for the overnight quarrel. It would be a matter of chance whether he would select the role of offender or victim; what was certain was that he would smear a dreary mess of emotional personal relationship over the jewel-like clearness and brightness of the scene. A little to the right of Mr Barnstaple and in front of him were wide steps leading down towards the lake. Three strides and he was going down these steps two at a time. It may have been his hectic fancy, but it seemed to him that he heard the voice of Father Amerton, 'Mr *Barn* – Staple,' in pursuit.

Mr Barnstaple doubled and doubled again and crossed a bridge across an avalanche gully, a bridge with huge masonry in back and roof and with delicate pillars of prismatic glass towards the lake. The sunlight entangled in these pillars broke into splashes of red and blue and golden light. Then at a turfy corner gay with blue gentians, he narrowly escaped a collision with Mr Rupert Catskill. Mr Catskill was in the same costume that he had worn on the previous day except that he was without his grey top hat. He walked with his hands clasped behind him.

'Hullo!' he said. 'What's the hurry? We seem to be the first people up.'

'I saw Father Amerton—'

'That accounts for it. You were afraid of being caught up in a service, Matins or Prime or whatever he calls it. Wise man to run. He shall pray for the lot of us. Me too.'

He did not wait for any endorsement from Mr Barnstaple, but went on talking.

'You have slept well? What did you think of the old fellow's answer to my speech. Eh? Evasive clichés. When in doubt, abuse the plaintiff's attorney. We don't agree with him because we have bad hearts.'

'What old fellow do you mean?'

'The worthy gentleman who spoke after me.'

'Urthred! But he's not forty.'

'He's seventy-three. He told us afterwards. They live long here, a lingering business. Our lives are a fitful hectic fever from their point of view. But as Tennyson said, "Better fifty years of Europe than a cycle of Cathay!" H'm? He evaded my points. This is Lotus Land, Sunset Land; we shan't be thanked for disturbing its slumbers.'

'I doubt their slumbers.'

'Perhaps the Socialist bug has bit you too. Yes – I see it has! Believe me this is the most complete demonstration of decadence it would be possible to imagine. Complete. And we *shall* disturb their slumbers, never fear. Nature, you will see, is on our side – in a way no one has thought of yet.'

'But I don't see the decadence,' said Mr Barnstaple.

'None so blind as those who won't see. It's everywhere. Their large flushed pseudo-health. Like fatted cattle. And their treatment of Barralonga. They don't know how to treat him. They don't even arrest him. They've never arrested anyone for a thousand years. He careers through their land, killing and slaying and frightening and disturbing and they're flabbergasted, Sir, simply flabbergasted. It's like a dog running amuck in a world full of sheep. If he hadn't had a side-slip I believe he would be hooting and snorting and careering along now – killing people. They've lost the instinct of social defence.'

'I wonder.'

'A very good attitude of mind. If indulged in, in moderation. But when your wondering is over, you will begin to see that I am right. H'm? Ah! There on that terrace! Isn't that my Lord Barralonga and his French acquaintance? It is. Inhaling the morning air. I think with your permission I will go on and have a word with them. Which way did you say Father Amerton was? I don't want to disturb his devotions. This way? Then if I go to the right—'

He grimaced amiably over his shoulder.

4

Mr Barnstaple came upon two Utopians gardening.

They had two light silvery wheelbarrows, and they were cutting out old wood and overblown clusters from a line of thickets that sprawled over a rough-heaped ridge of rock and foamed with crimson and deep red roses. These gardeners had great leather gauntlets and aprons of tanned skin, and they carried hooks and knives.

Mr Barnstaple had never before seen such roses as they were tending here; their fragrance filled the air. He did not know that double roses could be got in mountains; bright red single sorts he had seen high up in Switzerland, but not such huge loose-flowered monsters as these. They dwarfed their leaves. Their wood was in long, thorny, snaky-red streaked stems that writhed wide and climbed to the rocky lumps over which they grew. Their great petals fell like red snow and like drifting moths and like blood upon the soft soil that sheltered amidst the brown rocks.

'You are the first Utopians I have actually seen at work,' he said.

'This isn't our work,' smiled the nearer of the two, a fair-haired, freckled, blue-eyed youth. 'But as we are for these roses we have to keep them in order.'

'Are they your roses?'

'Many people think these double mountain roses too much trouble and a nuisance with their thorns and sprawling branches, and many people think only the single sorts of roses ought to be grown in these high places and that this lovely sort ought to be left to die out up here. Are you for our roses?'

'Such roses as these?' said Mr Barnstaple. 'Altogether.'

'Good! Then just bring me up my barrow closer for all this litter. We're responsible for the good behaviour of all this thicket reaching right down there almost to the water.'

'And you have to see to it yourselves?'

'Who else?'

'But couldn't you get someone – pay someone to see to it for you?'

'Oh, hoary relic from the ancient past!' the young man replied. 'Oh, fossil ignoramus from a barbaric universe! Don't you realize that there is no working class in Utopia? It died out fifteen hundred years or so ago. Wages-slavery, pimping and so forth are done with. We read about them in books. Who loves the rose must serve the rose – himself.'

'But you work.'

'Not for wages. Not because anyone else loves or desires something else and is too lazy to serve it or get it himself. We work, part of the brain, part of the will, of Utopia.'

'May I ask at what?'

'I explore the interior of our planet. I study high-pressure chemistry. And my friend—'

He interrogated his friend, whose dark face and brown eyes appeared suddenly over a foam of blossom. 'I do Food.'

'A cook?'

'Of sorts. Just now I am seeing to your Earthling dietary. It's most interesting and curious – but I should think rather destructive. I plan your meals. . . . I see you look anxious, but I saw to your breakfast last night.' He glanced at a minute wrist-watch under the gauntlet of his gardening glove. 'It will be ready in about an hour. How was the early tea?'

'Excellent,' said Mr Barnstaple.

'Good,' said the dark young man. 'I did my best. I hope the breakfast will be as satisfactory. I had to fly two hundred kilometres for a pig last night and kill it and cut it up myself, and find out how to cure it. Eating bacon has gone out of fashion in Utopia. I hope you will find my rashers satisfactory.'

'It seems very rapid curing – for a rasher,' said Mr Barnstaple. 'We could have done without it.'

'Your spokesman made such a point of it.'

The fair young man struggled out of the thicket and wheeled his barrow away. Mr Barnstaple wished the dark young man 'Good morning.'

'Why shouldn't it be?' asked the dark young man.

5

He discovered Ridley and Penk approaching him. Ridley's face and ear were still adorned with sticking-plaster and his bearing was eager and anxious. Penk followed a little way behind him, holding one hand to the side of his face. Both were in their professional dress, white-topped caps, square-cut leather coats and black gaiters; they had made no concessions to Utopian laxity.

Ridley began to speak as soon as he judged Mr Barnstaple was within earshot.

'You don't 'appen to know, Mister, where these 'ere decadents shoved our car?'

'I thought your car was all smashed up.'

'Not a Rolls-Royce – not like that. Windscreen, mud-guards and the on-footboard perhaps. We went over sideways. I want to 'ave a look at it. And I didn't turn the petrol off. The carburettor was leaking a bit. My fault. I 'adn't been careful enough with the strainer. If she runs out of petrol, where's one to get more of it in this blasted Elysium? I ain't seen a sign anywhere. I know if I don't get that car into running form before Lord Barralonga wants it there's going to be trouble.'

Mr Barnstaple had no idea where the cars were.

''Aven't you a car of your own?' asked Ridley reproachfully.

'I have. But I've never given it a thought since I got out of it.'

'Owner-driver,' said Ridley bitterly.

'Anyhow, I can't help you find your cars. Have you asked any of the Utopians?'

'Not us. We don't like the style of 'em,' said Ridley.

'They'll tell you.'

'And watch us – whatever we do to our cars. They don't get a chance of looking into a Rolls-Royce every day in the year. Next thing we shall have them driving off in 'em. I don't like the place, and I don't like these people. They're queer. They ain't decent. His lordship says they're a lot of degenerates, and it seems to me his lordship is about right. I ain't a Puritan, but all this running about without clothes is a bit too thick for me. I wish I knew where they'd stowed those cars.'

Mr Barnstaple was considering Penk. 'You haven't hurt your face?' he asked.

'Nothing to speak of,' said Penk. 'I suppose we ought to be getting on.'

Ridley looked at Penk and then at Mr Barnstaple. 'He's had a bit of a contoosion,' he remarked, a faint smile breaking through his sourness.

'We better be getting on if we're going to find those cars,' said Penk.

A grin of intense enjoyment appeared upon Ridley's face, ''E's bumped against something.'

'*Oh – shut it!*' said Penk.

But the thing was too good to keep back. 'One of these girls 'it 'im.'

'What do you mean?' said Mr Barnstaple. 'You haven't been taking liberties—?'

'I 'ave *not*,' said Penk. 'But as Mr Ridley's been so obliging as to start the topic I suppose I got to tell wot 'appened. It jest illustrates the uncertainties of being among a lot of arf-savage, arf-crazy people, like we got among.'

Ridley smiled and winked at Mr Barnstaple. 'Regular 'ard clout she gave 'im. Knocked him over. 'E put 'is 'and on 'er shoulder and *clop!* over 'e went. Never saw anything like it.'

'Rather unfortunate,' said Mr Barnstaple.

'It all 'appened in a second like.'

'It's a pity it happened.'

'Don't you go making any mistake about it, Mister, and don't you go running off with any false ideas about it,' said Penk. 'I don't want the story to get about – it might do me a lot of 'arm with Mr Burleigh. Pity Mr Ridley couldn't 'old 'is tongue. What provoked her I do not know. She came into my room as I was getting up, and she wasn't what you might call wearing anything, and she looked a bit saucy, to my way of thinking, and – well, something come into my head to say to her, something – well, just the least little bit sporty, so to speak. One can't always control one's thoughts – can one? A man's a man. If a man's expected to be civil in his private thoughts to girls without a stitch, so to speak – *well!* I dunno. I really do not know. It's against nature. I never said it, whatever it was I thought of. Mr Ridley 'ere will bear me out. I never said a word to her. I 'adn't opened my lips when she hit me. Knocked me over, she did – like a ninepin. Didn't even seem angry about it. A 'ook-'it – sideways. It was surprise as much as anything floored me.'

'But Ridley says you touched her.'

'Laid me 'and on 'er shoulder perhaps, in a sort of fatherly way. As she was turning to go – not being sure whether I wasn't going to speak to her, I admit. And there you are! If I'm to get into trouble because I was wantonly 'it—'

Penk conveyed despair of the world by an eloquent gesture.

Mr Barnstaple considered. 'I shan't make trouble,' he said. 'But all the same I think we must all be very careful with these Utopians. Their ways are not our ways.'

'Thank God!' said Ridley. 'The sooner I get out of this world back to Old England, the better I shall like it.'

He turned to go.

'You should 'ear 'is lordship,' said Ridley over his shoulder. ''E says it's just a world of bally degenerates – rotten degenerates – in fact, if you'll excuse me – § § * ! * ! * †* † ! degenerates. Eh? That about gets 'em.'

'The young woman's arm doesn't seem to have been very degenerate,' said Mr Barnstaple, standing the shock bravely.

'Don't it? ' said Ridley bitterly. 'That's all *you* know. Why! if there's one sign more sure than another about degeneration it's when women take to knocking men about. It's against instink. In any respectable decent world such a thing couldn't possibly 'ave 'appened. No 'ow!'

'No – 'ow,' echoed Penk.

'In *our* world, such a girl would jolly soon 'ave 'er lesson. Jolly soon. See?'

But Mr Barnstaple's roving eye had suddenly discovered Father Amerton approaching very rapidly across a wide space of lawn and making arresting gestures. Mr Barnstaple perceived he must act at once.

'Now here's someone who will certainly be able to help you find your cars, if he cares to do so. He's a most helpful man – Father Amerton. And the sort of views he has about women are the sort of views you have. You are bound to get on together. If you will stop him and put the whole case to him – plainly and clearly. . . .'

He set off at a brisk pace towards the lake shore.

He could not be far now from the little summerhouse that ran out over the water against which the gaily coloured boats were moored.

If he were to get into one of these and pull out into the lake he would have Father Amerton at a very serious disadvantage. Even if that good man followed suit. One cannot have a really eloquent emotional scene when one is pulling hard in pursuit of another boat.

6

As Mr Barnstaple untied the bright white canoe with the big blue eye painted at its prow that he had chosen, Lady Stella appeared on the landing-stage. She came out of the pavilion that stood over the water, and something in her quick movement as she emerged suggested to Mr Barnstaple's mind that she had been hiding there. She glanced about her and spoke very eagerly. 'Are you going to row out upon the lake, Mr Bastable? May I come?'

She was attired, he noted, in a compromise between the Earthly and the Utopian style. She was wearing what might have been either a very simple custard-coloured tea robe or a very sophisticated bath wrap; it left her slender, pretty arms bare and free except for a bracelet of amber and gold, and on her bare feet – and they were unusually shapely feet – were sandals. Her head was bare, and her dark hair very simply done with a little black and gold fillet round it that suited her intelligent face. Mr Barnstaple was an ignoramus about feminine costume, but he appreciated the fact that she had been clever in catching the Utopian note.

He helped her into the canoe. 'We will paddle right out – a good way,' she said with another glance over her shoulder, and sat down.

For a time Mr Barnstaple paddled straight out so that he had nothing before him but sunlit water and sky, the low hills that closed in the lake towards the great plain, the huge pillars of the distant dam, and Lady Stella. She affected to be overcome by the beauty of the Conference garden slope with its houses and terraces behind him, but he could see that she was not really looking at the scene as a whole, but searching it restlessly for some particular object or person.

She made conversational efforts, on the loveliness of the morning and on the fact that birds were singing – 'in July'.

'But here it is not necessarily July,' said Mr Barnstaple.

'How stupid of me! Of course not.'

'We seem to be in a fine May.'

'It is probably very early,' she said. 'I forgot to wind my watch.'

'Oddly enough we seem to be at about the same hours in our two worlds,' said Mr Barnstaple. 'My wrist-watch says seven.'

'No,' said Lady Stella, answering her own thoughts and with her eyes on the distant gardens. 'That is a Utopian girl. Have you met any others – of our party – this morning?'

Mr Barnstaple brought the canoe round so that he too could look at the shore. From here they could see how perfectly the huge terraces and avalanche walls and gullies mingled and interwove with the projecting ribs and cliffs of the mountain masses behind. The shrub tangles passed up into hanging pinewoods; the torrents and cascades from the snowfield above were caught and distributed amidst the emerald slopes and gardens of the Conference Park. The terraces that retained the soil and held the whole design spread out on either hand to a great distance and were continued up into the mountain substance; they were built of a material that ranged through a wide variety of colours from a deep red to a purple-veined white, and they were diversified by great arches over torrents and rock gullies, by huge round openings that spouted water and by cascades of steps. The buildings of the place were distributed over these terraces and over the grassy slopes they contained, singly or in groups and clusters, buildings of purple and blue and white as light and delicate as the Alpine flowers about them. For some moments Mr Barnstaple was held silent by this scene, and then he attended to Lady Stella's question. 'I met Mr Rupert Catskill and the two chauffeurs,' he said, 'and I saw Father Amerton and Lord Barralonga and M. Dupont in the distance. I've seen nothing of Mr Mush or Mr Burleigh.'

'Mr Cecil won't be about for hours yet. He will lie in bed until ten or eleven. He always takes a good rest in the morning when there is any great mental exertion before him.'

The lady hesitated and then asked: 'I suppose you haven't seen Miss Greeta Grey?'

'No,' said Mr Barnstaple. 'I wasn't looking for our people. I was just strolling about – and avoiding somebody.'

'The censor of manners and costumes?'

'Yes. . . . That, in fact, is why I took to this canoe.'

The lady reflected and decided on a confidence.

'I was running away from someone too.'

'Not the preacher?'

'Miss Grey!'

Lady Stella apparently went off at a tangent. 'This is going to be a very difficult world to stay in. These people have very delicate taste. We may easily offend them.'

'They are intelligent enough to understand.'

'Do people who understand necessarily forgive? I've always doubted that proverb.'

Mr Barnstaple did not wish the conversation to drift away into generalities, so he paddled and said nothing.

'You see Miss Grey used to play Phryne in a Revue.'

'I seem to remember something about it. There was a fuss in the newspapers.'

'That perhaps gave her a bias.'

Three long sweeps with the paddle.

'But this morning she came to me and told me that she was going to wear complete Utopian costume.'

'Meaning?'

'A little rouge and face powder. It doesn't suit her the least little bit, Mr Bastaple. It's a faux pas. It's indecent. But she's running about the gardens—. She might meet anyone. It's lucky Mr Cecil isn't up. If she meets Father Amerton–! But it's best not to think of that. You see, Mr Bastaple, these Utopians and their sun-brown bodies – and everything, are in the picture. They don't embarrass me. But Miss Grey—. An earthly civilized woman taken out of her clothes *looks* taken out of her clothes. Peeled. A sort of *bleached* white. That nice woman who seems to hover round us, Lychnis, when she advised me what to wear, never for one moment suggested anything of the sort. . . . But, of course, I don't know Miss Grey well enough to talk to her and besides, one never knows how a woman of that sort is going to take a thing. . . .'

Mr Barnstaple stared shoreward. Nothing was to be seen of an excessively visible Miss Greeta Grey. Then he had a conviction. 'Lychnis will take care of her,' he said.

'I hope she will. Perhaps, if we stay out here for a time—'

'She will be looked after,' said Mr Barnstaple. 'But I think Miss Grey and Lord Barralonga's party generally are going to make trouble for us. I wish they hadn't come through with us.'

'Mr Cecil thinks that,' said Lady Stella.

'Naturally we shall all be thrown very much together and judged in a lump.'

'Naturally,' Lady Stella echoed.

She said no more for a little while. But it was evident that she had more to say. Mr Barnstaple paddled slowly.

'Mr Bastable,' she began presently.

Mr Barnstaple's paddle became still.

'Mr Bastable – are you *afraid?*'

Mr Barnstaple judged himself. 'I have been too full of wonder to be afraid.'

Lady Stella decided to confess. 'I *am* afraid,' she said. 'I wasn't at first. Everything seemed to go so easily and simply. But in the night I woke up – horribly afraid.'

'No,' considered Mr Barnstaple. 'No. It hasn't taken me like that – yet. . . . Perhaps it will.'

Lady Stella leant forward and spoke confidentially, watching the effect of her words on Mr Barnstaple. 'These Utopians – I thought at first they were just simple, healthy human beings, artistic and innocent. But they are not, Mr Bastable. There is something hard and complicated about them, something that goes beyond us and that we don't understand. And they don't care for us. They look at us with heartless eyes. Lychnis is kind, but hardly any of the others are the least bit kind. And I think they find us inconvenient.'

Mr Barnstaple thought it over. 'Perhaps they do. I have been so preoccupied with admiration – so much of this is fine beyond dreaming – that I have not thought very much how we affected them. But – yes – they seem to be busy about other things and not very attentive to us. Except the ones who have evidently been assigned to watch and study us. And Lord Barralonga's headlong rush through the country must certainly have been inconvenient.'

'He killed a man.'

'I know.'

They remained thoughtfully silent for some moments.

'And there are other things,' Lady Stella resumed. 'They think quite differently from our way of thinking. I believe they despise us already. I noted something. . . . Last evening you were not with us by the lake when Mr Cecil asked them about their philosophy. He told them things about Hegel and Bergson and Lord Haldane and his own wonderful scepticism. He opened out – unusually. It was very interesting – to me. But I was watching Urthred and Lion and in the midst of it I saw – I am convinced – they were talking to each other in that silent way they have, about something quite different. They were just *shamming* attention. And when Freddy Mush tried to interest them in Neo-Georgian poetry and the effect of the war upon literature, and how he hoped that they had something *half* as beautiful as the Iliad in Utopia, though he confessed he couldn't believe they had, they didn't even pretend to listen. They did not answer him at all. . . . Our minds don't matter a bit to them.'

'In these subjects. They are three thousand years further on. But we might be interesting as learners.'

'Would it have been interesting to have taken a Hottentot about London explaining things to him – after one had got over the first fun of showing off his ignorance? Perhaps it would. But I don't think they want us here very much and I don't think they are going to like us very much, and I don't know what they are likely to do to us if we give too much trouble. And so I am afraid.'

She broke out in a new place. 'In the night I was reminded of my sister Mrs Kelling's monkeys.

'It's a mania with her. They run about the gardens and come into the house and the poor things are always in trouble. They don't quite know what they may do and what they may not do; they all look frightfully worried and they get slapped and carried to the door and thrown out and all sorts of things like that. They spoil things and make her guests uneasy. You never seem to know what a monkey's going to do. And everybody hates to have them about except my sister. And she keeps on scolding them. 'Come *down*, Jacko! Put that *down*, Sadie'!'

Mr Barnstaple laughed. 'It isn't going to be quite so bad as that with us, Lady Stella. We are not monkeys.'

She laughed too. 'Perhaps it isn't. But all the same – in the night – I felt it might be. We are inferior creatures. One has to admit it. . . .'

She knitted her brows. Her pretty face expressed great intellectual effort. 'Do you realize how we are cut off? . . . Perhaps you will think it silly of me, Mr Bastable, but last night before I went to bed I sat down to write my sister a letter and tell her all about things while they

303

were fresh in my mind. And suddenly I realized I might as well write –
to Julius Caesar.'

Mr Barnstaple hadn't thought of that.

'That's a thing I can't get out of my head, Mr Bastable – no letters,
no telegrams, no newspapers, no Bradshaw in Utopia. All the things
we care for really – All the people we live for. Cut off! I don't know for
how long. But completely cut off. .... How long are they likely to keep
us here?'

Mr Barnstaple's face became speculative.

'Are you *sure* they can ever send us back?' the lady asked.

'There seems to be some doubt. But they are astonishingly clever
people.'

'It seemed so easy coming here – just as if one walked round a
corner – but, of course, properly speaking we are out of space and
time. .... More out of it even than dead people. .... The North Pole or
Central Africa is a whole universe nearer home than we are. .... It's
hard to grasp that. In this sunlight it all seems so bright and familiar.
.... Yet last night there were moments when I wanted to scream. ....'

She stopped short and scanned the shore. Then very deliberately
she sniffed.

Mr Barnstaple became aware of a peculiarly sharp and appetizing
smell drifting across the water to him.

'Yes,' he said.

'It's breakfast bacon!' cried Lady Stella with a squeak in her voice.

'Exactly as Mr Burleigh told them,' said Mr Barnstaple, mechanically turning the canoe shoreward.

'Breakfast bacon! That's the most reassuring thing that has happened
yet. .... Perhaps after all it was silly to feel frightened. And there they
are signalling to us!' She waved her arm.

'Greeta in a white robe – as you prophesied – and Mr Mush in a
sort of toga talking to her. .... Where could he have got that toga?'

A faint sound of voices calling reached them.

'Com–*ing!*' cried Lady Stella.

'I hope I haven't been pessimistic,' said Lady Stella. 'But I felt *horrid*
in the night.'

BOOK THE SECOND

Quarantine Crag

CHAPTER THE FIRST

The Epidemic

I

The shadow of the great epidemic in Utopia fell upon our little band of Earthlings in the second day after their irruption. For more than twenty centuries the Utopians had had the completest freedom from infectious and contagious disease of all sorts. Not only had the graver epidemic fevers and all sorts of skin diseases gone out of the lives of animals and men, but all the minor infections of colds, coughs, influenzas and the like had also been mastered and ended. By isolation, by the control of carriers, and so forth, the fatal germs had been cornered and obliged to die out.

And there had followed a corresponding change in the Utopian physiology. Secretions and reactions that had given the body resisting power to infection had diminished; the energy that produced them had been withdrawn to other more serviceable applications. The Utopian physiology, relieved of these merely defensive necessities, had simplified itself and become more direct and efficient. This cleaning up of infections was such ancient history in Utopia that only those who specialized in the history of pathology understood anything of the miseries mankind had suffered under from this source, and even these specialists do not seem to have had any idea of how far the race had lost its former resistance to infection. The first person to think of this lost resisting power seems to have been Mr Rupert Catskill. Mr Barnstaple recalled that when they had met early on the first morning of their stay in the Conference Gardens, he had been hinting that Nature was in some unexplained way on the side of the Earthlings.

If making them obnoxious was being on their side then certainly Nature was on their side. By the evening of the second day after their arrival nearly everybody who had been in contact with the Earthlings, with the exception of Lychnis, Serpentine and three or four others who had retained something of their ancestral antitoxins, was in a fever with cough, sore throat, aching bones, headache and such physical depression and misery as Utopia had not known for twenty centuries. The first inhabitant of Utopia to die was that leopard which had sniffed at Mr Rupert Catskill on his first arrival. It was found unaccountably dead on the second morning after that encounter. In the afternoon of the same day one of the girls who had helped Lady Stella to unpack her bags sickened suddenly and died. ...

Utopia was even less prepared for the coming of these disease germs than for the coming of the Earthlings who brought them. The monstrous multitude of general and fever hospitals, doctors, drug shops, and so forth that had existed in the last Age of Confusion had long since passed out of memory; there was a surgical service for accidents and a watch kept upon the health of the young, and there were places of rest at which those who were extremely old were assisted, but there remained scarcely anything of the hygienic organization that had formerly struggled against disease. Abruptly the Utopian intelligence had to take up again a tangle of problems long since solved and set aside, to improvise forgotten apparatus and organizations for disinfection and treatment, and to return to all the disciplines of the war against diseases that had marked an epoch in its history twenty centuries before. In one respect indeed that war had left Utopia with certain permanent advantages. Nearly all the insect disease carriers had been exterminated, and rats and mice and the untidier sorts of small bird had passed out of the problem of sanitation. That set very definite limits to the spread of the new infections and to the nature of the infections that could be spread. It enabled the Earthlings only to communicate such ailments as could be breathed across an interval, or conveyed by a contaminating touch. Though not one of them was ailing at all, it became clear that some one among them had brought latent measles into the Utopian universe, and that three or four of them had liberated a long suppressed influenza. Themselves too tough to suffer, they remained at the focus of these two epidemics, while their victims coughed and sneezed and kissed and whispered them about the Utopian planet. It was not until the afternoon of the second day after the irruption that Utopia realized what had happened, and set itself to deal with this relapse into barbaric solicitudes.

2

Mr Barnstaple was probably the last of the Earthlings to hear of the epidemic. He was away from the rest of the party upon an expedition of his own.

It was early clear to him that the Utopians did not intend to devote any considerable amount of time or energy to the edification of their Earthling visitors. After the *éclaircissement* of the afternoon of the irruption there were no further attempts to lecture to the visitors upon the constitution and methods of Utopia and only some very brief questioning upon the earthly state of affairs. The Earthlings were left very much together to talk things out among themselves. Several Utopians were evidently entrusted with their comfort and well-being, but they did not seem to think that their functions extended to edification. Mr Barnstaple found much to irritate him in the ideas and comments of several of his associates, and so he obeyed his natural inclination to explore Utopia for himself. There was something that stirred his imagination in the vast plain below the lake that he had glimpsed before his aeroplane descended into the valley of the Conference, and on his second morning he had taken a little boat and rowed out across the lake to examine the dam that retained its waters and to get a view of the great plain from the parapet of the dam.

The lake was much wider than he had thought it and the dam much larger. The water was crystalline clear and very cold, and there were but few fish in it. He had come out immediately after his breakfast, but it was near midday before he had got to the parapet of the great dam and could look down the lower valley to the great plain.

The dam was built of huge blocks of red and gold-veined rock, but steps at intervals gave access to the roadway along its crest. The great seated figures which brooded over the distant plain had been put there, it would seem, in a mood of artistic lightheartedness. They sat as if they watched or thought, vast rude shapes, half mountainous, half human. Mr Barnstaple guessed them to be perhaps two hundred feet high; by pacing the distance between two of them and afterwards counting the number of them, he came to the conclusion that the dam was between seven and ten miles long. On the far side it dropped sheerly for perhaps five hundred feet, and it was sustained by a series of enormous buttresses that passed almost insensibly into native rock. In the bays between these buttresses hummed great batteries of water turbines, and then, its first task done, the water dropped foaming and dishevelled and gathered in another broad lake retained by a second great dam two miles or so away and perhaps a thousand feet lower. Far away was a third lake and a third dam and then the plain. Only three or four minute-looking Utopians were visible amidst all this Titanic engineering.

Mr Barnstaple stood, the smallest of objects, in the shadow of a brooding Colossus, and peered over these nearer things at the hazy levels of the plain beyond.

What sort of life was going on there? The relationship of plain to mountain reminded him very strongly of the Alps and the great plain of Northern Italy, down into which he had walked as the climax of many a summer holiday in his youth. In Italy he knew that those distant levels would be covered with clustering towns and villages and carefully irrigated and closely cultivated fields. A dense population would be toiling with an ant-like industry in the production of food; for ever increasing its numbers until those inevitable consequences of overcrowding, disease and pestilence established a sort of balance between the area of the land and the number of families scraping at it for nourishment. As a toiling man can grow more food than he can actually eat, and as virtuous women can bear more children than the land can possibly employ, a surplus of landless population would be gathered in wen-like towns and cities, engaged there in legal and financial operations against the agriculturalist or in the manufacture of just plausible articles for sale.

Ninety-nine out of every hundred of this population would be concentrated from childhood to old age upon the difficult task which is known as 'getting a living'. Amidst it, sustained by a pretence of magical propitiations, would rise shrines and temples, supporting a parasitic host of priests and monks and nuns. Eating and breeding, the simple routines of the common life since human societies began, complications of food-getting, elaborations of acquisitiveness and a tribute paid to fear; such would be the spectacle that any warm and fertile stretch of earth would still display. There would be gleams of laughter and humour there, brief interludes of holiday, flashes of youth before its extinction in adult toil; but a driven labour, the spite and hates of overcrowding, the eternal uncertainty of destitution, would dominate the scene. Decrepitude would come by sixty; women would be old and worn out by forty. But this Utopian plain below, sunlit and fertile though it was, was under another law. Here that common life of mankind, its ancient traditions, its hoary jests and tales repeated generation after generation, its seasonal festivals, its pious fears and spasmodic indulgences, its limited yet incessant and pitifully childish hoping, and its abounding misery and tragic futility, had come to an end. It had passed for ever out of this older world. That high tide of common living had receded and vanished while the soil was still productive and the sun still shone.

It was with something like awe that Mr Barnstaple realized how clean a sweep had been made of the common life in a mere score of centuries, how boldly and dreadfully the mind of man had taken hold, soul and body and destiny, of the life and destiny of the race. He knew himself now for the creature of transition he was, so deep in the habits of the old, so sympathetic with the idea of the new that has still but scarcely dawned on earth. For long he had known how intensely he loathed and despised that reeking peasant life which is our past; he realized now for the first time how profoundly he feared the high austere Utopian life which lies before us. This world he looked out upon seemed very clean and dreadful to him. What were they doing upon those distant plains? What daily life did they lead there?

He knew enough of Utopia now to know that the whole land would be like a garden, with every natural tendency to beauty seized upon and developed and every innate ugliness corrected and overcome. These people could work and struggle for loveliness, he knew, for his two rose growers had taught him as much. And to and fro the food folk and the housing people and those who ordered the general life went, keeping the economic machine running so smoothly that one heard nothing of the jangling and jarring and internal breakages that constitute the dominant melody in our Earth's affairs. The ages of economic disputes and experiments had come to an end; the right way to do things had been found. And the population of this Utopia, which had shrunken at one time to only two hundred million, was now increasing again to keep pace with the constant increase in human resources. Having freed itself from a thousand evils that would otherwise have grown with its growth, the race could grow indeed.

And down there under the blue haze of the great plain almost all those who were not engaged in the affairs of food and architecture, health, education and the correlation of activities, were busied upon creative work; they were continually exploring the world without or the world within, through scientific research and artistic creation. They were continually adding to their collective power over life or to the realized worth of life.

Mr Barnstaple was accustomed to think of our own world as a wild rush of inventions and knowledge, but all the progress of earth for a hundred years could not compare, he knew, with the forward swing of these millions of associated intelligences in one single year. Knowledge swept forward here and darkness passed as the shadow of a cloud passes on a windy day. Down there they were assaying the minerals that lie in the heart of their planet, and weaving a web to capture the sun and the stars. Life marched here; it was terrifying to think with what strides. Terrifying – because at the back of Mr Barnstaple's mind, as at the back of so many intelligent minds in our world still, had been the persuasion that presently everything would be known and the scientific process come to an end. And then we should be happy for ever after.

He was not really acclimatized to progress. He had always thought of Utopia as a tranquillity with everything settled for good. Even today it seemed tranquil under that level haze, but he knew that this quiet was the steadiness of a mill-race, which seems almost motionless in its quiet onrush until a bubble or a fleck of foam or some stick or leaf shoots along it and reveals its velocity.

And how did it feel to be living in Utopia? The lives of the people must be like the lives of very successful artists or scientific workers in this world, a continual refreshing discovery of new things, a constant adventure into the unknown and untried. For recreation they went about their planet, and there was much love and laughter and friend-ship in Utopia and an abundant easy informal social life. Games that did not involve bodily exercise, those substitutes of the half-witted for research and mental effort, had gone entirely out of life, but many active games were played for the sake of fun and bodily vigour. ... It must be a good life for those who had been educated to live it, indeed a most enviable life.

And pervading it all must be the happy sense that it mattered; it went on to endless consequences. And they loved no doubt – subtly and deliciously – but perhaps a little hardly. Perhaps in those distant plains there was not much pity nor tenderness. Bright and lovely beings they were – in no way pitiful. There would be no need for those qualities. ...

Yet the woman Lychnis looked kind. ...

Did they keep faith or need to keep faith as earthly lovers do? What was love like in Utopia? Lovers still whispered in the dusk. ... What was the essence of love? A preference, a sweet pride, a delightful gift won, the most exquisite reassurance of body and mind. ...

What could it be like to love and be loved by one of these Utopian women? – to have her glowing face close to one's own – to be quickened into life by her kiss? ...

Mr Barnstaple sat in his flannels, bare-footed, in the shadow of a stone Colossus. He felt like some minute stray insect perched upon the big dam. It seemed to him that it was impossible that this triumphant Utopian race could ever fall back again from its magnificent attack upon the dominion of all things. High and tremendously this world had clambered and was still clambering. Surely it was safe now in its attainment. Yet all this stupendous security and mastery of nature had come about in the little space of three thousand years. . . .

The race could not have altered fundamentally in that brief interval. Essentially it was still a stone-age race, it was not twenty thousand years away from the days when it knew nothing of metals and could not read nor write. Deep in its nature, arrested and undeveloped, there still lay the seeds of anger and fear and dissension. There must still be many uneasy and insubordinate spirits in this Utopia. Eugenics had scarcely begun here. He remembered the keen sweet face of the young girl who had spoken to him in the starlight on the night of his arrival, and the note of romantic eagerness in her voice when she had asked if Lord Barralonga was not a very vigourous and cruel man.

Did the romantic spirit still trouble imaginations here? Possibly only adolescent imaginations.

Might not some great shock or some phase of confusion still be possible to this immense order? Might not its system of education become wearied by its task of discipline and fall a prey to the experimental spirit? Might not the unforeseen be still lying in wait for this race? Suppose there should prove to be an infection in Father Amerton's religious fervour or Rupert Catskill's incurable craving for fantastic enterprises!

No! It was inconceivable. The achievement of this world was too calmly great and assured.

Mr Barnstaple stood up and made his way down the steps of the great dam to where, far below, his little skiff floated like a minute flower-petal upon the clear water.

3

He became aware of a considerable commotion in the Conference places.

There were more than thirty aeroplanes circling in the air and descending and ascending from the park, and a great number of big white vehicles were coming and going by the pass road. Also people seemed to be moving briskly among the houses, but it was too far off to distinguish what they were doing. He stared for a time and then got into his little boat.

He could not watch what was going on as he returned across the lake because his back was towards the slopes, but once an aeroplane came down very close to him, and he saw its occupant looking at him as he rowed. And once when he rested from rowing and sat round to look he saw what he thought was a litter carried by two men.

As he drew near the shore a boat put off to meet him. He was astonished to see that its occupants were wearing what looked like helmets of glass with white pointed visors. He was enormously astonished and puzzled.

As they approached their message resonated into his mind 'Quarantine. You have to go into quarantine. You Earthlings have started an epidemic and it is necessary to put you into quarantine.'

Then these glass helmets must be a sort of gas-mask!

When they came alongside him he saw that this was so. They were made of highly flexible and perfectly translucent material. . . .

4

Mr Barnstaple was taken past some sleeping loggias where Utopians were lying in beds, while others who wore gas-masks waited upon them. He found that all the Earthlings and all their possessions, except their cars, were assembled in the hall of the first day's Conference. He was told that the whole party were to be removed to a new place where they could be isolated and treated.

The only Utopians with the party were two who wore gas-masks and lounged in the open portico in attitudes disagreeably suggestive of sentries or custodians.

The Earthlings sat about in little groups among the seats, except for Mr Rupert Catskill, who was walking up and down in the apse talking. He was hatless, flushed and excited, with his hair in some disorder.

'It's what I foresaw would happen all along,' he repeated. 'Didn't I tell you Nature was on our side? Didn't I say it?'

Mr Burleigh was shocked and argumentative. 'For the life of me I can't see the logic of it,' he declared. 'Here are we – absolutely the only perfectly immune people here – and we – *we* are to be isolated.'

'They say they catch things from us,' said Lady Stella.

'Very well,' said Mr Burleigh, making his point with his long white hand. 'Very well, then let *them* be isolated! This is – Chinese; this is topsy-turvy. I'm disappointed in them.'

'I suppose it's their world,' said Mr Hunker, 'and we've got to do things their way.'

Mr Catskill concentrated upon Lord Barralonga and the two chauffeurs. 'I welcome this treatment. I welcome it.'

'What's your idea, Rupert?' said his lordship. 'We lose our freedom of action.'

'Not at all,' said Mr Catskill. 'Not at all. We gain it. We are to be isolated. We are to be put by ourselves in some island or mountain. Well and good. Well and good. This is only the beginning of our adventures. We shall see what we shall see.'

'But how?'

'Wait a little. Until we can speak more freely. . . . These are panic measures. This pestilence is only in its opening stage. Everything is just beginning. Trust me.'

Mr Barnstaple sat sulkily by his valise, avoiding the challenge of Mr Catskill's eye.

CHAPTER THE SECOND

The Castle on the Crag

I

The quarantine place to which the Earthlings were taken must have been at a very considerable distance from the place of the Conference, because they were nearly six hours upon their journey, and all the time they were flying high and very swiftly. They were all together in one flying ship; it was roomy and comfortable and could have held perhaps four times as many passengers. They were accompanied by about thirty Utopians in gas-masks, among whom were two women. The aviators wore dresses of a white fleecy substance that aroused the interest and envy of both Miss Grey and Lady Stella. The flying ship passed down the valley and over the great plain and across a narrow sea and another land with a rocky coast and dense forests, and across a great space of empty sea. There was scarcely any shipping to be seen upon this sea at all; it seemed to Mr Barnstaple that no earthly ocean would be so untravelled; only once or twice did he see very big drifting vessels quite unlike any earthly ships, huge rafts or platforms they seemed to be rather than ships, and once or twice he saw what was evidently a cargo boat – one with rigged masts and sails. And the air was hardly more frequented. After he was out of sight of land he saw only three aeroplanes until the final landfall.

They crossed a rather thickly inhabited, very delightful-looking coastal belt and came over what was evidently a rainless desert country, given over to mining and to vast engineering operations. Far away were very high snowy mountains, but the aeroplane descended before it came to these. For a time the Earthlings were flying over enormous heaps of slaggy accumulations, great mountains of them, that seemed to be derived from a huge well-like excavation that went down into the earth to an unknown depth. A tremendous thunder of machinery came out of this pit and much smoke. Here there were crowds of workers and they seemed to be living in camps among the debris. Evidently the workers came to this place merely for spells of work; there were no signs of homes. The aeroplane of the Earthlings skirted this region and flew on over a rocky and almost treeless desert deeply cut by steep gorges of the canyon type. Few people were to be seen, but there were abundant signs of engineering activity. Every torrent, every cataract was working a turbine, and great cables followed the cliffs of the gorges and were carried across the desert spaces. In the wider places of the gorges there were pine woods and a fairly abundant vegetation.

The high crag which was their destination stood out, an almost completely isolated headland, in the fork between two convergent canyons. It towered up to a height of perhaps two thousand feet above the foaming clash of the torrents below, a great mass of pale greenish and purple rocks, jagged and buttressed and cleft deeply by joint planes and white crystalline veins. The gorge on one side of it was much steeper than that on the other, it was so overhung indeed as to be darkened like a tunnel, and here within a hundred feet or so of the brow a slender metallic bridge had been flung across the gulf. Some yards above it were projections that might have been the remains of an earlier bridge of stone. Behind, the crag fell steeply for some hundreds of feet to a long slope covered with a sparse vegetation which rose again to the main masses of the mountain, a wall of cliffs with a level top.

It was on this slope that the aeroplane came down alongside of three or four smaller machines. The crag was surmounted by the tall ruins of an ancient castle, within the circle of whose walls clustered a number of buildings which had recently harboured a group of chemical students. Their researches, which had been upon some question of atomic structure quite incomprehensible to Mr Barnstaple, were finished now and the place had become vacant. Their labouratory was still stocked with apparatus and material; and water and power were supplied to it from higher up the gorge by means of pipes and cables. There was also an abundant store of provisions. A number of Utopians were busily adapting the place to its new purpose of isolation and disinfection when the Earthlings arrived.

Serpentine appeared in the company of a man in a gas-mask whose name was Cedar. This Cedar was a cytologist, and he was in charge of the arrangements for this improvised sanatorium.

Serpentine explained that he himself had flown to the crag in advance, because he understood the equipment of the place and the research that had been going on there, and because his knowledge of the Earthlings and his comparative immunity to their infections made him able to act as an intermediary between them and the medical men who would now take charge of their case. He made these explanations to Mr Burleigh, Mr Barnstaple, Lord Barralonga and Mr Hunker. The other Earthlings stood about in small groups beside the aeroplane from which they had alighted, regarding the castellated summit of the crag, the scrubby bushes of the bleak upland about them and the towering cliffs of the adjacent canyons with no very favourable expressions.

Mr Catskill had gone apart nearly to the edge of the great canyon, and was standing with his hands behind his back in an attitude almost Napoleonic, lost in thought, gazing down into those sunless depths. The roar of the unseen waters below, now loud, now nearly inaudible, quivered in the air.

Miss Greeta Grey had suddenly produced a Kodak camera; she had been reminded of its existence when packing for this last journey, and she was taking a snapshot of the entire party.

Cedar said that he would explain the method of treatment he proposed to follow, and Lord Barralonga called 'Rupert!' to bring Mr Catskill into the group of Cedar's hearers.

Cedar was as explicit and concise as Urthred had been. It was evident, he said, that the Earthlings were the hosts of a variety of infectious organisms which were kept in check in their bodies by immunizing counter substances, but against which the Utopians had no defences ready and could hope to secure immunity only after a painful and disastrous epidemic. The only way to prevent this epidemic devastating their whole planet, indeed, was firstly to gather together and cure all the cases affected, which was being done by converting the Conference Park into a big hospital, and next to take the Earthlings in hand and isolate them absolutely from the Utopians until they could be cleaned of their infections. It was, he confessed, an inhospitable thing to do to the Earthlings, but it seemed the only possible thing to do, to bring them into this peculiarly high and dry desert air and there to devise methods for their complete physical cleansing. If that was possible it would be done, and then the Earthlings would again be free to go and come as they pleased in Utopia.

'But suppose it is not possible?' said Mr Catskill abruptly.

'I think it will be.'

'But if you fail?'

Cedar smiled at Serpentine. 'Physical research is taking up the work in which Arden and Greenlake were foremost, and it will not be long before we are able to repeat their experiment. And then to reverse it.'

'With us as your raw material?'

'Not until we are fairly sure of a safe landing for you.'

'You mean,' said Mr Mush, who had joined the circle about Cedar and Serpentine, 'that you are going to send us back?'

'If we cannot keep you,' said Cedar, smiling.

'Delightful prospect!' said Mr Mush unpleasantly. 'To be shot across space in a gun. Experimentally.'

'And may I ask,' came the voice of Father Amerton, 'may I ask the nature of this *treatment* of yours, these experiments of which we are to be the – guinea pigs, so to speak? Is it to be anything in the nature of vaccination?'

'Injections,' explained Mr Barnstaple.

'I have hardly decided yet,' said Cedar. 'The problem raises questions this world has forgotten for ages.'

'I may say at once that I am a confirmed antivaccinationist,' said Father Amerton. 'Absolutely. Vaccination is an outrage on nature. If I had any doubts before I came into this world of – of *vitiation*, I have no doubts now. Not a doubt! If God had meant us to have these serums and ferments in our bodies He would have provided more natural and dignified means of getting them there than a squirt.'

Cedar did not discuss the point. He went on to further apologies. For a time he must ask the Earthlings to keep within certain limits, to confine themselves to the crag and the slopes below it as far as the mountain cliffs. And further, it was impossible to set young people to attend to them as had hitherto been done. They must cook for themselves and see to themselves generally. The appliances were all to be found above upon the crest of the crag and he and Serpentine would make any explanations that were needful. They would find there was ample provision for them.

'Then are we to be left alone here?' asked Mr Catskill.

'For a time. When we have our problem clearer we will come again and tell you what we mean to do.'

'Good,' said Mr Catskill. 'Good.'

'I wish I hadn't sent my maid by train,' said Lady Stella.

'I have come to my last clean collar,' said M. Dupont with a little humourous grimace 'It is no joke this week-end with Lord Barralonga.'

Lord Barralonga turned suddenly to his particular minion. 'I believe that Ridley has the makings of a very good cook.'

'I don't mind trying my hand,' said Ridley. 'I've done most things – and once I used to look after a steam car.'

'A man who can keep one of those – those things in order can do anything,' said Mr Penk with unusual emotion. 'I've no objection to being a temporary general utility along of Mr Ridley. I began my career in the pantry and I ain't ashamed to own it.'

'If this gentleman will show us the gadgets,' said Mr Ridley, indicating Serpentine.

'Exactly,' said Mr Penk.

'And if all of us give as little trouble as possible,' said Miss Greeta bravely.

'I think we shall be able to manage,' said Mr Burleigh to Cedar. 'If at first you can spare us a little advice and help.'

2

Cedar and Serpentine remained with the Earthlings upon Quarantine Crag until late in the afternoon. They helped to prepare a supper and set it out in the courtyard of the castle. They departed with a promise to return on the morrow, and the Earthlings watched them and their accompanying aeroplanes soar up into the sky.

Mr Barnstaple was surprised to find himself distressed at their going. He had a feeling that mischief was brewing amongst his companions and that the withdrawal of these Utopians removed a check upon this mischief. He had helped Lady Stella in the preparation of an omelette; he had to carry back a dish and a frying-pan to the kitchen after it was served, so that he was the last to seat himself at the supper-table. He found the mischief he dreaded well afoot.

Mr Catskill had finished his supper already and was standing with his foot upon a bench orating to the rest of the company.

'I ask you, Ladies and Gentlemen,' Mr Catskill was saying; 'I ask you: Is not Destiny writ large upon this day's adventure? Not for nothing was this place a fortress in ancient times. Here it is ready to be a fortress again. M'm – a fortress. . . . In such an adventure as will make the stories of Cortez and Pizarro pale their ineffectual fires!'

'My dear Rupert!' cried Mr Burleigh. 'What have you got in that head of yours now?'

Mr Catskill waved two fingers dramatically. 'The conquest of a world!'

'Good God!' cried Mr Barnstaple. 'Are you mad?'

'As Clive,' said Mr Catskill, 'or Sultan Baber when he marched to Panipat.'

'It's a tall proposition,' said Mr Hunker, who seemed to have had his mind already prepared for these suggestions, 'but I'm inclined to give it a hearing. The alternative so far as I can figure it out is to be scoured and whitewashed inside and out and then fired back into our own world – with a chance of hitting something hard on the way. You tell them, Mr Catskill.'

'Tell them,' said Lord Barralonga, who had also been prepared. 'It's a gamble, I admit. But there's situations when one has to gamble – or be gambled with. I'm all for the active voice.'

'It's a gamble – certainly,' said Mr Catskill. 'But upon this narrow peninsula, upon this square mile or so of territory, the fate, Sir, of two universes awaits decision. This is no time for the faint heart and the paralysing touch of discretion. Plan swiftly – act swiftly. . . .'

'This is simply *thrilling!*' cried Miss Greeta Grey clasping her hands about her knees and smiling radiantly at Mr Mush.

'These people,' Mr Barnstaple interrupted, 'are three thousand years ahead of us. We are like a handful of Hottentots in a showman's van at Earl's Court, planning the conquest of London.'

Mr Catskill, hands on hips, turned with extraordinary good humour upon Mr Barnstaple. 'Three thousand years away from us – *yes!* Three thousand years ahead of us – *no!* That is where you and I join issue. You say these people are super-men. M'm – super-men. . . . I say they are degenerate men. Let me call your attention to my reasons for this belief – in spite of their beauty, their very considerable material and intellectual achievements and so forth. Ideal people, I admit. . . . What then? . . . My case is that they have reached a summit – and passed it, that they are going on by inertia and that they have lost the power not only of resistance to disease – that weakness we shall see develop more and more – but also of meeting strange and distressing emergencies. They are gentle. Altogether too gentle. They are ineffectual. They do not know what to do. Here is Father Amerton. He disturbed that first meeting in the most insulting way. (You know you did, Father Amerton. I'm not blaming you. You are morally – sensitive. And there were things to outrage you.) He was threatened – as a little boy is threatened by a feeble old woman. Something was to be done to him. Has anything been done to him?'

'A man and a woman came and talked to me,' said Father Amerton.

'And what did you do?'

'Simply confuted them. Lifted up my voice and confuted them.'

'What did they say?'

'What *could* they say?'

'We all thought tremendous things were going to be done to poor Father Amerton. Well, and now take a graver case. Our friend Lord Barralonga ran amuck with his car – and killed a man. M'm. Even at home they'd have endorsed your licence you know. And fined your man. But here? ... The thing has scarcely been mentioned since. Why? Because they don't know what to say about it or do about it. And now they have put us here and begged us to be good. Until they are ready to come and try experiments upon us and inject things into us and I don't know what. And if we submit, Sir, if we submit, we lose one of our greatest powers over these people, our power of at once giving and resisting malaise, and in addition, I know not what powers of initiative that may very well be associated with that physiological toughness of which we are to be robbed. They may trifle with our ductless glands. But Science tells us that these very glands secrete our personalities. Mentally, morally we shall be dissolved. If we submit, Sir – if we submit. But suppose we do not submit; what then?'

'Well,' said Lord Barralonga, 'what then?'

'They will not know what to do. Do not be deceived by any outward shows of beauty and prosperity. These people are living, as the ancient Peruvians were living in the time of Pizarro, in an enervating dream. They have drunken the debilitating draught of Socialism and, as in ancient Peru, there is no health nor power of will left in them any more. A handful of resolute men and women who can dare – may not only dare but triumph in the face of such a world. And thus it is I lay my plans before you.'

'You mean to jump this entire Utopian planet?' said Mr Hunker.

'Big order,' said Lord Barralonga.

'I mean, Sir, to assert the rights of a more vigourous form of social life over a less vigourous form of social life. Here we are – in a fortress. It is a real fortress and quite defensible. While you others have been unpacking, Barralonga and Hunker and I have been seeing to that. There is a sheltered well so that if need arises we can get water from the canyon below. The rock is excavated into chambers and shelters; the wall on the land side is sound and high, glazed so that it cannot be scaled. This great archway can easily be barricaded when the need arises. Steps go down through the rock to that little bridge which can if necessary be cut away. We have not yet explored all the excavations. In Mr Hunker we have a chemist – he was a chemist before the movie picture claimed him as its master – and he says there is ample material in the labouratory for a store of bombs. This party, I find, can muster five revolvers with ammunition. I scarcely dared hope for that. We have food for many days.'

'Oh! This is ridiculous!' cried Mr Barnstaple standing up and then sitting down again. 'This is preposterous! To turn on these friendly people! But they can blow this little headland to smithereens whenever they want to.'

'Ah!' said Mr Catskill and held him with his outstretched finger. 'We've thought of that. But we can take a leaf from the book of Cortez – who, in the very centre of Mexico, held Montezuma as his prisoner and hostage. We too will have our hostage. Before we lift a finger—. First our hostage. . . .'

'Aerial bombs!'

'Is there such a thing in Utopia? Or such an idea? And again – we must have our hostage.'

'Somebody of importance,' said Mr Hunker.

'Cedar and Serpentine are both important people,' said Mr Burleigh in tones of disinterested observation.

'But surely, Sir, you do not countenance this schoolboy's dream of piracy!' cried Mr Barnstaple, sincerely shocked.

'Schoolboys!' cried Father Amerton. 'A cabinet minister, a peer and a great entrepreneur!'

'My dear Sir,' said Mr Burleigh, 'we are, after all, only envisaging eventualities. For the life of me, I do not see why we should not thresh out these possibilities. Though I pray to Heaven we may never have to realize them. You were saying, Rupert—?'

'We have to establish ourselves here and assert our independence and make ourselves *felt* by these Utopians.'

''Ear, 'ear!' said Mr Ridley cordially. 'One or two I'd like to make feel personally.'

'We have to turn this prison into a capitol, into the first foothold of mankind in this world. It is like a foot thrust into a reluctant door that must never more close upon our race.'

'It is closed,' said Mr Barnstaple. 'Except by the mercy of these Utopians we shall never see our world again. And even with their mercy, it is doubtful.'

'That's been keeping me awake nights,' said Mr Hunker.

'It's an idea that must have occurred to all of us,' said Mr Burleigh.

'And it's an idea that's so thundering disagreeable that one hasn't cared to talk about it,' said Lord Barralonga.

'I never 'ad it until this moment,' said Penk. 'You don't reely mean to say, Sir, *we can't get back?*'

'Things will be as they will be,' said Mr Burleigh. 'That is why I am anxious to hear Mr Catskill's ideas.'

Mr Catskill rested his hands on his hips and his manner became very solemn. 'For once,' he said, 'I am in agreement with Mr Barnaby. I believe that the chances are *against* our ever seeing the dear cities of our world again.'

'I felt that,' said Lady Stella, with white lips. 'I *knew* that two days ago.'

'And so behold my week-end expand to an eternity!' said M. Dupont, and for a time no one said another word.

'It's as if—' Penk said at last. 'Why! One might be dead!'

'But I *murst* be back,' Miss Greeta Grey broke out abruptly, as one who sets aside a foolish idea. 'It's absurd. I have to go on at the Alhambra on September the 2nd. It's imperative. We came here quite easily; it's ridiculous to say I can't go back in the same way.'

Lord Barralonga regarded her with affectionate malignity. 'You wait,' he said.

'But I murst!' she sang.

'There's such things as impossibilities – even for Miss Greeta Grey.'

'Charter a special aeroplane!' she said. 'Anything.'

He regarded her with an elfin grin and shook his head.

'My dear man,' she said, 'you've only seen me in a holiday mood, so far. Work is serious.'

'My dear girl, that Alhambra of yours is about as far from us now as the Court of King Nebuchadnezzar. .... It can't be done.'

'But it *murst*,' she said in her queenly way. 'And that's all about it.'

3

Mr Barnstaple got up from the table and walked apart to where a gap in the castle wall gave upon the darkling wilderness without. He sat down there. His eyes went from the little group talking around the supper-table to the sunlit crest of the cliffs across the canyon and to the wild and lonely mountain slopes below the headland. In this world he might have to live out the remainder of his days.

And those days might not be very numerous if Mr Catskill had his way. Sydenham, and his wife and the boys were indeed as far – 'as the Court of King Nebuchadnezzar'.

He had scarcely given his family a thought since he had posted his letter at Victoria. Now he felt a queer twinge of desire to send them some word or token – if only he could. Queer that they would never hear from him or of him again! How would they get on without him?

Would there be any difficulty about the account at the bank? Or about the insurance money? He had always intended to have a joint and several account with his wife at the bank, and he had never quite liked to do it. Joint and several. . . . A thing every man ought to do. . . . His attention came back to Mr Catskill unfolding his plans.

'We have to make up our minds to what may be a prolonged, a very prolonged stay here. Do not let us deceive ourselves upon that score. It may last for years – it may last for generations.'

Something struck Penk in that. 'I don't 'ardly see,' he said, 'how that can be – *generations?*'

'I am coming to that,' said Mr Catskill.

'Un'appily,' said Mr Penk, and became profoundly restrained and thoughtful with his eyes on Lady Stella.

'We have to remain, a little alien community, in this world until we dominate it, as the Romans dominated the Greeks, and until we master its science and subdue it to our purpose. That may mean a long struggle. It may mean a very long struggle indeed. And meanwhile we must maintain ourselves as a community; we must consider ourselves a colony, a garrison, until that day of reunion comes. We must hold our hostages, Sir, and not only our hostages. It may be necessary for our purpose, and if it is necessary for our purpose, so be it – to get in others of these Utopians, to catch them young, before this so-called education of theirs unfits them for our purpose, to train them in the great traditions of our Empire and our race.'

Mr Hunker seemed on the point of saying something but refrained. M. Dupont got up sharply from the table, walked four paces away, returned and stood still, watching Mr Catskill.

'Generations?' said Mr Penk.

'Yes,' said Mr Catskill. 'Generations. For here we are strangers – strangers, like that other little band of adventurers who established their citadel five-and-twenty centuries ago upon the Capitol beside the rushing Tiber. This is our Capitol. A greater Capitol – of a greater Rome – in a vaster world. And like that band of Roman adventurers we too may have to reinforce our scanty numbers at the expense of the Sabines about us, and take to ourselves servants and helpers and – *mates!* No sacrifice is too great for the high possibilities of this adventure.'

M. Dupont seemed to nerve himself for the sacrifice.

'Duly married,' injected Father Amerton.

'Duly married,' said Mr Catskill in parenthesis. 'And so, Sir, we will hold out here and maintain ourselves and dominate this desert countryside and spread our prestige and our influence and our spirit into the inert body of this decadent Utopian world. Until at last we are able to master the secret that Arden and Greenlake were seeking and recover the way back to our own people, opening to the crowded millions of our Empire—'

<h2 style="text-align:center">4</h2>

'Just a moment,' said Mr Hunker. 'Just a moment! About this empire—!'

'Exactly,' said M. Dupont, recalled abruptly from some romantic day-dream. 'About your Empire!'

Mr Catskill regarded them thoughtfully and defensively. 'When I say Empire I mean it in the most general sense.'

'Exactly,' snapped M. Dupont.

'I was thinking generally of our – Atlantic civilization.'

'Before, Sir, you go on to talk of Anglo-Saxon unity and the English-speaking race,' said M. Dupont, with a rising note of bitterness in his voice, 'permit me to remind you, Sir, of one very important fact that you seem to be overlooking. The language of Utopia, Sir, is French. I want to remind you of that. I want to recall it to your mind. I will lay no stress here on the sacrifices and martyrdoms that France has endured in the cause of Civilization—'

The voice of Mr Burleigh interrupted. 'A very natural mis-conception. But, if you will pardon the correction, the language of Utopia is *not* French.'

Of course, Mr Barnstaple reflected, M. Dupont had not heard the explanation of the language difficulty.

'Permit me, Sir, to believe the evidence of my own ears,' the French-man replied with dignified politeness. 'These Utopians, I can assure you, speak French and nothing but French – and very excellent French it is.'

'They speak no language at all,' said Mr Burleigh.

'Not even English?' sneered M. Dupont.

'Not even English.'

'Not League of Nations, perhaps? But – Bah! Why do I argue? They speak French. Not even a Bosch would deny it. It needs an Englishman—'

A beautiful wrangle, thought Mr Barnstaple. There was no Utopian present to undeceive M. Dupont and he stuck to his belief mag-nificently. With a mixture of pity and derision and anger, Mr Barnsta-ple listened to this little band of lost human beings, in the twilight of a vast, strange and possibly inimical world, growing more and more fierce and keen in a dispute over the claims of their three nations to 'dominate' Utopia, claims based entirely upon greeds and misconceptions. Their voices rose to shouts and sank to passionate intensity as their lifelong habits of national egotism reasserted themselves. Mr Hunker would hear nothing of any 'Empire'; M. Dupont would hear of nothing but the supreme claim of France. Mr Catskill twisted and turned. To Mr Barnstaple this conflict of patriotic prepossessions seemed like a dog-fight on a sinking ship. But at last Mr Catskill, persistent and ingenious, made headway against his two antagonists.

He stood at the end of the table explaining that he had used the word Empire loosely, apologizing for using it, explaining that when he said Empire he had all Western Civilization in mind. 'When I said it,' he said, turning to Mr Hunker, 'I meant a common brotherhood of understanding.' He faced towards M. Dupont. 'I meant our tried and imperishable Entente.'

'There are at least no Russians here,' said M. Dupont. 'And no Germans.'

'True,' said Lord Barralonga. 'We start ahead of the Hun here, and we can keep ahead.'

'And I take it,' said Mr Hunker, 'that Japanese are barred.'

'No reason why we shouldn't start clean with a complete colour bar,' reflected Lord Barralonga. 'This seems to me a White Man's World.'

'At the same time,' said M. Dupont, coldly and insistently, 'you will forgive me if I ask you for some clearer definition of our present relationship and for some guarantee, some effective guarantee, that the immense sacrifices France has made and still makes in the cause of civilized life, will receive their proper recognition and their due reward in this adventure. . . .

'I ask only for justice,' said M. Dupont.

5

Indignation made Mr Barnstaple bold. He got down from his perch upon the wall and came up to the table.

'Are you mad,' he said, 'or am I?

'This squabble over flags and countries and fanciful rights and deserts – it is hopeless folly. Do you not realize even now the position we are in?'

His breath failed him for a moment and then he resumed.

'Are you incapable of thinking of human affairs except in terms of flags and fighting and conquest and robbery? Cannot you realize the proportion of things and the quality of this world into which we have fallen? As I have said already, we are like some band of savages in a show at Earl's Court, plotting the subjugation of London. We are like suppressed cannibals in the heart of a great city dreaming of a revival of our ancient and forgotten filthiness. What are our chances in this fantastic struggle?'

Mr Ridley spoke reprovingly. 'You're forgetting everythink you just been told. Everythink. 'Arf their population is laid out with flu and measles. And there's no such thing as a 'ealthy fighting will left in all Utopia.'

'Precisely,' said Mr Catskill.

'Well, suppose you have chances? If that makes your scheme the more hopeful, it also makes it the more horrible. Here we are lifted up out of the troubles of our time to a vision, to a reality of civilization such as our own world can only hope to climb to in scores of centuries! Here is a world at peace, splendid, happy, full of wisdom and hope! If our puny strength and base cunning can contrive it, we are to shatter it all! We are proposing to wreck a world! I tell you it is not an adventure. It is a crime. It is an abomination. I will have no part in it. I am against you in this attempt.'

Father Amerton would have spoken but Mr Burleigh arrested him by a gesture.

'What would *you* have us do?' asked Mr Burleigh.

'Submit to their science. Learn what we can from them. In a little while we may be cured of our inherent poisons and we may be permitted to return from this outlying desert of mines and turbines and rock, to those gardens of habitation we have as yet scarcely seen. There we too may learn something of civilization. ... In the end we may even go back to our own disordered world – with knowledge, with hope and help, missionaries of a new order.'

'But why—?' began Father Amerton.

Again Mr Burleigh took the word. 'Everything you say,' he remarked, 'rests on unproven assumptions. You choose to see this Utopia through rose-tinted glasses. We others – for it is' – he counted – 'eleven to one against you – see things without such favourable preconceptions.'

'And may I ask, Sir,' said Father Amerton, springing to his feet and hitting the table a blow that set all the glasses talking. 'May I ask, who you are, to set yourself up as a judge and censor of the common opinion of mankind? For I tell you, Sir, that here in this lonely and wicked and strange world, we here, we twelve, do represent mankind. We are the advance guard, the pioneers – in the new world that God has given us, even as He gave Canaan to Israel His chosen, three thousand years ago. Who are *you*—'

'Exactly,' said Penk. 'Who are you?'

And Mr Ridley reinforced him with a shout: 'Oo the 'ell are *you?*'

Mr Barnstaple had no platform skill to meet so direct an attack. He stood helpless. Astonishingly Lady Stella came to his rescue.

'That isn't fair, Father Amerton,' she said. 'Mr Barnstaple, whoever he is, has a perfect right to express his own opinion.'

'And having expressed it,' said Mr Catskill, who had been walking up and down on the other side of the table to that on which Mr Barnstaple stood, 'M'm, having expressed it, to allow us to proceed with the business in hand. I suppose it was inevitable that we should find the conscientious objector in our midst – even in Utopia. The rest of us, I take it, are very much of one mind about our situation.'

'We are,' said Mr Mush, regarding Mr Barnstaple with a malevolent expression.

'Very well. Then I suppose we must follow the precedents established for such cases. We will not ask Mr – Mr Bastaple to share the dangers – and the honours – of a combatant. We will ask him merely to do civilian work of a helpful nature—'

Mr Barnstaple held up his hand. 'No,' he said. 'I am not disposed to be helpful. I do not recognize the analogy of the situation to the needs of the Great War, and, anyhow, I am entirely opposed to this project – this brigandage of a civilization. You cannot call me a conscientious objector to fighting, because I do not object to fighting in a just cause. But this adventure of yours is not a just cause. ... I implore you, Mr Burleigh, you who are not merely a politician, but a man of culture and a philosopher, to reconsider what it is we are being urged towards – towards acts of violence and mischief from which there will be no drawing back!'

'Mr Barnstaple,' said Mr Burleigh with grave dignity and something like a note of reproach in his voice, 'I *have* considered. But I think I may venture to say that I am a man of some experience, some traditional experience, in human affairs. I may not altogether agree with my friend Mr Catskill. Nay! I will go further and say that in many respects I do *not* agree with him. If I were the autocrat here I would say that we have to offer these Utopians resistance – for our self-respect – but not to offer them the violent and aggressive resistance that he contemplates. I think we could be far more subtle, far more elaborate, and far more successful than Mr Catskill is likely to be. But that is my own opinion. Neither Mr Hunker nor Lord Barralonga, nor Mr Mush, nor M. Dupont shares it. Nor do Mr – our friends, the ah! – technical engineers here share it. And what I do perceive to be imperative upon our little band of Earthlings, lost here in a strange universe, is *unity of action*. Whatever else betide, dissension must not betray us. We must hold together and act together as one body. Discuss if you will, when there is any time for discussion, but in the end *decide*. And having decided abide loyally by the decision. Upon the need of securing a hostage or two I have no manner of doubt whatever. Mr Catskill is right.'

Mr Barnstaple was a bad debater. 'But these Utopians are as human as we are,' he said. 'All that is most sane and civilized in ourselves is with them.'

Mr Ridley interrupted in a voice designedly rough. 'Oh Lord!' he said. 'We can't go on jawing 'ere for ever. It's sunset, and Mr – this gentleman 'as 'ad 'is say, and more than 'is say. We ought to have our places and know what is expected of us before night. May I propose that we elect Mr Catskill our Captain with full military powers?'

'I second that,' said Mr Burleigh with grave humility.

'Perhaps M. Dupont,' said Mr Catskill, 'will act with me as associated Captain, representing our glorious ally, his own great country.'

'In the absence of a more worthy representative,' acquiesced M. Dupont, 'and to see that French interests are duly respected.'

'And if Mr Hunker would act as my lieutenant? . . . Lord Barralonga will be our quartermaster and Father Amerton our chaplain and censor. Mr Burleigh, it goes without saying, will be our civil head.'

Mr Hunker coughed. He frowned with the expression of one who makes a difficult explanation. 'I won't be exactly lieutenant,' he said. 'I'll take no official position. I've a sort of distaste for – foreign entanglements. I'll be a looker-on – who helps. But I think you will find you can count on me, Gentlemen – when help is needed.'

Mr Catskill seated himself at the head of the table and indicated the chair next to his for M. Dupont. Miss Greeta Grey seated herself on his other hand between him and Mr Hunker. Mr Burleigh remained in his place, a chair or so from Mr Hunker. The rest came and stood round the Captain except Lady Stella and Mr Barnstaple.

Almost ostentatiously Mr Barnstaple turned his back on the new command. Lady Stella, he saw, remained seated far down the table, looking dubiously at the little crowd of people at the end. Then her eyes went to the desolate mountain crest beyond.

She shivered violently and stood up. 'It's going to be very cold here after sunset,' she said, with nobody heeding her. 'I shall go and unpack a wrap.'

She walked slowly to her quarters and did not reappear.

Mr Barnstaple did not want to seem to listen to this Council of War. He walked to the wall of the old castle and up a flight of stone steps and along the rampart to the peak of the headland. Here the shattering and beating sound of the waters in the two convergent canyons was very loud.

There was still a bright upper rim of sunlit rock on the mountain face behind, but all the rest of the world was now in a deepening blue shadow, and a fleecy white mist was gathering in the canyons below and hiding the noisy torrents. It drifted up almost to the level of the little bridge that spanned the narrower canyon to a railed stepway from the crest on the further side. For the first time since he had arrived in Utopia Mr Barnstaple felt a chill in the air. And loneliness like a pain.

Up the broader of the two meeting canyons some sort of engineering work was going on and periodic flashes lit the drifting mist. Far away over the mountains a solitary aeroplane, very high, caught the sun's rays ever and again and sent down quivering flashes of dazzling golden light, and then, as it wheeled about, vanished again in the deepening blue.

He looked down into the great courtyard of the ancient castle below him. The modern buildings in the twilight looked like phantom pavilions amidst the archaic masonry. Someone had brought a light, and Captain Rupert Catskill, the new Cortez, was writing orders, while his Commando stood about him

The light shone on the face and shoulders and arms of Miss Greeta Grey; she was peering over the Captain's arm to see what he was writing. And as Mr Barnstaple looked he saw her raise her hand suddenly to conceal an involuntary yawn.

CHAPTER THE THIRD

Mr Barnstaple as a Traitor to Mankind

I

Mr Barnstaple spent a large part of the night sitting upon his bed and brooding over the incalculable elements of the situation in which he found himself.

What could he do? What ought he to do? Where did his loyalty lie? The dark traditions and infections of the Earth had turned this wonderful encounter into an ugly and dangerous antagonism far too swiftly for him to adjust his mind to the new situation. Before him now only two possibilities seemed open. Either the Utopians would prove themselves altogether the stronger and the wiser and he and all his fellow pirates would be crushed and killed like vermin, or the desperate ambitions of Mr Catskill would be realized and they would become a spreading sore in the fair body of this noble civilization, a band of robbers and destroyers, dragging Utopia year by year and age by age back to terrestrial conditions. There seemed only one escape from the dilemma; to get away from this fastness to the Utopians, to reveal the whole scheme of the Earthlings to them, and to throw himself and his associates upon their mercy. But this must be done soon, before the hostages were seized and bloodshed began.

But in the first place it might be very difficult now to get away from the Earthling band. Mr Catskill would already have organized watchers and sentinels, and the peculiar position of the crag exposed every avenue of escape. And in the next place Mr Barnstaple had a lifelong habit of mind which predisposed him against tale-bearing and dissentient action. His school training had moulded him into sub-

335

servience to any group or gang in which he found himself; his form, his side, his house, his school, his club, his party and so forth. Yet his intelligence and his limitless curiosities had always been opposed to these narrow conspiracies against the world at large. His spirit had made him an uncomfortable rebel throughout his whole earthly existence. He loathed political parties and political leaders, he despised and rejected nationalism and imperialism and all the tawdry loyalties associated with them; the aggressive conqueror, the grabbing financier, the shoving business man, he hated as he hated wasps, rats, hyenas, sharks, fleas, nettles and the like: all his life he had been a citizen of Utopia exiled upon Earth. After his fashion he had sought to serve Utopia. Why should he not serve Utopia now? Because his band was a little and desperate band, that was no reason why he should serve the things he hated. If they were a desperate crew, the fact remained that they were also, as a whole, an evil crew. There is no reason why liberalism should degenerate into a morbid passion for minorities. . . .

Only two persons among the Earthlings, Lady Stella and Mr Burleigh, held any of his sympathy. And he had his doubts about Mr Burleigh. Mr Burleigh was one of those strange people who seem to understand everything and feel nothing. He impressed Mr Barnstaple as being intelligently irresponsible. Wasn't that really more evil than being unintelligently adventurous like Hunker or Barralonga?

Mr Barnstaple's mind returned from a long excursion in ethics to the realities about him. Tomorrow he would survey the position and make his plans, and perhaps in the twilight he would slip away.

It was entirely in his character to defer action in this way for the better part of the day. His life had been one of deferred action almost from the beginning.

2

But events could not wait for Mr Barnstaple.

He was called at dawn by Penk, who told him that henceforth the garrison would be aroused every morning by an electric hooter he and Ridley had contrived. As Penk spoke a devastating howl from this contrivance inaugurated the new era. He handed Mr Barnstaple a slip of paper torn from a note-book on which Mr Catskill had written: —

'Non-comb. Barnaby. To assist Ridley prepare breakfast, lunch and dinner, times and menu on mess-room wall, clear away and wash up smartly and at other times to be at disposal of Lt. Hunker, in chemical labouratory for experimenting and bomb-making. Keep labouratory clean.'

'That's your job,' said Penk. 'Ridley's waitin' for you.'

'Well,' said Mr Barnstaple, and got up. It was no use precipitating a quarrel if he was to escape. So he went to the scarred and bandaged Ridley, and they produced a very good imitation of a British military kitchen in that great raw year, 1914.

Everyone was turned out to breakfast at half-past six by a second solo on the hooter. The men were paraded and inspected by Mr Catskill, with M. Dupont standing beside him; Mr Hunker stood parallel with these two and a few yards away; all the other men fell in except Mr Burleigh, who was to be civil commander in Utopia, and was, in that capacity, in bed, and Mr Barnstaple the non-combatant. Miss Greeta Grey and Lady Stella sat in a sunny corner of the courtyard sewing at a flag. It was to be a blue flag with a white star, a design sufficiently unlike any existing national flag to avoid wounding the patriotic susceptibilities of any of the party. It was to represent the Earthling League of Nations.

After the parade the little garrison dispersed to its various posts and duties, M. Dupont assumed the chief command, and Mr Catskill, who had watched all night, went to lie down. He had the Napoleonic quality of going off to sleep for an hour or so at any time in the day.

Mr Penk went up to the top of the castle, where the hooter was installed, to keep a look out.

There were some moments to be snatched between the time when Mr Barnstaple had finished with Ridley and the time when Hunker would discover his help was available, and this time he devoted to an inspection of the castle wall on the side of the slopes. While he was standing on the old rampart, weighing his chances of slipping away that evening in the twilight, an aeroplane appeared above the crag and came down upon the nearer slope. Two Utopians descended, talked with their aviator for a time, and then turned their faces towards the fastness of the Earthlings.

A single note of the hooter brought out Mr Catskill upon the rampart beside Mr Barnstaple. He produced a field-glass and surveyed the approaching figures.

'Serpentine and Cedar,' he said, lowering his field-glass. 'And they come alone. Good.'

He turned round and signalled with his hand to Penk, who responded with two short whoops of his instrument. This was the signal for a general assembly.

Down below in the courtyard appeared the rest of the Allied force and Mr Hunker and fell in with a reasonable imitation of discipline.

Mr Catskill passed Mr Barnstaple without taking any notice of him, joined M. Dupont, Mr Hunker and their subordinates below and proceeded to instruct them in his plans for the forthcoming crisis. Mr Barnstaple could not hear what was said. He noted with sardonic disapproval that each man, as Mr Catskill finished with him, clicked his heels together and saluted. Then at a word of command they dispersed to their posts.

There was a partly ruined flight of steps leading down from the general level of the courtyard through this great archway in the wall that gave access to and from the slopes below. Ridley and Mush went down to the right of these steps and placed themselves below a projecting mass of masonry so as to be hidden from anyone approaching from below. Father Amerton and Mr Hunker concealed themselves similarly to the left. Father Amerton, Mr Barnstaple noted, had been given a coil of rope, and then his roving eye discovered Mr Mush glancing at a pistol in his hand and then replacing it in his pocket. Lord Barralonga took up a position for himself some steps above Mr Mush and produced a revolver which he held in his one efficient hand. Mr Catskill remained at the head of the stairs. He also was holding a revolver. He turned to the citadel, considered the case of Penk for a moment, and then motioned him down to join the others. M. Dupont, armed with a stout table leg, placed himself at Mr Catskill's right hand.

For a time Mr Barnstaple watched these dispositions without any realization of their significance. Then his eyes went from the crouching figures within the castle to the two unsuspecting Utopians who were coming up towards them, and he realized that in a couple of minutes Serpentine and Cedar would be struggling in the grip of their captors.
. . .

He perceived he had to act. And his had been a contemplative, critical life with no habit of decision.

He found himself trembling violently.

3

He still desired some mediatory intervention even in these fatal last moments. He raised an arm and cried 'Hi!' as much to the Earthlings below as to the Utopians without. No one noticed either his gesture or his feeble cry.

Then his will seemed to break through a tangle of obstacles to one simple idea. Serpentine and Cedar must not be seized. He was amazed and indignant at his own vacillation. Of course they must not be seized! This foolery must be thwarted forthwith. In four strides he was on the wall above the archway and now he was shouting loud and clear. 'Danger!' he shouted. 'Danger!' and again 'Danger!'

He heard Catskill's cry of astonishment and then a pistol bullet whipped through the air close to him.

Serpentine stopped short and looked up, touched Cedar's arm and pointed.

'These Earthlings want to imprison you. Don't come here! Danger!' yelled Mr Barnstaple waving his arms and '*pat, pat, pat,*' Mr Catskill experienced the disappointments of revolver shooting.

Serpentine and Cedar were turning back – but slowly and hesitatingly.

For a moment Mr Catskill knew not what to do. Then he flung himself down the steps, crying, 'After them! Stop them! Come on!'

'Go back!' cried Mr Barnstaple to the Utopians. 'Go back! Quickly! Quickly!'

Came a clatter of feet from below and then the eight men who constituted the combatant strength of the Earthling forces in Utopia emerged from under the archway running towards the two astonished Utopians. Mr Mush led, with Ridley at his heels; he was pointing his revolver and shouting. Next came M. Dupont zealous and active. Father Amerton brought up the rear with the rope.

'Go back!' screamed Mr Barnstaple, with his voice breaking.

Then he stopped shouting and watched – with his hands clenched.

The aviator was running down the slope from his machine to the assistance of Serpentine and Cedar. And above out of the blue two other aeroplanes had appeared.

The two Utopians disdained to hurry and in a few seconds their pursuers had come up with them. Hunker, Ridley and Mush led the attack. M. Dupont, flourishing his stick, was abreast with them but running out to the right as though he intended to get between them and the aviator. Mr Catskill and Penk were a little behind the leading three; the one-armed Barralonga was perhaps ten yards behind and Father Amerton had halted to re-coil his rope more conveniently.

There seemed to be a moment's parley and then Serpentine had moved quickly as if to seize Hunker. A pistol cracked and then another went off rapidly three times. 'Oh God!' cried Mr Barnstaple. 'Oh God!' as he saw Serpentine throw up his arms and fall backward, and then Cedar had grasped and lifted up Mush and hurled him at Mr Catskill and Penk, bowling both of them over into one indistinguishable heap. With a wild cry M. Dupont closed in on Cedar but not quickly enough. His club shot into the air as Cedar parried his blow, and then the Utopian stooped, caught him by a leg, overthrew him, lifted him and whirled him round as one might whirl a rabbit, to inflict a stunning blow on Mr Hunker.

Lord Barralonga ran back some paces and began shooting at the approaching aviator.

The confusion of legs and arms on the ground became three separate people again. Mr Catskill, shouting directions, made for Cedar, followed by Penk and Mush and, a moment after, by Hunker and Dupont. They clung to Cedar as hounds will cling to a boar. Time after time he flung them off him. Father Amerton hovered unhelpfully with his rope.

For some moments Mr Barnstaple's attention was concentrated upon this swaying and staggering attempt to overpower Cedar, and then he became aware of other Utopians running down the slope to join the fray. . . . The other two aeroplanes had landed.

Mr Catskill realized the coming of these reinforcements almost as soon as Mr Barnstaple. His shouts of 'Back! Back to the castle!' reached Mr Barnstaple's ears. The Earthlings scattered away from the tall dishevelled figure, hesitated, and began to walk and then run back towards the Castle.

And then Ridley turned and very deliberately shot Cedar, who clutched at his breast and fell into a sitting position.

The Earthlings retreated to the foot of the steps that led up through the archway into the castle, and stood there in a panting, bruised and ruffled group. Fifty yards away Serpentine lay still, the aviator whom Barralonga had shot writhed and moaned, and Cedar sat up with blood upon his chest trying to feel his back. Five other Utopians came hurrying to their assistance.

'What is all this firing?' said Lady Stella, suddenly at Mr Barnstaple's elbow.

'Have they caught their hostages?' asked Miss Greeta Grey.

'For the life of me!' said Mr Burleigh, who had come out upon the wall a yard or so away, 'this ought never to have happened. How did this get – *muffed*, Lady Stella?'

'I called out to them,' said Mr Barnstaple.

'*You* – called – out to them!' said Mr Burleigh incredulous.

'Treason I did not calculate upon,' came the wrathful voice of Mr Catskill ascending out of the archway.

4

For some moments Mr Barnstaple made no attempt to escape the danger that closed in upon him. He had always lived a life of very

340

great security and with him, as with so many highly civilized types, the power of apprehending personal danger was very largely atrophied. He was a spectator by temperament and training alike. He stood now as if he looked at himself, the central figure of a great and hopeless tragedy. The idea of flight came belatedly, in a reluctant and apologetic manner into his mind

'Shot as a traitor,' he said aloud. 'Shot as a traitor.'

There was that bridge over the narrow gorge. He might still get over that, if he went for it at once. If he was quick – quicker than they were. He was too intelligent to dash off for it; that would certainly have set the others running. He walked along the wall in a leisurely fashion past Mr Burleigh, himself too civilized to intervene. In a quickening stroll he gained the steps that led to the citadel. Then he stood still for a moment to survey the situation. Catskill was busy setting sentinels at the gate. Perhaps he had not thought yet of the little bridge and imagined that Mr Barnstaple was at his disposal at any time that suited him. Up the slope the Utopians were carrying off the dead or wounded men.

Mr Barnstaple ascended the steps as if buried in thought and stood on the citadel for some seconds, his hands in his trouser pockets, as if he surveyed the view. Then he turned to the winding staircase that went down to a sort of guard-room below. As soon as he was surely out of sight he began to think and move very quickly.

The guard-room was perplexing. It had five doors, any one of which except the one by which he had just entered the room might lead down to the staircase. Against one, however, stood a pile of neat packing-cases. That left three to choose from. He ran from one to the other leaving each door open. In each case stone steps ran down to a landing and a turning place. He stood hesitating at the third and noted that a cold draught came blowing up it. Surely that meant that this went down to the cliff face, or whence came the air? Surely this was it!

Should he shut the doors he had opened? No! Leave them all open.

He heard a clatter coming down the staircase from the citadel. Softly and swiftly he ran down the steps and halted for a second at the corner landing. He was compelled to stop and listen to the movements of his pursuers. 'This is the door to the bridge, Sir!' he heard Ridley cry, and then he heard Catskill say, 'The Tarpeian Rock,' and Barralonga, 'Exactly! Why should we waste a cartridge? Are you sure this goes to the bridge, Ridley?'

The footsteps pattered across the guard-room and passed – down one of the other staircases.

'A reprieve!' whispered Mr Barnstaple and then stopped aghast.

He was trapped! The staircase they were on was the staircase to the bridge!

They would go down as far as the bridge and as soon as they got to it they would see that he was neither on it nor on the steps on the opposite side of the gorge and that therefore he could not possibly have escaped. They would certainly bar that way either by closing and fastening any door there might be or, failing such a barrier, by setting a sentinel, and then they would come back and hunt for him at their leisure.

What was it Catskill had been saying? The Tarpeian Rock? . . .

Horrible!

They mustn't take him alive. . . .

He must fight like a rat in a corner and oblige them to shoot him. . . .

He went on down the staircase. It became very dark and then grew light again. It ended in an ordinary big cellar, which may once have been a gun-pit or magazine. It was fairly well lit by two unglazed windows cut in the rock. It now contained a store of provisions. Along one side stood an array of the flask-like bottles that were used for wine in Utopia; along the other was a miscellany of packing-cases and cubes wrapped in gold-leaf. He lifted one of the glass flasks by its neck. It would make an effective club. Suppose he made a sort of barrier of the packing-cases across the entrance and stood beside it and clubbed the pursuers as they came in! Glass and wine would smash over their skulls. . . . It would take time to make the barrier. . . . He chose and carried three of the larger flasks to the doorway where they would be handy for him. Then he had an inspiration and looked at the window.

He listened at the door of the staircase for a time. Not a sound came from above. He went to the window and lay down in the deep embrasure and wriggled forward until he could see out and up and down. The cliff below fell sheer; he could have spat on to the brawling torrent fifteen hundred feet perhaps below. The crag here was made up of almost vertical strata which projected and receded; a big buttress hid almost all of the bridge except the far end which seemed to be about twenty or thirty yards lower than the opening from which Mr Barnstaple was looking. Mr Catskill appeared upon this bridge, very small and distant, scrutinizing the rocky stair-way beyond the bridge. Mr Barnstaple withdrew his head hastily. Then very discreetly he peeped again. Mr Catskill was no longer to be seen. He was coming back.

To business! There was not much time.

In his earlier days before the great war had made travel dear and uncomfortable Mr Barnstaple had done some rock climbing in Switzerland and he had also had some experience in Cumberland and Wales. He surveyed now the rocks close at hand with an intelligent expertness. They were cut by almost horizontal joint planes into which there had been a considerable infiltration chiefly of white crystalline material. This stuff, which he guessed was calcite, had weathered more rapidly than the general material of the rock, leaving a series of irregular horizontal grooves. With luck it might be possible to work along the cliff face, turn the buttress and scramble to the bridge.

And then came an even more hopeful idea. He could easily get along the cliff face to the first recess, flatten himself there and remain until the Earthlings had searched his cellar. After they had searched he might creep back to the cellar. Even if they looked out of the window they would not see him and even if he left finger marks and so forth in the embrasure, they would be likely to conclude that he had either jumped or fallen down the crag into the gorge below. But at first it might be slow work negotiating the cliff face. . . . And this would cut him off from his weapons, the flasks. . . .

But the idea of hiding in the recess had taken a strong hold upon his imagination. Very cautiously he got out of the window, found a handhold, got his feet on to his ledge and began to work his way along towards his niche.

But there were unexpected difficulties, a gap of nearly five yards in the handhold – nothing. He had to flatten himself and trust to his feet and for a time he remained quite still in that position.

Further on was a rotten lump of the vein mineral and it broke away under him very disconcertingly, but happily his fingers had a grip and the other foot was firm. The detached crystals slithered down the rock face for a moment and then made no further sound. They had dropped into the void. For a time he was paralysed.

'I'm not in good form,' whispered Mr Barnstaple. 'I'm not in good form.'

He clung motionless and prayed.

With an effort he resumed his traverse.

He was at the very corner of the recess when some faint noise drew his eyes to the window from which he had emerged. Ridley's face was poked out slowly and cautiously, his eye red and fierce among his white bandages.

5

He did not at first see Mr Barnstaple. 'Gawd!' he said when he did so and withdrew his head hastily.

Came a sound of voices saying indistinguishable things.

Some inappropriate instinct kept Mr Barnstaple quite still, though he could have got into cover in the recess quite easily before Mr Catskill looked out revolver in hand.

For some moments they stared at each other in silence.

'Come back or I shoot,' said Mr Catskill unconvincingly.

'Shoot!' said Mr Barnstaple after a moment's reflection.

Mr Catskill craned his head out and stared down into the shadowy blue depths of the canyon. 'It isn't necessary,' he answered. 'We have to save cartridges.'

'You haven't the guts,' said Mr Barnstaple.

'It's not quite that,' said Mr Catskill.

'No,' said Mr Barnstaple, 'it isn't. You are fundamentally a civilized man.'

Mr Catskill scowled at him without hostility.

'You have a very good imagination,' Mr Barnstaple reflected. 'The trouble is that you have been so damnably educated. What is the trouble with you? You are be-Kiplinged. Empire and Anglo-Saxon and boy-scout and sleuth are the stuff in your mind. If I had gone to Eton I might have been the same as you are, I suppose.'

'Harrow,' corrected Mr Catskill.

'A perfectly *beastly* public school. Suburban place where the boys wear chignons and straw haloes. I might have guessed Harrow. But it's queer I bear you no malice. Given decent ideas you might have been very different from what you are. If I had been your schoolmaster – But it's too late now.'

'It is,' said Mr Rupert Catskill, smiling genially, and cocked his eye down into the canyon.

Mr Barnstaple began to feel for his ledge round the corner with one foot.

'Don't go for a minute,' said Mr Catskill. 'I'm not going to shoot.'

A voice from within, probably Lord Barralonga's, said something about heaving a rock at Mr Barnstaple. Someone else, probably Ridley, approved ferociously.

'Not without due form of trial,' said Mr Catskill over his shoulder. His face was inscrutable, but a fantastic idea began to run about in Mr Barnstaple's mind that Mr Catskill did not want to have him killed. He had thought about things and he wanted him now to escape – to the Utopians and perhaps rig up some sort of settlement with them.

'We intend to try you, Sir,' said Mr Catskill. 'We intend to try you. We cite you to appear.'

Mr Catskill moistened his lips and considered. 'The court will sit almost at once.' His little bright brown eyes estimated the chances of Mr Barnstaple's position very rapidly. He craned towards the bridge. 'We shall not waste time over our procedure,' he said. 'And I have little doubt of our verdict. We shall condemn you to death. So – there you are, Sir. I doubt if we shall be more than a quarter of an hour before your fate is legally settled.'

He glanced up trying to see the crest of the crag. 'We shall probably throw rocks,' he said.

'*Moriturus te saluo*,' said Mr Barnstaple with an air of making a witty remark. 'If you will forgive me I will go on now to find a more comfortable position.'

Mr Catskill remained looking hard at him.

'I've never borne you any ill-will,' said Mr Barnstaple. 'Had I been your schoolmaster everything might have been different. Thanks for the quarter of an hour more you give me. And if by any chance—'

'Exactly,' said Mr Catskill.

They understood one another.

When Mr Barnstaple stepped round the bend into the recess Mr Catskill was still looking out and Lord Barralonga was faintly audible advocating the immediate heaving of rocks.

6

The ways of the human mind are past finding out. From desperation Mr Barnstaple's mood had passed to exhilaration. His first sick horror of climbing above this immense height had given place now to an almost boyish assurance. His sense of immediate death had gone. He was appreciating this adventure, indeed he was enjoying it, with an entire disregard now of how it was to end.

He made fairly good time until he got to the angle of the buttress, though his arms began to ache rather badly, and then he had a shock. He had now a full view of the bridge and up the narrow gorge. The ledge he was working along did not run to the bridge at all. It ran a good thirty feet below it. And what was worse, between himself and the bridge were two gullies and chimneys of uncertain depth. At this discovery he regretted for the first time that he had not stayed in the cellar and made a fight for it there.

He had some minutes of indecision – with the ache in his arms increasing.

He was roused from his inaction by what he thought at first was the shadow of a swift-flying bird on the rock. Presently it returned. He hoped he was not to be assailed by birds. He had read a story – but never mind that now.

Then came a loud crack overhead, and he glanced up to see a lump of rock which had just struck a little bulge above him fly to fragments. From which incident he gathered firstly that the court had delivered an adverse verdict rather in advance of Mr Catskill's time, and secondly that he was visible from above. He resumed his traverse towards the shelter of the gully with feverish energy.

The gully was better than he expected, a chimney; difficult, he thought, to ascend, but quite practicable downward. It was completely overhung. And perhaps a hundred feet below there was a sort of step in it that gave a quite broad recess, sheltered from above and with room enough for a man to sprawl on it if he wanted to do so. There would be rest for Mr Barnstaple's arms, and without any needless delay he clambered down to it and abandoned himself to the delightful sensation of not holding on to anything. He was out of sight and out of reach of his Earthling pursuers.

In the back of the recess was a trickle of water. He drank and began to think of food and to regret that he had not brought some provision with him from the store in the cellar. He might have opened one of those gold-leaf-covered cubes or pocketed a small flask of wine. Wine would be very heartening just now. But it did not do to think of that. He stayed for a long time, as it seemed to him, on this precious shelf, scrutinizing the chimney below very carefully. It seemed quite practicable for a long way down. The sides became very smooth, but they seemed close enough together to get down with his back against one side and his feet against the other.

He looked at his wrist-watch. It was still not nine o'clock in the morning – it was about ten minutes to nine. He had been called by Ridley before half-past five. At half-past six he had been handing out breakfast in the courtyard. Serpentine and Cedar must have appeared about eight o'clock. In about ten minutes Serpentine had been murdered. Then the flight and the pursuit. How quickly things had happened! . . .

He had all day before him. He would resume his descent at half-past nine. Until then he would rest. . . . It was absurd to feel hungry yet. . . .

He was climbing again before half-past nine. For perhaps a hundred feet it was easy. Then by imperceptible degrees the gully broadened. He only realized it when he found himself slipping. He slipped, struggling furiously, for perhaps twenty feet, and then fell outright another ten and struck a rock and was held by a second shelf much broader than the one above. He came down on it with a jarring concussion and rolled – happily he rolled inward. He was bruised, but not seriously hurt. 'My luck,' he said. 'My luck holds good.'

He rested for a time, and then, confident that things would be all right, set himself to inspect the next stage of his descent. It was with a sort of incredulity that he discovered the chimney below his shelf was absolutely unclimbable. It was just a straight, smooth rock on either side for twenty yards at least and six feet wide. He might as well fling himself over at once as try to get down that. Then he saw that it was equally impossible to retrace his steps. He could not believe it; it seemed too silly. He laughed as one might laugh if one found one's own mother refusing to recognize one after a day's absence.

Then abruptly he stopped laughing.

He repeated every point in his examination. He fingered the smooth rocks about him. 'But this is absurd,' he said breaking out into a cold perspiration. There was no way out of this corner into which he had so painfully and labouriously got himself. He could neither go on nor go back. He was caught. His luck had given out.

7

At midday by his wrist-watch Mr Barnstaple was sitting in his recess as a weary invalid suffering from some incurable disease might sit up in an arm-chair during a temporary respite from pain, with nothing to do and no hope before him. There was not one chance in ten thousand that anything could happen to release him from this trap into which he had clambered. There was a trickle of water at the back but no food, not even a grass blade to nibble. Unless he saw fit to pitch himself over into the gorge, he must starve to death. .... It would perhaps be cold at nights but not cold enough to kill him.

To this end he had come then out of the worried journalism of London and the domesticities of Sydenham.

Queer journey it was that he and the Yellow Peril had made! – Camberwell, Victoria, Hounslow, Slough, Utopia, the mountain paradise, a hundred fascinating and tantalizing glimpses of a world of real happiness and order, that long, long aeroplane flight half round a world. .... And now – death.

The idea of abbreviating his sufferings by jumping over had no appeal for him. He would stay here and suffer such suffering as there might be before the end. And three hundred yards away or so were his fellow Earthlings, also awaiting their fate. .... It was amazing. It was prosaic. ....

After all to this or something like this most humanity had to come.

Sooner or later people had to lie and suffer, they had to think and then think feverishly and then weakly, and so fade to a final cessation of thought.

On the whole, he thought, it was preferable to die in this fashion, preferable to a sudden death, it was worth while to look death in the face for a time, to have leisure to write *finis* in one's mind, to think over life and such living as one had done and to think it over with a detachment, an independence, that only an entire inability to alter one jot of it now could give.

At present his mind was clear and calm; a bleak serenity like a clear winter sky possessed him. There was suffering ahead, he knew, but he did not believe it would be intolerable suffering. If it proved intolerable the canyon yawned below. In that respect this shelf or rock was a better death bed than most, a more convenient death bed. Your sick bed presented pain with a wide margin, set it up for your too complete examination. But to starve was not so very dreadful, he had read; hunger and pain there would be, most distressful about the third day, and after that one became feeble and did not feel so much. It would not be like the torture of many cancer cases or the agony of brain fever; it would not be one tithe as bad as that. Lonely it would be. But is one much less lonely on a death bed at home? They come and say, 'There! there!' and do little serviceable things – but are there any other interchanges? . . . You go your solitary way, speech and movement and the desire to speak or move passing from you, and their voices fade. . . . Everywhere death is a very solitary act, a going apart. . . .

A younger man would probably have found this loneliness in the gorge very terrible, but Mr Barnstaple had outlived the intenser delusions of companionship. He would have liked a last talk with his boys and to have put his wife into a good frame of mind, but even these desires were perhaps more sentimental than real. When it came to talks with his boys he was apt to feel shy. As they had come to have personalities of their own and to grow through adolescence, he had felt more and more that talking intimately to them was an invasion of their right to grow up along their own lines. And they too he felt were shy with him, defensively shy. Perhaps later on sons came back to a man – that was a later on that he would never know now. But he wished he could have let them know what had happened to him. That troubled him. It would set him right in their eyes, it would perhaps be better for their characters, if they did not think – as they were almost bound to think – that he had run away from them or lapsed mentally or even fallen into bad company and been made away with.

As it was they might be worried and ashamed, needlessly, or put to expense to find out where he was, and that would be a pity.

One had to die. Many men had died as he was going to die, fallen into strange places, lost in dark caverns, marooned on desert islands, astray in the Australian bush, imprisoned and left to perish. It was good to die without great anguish or insult. He thought of the myriads of men who had been crucified by the Romans – was it eight thousand or was it ten thousand of the army of Spartacus that they killed in that fashion along the Appian Way? – of negroes hung in chains to starve, and of an endless variety of such deaths. Shocking to young imaginations such things were and more fearful in thought than in reality. It is all a matter of a little more pain or a little less pain – but God will not have any great waste of pain. Cross, wheel, electric chair or bed of suffering – the thing is, you *die and have done.*

It was pleasant to find that one could think stoutly of these things. It was good to be caught and to find that one was not frantic. And Mr Barnstaple was surprised to find how little he cared, now that he faced the issue closely, whether he was immortal or whether he was not. He was quite prepared to find himself immortal or at least not ending with death, in whole or in part. It was ridiculous to be dogmatic and say that a part, an impression, of his conscience and even of his willing life might not go on in some fashion. But he found it impossible to imagine how that could be. It was unimaginable. It was not to be anticipated. He had no fear of that continuation. He had no thought nor fear of the possibility of punishment or cruelty. The universe had at times seemed to him to be very carelessly put together, but he had never believed that it was the work of a malignant imbecile. It impressed him as immensely careless but not as dominatingly cruel. He had been what he had been, weak and limited and sometimes silly, but the punishment of these defects lay in the defects themselves.

He ceased to think about his own death. He began to think of life generally, its present lowliness, its valiant aspiration. He found himself regretting bitterly that he was not to see more of this Utopian world, which was in so many respects so near an intimation of what our own world may become. It had been very heartening to see human dreams and human ideals vindicated by realization, but it was distressing to have had the vision snatched away while he was still only beginning to examine it. He found himself asking questions that had no answers for him, about economics, about love and struggle. Anyhow, he was glad to have seen as much as he had. It was good to have been purged by this vision and altogether lifted out of the dreary hopelessness of Mr Peeve, to have got life into perspective again.

The passions and conflicts and discomforts of AD 1921 were the discomforts of the fever of an uninoculated world. The Age of Confusion on the Earth also would, in its own time, work itself out, thanks to a certain obscure and indomitable righteousness in the blood of the human type. Squatting in a hole in the cliff of the great crag, with unclimbable heights and depths above him and below, chilly, hungry and uncomfortable, this thought was a profound comfort to the strangely constituted mind of Mr Barnstaple.

But how miserably had he and his companions failed to rise to the great occasions of Utopia! No one had raised an effectual hand to restrain the puerile imaginations of Mr Catskill and the mere brutal aggressiveness of his companions. How invincibly had Father Amerton headed for the rôle of the ranting, hating, persecuting, quarrel-making priest. How pitifully weak and dishonest Mr Burleigh – and himself scarcely better! disapproving always and always in ineffective opposition. What an unintelligent beauty-cow that woman Greeta Grey was, receptive, acquisitive, impenetrable to any idea but the idea of what was due to her as a yielding female! Lady Stella was of finer clay, but fired to no service. Women, he thought, had not been well represented in this chance expedition, just one waster and one ineffective. Was that a fair sample of Earth's womankind?

All the use these Earthlings had had for Utopia was to turn it back as speedily as possible to the aggressions, subjugations, cruelties and disorders of the Age of Confusion to which they belonged. Serpentine and Cedar, the man of scientific power and the man of healing, they had sought to make hostages to disorder, and failing that they had killed or sought to kill them.

They had tried to bring back Utopia to the state of Earth, and indeed but for the folly, malice and weakness of men Earth was now Utopia. Old Earth was Utopia now, a garden and a glory, the Earthly Paradise, except that it was trampled to dust and ruin by its Catskills, Hunkers, Barralongas, Ridleys, Duponts and their kind. Against their hasty trampling folly nothing was pitted, it seemed, in the whole wide world at present but the whinings of the Peeves, the acquiescent disapproval of the Burleighs and such immeasurable ineffectiveness as his own protest. And a few writers and teachers who produced results at present untraceable.

Once more Mr Barnstaple found himself thinking of his old friend, the school inspector and schoolbook writer, who had worked so steadfastly and broken down and died so pitifully. He had worked for Utopia all his days. Were there hundreds or thousands of such Utopians yet on earth? What magic upheld them?

'I wish I could get some message through to them,' said Mr Barnstaple, 'to hearten them.'

For it was true, though he himself had to starve and die like a beast fallen into a pit, nevertheless Utopia triumphed and would triumph. The grabbers and fighters, the persecutors and patriots, the lynchers and boycotters and all the riff-raff of shortsighted human violence, crowded on to final defeat. Even in their lives they know no happiness, they drive from excitement to excitement and from gratification to exhaustion. Their enterprises and successes, their wars and glories, flare and pass. Only the true thing grows, the truth, the clear idea, year by year and age by age, slowly and invincibly as a diamond grows amidst the darkness and pressures of the earth, or as the dawn grows amidst the guttering lights of some belated orgy.

What would be the end of those poor little people up above there? Their hold on life was even more precarious than his own, for he might lie and starve here slowly for weeks before his mind gave its last flicker. But they had openly pitted themselves against the might and wisdom of Utopia, and even now the ordered power of that world must be closing in upon them. He still had a faint irrational remorse for his betrayal of Catskill's ambush. He smiled now at the passionate conviction he had felt at the time that if once Catskill could capture his hostages, Earth might prevail over Utopia. That conviction had rushed him into action. His weak cries had seemed to be all that was left to avert this monstrous disaster. But suppose he had not been there at all, or suppose he had obeyed the lingering instinct of fellowship that urged him to fight with the others; what then?

When he recalled the sight of Cedar throwing Mush about as one might throw a lap-dog about, and the height and shape of Serpentine, he doubted whether even upon the stairs in the archway it would have been possible for the Earthlings to have overpowered these two. The revolvers would have come into use just as they had come into use upon the slope, and Catskill would have got no hostages but only two murdered men.

How unutterably silly the whole scheme of Catskill had been! But it was no sillier than the behaviour of Catskill, Burleigh and the rest of the world's statesmen had been on earth, during the last few years. At times during the world agony of the great war it had seemed that Utopia drew near to earth. The black clouds and smoke of these dark years had been shot with the light of strange hopes, with the promise of a world reborn. But the nationalists, financiers, priests and patriots had brought all those hopes to nothing. They had trusted to old poisons and infections and to the weak resistances of the civilized spirit. They had counted their weapons and set their ambushes and kept their women busy sewing flags of discord. ....

For a time they had killed hope, but only for a time. For Hope, the redeemer of mankind, there is perpetual resurrection.

'Utopia will win,' said Mr Barnstaple and for a time he sat listening to a sound he had heard before without heeding it very greatly, a purring throb in the rocks about him, like the running of some great machine. It grew louder and then faded down to the imperceptible again.

His thoughts came back to his erstwhile companions. He hoped they were not too miserable or afraid up there. He was particularly desirous that something should happen to keep up Lady Stella's courage. He worried affectionately about Lady Stella. For the rest it would be as well if they remained actively combative to the end. Possibly they were all toiling at some preposterous and wildly hopeful defensive scheme of Catskill's. Except Mr Burleigh who would be resting – convinced that for him at least there would still be a gentlemanly way out. And probably not much afraid if there wasn't. Amerton and possibly Mush might lapse into a religious revival – that would irritate the others a little, or possibly even provide a mental opiate for Lady Stella and Miss Greeta Grey. Then for Penk there was wine in the cellar. ....

They would follow the laws of their being, they would do the things that nature and habit would require of them. What else was possible?

Mr Barnstaple plunged into a metaphysical gulf. ....

Presently he caught himself looking at his wrist-watch. It was twenty minutes past twelve. He was looking at his watch more and more frequently – or time was going more slowly. .... Should he wind his watch or let it run down? He was already feeling very hungry. That could not be real hunger yet; it must be his imagination getting out of control.

The End of Quarantine Crag

I

Mr Barnstaple awoke slowly and reluctantly from a dream about cookery. He was Soyer, the celebrated chef of the Reform Club, and he was inventing and tasting new dishes. But in the pleasant way of dreamland he was not only Soyer, but at the same time he was a very clever Utopian biologist and also God Almighty. So that he could not only make new dishes, but also make new vegetables and meats to go into them. He was particularly interested in a new sort of fowl, the Chateaubriand breed of fowls, which was to combine the rich quality of very good beefsteak with the size and delicacy of a fowl's breast. And he wanted to stuff it with a blend of pimento, onion and mushroom – except that the mushroom wasn't quite the thing. The mushrooms – he tasted them – needed just the least little modification. And into the dream came an assistant cook, several assistant cooks, all naked as Utopians, bearing fowls from the pantry and saying that they had not kept, they had gone 'high' and they were going higher. In order to illustrate this idea of their going higher these assistant cooks lifted the fowls above their heads and then began to climb the walls of the kitchen, which were rocky and for a kitchen remarkably close together. Their figures became dark. They were thrown up in black outline against the luminous steam arising from a cauldron of boiling soup. It was boiling soup, and yet it was cold soup and cold steam.

Mr Barnstaple was awake.

In the place of luminous steam there was mist, brightly moonlit mist, filling the gorge. It threw up the figures of the two Utopians in black silhouette. . . .

What Utopians?

His mind struggled between dreaming and waking. He started up rigidly attentive. They moved with easy gestures, quite unaware of his presence so close to them. They had already got a thin rope ladder fixed to some point overhead, but how they had managed to do this he did not know. One still stood on the shelf, the other swayed above him stretched across the gully clinging to the rope with his feet against the rock. The head of a third figure appeared above the edge of the shelf. It swayed from side to side. He was evidently coming up by a second rope ladder. Some sort of discussion was in progress. It was borne in upon Mr Barnstaple that this last comer thought that he and his companions had clambered high enough, but that the uppermost man insisted they should go higher. In a few moments the matter was settled.

The uppermost Utopian became very active, lunged upward, swung out and vanished by jerks out of Mr Barnstaple's field of view. His companions followed him and one after the other was lost to sight, leaving nothing visible but the convulsively agitated rope ladder and a dangling rope that they seemed to be dragging up the crag with them.

Mr Barnstaple's taut muscles relaxed. He yawned silently, stretched his painful limbs and stood up very cautiously. He peered up the gully. The Utopians seemed to have reached the shelf above and to be busy there. The rope that had dangled became taut. They were hauling up something from below. It was a large bundle, possibly of tools or weapons or material wrapped in something that deadened its impacts against the rock. It jumped into view, hung spinning for a moment and was then snatched upward as the Utopians took in a fresh reef of rope. A period of silence followed.

He heard a metallic clang and then, thud, thud, a dull intermittent hammering. Then he jumped back as the end of a thin rope, apparently running over a pulley, dropped past him. The sounds from above now were like filing and then some bits of rock fell past him into the void.

2

He did not know what to do. He was afraid to call to these Utopians and make his presence known to them. After the murder of Serpentine he was very doubtful how a Utopian would behave to an Earthling found hiding in a dark corner.

He examined the rope ladder that had brought these Utopians to his level. It was held by a long spike the end of which was buried in the rock at the side of the gully. Possibly this spike had been fired at the rock from below while he was asleep. The ladder was made up of straight lengths and rings at intervals of perhaps two feet. It was of such light material that he would have doubted its capacity to bear a man if he had not seen the Utopians upon it. It occurred to him that he might descend by this now and take his chances with any Utopians who might be below. He could not very well bring himself to the attention of these three Utopians above except by some sudden and startling action which might provoke sudden and unpleasant responses, but if he appeared first clambering slowly from above, any Utopians beneath would have time to realize and consider the fact of his proximity before they dealt with him And also he was excessively eager to get down from this dreary ledge.

He gripped a ring, thrust a leg backwards over the edge of the shelf, listened for some moments to the little noises of the three workers above him, and then began his descent.

It was an enormous descent. Presently he found himself regretting that he had not begun counting the rings of the ladder. He must already have handed himself down hundreds. And still when he craned his neck to look down, the dark gulf yawned below. It had become very dark now. The moonlight did not cut down very deeply into the canyon and the faint reflection from the thin mists above was all there was to break the blackness. And even overhead the moonlight seemed to be passing.

Now he was near the rock, now it fell away and the rope ladder seemed to fall plumb into lightless bottomless space. He had to feel for each ring, and his bare feet and hands were already chafed and painful. And a new and disagreeable idea had come into his head – that some Utopian might presently come rushing up the ladder. But he would get notice of that because the rope would tighten and quiver, and he would be able to cry out, 'I am an Earthling coming down. I am a harmless Earthling.'

He began to cry out these words experimentally. The gorge re-echoed them, and there was no answering sound.

He became silent again, descending grimly and as steadily as possible, because now an intense desire to get off this infernal rope ladder and rest his hot hands and feet was overmastering every other motive.

Clang, clang and a flash of green light.

He became rigid peering into the depths of the canyon. Came the green flash again. It revealed the depths of the gorge, still as it seemed an immense distance below him. And up the gorge – something; he could not grasp what it was during that momentary revelation. At first he thought it was a huge serpent writhing its way down the gorge, and then he concluded it must be a big cable that was being brought along the gorge by a handful of Utopians. But how the three or four figures he had indistinctly seen could move this colossal rope he could not imagine. The head of this cable serpent seemed to be lifting itself obliquely up the cliff. Perhaps it was being dragged up by ropes he had not observed. He waited for a third flash, but none came. He listened. He could hear nothing but a throbbing sound he had already noted before, like the throbbing of an engine running very smoothly.

He resumed his descent.

When at last he reached a standing place it took him by surprise. The rope ladder fell past it for some yards and ended. He was swaying more and more and beginning to realize that the rope ladder came to an end, when he perceived the dim indication of a nearly horizontal gallery cut along the rock face. He put out a foot and felt an edge and swung away out from it. He was now so weary and exhausted that for a time he could not relinquish his grip on the rope ladder and get a footing on the shelf. At last he perceived how this could be done. He released his feet and gave himself a push away from the rock with them. He swung back into a convenient position for getting a foothold. He repeated this twice, and then had enough confidence to abandon his ladder and drop on to the shelf. The ladder dangled away from him into the darkness and then came wriggling back to tap him playfully and startlingly on the shoulder blade.

The gallery he found himself in seemed to follow a great vein of crystalline material along the cliff face. Borings as high as a man ran into the rock. He peered and felt his way along the gallery for a time. Manifestly if this was a mine there would be some way of ascending to it and descending from it into the gorge. The sound of the torrent was much louder now, and he judged he had perhaps come down two-thirds of the height of the crag. He was inclined to wait for daylight. The illuminated dial of his wrist-watch told him it was now four o'clock. It would not be long before dawn. He found a comfortable face of rock for his back and squatted down.

Dawn seemed to come very quickly, but in reality he dozed away the interval. When he glanced at his watch again it was half-past five.

He went to the edge of the gallery and peered up the gorge to where he had seen the cable. Things were pale and dim and very black and white, but perfectly clear. The walls of the canyon seemed to go up for ever and vanish at last in cloud. He had a glimpse of a Utopian below, who was presently hidden by the curve of the gorge. He guessed that the great cable must have been brought so close up to the Quarantine Crag as to be invisible to him.

He could find no down-going steps from the gallery, but some thirty or forty yards off were five or six cable ways running at a steep angle from the gallery to the opposite side of the gorge. They looked very black and distinct. He went along to them. Each was a carrier cable on which ran a small carrier trolley with a big hook below. Three of the carrier cables were empty, but on two the trolley was hauled up. Mr Barnstaple examined the trolleys and found a catch retained them. He turned over one of these catches and the trolley ran away promptly, nearly dropping him into the gulf. He saved himself by clutching the carrier cable. He watched the trolley swoop down like a bird to a broad stretch of sandy beach on the other side of the torrent and come to rest there. It seemed all right. Trembling violently, he turned to the remaining trolley.

His nerves and will were so exhausted now that it was a long time before he could bring himself to trust to the hook of the remaining trolley and to release its catch. Then smoothly and swiftly he swept across the gorge to the beach below. There were big heaps of crystalline mineral on this beach and a cable – evidently for raising it – came down out of the mists above from some invisible crane, but not a Utopian was in sight. He relinquished his hold and dropped safely on his feet. The beach broadened down-stream and he walked along it close to the edge of the torrent.

The light grew stronger as he went. The world ceased to be a world of greys and blacks; colour came back to things. Everything was heavily bedewed. And he was hungry and almost intolerably weary. The sand changed in its nature and became soft and heavy for his feet. He felt he could walk no further. He must wait for help. He sat down on a rock and looked up towards Quarantine Crag towering overhead.

3

Sheer and high the great headland rose like the prow of some gigantic ship behind the two deep blue canyons; a few wisps and layers of mist still hid from Mr Barnstaple its crest and the little bridge across the narrower gorge. The sky above between the streaks of mist was now an intense blue. And even as he gazed the mists swirled and dissolved, the rays of the rising sun smote the old castle to blinding gold, and the fastness of the Earthlings stood out clear and bright.

The bridge and the castle were very remote and all that part of the crag was like a little cap on the figure of a tall upstanding soldier.

Round beneath the level of the bridge at about the height at which the three Utopians had worked or were still working ran something dark, a rope-like band. He jumped to the conclusion that this must be the cable he had seen lit up by those green flashes in the night. Then he noted a peculiar body upon the crest of the more open of the two gorges. It was an enormous vertical coil, a coil flattened into a disc, which had appeared on the edge of the cliff opposite to Coronation Crag. Less plainly seen because of a projecting mass of rock, was a similar coil in the narrower canyon close to the steps that led up from the little bridge. Two or three Utopians, looking very small because they were so high and very squat because they were so fore-shortened, were moving along the cliff edge and handling something that apparently had to do with these coils.

Mr Barnstaple stared at these arrangements with much the same uncomprehending stare as that with which some savage who had never heard a shot fired in anger might watch the loading of a gun.

Came a familiar sound, faint and little. It was the hooter of Quarantine Castle sounding the reveille. And almost simultaneously the little Napoleonic figure of Mr Rupert Catskill emerged against the blue. The head and shoulders of Penk rose and halted and stood at attention behind him. The captain of the Earthlings produced his field-glasses and surveyed the coils through them.

'I wonder what he makes of them,' said Mr Barnstaple.

Mr Catskill turned and gave some direction to Penk, who saluted and vanished.

A click from the nearer gorge jerked his attention back to the little bridge. It had gone. His eye dropped and caught it up within a few yards of the water. He saw the water splash and the metal framework crumple up and dance two steps and lie still, and then a moment later the crash and clatter of the fall reached his ears.

'Now who did that?' asked Mr Barnstaple and Mr Catskill answered his question by going hastily to that corner of the castle and staring down. Manifestly he was surprised. Manifestly therefore it was the Utopians who had cut the bridge.

Mr Catskill was joined almost immediately by Mr Hunker and Lord Barralonga. Their gestures suggested an animated discussion.

The sunlight was creeping by imperceptible degrees down the front of Quarantine Crag. It had now got down to the cable that encircled the crest; in the light this shone with a coppery sheen. The three Utopians who had awakened Mr Barnstaple in the night became visible descending the rope ladder very rapidly. And once more Mr Barnstaple was aware of that humming sound he had heard ever and again during the night, but now it was much louder and it sounded everywhere about him, in the air, in the water, in the rocks and in his bones.

Abruptly something black and spear-shaped appeared beside the little group of Earthlings above. It seemed to jump up beside them, it paused and jumped again half the height of a man and jumped again. It was a flag being hauled up a flag staff, that Mr Barnstaple had not hitherto observed. It reached the top of the staff and hung limp.

Then some eddy in the air caught it. It flapped out for a moment, displayed a white star on a blue ground and dropped again.

This was the flag of Earth – this was the flag of the crusade to restore the blessings of competition, conflict and warfare to Utopia. Beneath it appeared the head of Mr Burleigh, examining the Utopian coils through his glasses.

4

The throbbing and humming in Mr Barnstaple's ears grew rapidly louder and rose acutely to an extreme intensity. Suddenly great flashes of violet light leapt across from coil to coil, passing through Quarantine Castle as though it was not there.

For a moment longer it *was* there.

The flag flared out madly and was torn from its staff. Mr Burleigh lost his hat. A half length of Mr Catskill became visible struggling with his coat tails which had blown up and enveloped his head. At the same time Mr Barnstaple saw the castle rotating upon the lower part of the crag, exactly as though some invisible giant had seized the upper tenth of the headland and was twisting it round. And then it vanished.

As it did so, a great column of dust poured up into its place; the waters in the gorge sprung into the air in tall fountains and were splashed to spray, and a deafening thud smote Mr Barnstaple's ears. Aerial powers picked him up and tossed him a dozen yards and he fell amidst a rain of dust and stones and water. He was bruised and stunned.

'My God!' he cried, 'My God,' and struggled to his knees, feeling violently sick.

He had a glimpse of the crest of Quarantine Crag, truncated as neatly as though it had been cheese cut with a sharp knife. And then fatigue and exhaustion had their way with him and he sprawled forward and lay insensible.

BOOK THE THIRD
A Neophyte in Utopia

The Peaceful Hills beside the River

I

'God has made more universes than there are pages in all the libraries of earth; man may learn and grow for ever amidst the multitude of His worlds.'

Mr Barnstaple had a sense of floating from star to star and from plane to plane, through an incessant variety and wonder of existences. He passed over the edge of being; he drifted for ages down the faces of immeasurable cliffs; he travelled from everlasting to everlasting in a stream of innumerable little stars. At last came a phase of profound restfulness. There was a sky of level clouds, warmed by the light of a declining sun, and a skyline of gently undulating hills, golden grassy upon their crests and carrying dark purple woods and thickets and patches of pale yellow like ripening corn upon their billowing slopes. Here and there were domed buildings and terraces, flowering gardens and little villas and great tanks of gleaming water.

There were many trees like the eucalyptus – only that they had darker leaves – upon the slopes immediately below and round and about him; and all the land fell at last towards a very broad valley down which a shining river wound leisurely in great semicircular bends until it became invisible in the evening haze.

A slight movement turned his eyes to discover Lychnis seated beside him. She smiled at him and put her finger on her lips. He had a vague desire to address her, and smiled faintly and moved his head. She got up and slipped away from him past the head of his couch. He was too feeble and incurious to raise his head and look to see where she had gone. But he saw that she had been sitting at a white table on which was a silver bowl full of intensely blue flowers, and the colour of the flowers held him and diverted his first faint impulse of curiosity.

He wondered whether colours were really brighter in this Utopian world or whether something in the air quickened and clarified his apprehension.

Beyond the table were the white pillars of the loggia. A branch of one of these eucalyptus-like trees, with leaves bronze black, came very close outside.

And there was music. It was a little trickle of sound, that dripped and ran, a mere unobtrusive rivulet of little clear notes upon the margin of his consciousness, the song of some fairyland Debussy.

Peace. . . .

2

He was awake again.

He tried hard to remember.

He had been knocked over and stunned in some manner too big and violent for his mind to hold as yet.

Then people had stood about him and talked about him. He remembered their feet. He must have been lying on his face with his face very close to the ground. Then they had turned him over, and the light of the rising sun had been blinding in his eyes.

Two gentle goddesses had given him some restorative in a gorge at the foot of high cliffs. He had been carried in a woman's arms as a child is carried. After that there were cloudy and dissolving memories of a long journey, a long flight through the air. There was something next to this, a vision of huge complicated machinery that did not join on to anything else. For a time his mind held this up in an interrogative fashion and then dropped it wearily. There had been voices in consultation, the prick of an injection and some gas that he had had to inhale. And sleep – or sleeps, spells of sleep interspersed with dreams. . . .

Now with regard to that gorge; how had he got there?

The gorge – in another light, a greenish light – with Utopians who struggled with a great cable.

Suddenly hard and clear came the vision of the headland of Coronation Crag towering up against the bright blue morning sky, and then the crest of it grinding round, with its fluttering flags and its dishevelled figures, passing slowly and steadily, as some great ship passes out of a dock, with its flags and passengers into the invisible and unknown. All the wonder of his great adventure returned to Mr Barnstaple's mind.

3

He sat up in a state of interrogation and Lychnis reappeared at his elbow.

She seated herself on his bed close to him, shook up some pillows behind him and persuaded him to lie back upon them. She conveyed to him that he was cured of some illness and no longer infectious, but that he was still very weak. Of what illness? he asked himself. More of the immediate past became clear to him.

'There was an epidemic,' he said. 'A sort of mixed epidemic – of all our infections.'

She smiled reassuringly. It was over. The science and organization of Utopia had taken the danger by the throat and banished it. Lychnis, however, had had nothing to do with the preventive and cleansing work that had ended the career of these invading microbes so speedily; her work had been the help and care of the sick. Something came through to the intelligence of Mr Barnstaple that made him think that she was faintly sorry that this work of pity was no longer necessary. He looked up into her beautiful kindly eyes and met her affectionate solicitude. She was not sorry Utopia was cured again; that was incredible; but it seemed to him that she was sorry that she could no longer spend herself in help and that she was glad that he at least was still in need of assistance.

'What became of those people on the rock?' he asked. 'What became of the other Earthlings?'

She did not know. They had been cast out of Utopia, she thought.

'Back to earth?'

She did not think they had gone back to earth. They had perhaps gone into yet another universe. But she did not know. She was one of those who had no mathematical aptitudes, and physico-chemical science and the complex theories of dimensions that interested so many people in Utopia were outside her circle of ideas. She believed that the crest of Coronation Crag had been swung out of the Utopian universe altogether. A great number of people were now intensely interested in this experimental work upon the unexplored dimensions into which physical processes might be swung, but these matters terrified her. Her mind recoiled from them as one recoils from the edge of a cliff. She did not want to think where the Earthlings had gone, what deeps they had reeled over, what immensities they had seen

365

and swept down into. Such thoughts opened dark gulfs beneath her feet where she had thought everything fixed and secure. She was a conservative in Utopia. She loved life as it was and as it had been. She had given herself to the care of Mr Barnstaple when she had found that he had escaped the fate of the other Earthlings, and she had not troubled very greatly about the particulars of that fate. She had avoided thinking about it.

'But where are they? Where have they gone?'

She did not know.

She conveyed to him haltingly and imperfectly her own halting and unsympathetic ideas of these new discoveries that had inflamed the Utopian imagination. The crucial moment had been the experiment of Arden and Greenlake that had brought the Earthlings into Utopia. That had been the first rupture of the hitherto invincible barriers that had held their universe in three spatial dimensions. That had opened these abysses. That had been the moment of release for all the new work that now filled Utopia. That had been the first achievement of practical results from an intricate network of theory and deduction. It sent Mr Barnstaple's mind back to the humbler discoveries of earth, to Franklin snapping the captive lightning from his kite and Galvani, with his dancing frog's legs, puzzling over the miracle that brought electricity into the service of men. But it had taken a century and a half for electricity to make any sensible changes in human life because the earthly workers were so few and the ways of the world so obstructive and slow and spiteful. In Utopia to make a novel discovery was to light an intellectual conflagration. Hundreds of thousands of experimentalists in free and open cooperation were now working along the fruitful lines that Arden and Greenlake had made manifest. Every day, every hour now, new and hitherto fantastic possibilities of interspatial relationship were being made plain to the Utopians.

Mr Barnstaple rubbed his head and eyes with both hands and then lay back, blinking at the great valley below him, growing slowly golden as the sun sank. He felt himself to be the most secure and stable of beings at the very centre of a sphere of glowing serenity. And that effect of an immense tranquillity was a delusion; that still evening peace was woven of incredible billions of hurrying and clashing atoms.

All the peace and fixity that man has ever known or will ever know is but the smoothness of the face of a torrent that flies along with incredible speed from cataract to cataract. Time was when men could talk of everlasting hills. Today a schoolboy knows that they dissolve under the frost and wind and rain and pour seaward, day by day and hour by hour. Time was when men could speak of Terra Firma and feel the earth fixed, adamantine beneath their feet. Now they know that it whirls through space eddying about a spinning, blindly driven sun amidst a sheeplike drift of stars. And this fair curtain of appearance before the eyes of Mr Barnstaple, this still and level flush of sunset and the great cloth of starry space that hung behind the blue; that too was now to be pierced and torn and rent asunder. . . .

The extended fingers of his mind closed on the things that concerned him most.

'But where are my people?' he asked. 'Where are their bodies? Is it just possible they are still alive?'

She could not tell him.

He lay thinking. . . . It was natural that he should be given into the charge of a rather backward-minded woman. The active-minded here had no more use for him in their lives than active-minded people on earth have for pet animals. She did not want to think about these spatial relations at all; the subject was too difficult for her; she was one of Utopia's educational failures. She sat beside him with a divine sweetness and tranquillity upon her face, and he felt his own judgment upon her like a committed treachery. Yet he wanted to know very badly the answer to his question.

He supposed the crest of Coronation Crag had been twisted round and flung off into some outer space. It was unlikely that this time the Earthlings would strike a convenient planet again. In all probability they had been turned off into the void, into the interstellar space of some unknown universe. . . .

What would happen then? They would freeze. The air would instantly diffuse right out of them. Their own gravitation would flatten them out, crush them together, collapse them! At least they would have no time to suffer. A gasp, like someone flung into ice-cold water. . . .

He contemplated these possibilities.

'Flung out!' he said aloud. 'Like a cageful of mice thrown over the side of a ship!'

'I don't understand,' said Lychnis, turning to him.

He appealed to her. 'And now – tell me. What is to become of me?'

4

For a time Lychnis gave him no answer. She sat with her soft eyes upon the blue haze into which the great river valley had now dissolved. Then she turned to him with a question:

'You want to stay in this world?'

'Surely any Earthling would want to stay in this world. My body has been purified. Why should I not stay?'

'It seems a good world to you?'

'Loveliness, order, health, energy and wonder; it has all the good things for which my world groans and travails.'

'And yet our world is not content.'

'I could be contented.'

'You are tired and weak still.'

'In this air I could grow strong and vigourous. I could almost grow young in this world. In years, as you count them here, I am still a young man.'

Again she was silent for a time. The mighty lap of the landscape was filled now with indistinguishable blue, and beyond the black silhouettes of the trees upon the hillside only the skyline of the hills was visible against the yellow green and pale yellow of the evening sky. Never had Mr Barnstaple seen so peaceful a nightfall. But her words denied that peace. 'Here,' she said, 'there is no rest. Every day men and women awake and say: What new thing shall we do to-day? What shall we change?'

'They have changed a wild planet of disease and disorder into a sphere of beauty and safety. They have made the wilderness of human motives bear union and knowledge and power.'

'And research never rests, and curiosity and the desire for more power and still more power consumes all our world.'

'A healthy appetite. I am tired now, as weak and weary and soft as though I had just been born; but presently when I have grown stronger I too may share in that curiosity and take a part in these great discoveries that now set Utopia astir. Who knows?'

He smiled at her kind eyes.

'You will have much to learn,' she said.

She seemed to measure her own failure as she said these words.

Some sense of the profound differences that three thousand years of progress might have made in the fundamental ideas and ways of thinking of the race dawned upon Mr Barnstaple's mind. He remembered that in Utopia he heard only the things he could understand, and that all that found no place in his terrestrial circle of ideas was inaudible to his mind. The gulfs of misunderstanding might be wider and deeper than he was assuming. A totally illiterate Gold Coast negro trying to master thermoelectricity would have set himself a far more hopeful task.

'After all it is not the new discoveries that I want to share,' he said; 'quite possibly they are altogether beyond me; it is this perfect, beautiful daily life, this life of all the dreams of my own time come true, that I want. I just want to be alive here. That will be enough for me.'

'You are weak and tired yet,' said Lychnis. 'When you are stronger you may face other ideas.'

'But what other ideas—?'

'Your mind may turn back to your own world and your own life.'

'Go back to Earth!'

Lychnis looked out at the twilight again for a while before she turned to him with, 'You are an Earthling born and made. What else can you be?'

'What else can I be?' Mr Barnstaple's mind rested upon that, and he lay feeling rather than thinking amidst its implications as the pinpoint lights of Utopia pricked the darkling blue below and ran into chains and groups and coalesced into nebulous patches.

He resisted the truth below her words. This glorious world of Utopia, perfect and assured, poised ready for tremendous adventures amidst untravelled universes, was a world of sweet giants and uncompanionable beauty, a world of enterprises in which a poor muddy-witted, weak-willed Earthling might neither help nor share. They had plundered their planet as one empties a purse; they thrust out their power amidst the stars. . . . They were kind. They were very kind. . . . But they were different. . . .

A Loiterer in a Living World

I

In a few days Mr Barnstaple had recovered strength of body and mind. He no longer lay in bed in a loggia, filled with self-pity and the beauty of a world subdued; he went about freely and was soon walking long distances over the Utopian countryside, seeking acquaintances and learning more and more of this wonderland of accomplished human desires.

For that is how it most impressed him. Nearly all the greater evils of human life had been conquered; war, pestilence and malaise, famine and poverty had been swept out of human experience. The dreams of artists, of perfected and lovely bodies and of a world transfigured to harmony and beauty had been realized; the spirits of order and organization ruled triumphant. Every aspect of human life had been changed by these achievements.

The climate of this Valley of Rest was bland and sunny like the climate of South Europe, but nearly everything characteristic of the Italian or Spanish scene had gone. Here were no bent and aged crones tallying burthens, no chattering pursuit by beggars, no ragged workers lowering by the wayside. The puny terracing, the distressing accumulations of hand cultivation, the gnarled olives, hacked vines, the little patches of grain or fruit, and the grudged litigious irrigation of those primitive conditions, gave place to sweeping schemes of conservation, to a broad and subtle handling of slope and soil and sunshine. No meagre goats nor sheep, child-tended, cropped among the stones, no tethered cattle ate their apportioned circles of herbage and no more. There were no hovels by the wayside, no shrines with tortured, blood-oozing images, no slinking misbegotten curs nor beaten beasts sweating and panting between their overloaded panniers at the steeper places of rutted, rock-strewn and dung-strewn roads. Instead the great smooth indestructible ways swept in easy gradients through the land, leaping gorges and crossing valleys upon wide-arched viaducts, piercing cathedral-like aisles through the hillsides, throwing off bastions to command some special splendour of the land. Here were resting places and shelters, stairways clambering to pleasant arbours and summer-houses where friends might talk and lovers shelter and rejoice. Here were groves and avenues of such trees as he had never seen before. For on earth as yet there is scarcely such a thing as an altogether healthy fully grown tree, nearly all our trees are bored and consumed by parasites, rotten and tumorous with fungi, more gnarled and crippled and disease-twisted even than mankind.

The landscape had absorbed the patient design of five-and-twenty centuries. In one place Mr Barnstaple found great works in progress; a bridge was being replaced, not because it was outworn, but because someone had produced a bolder, more delightful design.

For a time he did not observe the absence of telephonic or tele-graphic communication; the posts and wires that mark a modern countryside had disappeared. The reasons for that difference he was to learn later. Nor did he at first miss the railway, the railway station and the wayside inn. He perceived that the frequent buildings must have specific functions, that people came and went from them with an appearance of interest and preoccupation, that from some of them seemed to come a hum and whir of activity; work of many sorts was certainly in progress; but his ideas of the mechanical organization of this new world were too vague and tentative as yet for him to attempt to fix any significance to this sort of place or that. He walked agape like a savage in a garden.

He never came to nor saw any towns. The reason for any such close accumulations of human beings had largely disappeared. In certain places, he learnt, there were gatherings of people for studies, mutual stimulation, or other convenient exchanges, in great series of com-municating buildings; but he never visited any of these centres.

And about this world went the tall people of Utopia, fair and wonderful, smiling or making some friendly gesture as they passed him but giving him little chance for questions or intercourse. They travelled swiftly in machines upon the high road or walked, and ever and again the shadow of a silent soaring aeroplane would pass over him. He went a little in awe of these people and felt himself a queer creature when he met their eyes. For like the gods of Greece and Rome theirs was a cleaned and perfected humanity, and it seemed to him that they were gods. Even the great tame beasts that walked freely about this world had a certain divinity that checked the expression of Mr Barnstaple's friendliness.

2

Presently he found a companion for his rambles, a boy of thirteen, a cousin of Lychnis, named Crystal. He was a curly-headed youngster, brown-eyed as she was; and he was reading history in a holiday stage of his education.

So far as Mr Barnstaple could gather the more serious part of his intellectual training was in mathematical work interrelated to physical and chemical science, but all that was beyond an Earthling's range of ideas. Much of this work seemed to be done in co-operation with other boys, and to be what we should call research on earth. Nor could Mr Barnstaple master the nature of some other sort of study which seemed to turn upon refinements of expression. But the history brought them together. The boy was just learning about the growth of the Utopian social system out of the efforts and experiences of the Ages of Confusion. His imagination was alive with the tragic struggles upon which the present order of Utopia was founded, he had a hundred questions for Mr Barnstaple, and he was full of explicit information which was destined presently to sink down and become part of the foundations of his adult mind. Mr Barnstaple was as good as a book to him, and he was as good as a guide to Mr Barnstaple. They went about together talking upon a footing of the completest equality, this rather exceptionally intelligent Earthling and this Utopian stripling, who topped him by perhaps an inch when they stood side by side.

The boy had the broad facts of Utopian history at his fingers' ends. He could explain and find an interest in explaining how artificial and upheld the peace and beauty of Utopia still were. Utopians were in essence, he said, very much what their ancestors had been in the beginnings of the newer stone age, fifteen thousand or twenty thousand years ago. They were still very much what Earthlings had been in the corresponding period. Since then there had been only 600 or 700 generations and no time for any very fundamental changes in the race. There had not been even a general admixture of races. On Utopia as on earth there had been dusky and brown peoples, and they remained distinct. The various races mingled socially but did not interbreed very much; rather they purified and intensified their racial gifts and beauties. There was often very passionate love between people of contrasted race, but rarely did such love come to procreation. There had been a certain deliberate elimination of ugly, malignant, narrow, stupid and gloomy types during the past dozen centuries or so; but except for the fuller realization of his latent possibilities, the common man in Utopia was very little different from the ordinary energetic and able people of a later stone-age or early bronze-age community. They were infinitely better nourished, trained and educated, and mentally and physically their condition was clean and fit, but they were the same flesh and nature as we are.

'But,' said Mr Barnstaple, and struggled with that idea for a time. 'Do you mean to tell me that half the babies born on earth to-day might grow to be such gods as these people I meet?'

'Given our air, given our atmosphere.'

'Given your heritage.'

'Given our freedom.'

In the past of Utopia, in the Age of Confusion, Mr Barnstaple had to remember, everyone had grown up with a crippled or a thwarted will, hampered by vain restrictions or misled by plausible delusions. Utopia still bore it in mind that human nature was fundamentally animal and savage and had to be adapted to social needs, but Utopia had learnt the better methods of adaptation – after endless failures of compulsion, cruelty and deception. 'On Earth we tame our animals with hot irons and our fellow men by violence and fraud,' said Mr Barnstaple, and described the schools and books, newspapers and public discussions of the early twentieth century to his incredulous companion. 'You cannot imagine how beaten and fearful even decent people are upon Earth. You learn of the Age of Confusion in your histories but you do not know what the realities of a bad mental atmosphere, an atmosphere of feeble laws, hates and superstitions, are. As night goes round the Earth always there are hundreds of thousands of people who should be sleeping, lying awake, fearing a bully, fearing a cruel competition, dreading lest they cannot make good, ill of some illness they cannot comprehend, distressed by some irrational quarrel, maddened by some thwarted instinct or some suppressed and perverted desire.' . . .

Crystal admitted that it was hard to think now of the Age of Confusion in terms of misery. Much of the every-day misery of Earth was now inconceivable. Very slowly Utopia had evolved its present harmony of law and custom and education. Man was no longer crippled and compelled; it was recognized that he was fundamentally an animal and that his daily life must follow the round of appetites satisfied and instincts released. The daily texture of Utopian life was woven of various and interesting foods and drinks, of free and entertaining exercise and work, of sweet sleep and of the interest and happiness of fearless and spiteless love-making. Inhibition was at a minimum. But where the power of Utopian education began was after the animal had been satisfied and disposed of. The jewel on the reptile's head that had brought Utopia out of the confusions of human life was curiosity, the play impulse, prolonged and expanded in adult life into an insatiable appetite for knowledge and an habitual creative urgency. All Utopians had become as little children, learners and makers.

It was strange to hear this boy speaking so plainly and clearly of the educational process to which he was being subjected, and particularly to find he could talk so frankly of love.

An earthly bashfulness almost prevented Mr Barnstaple from asking, 'But you —. You do not make Love?'

'I have had curiosities,' said the boy, evidently saying what he had been taught to say. 'But it is not necessary nor becoming to make love too early in life nor to let desire take hold of one. It weakens youth to become too early possessed by desire – which often will not leave one again. It spoils and cripples the imagination. I want to do good work as my father has done before me.'

Mr Barnstaple glanced at the beautiful young profile at his side and was suddenly troubled by memories of a certain study number four at school, and of some ugly phases of his adolescence, the stuffy, secret room, the hot and ugly fact. He felt a beastlier Earthling than ever. 'Heigho!' he sighed. 'But this world of yours is as clean as starlight and as sweet as cold water on a dusty day.'

'Many people I love,' said the boy, 'but not with passion. Some day that will come. But one must not be too eager and anxious to meet passionate love or one might make-believe and give or snatch at a sham. .... There is no hurry. No one will prevent me when my time comes. All good things come to one in this world in their own good time.'

But work one does not wait for; one's work, since it concerns one's own self only, one goes to meet. Crystal thought very much about the work that he might do. It seemed to Mr Barnstaple that work, in the sense of uncongenial toil, had almost disappeared from Utopia. Yet all Utopia was working. Everyone was doing work that fitted natural aptitudes and appealed to the imagination of the worker. Everyone worked happily and eagerly – as those people we call geniuses do on our Earth.

For suddenly Mr Barnstaple found himself telling Crystal of the happiness of the true artist, of the true scientific worker, of the original man even on earth as it is today. They, too, like the Utopians, do work that concerns themselves and is in their own nature for great ends. Of all Earthlings they are the most enviable.

'If such men are not happy on earth,' said Mr Barnstaple, 'it is because they are touched with vulgarity and still heed the soiled successes and honours and satisfactions of vulgar men, still feel neglect and limitation that should concern them no more. But to him who has seen the sun shine in Utopia surely the utmost honour and glory of earth can signify no more and be no more desirable than the complimentary spittle of the chieftain and a string of barbaric beads.'

3

Crystal was still of an age to be proud of his *savoir faire*. He showed Mr Barnstaple his books and told him of his tutors and exercises.

Utopia still made use of printed books; books were still the simplest, clearest way of bringing statement before a tranquil mind. Crystal's books were very beautifully bound in flexible leather that his mother had tooled for him very prettily, and they were made of hand-made paper. The lettering was some fluent phonetic script that Mr Barnstaple could not understand. It reminded him of Arabic; and frequent sketches, outline maps and diagrams were interpolated. Crystal was advised in his holiday reading by a tutor for whom he prepared a sort of exercise report, and he supplemented his reading by visits to museums; but there was no educational museum convenient in the Valley of Peace for Mr Barnstaple to visit.

Crystal had passed out of the opening stage of education which was carried on, he said, upon large educational estates given up wholly to the lives of children. Education up to eleven or twelve seemed to be much more carefully watched and guarded and taken care of in Utopia than upon earth. Shocks to the imagination, fear and evil suggestions were warded off as carefully as were infection and physical disaster; by eight or nine the foundations of a Utopian character were surely laid, habits of cleanliness, truth, candour and helpfulness, confidence in the world, fearlessness and a sense of belonging to the great purpose of the race.

Only after nine or ten did the child go outside the garden of its early growth and begin to see the ordinary ways of the world. Until that age the care of the children was largely in the hands of nurses and teachers, but after that time the parents became more of a factor than they had been in a youngster's life. It was always a custom for the parents of a child to be near and to see that child in its nursery days, but just when earthly parents tended to separate from their children as they went away to school or went into business, Utopian parentage grew to be something closer. There was an idea in Utopia that between parent and child there was a necessary temperamental sympathy; children looked forward to the friendship and company of their parents, and parents looked forward to the interest of their children's adolescence, and though a parent had practically no power over a son or daughter, he or she took naturally the position of advocate, adviser and sympathetic friend. The friendship was all the franker and closer because of that lack of power, and all the easier because age for age the Utopians were so much younger and fresher-minded than Earthlings. Crystal it seemed had a very great passion for his mother. He was very proud of his father, who was a wonderful painter and designer; but it was his mother who possessed the boy's heart.

On his second walk with Mr Barnstaple he said he was going to hear from his mother, and Mr Barnstaple was shown the equivalent of correspondence in Utopia. Crystal carried a little bundle of wires and light rods; and presently coming to a place where a pillar stood in the midst of a lawn he spread this affair out like a long cat's cradle and tapped a little stud in the pillar with a key that he carried on a light gold chain about his neck. Then he took up a receiver attached to his apparatus, and spoke aloud and listened and presently heard a voice.

It was a very pleasant woman's voice; it talked to Crystal for a time without interruption, and then Crystal talked back, and afterwards there were other voices, some of which Crystal answered and some which he heard without replying. Then he gathered up his apparatus again.

This Mr Barnstaple learnt was the Utopian equivalent of letter and telephone. For in Utopia, except by previous arrangement, people do not talk together on the telephone. A message is sent to the station of the district in which the recipient is known to be, and there it waits until he chooses to tap his accumulated messages. And any that one wishes to repeat can be repeated. Then he talks back to the senders and dispatches any other messages he wishes. The transmission is wireless. The little pillars supply electric power for transmission or for any other purpose the Utopians require. For example, the gardeners resort to them to run their mowers and diggers and rakes and rollers.

Far away across the valley Crystal pointed out the district station at which this correspondence gathered and was dispersed. Only a few people were on duty there; almost all the connexions were automatic. The messages came and went from any part of the planet.

This set Mr Barnstaple going upon a long string of questions.

He discovered for the first time that the message organization of Utopia had a complete knowledge of the whereabouts of every soul upon the planet. It had a record of every living person and it knew in what message district he was. Everyone was indexed and noted.

To Mr Barnstaple, accustomed to the crudities and dishonesties of earthly governments, this was an almost terrifying discovery. 'On earth that would be the means of unending blackmail and tyranny,' he said. 'Everyone would lie open to espionage. We had a fellow at Scotland Yard. If he had been in your communication department he would have made life in Utopia intolerable in a week. You cannot imagine the nuisance he was.' . . .

Mr Barnstaple had to explain to Crystal what blackmail meant. It was like that in Utopia to begin with, Crystal said. Just as on earth so in Utopia there was the same natural disposition to use knowledge and power to the disadvantage of one's fellows, and the same jealousy of having one's personal facts known. In the Stone Age in Utopia men kept their true names secret and could only be spoken of by nicknames. They feared magic abuses. 'Some savages still do that on earth,' said Mr Barnstaple. It was only very slowly that Utopians came to trust doctors and dentists and only very slowly that doctors and dentists became trustworthy. It was a matter of scores of centuries before the chief abuses of the confidences and trusts necessary to a modern social organization could be effectively corrected.

Every young Utopian had to learn the Five Principles of Liberty, without which civilization is impossible. The first was the Principle of Privacy. This is that all individual personal facts are private between the citizen and the public organization to which he entrusts them, and can be used only for his convenience and with his sanction. Of course all such facts are available for statistical uses, but not as individual personal facts. And the second principle is the Principle of Free Movement. A citizen, subject to the due discharge of his public obligations, may go without permission or explanation to any part of the Utopian planet. All the means of transport are freely at his service. Every Utopian may change his surroundings, his climate and his social atmosphere as he will. The third principle is the Principle of Unlimited Knowledge. All that is known in Utopia, except individual personal facts about living people, is on record and as easily available as a perfected series of indices, libraries, museums, and inquiry offices can make it. Whatever the Utopian desires to know he may know with the utmost clearness, exactness and facility so far as his powers of knowing and his industry go. Nothing is kept from him and nothing is misrepresented to him. And that brought Mr Barnstaple to the fourth Principle of Liberty, which was that Lying is the Blackest Crime.

Crystal's definition of lying was a sweeping one; the inexact statement of facts, even the suppression of a material fact, was lying.

'Where there are lies there cannot be freedom.'

Mr Barnstaple was mightily taken by this idea. It seemed at once quite fresh to him and one that he had always unconsciously entertained. Half the difference between Utopia and our world he asserted lay in this, that our atmosphere was dense and poisonous with lies and shams.

'When one comes to think of it,' said Mr Barnstaple, and began to expatiate to Crystal upon all the falsehoods of human life. The fundamental assumptions of earthly associations were still largely lies, false assumptions of necessary and unavoidable differences in flags and nationality, pretences of function and power in monarchy; impostures of organized learning, religious and moral dogmas and shams. And one must live in it; one is a part of it. You are restrained, taxed, distressed and killed by these insane unrealities. 'Lying the Primary Crime! How simple that is! How true and necessary it is! That dogma is the fundamental distinction of the scientific world-state from all preceding states.' And going on from that Mr Barnstaple launched out into a long and loud tirade against the suppression and falsifications of earthly newspapers.

It was a question very near his heart. The London newspapers had ceased to be impartial vehicles of news; they omitted, they mutilated, they misstated. They were no better than propaganda rags. Rags! *Nature*, within its field, was shiningly accurate and full, but that was a purely scientific paper; it did not touch the every-day news. The Press, he held, was the only possible salt of contemporary life, and if the salt had lost its savour—!

The poor man found himself orating as though he was back at his Sydenham breakfast-table after a bad morning's paper.

'Once upon a time Utopia was in just such a tangle,' said Crystal consolingly. 'But there is a proverb, "Truth comes back where once she has visited." You need not trouble so much as you do. Some day even your press may grow clear.'

'How do *you* manage about newspapers and criticism?' said Mr Barnstaple.

Crystal explained that there was a complete distinction between news and discussion in Utopia. There were houses – one was in sight – which were used as reading-rooms. One went to these places to learn the news. Thither went the reports of all the things that were happening on the planet, things found, things discovered, things done. The reports were made as they were needed; there were no advertisement contracts to demand the same bulk of news every day. For some time Crystal said the reports had been very full and amusing about the Earthlings, but he had not been reading the paper for many days because of the interest in history the Earthling affair had aroused in him. There was always news of fresh scientific discoveries that stirred the imagination. One frequent item of public interest and excitement was the laying out of some wide scheme of research. The new spatial work that Arden and Greenlake had died for was producing much news. And when people died in Utopia it was the custom to tell the story of their lives. Crystal promised to take Mr Barnstaple to a news place and entertain him by reading him some of the Utopian descriptions of earthly life which had been derived from the Earthlings, and Mr Barnstaple asked that when this was done he might also hear about Arden and Greenlake, who had been not only great discoverers, but great lovers, and of Serpentine and Cedar, for whom he had conceived an intense admiration. Utopian news lacked of course the high spice of an earthly newspaper; the intriguing murders and amusing misbehaviours, the entertaining and exciting consequences of sexual ignorance and sexual blunderings, the libel cases and detected swindles, the great processional movements of Royalty across the general traffic, and the romantic fluctuations of the stock exchange and sport. But where the news of Utopia lacked liveliness, the liveliness of discussion made up for it. For the Fifth Principle of Liberty in Utopia was Free Discussion and Criticism.

Any Utopian was free to criticize and discuss anything in the whole universe provided he told no lies about it directly or indirectly; he could be as respectful or disrespectful as he pleased; he could propose anything however subversive. He could break into poetry or fiction as he chose. He could express himself in any literary form he liked or by sketch or caricature as the mood took him. Only he must refrain from lying; that was the one rigid rule of controversy. He could get what he had to say printed and distributed to the news rooms. There it was read or neglected as the visitors chanced to approve of it or not. Often if they liked what they read they would carry off a copy with them. Crystal had some new fantastic fiction about the exploration of space among his books; imaginative stories that boys were reading very eagerly; they were pamphlets of thirty or forty pages printed on a beautiful paper that he said was made directly from flax and certain reeds. The librarians noted what books and papers were read and taken away, and these they replaced with fresh copies. The piles that went unread were presently reduced to one or two copies and the rest went back to the pulping mills. But many of the poets and philosophers and story-tellers whose imaginations found no wide popularity were nevertheless treasured and their memories kept alive by a few devoted admirers.

4

'I am not at all clear in my mind about one thing,' said Mr Barnstaple. 'I have seen no coins and nothing like money passing in this world. By all outward appearance this might be a Communism such as was figured in a book we used to value on Earth, a book called *News from Nowhere* by an Earthling named William Morris. It was a graceful impossible book. In that dream everyone worked for the joy of working and took what he needed. But I have never believed in Communism because I recognize, as here in Utopia you seem to recognize, the natural fierceness and greediness of the untutored man. There is joy in creation for others to use, but no natural joy in unrequited service. The sense of justice to himself is greater in man than the sense of service. Somehow here you must balance the work anyone does for Utopia against what he destroys or consumes. How do you do it?'

Crystal considered. 'There were Communists in Utopia in the Last Age of Confusion. In some parts of our planet they tried to abolish money suddenly and violently and brought about great economic confusion and want and misery. To step straight to communism failed – very tragically. And yet Utopia today is practically a communism, and except by way of curiosity I have never had a coin in my hand in all my life.'

In Utopia just as upon earth, he explained, money came as a great discovery; as a method of freedom. Hitherto, before the invention of money, all service between man and man had been done through bondage or barter. Life was a thing of slavery and narrow choice. But money opened up the possibility of giving a worker a free choice in his reward. It took Utopia three thousand years and more to realize that possibility. The idea of money abounded in pitfalls and was easily corruptible; Utopia floundered its way to economic lucidity through long centuries of credit and debt, false and debased money; extravagant usury and every possibility of speculative abuse. In the matter of money more than in any other human concern, human cunning has set itself most vilely and treacherously to prey upon human necessity. Utopia once carried, as earth carries now, a load of parasitic souls, speculators, forestallers, gamblers and bargain-pressing Shylocks, exacting every conceivable advantage out of the weaknesses of the monetary system; she had needed centuries of economic sanitation. It was only when Utopia had got to the beginnings of world-wide political unity and when there were sufficiently full statistics of world resources and world production, that human society could at last give the individual worker the assurance of a coin of steadfast significance, a coin that would mean for him today or tomorrow or at any time the certainty of a set quantity of elemental values. And with peace throughout the planet and increasing social stability, interest, which is the measure of danger and uncertainty, dwindled at last to nothing. Banking became a public service perforce, because it no longer offered profit to the individual banker. 'Rentier classes,' Crystal conveyed, 'are not a permanent element in any community. They mark a phase of transition between a period of insecurity and high interest and a period of complete security and no interest. They are a dawn phenomenon.'

Mr Barnstaple digested this statement after an interval of incredulity. He satisfied himself by a few questions that young Utopia really had some idea of what a rentier class was, what its moral and imaginative limitations were likely to be and the role it may have played in the intellectual development of the world by providing a class of independent minds.

'Life is intolerant of all independent classes,' said Crystal, evidently repeating an axiom. 'Either you must earn or you must rob. . . . We have got rid of robbing.'

The youngster still speaking by his book went on to explain how the gradual disuse of money came about. It was an outcome of the general progressive organization of the economic system, the substitution of collective enterprises for competitive enterprises and of wholesale for retail dealing. There had been a time in Utopia when money changed hands at each little transaction and service. One paid money if one wanted a newspaper or a match or a bunch of flowers or a ride on a street conveyance. Everybody went about the world with pockets full of small coins paying on every slight occasion. Then as economic science became more stable and exact the methods of the club and the covering subscription extended. People were able to buy passes that carried them by all the available means of transport for a year or for ten years or for life. The State learnt from clubs and hotels to provide matches, newspapers, stationery and transport for a fixed annual charge. The same inclusive system spread from small and incidental things to great and essential matters, to housing and food and even clothing. The State postal system, which knew where every Utopian citizen was, was presently able in conjunction with the public banking system to guarantee his credit in any part of the world. People ceased to draw coin for their work; the various departments of service, and of economic, educational and scientific activity would credit the individual with his earnings in the public bank and debit him with his customary charges for all the normal services of life.

'Something of this sort is going on on earth even now,' said Mr Barnstaple. 'We use money in the last resort, but a vast volume of our business is already a matter of book-keeping.'

Centuries of unity and energy had given Utopia a very complete control of many fountains of natural energy upon the planet, and this was the heritage of every child born therein. He was credited at his birth with a sum sufficient to educate and maintain him up to four- or five-and-twenty, and then he was expected to choose some occupation to replenish his account.

'But if he doesn't?' said Mr Barnstaple.

'Everyone does.'

'But if he didn't?'

'He'd be miserable and uncomfortable. I've never heard of such a case. I suppose he'd be discussed. Psychologists might examine him. ... But one must do something.'

'But suppose Utopia had no work for him to do?'

Crystal could not imagine that. 'There is always something to be done.'

'But in Utopia once, in the old times, you had unemployment?'

'That was part of the Confusion. There was a sort of hypertrophy of debt; it had become paralysis. Why, when they had unemployment at that same time there was neither enough houses nor food nor clothing. They had unemployment and shortage at one and the same time. It is incredible.'

'Does everyone earn about the same amount of pay?'

'Energetic and creative people are often given big grants if they seem to need the help of others or a command of natural resources. ... And artists sometimes grow rich if their work is much desired.'

'Such a gold chain as yours you had to buy?'

'From the maker in his shop. My mother bought it.'

'Then there are shops?'

'You shall see some. Places where people go to see new and delightful things.'

'And if an artist grows rich, what can he do with his money?'

'Take time and material to make some surpassingly beautiful thing to leave the world. Or collect and help with the work of other artists. Or do whatever else he pleases to teach and fine the common sense of beauty in Utopia. Or just do nothing. . . . Utopia can afford it – if he can.'

5

'Cedar and Lion,' said Mr Barnstaple, 'explained to the rest of us how it is that your government is as it were broken up and dispersed among the people who have special knowledge of the matters involved. The balance between interests, we gathered, was maintained by those who studied the general psychology and the educational organization of Utopia. At first it was very strange to our earthly minds that there should be nowhere a pretended omniscience and a practical omnipotence, that is to say a sovereign thing, a person or an assembly whose *fiat* was final. Mr Burleigh and Mr Catskill thought that such a thing was absolutely necessary, and so, less surely, did I. "Who will decide?" was their riddle. They expected to be taken to see the President or the Supreme Council of Utopia. I suppose it seems to you the most natural of things that there should be nothing of the sort, and that a question should go simply and naturally to the man who knows best about it.'

'Subject to free criticism,' said Crystal.

'Subject to the same process that has made him eminent and responsible. But don't people thrust themselves forward even here – out of vanity? And don't people get thrust forward in front of the best – out of spite?'

'There is plenty of spite and vanity in every Utopian soul,' said Crystal. 'But people speak very plainly and criticism is very searching and free. So that we learn to search our motives before we praise or question.'

'What you say and do shows up here plainly at its true value,' said Mr Barnstaple. 'You cannot throw mud in the noise and darkness unchallenged or get a false claim acknowledged in the disorder.'

'Some years ago there was a man, an artist, who made a great trouble about the work of my father. Often artistic criticism is very bitter here, but he was bitter beyond measure. He caricatured my father and abused him incessantly. He followed him from place to place. He tried to prevent the allocation of material to him. He was quite ineffective. Some people answered him, but for the most part he was disregarded. . . .'

The boy stopped short.

'Well?'

'He killed himself. He could not escape from his own foolishness. Everyone knew what he had said and done. . . .'

383

'But in the past there were kings and councils and conferences in Utopia,' said Mr Barnstaple, returning to the main point.

'My books teach me that our state could have grown up in no other way. We had to have these general dealers in human relationship, politicians and lawyers, as a necessary stage in political and social development. Just as we had to have soldiers and policemen to save people from mutual violence. It was only very slowly that politicians and lawyers came to admit the need for special knowledge in the things they had to do. Politicians would draw boundaries without any proper knowledge of ethnology or economic geography, and lawyers decide about will and purpose with the crudest knowledge of psychology. They produced the most preposterous and unworkable arrangements in the gravest fashion.'

'Like Tristram Shandy's parish bull – which set about begetting the peace of the world at Versailles,' said Mr Barnstaple.

Crystal looked puzzled.

'A complicated allusion to a purely earthly matter,' said Mr Barnstaple. 'This complete diffusion of the business of politics and law among the people with knowledge, is one of the most interesting things of all to me in this world. Such a diffusion is beginning upon earth. The people who understand world-health for instance are dead against political and legal methods, and so are many of our best economists. And most people never go into a law court, and wouldn't dream of doing so upon business of their own, from their cradles to their graves. What became of your politicians and lawyers? Was there a struggle?'

'As light grew and intelligence spread they became more and more evidently unnecessary. They met at last only to appoint men of know-ledge as assessors and so forth, and after a time even these appointments became foregone conclusions. Their activities melted into the general body of criticism and discussion. In places there are still old buildings that used to be council chambers and law courts. The last politician to be elected to a legislative assembly died in Utopia about a thousand years ago. He was an eccentric and garrulous old gentleman; he was the only candidate and one man voted for him, and he insisted upon assembling in solitary state and having all his speeches and proceedings taken down in shorthand. Boys and girls who were learning stenography used to go to report him. Finally he was dealt with as a mental case.'

'And the last judge?'

'I have not learnt about the last judge,' said Crystal. 'I must ask my tutor. I suppose there was one, but I suppose nobody asked him to judge anything. So he probably got something more respectable to do.'

6

'I begin to apprehend the daily life of this world,' said Mr Barnstaple. 'It is a life of demi-gods, very free, strongly individualized, each following an individual bent, each contributing to great racial ends. It is not only cleanly naked and sweet and lovely but full of personal dignity. It is, I see, a practical communism, planned and led up to through long centuries of education and discipline and collectivist preparation. I had never thought before that socialism could exalt and ennoble the individual and individualism degrade him, but now I see plainly that here the thing is proved. In this fortunate world – it is indeed the crown of all its health and happiness – there is no Crowd. The old world, the world to which I belong, was and in my universe alas still is, the world of the Crowd, the world of that detestable crawling mass of un-featured, infected human beings.

'You have never seen a Crowd, Crystal; and in all your happy life you never will. You have never seen a Crowd going to a football match or a race meeting or a bull-fight or a public execution or the like crowd joy; you have never watched a Crowd wedge and stick in a narrow place or hoot or howl in a crisis. You have never watched it stream sluggishly along the streets to gape at a King, or yell for a war, or yell quite equally for a peace. And you have never seen the Crowd, struck by some Panic breeze, change from Crowd proper to Mob and begin to smash and hunt. All the Crowd celebrations have gone out of this world; all the Crowd's gods, there is no Turf here, no Sport, no war demonstrations, no Coronations and Public Funerals, no great shows, but only your little theatres. . . . Happy Crystal! who will never see a Crowd!'

'But I have seen Crowds,' said Crystal.

'Where?'

'I have seen cinematograph films of Crowds, photographed thirty centuries ago and more. They are shown in our history museums. I have seen Crowds streaming over downs after a great race meeting, photographed from an aeroplane, and Crowds rioting in some public square and being dispersed by the police. Thousands and thousands of swarming people. But it is true what you say. There are no more Crowds in Utopia. Crowds and the crowd-mind have gone for ever.'

7

When after some days Crystal had to return to his mathematical studies, his departure left Mr Barnstaple very lonely. He found no other companion. Lychnis seemed always near him and ready to be with him, but her want of active intellectual interests, so remarkable in this world of vast intellectual activities, estranged him from her. Other Utopians came and went, friendly, amused, polite, but intent upon their own business. They would question him curiously, attend perhaps to a question or so of his own, and depart with an air of being called away.

Lychnis, he began to realize, was one of Utopia's failures. She was a lingering romantic type and she cherished a great sorrow in her heart. She had had two children whom she had loved passionately. They were adorably fearless, and out of foolish pride she had urged them to swim out to sea and they had been taken by a current and drowned. Their father had been drowned in attempting their rescue and Lychnis had very nearly shared their fate. She had been rescued. But her emotional life had stopped short at that point, had, as it were, struck an attitude and remained in it. Tragedy possessed her. She turned her back on laughter and gladness and looked for distress. She had rediscovered the lost passion of pity, first pity for herself and then a desire to pity others. She took no interest any more in vigourous and complete people, but her mind concentrated upon the consolation to be found in consoling pain and distress in others. She sought her healing in healing them. She did not want to talk to Mr Barnstaple of the brightness of Utopia; she wanted him to talk to her of the miseries of earth and of his own miseries. That she might sympathize. But he would not tell her of his own miseries because indeed, such was his temperament, he had none; he had only exasperations and regrets.

She dreamt, he perceived, of being able to come to earth and give her beauty and tenderness to the sick and poor. Her heart went out to the spectacle of human suffering and weakness. It went out to these things hungrily and desirously. . . .

Before he detected the drift of her mind he told her many things about human sickness and poverty. But he spoke of these matters not with pity but indignation, as things that ought not to be. And when he perceived how she feasted on these things he spoke of them hardly and cheerfully as things that would presently be swept away. 'But they will still have suffered,' she said. . . .

Since she was always close at hand, she filled for him perhaps more than her legitimate space in the Utopian spectacle. She lay across it like a shadow. He thought very frequently about her and about the pity and resentment against life and vigour that she embodied. In a world of fear, weakness, infection, darkness and confusion, pity, the act of charity, the alms and the refuge, the deed of stark devotion, might show indeed like sweet and gracious presences; but in this world of health and brave enterprises, pity betrayed itself a vicious desire. Crystal, Utopian youth, was as hard as his name. When he had slipped one day on some rocks and twisted and torn his ankle, he had limped but he had laughed. When Mr Barnstaple was winded on a steep staircase Crystal was polite rather than sympathetic. So Lychnis had found no confederate in the dedication of her life to sorrow; even from Mr Barnstaple she could win no sympathy. He perceived that indeed so far as temperament went he was a better Utopian than she was. To him as to Utopia it seemed rather an occasion for gladness than sorrow that her man and her children had met death fearlessly. They were dead; a brave stark death; the waters still glittered and the sun still shone. But her loss had revealed some underlying racial taint in her, something very ancient in the species, something that Utopia was still breeding out only very slowly, the dark sacrificial disposition that bows and responds to the shadow. It was strange and yet perhaps it was inevitable that Mr Barnstaple should meet again in Utopia that spirit which Earth knows so well, the spirit that turns from the Kingdom of Heaven to worship the thorns and the nails, which delights to represent its God not as the Resurrection and the Life but as a woeful and defeated cadaver.

She would talk to him of his sons as if she envied him because of the loss of her own, but all she said reminded him of the educational disadvantages and narrow prospects of his boys and how much stouter and finer and happier their lives would have been in Utopia. He would have risked drowning them a dozen times to have saved them from being clerks and employees of other men. Even by earthly standards he felt now that he had not done his best by them; he had let many things drift in their lives and in the lives of himself and his wife that he now felt he ought to have controlled. Could he have his time over again he felt that he would see to it that his sons took a livelier interest in politics and science and were not so completely engulfed in the trivialities of suburban life, in tennis playing, amateur theatricals, inane flirtations and the like. They were good boys in substance he felt, but he had left them to their mother; and he had left their mother too much to herself instead of battling with her for the sake of his own ideas. They were living trivially in the shadow of one great catastrophe and with no security against another; they were living in a world of weak waste and shabby insufficiency. And his own life also had been – weak waste.

His life at Sydenham began to haunt him. 'I criticized everything but I altered nothing,' he said. 'I was as bad as Peeve. Was I any more use in that world than I am in this? But on Earth we are all wasters. . . .'

He avoided Lychnis for a day or so and wandered about the valley alone. He went into a great reading-room and fingered books he could not read; he was suffered to stand in a workshop, and he watched an artist make a naked girl of gold more lovely than any earthly statuette and melt her again dissatisfied; here he came upon men building, and here was work upon the fields, here was a great shaft in the hillside and something deep in the hill that flashed and scintillated strangely; they would not let him go in to it; he saw a thousand things he could not understand. He began to feel as perhaps a very intelligent dog must sometimes feel in the world of men, only that he had no master and no instincts that could find a consolation in canine abjection. The Utopians went about their business in the day-time, they passed him smiling and they filled him with intolerable envy. They knew what to do. They belonged. They went by in twos and threes in the evening, communing together and sometimes singing together. Lovers would pass him, their sweetly smiling faces close together, and his loneliness became an agony of hopeless desires.

Because, though he fought hard to keep it below the threshold of his consciousness, Mr Barnstaple desired greatly to love and be loved in Utopia. The realization that no one of these people could ever conceive of any such intimacy of body or spirit with him was a humiliation more fundamental even than his uselessness. The love-liness of the Utopian girls and women who glanced at him curiously or passed him with a serene indifference, crushed down his self-respect and made the Utopian world altogether intolerable to him. Mutely, unconsciously, these Utopian goddesses concentrated upon him the uttermost abasement of caste and race inferiority. He could not keep his thoughts from love where everyone it seemed had a lover, and in this Utopian world love for him was a thing grotesque and incon-ceivable. . . .

Then one night as he lay awake distressed beyond measure by the thought of such things, an idea came to him whereby it seemed to him he might restore his self-respect and win a sort of citizenship in Utopia.

So that they might even speak of him and remember him with interest and sympathy.

CHAPTER THE THIRD

The Service of the Earthling

I

The man to whom Mr Barnstaple, after due inquiries, went to talk was named Sungold. He was probably very old, because there were lines of age about his eyes and over his fine brow. He was a ruddy man, bearded with an auburn beard that had streaks of white, and his eyes were brown and nimble under his thick eyebrows. His hair had thinned but little and flowed back like a mane, but its copper-red colour had gone. He sat at a table with papers spread before him, making manuscript notes. He smiled at Mr Barnstaple, for he had been expecting him, and indicated a seat for him with his stout and freckled hand. Then he waited smilingly for Mr Barnstaple to begin.

'This world is one triumph of the desire for order and beauty in men's minds,' said Mr Barnstaple. 'But it will not tolerate one useless soul in it. Everyone is happily active. Everyone but myself. . . . I belong nowhere. I have nothing to do. And no one – is related to me.'

Sungold moved his head slightly to show that he understood.

'It is hard for an Earthling, with an earthly want of training, to fall into any place here. Into any usual work or any usual relationship. One is – a stranger. . . . But it is still harder to have no place at all. In the new work, of which I am told you know most of anyone and are indeed the centre and regulator, it has occurred to me that I might be of some use, that I might indeed be as good as a Utopian. . . . If so, I want to be of use. You may want someone just to risk death – to take the danger of going into some strange place – someone who desires to serve Utopia – and who need not have skill or knowledge – or be a beautiful or able person?'

Mr Barnstaple stopped short.

Sungold conveyed the completest understanding of all that was in Mr Barnstaple's mind.

Mr Barnstaple sat interrogative while for a time Sungold thought.

Then words and phrases began to string themselves together in Mr Barnstaple's mind.

Sungold wondered if Mr Barnstaple understood either the extent or the limitations of the great discoveries that were now being made in Utopia. Utopia, he said, was passing into a phase of intense intellectual exaltation. New powers and possibilities intoxicated the imagination of the race, and it was indeed inconceivable that an unteachable and perplexed Earthling could be anything but distressed and uncomfortable amidst the vast strange activities that must now begin. Even many of their own people, the more backward Utopians, were disturbed. For centuries Utopian philosophers and experimentalists had been criticizing, revising and reconstructing their former instinctive and traditional ideas of space and time, of form and substance, and now very rapidly the new ways of thinking were becoming clear and simple and bearing fruit in surprising practical applications. The limitations of space which had seemed for ever insurmountable were breaking down; they were breaking down in a strange and perplexing way but they were breaking down. It was now theoretically possible, it was rapidly becoming practicably possible, to pass from the planet Utopia to which the race had hitherto been confined, to other points in its universe of origin, that is to say to remote planets and distant stars. ... That was the gist of the present situation.

'I cannot imagine that,' said Mr Barnstaple.

'You cannot imagine it,' Sungold agreed, quite cordially 'But it is so. A hundred years ago it was inconceivable – here.'

'Do you get there by some sort of backstairs in another dimension?' said Mr Barnstaple.

Sungold considered this guess. It was a grotesque image, he said, but from the point of view of an Earthling it would serve. That conveyed something of its quality. But it was so much more wonderful. ...

'A new and astounding phase has begun for life here. We learnt long ago the chief secrets of happiness upon this planet. Life is good in this world. You find it good? ... For thousands of years yet it will be our fastness and our home. But the wind of a new adventure blows through

390

our life. All this world is in a mood like striking camp in the winter quarters when spring approaches.'

He leant over his papers towards Mr Barnstaple, and held up a finger and spoke audible words as if to make his meaning plainer. It seemed to Mr Barnstaple that each word translated itself into English as he spoke it. At any rate Mr Barnstaple understood. 'The collision of our planet Utopia with your planet Earth was a very curious accident, but an unimportant accident, in this story. I want you to understand that. Your universe and ours are two out of a great number of gravitation-time universes, which are translated together through the inexhaustible infinitude of God. They are similar throughout, but they are identical in nothing. Your planet and ours happen to be side by side, so to speak, but they are not travelling at exactly the same pace nor in a strictly parallel direction. They will drift apart again and follow their several destinies. When Arden and Greenlake made their experiment the chances of their hitting anything in your universe were infinitely remote. They had disregarded it, they were merely rotating some of our matter out of and then back into our universe. You fell into us — as amazingly for us as for you. The importance of our discoveries for us lies in our own universe and not in yours. We do not want to come into your universe nor have more of your world come into ours. You are too like us, and you are too dark and troubled and diseased – you are too contagious – and we, we cannot help you yet because we are not gods but men.'

Mr Barnstaple nodded.

'What could Utopians do with the men of Earth? We have no strong instinct in us to teach or dominate other adults. That has been bred out of us by long centuries of equality and free co-operation. And you would be too numerous for us to teach and much of your population would be grown up and set in bad habits. Your stupidities would get in our way, your quarrels and jealousies and traditions, your flags and religions and all your embodied spites and suppressions, would hamper us in everything we should want to do. We should be impatient with you, unjust, overbearing. You are too like us for us to be patient with your failures. It would be hard to remember constantly how ill-bred you were. In Utopia we found out long ago that no race of human beings was sufficiently great, subtle and powerful to think and act for any other race. Perhaps already you are finding out the same thing on Earth as your races come into closer contact. And much more would this be true between Utopia and Earth. From what I know of your people and their ignorance and obstinacies it is clear our people would despise you; and contempt is the cause of all injustice. We might end by exterminating you. ... But why should we make that possible? ... We must leave you alone. We cannot trust ourselves with you. ... Believe me this is the only reasonable course for us.'

Mr Barnstaple assented silently.

'You and I – two individuals – can be friends and understand.'

'What you say is true,' said Mr Barnstaple. 'It is true. But it grieves me it is true. ... Greatly. ... Nevertheless, I gather, I at least may be of service in Utopia?'

'You can.'

'How?'

'By returning to your own world.'

Mr Barnstaple thought for some moments. It was what he had feared. But he had offered himself. 'I will do that.'

'By attempting to return, I should say. There is risk. You may be killed.'

'I must take that.'

'We want to verify all the data we have of the relations of our universe to yours. We want to reverse the experiment of Arden and Greenlake and see if we can return a living being to your world. We are almost certain now that we can do so. And that human being must care for us enough and care for his own world enough to go back and give us a sign that he has got there.'

Mr Barnstaple spoke huskily. 'I can do that,' he said.

'We can put you into that machine of yours and into the clothes you wore. You can be made again exactly as you left your world.'

'Exactly. I understand.'

'And because your world is vile and contentious and yet has some strangely able brains in it, here and there, we do not want your people to know of us, living so close to you – for we shall be close to you yet for some hundreds of years at least – we do not want them to know for fear that they should come here presently, led by some poor silly genius of a scientific man, come in their greedy, foolish, breeding swarms, hammering at our doors, threatening our lives, and spoiling our high adventures, and so have to be beaten off and killed like an invasion of rats or parasites.'

'Yes,' said Mr Barnstaple. 'Before men can come to Utopia, they must learn the way here. Utopia, I see, is only a home for those who have learnt the way.'

He paused and answered some of his own thoughts. 'When I have returned,' he said, 'shall I begin to forget Utopia?'

Sungold smiled and said nothing.

'All my days the nostalgia of Utopia will distress me.'

'And uphold you.'

'I shall take up my earthly life at the point where I laid it down, but – on Earth – I shall be a Utopian. For I feel that having offered my service and had it accepted, that I am no longer an outcast in Utopia. I belong. ...'

'Remember you may be killed. You may die in the trial.'

'As it may happen.'

'Well – Brother!'

The friendly paw took Mr Barnstaple's and pressed it and the deep eyes smiled.

'After you have returned and given us your sign, several of the other Earthlings may also be sent back.'

Mr Barnstaple sat up. '*But!*' he gasped. His voice rose high in amazement. 'I thought they were hurled into the blank space of some outer universe and altogether destroyed!'

'Several were killed. They killed themselves by rushing down the side of the old fortress in the outer darkness as the Crag rotated. The men in leather. The man you call Long Barrow—'

'Barralonga?'

'Yes. And the man who shrugged his shoulders and said, "What would you?" The others came back as the rotation was completed late in the day – asphyxiated and frozen but not dead. They have been restored to life, and we are puzzled now how to dispose of them. ... They are of no use whatever in this world. They encumber us.'

'It is only too manifest,' said Mr Barnstaple.

'The man you call Burleigh seems to be of some importance in your earthly affairs. We have searched his mind. His powers of belief are very small. He believes in very little but the life of a cultivated wealthy gentleman who holds a position of modest distinction in the councils of a largely fictitious empire. It is doubtful if he will believe in the reality of any of this experience. We will make sure anyhow that he thinks it has been an imaginative dream. He will consider it too fantastic to talk about because it is plain he is already very afraid of his imagination. He will find himself back in your world a few days after you reach it and he will make his way to his own home unobtrusively. He will come next after you. You will see him reappear in political affairs. Perhaps a little wiser.'

'It might well be,' said Mr Barnstaple.

'And – what are the sounds of his name? – Rupert Catskill; he too will return. Your world would miss him.'

'Nothing will make *him* wiser,' said Mr Barnstaple with conviction.

'Lady Stella will come.'

'I am glad she has escaped. She will say nothing about Utopia. She is very discreet.'

'The priest is mad. His behaviour became offensive and obscene and he is under restraint.'

'What did he do?'

'He made a number of aprons of black silk and set out with them to attack our young people in an undignified manner.'

'You can send him back,' said Mr Barnstaple after reflection.

'But will your world allow that sort of thing?'

'*We* call that sort of thing Purity,' said Mr Barnstaple. 'But of course if you like to keep him. . . .'

'He shall come back,' said Sungold.

'The others you can keep,' said Mr Barnstaple. 'In fact you will have to keep them. Nobody on Earth will trouble about them very much. In our world there are so many people that always a few are getting lost. As it is, returning even the few you propose to do may excite attention. Local people may begin to notice all these wanderers coming from nowhere in particular and asking their way home upon the Maidenhead Road. They might give way under questions. . . . You cannot send any more. Put the rest on an island. Or something of that sort. I wish I could advise you to keep the priest also. But many people would miss him. They would suffer from suppressed Purity and begin to behave queerly. The pulpit of St Barnabas satisfies a recognized craving. And it will be quite easy to persuade him that Utopia is a dream and delusion. All priests believe that naturally of all Utopias. He will think of it, if he thinks of it at all, as – what would he call it? – as a moral nightmare.'

2

Their business was finished, but Mr Barnstaple was loth to go.

He looked Sungold in the eye and found something kindly there.

'You have told me all that I have to do,' he said, 'and it is fully time that I went away from you, for any moment in your life is more precious than a day of mine. Yet because I am to go so soon and so obediently out of this vast and splendid world of yours back to my native disorders, I could find it in my heart to ask you to unbend if you could, to come down to me a little, and to tell me simply and plainly of the greater days and greater achievements that are now dawning upon this planet. You speak of your being able presently to go out of this Utopia to remote parts in your universe. That perplexes my mind. Probably I am unfitted to grasp that idea, but it is very important to me. It has been a belief in our world that at last there must be an end to life because our sun and planets are cooling, and there seems no hope of escape from the little world upon which we have arisen. We were born with it and we must die with it. That robbed many of us of hope and energy: for why should we work for progress in a world that must freeze and die?'

Sungold laughed. 'Your philosophers concluded too soon.'

He sprawled over the table towards his hearer and looked him earnestly in the face.

'Your earthly science has been going on for how long?'

'Two hundred – three hundred years.'

Sungold held up two fingers. 'And men? How many men?'

'A few hundred who mattered in each generation.'

'We have gone on for three thousand years now, and a hundred million good brains have been put like grapes into the wine-press of science. And we know today – how little we know. There is never an observation made but a hundred observations are missed in the making of it ; there is never a measurement but some impish truth mocks us and gets away from us in the margin of error. I know something of where your scientific men are, all power to the poor savages! because I have studied the beginnings of our own science in the long past of Utopia. How can I express our distances? Since those days we have examined and tested and tried and retried a score of new ways of thinking about space, of which time is only a specialized form. We have forms of expression that we cannot get over to you so that things that used to seem difficult and paradoxical to us – that probably seem hopelessly difficult and paradoxical to you, lose all their difficulty in our minds. It is hard to convey to you. We think in terms of a space in which the space and time system, in terms of which you think, is only a specialized case. So far as our feelings and instincts and daily habits go we too live in another such system as you do – but not so far as our knowledge goes, not so far as our powers go. Our minds have exceeded our lives – as yours will. We are still flesh and blood, still hope and desire, we go to and fro and look up and down, but things that seemed remote are brought near, things that were inaccessible bow down, things that were insurmountable lie under the hollows of our hands.'

'And you do not think your race nor, for the matter of that, ours, need ever perish?'

'Perish! We have hardly begun!'

The old man spoke very earnestly. Unconsciously he parodied Newton. 'We are like little children who have been brought to the shores of a limitless ocean. All the knowledge we have gathered yet in the few score generations since first we began to gather knowledge, is like a small handful of pebbles gathered upon the shore of that limitless sea.

'Before us lies knowledge, endlessly, and we may take and take, and as we take, grow. We grow in power, we grow in courage. We renew our youth. For mark what I say, our worlds grow younger. The old generations of apes and sub-men before us had aged minds; their narrow reluctant wisdom was the meagre profit, hoarded and stale and sour, of innumerable lives. They dreaded new things; so bitterly did they value the bitterly won old. But to learn is, at length, to become young again, to be released, to begin afresh. Your world, compared with ours, is a world of unteachable encrusted souls, of bent and droning traditions, of hates and injuries and such-like unforgettable things. But some day you too will become again like little children, and it will be you who will find your way through to us – to us, who will be waiting for you. Two universes will meet and embrace, to beget a yet greater universe. ... You Earthlings do not begin to realize yet the significance of life. Nor we Utopians – scarcely more. ... Life is still only a promise, still waits to be born, out of such poor stirrings in the dust as we. ...

'Some day here and everywhere, Life of which you and I are but anticipatory atoms and eddies, Life will awaken indeed, one and whole and marvellous, like a child awaking to conscious life. It will open its drowsy eyes and stretch itself and smile, looking the mystery of God in the face as one meets the morning sun. We shall be there then, all that matters of us, you and I. ...

'And it will be no more than a beginning, no more than a beginning. ...'

CHAPTER THE FOURTH

The Return of the Earthling

I

Too soon the morning came when Mr Barnstaple was to look his last upon the fair hills of Utopia and face the great experiment to which he had given himself. He had been loth to sleep and he had slept little that night, and in the early dawn he was abroad, wearing for the last time the sandals and the light white robe that had become his Utopian costume. Presently he would have to struggle into socks and boots and trousers and collar; the strangest gear. It would choke him he felt, and he stretched his bare arms to the sky and yawned and breathed his lungs full. The valley below still drowsed beneath a coverlet of fleecy mists; he turned his face uphill, the sooner to meet the sun.

Never before had he been out among the Utopian flowers at such an early hour; it was amusing to see how some of the great trumpets still drooped asleep and how many of the larger blossoms were furled and hung. Many of the leaves too were wrapped up, as limp as new-hatched moths. The gossamer spiders had been busy and everything was very wet with dew. A great tiger came upon him suddenly out of a side path and stared hard at him for some moments with round yellow eyes. Perhaps it was trying to remember the forgotten instincts of its breed.

Some way up the road he passed under a vermilion archway and went up a flight of stone stairs that promised to bring him earlier to the crest.

A number of friendly little birds, very gaily coloured, flew about him for a time and one perched impudently upon his shoulder, but when he put up his hand to caress it it evaded him and flew away. He was still ascending the staircase when the sun rose. It was as if the hillside slipped off a veil of grey and blue and bared the golden beauty of its body.

Mr Barnstaple came to a landing place upon the staircase and stopped, and stood very still watching the sunrise search and quicken the brooding deeps of the valley below.

Far away, like an arrow shot from east to west, appeared a line of dazzling brightness on the sea.

2

'Serenity,' he murmured. 'Beauty. All the works of men – in perfect harmony … minds brought to harmony. …'

According to his journalistic habit he tried over phrases. 'An energetic peace … confusions dispersed. … A world of spirits, crystal clear. …'

What was the use of words?

For a time he stood quite still listening, for from some slope above a lark had gone heavenward, spraying sweet notes. He tried to see that little speck of song and was blinded by the brightening blue of the sky.

Presently the lark came down and ceased. Utopia was silent, except for a burst of childish laughter somewhere on the hillside below.

It dawned upon Mr Barnstaple how peaceful was the Utopian air in comparison with the tormented atmosphere of Earth. Here was no yelping and howling of tired or irritated dogs, no braying, bellowing, squealing and distressful outcries of uneasy beasts, no farmyard clamour, no shouts of anger, no barking and coughing, no sounds of hammering, beating, sawing, grinding, mechanical hooting, whistling, screaming and the like, no clattering of distant trains, clanking of automobiles or other ill-contrived mechanisms; the tiresome and ugly noises of many an unpleasant creature were heard no more. In Utopia the ear like the eye was at peace. The air which had once been a mud of felted noises was now – a purified silence. Such sounds as one heard lay upon it like beautiful printing on a generous sheet of fine paper.

His eyes returned to the landscape below as the last fleecy vestiges of mist dissolved away. Watertanks, roads, bridges, buildings, embankments, colonnades, groves, gardens, channels, cascades and fountains grew multitudinously clear, framed under a branch of dark foliage from a white-stemmed tree that gripped a hold among the rocks at his side.

'Three thousand years ago this was a world like ours. … Think of it – in a hundred generations. .... In three thousand years we might make our poor waste of an Earth, jungle and desert, slag-heap and slum, into another such heaven of beauty and power. ....

'Worlds they are – similar, but not the same. ....

'If I could tell them what I have seen! ...

'Suppose all men could have this vision of Utopia. ....

'They would not believe it if I told them. No. ....

'They would bray like asses at me and bark like dogs! ... They will have no world but their own world. It hurts them to think of any world but their own. Nothing can be done that has not been done already. To think otherwise would be humiliation. ... Death, torture, futility – anything but humiliation! So they must sit among their weeds and excrement, scratching and nodding sagely at one another, hoping for a good dog-fight and to gloat upon pain and effort they do not share, sure that mankind stank, stinks and must always stink, that stinking is very pleasant indeed, and that there is nothing new under the sun. ...'

His thoughts were diverted by two young girls who came running one after the other up the staircase. One was dark even to duskiness and her hands were full of blue flowers; the other who pursued her was a year or so younger and golden fair. They were full of the limitless excitement of young animals at play. The former one was so intent upon the other that she discovered Mr Barnstaple with a squeak of surprise after she had got to his landing. She stared at him with a quick glance of inquiry, flashed into impudent roguery, flung two blue flowers in his face and was off up the steps above. Her companion, intent on capture, flew by. They flickered up the staircase like two butterflies of buff and pink; halted far above and came together for a momentary consultation about the stranger, waved hands to him and vanished.

Mr Barnstaple returned their greeting and remained cheered.

3

The view-point to which Lychnis had directed Mr Barnstaple stood out on the ridge between the great valley in which he had spent the last few days and a wild and steep glen down which ran a torrent that was destined after some hundred miles of windings to reach the river of the plain. The view-point was on the crest of a crag, it had been built out upon great brackets so that it hung sheer over a bend in the torrent below; on the one hand was mountainous scenery and a rich and picturesque foam of green vegetation in the depths, on the other spread the broad garden spaces of a perfected landscape. For a time Mr Barnstaple scrutinized this glen into which he looked for the first time. Five hundred feet or so below him, so that he felt that he could have dropped a pebble upon its outstretched wings, a bustard was soaring.

Many of the trees below he thought must be fruit trees, but they were too far off to see distinctly. Here and there he could distinguish a footpath winding up among the trees and rocks, and among the green masses were little pavilions in which he knew the wayfarer might rest and make tea for himself and find biscuits and such-like refreshment and possibly a couch and a book. The whole world, he knew, was full of such summer-houses and kindly shelters. . . .

After a time he went back to the side of this view-place up which he had come, and regarded the great valley that went out towards the sea. The word Pisgah floated through his mind. For indeed below him was the Promised Land of human desires. Here at last, established and secure, were peace, power, health, happy activity, length of days and beauty. All that we seek was found here and every dream was realized.

How long would it be yet – how many centuries or thousands of years – before a man would be able to stand upon some high place on earth also and see mankind triumphant and wholly and for ever at peace? . . .

He folded his arms under him upon the parapet and mused profoundly.

There was no knowledge in this Utopia of which Earth had not the germs, there was no power used here that Earthlings might not use. Here, but for ignorance and darkness and the spites and malice they permit, was Earth to-day. . . .

Towards such a world as this Utopia Mr Barnstaple had been striving weakly all his life. If the experiment before him succeeded, if presently he found himself alive again on Earth, it would still be towards Utopia that his life would be directed. And he would not be alone. On Earth there must be thousands, tens of thousands, perhaps hundreds of thousands, who were also struggling in their minds and acts to find a way of escape for themselves and for their children from the disorders and indignities of the Age of Confusion, hundreds of thousands who wanted to put an end to wars and waste, to heal and educate and restore, to set up the banner of Utopia over the shams and divisions that waste mankind.

'Yes, but we fail,' said Mr Barnstaple and walked fretfully to and fro. 'Tens and hundreds of thousands of men and women! And we achieve so little! Perhaps every young man and every young woman has had some dream at least of serving and bettering the world. And we are scattered and wasted, and the old things and the foul things, customs, delusions, habits, tolerated treasons, base immediacies, triumph over us!'

He went to the parapet again and stood with his foot on a seat, his elbow on his knee and his chin in his hand, staring at the loveliness of this world he was to leave so soon. . . .

'We could do it.'

And suddenly it was borne in upon Mr Barnstaple that he belonged now soul and body to the Revolution, to the Great Revolution that is afoot on Earth; that marches and will never desist nor rest again until old Earth is one city and Utopia set up therein. He knew clearly that this Revolution is life, and that all other living is a trafficking of life with death. And as this crystallized out in his mind he knew instantly that so presently it would crystallize out in the minds of countless others of those hundreds of thousands of men and women on Earth whose minds are set towards Utopia.

He stood up. He began walking to and fro. 'We shall do it,' he said.

Earthly thought was barely awakened as yet to the task and possibilities before mankind. All human history so far had been no more than the stirring of a sleeper, a gathering discontent, a rebellion against the limitations set upon life, the unintelligent protest of thwarted imaginations. All the conflicts and insurrections and revolutions that had ever been on Earth were but indistinct preludes of the revolution that has still to come. When he had started out upon this fantastic holiday Mr Barnstaple realized he had been in a mood of depression; earthly affairs had seemed utterly confused and hopeless to him; but now from the view-point of Utopia achieved, and with his health renewed, he could see plainly enough how steadily men on earth were feeling their way now, failure after failure, towards the opening drive of the final revolution. He could see how men in his own lifetime had been struggling out of such entanglements as the lie of monarchy, the lies of dogmatic religion and dogmatic morality towards public self-respect and cleanness of mind and body. They struggled now also towards international charity and the liberation of their common economic life from a network of pretences, dishonesties and impostures. There is confusion in all struggles; retractions and defeats; but the whole effect seen from the calm height of Utopia was one of steadfast advance. . . .

There were blunders, there were set-backs, because the forces of revolution still worked in the twilight. The great effort and the great failure of the socialist movement to create a new state in the world had been contemporaneous with Mr Barnstaple's life; socialism had been the gospel of his boyhood; he had participated in its hopes, its doubts, its bitter internal conflicts. He had seen the movement losing sweetness and gathering force in the narrowness of the Marxist formula. He had seen it sacrifice its constructive power for militant intensity. In Russia he had marked its ability to overthrow and its inability to plan or build. Like every liberal spirit in the world he had shared the chill of Bolshevik presumption and Bolshevik failure, and for a time it had seemed to him that this open bankruptcy of a great creative impulse was no less and no more than a victory for reaction, that it gave renewed life to all the shams, impostures, corruptions, traditional anarchies and ascendancies that restrain and cripple human life. ... But now from this high view-point in Utopia he saw clearly that the Phoenix of Revolution flames down to ashes only to be born again. While the noose is fitted round the Teacher's neck the youths are reading his teaching; Revolutions arise and die; the Great Revolution comes – incessantly and inevitably.

The time was near – and in what life was left to him, he himself might help to bring it nearer – when the forces of that last and real revolution would work no longer in the twilight but in the dawn, and a thousand sorts of men and women now far apart and unorganized and mutually antagonistic would be drawn together by the growth of a common vision of the world desired. The Marxist had wasted the forces of revolution for fifty years; he had had no vision; he had had only a condemnation for established things. He had estranged all scientific and able men by his pompous affectation of the scientific; he had terrified them by his intolerant orthodoxy; his delusion that all ideas are begotten by material circumstances had made him negligent of education and criticism. He had attempted to build social unity on hate and rejected every other driving force for the bitterness of a class war. But now, in its days of doubt and exhaustion, vision was returning to Socialism, and the dreary spectacle of a proletarian dictatorship gave way once more to Utopia, to the demand for a world fairly and righteously at peace, its resources husbanded and exploited for the common good, its every citizen freed not only from servitude but from ignorance, and its surplus energies directed steadfastly to the increase of knowledge and beauty. The attainment of that vision by more and more minds was a thing now no longer to be prevented. Earth would tread the path Utopia had trod. She too would weave law, duty and education into a larger sanity than man has ever known. Men also would presently laugh at the things they had feared, and brush aside the impostures that had overawed them and the absurdities that had tormented and crippled their lives. And as this great revolution was achieved and earth wheeled into daylight, the burthen of human miseries would lift, and courage oust sorrow from the hearts of men. Earth, which was now no more than a wilderness, sometimes horrible and at best picturesque, a wilderness interspersed with weedy scratchings for food and with hovels and slums and slag-heaps, Earth too would grow rich with loveliness and fair as this great land was fair. The sons of Earth also, purified from disease, sweet-minded and strong and beautiful, would go proudly about their conquered planet and lift their daring to the stars.

'Given the will,' said Mr Barnstaple. 'Given only the will.' ...

4

From some distant place came the sound of a sweet-toned bell striking the hour.

The time for the service to which he was dedicated was drawing near. He must descend, and be taken to the place where the experiment was to be made.

He took one last look at the glen and then went back to the broad prospect of the great valley, with its lakes and tanks and terraces, its groves and pavilions, its busy buildings and high viaducts, its wide slopes of sunlit cultivation, its universal gracious amenity. 'Farewell, Utopia,' he said, and was astonished to discover how deeply his emotions were stirred.

'Dear Dream of Hope and Loveliness, Farewell!'

He stood quite still in a mood of sorrowful deprivation too deep for tears.

It seemed to him that the spirit of Utopia bent down over him like a goddess, friendly, adorable – and inaccessible.

His very mind stood still.

'Never,' he whispered at last, 'for me ... Except to serve. ... No. ...'

Presently he began to descend the steps that wound down from the view-point. For a time he noted little of the things immediately about him. Then the scent of roses invaded his attention, and he found himself walking down a slanting pergola covered with great white roses and very active with little green birds. He stopped short and stood looking up at the leaves, light-saturated, against the sky. He put up his hands and drew down one of the great blossoms until it touched his cheek.

They took Mr Barnstaple back by aeroplane to the point upon the glassy road where he had first come into Utopia. Lychnis came with him and Crystal, who was curious to see what would be done.

A group of twenty or thirty people, including Sungold, awaited him. The ruined labouratory of Arden and Greenlake had been replaced by fresh buildings, and there were additional erections on the further side of the road; but Mr Barnstaple could recognize quite clearly the place where Mr Catskill had faced the leopard and where Mr Burleigh had accosted him. Several new kinds of flowers were now out, but the blue blossoms that had charmed him on arrival still prevailed. His old car, the Yellow Peril, looking now the clumsiest piece of ironmongery conceivable, stood in the road. He went and examined it. It seemed to be in perfect order; it had been carefully oiled and the petrol tank was full.

In a little pavilion were his bag and all his earthly clothes. They were very clean and they had been folded and pressed, and he put them on. His shirt seemed tight across his chest and his collar decidedly tight, and his coat cut him a little under the arms. Perhaps these garments had shrunken when they were disinfected. He packed his bag and Crystal put it in the car for him.

Sungold explained very simply all that Mr Barnstaple had to do. Across the road, close by the restored labouratory, stretched a line as thin as gossamer. 'Steer your car to that and break it,' he said. 'That is all you have to do. Then take this red flower and put it down exactly where your wheel tracks show you have entered your own world.'

Mr Barnstaple was left beside the car. The Utopians went back twenty or thirty yards and stood in a circle about him. For a few moments everyone was still.

6

Mr Barnstaple got into his car, started his engine, let it throb for a minute and then put in the clutch. The yellow car began to move towards the line of gossamer. He made a gesture with one hand which Lychnis answered. Sungold and others of the Utopians also made friendly movements. But Crystal was watching too intently for any gesture.

'Good-bye, Crystal!' cried Mr Barnstaple, and the boy responded with a start.

Mr Barnstaple accelerated, set his teeth and, in spite of his will to keep them open, shut his eyes as he touched the gossamer line. Came that sense again of unendurable tension and that sound like the snapping of a bow-string. He had an irresistible impulse to stop – go back. He took his foot from the accelerator, and the car seemed to fall a foot or so and stopped so heavily and suddenly that he was jerked forward against the steering wheel. The oppression lifted. He opened his eyes and looked about him.

The car was standing in a field from which the hay had recently been carried. He was tilted on one side because of a roll in the ground. A hedge in which there was an open black gate separated this hay-field from the high road. Close at hand was a board advertisement of some Maidenhead hotel. On the far side of the road were level fields against a background of low wooded hills. Away to the left was a little inn. He turned his head and saw Windsor Castle in the remote distance rising above poplar-studded meadows. It was not, as his Utopians had promised him, the exact spot of his departure from our Earth, but it was certainly less than a hundred yards away.

He sat still for some moments, mentally rehearsing what he had to do. Then he started the Yellow Peril again and drove it close up to the black gate.

He got out and stood with the red flower in his hand. He had to go back to the exact spot at which he had re-entered this universe and put that flower down there. It would be quite easy to determine that point by the track the car had made in the stubble. But he felt an extraordinary reluctance to obey these instructions. He wanted to keep this flower. It was the last thing, the only thing, he had now from that golden world. That and the sweet savour on his hands.

It was extraordinary that he had brought no more than this with him. Why had he not brought a lot of flowers? Why had they given him nothing, no little thing, out of all their wealth of beauty? He wanted intensely to keep this flower. He was moved to substitute a spray of honeysuckle from the hedge close at hand. But then he remembered that that would be infected stuff for them. He must do as he was told. He walked back along the track of his car to its beginning, stood for a moment hesitating, tore a single petal from that glowing bloom, and then laid down the rest of the great flower carefully in the very centre of his track. The petal he put in his pocket. Then with a heavy heart he went back slowly to his car and stood beside it, watching that star of almost luminous red.

His grief and emotion were very great. He was bitterly sorrowful now at having left Utopia.

It was evident the great drought was still going on, for the field and the hedges were more parched and brown than he had ever seen an English field before. Along the road lay a thin cloud of dust that passing cars continually renewed. This old world seemed to him to be full of unlovely sights and sounds and odours already half forgotten. There was the honking of distant cars, the uproar of a train, a thirsty cow mourning its discomfort; there was the irritation of dust in his nostrils and the smell of sweltering tar; there was barbed wire in the hedge near by and along the top of the black gate, and horse-dung and scraps of dirty paper at his feet. The lovely world from which he had been driven had shrunken now to a spot of shining scarlet.

Something happened very quickly. It was as if a hand appeared for a moment and took the flower. In a moment it had gone. A little eddy of dust swirled and drifted and sank. . . .

It was the end.

At the thought of the traffic on the main road Mr Barnstaple stooped down so as to hide his face from the passers-by. For some minutes he was unable to regain his self-control. He stood with his arm covering his face, leaning against the shabby brown hood of his car. . . .

At last this gust of sorrow came to an end and he could get in again, start up the engine and steer into the main road.

He turned eastward haphazard. He left the black gate open behind him. He went along very slowly for as yet he had formed no idea of whither he was going. He began to think that probably in this old world of ours he was being sought for as a person who had mysteriously disappeared. Someone might discover him and he would become the focus of a thousand impossible questions. That would be very tiresome and disagreeable. He had not thought of this in Utopia. In Utopia it had seemed quite possible that he could come back into Earth unobserved. Now on earth that confidence seemed foolish. He saw ahead of him the board of a modest tea-room. It occurred that he might alight there, see a newspaper, ask a discreet question or so, and find out what had been happening to the world and whether he had indeed been missed.

He found a table already laid for tea under the window. In the centre of the room a larger table bore an aspidistra in a big green pot and a selection of papers, chiefly out-of-date illustrated papers. But there was also a copy of the morning's *Daily Express*.

He seized upon this eagerly, fearful that he would find it full of the mysterious disappearance of Mr Burleigh, Lord Barralonga, Mr Rupert Catskill, Mr Hunker, Father Amerton and Lady Stella, not to mention the lesser lights. . . . Gradually as he turned it over his fears vanished. There was not a word about any of them!

'But surely,' he protested to himself, now clinging to his idea, 'their friends must have missed them!'

He read through the whole paper. Of one only did he find mention and that was the last name he would have expected to find – Mr Freddy Mush. The Princess de Modena-Frascati (*née* Higgisbottom) Prize for English literature had been given away to nobody in particular by Mr Graceful Gloss owing to 'the unavoidable absence of Mr Freddy Mush abroad'.

The problem of why there had been no hue and cry for the others opened a vast field of worldly speculation to Mr Barnstaple in which he wandered for a time. His mind went back to that bright red blossom lying among the cut stems of the grass in the mown field and to the hand that had seemed to take it. With that the door that had opened so marvellously between that strange and beautiful world and our own had closed again.

Wonder took possession of Mr Barnstaple's mind. That dear world of honesty and health was beyond the utmost boundaries of our space, utterly inaccessible to him now for evermore; and yet, as he had been told, it was but one of countless universes that move together in time, that lie against one another, endlessly like the leaves of a book. And all of them are as nothing in the endless multitudes of systems and dimensions that surround them. 'Could I but rotate my arm out of the limits set to it,' one of the Utopians had said to him; 'I could thrust it into a thousand universes.' . . .

A waitress with his teapot recalled him to mundane things.

The meal served to him seemed tasteless and unclean. He drank the queer brew of the tea because he was thirsty but he ate scarcely a mouthful.

Presently he chanced to put his hand in his pocket and touched something soft. He drew out the petal he had torn from the red flower. It had lost its glowing red, and as he held it out in the stuffy air of the room it seemed to writhe as it shrivelled and blackened; its delicate scent gave place to a mawkish odour.

'Manifestly,' he said. 'I should have expected this.'

He dropped the lump of decay on his plate, then picked it up again and thrust it into the soil in the pot of the aspidistra.

He took up the *Daily Express* again and turned it over, trying to recover his sense of this world's affairs.

7

For a long time Mr Barnstaple meditated over the *Daily Express* in the tea-room at Colnebrook. His thoughts went far so that presently the newspaper slipped to the ground unheeded. He roused himself with a sigh and called for his bill. Paying, he became aware of a pocket-book still full of pound notes. 'This will be the cheapest holiday I have ever had,' he thought. 'I've spent no money at all.' He inquired for the post-office, because he had a telegram to send.

Two hours later he stopped outside the gate of his little villa at Sydenham. He set it open – the customary bit of stick with which he did this was in its usual place – and steered the Yellow Peril with the dexterity of use and went past the curved flower-bed to the door of his shed. Mrs Barnstaple appeared in the porch.

'Alfred! You're back at last?'

'Yes, I'm back. You got my telegram?'

'Ten minutes ago. Where have you been all this time? It's more than a month.'

'Oh! just drifting about and dreaming. I've had a wonderful time.'

'You ought to have written. You really ought to have written. ....
You *did*, Alfred. ....'

'I didn't bother. The doctor said I wasn't to bother. I told you. Is there any tea going? Where are the boys?'

'The boys are out. Let me make you some fresh tea.' She did so and came and sat down in the cane chair in front of him and the tea-table. 'I'm glad to have you back. Though I could scold you. ....'

'You're looking wonderfully well,' she said. 'I've never seen your skin so clear and brown.'

'I've been in good air all the time.'

'Did you get to the Lakes?'

'Not quite. But it's been good air everywhere. Healthy air.'

'You never got lost?'

'Never.'

'I had ideas of you getting lost – losing your memory. Such things happen. You didn't?'

'My memory's as bright as a jewel.'

'But where did you go?'

'I just wandered and dreamt. Lost in a daydream. Often I didn't ask the name of the place where I was staying. I stayed in one place and then in another. I never asked their names. I left my mind passive. Quite passive. I've had a tremendous rest – from everything. I've hardly given a thought to politics or money or social questions – at least, the sort of thing we call social questions – or any of these worries, since I started. . . . Is that this week's *Liberal?*'

He took it, turned it over, and at last tossed it on to the sofa. 'Poor old Peeve,' he said. 'Of course I must leave that paper. He's like wall-paper on a damp wall. Just blotches and rustles and fails to stick. . . . Gives me mental rheumatics.'

Mrs Barnstaple stared at him doubtfully. 'But I always thought that the *Liberal* was such a safe job.'

'I don't want a safe job now. I can do better. There's other work before me. . . . Don't you worry. I can take hold of things surely enough after this rest. . . . How are the boys?'

'I'm a little anxious about Frankie.'

Mr Barnstaple had picked up the *Times*. An odd advertisement in the Agony column had caught his eye. It ran: 'Cecil. Your absence exciting remark. Would like to know what you wish us to tell people. Write fully Scotch address. Di. ill with worry. All instructions will be followed.'

'I beg your pardon, my dear?' he said putting the paper aside.

'I was saying that he doesn't seem to be settling down to business. He doesn't like it. I wish you could have a good talk to him. He's fretting because he doesn't *know* enough. He says he wants to be a science student at the Polytechnic and go on learning things.'

'Well, he can. Sensible boy! I didn't think he had it in him. I meant to have a talk to him. But this meets me half-way. Certainly he shall study science.'

'But the boy has to earn a living.'

'That will come. If he wants to study science he shall.'

Mr Barnstaple spoke in a tone that was altogether new to Mrs Barnstaple, a tone of immediate, quiet, and assured determination. It surprised her still more that he should use this tone without seeming to be aware that he had used it.

He bit his slice of bread-and-butter, and she could see that some-thing in the taste surprised and displeased him. He glanced doubtfully at the remnant of the slice in his hand. 'Of course,' he said. 'London butter. Three days' wear. Left about. Funny how quickly one's taste alters.'

He picked up the *Times* again and ran his eye over its columns.

'This world is really very childish,' he said. 'Very. I had forgotten. Imaginary Bolshevik plots. Sinn Fein proclamations. The Prince. Po-land. Obvious lies about the Chinese. Obvious lies about Egypt. People pulling Wickham Steed's leg. Sham-pious article about Trinity-Sunday. The Hitchin murder. . . . H'm! – rather a nasty one. . . . The Pomfort

Rembrandt. . . . Insurance. . . . Letter from indignant peer about Death Duties. . . . Dreary Sport. Boating, Tennis, Schoolboy cricket. Collapse of Harrow! As though such things were of the slightest importance! . . . How silly it is – all of it! It's like coming back to the quarrels of servants and the chatter of children.'

He found Mrs Barnstaple regarding him intently. 'I haven't seen a paper from the day I started until this morning,' he explained.

He put down the paper and stood up. For some minutes Mrs Barnstaple had been doubting whether she was not the victim of an absurd hallucination. Now she realized that she was in the presence of the most amazing fact she had ever observed.

'Yes,' she said. 'It is so. Don't move! Keep like that. I know it sounds ridiculous, William, but you have grown taller. It's not simply that your stoop has gone. You have grown oh ! – two or three inches.'

Mr Barnstaple stared at her, and then held out his arm. Certainly he was showing an unusual length of wrist. He tried to judge whether his trousers had also the same grown-out-of look.

Mrs Barnstaple came up to him almost respectfully. She stood beside him and put her shoulder against his arm. 'Your shoulder used to be exactly level with mine,' she said. 'See where we are now!'

She looked up into his eyes. As though she was very glad indeed to have him back with her.

But Mr Barnstaple remained lost in thought. 'It must be the extreme freshness of the air. I have been in some wonderful air. . . . Wonderful! . . . But at my age! To have grown! And I *feel* as though I'd grown, inside and out, mind and body.'

Mrs Barnstaple presently began to put the tea-things together for removal.

'You seem to have avoided the big towns.'

'I did.'

'And kept to the country roads and lanes.'

'Practically. . . . It was all new country to me. . . . Beautiful. . . . Wonderful. . . .'

His wife still watched him.

'You must take *me* there some day,' she said. 'I can see that it has done you a world of good.'

THE SLEEPER AWAKES

I

Insomnia

One afternoon at low water Mr Isbister, a young artist lodging at Boscastle, walked from that place to the picturesque cove of Pentargen, desiring to examine the caves there. Halfway down the precipitous path to the Pentargen beach he came suddenly upon a man sitting in an attitude of profound distress beneath a projecting mass of rock. The hands of this man hung limply over his knees, his eyes were red and staring before him, and his face was wet with tears.

He glanced round at Isbister's footfall. Both men were disconcerted, Isbister the more so, and to override the awkwardness of his involuntary pause he remarked, with an air of mature conviction, that the weather was hot for the time of year.

'Very,' answered the stranger shortly, hesitated a second, and added in a colourless tone, 'I can't sleep.'

Isbister stopped abruptly. 'No?' was all he said, but his bearing conveyed his helpful impulse.

'It may sound incredible,' said the stranger, turning weary eyes to Isbister's face and emphasizing his words with a languid hand, 'but I have had no sleep – no sleep at all for six nights.'

'Had advice?'

'Yes. Bad advice for the most part. Drugs. My nervous system. . . . They are all very well for the run of people. It's hard to explain. I dare not take . . . sufficiently powerful drugs.'

'That makes it difficult,' said Isbister.

He stood helplessly in the narrow path, perplexed what to do. Clearly the man wanted to talk. An idea natural enough under the circumstances, prompted him to keep the conversation going. 'I've never suffered from sleeplessness myself,' he said in a tone of commonplace gossip, 'but in those cases I have known, people have usually found something—'

'I dare make no experiments.'

He spoke wearily. He gave a gesture of rejection, and for a space both men were silent.

'Exercise?' suggested Isbister diffidently, with a glance from his interlocutor's face of wretchedness to the touring costume he wore.

'That is what I have tried. Unwisely perhaps. I have followed the coast, day after day – from Newquay. It has only added muscular fatigue to the mental. The cause of this unrest was overwork – trouble. There was something—'

He stopped as if from sheer fatigue. He rubbed his forehead with a lean hand. He resumed speech like one who talks to himself.

'I am a lone wolf, a solitary man, wandering through a world in which I have no part. I am wifeless – childless – who is it speaks of the childless as the dead twigs on the tree of life? I am wifeless, childless – I could find no duty to do. No desire even in my heart. One thing at last I set myself to do.

'I said, I *will* do this; and to do it, to overcome the inertia of this dull body, I resorted to drugs. Great God, I've had enough of drugs! I don't know if *you* feel the heavy inconvenience of the body, its exasperating demand of time from the mind – time – life! Live! We only live in patches. We have to eat, and then come the dull digestive complacencies – or irritations. We have to take the air or else our thoughts grow sluggish, stupid, run into gulfs and blind alleys. A thousand distractions arise from within and without, and then come drowsiness and sleep. Men seem to live for sleep. How little of a man's day is his own – even at the best! And then come those false friends, those Thug helpers, the alkaloids that stifle natural fatigue and kill rest – black coffee, cocaine—'

'I see,' said Isbister.

'I did my work,' said the sleepless man with a querulous intonation.

'And this is the price?'

'Yes.'

For a little while the two remained without speaking.

'You cannot imagine the craving for rest that I feel – a hunger and thirst. For six long days, since my work was done, my mind has been a whirlpool, swift, unprogressive and incessant, a torrent of thoughts leading nowhere, spinning round swift and steady—'

He paused. 'Towards the gulf.'

414

'You must sleep,' said Isbister decisively, and with an air of a remedy discovered. 'Certainly you must sleep.'

'My mind is perfectly lucid. It was never clearer. But I know I am drawing towards the vortex. Presently—'

'Yes?'

'You have seen things go down an eddy? Out of the light of the day, out of this sweet world of sanity – down—'

'But,' expostulated Isbister.

The man threw out a hand towards him, and his eyes were wild, and his voice suddenly high. 'I shall kill myself. If in no other way – at the foot of yonder dark precipice there, where the waves are green, and the white surge lifts and falls, and that little thread of water trembles down. There at any rate is . . . sleep.'

'That's unreasonable,' said Isbister, startled at the man's hysterical gust of emotion. 'Drugs are better than that.'

'There at any rate is sleep,' repeated the stranger, not heeding him.

Isbister looked at him. 'It's not a cert, you know,' he remarked. 'There's a cliff like that at Lulworth Cove – as high, anyhow – and a little girl fell from top to bottom. And lives today – sound and well.'

'But those rocks there?'

'One might lie on them rather dismally through a cold night, broken bones grating as one shivered, chill water splashing over you. Eh?'

Their eyes met. 'Sorry to upset your ideals,' said Isbister with a sense of devil-may-careish brilliance. 'But a suicide over that cliff (or any cliff for the matter of that), really, as an artist—' He laughed. 'It's so damned amateurish.'

'But the other thing,' said the sleepless man irritably, 'the other thing. No man can keep sane if night after night—'

'Have you been walking along this coast alone?'

'Yes.'

'Silly sort of thing to do. If you'll excuse my saying so. Alone! As you say; body fag is no cure for brain fag. Who told you to? No wonder; walking! And the sun on your head, heat, fag, solitude, all the day long, and then, I suppose, you go to bed and try very hard – eh?'

Isbister stopped short and looked at the sufferer doubtfully.

'Look at these rocks!' cried the seated man with a sudden force of gesture. 'Look at that sea that has shone and quivered there for ever! See the white spume rush into darkness under that great cliff. And this blue vault, with the blinding sun pouring from the dome of it. It is your world. You accept it, you rejoice in it. It warms and supports and delights you. And for me—'

He turned his head and showed a ghastly face, bloodshot pallid eyes and bloodless lips. He spoke almost in a whisper. 'It is the garment of my misery. The whole world . . . is the garment of my misery.'

Isbister looked at all the wild beauty of the sunlit cliffs about them and back to that face of despair. For a moment he was silent.

He started, and made a gesture of impatient rejection. 'You get a night's sleep,' he said, 'and you won't see much misery out here. Take my word for it.'

He was quite sure now that this was a providential encounter. Only half an hour ago he had been feeling horribly bored. Here was employment the bare thought of which was righteous self-applause. He took possession forthwith. The first need of this exhausted being was companionship. He flung himself down on the steeply sloping turf beside the motionless seated figure, and threw out a skirmishing line of gossip.

His hearer lapsed into apathy; he stared dismally seaward, and spoke only in answer to Isbister's direct questions – and not to all of those. But he made no objection to this benevolent intrusion upon his despair.

He seemed even grateful, and when presently Isbister, feeling that his unsupported talk was losing vigour, suggested that they should reascend the steep and go towards Boscastle, alleging the view into Blackapit, he submitted quietly. Halfway up he began talking to himself, and abruptly turned a ghastly face on his helper. 'What can be happening?' he asked with a gaunt illustrative hand. 'What can be happening? Spin, spin, spin, spin. It goes round and round, round and round for evermore.'

He stood with his hand circling.

'It's all right, old chap,' said Isbister with the air of an old friend. 'Don't worry yourself. Trust to me.'

The man dropped his hand. They went over the brow and to the headland beyond Penally, with the sleepless man gesticulating ever and again, and speaking fragmentary things concerning his whirling brain. At the headland they stood by the seat that looks into the dark mysteries of Blackapit, and then he sat down. Isbister had resumed his talk whenever the path had widened sufficiently for them to walk abreast. He was enlarging upon the complex difficulty of making Boscastle Harbour in bad weather, when suddenly and quite irrelevantly his companion interrupted him again.

'My head is not like what it was,' he said. 'It's not like what it was. There is a sort of oppression, a weight. No – not drowsiness, would God it were! It is like a shadow, a deep shadow falling suddenly and swiftly across something busy. Spin, spin into the darkness. The tumult of thought, the confusion, the eddy and eddy. I can't express it. I can hardly keep my mind on it – steadily enough to tell you.'

He stopped feebly.

'Don't trouble, old chap,' said Isbister. 'I think I can understand. At any rate, it don't matter very much just at present about telling me, you know.'

The sleepless man thrust his knuckles into his eyes and rubbed them. Isbister talked while this rubbing continued, and then he had a fresh idea. 'Come down to my room,' he said, 'and try a pipe. I can show you some sketches of this Blackapit. If you'd care?'

The other rose obediently and followed him down the steep.

Several times Isbister heard him stumble as they came down, and his movements were slow and hesitating. 'Come in with me,' said Isbister, 'and try some cigarettes and the blessed gift of alcohol. If you take alcohol?'

The stranger hesitated at the garden gate. He seemed no longer aware of his actions. 'I don't drink,' he said slowly, coming up the garden path, and after a moment's interval repeated absently, 'No – I don't drink. It goes round. Spin, it goes – spin—'

He stumbled at the doorstep and entered the room with the bearing of one who sees nothing.

Then he sat down heavily in the easy chair. He leant forward with his brows on his hands and became motionless. Presently there was a faint sound in his throat.

Isbister moved about the room with the nervousness of an inexperienced host, making little remarks that scarcely required answering. He crossed the room to his portfolio, placed it on the table and noticed the mantel clock.

'I don't know if you'd care to have supper with me,' he said with an unlighted cigarette in his hand, his mind troubled with ideas of a furtive administration of chloral. 'Only cold mutton, you know, but passing sweet. Welsh. And a tart, I believe.' He repeated this after momentary silence.

The seated man made no answer. Isbister stopped, match in hand, regarding him.

The stillness lengthened. The match went out, the cigarette was put down unlit. The man was certainly very still. Isbister took up the portfolio, opened it, put it down, hesitated. 'Perhaps,' he whispered doubtfully. Presently he glanced at the door and back to the figure. Then he stole on tiptoe out of the room, glancing at his companion after each elaborate pace.

He closed the door noiselessly. The house door was standing open, and he went out beyond the porch, and stood where the monkshood rose at the corner of the garden bed. From this point he could see the stranger through the open window, still and dim, sitting head on hand. He had not moved.

A number of children going along the road stopped and regarded the artist curiously. A boatman exchanged civilities with him. He felt that possibly his circumspect attitude and position looked peculiar and unaccountable. Smoking, perhaps, might seem more natural. He drew pipe and pouch from his pocket, filled the pipe slowly.

'I wonder,' ... he said, with a scarcely perceptible loss of complacency. 'At any rate one must give him a chance.' He struck a match in the virile way, and proceeded to light his pipe.

He heard his landlady behind him, coming with his lamp lit from the kitchen. He turned, gesticulating with his pipe, and stopped her at the door of his sitting room. He had some difficulty in explaining the situation in whispers, for she did not know he had a visitor. She retreated again with the lamp, still a little mystified to judge from her manner, and he resumed his hovering at the corner of the porch, flushed and less at his ease.

Long after he had smoked out his pipe, and when the bats were abroad, curiosity dominated his complex hesitations, and he stole back into his darkling sitting room. He paused in the doorway. The stranger was still in the same attitude, dark against the window. Save for the singing of some sailors aboard one of the little slate-carrying ships in the harbour the evening was very still. Outside, the spikes of monkshood and delphinium stood erect and motionless against the shadow of the hillside. Something flashed into Isbister's mind; he started, and leaning over the table, listened. An unpleasant suspicion grew stronger; became conviction. Astonishment seized him and became – dread!

No sound of breathing came from the seated figure!

He crept slowly and noiselessly round the table, pausing twice to listen. At last he could lay his hand on the back of the armchair. He bent down until the two heads were ear to ear.

Then he bent still lower to look up at his visitor's face. He started violently and uttered an exclamation. The eyes were void spaces of white.

He looked again and saw that they were open and with the pupils rolled under the lids. He was afraid. He took the man by the shoulder and shook him. 'Are you asleep?' he said, with his voice jumping, and again, 'Are you asleep?'

A conviction took possession of his mind that this man was dead.

He became active and noisy, strode across the room, blundering against the table as he did so, and rang the bell.

'Please bring a light at once,' he said in the passage. 'There is something wrong with my friend.'

He returned to the motionless seated figure, grasped the shoulder, shook it, shouted. The room was flooded with yellow glare as his landlady entered with the light. His face was white as he turned blinking towards her. 'I must fetch a doctor,' he said. 'It is either death or a fit. Is there a doctor in the village? Where is a doctor to be found?'

2

The Trance

The state of cataleptic rigour into which this man had fallen, lasted for an unprecedented length of time, and then he passed slowly to the flaccid state, to a lax attitude suggestive of profound repose. Then it was his eyes could be closed.

He was removed from the hotel to the Boscastle surgery, and from the surgery, after some weeks, to London. But he still resisted every attempt at reanimation. After a time, for reasons that will appear later, these attempts were discontinued. For a great space he lay in that strange condition, inert and still – neither dead nor living but, as it were, suspended, hanging midway between nothingness and existence. His was a darkness unbroken by a ray of thought or sensation, a dreamless inanition, a vast space of peace. The tumult of his mind had swelled and risen to an abrupt climax of silence. Where was the man? Where is any man when insensibility takes hold of him?

'It seems only yesterday,' said Isbister. 'I remember it all as though it happened yesterday – clearer, perhaps, than if it had happened yesterday.'

It was the Isbister of the last chapter, but he was no longer a young man. The hair that had been brown and a trifle in excess of the fashionable length, was iron grey and clipped close, and the face that had been pink and white was buff and ruddy. He had a pointed beard shot with grey. He talked to an elderly man who wore a summer suit of drill (the summer of that year was unusually hot). This was Warming, a London solicitor and next of kin to Graham, the man who had fallen into the trance. And the two men stood side by side in a room in a house in London regarding his recumbent figure.

It was a yellow figure lying lax upon a water-bed and clad in a flowing shirt, a figure with a shrunken face and a stubby beard, lean limbs and lank nails, and about it was a case of thin glass. This glass seemed to mark off the sleeper from the reality of life about him, he was a thing apart, a strange, isolated abnormality. The two men stood close to the glass, peering in.

'The thing gave me a shock,' said Isbister. 'I feel a queer sort of surprise even now when I think of his white eyes. They were white, you know, rolled up. Coming here again brings it all back to me.'

'Have you never seen him since that time?' asked Warming.

'Often wanted to come,' said Isbister; 'but business nowadays is too serious a thing for much holiday keeping. I've been in America most of the time.'

'If I remember rightly,' said Warming, 'you were an artist?'

'Was. And then I became a married man. I saw it was all up with black and white, very soon – at least for a mediocrity, and I jumped on to process. Those posters on the Cliffs at Dover are by my people.'

'Good posters,' admitted the solicitor, 'though I was sorry to see them there.'

'Last as long as the cliffs, if necessary,' exclaimed Isbister with satisfaction. 'The world changes. When he fell asleep, twenty years ago, I was down at Boscastle with a box of watercolours and a noble, old-fashioned ambition. I didn't expect that some day my pigments would glorify the whole blessed coast of England, from Land's End round again to the Lizard. Luck comes to a man very often when he's not looking.'

Warming seemed to doubt the quality of the luck. 'I just missed seeing you, if I recollect aright.'

'You came back by the trap that took me to Camelford railway station. It was close on the Jubilee, Victoria's Jubilee, because I remember the seats and flags in Westminster, and the row with the cabman at Chelsea.'

'The Diamond Jubilee, it was,' said Warming; 'the second one.'

'Ah, yes! At the proper Jubilee – the Fifty Year affair – I was down at Wookey – a boy. I missed all that. . . . What a fuss we had with him! My landlady wouldn't take him in, wouldn't let him stay – he looked so queer when he was rigid. We had to carry him in a chair up to the hotel. And the Boscastle doctor – it wasn't the present chap, but the GP before him – was at him until nearly two, with me and the landlord holding lights and so forth.'

'Do you mean – he was stiff and hard?'

'Stiff! – wherever you bent him he stuck. You might have stood him

421

on his head and he'd have stopped. I never saw such stiffness. Of course this' – he indicated the prostrate figure by a movement of his head – 'is quite different. And the little doctor – what was his name?'

'Smithers?'

'Smithers it was – was quite wrong in trying to fetch him round too soon, according to all accounts. The things he did! Even now it makes me feel all – ugh! Mustard, snuff, pricking. And one of those beastly little things, not dynamos—'

'Coils.'

'Yes. You could see his muscles throb and jump, and he twisted about. There were just two flaring yellow candles, and all the shadows were shivering, and the little doctor nervous and putting on side, and *him* – stark and squirming in the most unnatural ways. Well, it made me dream.'

Pause.

'It's a strange state,' said Warming.

'It's a sort of complete absence,' said Isbister. 'Here's the body, empty. Not dead a bit, and yet not alive. It's like a seat vacant and marked "engaged". No feeling, no digestion, no beating of the heart – not a flutter. *That* doesn't make me feel as if there was a man present. In a sense it's more dead than death, for these doctors tell me that even the hair has stopped growing. Now with the proper dead, the hair will go on growing—'

'I know,' said Warming, with a flash of pain in his expression.

They peered through the glass again. Graham was indeed in a strange state, in the flaccid phase of a trance, but a trance unprecedented in medical history. Trances had lasted for as much as a year before – but at the end of that time it had ever been a waking or a death; sometimes first one and then the other. Isbister noted the marks the physicians had made in injecting nourishment, for that had been resorted to to postpone collapse; he pointed them out to Warming, who had been trying not to see them.

'And while he has been lying here,' said Isbister, with the zest of a life freely spent, 'I have changed my plans in life; married, raised a family, my eldest lad – I hadn't begun to think of sons then – is an American citizen and looking forward to leaving Harvard. There's a touch of grey in my hair. And this man, not a day older nor wiser (practically) than I was in my downy days. It's curious to think of.'

Warming turned. 'And I have grown old too. I played cricket with him when I was still only a boy. And he looks a young man still. Yellow perhaps. But that *is* a young man nevertheless.'

'And there's been the War,' said Isbister.

'From beginning to end.'

'I've understood,' said Isbister after a pause, 'that he had some moderate property of his own?'

'That is so,' said Warming. He coughed primly. 'As it happens – I have charge of it.'

'Ah!' Isbister thought, hesitated and spoke: 'No doubt – his keep here is not expensive – no doubt it will have improved – accumulated?'

'It has. He will wake up very much better off – if he wakes – than when he slept.'

'As a businessman,' said Isbister, 'that thought has naturally been in my mind. I have indeed sometimes thought that, speaking commercially of course, this sleep may be a very good thing for him. That he knows what he is about, so to speak, in being insensible so long. If he had lived straight on—'

'I doubt if he would have premeditated as much,' said Warming. 'He was not a far-sighted man. In fact—'

'Yes?'

'We differed on that point. I stood to him somewhat in the relation of a guardian. You have probably seen enough of affairs to recognize that occasionally a certain friction – But even if that was the case, there is a doubt whether he will ever awake. This sleep exhausts slowly, but it exhausts. Apparently he is sliding slowly, very slowly and tediously, down a long slope, if you can understand me?'

'It will be a pity to lose his surprise. There's been a lot of change these twenty years. It's Rip Van Winkle come real.'

'There has been a lot of change certainly,' said Warming. 'And, among other changes, I have changed. I am an old man.'

Isbister hesitated, and then feigned a belated surprise. 'I shouldn't have thought it.'

'I was forty-three when his bankers – you remember you wired to his bankers – sent on to me.'

'I got their address from the cheque book in his pocket,' said Isbister.

'Well, the addition is not difficult,' said Warming.

There was another pause, and then Isbister gave way to an unavoidable curiosity. 'He may go on for years yet,' he said, and had a moment of hesitation. 'We have to consider that. His affairs, you know, may fall some day into the hands of – someone else, you know.'

'That, if you will believe me, Mr Isbister, is one of the problems most constantly before my mind. We happen to be – as a matter of fact, there are no very trustworthy connections of ours. It is a grotesque and unprecedented position.'

'Rather,' said Isbister.

'It seems to me it's a case of some public body, some practically undying guardian. If he really is going on living – as the doctors, some of them, think. As a matter of fact, I have gone to one or two public men about it. But so far nothing has been done.'

'It wouldn't be a bad idea to hand him over to some public body – the British Museum Trustees, or the Royal College of Physicians. Sounds a bit odd, of course, but the whole situation is odd.'

'The difficulty is to induce them to take him.'

'Red tape, I suppose?'

'Partly.'

Pause. 'It's a curious business, certainly,' said Isbister. 'And compound interest has a way of mounting up.'

'It has,' said Warming. 'And now the gold supplies are running short there is a tendency towards ... appreciation.'

'I've felt that,' said Isbister with a grimace. 'But it makes it better for *him*.'

'*If* he awakes.'

'If he awakes,' echoed Isbister. 'Do you notice the pinched-in look of his nose, and the way in which his eyelids sink?'

Warming looked and thought for a space. 'I doubt if he will awake,' he said at last.

'I never properly understood,' said Isbister, 'what it was brought this on. He told me something about overstudy. I've often been curious.'

'He was a man of considerable gifts, but spasmodic, emotional. He had grave domestic troubles, divorced his wife in fact, and it was as a relief from that, I think, that he took up politics of the rabid sort. He was a fanatical Radical – a Socialist – or typical Liberal, as they used to call themselves, of the advanced school. Energetic – flighty – undisciplined. Overwork upon a controversy did this for him. I remember the pamphlet he wrote – a curious production. Wild, whirling stuff. There were one or two prophecies. Some of them are already exploded, some of them are established facts. But for the most part to read such a thesis is to realize how full the world is of unanticipated things. He will have much to learn, much to unlearn, when he awakes. If ever an awakening comes.'

'I'd give anything to be there,' said Isbister, 'just to hear what he would say to it all.'

'So would I,' said Warming. 'Aye! so would I,' with an old man's sudden turn to self-pity. 'But I shall never see him awake.'

He stood looking thoughtfully at the waxen figure. 'He will never awake,' he said at last. He sighed. 'He will never awake again.'

3

The Awakening

But Warming was wrong in that. An awakening came.

What a wonderfully complex thing! this simple seeming unity – the self! Who can trace its reintegration as morning after morning we awaken, the flux and confluence of its countless factors interweaving, rebuilding, the dim first stirrings of the soul, the growth and synthesis of the unconscious to the subconscious, the subconscious to dawning consciousness, until at last we recognize ourselves again. And as it happens to most of us after the night's sleep, so it was with Graham at the end of his vast slumber. A dim mist of sensation taking shape, a cloudy dreariness, and he found himself vaguely somewhere, recumbent, faint, but alive.

The pilgrimage towards a personal being seemed to traverse vast gulfs, to occupy epochs. Gigantic dreams that were terrible realities at the time, left vague perplexing memories, strange creatures, strange scenery, as if from another planet. There was a distinct impression, too, of a momentous conversation, of a name – he could not tell what name – that was subsequently to recur, of some queer long-forgotten sensation of vein and muscle, of a feeling of vast hopeless effort, the effort of a man near drowning in darkness. Then came a panorama of dazzling unstable confluent scenes. . . .

Graham became aware that his eyes were open and regarding some unfamiliar thing.

It was something white, the edge of something, a frame of wood. He moved his head slightly, following the contour of this shape. It went up beyond the top of his eyes. He tried to think where he might be. Did it matter, seeing he was so wretched? The colour of his thoughts was a dark depression. He felt the featureless misery of one who wakes towards the hour of dawn. He had an uncertain sense of whispers and footsteps hastily receding.

The movement of his head involved a perception of extreme physical weakness. He supposed he was in bed in the hotel at the place in the valley – but he could not recall that white edge. He must have slept. He remembered now that he had wanted to sleep. He recalled the cliff and waterfall again, and then recollected something about talking to a passer-by. . . .

How long had he slept? What was that sound of pattering feet? And that rise and fall, like the murmur of breakers on pebbles? He put out a languid hand to reach his watch from the chair whereon it was his habit to place it, and touched some smooth hard surface like glass. This was so unexpected that it startled him extremely. Quite suddenly he rolled over, stared for a moment, and struggled into a sitting position. The effort was unexpectedly difficult, and it left him giddy and weak – and amazed.

He rubbed his eyes. The riddle of his surroundings was confusing but his mind was quite clear – evidently his sleep had benefited him. He was not in a bed at all as he understood the word, but lying naked on a very soft and yielding mattress, in a trough of dark glass. The mattress was partly transparent, a fact he observed with a sense of insecurity, and below it was a mirror reflecting him greyly. About his arm – and he saw with a shock that his skin was strangely dry and yellow – was bound a curious apparatus of rubber, bound so cunningly that it seemed to pass into his skin above and below. And this bed was placed in a case of greenish-coloured glass (as it seemed to him), a bar in the white framework of which had first arrested his attention. In the corner of the case was a stand of glittering and delicately made apparatus, for the most part quite strange appliances, though a maximum and minimum thermometer was recognizable.

The slightly greenish tint of the glass-like substance which surrounded him on every hand obscured what lay behind, but he perceived it was a vast apartment of splendid appearance, and with a very large and simple white archway facing him. Close to the walls of the cage were articles of furniture, a table covered with a silvery cloth, silvery like the side of a fish, a couple of graceful chairs, and on the table a number of dishes with substances piled on them, a bottle and two glasses. He realized that he was intensely hungry.

He could see no one, and after a period of hesitation scrambled off the translucent mattress and tried to stand on the clean white floor of his little apartment. He had miscalculated his strength, however, and staggered and put his hand against the glass-like pane before him to steady himself. For a moment it resisted his hand, bending outward like a distended bladder, then it broke with a slight report and vanished – a pricked bubble. He reeled out into the general space of the hall, greatly astonished. He caught at the table to save himself, knocking one of the glasses to the floor – it rang but did not break – and sat down in one of the armchairs.

When he had a little recovered he filled the remaining glass from the bottle and drank – a colourless liquid it was, but not water, with a pleasing faint aroma and taste and a quality of immediate support and stimulus. He put down the vessel and looked about him.

The apartment lost none of its size and magnificence now that the greenish transparency that had intervened was removed. The archway he saw led to a flight of steps, going downward without the intermediation of a door, to a spacious transverse passage. This passage ran between polished pillars of some white-veined substance of deep ultramarine, and along it came the sound of human movements, and voices and a deep undeviating droning note. He sat, now fully awake, listening alertly, forgetting the viands in his attention.

Then with a shock he remembered that he was naked, and casting about him for covering, saw a long black robe thrown on one of the chairs beside him. This he wrapped about him and sat down again, trembling.

His mind was still a surging perplexity. Clearly he had slept, and had been removed in his sleep. But where? And who were those people, the distant crowd beyond the deep blue pillars? Boscastle? He poured out and partially drank another glass of the colourless fluid.

What was this place? – this place that to his senses seemed subtly quivering like a thing alive? He looked about him at the clean and beautiful form of the apartment, unstained by ornament, and saw that the roof was broken in one place by a circular shaft full of light, and as he looked a steady, sweeping shadow blotted it out and passed, and came again and passed. 'Beat, beat,' that sweeping shadow had a note of its own in the subdued tumult that filled the air.

He would have called out, but only a little sound came into his throat. Then he stood up and, with the uncertain steps of a drunkard, made his way towards the archway. He staggered down the steps, tripped on the corner of the black cloak he had wrapped about himself, and saved himself by catching at one of the blue pillars.

The passage ran down a cool vista of blue and purple and ended remotely in a railed space like a balcony brightly lit and projecting into a space of haze, a space like the interior of some gigantic building.

427

Beyond and remote were vast and vague architectural forms. The tumult of voices rose now loud and clear, and on the balcony and with their backs to him, gesticulating and apparently in animated conversation, were three figures, richly dressed in loose and easy garments of bright soft colourings. The noise of a great multitude of people poured up over the balcony, and once it seemed the top of a banner passed, and once some brightly coloured object, a pale blue cap or garment thrown up into the air perhaps, flashed athwart the space and fell. The shouts sounded like English, there was a reiteration of 'wake!' He heard some indistinct shrill cry, and abruptly these three men began laughing.

'Ha, ha, ha!' laughed one – a red-haired man in a short purple robe. 'When the Sleeper wakes – *When!*'

He turned his eyes full of merriment along the passage. His face changed, the whole man changed, became rigid. The other two turned swiftly at his exclamation and stood motionless. Their faces assumed an expression of consternation, an expression that deepened into awe.

Suddenly Graham's knees bent beneath him, his arm against the pillar collapsed limply, he staggered forward and fell upon his face.

4

The Sound of a Tumult

Graham's last impression before he fainted was of the ringing of bells. He learnt afterwards that he was insensible, hanging between life and death, for the better part of an hour. When he recovered his senses he was back on his translucent couch, and there was a stirring warmth at heart and throat. The dark apparatus, he perceived, had been removed from his arm, which was bandaged. The white framework was still about him, but the greenish transparent substance that had filled it was altogether gone. A man in a deep violet robe, one of those who had been on the balcony, was looking keenly into his face.

Remote but insistent was a clamour of bells and confused sounds, that suggested to his mind the picture of a great number of people shouting together. Something seemed to fall across this tumult, a door suddenly closed.

Graham moved his head. 'What does this all mean?' he said slowly. 'Where am I?'

He saw the red-haired man who had been first to discover him. A voice seemed to be asking what he had said, and was abruptly stilled.

The man in violet answered in a soft voice, speaking English with a slightly foreign accent, or so at least it seemed to the Sleeper's ears. 'You are quite safe. You were brought hither from where you fell asleep. It is quite safe. You have been here some time – sleeping. In a trance.'

He said something further that Graham could not hear, and a little phial was handed across to him. Graham felt a cooling spray, a fragrant mist played over his forehead for a moment, and his sense of refreshment increased. He closed his eyes in satisfaction.

'Better?' asked the man in violet, as Graham's eyes reopened. He was a pleasant-faced man of thirty perhaps, with a pointed flaxen beard and a clasp of gold at the neck of his violet robe.

'Yes,' said Graham.

'You have been asleep some time. In a cataleptic trance. You have heard? Catalepsy? It may seem strange to you at first, but I can assure you everything is well.'

Graham did not answer, but these words served their reassuring purpose. His eyes went from face to face of the three people about him. They were regarding him strangely. He knew he ought to be somewhere in Cornwall, but he could not square these things with that impression.

A matter that had been in his mind during his last waking moments at Boscastle recurred, a thing resolved upon and somehow neglected. He cleared his throat.

'Have you wired my cousin?' he asked. 'E. Warming, 27, Chancery Lane?'

They were all assiduous to hear. But he had to repeat it. 'What an odd *blurr* in his accent!' whispered the red-haired man. 'Wire, sir?' said the young man with the flaxen beard, evidently puzzled.

'He means send an electric telegram,' volunteered the third, a pleasant-faced youth of nineteen or twenty. The flaxen-bearded man gave a cry of comprehension. 'How stupid of me! You may be sure everything shall be done, sir,' he said to Graham. 'I am afraid it would be difficult to – *wire* to your cousin. He is not in London now. But don't trouble about arrangements yet; you have been asleep a very long time and the important thing is to get over that, sir.' (Graham concluded the word was sir, but this man pronounced it '*Sire*.')

'Oh!' said Graham, and became quiet.

It was all very puzzling, but apparently these people in unfamiliar dress knew what they were about. Yet they were odd and the room was odd. It seemed he was in some newly established place. He had a sudden flash of suspicion! Surely this wasn't some hall of public exhibition! If it was he would give Warming a piece of his mind. But it scarcely had that character. And in a place of public exhibition he would not have discovered himself naked.

Then suddenly, he realized what had happened. There was no perceptible interval of suspicion, no dawn to his knowledge. Abruptly he knew that his trance had lasted for a vast interval; as if by some process of thought-reading he interpreted the awe in the faces that peered into his. He looked at them strangely, full of intense emotion. It seemed they read his eyes. He framed his lips to speak and could

430

not. A queer impulse to hide his knowledge came into his mind almost at the moment of his discovery. He looked at his bare feet, regarding them silently. His impulse to speak passed. He was trembling exceedingly.

They gave him some pink fluid with a greenish fluorescence and a meaty taste, and the assurance of returning strength grew.

'That – that makes me feel better,' he said hoarsely, and there were murmurs of respectful approval. He knew now quite clearly. He made to speak again, and again he could not.

He pressed his throat and tried a third time. 'How long?' he asked in a level voice. 'How long have I been asleep?'

'Some considerable time,' said the flaxen-bearded man, glancing quickly at the others.

'How long?'

'A very long time.'

'Yes – yes,' said Graham, suddenly testy. 'But I want – Is it – it is – some years? Many years? There was something – I forget what. I feel – confused. But you —' He sobbed. 'You need not fence with me. How long—?'

He stopped, breathing irregularly. He squeezed his eyes with his knuckles and sat waiting for an answer.

They spoke in undertones.

'Five or six?' he asked faintly. 'More?'

'Very much more than that.'

'More!'

'More.'

He looked at them and it seemed as though imps were twitching the muscles of his face. He looked his question.

'Many years,' said the man with the red beard.

Graham struggled into a sitting position. He wiped a rheumy tear from his face with a lean hand. 'Many years!' he repeated. He shut his eyes tight, opened them, and sat looking about him from one unfamiliar thing to another.

'How many years?' he asked.

'You must be prepared to be surprised.'

'Well?'

'More than a gross of years.'

He was irritated at the strange word. 'More than a *what*?'

Two of them spoke together. Some quick remarks that were made about 'decimal' he did not catch.

'How long did you say?' asked Graham. 'How long? Don't look like that. Tell me.'

Among the remarks in an undertone, his ear caught six words: 'More than a couple of centuries.'

'*What?*' he cried, turning on the youth who he thought had spoken. 'Who says –? What was that? A couple of *centuries!*'

'Yes,' said the man with the red beard. 'Two hundred years.'

Graham repeated the words. He had been prepared to hear of a vast repose, and yet these concrete centuries defeated him.

'Two hundred years,' he said again, with the figure of a great gulf opening very slowly in his mind; and then, 'Oh, but—!'

They said nothing.

'You – did you say—?'

'Two hundred years. Two centuries of years,' said the man with the red beard.

There was a pause. Graham looked at their faces and saw that what he had heard was indeed true.

'But it can't be,' he said querulously. 'I am dreaming. Trances – trances don't last. That is not right – this is a joke you have played upon me! Tell me – some days ago, perhaps, I was walking along the coast of Cornwall—?'

His voice failed him.

The man with the flaxen beard hesitated. 'I'm not very strong in history, sir,' he said weakly, and glanced at the others.

'That was it, sir,' said the youngster. 'Boscastle, in the old Duchy of Cornwall – it's in the south-west country beyond the dairy meadows. There is a house there still. I have been there.'

'Boscastle!' Graham turned his eyes to the youngster. 'That was it – Boscastle. Little Boscastle. I fell asleep – somewhere there. I don't exactly remember. I don't exactly remember.'

He pressed his brows and whispered, 'More than *two hundred years!*'

He began to speak quickly with a twitching face, but his heart was cold within him. 'But if it *is* two hundred years, every soul I know, every human being that ever I saw or spoke to before I went to sleep, must be dead.'

They did not answer him.

'The Queen and the Royal Family, her Ministers, Church and State. High and low, rich and poor, one with another ... Is there England still? ...

'That's a comfort! Is there London? ...

'This *is* London, eh? And you are my assistant-custodian; assistant-custodian. And these—? Eh? Assistant-custodians too!'

He sat with a gaunt stare on his face. 'But why am I here? No! Don't talk. Be quiet. Let me—'

He sat silent, rubbed his eyes, and, uncovering them, found another little glass of pinkish fluid held towards him. He took the dose. Directly he had taken it he began to weep naturally and refreshingly.

Presently he looked at their faces, suddenly laughed through his tears, a little foolishly. 'But – two – hun – dred – years!' he said. He grimaced hysterically and covered his face again.

After a space he grew calm. He sat up, his hands hanging over his knees in almost precisely the same attitude in which Isbister had found him on the cliff at Pentargen. His attention was attracted by a thick domineering voice, the footsteps of an advancing personage. 'What are you doing? Why was I not warned? Surely you could tell? Someone will suffer for this. The man must be kept quiet. Are the doorways closed? All the doorways? He must be kept perfectly quiet. He must not be told. Has he been told anything?'

The man with the fair beard made some inaudible remark, and Graham looking over his shoulder saw approaching a short, fat and thickset beardless man, with aquiline nose and heavy neck and chin. Very thick black and slightly sloping eyebrows that almost met over his nose and overhung deep grey eyes, gave his face an oddly formidable expression. He scowled momentarily at Graham and then his regard returned to the man with the flaxen beard. 'These others,' he said in a voice of extreme irritation. 'You had better go.'

'Go?' said the red-bearded man.

'Certainly – go now. But see the doorways are closed as you go.'

The two men addressed turned obediently, after one reluctant glance at Graham, and instead of going through the archway as he expected, walked straight to the dead wall of the apartment opposite the archway. A long strip of this apparently solid wall rolled up with a snap, hung over the two retreating men and fell again, and immediately Graham was alone with the newcomer and the purple-robed man with the flaxen beard.

For a space the thickset man took not the slightest notice of Graham, but proceeded to interrogate the other – obviously his subordinate – upon the treatment of their charge. He spoke clearly, but in phrases only partially intelligible to Graham. The awakening seemed not only a matter of surprise but of consternation and annoyance to him. He was evidently profoundly excited.

'You must not confuse his mind by telling him things,' he repeated again and again. 'You must not confuse his mind.'

His questions answered, he turned quickly and eyed the awakened sleeper with an ambiguous expression.

'Feel queer?' he asked.

'Very.'

'The world, what you see of it, seems strange to you?'

'I suppose I have to live in it, strange as it seems.'

'I suppose so, now.'

'In the first place, hadn't I better have some clothes?'

'They —' said the thickset man and stopped, and the flaxen-bearded man met his eye and went away. 'You will very speedily have clothes,' said the thickset man.

'Is it true indeed, that I have been asleep two hundred –?' asked Graham.

'They have told you that, have they? Two hundred and three, as a matter of fact.'

Graham accepted the indisputable now with raised eyebrows and depressed mouth. He sat silent for a moment, and then asked a question, 'Is there a mill or dynamo near here?' He did not wait for an answer. 'Things have changed tremendously, I suppose?' he said.

'What is that shouting?' he asked abruptly.

'Nothing,' said the thickset man impatiently. 'It's people. You'll understand better later – perhaps. As you say, things have changed.' He spoke shortly, his brows were knit, and he glanced about him like a man trying to decide in an emergency. 'We must get you clothes and so forth, at any rate. Better wait here until they can be procured. No one will come near you. You want shaving.'

Graham rubbed his chin.

The man with the flaxen beard came back towards them, turned suddenly, listened for a moment, lifted his eyebrows at the older man, and hurried off through the archway towards the balcony. The tumult of shouting grew louder, and the thickset man turned and listened also. He cursed suddenly under his breath, and turned his eyes upon Graham with an unfriendly expression. It was a surge of many voices, rising and falling, shouting and screaming, and once came a sound like blows and sharp cries, and then a snapping like the crackling of dry sticks. Graham strained his ears to draw some single thread of sound from the woven tumult.

Then he perceived, repeated again and again, a certain formula. For a time he doubted his ears. But surely these were the words: 'Show us the Sleeper! Show us the Sleeper!'

The thickset man rushed suddenly to the archway.

'Wild!' he cried. 'How do they know? Do they know? Or is it guessing?'

There was perhaps an answer.

434

'I can't come,' said the thickset man; 'I have *him* to see to. But shout from the balcony.'

There was an inaudible reply.

'Say he is not awake. Anything! I leave it to you.'

He came hurrying back to Graham. 'You must have clothes at once,' he said. 'You cannot stop here – and it will be impossible to—'

He rushed away, Graham calling unanswered questions after him. In a moment he was back.

'I can't tell you what is happening. It is too complex to explain. In a moment you shall have your clothes made. Yes – in a moment. And then I can take you away from here. You will find out our troubles soon enough.'

'But those voices. They were shouting—?'

'Something about the Sleeper – that's you. They have some twisted idea. I don't know what it is. I know nothing.'

A shrill bell jetted acutely across the indistinct mingling of remote noises, and this brusque person sprang to a little group of appliances in the corner of the room. He listened for a moment, regarding a ball of crystal, nodded, and said a few words; then he walked to the wall through which the two men had vanished. It rolled up again like a curtain, and he stood waiting.

Graham lifted his arm and was astonished to find what strength the restoratives had given him. He thrust one leg over the side of the couch and then the other. His head no longer swam. He could scarcely credit his rapid recovery. He sat feeling his limbs.

The man with the flaxen beard re-entered from the archway, and as he did so the cage of a lift came sliding down in front of the thickset man, and a lean, grey-bearded man, carrying a roll and wearing a tightly fitting costume of dark green, appeared therein.

'This is the tailor,' said the thickset man with an introductory gesture. 'It will never do for you to wear that black. I cannot understand how it got here. But I shall. I shall. You will be as rapid as possible?' he said to the tailor.

The man in green bowed, and, advancing, seated himself by Graham on the bed. His manner was calm, but his eyes were full of curiosity. 'You will find the fashions altered, Sire,' he said. He glanced from under his brows at the thickset man.

He opened the roller with a quick movement, and a confusion of brilliant fabrics poured out over his knees. 'You lived, Sire, in a period essentially cylindrical – the Victorian. With a tendency to the hemisphere in hats. Circular curves always. Now —' He flicked out a little appliance the size and appearance of a keyless watch, whirled the

435

knob, and behold – a little figure in white appeared kinetoscope fashion on the dial, walking and turning. The tailor caught up a pattern of bluish white satin. 'That is my conception of your immediate treatment,' he said.

The thickset man came and stood by the shoulder of Graham.

'We have very little time,' he said.

'Trust me,' said the tailor. 'My machine follows. What do you think of this?'

'What is that?' asked the man from the nineteenth century.

'In your days they showed you a fashion-plate,' said the tailor, 'but this is our modern development. See here.' The little figure repeated its evolutions, but in a different costume. 'Or this,' and with a click another small figure in a more voluminous type of robe marched on to the dial. The tailor was very quick in his movements, and glanced twice towards the lift as he did these things.

It rumbled again, and a crop-haired anaemic lad with features of the Chinese type, clad in coarse pale blue canvas, appeared together with a complicated machine, which he pushed noiselessly on little castors into the room. Incontinently the little kinetoscope was dropped, Graham was invited to stand in front of the machine and the tailor muttered some instructions to the crop-haired lad, who answered in guttural tones and with words Graham did not recognize. The boy then went to conduct an incomprehensible monologue in the corner, and the tailor pulled out a number of slotted arms terminating in little discs, pulling them out until the discs were flat against the body of Graham, one at each shoulder blade, one at the elbows, one at the neck and so forth, so that at last there were, perhaps, two score of them upon his body and limbs. At the same time, some other person entered the room by the lift, behind Graham. The tailor set moving a mechanism that initiated a faint-sounding rhythmic movement of parts in the machine, and in another moment he was knocking up the levers and Graham was released. The tailor replaced his cloak of black, and the man with the flaxen beard proffered him a little glass of some refreshing fluid. Graham saw over the rim of the glass a pale-faced young man regarding him with a singular fixity.

The thickset man had been pacing the room fretfully, and now turned and went through the archway towards the balcony, from which the noise of a distant crowd still came in gusts and cadences. The crop-headed lad handed the tailor a roll of the bluish satin and the two began fixing this in the mechanism in a manner reminiscent of a roll of paper in a nineteenth-century printing machine. Then they ran the entire thing on its easy, noiseless bearings across the room to a remote corner where a twisted cable looped rather gracefully from the wall. They made some connection and the machine became energetic and swift.

'What is that doing?' asked Graham, pointing with the empty glass to the busy figures and trying to ignore the scrutiny of the newcomer. 'Is that – some sort of force – laid on?'

'Yes,' said the man with the flaxen beard.

'Who is *that*?' He indicated the archway behind him.

The man in purple stroked his little beard, hesitated, and answered in an undertone, 'He is Howard, your chief guardian. You see, Sire – it's a little difficult to explain. The Council appoints a guardian and assistants. This hall has under certain restrictions been public. In order that people might satisfy themselves. We have barred the doorways for the first time. But I think – if you don't mind, I will leave him to explain.'

'Odd!' said Graham. 'Guardian? Council?' Then turning his back on the newcomer, he asked in an undertone, 'Why is this man *glaring* at me? Is he a mesmerist?'

'Mesmerist! He is a capillotomist.'

'Capillotomist!'

'Yes – one of the chief. His yearly fee is sixdoz lions.'

It sounded sheer nonsense. Graham snatched at the last phrase with an unsteady mind. 'Sixdoz lions?' he said.

'Didn't you have lions? I suppose not. You had the old pounds? They are our monetary units.'

'But what was that you said – sixdoz?'

'Yes. Six dozen, Sire. Of course things, even these little things, have altered. You lived in the days of the decimal system, the Arab system – tens, and little hundreds and thousands. We have eleven numerals now. We have single figures for both ten and eleven, two figures for a dozen, and a dozen dozen makes a gross, a great hundred, you know, a dozen gross a dozand, and a dozand dozand a myriad. Very simple?'

'I suppose so,' said Graham. 'But about this cap – what was it?'

The man with the flaxen beard glanced over his shoulder.

'Here are your clothes!' he said. Graham turned round sharply and saw the tailor standing at his elbow smiling, and holding some palpably new garments over his arm. The crop-headed boy, by means of one finger, was impelling the complicated machine towards the lift by which he had arrived. Graham stared at the completed suit. 'You don't mean to say—!'

'Just made,' said the tailor. He dropped the garments at the feet of Graham, walked to the bed on which Graham had so recently been lying, flung out the translucent mattress, and turned up the looking-glass. As he did so a furious bell summoned the thickset man to the corner. The man with the flaxen beard rushed across to him and then hurried out by the archway.

The tailor was assisting Graham into a dark purple combination garment, stockings, vest and pants in one, as the thickset man came back from the corner to meet the man with the flaxen beard returning from the balcony. They began speaking quickly in an undertone, their bearing had an unmistakable quality of anxiety. Over the purple under-garment came a complex garment of bluish white, and Graham was clothed in the fashion once more and saw himself, sallow-faced, unshaven and shaggy still, but at least naked no longer, and in some indefinable unprecedented way graceful.

'I must shave,' he said regarding himself in the glass.

'In a moment,' said Howard.

The persistent stare ceased. The young man closed his eyes, reopened them, and with a lean hand extended, advanced on Graham. Then he stopped, with his hand slowly gesticulating, and looked about him.

'A seat,' said Howard impatiently, and in a moment the flaxen-bearded man had a chair behind Graham. 'Sit down, please,' said Howard.

Graham hesitated, and in the other hand of the wild-eyed man he saw the glint of steel.

'Don't you understand, Sire?' cried the flaxen-bearded man with hurried politeness. 'He is going to cut your hair.'

'Oh!' cried Graham enlightened. 'But you called him—'

'A capillotomist – precisely! He is one of the finest artists in the world.'

Graham sat down abruptly. The flaxen-bearded man disappeared. The capillotomist came forward, examined Graham's ears and surveyed him, felt the back of his head, and would have sat down again to regard him but for Howard's audible impatience. Forthwith with rapid movements and a succession of deftly handled implements he shaved Graham's chin, clipped his moustache, and cut and arranged his hair. All this he did without a word, with something of the rapt air of a poet inspired. And as soon as he had finished Graham was handed a pair of shoes.

Suddenly a loud voice shouted – it seemed from a piece of machinery in the corner – 'At once – at once. The people know all over the city. Work is being stopped. Work is being stopped. Wait for nothing, but come.'

438

This shout appeared to perturb Howard exceedingly. By his gestures it seemed to Graham that he hesitated between two directions. Abruptly he went towards the corner where the apparatus stood about the little crystal ball. As he did so the undertone of tumultuous shouting from the archway that had continued during all these occurrences rose to a mighty sound, roared as if it were sweeping past, and fell again as if receding swiftly. It drew Graham after it with an irresistible attraction. He glanced at the thickset man, and then obeyed his impulse. In two strides he was down the steps and in the passage, and in a score he was out upon the balcony upon which the three men had been standing.

5

The Moving Ways

He went to the railings of the balcony and stared upward. An exclamation of surprise at his appearance, and the movements of a number of people came from the great area below.

His first impression was of overwhelming architecture. The place into which he looked was an aisle of Titanic buildings, curving spaciously in either direction. Overhead mighty cantilevers sprang together across the huge width of the place, and a tracery of translucent material shut out the sky. Gigantic globes of cool white light shamed the pale sunbeams that filtered down through the girders and wires. Here and there a gossamer suspension bridge dotted with foot passengers flung across the chasm and the air was webbed with slender cables. A cliff of edifice hung above him, he perceived as he glanced upward, and the opposite façade was grey and dim and broken by great archings, circular perforations, balconies, buttresses, turret projections, myriads of vast windows and an intricate scheme of architectural relief. Athwart these ran inscriptions horizontally and obliquely in an unfamiliar lettering. Here and there close to the roof cables of a peculiar stoutness were fastened, and drooped in a steep curve to circular openings on the opposite side of the space, and even as Graham noted these a remote and tiny figure of a man clad in pale blue arrested his attention. This little figure was far overhead across the space beside the higher fastening of one of these festoons, hanging forward from a little ledge of masonry and handling some well-nigh invisible strings dependent from the line. Then suddenly, with a swoop that sent Graham's heart into his mouth, this man had rushed down the curve and vanished through a round opening on the hither side of the way.

Graham had been looking up as he came out upon the balcony, and the things he saw above and opposed to him had at first seized his attention to the exclusion of anything else. Then suddenly he discovered the roadway! It was not a roadway at all, as Graham understood such things, for in the nineteenth century the only roads and streets were beaten tracks of motionless earth, jostling rivulets of vehicles between narrow footways. But this roadway was three hundred feet across, and it moved; it moved, all save the middle, the lowest part. For a moment the motion dazzled his mind. Then he understood.

Under the balcony this extraordinary roadway ran swiftly to Graham's right, an endless flow rushing along as fast as a nineteenth-century express train, an endless platform of narrow transverse overlapping slats with little interspaces that permitted it to follow the curvatures of the street. Upon it were seats, and here and there little kiosks, but they swept by too swiftly for him to see what might be therein. From this nearest and swiftest platform a series of others descended to the centre of the space. Each moved to the right, each perceptibly slower than the one above it, but the difference in pace was small enough to permit anyone to step from any platform to the one adjacent, and so walk uninterruptedly from the swiftest to the motionless middle way. Beyond this middle way was another series of endless platforms rushing with varying pace to Graham's left. And seated in crowds upon the two widest and swiftest platforms, or stepping from one to another down the steps, or swarming over the central space, was an innumerable and wonderfully diversified multitude of people.

'You must not stop here,' shouted Howard suddenly at his side. 'You must come away at once.'

Graham made no answer. He heard without hearing. The platforms ran with a roar and the people were shouting. He saw women and girls with flowing hair, beautifully robed, with bands crossing between the breasts. These first came out of the confusion. Then he perceived that the dominant note in that kaleidoscope of costume was the pale blue that the tailor's boy had worn. He became aware of cries of 'The Sleeper. What has happened to the Sleeper?' and it seemed as though the rushing platforms before him were suddenly spattered with the pale buff of human faces, and then still more thickly. He saw pointing fingers. The motionless central area of this huge arcade just opposite to the balcony was densely crowded with blue-clad people. Some sort of struggle had sprung into life. People seemed to be pushed up the running platforms on either side, and carried away against their will.

441

They would spring off so soon as they were beyond the thick of the confusion, and run back towards the conflict.

'It is the Sleeper. Verily it is the Sleeper,' shouted voices. 'That is never the Sleeper,' shouted others. More and more faces were turned to him. At the intervals along this central area Graham noted openings, pits, apparently the heads of staircases going down with people ascending out of them and descending into them. The struggle centred about the one of these nearest to him. People were running down the moving platforms to this, leaping dexterously from platform to platform. The clustering people on the higher platforms seemed to divide their interest between this point and the balcony. A number of sturdy little figures clad in a uniform of bright red, and working methodically together, were employed in preventing access to this descending staircase. About them a crowd was rapidly accumulating. Their brilliant colour contrasted vividly with the whitish-blue of their antagonists, for the struggle was indisputable.

He saw these things with Howard shouting in his ear and shaking his arm. And then suddenly Howard was gone and he stood alone.

The cries of 'The Sleeper!' grew in volume, and the people on the nearer platform were standing up. The nearer platform he perceived was empty to the right of him, and far across the space the platform running in the opposite direction was coming crowded and passing away bare. With incredible swiftness a vast crowd had gathered in the central space before his eyes; a dense swaying mass of people, and the shouts grew from a fitful crying to a voluminous incessant clamour: 'The Sleeper! The Sleeper!' and yells and cheers, a waving of garments and cries of 'Stop the ways!' They were also crying another name strange to Graham. It sounded like 'Ostrog'. The slower platforms were soon thick with active people, running against the movement so as to keep themselves opposite to him.

'Stop the ways,' they cried. Agile figures ran up from the centre to the swift road nearest to him, were borne rapidly past him, shouting strange, unintelligible things, and ran back obliquely to the central way. One thing he distinguished: 'It is indeed the Sleeper. It is indeed the Sleeper,' they testified.

For a space Graham stood motionless. Then he became vividly aware that all this concerned him. He was pleased at his wonderful popularity, he bowed, and, seeking a gesture of longer range, waved his arm. He was astonished at the uproar this provoked. The tumult about the descending stairway rose to furious violence. He was aware of crowded balconies, of men sliding along ropes, of men in trapeze-like seats hurling athwart the space. He heard voices behind him, a number of people descending the steps through the archway; he suddenly perceived that his guardian Howard was back again and gripping his arm painfully, and shouting inaudibly in his ear.

He turned, and Howard's face was white. 'Come back,' he heard. 'They will stop the ways. The whole city will be in confusion.'

There appeared a number of men hurrying along the passage of blue pillars behind Howard, the red-haired man, the man with the flaxen beard, a tall man in vivid vermilion, a crowd of others in red carrying staves, and all these people had anxious eager faces.

'Get him away,' cried Howard.

'But why?' said Graham. 'I don't see—'

'You must come away!' said the man in red in a resolute voice. His face and eyes were resolute too. Graham's glances went from face to face, and he was suddenly aware of that most disagreeable flavour in life, compulsion. Someone gripped his arm. . . .

He was being dragged away. It seemed as though the tumult suddenly became two, as if half the shouts that had come in from this wonderful roadway had sprung into the passages of the great building behind him. Marvelling and confused, feeling an impotent desire to resist, Graham was half led, half thrust, along the passage of blue pillars, and suddenly he found himself alone with Howard in a lift and moving swiftly upward.

6

The Hall of the Atlas

From the moment when the tailor had bowed his farewell to the moment when Graham found himself in the lift, was altogether barely five minutes. As yet the haze of his vast interval of sleep hung about him, as yet the initial strangeness of his being alive at all in this remote age touched everything with wonder, with a sense of the irrational, with something of the quality of a realistic dream. He was still detached, an astonished spectator, still but half involved in life. What he had seen, and especially the last crowded tumult, framed in the setting of the balcony, had a spectacular turn like a thing witnessed from the box of a theatre. 'I don't understand,' he said. 'What was the trouble? My mind is in a whirl. Why were they shouting? What is the danger?'

'We have our troubles,' said Howard. His eyes avoided Graham's enquiry. 'This is a time of unrest. And, in fact, your appearance, your waking just now, has a sort of connection—'

He spoke jerkily, like a man not quite sure of his breathing. He stopped abruptly.

'I don't understand,' said Graham.

'It will be clearer later,' said Howard.

He glanced uneasily upward, as though he found the progress of the lift slow.

'I shall understand better, no doubt, when I have seen my way about a little,' said Graham puzzled. 'It will be – it is bound to be perplexing. At present it is all so strange. Anything seems possible. Anything. In the details even. Your counting, I understand, is different.'

The lift stopped, and they stepped out into a narrow but very long passage between high walls, along which ran an extraordinary number of tubes and big cables.

'What a huge place this is!' said Graham. 'Is it all one building? What place is it?'

'This is one of the city ways for various public services. Light and so forth.'

'Was it a social trouble – that – in the great roadway place? How are you governed? Have you still a police?'

'Several,' said Howard.

'Several?'

'About fourteen.'

'I don't understand.'

'Very probably not. Our social order will probably seem very complex to you. To tell you the truth, I don't understand it myself very clearly. Nobody does. You will, perhaps – by and by. We have to go to the Council.'

Graham's attention was divided between the urgent necessity of his enquiries and the people in the passages and halls they were traversing. For a moment his mind would be concentrated upon Howard and the halting answers he made, and then he would lose the thread in response to some vivid unexpected impression. Along the passages, in the halls, half the people seemed to be men in the red uniform. The pale blue canvas that had been so abundant in the aisle of moving ways did not appear. Invariably these men looked at him, and saluted him and Howard as they passed.

He had a clear vision of entering a long corridor, and there were a number of girls sitting on low seats, as though in a class. He saw no teacher, but only a novel apparatus from which he fancied a voice proceeded. The girls regarded him and his conductor, he thought, with curiosity and astonishment. But he was hurried on before he could form a clear idea of the gathering. He judged they knew Howard and not himself, and that they wondered who he might be. This Howard, it seemed, was a person of importance. But then he was merely Graham's guardian. That was odd.

There came a passage in twilight, and into this passage a footway hung so that he could see the feet and ankles of people going to and fro thereon, but no more of them. Then vague impressions of galleries and of casual astonished passers-by turning round to stare after the two of them with their red-clad guard.

The stimulus of the restoratives he had taken was only temporary. He was speedily fatigued by this excessive haste. He asked Howard to slacken his speed. Presently he was in a lift that had a window upon

445

the great street space, but this was glazed and did not open, and they were too high for him to see the moving platforms below. But he saw people going to and fro along cables and along strange, frail looking bridges.

Thence they passed across the street and at a vast height above it. They crossed by means of a narrow bridge closed in with glass, so clear that it made him giddy even to remember it. The floor of it also was of glass. From his memory of the cliffs between Newquay and Boscastle, so remote in time, and so recent in his experience, it seemed to him that they must be nearly four hundred feet above the moving ways. He stopped, looked down between his legs upon the swarming blue and red multitudes, minute and foreshortened, struggling and gesticulating still towards the little balcony far below, a little toy balcony, it seemed, where he had so recently been standing. A thin haze and the glare of the mighty globes of light obscured everything. A man seated in a little openwork cradle shot by from some point still higher than the little narrow bridge, rushing down a cable as swiftly almost as if he were falling. Graham stopped involuntarily to watch this strange passenger vanish below, and then his eyes went back to the tumultuous struggle.

Along one of the faster ways rushed a bunch of red spots. This broke up into individuals as it approached the balcony, and went pouring down the slower ways towards the dense struggling crowd on the central area. These men in red appeared to be armed with sticks or truncheons; they seemed to be striking and thrusting. A great shouting, cries of wrath, screaming, burst out and came up to Graham, faint and thin. 'Go on,' cried Howard, laying hands on him.

Another man rushed down a cable. Graham suddenly glanced up to see whence he came, and beheld through the glassy roof and the network of cables and girders, dim rhythmically passing forms like the vans of windmills, and between them glimpses of a remote and pallid sky. Then Howard had thrust him forward across the bridge, and he was in a little narrow passage decorated with geometrical patterns.

'I want to see more of that,' cried Graham, resisting.

'No, no,' cried Howard, still gripping his arm. 'This way. You must go this way.' And the men in red following them seemed ready to enforce his orders.

Some Negroes in a curious wasp-like uniform of black and yellow appeared down the passage, and one hastened to throw up a sliding shutter that had seemed a door to Graham, and led the way through it. Graham found himself in a gallery overhanging the end of a great chamber. The attendant in black and yellow crossed this, thrust up a second shutter and stood waiting.

This place had the appearance of an ante-room. He saw a number of people in the central space, and at the opposite end a large and imposing doorway at the top of a flight of steps, heavily curtained but giving a glimpse of some still larger hall beyond. He perceived white men in red and other Negroes in black and yellow standing stiffly about those portals.

As they crossed the gallery he heard a whisper from below, 'The Sleeper,' and was aware of a turning of heads, a hum of observation. They entered another little passage in the wall of this antechamber, and then he found himself on an iron-railed gallery of metal that passed round the side of the great hall he had already seen through the curtains. He entered the place at the corner, so that he received the fullest impression of its huge proportions. The black in the wasp uniform stood aside like a well-trained servant, and closed the valve behind him.

Compared with any of the places Graham had seen thus far, this second hall appeared to be decorated with extreme richness. On a pedestal at the remoter end, and more brilliantly lit than any other object, was a gigantic white figure of Atlas, strong and strenuous, the globe upon his bowed shoulders. It was the first thing to strike his attention, it was so vast, so patiently and painfully real, so white and simple. Save for this figure and for a dais in the centre, the wide floor of the place was a shining vacancy. The dais was remote in the greatness of the area; it would have looked a mere slab of metal had it not been for the group of seven men who stood about a table on it, and gave an inkling of its proportions. They were all dressed in white robes, they seemed to have arisen that moment from their seats, and they were regarding Graham steadfastly. At the end of the table he perceived the glitter of some mechanical appliances.

Howard led him along the end gallery until they were opposite this mighty labouring figure. Then he stopped. The two men in red who had followed them into the gallery came and stood on either hand of Graham.

'You must remain here,' murmured Howard, 'for a few moments,' and, without waiting for a reply, hurried away along the gallery.

'But, *why* –?' began Graham.

He moved as if to follow Howard, and found his path obstructed by one of the men in red. 'You have to wait here, Sire,' said the man in red.

'*Why?*'

'Orders, Sire.'

'Whose orders?'

'Our orders, Sire.'

Graham looked his exasperation.

'What place is this?' he said presently. 'Who are those men?'

'They are the lords of the Council, Sire.'

'What Council?'

'*The* Council.'

'Oh!' said Graham, and after an equally ineffectual attempt at the other man, went to the railing and stared at the distant men in white, who stood watching him and whispering together.

The Council? He perceived there were now eight, though how the newcomer had arrived he had not observed. They made no gestures of greeting; they stood regarding him as in the nineteenth century a group of men might have stood in the street regarding a distant balloon that had suddenly floated into view. What council could it be that gathered there, that little body of men beneath the significant white Atlas, secluded from every eavesdropper in this impressive spaciousness? And why should he be brought to them, and be looked at strangely and spoken of inaudibly? Howard appeared beneath, walking quickly across the polished floor towards them. As he drew near he bowed and performed certain peculiar movements, apparently of a ceremonious nature. Then he ascended the steps of the dais, and stood by the apparatus at the end of the table.

Graham watched that visible inaudible conversation. Occasionally one of the white-robed men would glance towards him. He strained his ears in vain. The gesticulation of two of the speakers became animated. He glanced from them to the passive faces of his attendants. ... When he looked again Howard was extending his hands and moving his head like a man who protests. He was interrupted, it seemed, by one of the white-robed men rapping the table.

The conversation lasted an interminable time to Graham's sense. His eyes rose to the still giant at whose feet the Council sat. Thence they wandered to the walls of the hall. It was decorated in long painted panels of a quasi-Japanese type, many of them very beautiful. These panels were grouped in a great and elaborate framing of dark metal, which passed into the metallic caryatidae of the galleries and the great structural lines of the interior. The facile grace of these panels enhanced the mighty white effort that laboured in the centre of the scheme. Graham's eyes came back to the Council, and Howard was descending the steps. As he drew nearer his features could be distinguished, and Graham saw that he was flushed and blowing out his cheeks. His countenance was still disturbed when presently he reappeared along the gallery.

'This way,' he said concisely, and they went on in silence to a little door that opened at their approach. The two men in red stopped on either side of this door. Howard and Graham passed in, and Graham, glancing back, saw the white-robed Council still standing in a close group and looking at him. Then the door closed behind him with a heavy thud, and for the first time since his awakening he was in silence. The floor, even, was noiseless to his feet.

Howard opened another door, and they were in the first of two contiguous chambers furnished in white and green. 'What Council was that?' began Graham. 'What were they discussing? What have they to do with me?' Howard closed the door carefully, heaved a huge sigh, and said something in an undertone. He walked slantingways across the room and turned, blowing out his cheeks again. 'Ugh!' he grunted, a man relieved.

Graham stood regarding him.

'You must understand,' began Howard abruptly, avoiding Graham's eyes, 'that our social order is very complex. A half explanation, a bare unqualified statement would give you false impressions. As a matter of fact – it is a case of compound interest partly – your small fortune, and the fortune of your cousin Warming which was left to you – and certain other beginnings – have become very considerable. And in other ways that will be hard for you to understand, you are become a person of significance – of immense legal significance – legal rather than practical – involved in the world's affairs.'

He stopped.

'Yes?' said Graham.

'We have grave social troubles.'

'Yes?'

'Things have come to such a pass that, in fact, it is advisable to seclude you here.'

'Keep me prisoner!' exclaimed Graham.

'Well – to ask you to keep in seclusion.'

Graham turned on him. 'This is strange!' he said.

'No harm will be done you.'

'No harm!'

'But you must be kept here—'

'While I learn my position, I presume.'

'Precisely.'

'Very well then. Begin. Why *harm*?'

'Not now.'

'Why not?'

'It is too long a story, Sire.'

'All the more reason I should begin at once. You say I am a person of importance. What was that shouting I heard? Why is a great multitude shouting and excited because my trance is over, and who are the men in white in that huge council chamber?'

'All in good time, Sire,' said Howard. 'But not crudely, not crudely. This is one of those flimsy times when no man has a settled mind. Your awakening – no one expected your awakening. The Council is consulting.'

'What council?'

'The Council you saw.'

Graham made a petulant movement. 'This is not right,' he said. 'I should be told what is happening.'

'You must wait. Really you must wait.'

Graham sat down abruptly. 'I suppose since I have waited so long to resume life,' he said, 'that I must wait a little longer.'

'That is better,' said Howard. 'Yes, that is much better. And I must leave you alone. For a space. While I attend the discussion in the Council. . . . I am sorry.'

He went towards the noiseless door, hesitated and vanished.

Graham walked to the door, tried it, found it securely fastened in some way he never came to understand, turned about, paced the room restlessly, made the circuit of the room, and sat down. He remained sitting for some time with folded arms and knitted brow, biting his fingernails and trying to piece together the kaleidoscopic impressions of this first hour of awakened life; the vast mechanical spaces, the endless series of chambers and passages, the great struggle that roared and splashed through these strange ways, the little group of remote unsympathetic men beneath the colossal Atlas, Howard's mysterious behaviour. There was an inkling of some great inheritance already in his mind – an inheritance perhaps misapplied – of some unprecedented importance and opportunity. What had he to do? And this room's secluded silence was eloquent of imprisonment!

It came into Graham's mind with irresistible conviction that this was all a dream. He tried to shut his eyes and succeeded, but that time-honoured device led to no awakening.

Presently he began to touch and examine all the unfamiliar appointments of the two small rooms in which he found himself.

In a long oval panel of mirror he saw himself and stopped astonished. He was clad in a graceful costume of purple and bluish white, with a little greyshot beard trimmed to a point, and his hair, its blackness streaked now with bands of grey, arranged over his forehead in an unfamiliar but pleasing manner. He seemed a man of five-and-forty perhaps. For a moment he did not perceive this was himself.

A flash of laughter came with the recognition. 'To call on old Warming like this!' he exclaimed, 'and make him take me out to lunch!'

Then he thought of meeting first one and then another of the few familiar acquaintances of his early manhood, and in the midst of his amusement realized that every soul with whom he might jest had died many score of years ago. The thought smote him abruptly and keenly; he stopped short, the expression of his face changed to a white consternation.

The tumultuous memory of the moving platforms and the huge façade of that wonderful street reasserted itself. The shouting multitudes came back, clear and vivid, and those remote, inaudible, unfriendly councillors in white. He felt himself a little figure, very small and ineffectual, pitifully conspicuous. And all about him, the world was – *strange*.

7

In the Silent Rooms

Presently Graham resumed his examination of his apartments. Curiosity kept him moving in spite of his fatigue. The inner room, he perceived, was high and its ceiling dome-shaped, with an oblong aperture in the centre opening into a funnel in which a wheel of broad vanes seemed to be rotating, apparently driving the air up the shaft. The faint humming note of its easy motion was the only clear sound in that quiet place. As these vanes sprang up one after the other, Graham could get transient glimpses of the sky. He was surprised to see a star.

This drew his attention to the fact that the bright lighting of these rooms was due to a multitude of very faint glow lamps set about the cornices. There were no windows. And he began to recall that along all the vast chambers and passages he had traversed with Howard he had observed no windows at all. Had there been windows? There were windows on the street indeed, but were they for light? Or was the whole city lit day and night for evermore, so that there was no night there?

And another thing dawned upon him. There was no fireplace in either room. Was the season summer, and were these merely summer apartments, or was the whole city uniformly heated or cooled? He became interested in these questions, began examining the smooth texture of the walls, the simply constructed bed, the ingenious arrangements by which the labour of bedroom service was practically abolished. And over everything was a curious absence of deliberate ornament, a bare grace of form and colour, that he found very pleasing to the eye. There were several comfortable chairs, a light table on silent runners carrying several bottles of fluids and glasses, and two plates bearing a clear substance like jelly. Then he noticed there were no books, no newspapers, no writing materials. 'The world has changed indeed,' he thought.

He observed one entire side of the outer room was set with rows of peculiar double cylinders inscribed with green lettering on white that harmonized with the decorative scheme of the room, and in the centre of this side projected a little apparatus about a yard square and having a white smooth face to the room. A chair faced this. He had a transitory idea that these cylinders might be books, or a modern substitute for books, but at first it did not seem so.

The lettering on the cylinders puzzled him. It seemed like Russian. Then he noticed a suggestion of mutilated English about certain of the words.

'Θi Man huwdbi Kiη,'

forced itself on him as 'The Man who would be King'. 'Phonetic spelling,' he said. He remembered reading a story with that title, then he recalled the story vividly, one of the best stories in the world. But this thing before him was not a book as he understood it. He puzzled out the titles of two adjacent cylinders. 'The Heart of Darkness' he had never heard of before nor 'The Madonna of the Future' – no doubt if they were indeed stories, they were by post-Victorian authors.

He puzzled over this peculiar cylinder for some time and replaced it. Then he turned to the square apparatus and examined that. He opened a sort of lid and found one of the double cylinders within, and on the upper edge a little stud like the stud of an electric bell. He pressed this and a rapid clicking began and ceased. He became aware of voices and music, and noticed a play of colour on the smooth front face. He suddenly realized what this might be, and stepped back to regard it.

On the flat surface was now a little picture, very vividly coloured, and in this picture were figures that moved. Not only did they move, but they were conversing in clear small voices. It was exactly like reality viewed through an inverted opera-glass and heard through a long tube. His interest was seized at once by the situation, which presented a man pacing up and down and vociferating angry things to a pretty but petulant woman. Both were in the picturesque costume that seemed so strange to Graham. 'I have worked,' said the man, 'but what have you been doing?'

'Ah!' said Graham. He forgot everything else, and sat down in the chair. Within five minutes he heard himself named, heard 'when the Sleeper wakes', used jestingly as a proverb for remote postponement, and passed himself by, a thing remote and incredible. But in a little while he knew those two people like intimate friends.

At last the miniature drama came to an end, and the square face of the apparatus was blank again.

It was a strange world into which he had been permitted to look, unscrupulous, pleasure-seeking, energetic, subtle, a world too of dire economic struggle; there were allusions he did not understand, incidents that conveyed strange suggestions of altered moral ideals, flashes of dubious enlightenment. The blue canvas that bulked so largely in his first impression of the city ways appeared again and again as the costume of the common people. He had no doubt the story was contemporary, and its intense realism was undeniable. And the end had been a tragedy that oppressed him. He sat staring at the blankness.

He started and rubbed his eyes. He had been so absorbed in the latter-day substitute for a novel, that he awoke to the little green and white room with more than a touch of the surprise of his first awakening.

He stood up, and abruptly he was back in his own wonderland. The clearness of the kinetoscope drama passed, and the struggle in the vast place of streets, the ambiguous Council, the swift phases of his waking hour, came back. These people had spoken of the Council with suggestions of a vague universality of power. And they had spoken of the Sleeper; it had not really struck him vividly at the time that he was the Sleeper. He had to recall precisely what they had said. . . .

He walked into the bedroom and peered up through the quick intervals of the revolving fan. As the fan swept round, a dim turmoil like the noise of machinery came in rhythmic eddies. All else was silence. Though the perpetual day still irradiated his apartments, he perceived the intermittent strip of sky was now deep blue – black almost, with a dust of little stars. . . .

He resumed his examination of the rooms. He could find no way of opening the padded door, no bell nor other means of calling for attendance. His feeling of wonder was in abeyance; but he was curious, anxious for information. He wanted to know exactly how he stood to these new things. He tried to compose himself to wait until someone came to him. Presently he became restless and eager for information, for distraction, for fresh sensations.

He went back to the apparatus in the other room, and had soon puzzled out the method of replacing the cylinders by others. As he did so, it came into his mind that it must be these little appliances had fixed the language so that it was still clear and understandable after two hundred years. The haphazard cylinders he substituted displayed a musical fantasia. At first it was beautiful, and then it was sensuous. He presently recognized what appeared to him to be an altered version of the story of Tannhäuser. The music was unfamiliar. But the rendering was realistic, and with a contemporary unfamiliarity. Tannhäuser did not go to a Venusberg, but to a Pleasure City. What was a Pleasure City? A dream, surely, the fancy of a fantastic, voluptuous writer.

He became interested, curious. The story developed with a flavour of strangely twisted sentimentality. Suddenly he did not like it. He liked it less as it proceeded.

He had a revulsion of feeling. These were no pictures, no idealizations, but photographed realities. He wanted no more of the twenty-second-century Venusberg. He forgot the part played by the model in nineteenth-century art, and gave way to an archaic indignation. He rose, angry and half ashamed at himself for witnessing this thing even in solitude. He pulled forward the apparatus, and with some violence sought for a means of stopping its action. Something snapped. A violet spark stung and convulsed his arm and the thing was still. When he attempted next day to replace these Tannhäuser cylinders by another pair, he found the apparatus broken. ...

He struck out a path oblique to the room and paced to and fro, struggling with intolerable vast impressions. The things he had derived from the cylinders and the things he had seen, conflicted, confused him. It seemed to him beyond measure incredible that in his thirty years of life he had never tried to shape a picture of these coming times. 'We were making the future,' he said, 'and hardly any of us troubled to think what future we were making. And here it is!

'What have they got to, what has been done? How do I come into the midst of it all?' The vastness of street and house he was prepared for, the multitudes of people. But conflicts in the city ways! And the systematized sensuality of a class of rich men!

He thought of Bellamy, the hero of whose Socialistic Utopia had so oddly anticipated this actual experience. But here was no Utopia, no Socialistic state. He had already seen enough to realize that the ancient antithesis of luxury, waste and sensuality on the one hand and abject poverty on the other, still prevailed. He knew enough of the essential factors of life to understand that correlation. And not only were the buildings of the city gigantic and the crowds in the street gigantic, but the voices he had heard in the ways, the uneasiness of Howard, the very atmosphere spoke of gigantic discontent. What country was he in? Still England it seemed, and yet strangely 'un-English'. His mind glanced at the rest of the world, and saw only an enigmatical veil.

He prowled about his apartment, examining everything as a caged animal might do. He was very tired, with that feverish exhaustion that does not admit of rest. He listened for long spaces under the ventilator to catch some distant echo of the tumults he felt must be proceeding in the city.

He began to talk to himself. 'Two hundred and three years!' he said to himself over and over again, laughing stupidly. 'Then I am two hundred and thirty-three years old! The oldest inhabitant. Surely they haven't reversed the tendency of our time and gone back to the rule of the oldest. My claims are indisputable. Mumble, mumble. I remember the Bulgarian atrocities as though it was yesterday. 'Tis a great age! Ha ha!' He was surprised at first to hear himself laughing, and then laughed again deliberately and louder. Then he realized that he was behaving foolishly. 'Steady,' he said. 'Steady!'

His pacing became more regular. 'This new world,' he said. 'I don't understand it. *Why?* . . . But it is all *why!*

'I suppose they can fly and do all sorts of things. Let me try and remember just how it began.'

He was surprised at first to find how vague the memories of his first thirty years had become. He remembered fragments, for the most part trivial moments, things of no great importance that he had observed. His boyhood seemed the most accessible at first, he recalled school books and certain lessons in mensuration. Then he revived the more salient features of his life, memories of the wife long since dead, her magic influence now gone beyond corruption, of his rivals and friends and betrayers, of the decision of this issue and that, and then of his last years of misery, of fluctuating resolves, and at last of his strenuous studies. In a little while he perceived he had it all again; dim perhaps, like metal long laid aside, but in no way defective or injured, capable of re-polishing. And the hue of it was a deepening misery. Was it worth re-polishing? By a miracle he had been lifted out of a life that had become intolerable. . . .

He reverted to his present condition. He wrestled with the facts in vain. It became an inextricable tangle. He saw the sky through the ventilator pink with dawn. An old persuasion came out of the dark recesses of his memory. 'I must sleep,' he said. It appeared as a delightful relief from this mental distress and from the growing pain and heaviness of his limbs. He went to the strange little bed, lay down and was presently asleep. . . .

He was destined to become very familiar indeed with these apartments before he left them, for he remained imprisoned for three days. During that time no one, except Howard, entered the rooms. The marvel of his fate mingled with and in some way minimized the marvel of his survival. He had awakened to mankind it seemed only to be snatched away into this unaccountable solitude. Howard came regularly with sustaining and nutritive fluids, and light and pleasant foods, quite strange to Graham. He always closed the door carefully as he entered. On matters of detail he was increasingly obliging, but the bearing of Graham on the great issues that were evidently being contested so closely beyond the sound-proof walls that enclosed him, he would not elucidate. He evaded, as politely as possible, every question on the position of affairs in the outer world.

And in those three days Graham's incessant thoughts went far and wide. All that he had seen, all this elaborate contrivance to prevent him seeing, worked together in his mind. Almost every possible interpretation of his position he debated – even, as it chanced, the right interpretation. Things that presently happened to him, became at least credible by virtue of this seclusion. When at length the moment of his release arrived, it found him prepared. . . .

Howard's bearing went far to deepen Graham's impression of his own strange importance; the door between its opening and closing seemed to admit with him a breath of momentous happening. His enquiries became more definite and searching. Howard retreated through protests and difficulties. The awakening was unforeseen, he repeated; it happened to have fallen in with the trend of a social convulsion. 'To explain it I must tell you the history of a gross and a half of years,' protested Howard.

'The thing is this,' said Graham. 'You are afraid of something I shall do. In some way I am arbitrator – I might be arbitrator.'

'It is not that. But you have – I may tell you this much – the automatic increase of your property puts great possibilities of interference in your hands. And in certain other ways you have influence, with your eighteenth-century notions.'

'Nineteenth-century,' corrected Graham.

'With your old-world notions, anyhow, ignorant as you are of every feature of our State.'

'Am I a fool?'

'Certainly not.'

'Do I seem to be the sort of man who would act rashly?'

'You were never expected to act at all. No one counted on your awakening. No one dreamt you would ever awake. The Council had surrounded you with antiseptic conditions. As a matter of fact, we thought that you were dead – a mere arrest of decay. And – but it is too complex. We dare not suddenly – while you are still half awake.'

'It won't do,' said Graham. 'Suppose it is as you say – why am I not being crammed night and day with facts and warnings and all the wisdom of the time to fit me for my responsibilities? Am I any wiser now than two days ago, if it is two days, when I awoke?'

Howard pulled his lip.

'I am beginning to feel – every hour I feel more clearly – a system of concealment of which you are the face. Is this Council, or committee, or whatever they are, cooking the accounts of my estate? Is that it?'

'That note of suspicion —' said Howard.

'Ugh!' said Graham. 'Now, mark my words, it will be ill for those who have put me here. It will be ill. I am alive. Make no doubt of it, I am alive. Every day my pulse is stronger and my mind clearer and more vigorous. No more quiescence. I am a man come back to life. And I want to *live*—'

'*Live!*'

Howard's face lit with an idea. He came towards Graham and spoke in an easy confidential tone.

'The Council secludes you here for your good. You are restless. Naturally – an energetic man! You find it dull here. But we are anxious that everything you may desire – every desire – every sort of desire ... There may be something. Is there any sort of company?'

He paused meaningly.

'Yes,' said Graham thoughtfully. 'There is.'

'Ah! *Now!* We have treated you neglectfully.'

'The crowds in yonder streets of yours.'

'That,' said Howard, 'I am afraid – But—'

Graham began pacing the room. Howard stood near the door watching him. The implication of Howard's suggestion was only half evident to Graham. Company? Suppose he were to accept the proposal, demand some sort of *company?* Would there be any possibilities of gathering from the conversation of this additional person some vague inkling of the struggle that had broken out so vividly at his waking moment? He meditated again, and the suggestion took colour. He turned on Howard abruptly.

'What do you mean by company?'

Howard raised his eyes and shrugged his shoulders. 'Human beings,' he said, with a curious smile on his heavy face.

'Our social ideas,' he said, 'have a certain increased liberality, perhaps, in comparison with your times. If a man wishes to relieve

461

such a tedium as this – by feminine society, for instance. We think it no scandal. We have cleared our minds of formulae. There is in our city a class, a necessary class, no longer despised – discreet—'

Graham stopped dead.

'It would pass the time,' said Howard. 'It is a thing I should perhaps have thought of before, but as a matter of fact so much is happening—'

He indicated the exterior world.

Graham hesitated. For a moment the figure of a possible woman dominated his mind with an intense attraction. Then he flashed into anger.

'*No!*' he shouted.

He began striding rapidly up and down the room. 'Everything you say, everything you do, convinces me – of some great issue in which I am concerned. I do not want to pass the time, as you call it. Yes, I know. Desire and indulgence are life in a sense – and death! Extinction! In my life before I slept I had worked out that pitiful question. I will not begin again. There is a city, a multitude – And meanwhile I am here like a rabbit in a bag.'

His rage surged high. He choked for a moment and began to wave his clenched fists. He gave way to an anger fit, he swore archaic curses. His gestures had the quality of physical threats.

'I do not know who your party may be. I am in the dark, and you keep me in the dark. But I know this, that I am secluded here for no good purpose. For no good purpose. I warn you, I warn you of the consequences. Once I come at my power—'

He realized that to threaten thus might be a danger to himself. He stopped. Howard stood regarding him with a curious expression.

'I take it this is a message to the Council,' said Howard. Graham had a momentary impulse to leap upon the man, fell or stun him. It must have shown upon his face; at any rate Howard's movement was quick. In a second the noiseless door had closed and the man from the nineteenth century was alone.

For a moment he stood rigid, with clenched hands half raised. Then he flung them down. 'What a fool I have been!' he said, and gave way to his anger, stamping about the room and shouting curses. ... For a long time he kept himself in a sort of frenzy, raging at his position, at his own folly, at the knaves who had imprisoned him. He did this because he did not want to look calmly at his position. He clung to his anger – because he was afraid of fear.

Presently he was reasoning with himself. This imprisonment was unaccountable, but no doubt the legal forms – new legal forms – of the time permitted it. It must of course be legal. These people were two hundred years further on in the march of civilization than the Victorian generation. It was not likely they would be less – humane. Yet they had cleared their minds of formulae! Was humanity a formula as well as chastity?

His imagination set to work to suggest things that might be done to him. The attempts of his reason to dispose of these suggestions, though for the most part logically valid, were quite unavailing. 'Why should anything be done to me?

'If the worst comes to the worst,' he found himself saying at last, 'I can give up what they want. But what do they want? And why don't they ask me for it instead of cooping me up?'

He returned to his former preoccupation with the Council's possible intentions. He began to reconsider the details of Howard's behaviour, sinister glances, inexplicable hesitations. Then for a time his mind circled about the idea of escaping from these rooms; but whither could he escape into this vast, crowded world? He would be worse off than a Saxon yeoman suddenly dropped into nineteenth-century London. And besides, how could anyone escape from these rooms?

'How can it benefit anyone if harm should happen to me?'

He thought of the tumult, the great social trouble of which he was so unaccountably the axis. A text, irrelevant enough and yet curiously insistent, came floating up out of the darkness of his memory. This also a Council had said:

'It is expedient for us that one man should die for the people.'

8

The Roof Spaces

As the fans in the circular aperture of the inner room rotated and permitted glimpses of the night, dim sounds drifted in thereby. And Graham, standing underneath, was startled by the sound of a voice.

He peered up and saw in the intervals of the rotation, dark and dim, the face and shoulders of a man regarding him. Then a dark hand was extended, the swift vane struck it, swung round and beat on with a little brownish patch on the edge of its thin blade, and something began to fall therefrom upon the floor, dripping silently.

Graham looked down, and there were spots of blood at his feet. He looked up again in a strange excitement. The figure had gone.

He remained motionless – his every sense intent upon the flickering patch of darkness. He became aware of some faint, remote, dark specks floating lightly through the outer air. They came down towards him, fitfully, eddyingly, and passed aside out of the uprush from the fan. A gleam of light flickered, the specks flashed white, and then the darkness came again. Warmed and lit as he was, he perceived that it was snowing within a few feet of him.

Graham walked across the room and came back to the ventilator again. He saw the head of a man pass near. There was a sound of whispering. Then a smart blow on some metallic substance, effort, voices, and the vanes stopped. A gust of snowflakes whirled into the room, and vanished before they touched the floor. 'Don't be afraid,' said a voice.

Graham stood under the van. 'Who are you?' he whispered.

For a moment there was nothing but a swaying of the fan, and then the head of a man was thrust cautiously into the opening. His face

464

appeared nearly inverted to Graham; his dark hair was wet with dissolving flakes of snow upon it. His arm went up into the darkness holding something unseen. He had a youthful face and bright eyes, and the veins of his forehead were swollen. He seemed to be exerting himself to maintain his position.

For several seconds neither he nor Graham spoke.

'You were the Sleeper?' said the stranger at last.

'Yes,' said Graham. 'What do you want with me?'

'I come from Ostrog, Sire.'

'Ostrog?'

The man in the ventilator twisted his head round so that his profile was towards Graham. He appeared to be listening. Suddenly there was a hasty exclamation, and the intruder sprang back just in time to escape the sweep of the released fan. And when Graham peered up there was nothing visible but the slowly falling snow.

It was perhaps a quarter of an hour before anything returned to the ventilator. But at last came the same metallic interference again; the fans stopped and the face reappeared. Graham had remained all this time in the same place, alert and tremulously excited.

'Who are you? What do you want?' he said.

'We want to speak to you, Sire,' said the intruder. 'We want – I can't hold the thing. We have been trying to find a way to you – these three days.'

'Is it rescue?' whispered Graham. 'Escape?'

'Yes, Sire. If you will.'

'You are my party – the party of the Sleeper?'

'Yes, Sire.'

'What am I to do?' said Graham.

There was a struggle. The stranger's arm appeared, and his hand was bleeding. His knees came into view over the edge of the funnel 'Stand away from me,' he said, and he dropped rather heavily on his hands and one shoulder at Graham's feet. The released ventilator whirled noisily. The stranger rolled over, sprang up nimbly and stood panting, hand to a bruised shoulder, and with his bright eyes on Graham.

'You are indeed the Sleeper,' he said. 'I saw you asleep. When it was the law that anyone might see you.'

'I am the man who was in a trance,' said Graham. 'They have imprisoned me here. I have been here since I awoke – at least three days.'

The intruder seemed about to speak, heard something, glanced swiftly at the door, and suddenly left Graham and ran towards it, shouting quick incoherent words. A bright wedge of steel flashed in his hand, and he began tap, tap, a quick succession of blows upon the hinges. 'Mind!' cried a voice. 'Oh!' The voice came from above.

Graham glanced up, saw the soles of two feet, ducked, was struck on the shoulder by one of them, and a heavy weight bore him to the ground. He fell on his knees and forward, and the weight went over his head. He knelt up and saw a second man from above seated before him.

'I did not see you, Sire,' panted the man. He rose and assisted Graham to rise. 'Are you hurt, Sire?' he panted. A succession of heavy blows on the ventilator began, something fell close to Graham's face, and a shivering edge of white metal danced, fell over, and lay flat upon the floor.

'What is this?' cried Graham, confused and looking at the ventilator. 'Who are you? What are you going to do? Remember, I understand nothing.'

'Stand back,' said the stranger, and drew him from under the ventilator as another fragment of metal fell heavily.

'We want you to come, Sire,' panted the newcomer, and Graham glancing at his face again, saw a new cut had changed from white to red on his forehead, and a couple of little trickles of blood were starting therefrom. 'Your people call for you.'

'Come where? My people?'

'To the hall above the markets. Your life is in danger here. We have spies. We learnt but just in time. The Council has decided – this very day – either to drug or kill you. And everything is ready. The people are drilled, the wind-vane police, the engineers, and half the way-gearers are with us. We have the halls crowded – shouting. The whole city shouts against the Council. We have arms.' He wiped the blood with his hand. 'Your life here is not worth—'

'But why arms?'

'The people have risen to protect you, Sire. What?'

He turned quickly as the man who had first come down made a hissing with his teeth. Graham saw the latter start back, gesticulate to them to conceal themselves, and move as if to hide behind the opening door.

As he did so Howard appeared, a little tray in one hand and his heavy face downcast. He started, looked up, the door slammed behind him, the tray tilted sideways, and the steel wedge struck him behind the ear. He went down like a felled tree, and lay as he fell athwart the floor of the outer room. The man who had struck him bent hastily,

466

studied his face for a moment, rose, and returned to his work at the door.

'Your poison!' said a voice in Graham's ear.

Then abruptly they were in darkness. The innumerable cornice lights had been extinguished. Graham saw the aperture of the ventilator with ghostly snow whirling above it and dark figures moving hastily. Three knelt on the fan. Some dim thing – a ladder – was being lowered through the opening, and a hand appeared holding a fitful yellow light.

He had a moment of hesitation. But the manner of these men, their swift alacrity, their words, marched so completely with his own fears of the Council, with his idea and hope of a rescue, that it lasted not a moment. And his people awaited him!

'I do not understand,' he said. 'I trust. Tell me what to do.'

The man with the cut brow gripped Graham's arm. 'Clamber up the ladder,' he whispered. 'Quick. They will have heard—'

Graham felt for the ladder with extended hands, put his foot on the lower rung and, turning his head, saw over the shoulder of the nearest man, in the yellow flicker of the light, the first-comer astride over Howard and still working at the door. Graham turned to the ladder again, and was thrust by his conductor and helped up by those above, and then he was standing on something hard and cold and slippery outside the ventilating funnel.

He shivered. He was aware of a great difference in the temperature. Half a dozen men stood about him, and light flakes of snow touched hands and face and melted. For a moment it was dark, then for a flash a ghastly violet white, and then everything was dark again.

He saw he had come out upon the roof of the vast city structure which had replaced the miscellaneous houses, streets and open spaces of Victorian London. The place upon which he stood was level, with huge serpentine cables lying athwart it in every direction. The circular wheels of a number of windmills loomed indistinct and gigantic through the darkness and snowfall, and roared with a varying loudness as the fitful wind rose and fell. Some way off an intermittent white light smote up from below, touched the snow eddies with a transient glitter, and made an evanescent spectre in the night; and here and there, low down, some vaguely outlined wind-driven mechanism flickered with livid sparks.

All this he appreciated in a fragmentary manner as his rescuers stood about him. Someone threw a thick soft cloak of fur-like texture about him, and fastened it by buckled straps at waist and shoulders. Things were said briefly, decisively. Someone thrust him forward.

467

Before his mind was yet clear a dark shape gripped his arm. 'This way,' said this shape, urging him along, and pointed Graham across the flat roof in the direction of a dim semicircular haze of light. Graham obeyed.

'Mind!' said a voice, as Graham stumbled against a cable. 'Between them and not across them,' said the voice. And, 'We must hurry.'

'Where are the people?' said Graham. 'The people you said awaited me?'

The stranger did not answer. He left Graham's arm as the path grew narrower, and led the way with rapid strides. Graham followed blindly. In a minute he found himself running. 'Are the others coming?' he panted, but received no reply. His companion glanced back and ran on. They came to a sort of pathway of open metalwork, transverse to the direction they had come, and they turned aside to follow this. Graham looked back, but the snowstorm had hidden the others.

'Come on!' said his guide. Running now, they drew near a little windmill spinning high in the air. 'Stoop,' said Graham's guide, and they avoided an endless band running roaring up to the shaft of the vane. 'This way!' and they were ankle deep in a gutter full of drifted thawing snow, between two low walls of metal that presently rose waist high. 'I will go first,' said the guide. Graham drew his cloak about him and followed. Then suddenly came a narrow abyss across which the gutter leapt to the snowy darkness of the further side. Graham peeped over the side once and the gulf was black. For a moment he regretted his flight. He dared not look again, and his brain spun as he waded through the half liquid snow.

Then out of the gutter they clambered and hurried across a wide flat space damp with thawing snow, and for half its extent dimly translucent to lights that went to and fro underneath. He hesitated at this unstable looking substance, but his guide ran on unheeding, and so they came to and clambered up slippery steps to the rim of a great dome of glass. Round this they went. Far below a number of people seemed to be dancing, and music filtered through the dome. ... Graham fancied he heard a shouting through the snowstorm, and his guide hurried him on with a new spurt of haste. They clambered panting to a space of huge windmills, one so vast that only the lower edge of its vanes came rushing into sight and rushed up again and was lost in the night and the snow. They hurried for a time through the colossal metallic tracery of its supports, and came at last above a place of moving platforms like the place into which Graham had looked from the balcony. They crawled across the sloping transparency that covered this street of platforms, crawling on hands and knees because of the slipperiness of the snowfall.

For the most part the glass was bedewed, and Graham saw only hazy suggestions of the forms below, but near the pitch of the transparent roof the glass was clear, and he found himself looking sheerly down upon it all. For a while, in spite of the urgency of his guide, he gave way to vertigo and lay spread-eagled on the glass, sick and paralysed. Far below, mere stirring specks and dots, went the people of the unsleeping city in their perpetual daylight, and the moving platforms ran on their incessant journey. Messengers and men on unknown businesses shot along the drooping cables and the frail bridges were crowded with men. It was like peering into a gigantic glass hive, and it lay vertically below him with only a tough glass of unknown thickness to save him from a fall. The street showed warm and lit, and Graham was wet now to the skin with thawing snow, and his feet were numbed with cold. For a space he could not move. 'Come on!' cried his guide, with terror in his voice. 'Come on!'

Graham reached the pitch of the roof by an effort.

Over the ridge, following his guide's example, he turned about and slid backward down the opposite slope very swiftly, amid a little avalanche of snow. While he was sliding he thought of what would happen if some broken gap should come in his way. At the edge he stumbled to his feet ankle deep in slush, thanking heaven for an opaque footing again. His guide was already clambering up a metal screen to a level expanse.

Through the spare snowflakes above this loomed another line of vast windmills, and then suddenly the amorphous tumult of the rotating wheels was pierced with a deafening sound. It was a mechanical shrilling of extraordinary intensity that seemed to come simultaneously from every point of the compass.

'They have missed us already!' cried Graham's guide in an accent of terror, and suddenly, with a blinding flash, the night became day.

Above the driving snow, from the summits of the wind-wheels, appeared vast masts carrying globes of livid light. They receded in illimitable vistas in every direction. As far as his eye could penetrate the snowfall they glared.

'Get on this,' cried Graham's conductor, and thrust him forward to a long grating of snowless metal that ran like a band between two slightly sloping expanses of snow. It felt warm to Graham's benumbed feet, and a faint eddy of steam rose from it.

'Come on!' shouted his guide ten yards off, and, without waiting, ran swiftly through the incandescent glare towards the iron supports of the next range of wind-wheels. Graham, recovering from his astonishment, followed as fast, convinced of his imminent capture. . . .

In a score of seconds they were within a tracery of glare and black shadows shot with moving bars beneath the monstrous wheels. Graham's conductor ran on for some time, and suddenly darted sideways and vanished into a black shadow in the corner of the foot of a huge support. In another moment Graham was beside him.

They cowered panting and stared out.

The scene upon which Graham looked was very wild and strange. The snow had now almost ceased; only a belated flake passed now and again across the picture. But the broad stretch of level before them was a ghastly white, broken only by gigantic masses and moving shapes and lengthy strips of impenetrable darkness, vast ungainly Titans of shadow. All about them huge metallic structures, iron girders, inhumanly vast as it seemed to him, interlaced, and the edges of wind-wheels, scarcely moving in the lull, passed in great shining curves more and more steeply up into a luminous haze. Wherever the snow-spangled light struck down, beams and girders, and incessant bands running with a halting, indomitable resolution, passed upward and downward into the black. And with all that mighty activity, with an omnipresent sense of motive and design, this snowclad desolation of mechanism seemed void of all human presence save themselves, seemed as trackless and deserted and unfrequented by men as some inaccessible Alpine snowfield.

'They will be chasing us,' cried the leader. 'We are scarcely halfway there yet. Cold as it is we must hide here for a space – at least until it snows more thickly again.'

His teeth chattered in his head.

'Where are the markets?' asked Graham staring out. 'Where are all the people?'

The other made no answer.

'*Look!*' whispered Graham, crouched close, and became very still.

The snow had suddenly become thick again, and sliding with the whirling eddies out of the black pit of the sky came something, vague and large and very swift. It came down in a steep curve and swept round, wide wings extended and a trail of white condensing steam behind it, rose with an easy swiftness and went gliding up the air, swept horizontally forward in a wide curve, and vanished again in the steaming specks of snow. And through the ribs of its body Graham saw two little men, very minute and active, searching the snowy areas about him, as it seemed to him, with field-glasses. For a second they were clear, then hazy through a thick whirl of snow, then small and distant, and in a minute they were gone.

'*Now!*' cried his companion. 'Come!'

He pulled Graham's sleeve, and incontinently the two were running headlong down the arcade of ironwork beneath the wind-wheels. Graham, running blindly, collided with his leader, who had turned back on him suddenly. He found himself within a dozen yards of a black chasm. It extended as far as he could see right and left. It seemed to cut off their progress in either direction.

'Do as I do,' whispered his guide. He lay down and crawled to the edge, thrust his head over and twisted until one leg hung. He seemed to feel for something with his foot, found it, and went sliding over the edge into the gulf. His head reappeared. 'It is a ledge,' he whispered. 'In the dark all the way along. Do as I did.'

Graham hesitated, went down upon all fours, crawled to the edge, and peered into a velvety blackness. For a sickly moment he had courage neither to go on nor retreat, then he sat and hung his leg down, felt his guide's hands pulling at him, had a horrible sensation of sliding over the edge into the unfathomable, splashed, and felt himself in a slushy gutter, impenetrably dark.

'This way,' whispered the voice, and he began crawling along the gutter through the trickling thaw, pressing himself against the wall. They continued along it for some minutes. He seemed to pass through a hundred stages of misery, to pass minute after minute through a hundred degrees of cold, damp and exhaustion. In a little while he ceased to feel his hands and feet.

The gutter sloped downwards. He observed that they were now many feet below the edge of the buildings. Rows of spectral white shapes like the ghosts of blind-drawn windows rose above them. They came to the end of a cable fastened above one of these white windows, dimly visible and dropping into impenetrable shadows. Suddenly his hand came against his guide's. '*Still!*' whispered the latter very softly.

He looked up with a start and saw the huge wings of the flying machine gliding slowly and noiselessly overhead athwart the broad band of snow-flecked grey-blue sky. In a moment it was hidden again.

'Keep still; they were just turning.'

For a while both were motionless, then Graham's companion stood up, and reaching towards the fastenings of the cable fumbled with some indistinct tackle.

'What is that?' asked Graham.

The only answer was a faint cry. The man crouched motionless. Graham peered and saw his face dimly. He was staring down the long

471

ribbon of sky, and Graham, following his eyes, saw the flying machine small and faint and remote. Then he saw that the wings spread on either side, that it headed towards them, that every moment it grew larger. It was following the edge of the chasm towards them.

The man's movements became convulsive. He thrust two cross bars into Graham's hand. Graham could not see them, he ascertained their form by feeling. They were slung by thin cords to the cable. On the cord were hand grips of some soft elastic substance. 'Put the cross between your legs,' whispered the guide hysterically, 'and grip the holdfasts. Grip tightly, grip!'

Graham did as he was told.

'Jump,' said the voice. 'In heaven's name, jump!'

For one momentous second Graham could not speak. He was glad afterwards that darkness hid his face. He said nothing. He began to tremble violently. He looked sideways at the swift shadow that swallowed up the sky as it rushed upon him.

'Jump! Jump – in God's name! Or they will have us,' cried Graham's guide, and in the violence of his passion thrust him forward.

Graham tottered convulsively, gave a sobbing cry, a cry in spite of himself, and then, as the flying machine swept over them, fell forward into the pit of that darkness, seated on the cross wood and holding the ropes with the clutch of death. Something cracked, something rapped smartly against a wall. He heard the pulley of the cradle hum on its rope. He heard the aeronauts shout. He felt a pair of knees digging into his back. ... He was sweeping headlong through the air, falling through the air. All his strength was in his hands. He would have screamed but he had no breath.

He shot into a blinding light that made him grip the tighter. He recognized the great passage with the running ways, the hanging lights and interlacing girders. They rushed upward and by him. He had a momentary impression of a great round mouth yawning to swallow him up.

He was in the dark again, falling, falling, gripping with aching hands, and behold! a clap of sound, a burst of light, and he was in a brightly lit hall with a roaring multitude of people beneath his feet. The people! His people! A proscenium, a stage rushed up towards him, and his cable swept down to a circular aperture to the right of this. He felt he was travelling slower, and suddenly very much slower. He distinguished shouts of 'Saved! The Master. He is safe!' The stage rushed up towards him with rapidly diminishing swiftness. Then—

He heard the man clinging behind him shout as if suddenly terrified, and this shout was echoed by a shout from below. He felt that he was

472

no longer gliding along the cable but falling with it. There was a tumult of yells, screams and cries. He felt something soft against his extended hand, and the impact of a broken fall quivering through his arm. . . .

He wanted to be still and the people were lifting him. He believed afterwards he was carried to the platform, but he was never sure. He did not notice what became of his guide. When his mind was clear again he was on his feet; eager hands were assisting him to stand. He was in a big alcove, occupying the position that in his previous experience had been devoted to the lower boxes. If this was indeed a theatre.

A mighty tumult was in his ears, a thunderous roar, the shouting of a countless multitude. 'It is the Sleeper! The Sleeper is with us!'

'The Sleeper is with us! The Master – the Owner! The Master is with us. He is safe.'

Graham had a surging vision of a great hall crowded with people. He saw no individuals, he was conscious of a froth of pink faces, of waving arms and garments, he felt the occult influence of a vast crowd pouring over him, buoying him up. There were balconies, galleries, great archways giving remoter perspectives, and everywhere people, a vast arena of people, densely packed and cheering. Across the nearer space lay the collapsed cable like a huge snake. It had been cut by the men of the flying machine at its upper end, and had crumpled down into the hall. Men seemed to be hauling this out of the way. But the whole effect was vague, the very buildings throbbed and leapt with the roar of the voices.

He stood unsteadily and looked at those about him. Someone supported him by one arm. 'Let me go into a little room,' he said, weeping; 'a little room,' and could say no more. A man in black stepped forward, took his disengaged arm. He was aware of officious men opening a door before him. Someone guided him to a seat. He staggered. He sat down heavily and covered his face with his hands; he was trembling violently, his nervous control was at an end. He was relieved of his cloak, he could not remember how; his purple hose he saw were black with wet. People were running about him, things were happening, but for some time he gave no heed to them.

He had escaped. A myriad cries told him that. He was safe. These were the people who were on his side. For a space he sobbed for breath, and then he sat still with his face covered. The air was full of the shouting of innumerable men.

9

The People March

He became aware of someone urging a glass of clear fluid upon his attention, looked up and discovered this was a dark young man in a yellow garment. He took the dose forthwith, and in a moment he was glowing. A tall man in a black robe stood by his shoulder, and pointed to the half-open door into the hall. This man was shouting close to his ear, and yet what was said was indistinct because of the tremendous uproar from the great theatre. Behind the man was a girl in a silvery grey robe, whom Graham, even in this confusion, perceived to be beautiful. Her dark eyes, full of wonder and curiosity, were fixed on him, her lips trembled apart. A partially opened door gave a glimpse of the crowded hall, and admitted a vast uneven tumult, a hammering, clapping and shouting that died away and began again and rose to a thunderous pitch, and so continued intermittently all the time that Graham remained in the little room. He watched the lips of the man in black and gathered that he was making some explanation.

He stared stupidly for some moments at these things and then stood up abruptly; he grasped the arm of this shouting person. 'Tell me!' he cried. 'Who am I? Who am I?'

The others came nearer to hear his words. 'Who am I?' His eyes searched their faces.

'They have told him nothing!' cried the girl.

'Tell me, tell me!' cried Graham.

'You are the Master of the Earth. You are owner of the world.'

He did not believe he heard aright. He resisted the persuasion. He pretended not to understand, not to hear. He lifted his voice again. 'I have been awake three days – a prisoner three days. I judge there is some struggle between a number of people in this city – it is London?'

'Yes,' said the younger man.

'And those who meet in the great hall with the white Atlas? How does it concern me? In some way it has to do with me. *Why*, I don't know. Drugs? It seems to me that while I have slept the world has gone mad. I have gone mad. . . . Who are those Councillors under the Atlas? Why should they try to drug me?'

'To keep you insensible,' said the man in yellow. 'To prevent your interference.'

'But *why*?'

'Because *you* are the Atlas, Sire,' said the man in yellow. 'The world is on your shoulders. They rule it in your name.'

The sounds from the hall had died into a silence threaded by one monotonous voice. Now suddenly, trampling on these last words, came a deafening tumult, a roaring and thundering, cheer crowded on cheer, voices hoarse and shrill, beating, overlapping, and while it lasted the people in the little room could not hear each other shout.

Graham stood, his intelligence clinging helplessly to the thing he had just heard. 'The Council,' he repeated blankly, and then snatched at a name that had struck him. 'But who is Ostrog?' he said.

'He is the organizer – the organizer of the revolt. Our Leader – in your name.'

'In my name? – And you? Why is he not here?'

'He – has deputed us. I am his brother – his half-brother, Lincoln. He wants you to show yourself to those people and then come on to him. That is why he was sent. He is at the wind-vane offices directing. The people are marching.'

'In your name,' shouted the younger man. 'They have ruled, crushed, tyrannized. At last even—'

'In my name! My name! Master?'

The younger man suddenly became audible in a pause of the outer thunder, indignant and vociferous, a high penetrating voice under his red aquiline nose and bushy moustache. 'No one expected you to wake. No one expected you to wake. They were cunning. Damned tyrants! But they were taken by surprise. They did not know whether to drug you, hypnotize you, kill you.'

Again the hall dominated everything.

'Ostrog is at the wind-vane offices ready – Even now there is a rumour of fighting beginning.'

The man who had called himself Lincoln came close to him. 'Ostrog has it planned. Trust him. We have our organizations ready. We shall seize the flying stages – Even now he may be doing that. Then—'

475

'This public theatre,' bawled the man in yellow, 'is only a contingent. We have five myriads of drilled men—'

'We have arms,' cried Lincoln. 'We have plans. A leader. Their police have gone from the streets and are massed in the —' (inaudible). 'It is now or never. The Council is rocking – They cannot trust even their drilled men—'

'Hear the people calling to you!'

Graham's mind was like a night of moon and swift clouds, now dark and hopeless, now clear and ghastly. He was Master of the Earth, he was a man sodden with thawing snow. Of all his fluctuating impressions the dominant ones presented an antagonism; on the one hand was the White Council, powerful, disciplined, few, the White Council from which he had just escaped; and on the other, monstrous crowds, packed masses of indistinguishable people clamouring his name, hailing him Master. The other side had imprisoned him, debated his death. These shouting thousands beyond the little doorway had rescued him. But why these things should be so he could not understand.

The door opened, Lincoln's voice was swept away and drowned, and a rush of people followed on the heels of the tumult. These intruders came towards him and Lincoln gesticulating. The voices without explained their soundless lips. 'Show us the Sleeper, show us the Sleeper!' was the burden of the uproar. Men were bawling for 'Order! Silence!'

Graham glanced towards the open doorway, and saw a tall, oblong picture of the hall beyond, a waving, incessant confusion of crowded, shouting faces, men and women together, waving pale blue garments, extended hands. Many were standing; one man in rags of dark brown, a gaunt figure, stood on the seat and waved a black cloth. He met the wonder and expectation of the girl's eyes. What did these people expect from him? He was dimly aware that the tumult outside had changed its character, was in some way beating, marching. His own mind, too, changed. For a space he did not recognize the influence that was transforming him. But a moment that was near to panic passed. He tried to make audible inquiries in vain.

Lincoln was shouting in his ear, but Graham was deafened to that. All the others save the woman gesticulated towards the hall. He perceived what had happened to the uproar. The whole mass of people was chanting together. It was not simply a song, the voices were gathered together and upborne by a torrent of instrumental music, music like the music of an organ, a woven texture of sounds, full of trumpets, full of flaunting banners, full of the march and pageantry of

476

opening war. And the feet of the people were beating time – tramp, tramp.

He was urged towards the door. He obeyed mechanically. The strength of that chant took hold of him, stirred him, emboldened him. The hall opened to him, a vast welter of fluttering colour swaying to the music.

'Wave your arm to them,' said Lincoln. 'Wave your arm to them.'

'This,' said a voice on the other side, 'he must have this.' Arms were about his neck detaining him in the doorway, and a black mantle hung from his shoulders. He threw his arm free of this and followed Lincoln. He perceived the girl in grey close to him, her face lit, her gesture onward. For the instant she became to him, flushed and eager as she was, an embodiment of the song. He emerged in the alcove again. Incontinently the mounting waves of the song broke upon his appearing, and flashed up into a foam of shouting. Guided by Lincoln's hand he marched obliquely across the centre of the stage facing the people.

The hall was a vast and intricate space – galleries, balconies, broad spaces of amphitheatral steps, and great archways. Far away, high up, seemed the mouth of a huge passage full of struggling humanity. The whole multitude was swaying in congested masses. Individual figures sprang out of the tumult, impressed him momentarily, and lost definition again. Close to the platform swayed a beautiful fair woman carried by three men, her hair across her face and brandishing a green staff. Next this group an old careworn man in blue canvas maintained his place in the crush with difficulty, and behind shouted a hairless face, a great cavity of toothless mouth. A voice called that enigmatical word 'Ostrog'. All his impressions were vague save the massive emotion of that trampling song. The multitude were beating time with their feet – marking time, tramp, tramp, tramp, tramp. The green weapons waved, flashed and slanted. Then he saw those nearest to him on a level space before the stage were marching in front of him, passing towards a great archway, shouting 'To the Council!' Tramp, tramp, tramp, tramp. He raised his arm, and the roaring was redoubled. He remembered he had to shout 'March!' His mouth shaped inaudible heroic words. He waved his arm again and pointed to the archway, shouting 'Onward!' They were no longer marking time, they were marching; tramp, tramp, tramp, tramp. In that host were bearded men, old men, youths, fluttering robed bare-armed women, girls. Men and women of the new age! Rich robes, grey rags fluttered together in the whirl of their movement amidst the dominant blue. A monstrous black banner jerked its way to the right. He perceived a blue-clad Negro, a shrivelled woman in yellow, then a group of tall fair-haired, white-faced, blue-clad men pushed theatrically past him. He noted two Chinamen. A tall, sallow, dark-haired, shining-eyed youth, white clad from top to toe, clambered up towards the platform shouting loyally, and sprang down again and receded, looking backward. Heads, shoulders, hands clutching weapons, all were swinging with those marching cadences.

Faces came out of the confusion to him as he stood there, eyes met his and passed and vanished. Men gesticulated to him, shouted inaudible personal things. Most of the faces were flushed, but many were ghastly white. And disease was there, and many a hand that waved to him was gaunt and lean. Men and women of the new age! Strange and incredible meeting! As the broad stream passed before him to the right, tributary gangways from the remote uplands of the hall thrust downward in an incessant replacement of people; tramp, tramp, tramp, tramp. The unison of the song was enriched and complicated by the massive echoes of arches and passages. Men and women mingled in the ranks; tramp, tramp, tramp, tramp. The whole world seemed marching. Tramp, tramp, tramp, tramp; his brain was tramping. The garments waved onward, the faces poured by more abundantly.

Tramp, tramp, tramp, tramp; at Lincoln's pressure he turned towards the archway, walking unconsciously in that rhythm, scarcely noticing his movement for the melody and stir of it. The multitude, the gesture and song, all moved in that direction, the flow of people smote downward until the upturned faces were below the level of his feet. He was aware of a path before him, of a suite about him, of guards and dignities and Lincoln on his right hand. Attendants intervened, and ever and again blotted out the sight of the multitude to the left. Before him went the backs of the guards in black – three and three and three. He was marched along a little railed way, and crossed above the archway with the torrent dipping to flow beneath and shouting up to him. He did not know whither he went; he did not want to know. He glanced back across a flaming spaciousness of hall. Tramp, tramp, tramp, tramp.

The Battle of the Darkness

He was no longer in the hall. He was marching along a gallery overhanging one of the great streets of the moving platforms that traversed the city. Before him and behind him tramped his guards. The whole concave of the moving ways below was a congested mass of people marching, tramping to the left, shouting, waving hands and arms, pouring along a huge vista, shouting as they came into view, shouting as they passed, shouting as they receded, until the globes of electric light receding in perspective dropped down it seemed and hid the swarming bare heads. Tramp, tramp, tramp, tramp.

The song roared up to Graham now, no longer upborne by music but coarse and noisy, and the beating of the marching feet, tramp, tramp, tramp, tramp, interwove with a thunderous irregularity of footsteps from the undisciplined rabble that poured along the higher ways.

Abruptly he noted a contrast. The buildings on the opposite side of the way seemed deserted, the cables and bridges that laced across the aisle were empty and shadowy. It came into Graham's mind that these also should have swarmed with people.

He felt a curious emotion – throbbing – very fast! He stopped again. The guards before him marched on; those about him stopped as he did. He saw anxiety and fear in their faces. The throbbing had something to do with the lights. He too looked up.

At first it seemed to him a thing that affected the lights simply, an isolated phenomenon having no bearing on the things below. Each huge globe of blinding whiteness was as it were clutched, compressed in a systole that was followed by a transitory diastole, and again

479

a systole like a tightening grip, darkness, light, darkness, in rapid alternation.

Graham became aware that this strange behaviour of the lights had to do with the people below. The appearance of the houses and ways, the appearance of the packed masses changed, became a confusion of vivid lights and leaping shadows. He saw a multitude of shadows had sprung into aggressive existence, seemed rushing up, broadening, widening, growing with steady swiftness – to leap suddenly back and return reinforced. The song and the tramping had ceased. The unanimous march, he discovered, was arrested, there were eddies, a flow sideways, shouts of 'The lights!' Voices were crying together one thing. 'The lights! The lights!' He looked down. In this dancing death of the lights the area of the street had suddenly become a monstrous struggle. The huge white globes became purple-white, purple with a reddish glow, flickered, flickered faster and faster, fluttered between light and extinction, ceased to flicker and became mere fading specks of glowing red in a vast obscurity. In ten seconds the extinction was accomplished, and there was only this roaring darkness, a black monstrosity that had suddenly swallowed up those glittering myriads of men.

He felt invisible forms about him; his arms were gripped. Something rapped sharply against his shin. A voice bawled in his ear, 'It is all right – all right.'

Graham shook off the paralysis of his first astonishment. He struck his forehead against Lincoln's and bawled, 'What is this darkness?'

'The Council has cut the currents that light the city. We must wait – stop. The people will go on. They will—'

His voice was drowned. There was an immense shouting, 'Save the Sleeper. Take care of the Sleeper.' A guard stumbled against Graham and hurt his hand by an inadvertent blow of his weapon. A wild tumult tossed and whirled about him, growing, as it seemed, louder, denser, more furious each moment. Fragments of recognizable sounds drove towards him, were whirled away from him as his mind reached out to grasp them. Men seemed to be shouting conflicting orders, others answered. There was suddenly a succession of piercing screams close beneath them.

A voice bawled in his ear, 'The red police,' and receded forthwith beyond his questions.

A crackling sound grew to distinctness, and therewith a leaping of faint flashes along the edge of the further ways. By their light Graham saw the heads and bodies of a number of men, armed with weapons like those of his guards, leap into an instant's dim visibility. The whole area began to crackle, to flash with little instantaneous streaks of light, and abruptly the darkness rolled back like a curtain.

A glare of light dazzled his eyes, a vast, seething expanse of struggling men confused his mind A shout, a burst of cheering, came across the ways. He looked up to see the source of the light. A man hung far overhead from the upper part of a cable, holding by a rope the blinding star that had driven the darkness back.

Graham's eyes fell to the ways again. A wedge of red a little way along the vista caught his eye. He saw it was a dense mass of red-clad men jammed on the higher further way, their backs against the pitiless cliff of building, and surrounded by a great crowd of antagonists. They were fighting. Weapons flashed and rose and fell, heads vanished at the edge of the contest, and other heads replaced them, the little flashes from the green weapons became little jets of smoky grey while the light lasted.

Abruptly the flare was extinguished and the ways were an inky darkness once more, a tumultuous mystery.

He felt something thrusting against him. He was being pushed along the gallery. Someone was shouting – it might be at him. He was too confused to hear. He was thrust against the wall, and a number of people blundered past him. It seemed to him that his guards were struggling with one another.

Suddenly the cable-hung star-holder appeared again, and the whole scene was white and dazzling. The band of red-coats seemed broader and nearer; its apex was halfway down the ways towards the central aisle. And raising his eyes Graham saw that a number of these men had also appeared now in the darkened lower galleries of the opposite building, and were firing over the heads of their fellows below at the boiling confusion of people on the lower ways. The meaning of these things dawned upon him. The march of the people had come upon an ambush at the very outset. Thrown into confusion by the extinction of the lights they were now being attacked by the red police. Then he became aware that he was standing alone, that his guards and Lincoln were some way off in the direction along which he had come before the darkness fell. He saw they were gesticulating to him wildly, running back towards him. A great shouting came from across the ways. Then it seemed as though the whole face of the darkened building opposite was lined and speckled with red-clad men. And they were pointing over to him and shouting. 'The Sleeper! Save the Sleeper!' shouted a multitude of throats.

Something struck the wall above his head. He looked up at the impact and saw a star-shaped splash of silvery metal. He saw Lincoln near him. Felt his arm gripped. Then, pat, pat; he had been missed twice.

For a moment he did not understand this. The street was hidden, everything was hidden, as he looked. The second flare had burned out.

Lincoln had gripped Graham by the arm, was lugging him along the gallery. 'Before the next light!' he cried. His haste was contagious. Graham's instinct of self-preservation overcame the paralysis of his incredulous astonishment. He became for a time the blind creature of the fear of death. He ran, stumbling because of the uncertainty of the darkness, blundered into his guards as they turned to run with him. Haste was his one desire, to escape this perilous gallery upon which he was exposed. A third glare came close on its predecessors. With it came a great shouting across the ways, an answering tumult from the ways. The red-coats below, he saw, had now almost gained the central passage. Their countless faces turned towards him, and they shouted. The white façade opposite was densely stippled with red. All these wonderful things concerned him, turned upon him as a pivot. These were the guards of the Council attempting to recapture him.

Lucky it was for him that these shots were the first fired in anger for a hundred and fifty years. He heard bullets whacking over his head, felt a splash of molten metal sting his ear, and perceived without looking that the whole opposite façade, an unmasked ambuscade of red police, was crowded and bawling and firing at him.

Down went one of his guards before him, and Graham, unable to stop, leapt the writhing body.

In another second he had plunged unhurt into a black passage, and incontinently someone, coming it may be in a transverse direction, blundered violently into him. He was hurling down a staircase in absolute darkness. He reeled, and was struck again, and came against a wall with his hands. He was crushed by a weight of struggling bodies, whirled round, and thrust to the right. A vast pressure pinned him. He could not breathe, his ribs seemed cracking. He felt a momentary relaxation, and then the whole mass of people moving together, bore him back towards the great theatre from which he had so recently come. There were moments when his feet did not touch the ground. Then he was staggering and shoving. He heard shouts of 'They are coming!' and a muffled cry close to him. His foot blundered against something soft, he heard a hoarse scream under foot. He heard shouts of 'The Sleeper!' but he was too confused to speak. He heard the green weapons crackling. For a space he lost his individual will, became an atom in a panic, blind, unthinking, mechanical. He thrust and pressed back and writhed in the pressure, kicked presently against a step, and found himself ascending a slope. And abruptly the faces all about him leapt out of the black, visible, ghastly-white and astonished, terrified, perspiring, in a livid glare. One face, a young man's, was very near to him, not twenty inches away. At the time it was but a passing incident of no emotional value, but afterwards it came back to him in his dreams. For this young man, wedged upright in the crowd for a time, had been shot and was already dead.

A fourth white star must have been lit by the man on the cable. Its light came glaring in through vast windows and arches and showed Graham that he was now one of a dense mass of flying black figures pressed back across the lower area of the great theatre. This time the picture was livid and fragmentary, slashed and barred with black shadows. He saw that quite near to him the red guards were fighting their way through the people. He could not tell whether they saw him. He looked for Lincoln and his guards. He saw Lincoln near the stage of the theatre surrounded by a crowd of black-badged revolutionaries, lifted up and staring to and fro as if seeking him. Graham perceived that he himself was near the opposite edge of the crowd, that behind him, separated by a barrier, sloped the now vacant seats of the theatre. A sudden idea came to him, and he began fighting his way towards the barrier. As he reached it the glare came to an end.

In a moment he had thrown off the great cloak that not only impeded his movements, but made him conspicuous, and had slipped it from his shoulders. He heard someone trip in its folds. In another he was scaling the barrier and had dropped into the blackness on the further side. Then feeling his way he came to the lower end of an ascending gangway. In the darkness the sound of firing ceased and the roar of feet and voices lulled. Then suddenly he came to an unexpected step and tripped and fell. As he did so pools and islands amidst the darkness about him leapt to vivid light again, the uproar surged louder and the glare of the fifth white star shone through the vast fenestrations of the theatre walls.

He rolled over among some seats, heard a shouting and the whirring rattle of weapons, struggled up and was knocked back again, perceived that a number of black-badged men were all about him firing at the reds below, leaping from seat to seat, crouching among the seats to reload. Instinctively he crouched amidst the seats, as stray shots ripped the pneumatic cushions and cut bright slashes on their soft metal frames. Instinctively he marked the direction of the gangways, the most plausible way of escape for him so soon as the veil of darkness fell again.

A young man in faded blue garments came vaulting over the seats. 'Hullo!' he said, with his flying feet within six inches of the crouching Sleeper's face.

He stared without any sign of recognition, turned to fire, fired, and shouting, 'To hell with the Council!' was about to fire again. Then it seemed to Graham that the half of this man's neck had vanished. A drop of moisture fell on Graham's cheek. The green weapon stopped half raised. For a moment the man stood still with his face suddenly expressionless, then he began to slant forward. His knees bent. Man and darkness fell together. At the sound of his fall Graham rose up and ran for his life until a step down to the gangway tripped him. He scrambled to his feet, turned up the gangway and ran on.

When the sixth star glared he was already close to the yawning throat of a passage. He ran on the swifter for the light, entered the passage and turned a corner into absolute night again. He was knocked sideways, rolled over, and recovered his feet. He found himself one of a crowd of invisible fugitives pressing in one direction. His one thought now was their thought also; to escape out of this fighting. He thrust and struck, staggered, ran, was wedged tightly, lost ground and then was clear again.

For some minutes he was running through the darkness along a winding passage, and then he crossed some wide and open space, passed down a long incline, and came at last down a flight of steps to a level place. Many people were shouting, 'They are coming! The guards are coming. They are firing. Get out of the fighting. The guards are firing. It will be safe in Seventh Way. Along here to Seventh Way!' There were women and children in the crowd as well as men.

The crowd converged on an archway, passed through a short throat and emerged on a wider space again, lit dimly. The black figures about him spread out and ran up what seemed in the twilight to be a gigantic series of steps. He followed. The people dispersed to the right and left. . . . He perceived that he was no longer in a crowd. He stopped near the highest step. Before him, on that level, were groups of seats and a little kiosk. He went up to this and, stopping in the shadow of its eaves, looked about him panting.

Everything was vague and grey, but he recognized that these great steps were a series of platforms of the 'ways', now motionless again. The platform slanted up on either side, and the tall buildings rose beyond, vast dim ghosts, their inscriptions and advertisements indistinctly seen, and up through the girders and cables was a faint interrupted ribbon of pallid sky. A number of people hurried by. From their shouts and voices, it seemed they were hurrying to join the fighting. Other less noisy figures flitted timidly among the shadows.

From very far away down the street he could hear the sound of a struggle. But it was evident to him that this was not the street into which the theatre opened. That former fight, it seemed, had suddenly dropped out of sound and hearing. And they were fighting for him!

For a space he was like a man who pauses in the reading of a vivid book, and suddenly doubts what he has been taking unquestionably. At that time he had little mind for details; the whole effect was a huge astonishment. Oddly enough, while the flight from the Council prison, the great crowd in the hall, and the attack of the red police upon the swarming people were clearly present in his mind, it cost him an effort to piece in his awakening and to revive the meditative interval of the Silent Rooms. At first his memory leapt these things and took him back to the cascade at Pentargen quivering in the wind, and all the sombre splendours of the sunlit Cornish coast. The contrast touched everything with unreality. And then the gap filled, and he began to comprehend his position.

It was no longer absolutely a riddle, as it had been in the Silent Rooms. At least he had the strange, bare outline now. He was in some way the owner of the world, and great political parties were fighting to possess him. On the one hand was the Council with its red police, set resolutely, it seemed, on the usurpation of his property and perhaps his murder; on the other, the revolution that had liberated him, with this unseen 'Ostrog' as its leader. And the whole of this gigantic city was convulsed by their struggle. Frantic development of his world! 'I do not understand,' he cried. 'I do not understand!'

He had slipped out between the contending parties into this liberty of the twilight. What would happen next? What was happening? He figured the red-clad men as busily hunting him, driving the black-badged revolutionists before them.

At any rate chance had given him a breathing space. He could lurk unchallenged by the passers-by, and watch the course of things. His eye followed up the intricate dim immensity of the twilight buildings, and it came to him as a thing infinitely wonderful that above there the sun was rising, and the world was lit and glowing with the old familiar light of day. In a little while he had recovered his breath. His clothing had already dried upon him from the snow.

He wandered for miles along these twilight ways, speaking to no one, accosted by no one – a dark figure among dark figures – the coveted man out of the past, the inestimable unintentional owner of the world. Wherever there were lights or dense crowds or exceptional excitement, he was afraid of recognition, and watched and turned back or went up and down by the middle stairways into some transverse system of ways at a lower or higher level. And though he came on no more fighting, the whole city stirred with battle. Once he had to run to avoid a marching multitude of men that swept the street. Everyone abroad seemed involved. For the most part they were men, and they carried what he judged were weapons. It seemed as though the struggle was concentrated mainly in the quarter of the city from which he came. Ever and again a distant roaring, the remote suggestion of that conflict, reached his ears. Then his caution and his curiosity struggled together. But his caution prevailed, and he continued wandering away from the fighting – so far as he could judge. He went unmolested, unsuspected through the dark. After a time he ceased to hear even a remote echo of the battle, fewer and fewer people passed him, until at last the streets became deserted. The frontages of the buildings grew plain and harsh; he seemed to have come to a district of vacant warehouses. Solitude crept upon him – his pace slackened.

He became aware of a growing fatigue. At times he would turn aside and sit down on one of the numerous benches of the upper ways. But a feverish restlessness, the knowledge of his vital implication in this struggle, would not let him rest in any place for long. Was the struggle on his behalf alone?

And then in a desolate place came the shock of an earthquake – a roaring and thundering – a mighty wind of cold air pouring through the city, the smash of glass, the slip and thud of falling masonry – a series of gigantic concussions. A mass of glass and ironwork fell from the remote roofs into the middle gallery not a hundred yards away from him, and in the distance were shouts and running. He, too, was startled to an aimless activity, and ran first one way and then as aimlessly back.

A man came running towards him. His self-control returned. 'What have they blown up?' asked the man breathlessly. 'That was an explosion,' and before Graham could speak he had hurried on.

The great buildings rose dimly, veiled by a perplexing twilight albeit the rivulet of sky above was now bright with day. He noted many strange features, understanding none at the time; he even spelt out many of the inscriptions in Phonetic lettering. But what profits it to decipher a confusion of odd-looking letters resolving itself, after painful strain of eye and mind, into 'Here is Eadhamite', or, 'Labour Bureau – Little Side'? Grotesque thought, that all these cliff-like houses were his!

The perversity of his experience came to him vividly. In actual fact he had made such a leap in time as romancers have imagined again and again. And that fact realized, he had been prepared. His mind had, as it were, seated itself for a spectacle. And no spectacle unfolded itself, but a great vague danger, unsympathetic shadows and veils of darkness. Somewhere through the labyrinthine obscurity his death sought him. Would he, after all, be killed before he saw? It might be that even at the next corner his destruction ambushed. A great desire to see, a great longing to know, arose in him.

He became fearful of corners. It seemed to him that there was safety in concealment. Where could he hide to be inconspicuous when the lights returned? At last he sat down upon a seat in a recess on one of the higher ways, conceiving he was alone there.

He squeezed his knuckles into his weary eyes. Suppose when he looked again he found the dark trough of parallel ways and that intolerable altitude of edifice gone. Suppose he were to discover the whole story of these last few days, the awakening, the shouting multitudes, the darkness and the fighting, a phantasmagoria, a new and more vivid sort of dream. It must be a dream; it was so inconsecutive, so reasonless. Why were the people fighting for him? Why should this saner world regard him as Owner and Master?

So he thought, sitting blinded; and then he looked again, half hoping in spite of his ears to see some familiar aspect of the life of the nineteenth century, to see, perhaps, the little harbour of Boscastle about him, the cliffs of Pentargen, or the bedroom of his home. But fact takes no heed of human hopes. A squad of men with a black banner tramped athwart the nearer shadows, intent on conflict, and beyond rose that giddy wall of frontage, vast and dark, with the dim incomprehensible lettering showing faintly on its face.

'It is no dream,' he said, 'no dream.' And he bowed his face upon his hands.

11

The Old Man Who Knew Everything

He was startled by a cough close at hand.

He turned sharply, and peering, saw a small, hunched-up figure sitting a couple of yards off in the shadow of the enclosure.

'Have ye any news?' asked the high-pitched wheezy voice of a very old man.

Graham hesitated. 'None,' he said.

'I stay here till the lights come again,' said the old man. 'These blue scoundrels are everywhere – everywhere.'

Graham's answer was inarticulate assent. He tried to see the old man but the darkness hid his face. He wanted very much to respond, to talk, but he did not know how to begin.

'Dark and damnable,' said the old man suddenly. 'Dark and damnable. Turned out of my room among all these dangers.'

'That's hard,' ventured Graham. 'That's hard on you.'

'Darkness. An old man lost in the darkness. And all the world gone mad. War and fighting. The police beaten and rogues abroad. Why don't they bring some Negroes to protect us? . . . No more dark passages for me. I fell over a dead man.'

'You're safer with company,' said the old man, 'if it's company of the right sort,' and peered frankly. He rose suddenly and came towards Graham.

Apparently the scrutiny was satisfactory. The old man sat down as if relieved to be no longer alone. 'Eh!' he said, 'but this is a terrible time! War and fighting, and the dead lying there – men, strong men, dying in the dark. Sons! I have three sons. God knows where they are tonight.'

The voice ceased. Then repeated quavering: 'God knows where they are tonight.'

Graham stood revolving a question that should not betray his ignorance. Again the old man's voice ended the pause.

'This Ostrog will win,' he said. 'He will win. And what the world will be like under him no one can tell. My sons are under the wind-vanes, all three. One of my daughters-in-law was his mistress for a while. His mistress! We're not common people. Though they've sent me to wander tonight and take my chance. . . . I knew what was going on. Before most people. But this darkness! And to fall over a dead body suddenly in the dark!'

His wheezy breathing could be heard.

'Ostrog!' said Graham.

'The greatest Boss the world has ever seen,' said the voice.

Graham ransacked his mind. 'The Council has few friends among the people,' he hazarded.

'Few friends. And poor ones at that. They've had their time. Eh! They should have kept to the clever ones. But twice they held election. And Ostrog – And now it has burst out and nothing can stay it, nothing can stay it. Twice they rejected Ostrog – Ostrog the Boss. I heard of his rages at the time – he was terrible. Heaven save them! For nothing on earth can now he has raised the Labour Companies upon them. No one else would have dared. All the blue canvas armed and marching! He will go through with it. He will go through.'

He was silent for a little while. 'This Sleeper,' he said, and stopped.

'Yes,' said Graham. 'Well?'

The senile voice sank to a confidential whisper, the dim, pale face came close. 'The real Sleeper—'

'Yes,' said Graham.

'Died years ago.'

'What?' said Graham, sharply.

'Years ago. Died. Years ago.'

'You don't say so!' said Graham.

'I do. I do say so. He died. This Sleeper who's woke up – they changed in the night. A poor, drugged insensible creature. But I mustn't tell all I know. I mustn't tell all I know.'

For a little while he muttered inaudibly. His secret was too much for him. 'I don't know the ones that put him to sleep – that was before my time – but I know the man who injected the stimulants and woke him again. It was ten to one – wake or kill. Wake or kill. Ostrog's way.'

Graham was so astonished that he had to interrupt, to make the old man repeat his words, to re-question vaguely, before he was sure of the meaning and folly of what he heard. And his awakening had not been natural! Was that an old man's senile superstition, too, or had it any truth in it? Feeling in the dark corners of his memory, he presently came on a dream of his arm being pierced that might conceivably be an impression of some such stimulating effect. It dawned upon him that he had happened upon a lucky encounter, that at last he might learn something of the new age. The old man wheezed a while and spat, and then the piping, reminiscent voice resumed:

'First they rejected him. I've followed it all.'

'Rejected whom?' said Graham. 'The Sleeper?'

'Sleeper? *No.* Ostrog. He was terrible – terrible! And he was promised then, promised certainly the next time. Fools they were – not to be more afraid of him. Now all the city's his millstone, and such as we, dust ground upon it. Dust ground upon it. Until he set to work – the workers cut each other's throats, and murdered a Chinaman or a Labour policeman now and then, and left the rest of us in peace. Dead bodies! Robbing! Darkness! Such a thing hasn't been this gross of years. Eh! – but 'tis ill on small folks when the great fall out! It's ill.'

'Did you say – there had not been – what? – for a gross of years?'

'Eh?' said the old man.

The old man grumbled at his way of clipping his words, and made him repeat this. 'Fighting and slaying, and weapons in hand, and fools bawling freedom and the like,' said the old man. 'Not in all my life has there been that. These are like the old days – for sure – when the Paris people broke out – three gross of years ago. That's what I mean hasn't been. But it's the world's way. It had to come back. I know. I know. This five years Ostrog has been working, and there has been trouble and trouble, and hunger and threats and high talk and arms. Blue canvas and murmurs. No one safe. Everything sliding and slipping. And now here we are! Revolt and fighting, and the Council come to its end.'

'You are rather well-informed on these things,' said Graham.

'I know what I hear. It isn't all Babble Machine with me.'

'No,' said Graham, wondering what Babble Machine might be. 'And you are certain this Ostrog – you are certain Ostrog organized this rebellion and arranged for the waking of the Sleeper? Just to assert himself – because he was not elected to the Council?'

'Everyone knows that, I should think,' said the old man. 'Except – just fools. He meant to be master somehow. In the Council or not. Everyone who knows anything knows that. And here we are with dead bodies lying in the dark! Why, where have you been if you haven't heard all about the trouble between Ostrog and the Verneys? And what do you think the troubles are about? The Sleeper? Eh? You think the Sleeper's real and woke of his own accord – eh?'

'I'm a dull man, older than I look, and forgetful,' said Graham. 'Lots of things that have happened – especially of late years – If I was the Sleeper, to tell you the truth, I couldn't know less about them.'

'Eh!' said the voice. 'Old, are you? You don't sound so very old! But it's not everyone keeps his memory to my time of life – truly. But these notorious things! But you're not so old as me – not nearly so old as me. Well! I ought not to judge other men by myself, perhaps. I'm young – for so old a man. Maybe you're old for so young.'

'That's it,' said Graham. 'And I've a queer history. I know very little. History! Practically I know no history. The Sleeper and Julius Caesar are all the same to me. It's interesting to hear you talk of these things.'

'I know a few things,' said the old man. 'I know a thing or two. But – Hark!'

The two men became silent, listening. There was a heavy thud, a concussion that made their seat shiver. The passers-by stopped, shouted to one another. The old man was full of questions; he shouted to a man who passed near. Graham, emboldened by his example, got up and accosted others. None knew what had happened.

He returned to the seat and found the old man muttering vague interrogations in an undertone. For a while they said nothing to one another.

The sense of this gigantic struggle, so near and yet so remote, oppressed Graham's imagination. Was this old man right, was the report of the people right, and were the revolutionaries winning? Or were they all in error, and were the red guards driving all before them? At any time the flood of warfare might pour into this silent quarter of the city and seize upon him again. It behoved him to learn all he could while there was time. He turned suddenly to the old man with a question and left it unsaid. But his motion moved the old man to speech again.

'Eh! but how things work together!' said the old man. 'This Sleeper that all the fools put their trust in! I've the whole history of it – I was always a good one for histories. When I was a boy – I'm that old – I used to read printed books. You'd hardly think it. Likely you've seen none – they rot and dust so – and the Sanitary Company burns them to make ashlarite. But they were convenient in their dirty way. One learnt a lot. These new-fangled Babble Machines – they don't seem new-fangled to you, eh? – they're easy to hear, easy to forget. But I've traced all the Sleeper business from the first.'

'You will scarcely believe it,' said Graham slowly, 'I'm so ignorant –

I've been so preoccupied in my own little affairs, my circumstances have been so odd – I know nothing of this Sleeper's history. Who was he?'

'Eh!' said the old man. 'I know, I know. He was a poor nobody, and set on a playful woman, poor soul! And he fell into a trance. There's the old things they had, those brown things – silver photographs – still showing him as he lay, a gross and a half years ago – a gross and a half of years.'

'Set on a playful woman, poor soul,' said Graham softly to himself, and then aloud, 'Yes – well, go on.'

'You must know he had a cousin named Warming, a solitary man without children, who made a big fortune speculating in roads – the first Eadhamite roads. But surely you've heard? No? Why, – he bought all the patent rights and made a big company. In those days there were grosses of grosses of separate businesses and business companies. Grosses of grosses! His roads killed the railroads – the old things – in two dozen years; he bought up and Eadhamited the tracks. And because he didn't want to break up his great property or let in share-holders, he left it all to the Sleeper, and put it under a Board of Trustees that he had picked and trained. He knew then the Sleeper wouldn't wake, that he would go on sleeping, sleeping till he died. He knew that quite well! And plump! a man in the United States, who had lost two sons in a boat accident, followed that up with another great bequest. His trustees found themselves with a dozen myriads of lions'-worth or more of property at the very beginning.'

'What was his name?'

'Graham.'

'No – I mean – that American's.'

'Isbister.'

'Isbister!' cried Graham. 'Why, I don't even know the name.'

'Of course not,' said the old man. 'Of course not. People don't learn much in the schools nowadays. But I know all about him. He was a rich American who went from England, and he left the Sleeper even more than Warming. How he made it? That I don't know. Something about pictures by machinery. But he made it and left it, and so the Council had its start. It was just a council of trustees at first.'

'And how did it grow?'

'Eh! – but you're not up to things. Money attracts money – and twelve brains are better than one. They played it cleverly. They worked politics with money, and kept on adding to the money by working currency and tariffs. They grew – they grew. And for years the twelve trustees hid the growing of the Sleeper's estate under double names and company titles and all that. The Council spread by title deed, mortgage, share; every political party, every newspaper they bought. If you listen to the old stories you will see the Council growing and growing. Billions and billions of lions at last – the Sleeper's estate. And all growing out of a whim – out of this Warming's will, and an accident to Isbister's sons.

'Men are strange,' said the old man. 'The strange thing to me is how the Council worked together so long. As many as twelve. But they worked in cliques from the first. And they've slipped back. In my young days speaking of the Council was like an ignorant man speaking of God. We didn't think they could do wrong. We didn't know of their women and all that! Or else I've got wiser.

'Men are strange,' said the old man. 'Here are you, young and ignorant, and me – sevendy years old, and I might reasonably be forgetting – explaining it all to you short and clear.

'Sevendy,' he said, 'sevendy, and I hear and see – hear better than I see. And reason clearly, and keep myself up to all the happenings of things. Sevendy!

'Life is strange. I was twaindy before Ostrog was a baby. I remember him long before he'd pushed his way to the head of the Wind Vanes Control. I've seen many changes. Eh! I've worn the blue. And at last I've come to see this crush and darkness and tumult and dead men carried by in heaps on the ways. And all his doing! All his doing!'

His voice died away in scarcely articulate praises of Ostrog.

Graham thought. 'Let me see,' he said, 'if I have it right.'

He extended a hand and ticked off points upon his fingers. 'The Sleeper has been asleep—'

'Changed,' said the old man.

'Perhaps. And meanwhile the Sleeper's property grew in the hands of Twelve Trustees, until it swallowed up nearly all the great ownership of the world. The Twelve Trustees – by virtue of this property have become masters of the world. Because they are the paying power – just as the old English Parliament used to be—'

'Eh!' said the old man. 'That's so – that's a good comparison. You're not so—'

'And now this Ostrog – has suddenly revolutionized the world by waking the Sleeper – who no one but the superstitious, common people had ever dreamt would wake again – raising the Sleeper to claim his property from the Council, after all these years.'

The old man endorsed this statement with a cough.

'It's strange,' he said, 'to meet a man who learns these things for the first time tonight.'

'Aye,' said Graham, 'it's strange.'

'Have you been in a Pleasure City?' said the old man. 'All my life I've longed —' He laughed. 'Even now,' he said, 'I could enjoy a little fun. Enjoy seeing things, anyhow.' He mumbled a sentence Graham did not understand.

'The Sleeper – when did he awake?' said Graham suddenly.

'Three days ago.'

'Where is he?'

'Ostrog has him. He escaped from the Council not four hours ago. My dear sir, where were you at the time? He was in the hall of the markets – where the fighting has been. All the city was screaming about it. All the Babble Machines. Everywhere it was shouted. Even the fools who speak for the Council were admitting it. Everyone was rushing off to see him – everyone was getting arms. Were you drunk or asleep? And even then! But you're joking! Surely you're pretending. It was to stop the shouting of the Babble Machines and prevent the people gathering that they turned off the electricity – and put this damned darkness upon us. Do you mean to say—?'

'I had heard the Sleeper was rescued,' said Graham. 'But – to come back a minute. Are you sure Ostrog has him?'

'He won't let him go,' said the old man.

'And the Sleeper. Are you sure he is not genuine? I have never heard—'

'So all the fools think. So they think. As if there wasn't a thousand things that were never heard. I know Ostrog too well for that. Did I tell you? In a way I'm a sort of relation of Ostrog's. A sort of relation. Through my daughter-in-law.'

'I suppose—'

'Well?'

'I suppose there's no chance of this Sleeper asserting himself. I suppose he's certain to be a puppet – in Ostrog's hands or the Council's, as soon as the struggle is over.'

'In Ostrog's hands – certainly. Why shouldn't he be a puppet? Look at his position. Everything done for him, every pleasure possible. Why should he want to assert himself?'

'What are these Pleasure Cities?' said Graham, abruptly.

The old man made him repeat the question. When at last he was assured of Graham's words, he nudged him violently. 'That's *too* much,' said he. 'You're poking fun at an old man. I've been suspecting you know more than you pretend.'

'Perhaps I do,' said Graham. 'But no! why should I go on acting? No, I do not know what a Pleasure City is.'

The old man laughed in an intimate way.

'What is more, I do not know how to read your letters, I do not know what money you use, I do not know what foreign countries there are. I do not know where I am. I cannot count. I do not know where to get food, nor drink, nor shelter.'

'Come, come,' said the old man, 'if you had a glass of drink now, would you put it in your ear or your eye?'

'I want you to tell me all these things.'

'He, he! Well, gentlemen who dress in silk must have their fun.' A withered hand caressed Graham's arm for a moment. 'Silk. Well, well! But, all the same, I wish I was the man who was put up as the Sleeper. He'll have a fine time of it. All the pomp and pleasure. He's a queer-looking face. When they used to let anyone go to see him, I've got tickets and been. The image of the real one, as the photographs show him, this substitute used to be. Yellow. But he'll get fed up. It's a queer world. Think of the luck of it. The luck of it. I expect he'll be sent to Capri. It's the best fun for a greener.'

His cough overtook him again. Then he began mumbling enviously of pleasures and strange delights. 'The luck of it, the luck of it! All my life I've been in London, hoping to get my chance.'

'But you don't know that the Sleeper died,' said Graham, suddenly.

The old man made him repeat his words.

'Men don't live beyond ten dozen. It's not in the order of things,' said the old man. 'I'm not a fool. Fools may believe it, but not me.'

Graham became angry with the old man's assurance. 'Whether you are a fool or not,' he said, 'it happens you are wrong about the Sleeper.'

'Eh?'

'You are wrong about the Sleeper. I haven't told you before, but I will tell you now. You are wrong about the Sleeper.'

'How do you know? I thought you didn't know anything – not even about Pleasure Cities.'

Graham paused.

'You don't know,' said the old man. 'How are you to know? It's very few men—'

'I *am* the Sleeper.'

He had to repeat it.

There was a brief pause. 'There's a silly thing to say, sir, if you'll excuse me. It might get you into trouble in a time like this,' said the old man.

Graham, slightly dashed, repeated his assertion.

'I was saying I was the Sleeper. That years and years ago I did indeed fall asleep in a little stone-built village, in the days when there were

495

hedgerows and villages and inns, and all the countryside cut up into little pieces, little fields. Have you never heard of those days? And it is I – I who speak to you – who awakened again these four days since.'

'Four days since! – the Sleeper! But they've *got* the Sleeper. They have him and they won't let him go. Nonsense! You've been talking sensibly enough up to now. I can see it as though I was there. There will be Lincoln like a keeper just behind him; they won't let him go about alone. Trust them. You're a queer fellow. One of these fun pokers. I see now why you have been clipping your words so oddly, but—'

He stopped abruptly, and Graham could see his gesture.

'As if Ostrog would let the Sleeper run about alone! No, you're telling that to the wrong man altogether. Eh! as if I should believe. What's your game? And besides, we've been talking of the Sleeper.'

Graham stood up. 'Listen,' he said. 'I am the Sleeper.'

'You're an odd man,' said the old man, 'to sit here in the dark, talking clipped, and telling a lie of that sort. But—'

Graham's exasperation fell to laughter. 'It is preposterous,' he cried. 'Preposterous. The dream must end. It gets wilder and wilder. Here am I – in this damned twilight – I never knew a dream in twilight before – an anachronism by two hundred years and trying to persuade an old fool that I am myself, and meanwhile – Ugh!'

He moved in gusty irritation and went striding. In a moment the old man was pursuing him. 'Eh! but don't go!' cried the old man. 'I'm an old fool, I know. Don't go. Don't leave me in all this darkness.'

Graham hesitated, stopped. Suddenly the folly of telling his secret flashed into his mind.

'I didn't mean to offend you – disbelieving you,' said the old man coming near. 'It's no manner of harm. Call yourself the Sleeper if it pleases you. 'Tis a foolish trick—'

Graham hesitated, turned abruptly and went on his way.

For a time he heard the old man's hobbling pursuit and his wheezy cries receding. But at last the darkness swallowed him, and Graham saw him no more.

12

Ostrog

Graham could now take a clearer view of his position. For a long time yet he wandered, but after the talk of the old man his discovery of this Ostrog was clear in his mind as the final inevitable decision. One thing was evident, those who were at the headquarters of the revolt had succeeded very admirably in suppressing the fact of his disappearance. But every moment he expected to hear the report of his death or of his recapture by the Council.

Presently a man stopped before him. 'Have you heard?' he said.

'No!' said Graham, starting.

'Near a dozand,' said the man, 'a dozand men!' and hurried on.

A number of men and a girl passed in the darkness, gesticulating and shouting: 'Capitulated! Given up!' 'A dozand of men.' 'Two dozand of men.' 'Ostrog, Hurrah! Ostrog, Hurrah!' These cries receded, became indistinct.

Other shouting men followed. For a time his attention was absorbed in the fragments of speech he heard. He had a doubt whether all were speaking English. Scraps floated to him, scraps like pigeon English, like 'nigger' dialect, blurred and mangled distortions. He dared accost no one with questions. The impression the people gave him jarred altogether with his preconceptions of the struggle and confirmed the old man's faith in Ostrog. It was only slowly could bring himself to believe that all these people were rejoicing at the defeat of the Council, that the Council which had pursued him with such power and vigour was after all the weaker of the two sides in conflict. And if that was so, how did it affect him? Several times he hesitated on the verge of fundamental questions. Once he turned and walked for a long way after a little man of rotund inviting outline, but he was unable to master confidence to address him.

It was only slowly that it came to him that he might ask for the 'wind-vane offices' whatever the 'wind-vane offices' might be. His first inquiry simply resulted in a direction to go on towards Westminster. His second led to the discovery of a short cut in which he was speedily lost. He was told to leave the ways to which he had hitherto confined himself – knowing no other means of transit – and to plunge down one of the middle staircases into the blackness of a cross-way. Thereupon came some trivial adventures; chief of these an ambiguous encounter with a gruff-voiced invisible creature speaking in a strange dialect that seemed at first a strange tongue, a thick flow of speech with the drifting corpses of English words therein, the dialect of the latter-day vile. Then another voice drew near, a girl's voice singing, 'tralala tralala'. She spoke to Graham, her English touched with something of the same quality. She professed to have lost her sister, she blundered needlessly into him he thought, caught hold of him and laughed. But a word of vague remonstrance sent her into the unseen again.

The sounds about him increased. Stumbling people passed him, speaking excitedly. 'They have surrendered!' 'The Council! Surely not the Council!' 'They are saying so in the Ways.' The passage seemed wider. Suddenly the wall fell away. He was in a great space and people were stirring remotely. He inquired his way of an indistinct figure. 'Strike straight across,' said a woman's voice. He left his guiding wall, and in a moment had stumbled against a little table on which were utensils of glass. Graham's eyes, now attuned to darkness, made out a long vista with tables on either side. He went down this. At one or two of the tables he heard a clang of glass and a sound of eating. There were people then cool enough to dine, or daring enough to steal a meal in spite of social convulsion and darkness. Far off and high up he presently saw a pallid light of a semicircular shape. As he approached this, a black edge came up and hid it. He stumbled at steps and found himself in a gallery. He heard a sobbing, and found two scared little girls crouched by a railing. These children became silent at the near sound of feet. He tried to console them, but they were very still until he left them. Then as he receded he could hear them sobbing again.

Presently he found himself at the foot of a staircase and near a wide opening. He saw a dim twilight above this and ascended out of the blackness into a street of moving Ways again. Along this a disorderly swarm of people marched shouting. They were singing snatches of the song of the revolt, most of them out of tune. Here and there torches flared, creating brief hysterical shadows. He asked his way and was twice puzzled by that same thick dialect. His third attempt won an answer he could understand. He was two miles from the wind-vane offices in Westminster, but the way was easy to follow.

When at last he did approach the district of the wind-vane offices it seemed to him, from the cheering processions that came marching along the Ways, from the tumult of rejoicing, and finally from the restoration of the lighting of the city, that the overthrow of the Council must already be accomplished. And still no news of his absence came to his ears.

The re-illumination of the city came with startling abruptness. Suddenly he stood blinking, all about him men halted dazzled, and the world was incandescent. The light found him already upon the outskirts of the excited crowds that choked the Ways near the wind-vane offices, and the sense of visibility and exposure that came with it turned his colourless intention of joining Ostrog to a keen anxiety.

He was jostled, obstructed and endangered by men hoarse and weary with cheering his name, some of them bandaged and bloody in his cause. The frontage of the wind-vane offices was illuminated by some moving picture, but what it was he could not see, because in spite of his strenuous attempts the density of the crowd prevented his approaching it. From the fragments of speech he caught, he judged it conveyed news of the fighting about the Council House. Ignorance and indecision made him slow and ineffective in his movements. For a time he could not conceive how he was to get within the unbroken façade of this place. He made his way into the midst of this mass of people, until he realized that the descending staircase of the central Way led to the interior of the buildings. This gave him a goal, but the crowding in the central path was so dense that it was long before he could reach it. And even then he encountered intricate obstruction, and had an hour of vivid argument first in this guard-room and then in that before he could get a note taken to the one man of all men who was most eager to see him. His story was laughed to scorn at one place, and wiser for that, when at last he reached a second stairway he professed simply to have news of extraordinary importance for Ostrog. What it was he would not say. They sent his note reluctantly. He waited in a little room at the foot of the lift shaft, and thither at last came Lincoln, eager, apologetic, astonished. He stopped in the doorway scrutinizing Graham, then rushed forward effusively.

'Yes,' he cried. 'It is you. And you are not dead!'

'My brother is waiting,' explained Lincoln. 'He is alone in the wind-vane offices. We feared you had been killed in the theatre. He doubted – and things are very urgent still in spite of what we are telling them *there* – or he would have come to you.'

They ascended a lift, passed along a narrow passage, crossed a great hall, empty save for two hurrying messengers, and entered a comparatively little room, whose only furniture was a long settee and a large oval disc of cloudy, shifting grey, hung by cables from the wall. There Lincoln left Graham for a space, and he remained alone without understanding the smoky shapes that drove slowly across this disc.

His attention was arrested by a sound that began abruptly. It was cheering, the frantic cheering of a vast but very remote crowd, a roaring exultation. This ended as sharply as it had begun, like a sound heard between the opening and shutting of a door. In the outer room was a noise of hurrying steps and a melodious clinking as if a loose chain was running over the teeth of a wheel.

Then he heard the voice of a woman, the rustle of unseen garments. 'It is Ostrog!' he heard her say. A little bell rang fitfully, and then everything was still again.

Presently came voices, footsteps and movement without. The footsteps of some one person detached itself from the other sounds, and drew near, firm, evenly measured steps. The curtain lifted slowly. A tall, white-haired man, clad in garments of cream-coloured silk, appeared, regarding Graham from under his raised arm.

For a moment the white form remained holding the curtain, then dropped it and stood before it. Graham's first impression was of a very broad forehead, very pale blue eyes deep sunken under white brows, an aquiline nose, and a heavily lined resolute mouth. The folds of flesh over the eyes, the drooping of the corners of the mouth contradicted the upright bearing, and said the man was old. Graham rose to his feet instinctively, and for a moment the two men stood in silence, regarding each other.

'You are Ostrog?' said Graham.

'I am Ostrog.'

'The Boss?'

'So I am called.'

Graham felt the inconvenience of the silence. 'I have to thank you chiefly, I understand, for my safety,' he said presently.

'We were afraid you were killed,' said Ostrog. 'Or sent to sleep again – for ever. We have been doing everything to keep our secret – the secret of your disappearance. Where have you been? How did you get here?'

Graham told him briefly.

Ostrog listened in silence.

He smiled faintly. 'Do you know what I was doing when they came to tell me you had come?'

'How can I guess?'

'Preparing your double.'

'My double?'

'A man as like you as we could find. We were going to hypnotize him, to save him the difficulty of acting. It was imperative. The whole of this revolt depends on the idea that you are awake, alive, and with us. Even now a great multitude of people has gathered in the theatre clamouring to see you. They do not trust. . . . You know, of course – something of your position?'

'Very little,' said Graham.

'It is like this.' Ostrog walked a pace or two into the room and turned. 'You are absolute owner,' he said, 'of the world. You are King of the Earth. Your powers are limited in many intricate ways, but you are the figurehead, the popular symbol of government. This White Council, the Council of Trustees as it is called—'

'I have heard the vague outline of these things.'

'I wondered.'

'I came upon a garrulous old man.'

'I see . . . Our masses – the word comes from your days – you know, of course, that we still have masses – regard you as our actual ruler. Just as a great number of people in your days regarded the Crown as the ruler. They are discontented – the masses all over the earth – with the rule of your Trustees. For the most part it is the old discontent, the old quarrel of the common man with his commonness – the misery of work and discipline and unfitness. But your Trustees have ruled ill. In certain matters, in the administration of the Labour Companies, for example, they have been unwise. They have given endless opportunities. Already we of the popular party were agitating for reforms – when your waking came. Came! If it had been contrived it could not have come more opportunely.' He smiled. 'The public mind, making no allowance for your years of quiescence, had already hit on the thought of waking you and appealing to you, and – Flash!'

He indicated the outbreak by a gesture, and Graham moved his head to show that he understood.

'The Council muddled – quarrelled. They always do. They could not decide what to do with you. You know how they imprisoned you?'

'I see. I see. And now – we win?'

'We win. Indeed we win. Tonight, in five swift hours. Suddenly we struck everywhere. The wind-vane people, the Labour Company and its millions, burst the bonds. We got the pull of the aeroplanes.'

'Yes,' said Graham.

'That was, of course, essential. Or they could have got away. All the city rose, every third man almost was in it! All the blue, all the public services, save only just a few aeronauts and about half the red police. You were rescued, and their own police of the Ways – not half of them could be massed at the Council House – have been broken up, disarmed or killed. All London is ours – now. Only the Council House remains.

'Half of those who remain to them of the red police were lost in that foolish attempt to recapture you. They lost their heads when they lost you. They flung all they had at the theatre. We cut them off from the Council House there. Truly tonight has been a night of victory. Everywhere your star has blazed. A day ago – the White Council ruled as it has ruled for a gross of years, for a century and a half of years, and then, with only a little whispering, a covert arming here and there, suddenly – So!'

'I am very ignorant,' said Graham. 'I suppose – I do not clearly understand the conditions of this fighting. If you could explain. Where is the Council? Where is the fight?'

Ostrog stepped across the room, something clicked, and suddenly, save for an oval glow, they were in darkness. For a moment Graham was puzzled.

Then he saw that the cloudy grey disc had taken depth and colour, had assumed the appearance of an oval window looking out upon a strange unfamiliar scene.

At the first glance he was unable to guess what this scene might be. It was a daylight scene, the daylight of a wintry day, grey and clear. Across the picture, and halfway as it seemed between him and the remoter view, a stout cable of twisted white wire stretched vertically. Then he perceived that the rows of great wind-wheels he saw, the wide intervals, the occasional gulfs of darkness, were akin to those through which he had fled from the Council House. He distinguished an orderly file of red figures marching across an open space between files of men in black, and realized before Ostrog spoke that he was looking down on the upper surface of latter-day London. The overnight snows had gone. He judged that this mirror was some modern replacement of the camera obscura, but that matter was not explained to him. He saw that though the file of red figures was trotting from left to right, yet they were passing out of the picture to the left. He wondered momentarily, and then saw that the picture was passing silently, panorama fashion, across the oval.

'In a moment you will see the fighting,' said Ostrog at his elbow. 'Those fellows in red you notice are prisoners. This is the roof space of London – all the houses are practically continuous now. The streets and public squares are covered in. The gaps and chasms of your time have disappeared.'

Something out of focus obliterated half the picture. Its form suggested a man. There was a gleam of metal, a flash, something that swept across the oval, as the eyelid of a bird sweeps across its eye, and the picture was clear again. And now Graham beheld men running down among the wind-wheels, pointing weapons from which jetted out little smoky flashes. They swarmed thicker and thicker to the right, gesticulating – it might be they were shouting, but of that the picture told nothing. They and the wind-wheels passed slowly and steadily across the field of the mirror.

'Now,' said Ostrog, 'comes the Council House,' and a black edge crept into view and gathered Graham's attention. Soon it was no longer an edge but a cavity, a huge blackened space amidst the clustering edifices, and from it thin spires of smoke rose into the pallid winter sky. Gaunt ruinous masses of the building, mighty truncated piers and girders, rose dismally out of this cavernous darkness. And over these vestiges of some splendid place, countless minute men were clambering, leaping, swarming.

'This is the Council House,' said Ostrog. 'Their last stronghold. And the fools wasted enough ammunition to hold out for a month in blowing up the buildings all about them – to stop our attack. You heard the smash? It shattered half the brittle glass in the city.'

And while he spoke, Graham saw that beyond this area of ruins, overhanging it and rising to a great height, was a ragged mass of white building. This mass had been isolated by the ruthless destruction of its surroundings. Black gaps marked the passages the disaster had torn apart; big halls had been slashed open and the decoration of their interiors showed dismally in the wintry dawn, and down the jagged walls hung festoons of divided cables and twisted ends of lines and metallic rods. And amidst all the vast details moved little red specks, the red-clothed defenders of the Council. Every now and then faint flashes illuminated the bleak shadows. At the first sight it seemed to Graham that an attack upon this isolated white building was in progress, but then he perceived that the party of the revolt was not advancing but, sheltered amidst the colossal wreckage that encircled this last ragged stronghold of the red-garbed men, was keeping up a fitful firing.

And not ten hours ago he had stood beneath the ventilating fans in a little chamber within that remote building wondering what was happening in the world!

Looking more attentively as this warlike episode moved silently across the centre of the mirror, Graham saw that the white building was surrounded on every side by ruins, and Ostrog proceeded to describe in concise phrases how its defenders had sought by such destruction to isolate themselves from a storm. He spoke of the loss of men that huge downfall had entailed in an indifferent tone. He indicated an improvised mortuary among the wreckage, showed ambulances swarming like cheese-mites along a ruinous groove that had once been a street of moving ways. He was more interested in pointing out the parts of the Council House, the distribution of the besiegers. In a little while the civil contest that had convulsed London was no longer a mystery to Graham. It was no tumultuous revolt had occurred that night, no equal warfare, but a splendidly organized *coup d'état*. Ostrog's grasp of details was astonishing; he seemed to know the business of even the smallest knot of black and red specks that crawled amidst these places.

He stretched a huge black arm across the luminous picture, and showed the room whence Graham had escaped, and across the chasm of ruins the course of his flight. Graham recognized the gulf across which the gutter ran, and the wind-wheels where he had crouched from the flying machine. The rest of his path had succumbed to the explosion. He looked again at the Council House, and it was already half hidden, and on the right a hillside with a cluster of domes and pinnacles, hazy, dim and distant, was gliding into view.

'And the Council is really overthrown?' he said.

'Overthrown,' said Ostrog.

'And I – Is it indeed true that I—?'

'You are Master of the World.'

'But that white flag—'

'That is the flag of the Council – the flag of the Rule of the World. It will fall. The fight is over. Their attack on the theatre was their last frantic struggle. They have only a thousand men or so, and some of these men will be disloyal. They have little ammunition. And we are reviving the ancient arts. We are casting guns.'

'But – help. Is this city the world?'

'Practically this is all they have left to them of their empire. Abroad the cities have either revolted with us or wait the issue. Your awakening has perplexed them, paralysed them.'

'But haven't the Council flying machines? Why is there no fighting with them?'

'They had. But the greater part of the aeronauts were in the revolt with us. They wouldn't take the risk of fighting on our side, but they would not stir against us. We *had* to get a pull with the aeronauts.

504

Quite half were with us, and the others knew it. Directly they knew you had got away, those looking for you dropped. We killed the man who shot at you – an hour ago. And we occupied the flying stages at the outset in every city we could, and so stopped and captured the greater aeroplanes, and as for the little flying machines that turned out – for some did – we kept up too straight and steady a fire for them to get near the Council House. If they dropped they couldn't rise again, because there's no clear space about there for them to get up. Several we have smashed, several others have dropped and surrendered, the rest have gone off to the Continent to find a friendly city if they can before their fuel runs out. Most of these men were only too glad to be taken prisoner and kept out of harm's way. Upsetting in a flying machine isn't a very attractive prospect. There's no chance for the Council that way. Its days are done.'

He laughed and turned to the oval reflection again to show Graham what he meant by flying stages. Even the four nearer ones were remote and obscured by a thin morning haze. But Graham could perceive they were very vast structures, judged even by the standard of the things about them.

And then as these dim shapes passed to the left there came again the sight of the expanse across which the disarmed men in red had been marching. And then the black ruins, and then again the belea-guered white fastness of the Council. It appeared no longer a ghostly pile, but glowing amber in the sunlight, for a cloud shadow had passed. About it the pigmy struggle still hung in suspense, but now the red defenders were no longer firing.

So, in a dusky stillness, the man from the nineteenth century saw the closing scene of the great revolt, the forcible establishment of his rule. With a quality of startling discovery it came to him that this was his world, and not that other he had left behind; that this was no spectacle to culminate and cease; that in this world lay whatever life was still before him, lay all his duties and dangers and responsibilities. He turned with fresh questions. Ostrog began to answer them, and then broke off abruptly. 'But these things I must explain more fully later. At present there are – things to be done. The people are coming by the moving ways towards this ward from every part of the city – the markets and theatres are densely crowded. You are just in time for them. They are clamouring to see you. And abroad they want to see you. Paris, New York, Chicago, Denver, Capri – thousands of cities are up and in a tumult, undecided, and clamouring to see you. They have clamoured that you should be awakened for years, and now it is done they will scarcely believe—'

505

'But surely – I can't go . . .'

Ostrog answered from the other side of the room, and the picture on the oval disc paled and vanished as the light jerked back again. 'There are kinetotelephotographs,' he said. 'As you bow to the people here – all over the world myriads of myriads of people, packed and still in darkened halls, will see you also. In black and white, of course – not like this. And you will hear their shouts reinforcing the shouting in the hall.

'And there is an optical contrivance we have,' said Ostrog, 'used by some of the posturers and women dancers. It may be novel to you. You stand in a very bright light, and they see not you but a magnified image of you thrown on a screen – so that even the farthest man in the remotest gallery can, if he chooses, count your eyelashes.'

Graham clutched desperately at one of the questions in his mind. 'What is the population of London?' he said.

'Eight and twaindy myriads.'

'Eight and what?'

'More than thirty-three millions.'

These figures went beyond Graham's imagination.

'You will be expected to say something,' said Ostrog. 'Not what you used to call a Speech, but what our people call a Word – just one sentence, six or seven words. Something formal. If I might suggest – "I have awakened and my heart is with you." That is the sort of thing they want.'

'What was that?' asked Graham.

'"I am awakened and my heart is with you." And bow – bow royally. But first we must get you black robes – for black is your colour. Do you mind? And then they will disperse to their homes.'

Graham hesitated. 'I am in your hands,' he said.

Ostrog was clearly of that opinion. He thought for a moment, turned to the curtain and called brief directions to some unseen attendants. Almost immediately a black robe, the very fellow of the black robe Graham had worn in the theatre, was brought. And as he threw it about his shoulders there came from the room without the shrilling of a high-pitched bell. Ostrog turned in interrogation to the attendant, then suddenly seemed to change his mind, pulled the curtain aside and disappeared.

Graham stood with the deferential attendant listening to Ostrog's retreating steps. There was a sound of quick question and answer and of men running. The curtain was snatched back and Ostrog reappeared, his massive face glowing with excitement. He crossed the room in a stride, clicked the room into darkness, gripped Graham's arm and pointed to the mirror.

'Even as we turned away,' he said.

Graham saw his index finger, black and colossal, above the mirrored Council House. He did not understand immediately. And then he perceived that the flagstaff that had carried the white banner was bare.

'Do you mean –?' he began.

'The Council has surrendered. Its rule is at an end for evermore.

'Look!' and Ostrog pointed to a coil of black that crept in little jerks up the vacant flagstaff, unfolding as it rose.

The oval picture paled as Lincoln pulled the curtain aside and entered.

'They are clamorous,' he said.

Ostrog kept his grip of Graham's arm.

'We have raised the people,' he said. 'We have given them arms. For today at least their wishes must be law.'

Lincoln held the curtain open for Graham and Ostrog to pass through. . . .

On his way to the markets Graham had a transitory glance of a long narrow white-walled room in which men in the universal blue canvas were carrying covered things like biers, and about which men in medical purple hurried to and fro. From this room came groans and wailing. He had an impression of an empty bloodstained couch, of men on other couches, bandaged and bloodstained. It was just a glimpse from a railed footway and then a buttress hid the place and they were going on towards the markets. . . .

The roar of the multitude was near now: it leapt to thunder. And, arresting his attention, a fluttering of black banners, the waving of blue canvas and brown rags, and the swarming vastness of the theatre near the public markets came into view down a long passage. The picture opened out. He perceived they were entering the great theatre of his first appearance, the great theatre he had last seen as a chequer-work of glare and blackness in his flight from the red police. This time he entered it along a gallery at a level high above the stage. The place was now brilliantly lit again. His eyes sought the gangway up which he had fled, but he could not tell it from among its dozens of fellows; nor could he see anything of the smashed seats, deflated cushions, and such like traces of the fight because of the density of the people. Except the stage the whole place was closely packed. Looking down the effect was a vast area of stippled pink, each dot a still upturned face regarding him. At his appearance with Ostrog the cheering died away, the singing died away, a common interest stilled and unified the disorder. It seemed as though every individual of those myriads was watching him.

507

13

The End of the Old Order

So far as Graham was able to judge, it was near midday when the white banner of the Council fell. But some hours had to elapse before it was possible to effect the formal capitulation, and so after he had spoken his 'Word' he retired to his new apartments in the wind-vane offices. The continuous excitement of the last twelve hours had left him inordinately fatigued, even his curiosity was exhausted; for a space he sat inert and passive with open eyes, and for a space he slept. He was roused by two medical attendants, come prepared with stimulants to sustain him through the next occasion. After he had taken their drugs and bathed by their advice in cold water, he felt a rapid return of interest and energy, and was presently able and willing to accompany Ostrog through several miles (as it seemed) of passages, lifts, and slides to the closing scene of the White Council's rule.

The way ran deviously through a maze of buildings. They came at last to a passage that curved about, and showed broadening before him an oblong opening, clouds hot with sunset, and the ragged skyline of the ruinous Council House. A tumult of shouts came drifting up to him. In another moment they had come out high up on the brow of the cliff of torn buildings that overhung the wreckage. The vast area opened to Graham's eyes, none the less strange and wonderful for the remote view he had had of it in the oval mirror.

This rudely amphitheatral space seemed now the better part of a mile to its outer edge. It was gold-lit on the left hand, catching the sunlight, and below and to the right clear and cold in the shadow. Above the shadowy grey Council House that stood in the midst of it, the great black banner of the surrender still hung in sluggish folds against the blazing sunset. Severed rooms, halls and passages gaped strangely, broken masses of metal projected dismally from the complex wreckage, vast masses of twisted cable dropped like tangled seaweed, and from its base came a tumult of innumerable voices, violent concussions and the sound of trumpets. All about this great white pile was a ring of desolation; the smashed and blackened masses, the gaunt foundations and ruinous lumber of the fabric that had been destroyed by the Council's orders, skeletons of girders, Titanic masses of wall, forests of stout pillars. Amongst the sombre wreckage beneath, running water flashed and glistened, and far away across the space, out of the midst of a vague vast mass of buildings, there thrust the twisted end of a water-main, two hundred feet in the air, thunderously spouting a shining cascade. And everywhere great multitudes of people.

Wherever there was space and foothold, people swarmed, little people, small and minutely clear except where the sunset touched them to indistinguishable gold. They clambered up the tottering walls, they clung in wreaths and groups about the high-standing pillars. They swarmed along the edges of the circle of ruins. The air was full of their shouting, and they were pressing and swaying towards the central space.

The upper storeys of the Council House seemed deserted, not a human being was visible. Only the drooping banner of the surrender hung heavily against the light. The dead were within the Council House, or hidden by the swarming people, or carried away. Graham could see only a few neglected bodies in gaps and corners of the ruins, and amidst the flowing water.

'Will you let them see you, Sire?' said Ostrog. 'They are very anxious to see you.'

Graham hesitated, and then walked forward to where the broken verge of wall dropped sheer. He stood looking down, a lonely, tall, black figure against the sky.

Very slowly the swarming ruins became aware of him. And as they did so little bands of black-uniformed men appeared remotely, thrusting through the crowds towards the Council House. He saw little black heads become pink, looking at him, saw by that means a wave of recognition sweep across the space. It occurred to him that he should accord them some recognition. He held up his arm, then pointed to the Council House and dropped his hand. The voices below became unanimous, gathered volume, came up to him as multitudinous wavelets of cheering.

The western sky was a pallid bluish green and Jupiter shone high in the south, before the capitulation was accomplished. Above was a slow insensible change, the advance of night serene and beautiful; below was hurry, excitement, conflicting orders, pauses, spasmodic developments of organization, a vast ascending clamour and confusion. Before the Council came out, toiling perspiring men, directed by a conflict of shouts, carried forth hundreds of those who had perished in the hand-to-hand conflict within those long passages and chambers. . . .

Guards in black lined the way that the Council would come and as far as the eye could reach into the hazy blue twilight of the ruins, and swarming now at every possible point in the captured Council House and along the shattered cliff of its circumadjacent buildings, were innumerable people, and their voices, even when they were not cheering, were as the soughing of the sea upon a pebble beach. Ostrog had chosen a huge commanding pile of crushed and overthrown masonry, and on this a stage of timbers and metal girders was being hastily constructed. Its essential parts were complete, but humming and clangorous machinery still glared fitfully in the shadows beneath this temporary edifice.

The stage had a small higher portion on which Graham stood with Ostrog and Lincoln close beside him, a little in advance of a group of minor officers. A broader lower stage surrounded this quarter-deck, and on this were the black-uniformed guards of the revolt armed with the little green weapons whose very names Graham still did not know. Those standing about him perceived that his eyes wandered perpetually from the swarming people in the twilight ruins about him to the darkling mass of the White Council House, whence the Trustees would presently come, and to the gaunt cliffs of ruin that encircled him, and so back to the people. The voices of the crowd swelled to a deafening tumult.

He saw the Councillors first afar off in the glare of one of the temporary lights that marked their path, a little group of white figures in a black archway. In the Council House they had been in darkness. He watched them approaching, drawing nearer past first this blazing electric star and then that; the minatory roar of the crowd over whom their power had lasted for a hundred and fifty years marched along beside them. As they drew still nearer their faces came out weary, white and anxious. He saw them blinking up through the glare about him and Ostrog. He contrasted their strange cold looks in the Hall of Atlas. . . . Presently he could recognize several of them; the man who had rapped the table at Howard, a burly man with a red beard, and one delicate-featured, short, dark man with a peculiarly long skull. He noted that two were whispering together and looking behind him at

Ostrog. Next there came a tall, dark and handsome man, walking downcast. Abruptly he glanced up, his eyes touched Graham for a moment, and passed beyond him to Ostrog. The way that had been made for them was so contrived that they had to march past and curve about before they came to the sloping path of planks that ascended to the stage where their surrender was to be made.

'The Master, the Master! God and the Master,' shouted the people. 'To hell with the Council!' Graham looked at their multitudes, receding beyond counting into a shouting haze, and then at Ostrog beside him, white and steadfast and still. His eye went again to the group of White Councillors. And then he looked up at the familiar quiet stars overhead. The marvellous element in his fate was suddenly vivid. Could that be his indeed, that little life in his memory two hundred years gone by – and this as well?

14

From the Crow's Nest

And so after strange delays and through an avenue of doubt and battle, this man from the nineteenth century came at last to his position at the head of that complex world.

At first when he rose from the long deep sleep that followed his rescue and the surrender of the Council, he did not recognize his surroundings. By an effort he gained a clue in his mind, and all that had happened came back to him, with a quality of insincerity like a story heard, like something read out of a book. And even before his memories were clear, the exultation of his escape, the wonder of his prominence were back in his mind. He was owner of the world; Master of the Earth. This new great age was in the completest sense his. He no longer hoped to discover his experiences a dream; he became anxious now to convince himself that they were real.

An obsequious valet assisted him to dress under the direction of a dignified chief attendant, a little man whose face proclaimed him Japanese, albeit he spoke English like an Englishman. From the latter he learnt something of the state of affairs. Already the revolution was an accepted fact; already business was being resumed throughout the city. Abroad the downfall of the Council had been received for the most part with delight. Nowhere was the Council popular, and the thousand cities of Western America, after two hundred years still jealous of New York, London, and the East, had risen almost unanimously two days before at the news of Graham's imprisonment. Paris was fighting within itself. The rest of the world hung in suspense.

While he was breaking his fast, the sound of a telephone bell jetted from a corner, and his chief attendant called his attention to the voice of Ostrog making polite inquiries. Graham interrupted his refreshment to reply. Very shortly Lincoln arrived, and Graham at once expressed a strong desire to talk to people and to be shown more of the new life that was opening before him. Lincoln informed him that in three hours' time a representative gathering of officials and their wives would be held in the state apartments of the wind-vane Chief. Graham's desire to traverse the ways of the city was, however, at present impossible, because of the enormous excitement of the people. It was, however, quite possible for him to take a bird's-eye view of the city from the crow's nest of the wind-vane keeper. To this accordingly Graham was conducted by his attendant. Lincoln, with a graceful compliment to the attendant, apologized for not accompanying them, on account of the present pressure of administrative work.

Higher even than the most gigantic wind-wheels hung this crow's nest, a clear thousand feet above the roofs, a little disc-shaped speck on a spear of metallic filigree, cable stayed. To its summit Graham was drawn in a little wire-hung cradle. Halfway down the frail-seeming stem was a light gallery about which hung a cluster of tubes – minute they looked from above – rotating slowly on the ring of its outer rail. These were the specula, *en rapport* with the wind-vane keeper's mirrors, in one of which Ostrog had shown him the coming of his rule. His Japanese attendant ascended before him and they spent nearly an hour asking and answering questions.

It was a day full of the promise and quality of spring. The touch of the wind warmed. The sky was an intense blue and the vast expanse of London shone dazzling under the morning sun. The air was clear of smoke and haze, sweet as the air of a mountain glen.

Save for the irregular oval of ruins about the House of the Council and the black flag of the surrender that fluttered there, the mighty city seen from above showed few signs of the swift revolution that had, to his imagination, in one night and one day changed the destinies of the world. A multitude of people still swarmed over these ruins, and the huge openwork stagings in the distance from which started in times of peace the service of aeroplanes to the various great cities of Europe and America, were also black with the victors. Across a narrow way of planking raised on trestles that crossed the ruins a crowd of workmen were busy restoring the connection between the cables and wires of the Council House and the rest of the city, preparatory to the transfer thither of Ostrog's headquarters from the wind-vane buildings.

For the rest the luminous expanse was undisturbed. So vast was its serenity in comparison with the areas of disturbance, that presently Graham, looking beyond them, could almost forget the thousands of men lying out of sight in the artificial glare within the quasi-subterranean labyrinth, dead or dying of their overnight wounds, forget the improvised wards with the hosts of surgeons, nurses, and bearers feverishly busy, forget, indeed, all the wonder, consternation and novelty under the electric lights. Down there in the hidden ways of the anthill he knew that the revolution triumphed, that black everywhere carried the day, black favours, black banners, black festoons across the streets. And out here under the fresh sunlight, beyond the crater of the fight, as if nothing had happened to the earth, the forest of wind-vanes that had grown from one or two while the Council had ruled, roared peacefully upon their incessant duty.

Far away, spiked, jagged and indented by the wind-vanes, the Surrey Hills rose blue and faint; to the north and nearer, the sharp contours of Highgate and Muswell Hill were similarly jagged. And all over the countryside, he knew, on every crest and hill where once the hedges had interlaced, and cottages, churches, inns and farmhouses had nestled among their trees, wind-wheels similar to those he saw and bearing like them vast advertisements, gaunt and distinctive symbols of the new age, cast their whirling shadows and stored incessantly the energy that flowed away incessantly through all the arteries of the city. And underneath these wandered the countless flocks and herds of the British Food Trust, his property, with their lonely guards and keepers.

Not a familiar outline anywhere broke the cluster of gigantic shapes below. St Paul's he knew survived, and many of the old buildings in Westminster, embedded out of sight, arched over and covered in among the giant growths of this great age. The Thames, too, made no fall and gleam of silver to break the wilderness of the city; the thirsty water mains drank up every drop of its waters before they reached the walls. Its bed and estuary, scoured and sunken, was now a canal of sea water, and a race of grimy bargemen brought the heavy materials of trade from the Pool thereby beneath the very feet of the workers. Faint and dim in the eastward between earth and sky hung the clustering masts of the colossal shipping in the Pool. For all the heavy traffic, for which there was no need of haste, came in gigantic sailing ships from the ends of the earth, and the heavy goods for which there was urgency in mechanical ships of a smaller swifter sort.

And to the south over the hills came vast aqueducts with sea water for the sewers, and in three separate directions ran pallid lines – the roads, stippled with moving grey specks. On the first occasion that offered he was determined to go out and see these roads. That would come after the flying ship he was presently to try. His attendant officer described them as a pair of gently curving surfaces a hundred yards wide, each one for the traffic going in one direction, and made of a substance called Eadhamite – an artificial substance, so far as he could gather, resembling toughened glass. Along this shot a strange traffic of narrow rubber-shod vehicles, great single wheels, two- and four-wheeled vehicles, sweeping along at velocities of from one to six miles a minute. Railroads had vanished; a few embankments remained as rust-crowned trenches here and there. Some few formed the cores of Eadhamite ways.

Among the first things to strike his attention had been the great fleets of advertisement balloons and kites that receded in irregular vistas northward and southward along the lines of the aeroplane journeys. No great aeroplanes were to be seen. Their passages had ceased, and only one little-seeming monoplane circled high in the blue distance above the Surrey Hills, an unimpressive soaring speck.

A thing Graham had already learnt, and which he found very hard to imagine, was that nearly all the towns in the country and almost all the villages had disappeared. Here and there only, he understood, a gigantic hotel-like edifice stood amid square miles of some single cultivation and preserved the name of a town – as Bournemouth, Wareham or Swanage. Yet the officer had speedily convinced him how inevitable such a change had been. The old order had dotted the country with farmhouses, and every two or three miles was the ruling landlord's estate, and the place of the inn and cobbler, the grocer's shop and church – the village. Every eight miles or so was the country town, where lawyer, corn merchant, wool-stapler, saddler, veterinary surgeon, doctor, draper, milliner and so forth lived. Every eight miles – simply because that eight-mile marketing journey, four there and back, was as much as was comfortable for the farmer. But directly the railways came into play, and after them the light railways, and all the swift new motor cars that had replaced wagons and horses, and so soon as the high roads began to be made of wood and rubber and Eadhamite and all sorts of elastic durable substances – the necessity of having such frequent market towns disappeared. And the big towns grew. They drew the worker with the gravitational force of seemingly endless work, the employer with their suggestion of an infinite ocean of labour.

And as the standard of comfort rose, as the complexity of the mechanism of living increased, life in the country had become more and more costly, or narrow and impossible. The disappearance of vicar and squire, the extinction of the general practitioner by the city specialist, had robbed the village of its last touch of culture. After telephone, kinematograph and phonograph had replaced newspaper, book, schoolmaster and letter, to live outside the range of the electric

515

cables was to live an isolated savage. In the country were neither means of being clothed nor fed (according to the refined conceptions of the time), no efficient doctors for an emergency, no company and no pursuits.

Moreover, mechanical appliances in agriculture made one engineer the equivalent of thirty labourers. So, inverting the condition of the city clerk in the days when London was scarce inhabitable because of the coaly foulness of its air, the labourers now came to the city and its life and delights at night to leave it again in the morning. The city had swallowed up humanity; man had entered upon a new stage in his development. First had come the nomad, the hunter, then had followed the agriculturist of the agricultural state, whose towns and cities and ports were but the headquarters and markets of the countryside. And now, logical consequence of an epoch of invention, was this huge new aggregation of men.

Such things as these, simple statements of fact though they were to contemporary men, strained Graham's imagination to picture. And when he glanced 'over beyond there' at the strange things that existed on the Continent, it failed him altogether.

He had a vision of city beyond city; cities on great plains, cities beside great rivers, vast cities along the sea margin, cities girdled by snowy mountains. Over a great part of the earth the English tongue was spoken; taken together with its Spanish-American and Hindoo and Negro and 'Pidgin' dialects, it was the everyday language of two-thirds of humanity. On the Continent, save as remote and curious survivals, three other languages alone held sway – German, which reached to Antioch and Genoa and jostled Spanish-English at Cadiz, a Gallicized Russian which met the Indian English in Persia and Kurdistan and the 'Pidgin' English in Pekin, and French still clear and brilliant, the language of lucidity, which shared the Mediterranean with the Indian English and German and reached through a Negro dialect to the Congo.

And everywhere now through the city-set earth, save in the administered 'black belt' territories of the tropics, the same cosmopolitan social organization prevailed, and everywhere from Pole to Equator his property and his responsibilities extended. The whole world was civilized; the whole world dwelt in cities; the whole world was his property. . . .

Out of the dim south-west, glittering and strange, voluptuous, and in some way terrible, shone those Pleasure Cities of which the kinematograph-phonograph and the old man in the street had spoken. Strange places reminiscent of the legendary Sybaris, cities of art and beauty, mercenary art and mercenary beauty, sterile wonderful cities of motion and music, whither repaired all who profited by the fierce, inglorious, economic struggle that went on in the glaring labyrinth below.

Fierce he knew it was. How fierce he could judge from the fact that these latter-day people referred back to the England of the nineteenth century as the figure of an idyllic easy-going life. He turned his eyes to the scene immediately before him again, trying to conceive the big factories of that intricate maze. . . .

15

Prominent People

The state apartments of the wind-vane keeper would have astonished Graham had he entered them fresh from his nineteenth-century life, but already he was growing accustomed to the scale of the new time. He came out through one of the now familiar sliding panels upon a plateau of landing at the head of a flight of very broad and gentle steps, with men and women far more brilliantly dressed than any he had hitherto seen, ascending and descending. From this position he looked down a vista of subtle and varied ornament in lustreless white and mauve and purple, spanned by bridges that seemed wrought of porcelain and filigree, and terminating far off in a cloudy mystery of perforated screens.

Glancing upward, he saw tier above tier of ascending galleries with faces looking down upon him. The air was full of the babble of innumerable voices and of a music that descended from above, a gay and exhilarating music whose source he did not discover.

The central aisle was thick with people, but by no means uncomfortably crowded; altogether that assembly must have numbered many thousands. They were brilliantly, even fantastically dressed, the men as fancifully as the women, for the sobering influence of the Puritan conception of dignity upon masculine dress had long since passed away. The hair of the men, too, though it was rarely worn long, was commonly curled in a manner that suggested the barber, and baldness had vanished from the earth. Frizzy straight-cut masses that would have charmed Rossetti abounded, and one gentleman, who was pointed out to Graham under the mysterious title of an 'amorist', wore his hair in two becoming plaits *à la* Marguerite. The pigtail was in evidence; it

518

would seem that citizens of Manchurian extraction were no longer ashamed of their race. There was little uniformity of fashion apparent in the forms of clothing worn. The more shapely men displayed their symmetry in trunk hose, and here were puffs and slashes, and there a cloak and there a robe. The fashions of the days of Leo the Tenth were perhaps the prevailing influence, but the aesthetic conceptions of the Far East were also patent. Masculine embonpoint, which in Victorian times would have been subjected to the buttoned perils, the ruthless exaggeration of tight-legged, tight-armed evening dress, now formed but the basis of a wealth of dignity and drooping folds. Graceful slenderness abounded also. To Graham, a typically stiff man from a typically stiff period, not only did these men seem altogether too graceful in person, but altogether too expressive in their vividly expressive faces. They gesticulated, they expressed surprise, interest, amusement, above all they expressed the emotions excited in their minds by the ladies about them with astonishing frankness. Even at the first glance it was evident that women were in a great majority.

The ladies in the company of these gentlemen displayed in dress, bearing and manner alike, less emphasis and more intricacy. Some affected a classical simplicity of robing and subtlety of fold, after the fashion of the First French Empire, and flashed conquering arms and shoulders as Graham passed. Others had closely fitting dresses without seam or belt at the waist, sometimes with long folds falling from the shoulders. The delightful confidences of evening dress had not been diminished by the passage of two centuries.

Everyone's movements seemed graceful. Graham remarked to Lincoln that he saw men as Raphael's cartoons' walking, and Lincoln told him that the attainment of an appropriate set of gestures was part of every rich person's education. The Master's entry was greeted with a sort of tittering applause, but these people showed their distinguished manners by not crowding upon him nor annoying him by any persistent scrutiny, as he descended the steps towards the floor of the aisle.

He had already learnt from Lincoln that these were the leaders of existing London society; almost every person there that night was either a powerful official or the immediate connection of a powerful official. Many had returned from the European Pleasure Cities expressly to welcome him. The aeronautic authorities, whose defection had played a part in the overthrow of the Council only second to Graham's, were very prominent, and so, too, was the Wind-Vane Control. Amongst others there were several of the more prominent officers of the Food Department; the controller of the European Piggeries had a particularly melancholy and interesting countenance and a daintily cynical manner. A bishop in full canonicals passed athwart Graham's vision, conversing with a gentleman dressed exactly like the traditional Chaucer, including even the laurel wreath.

'Who is that?' he asked almost involuntarily.

'The Bishop of London,' said Lincoln.

'No – the other, I mean.'

'Poet Laureate.'

'You still—?'

'He doesn't make poetry, of course. He's a cousin of Wotton – one of the Councillors. But he's one of the Red Rose Royalists – a delightful club – and they keep up the tradition of these things.'

'Asano told me there was a King.'

'The King doesn't belong. They had to expel him. It's the Stuart blood, I suppose; but really—'

'Too much?'

'Far too much.'

Graham did not quite follow all this, but it seemed part of the general inversion of the new age. He bowed condescendingly to his first introduction. It was evident that subtle distinctions of class prevailed even in this assembly, that only to a small proportion of the guests, to an inner group, did Lincoln consider it appropriate to introduce him. This first introduction was the Master Aeronaut, a man whose sun-tanned face contrasted oddly with the delicate complexions about him. Just at present his critical defection from the Council made him a very important person indeed.

His manner contrasted favourably, according to Graham's ideas, with the general bearing. He offered a few commonplace remarks, assurances of loyalty and frank enquiries about the Master's health. His manner was breezy, his accent lacked the easy staccato of latter-day English. He made it admirably clear to Graham that he was a bluff 'aerial dog' – he used that phrase – that there was no nonsense about him, that he was a thoroughly manly fellow and old-fashioned at that, that he didn't profess to know much, and that what he did not know was not worth knowing. He made a curt bow, ostentatiously free from obsequiousness, and passed.

'I am glad to see that type endures,' said Graham.

'Phonographs and kinematographs,' said Lincoln, a little spitefully. 'He has studied from the life.' Graham glanced at the burly form again. It was oddly reminiscent.

'As a matter of fact we bought him,' said Lincoln. 'Partly. And partly he was afraid of Ostrog. Everything rested with him.'

He turned sharply to introduce the Surveyor-General of the Public

Schools. This person was a willowy figure in a blue-grey academic gown, he beamed down upon Graham through *pince-nez* of a Victorian pattern, and illustrated his remarks by gestures of a beautifully manicured hand. Graham was immediately interested in this gentleman's functions, and asked him a number of singularly direct questions. The Surveyor-General seemed quietly amused at the Master's fundamental bluntness. He was a little vague as to the monopoly of education his Company possessed; it was done by contract with the syndicate that ran the numerous London Municipalities, but he waxed enthusiastic over educational progress since the Victorian times. 'We have conquered Cram,' he said, 'completely conquered Cram – there is not an examination left in the world. Aren't you glad?'

'How do you get the work done?' asked Graham.

'We make it attractive – as attractive as possible. And if it does not attract then – we let it go. We cover an immense field.'

He proceeded to details, and they had a lengthy conversation. Graham learnt that University Extension still existed in a modified form. 'There is a certain type of girl, for example,' said the Surveyor-General, dilating with a sense of his usefulness, 'with a perfect passion for severe studies – when they are not too difficult, you know. We cater for them by the thousand. At this moment,' he said with a Napoleonic touch, 'nearly five hundred phonographs are lecturing in different parts of London on the influence exercised by Plato and Swift on the love affairs of Shelley, Hazlitt and Burns. And afterwards they write essays on the lectures, and their names in order of merit are put in conspicuous places. You see how your little germ has grown? The illiterate middle-class of your days has quite passed away.'

'About the public elementary schools,' said Graham. 'Do you control them?'

The Surveyor-General did, 'entirely'. Now Graham in his later democratic days had taken a keen interest in these, and his questioning quickened. Certain casual phrases that had fallen from the old man with whom he had talked in the darkness recurred to him. The Surveyor-General in effect endorsed the old man's words. 'We try and make the elementary schools pleasant for the little children. They will have to work so soon. Just a few simple principles – obedience – industry.'

'You teach them very little?'

'Why should we? It only leads to trouble and discontent. We amuse them. Even as it is – there are troubles – agitations. Where the labourers get the ideas, one cannot tell. They tell one another. There are socialistic dreams – anarchy even! Agitators *will* get to work among them. I take it – I have always taken it – that my foremost duty is to fight against popular discontent. Why should people be made unhappy?'

'I wonder,' said Graham thoughtfully. 'But there are a great many things I want to know.'

Lincoln, who had stood watching Graham's face throughout the conversation, intervened. 'There are others,' he said in an undertone.

The Surveyor-General of Schools gesticulated himself away. 'Perhaps,' said Lincoln, intercepting a casual glance, 'you would like to know some of these ladies?'

The daughter of the Manager of the Piggeries was a particularly charming little person with red hair and animated blue eyes. Lincoln left him a while to converse with her, and she displayed herself as quite an enthusiast for the 'dear old days', as she called them, that had seen the beginning of his trance. As she talked she smiled, and her eyes smiled in a manner that demanded reciprocity.

'I have tried,' she said, 'countless times – to imagine those old romantic days. And to you – they are memories. How strange and crowded the world must seem to you! I have seen photographs and pictures of the past, the little isolated houses built of bricks made out of burnt mud and all black with soot from your fires, the railway bridges, the simple advertisements, the solemn savage Puritanical men in strange black coats and those tall hats of theirs, iron railway trains on iron bridges overhead, horses and cattle, and even dogs running half wild about the streets. And suddenly, you have come into this!'

'Into this,' said Graham.

'Out of your life – out of all that was familiar.'

'The old life was not a happy one,' said Graham. 'I do not regret that.'

She looked at him quickly. There was a brief pause. She sighed encouragingly. 'No?'

'No,' said Graham. 'It was a little life – and unmeaning. But this – We thought the world complex and crowded and civilized enough. Yet I see – although in this world I am barely four days old – looking back on my own time, that it was a queer, barbaric time – the mere beginning of this new order. The mere beginning of this new order. You will find it hard to understand how little I know.'

'You may ask me what you like,' she said, smiling at him.

'Then tell me who these people are. I'm still very much in the dark about them. It's puzzling Are there any Generals?'

'Men in hats and feathers?'

'Of course not. No. I suppose they are the men who control the great public businesses. Who is that distinguished-looking man?'

'That? He's a most important officer. That is Morden. He is managing director of the Antibilious Pill Department. I have heard that his workers sometimes turn out a myriad myriad pills a day in the twenty-four hours. Fancy a myriad myriad!'

'A myriad myriad. No wonder he looks proud,' said Graham. 'Pills! What a wonderful time it is! That man in purple?'

'He is not quite one of the inner circle, you know. But we like him. He is really clever and very amusing. He is one of the heads of the Medical Faculty of our London University. All medical men, you know, wear that purple. But of course people who are paid by fees for *doing* something —' She smiled away the social pretensions of all such people.

'Are any of your great artists or authors here?'

'No authors. They are mostly such queer people – and so preoccupied about themselves. And they quarrel so dreadfully! They will fight, some of them, for precedence on staircases! Dreadful, isn't it? But I think Wraysbury, the fashionable capillotomist, is here. From Capri.'

'Capillotomist,' said Graham. 'Ah! I remember. An artist! Why not?'

'We have to cultivate him,' she said apologetically. 'Our heads are in his hands.' She smiled.

Graham hesitated at the invited compliment, but his glance was expressive. 'Have the arts grown with the rest of civilized things?' he said. 'Who are your great painters?'

She looked at him doubtfully. Then laughed. 'For a moment,' she said, 'I thought you meant —' She laughed again. 'You mean, of course, those good men you used to think so much of because they could cover great spaces of canvas with oil-colours? Great oblongs. And people used to put the things in gilt frames and hang them up in rows in their square rooms. We haven't any. People grew tired of that sort of thing.'

'But what did you think I meant?'

She put a finger significantly on a cheek whose glow was above suspicion, and smiled and looked very arch and pretty and inviting. 'And here,' and she indicated her eyelid.

Graham had an adventurous moment. Then a grotesque memory of a picture he had somewhere seen of Uncle Toby and the Widow flashed across his mind. An archaic shame came upon him. He became acutely aware that he was visible to a great number of interested people. 'I see,' he remarked inadequately. He turned awkwardly away from her fascinating facility. He looked about him to meet a number of eyes that immediately occupied themselves with other things. Possibly he coloured a little. 'Who is that talking with the lady in saffron?' he asked, avoiding her eyes.

The person in question he learnt was one of the great organizers of the American theatres just fresh from a gigantic production in Mexico. His face reminded Graham of a bust of Caligula. Another striking-looking man was the Black Labour Master. The phrase at the time made no deep impression, but afterwards it recurred; – the Black Labour Master? The little lady, in no degree embarrassed, pointed out to him a charming little woman as one of the subsidiary wives of the Anglican Bishop of London. She added encomiums on the episcopal courage – hitherto there had been a rule of clerical monogamy – 'neither a natural nor an expedient condition of things. Why should the natural development of the affections be dwarfed and restricted because a man is a priest?

'And by-the-by,' she added, 'are you an Anglican?' Graham was on the verge of hesitating enquiries about the status of a 'subsidiary wife', apparently an euphemistic phrase, when Lincoln's return broke off this very suggestive and interesting conversation. They crossed the aisle to where a tall man in crimson and two charming persons in Burmese costume (as it seemed to him) awaited him diffidently. From their civilities he passed to other presentations.

In a little while his multitudinous impressions began to organize themselves into a general effect. At first the glitter of the gathering had raised all the democrat in Graham; he had felt hostile and satirical. But it is not in human nature to resist an atmosphere of courteous regard. Soon the music, the light, the play of colours, the shining arms and shoulders about him, the touch of hands, the transient interest of smiling faces, the frothing sound of skilfully modulated voices, the atmosphere of compliment, interest and respect, had woven together into a fabric of indisputable pleasure. Graham for a time forgot his spacious resolutions. He gave way insensibly to the intoxication of the position that was conceded him, his manner became more con-vincingly regal, his feet walked assuredly, the black robe fell with a bolder fold and pride ennobled his voice. After all, this was a brilliant, interesting world.

He looked up and saw passing across a bridge of porcelain and looking down upon him, a face that was almost immediately hidden, the face of the girl he had seen overnight in the little room beyond the theatre after his escape from the Council. And she was watching him.

For the moment he did not remember where he had seen her, and then came a vague memory of the stirring emotions of their first encounter. But the dancing web of melody about him kept the air of that great marching song from his memory.

The lady to whom he talked repeated her remark, and Graham recalled himself to the quasi-regal flirtation upon which he was engaged.

Yet unaccountably a vague restlessness, a feeling that grew to dissatisfaction, came into his mind. He was troubled as if by some half-forgotten duty, by the sense of things important slipping from him amidst this light and brilliance. The attraction that these ladies who crowded about him were beginning to exercise ceased. He no longer gave vague and clumsy responses to the subtly amorous advances that he was now assured were being made to him, and his eyes wandered for another sight of the girl of the first revolt.

Where precisely had he seen her? . . .

Graham was in one of the upper galleries in conversation with a bright-eyed lady on the subject of Eadhamite – the subject was his choice and not hers. He had interrupted her warm assurances of personal devotion with a matter-of-fact inquiry. He found her, as he had already found several other latter-day women that night, less well informed than charming. Suddenly, struggling against the eddying drift of nearer melody, the song of the Revolt, the great song he had heard in the Hall, hoarse and massive, came beating down to him.

Ah! Now he remembered!

He glanced up startled, and perceived above him an *oeil de boeuf* through which this song had come, and beyond, the upper courses of cable, the blue haze, and the pendant fabric of the lights of the public ways. He heard the song break into a tumult of voices and cease. He perceived quite clearly the drone and tumult of the moving platforms and a murmur of many people. He had a vague persuasion that he could not account for, a sort of instinctive feeling that outside in the ways a huge crowd must be watching this place in which their Master amused himself.

Though the song had stopped so abruptly, though the special music of this gathering reasserted itself, the *motif* of the marching song, once it had begun, lingered in his mind.

The bright-eyed lady was still struggling with the mysteries of Eadhamite when he perceived the girl he had seen in the theatre again. She was coming now along the gallery towards him; he saw her first before she saw him. She was dressed in a faintly luminous grey, her dark hair about her brows was like a cloud, and as he saw her the cold light from the circular opening into the ways fell upon her downcast face.

The lady in trouble about the Eadhamite saw the change in his expression, and grasped her opportunity to escape. 'Would you care to know that girl, Sire?' she asked boldly. 'She is Helen Wotton – a niece of Ostrog's. She knows a great many serious things. She is one of the most serious persons alive. I am sure you will like her.'

In another moment Graham was talking to the girl, and the bright-eyed lady had fluttered away.

'I remember you quite well,' said Graham. 'You were in that little room. When all the people were singing and beating time with their feet. Before I walked across the Hall.'

Her momentary embarrassment passed. She looked up at him, and her face was steady. 'It was wonderful,' she said, hesitated, and spoke with a sudden effort. 'All those people would have died for you, Sire. Countless people did die for you that night.'

Her face glowed. She glanced swiftly aside to see that no other heard her words.

Lincoln appeared some way off along the gallery, making his way through the press towards them. She saw him and turned to Graham strangely eager, with a swift change to confidence and intimacy. 'Sire,' she said quickly, 'I cannot tell you now and here. But the common people are very unhappy; they are oppressed – they are misgoverned. Do not forget the people, who faced death – death that you might live.'

'I know nothing —' began Graham.

'I cannot tell you now.'

Lincoln's face appeared close to them. He bowed an apology to the girl.

'You find the new world amusing, Sire?' asked Lincoln with smiling deference, and indicating the space and splendour of the gathering by one comprehensive gesture. 'At any rate, you find it changed.'

'Yes,' said Graham, 'changed. And yet, after all, not so greatly changed.'

'Wait till you are in the air,' said Lincoln. 'The wind has fallen; even now an aeroplane awaits you.'

The girl's attitude awaited dismissal.

Graham glanced at her face, was on the verge of a question, found a warning in her expression, bowed to her and turned to accompany Lincoln.

16

The Monoplane

The Flying Stages of London were collected together in an irregular crescent on the southern side of the river. They formed three groups of two each and retained the names of ancient suburban hills or villages. They were named in order, Roehampton, Wimbledon Park, Streatham, Norwood, Blackheath and Shooter's Hill. They were uniform structures rising high above the general roof surfaces. Each was about four thousand yards long and a thousand broad, and constructed of the compound of aluminium and iron that had replaced iron in architecture. Their higher tiers formed an openwork of girders through which lifts and staircases ascended. The upper surface was a uniform expanse, with portions – the starting carriers – that could be raised and were then able to run on very slightly inclined rails to the end of the fabric.

Graham went to the flying stages by the public ways. He was accompanied by Asano, his Japanese attendant. Lincoln was called away by Ostrog, who was busy with his administrative concerns. A strong guard of the wind-vane police awaited the Master outside the wind-vane offices, and they cleared a space for him on the upper moving platform. His passage to the flying stages was unexpected, nevertheless a considerable crowd gathered and followed him to his destination. As he went along, he could hear the people shouting his name, and saw numberless men and women and children in blue come swarming up the staircases in the central path, gesticulating and shouting. He could not hear what they shouted. He was struck again by the evident existence of a vulgar dialect among the poor of the city. When at last he descended, his guards were immediately surrounded by a dense excited crowd. Afterwards it occurred to him that some had attempted to reach him with petitions. His guards cleared a passage for him with difficulty.

He found a monoplane in charge of an aeronaut awaiting him on the westward stage. Seen close this mechanism was no longer small. As it lay on its launching carrier upon the wide expanse of the flying stage, its aluminium body skeleton was as big as the hull of a twenty-ton yacht. Its lateral supporting sails, braced and stayed with metal nerves almost like the nerves of a bee's wing and made of some sort of glassy artificial membrane, cast their shadow over many hundreds of square yards. The chairs for the engineer and his passenger hung free to swing by a complex tackle within the protecting ribs of the frame and well abaft the middle. The passenger's chair was protected by a windguard and guarded about with metallic rods carrying air cushions. It could, if desired, be completely closed in, but Graham was anxious for novel experiences and desired that it should be left open. The aeronaut sat behind a glass that sheltered his face. The passenger could secure himself firmly in his seat, and this was almost unavoidable on landing, or he could move along by means of a little rail and rod to a locker at the stem of the machine where his personal luggage, his wraps and restoratives were placed, and which also with the seats, served as a makeweight to the parts of the central engine that projected to the propeller at the stern.

The flying stage about him was empty save for Asano and their suite of attendants. Directed by the aeronaut he placed himself in his seat. Asano stepped through the bars of the hull, and stood below on the stage waving his hand. He seemed to slide along the stage to the right and vanish.

The engine was humming loudly, the propeller spinning, and for a second the stage and the buildings beyond were gliding swiftly and horizontally past Graham's eye; then these things seemed to tilt up abruptly. He gripped the little rods on either side of him instinctively. He felt himself moving upward, heard the air whistle over the top of the windscreen. The propeller screw moved round with powerful rhythmic impulses – one, two, three, pause; one, two, three – which the engineer controlled very delicately. The machine began a quivering vibration that continued throughout the flight, and the roof areas seemed running away to starboard very quickly and growing rapidly smaller. He looked from the face of the engineer through the ribs of the machine. Looking sideways, there was nothing very startling in what he saw – a rapid funicular railway might have given the same sensations. He recognized the Council House and the Highgate Ridge. And then he looked straight down between his feet.

Physical terror possessed him, a passionate sense of insecurity. He held tight. For a second or so he could not lift his eyes. Some hundred feet or more sheer below him was one of the big wind-vanes of south-west London, and beyond it the southernmost flying stage crowded with little black dots. These things seemed to be falling away from him. For a second he had an impulse to pursue the earth. He set his teeth, he lifted his eyes by a muscular effort, and the moment of panic passed.

He remained with his teeth set hard, his eyes staring into the sky. Throb, throb, throb – beat, went the engine; throb, throb, throb – beat. He gripped his bars tightly, glanced at the aeronaut, and saw a smile upon his sun-tanned face. He smiled in return – perhaps a little artificially. 'A little strange at first,' he shouted before he recalled his dignity. But he dared not look down again for some time. He stared over the aeronaut's head to where a rim of vague blue horizon crept up the sky. He could not banish the thought of possible accidents from his mind. Throb, throb, throb – beat; suppose some trivial screw went wrong in that supporting engine! Suppose—! He made a grim effort to dismiss all such suppositions. He did at least drive them from the foreground of his thoughts. And up he went steadily, higher and higher into the clear air.

Once the mental shock of moving unsupported through the air was over, his sensations ceased to be unpleasant, became very speedily pleasurable. He had been warned of air sickness. But he found the pulsating movement of the monoplane as it drove up the faint south-west breeze was very little in excess of the pitching of a boat head on to broad rollers in a moderate gale, and he was constitutionally a good sailor. And the keenness of the more rarefied air into which they ascended produced a sense of lightness and exhilaration. He looked up and saw the blue sky above fretted with cirrus clouds. His eye came cautiously down through the ribs and bars to a shining flight of white birds that hung in the lower sky. Then going lower and less apprehensively, he saw the slender figure of the wind-vane keeper's crow's nest shining golden in the sunlight and growing smaller every moment. As his eye fell with more confidence now, there came a blue line of hills, and then London, already to leeward, an intricate space of roofing. Its near edge came sharp and clear, and banished his last apprehensions in a shock of surprise. For the boundary of London was like a wall, like a cliff, a steep fall of three or four hundred feet, a frontage broken only by terraces here and there, a complex decorative façade.

That gradual passage of town into country through an extensive sponge of suburbs, which was so characteristic a feature of the great cities of the nineteenth century, existed no longer. Nothing remained of it here but a waste of ruins, variegated and dense with thickets of the heterogeneous growths that had once adorned the gardens of the belt, interspersed among levelled brown patches of sown ground, and verdant stretches of winter greens. The latter even spread among the vestiges of houses. But for the most part the reefs and skerries of ruins, the wreckage of suburban villas, stood among their streets and roads, queer islands amidst the levelled expanses of green and brown, abandoned indeed by the inhabitants years since, but too substantial, it seemed, to be cleared out of the way of the wholesale horticultural mechanisms of the time.

The vegetation of this waste undulated and frothed amidst the countless cells of crumbling house walls, and broke along the foot of the city wall in a surf of bramble and holly and ivy and teazle and tall grasses. Here and there gaudy pleasure palaces towered amidst the puny remains of Victorian times, and cable ways slanted to them from the city. That winter day they seemed deserted. Deserted, too, were the artificial gardens among the ruins. The city limits were indeed as sharply defined as in the ancient days when the gates were shut at nightfall and the robber foeman prowled to the very walls. A huge semi-circular throat poured out a vigorous traffic upon the Eadhamite Bath Road. So the first prospect of the world beyond the city flashed on Graham, and dwindled. And when at last he could look vertically downward again, he saw below him the vegetable fields of the Thames valley – innumerable minute oblongs of ruddy brown, intersected by shining threads, the sewage ditches.

His exhilaration increased rapidly, became a sort of intoxication. He found himself drawing deep breaths of air, laughing aloud, desiring to shout. That desire became too strong for him, and he shouted. They curved about towards the south. They drove with a slight list to leeward, and with a slow alternation of movement, first a short, sharp ascent and then a long downward glide that was very swift and pleasing. During these downward glides the propeller was inactive altogether. These ascents gave Graham a glorious sense of successful effort; the descents through the rarefied air were beyond all experience. He wanted never to leave the upper air again.

For a time he was intent upon the landscape that ran swiftly northward beneath him. Its minute, clear detail pleased him exceedingly.

He was impressed by the ruin of the houses that had once dotted the country, by the vast treeless expanse of country from which all farms and villages had gone, save for crumbling ruins. He had known the thing was so, but seeing it so was an altogether different matter. He tried to make out familiar places within the hollow basin of the world below, but at first he could distinguish no data now that the Thames valley was left behind. Soon, however, they were driving over a sharp chalk hill that he recognized as the Guildford Hog's Back, because of the familiar outline of the gorge at its eastward end, and because of the ruins of the town that rose steeply on either lip of this gorge. And from that he made out other points, Leith Hill, the sandy wastes of Aldershot, and so forth. Save where the broad Eadhamite Portsmouth Road, thickly dotted with rushing shapes, followed the course of the old railway, the gorge of the Wey was choked with thickets.

The whole expanse of the Downs escarpment, so far as the grey haze permitted him to see, was set with wind-wheels to which the largest of the city was but a younger brother. They stirred with a stately motion before the south-west wind. And here and there were patches dotted with the sheep of the British Food Trust, and here and there a mounted shepherd made a spot of black. Then rushing under the stern of the monoplane came the Wealden Heights, the line of Hindhead, Pitch Hill and Leith Hill, with a second row of wind-wheels that seemed striving to rob the downland whirlers of their share of breeze. The purple heather was speckled with yellow gorse, and on the further side a drove of black oxen stampeded before a couple of mounted men. Swiftly these swept behind, and dwindled and lost colour, and became scarce moving specks that were swallowed up in haze.

And when these had vanished in the distance Graham heard a peewit wailing close at hand. He perceived he was now above the South Downs, and staring over his shoulder saw the battlements of Portsmouth Landing Stage towering over the ridge of Portsdown Hill. In another moment there came into sight a spread of shipping like floating cities, the little white cliffs of the Needles dwarfed and sunlit, and the grey and glittering waters of the narrow sea. They seemed to leap the Solent in a moment, and in a few seconds the Isle of Wight was running past; and then beneath him spread a wider and wider extent of sea, here purple with the shadow of a cloud, here grey, here a burnished mirror, and here a spread of cloudy greenish blue. The Isle of Wight grew smaller and smaller. In a few more minutes a strip of grey haze detached itself from other strips that were clouds, descended out of the sky and became a coastline – sunlit and pleasant – the coast of northern France. It rose, it took colour, became definite and detailed, and the counterpart of the Downland of England was speeding by below.

In a little time, as it seemed, Paris came above the horizon, and hung there for a space, and sank out of sight again as the monoplane circled about to the north. But he perceived the Eiffel Tower still standing, and beside it a huge dome surmounted by a pinpoint Colossus. And he perceived, too, though he did not understand it at the time, a slanting drift of smoke. The aeronaut said something about 'trouble in the underways', that Graham did not heed. But he marked the minarets and towers and slender masses that streamed skyward above the city wind-vanes, and knew that in the matter of grace at least Paris still kept in front of her larger rival. And even as he looked˙ a pale-blue shape ascended very swiftly from the city like a dead leaf driving up before a gale. It curved round and soared towards them, growing rapidly larger and larger. The aeronaut was saying something. 'What?' said Graham, loth to take his eyes from this. 'London aeroplane, Sire,' bawled the aeronaut, pointing.

They rose and curved about northward as it drew nearer. Nearer it came and nearer, larger and larger. The throb, throb, throb – beat, of the monoplane's flight, that had seemed so potent and so swift, suddenly appeared slow by comparison with this tremendous rush. How great the monster seemed, how swift and steady! It passed quite closely beneath them, driving along silently, a vast spread of wire-netted translucent wings, a thing alive. Graham had a momentary glimpse of the rows and rows of wrapped-up passengers, slung in their little cradles behind windscreens, of a white-clothed engineer crawling against the gale along a ladder way, of spouting engines beating together, of the whirling wind-screw, and of a wide waste of wing. He exulted in the sight. And in an instant the thing had passed.

It rose slightly and their own little wings swayed in the rush of its flight. It fell and grew smaller. Scarcely had they moved, as it seemed, before it was again only a flat blue thing that dwindled in the sky. This was the aeroplane that went to and fro between London and Paris. In fair weather and in peaceful times it came and went four times a day.

They beat across the Channel, slowly as it seemed now to Graham's enlarged ideas, and Beachy Head rose greyly to the left of them.

'Land,' called the aeronaut, his voice small against the whistling of the air over the windscreen.

'Not yet,' bawled Graham, laughing. 'Not land yet. I want to learn more of this machine.'

'I meant —' said the aeronaut.

'I want to learn more of this machine,' repeated Graham.

'I'm coming to you,' he said, and had flung himself free of his chair and taken a step along the guarded rail between them. He stopped for a moment, and his colour changed and his hands tightened. Another step and he was clinging close to the aeronaut. He felt a weight on his shoulder, the pressure of the air. His hat was a whirling speck behind. The wind came in gusts over his windscreen and blew his hair in streamers past his cheek. The aeronaut made some hasty adjustments for the shifting of the centres of gravity and pressure.

'I want to have these things explained,' said Graham. 'What do you do when you move that engine forward?'

The aeronaut hesitated. Then he answered, 'They are complex, Sire.'

'I don't mind,' shouted Graham. 'I don't mind.'

There was a moment's pause. 'Aeronautics is the secret – the privilege—'

'I know. But I'm the Master, and I mean to know.' He laughed, full of this novel realization of power that was his gift from the upper air.

The monoplane curved about, and the keen fresh wind cut across Graham's face and his garment lugged at his body as the stem pointed round to the west. The two men looked into each other's eyes.

'Sire, there are rules—'

'Not where I am concerned,' said Graham. 'You seem to forget.'

The aeronaut scrutinized his face. 'No,' he said. 'I do not forget, Sire. But in all the earth – no man who is not a sworn aeronaut – has ever a chance. They come as passengers—'

'I have heard something of the sort. But I'm not going to argue these points. Do you know why I have slept two hundred years? To fly!'

'Sire,' said the aeronaut, 'the rules – if I break the rules—'

Graham waved the penalties aside.

'Then if you will watch me—'

'No,' said Graham, swaying and gripping tight as the machine lifted its nose again for an ascent. 'That's not my game. I want to do it myself. Do it myself if I smash for it! No! I will. See I am going to clamber by this – to come and share your seat. Steady! I mean to fly of my own accord if I smash at the end of it. I will have something to pay for my sleep. Of all other things – In my past it was my dream to fly. Now – keep your balance.'

'A dozen spies are watching me, Sire!'

Graham's temper was at end. Perhaps he chose it should be. He swore. He swung himself round the intervening mass of levers and the monoplane swayed.

'Am I Master of the Earth?' he said. 'Or is your Society? Now. Take your hands off those levers, and hold my wrists. Yes – so. And now, how do we turn her nose down to the glide?'

'Sire,' said the aeronaut.

'What is it?'

'You will protect me?'

'Lord! Yes! If I have to burn London. Now!'

And with that promise Graham bought his first lesson in aerial navigation. 'It's clearly to your advantage, this journey,' he said with a loud laugh – for the air was like strong wine – 'to teach me quickly and well. Do I pull this? Ah! So! Hullo!'

'Back, Sire! Back!'

'Back – right. One – two – three – good God! Ah! Up she goes! But this is living!'

And now the machine began to dance the strangest figures in the air. Now it would sweep round a spiral of scarcely a hundred yards diameter, now rush up into the air and swoop down again, steeply, swiftly, falling like a hawk, to recover in a rushing loop that swept it high again. In one of these descents it seemed driving straight at the drifting park of balloons in the south-east, and only curved about and cleared them by a sudden recovery of dexterity. The extraordinary swiftness and smoothness of the motion, the extraordinary effect of the rarefied air upon his constitution, threw Graham into a careless fury.

But at last a queer incident came to sober him, to send him flying down once more to the crowded life below with all its dark insoluble riddles. As he swooped, came a tap and something flying past, and a drop like a drop of rain. Then as he went on down he saw something like a white rag whirling down in his wake. 'What was that?' he asked. 'I did not see.'

The aeronaut glanced, and then clutched at the lever to recover, for they were sweeping down. When the monoplane was rising again he drew a deep breath and replied, 'That,' and he indicated the white thing still fluttering down, 'was a swan.'

'I never saw it,' said Graham.

The aeronaut made no answer, and Graham saw little drops upon his forehead.

They drove horizontally while Graham clambered back to the passenger's place out of the lash of the wind. And then came a swift rush down, with the wind-screw whirling to check their fall, and the flying stage growing broad and dark before them. The sun, sinking over the chalk hills in the west, fell with them, and left the sky a blaze of gold.

Soon men could be seen as little specks. He heard a noise coming up to meet him, a noise like the sound of waves upon a pebbly beach, and saw that the roofs about the flying stage were dense with his people rejoicing over his safe return. A black mass was crushed together under the stage, a darkness stippled with innumerable faces, and quivering with the minute oscillation of waved white handkerchiefs and waving hands.

17

Three Days

Lincoln awaited Graham in an apartment beneath the flying stages. He seemed curious to learn all that had happened, pleased to hear of the extraordinary delight and interest which Graham took in flying. Graham was in a mood of enthusiasm. 'I must learn to fly,' he cried. 'I must master that. I pity all poor souls who have died without this opportunity. The sweet swift air! It is the most wonderful experience in the world.'

'You will find our new times full of wonderful experiences,' said Lincoln. 'I do not know what you will care to do now. We have music that may seem novel.'

'For the present,' said Graham, 'flying holds me. Let me learn more of that. Your aeronaut was saying there is some trades union objection to one's learning.'

'There is, I believe,' said Lincoln. 'But for you – ! If you would like to occupy yourself with that, we can make you a sworn aeronaut tomorrow.'

Graham expressed his wishes vividly and talked of his sensations for a while. 'And as for affairs,' he asked abruptly. 'How are things going on?'

Lincoln waved affairs aside. 'Ostrog will tell you that tomorrow,' he said. 'Everything is settling down. The Revolution accomplishes itself all over the world. Friction is inevitable here and there, of course; but your rule is assured. You may rest secure with things in Ostrog's hands.'

'Would it be possible for me to be made a sworn aeronaut, as you call it, forthwith – before I sleep?' said Graham, pacing. 'Then I could be at it the very first thing tomorrow again.' . . .

'It would be possible,' said Lincoln thoughtfully. 'Quite possible. Indeed, it shall be done.' He laughed. 'I came prepared to suggest amusements, but you have found one for yourself. I will telephone to the aeronautical offices from here and we will return to your apartments in the Wind-Vane Control. By the time you have dined the aeronauts will be able to come. You don't think that after you have dined you might prefer—?' He paused.

'Yes?' said Graham.

'We had prepared a show of dancers – they have been brought from the Capri theatre.'

'I hate ballets,' said Graham, shortly. 'Always did. That other – That's not what I want to see. We had dancers in the old days. For the matter of that, they had them in ancient Egypt. But flying—'

'True,' said Lincoln. 'Though our dancers—'

'They can afford to wait,' said Graham; 'they can afford to wait. I know. I'm not a Latin. There's questions I want to ask some expert – about your machinery. I'm keen. I want no distractions.'

'You have the world to choose from,' said Lincoln: 'whatever you want is yours.'

Asano appeared, and under the escort of a strong guard they returned through the city streets to Graham's apartments. Far larger crowds had assembled to witness his return than his departure had gathered, and the shouts and cheering of these masses of people sometimes drowned Lincoln's answers to the endless questions Graham's aerial journey had suggested. At first Graham had acknowledged the cheering and cries of the crowd by bows and gestures, but Lincoln warned him that such a recognition would be considered incorrect behaviour. Graham, already a little wearied by rhythmic civilities, ignored his subjects for the remainder of his public progress.

Directly they arrived at his apartments Asano departed in search of kinematographic renderings of machinery in motion, and Lincoln despatched Graham's commands for models of machines and small machines to illustrate the various mechanical advances of the last two centuries. The little group of appliances for telegraphic communication attracted the Master so strongly that his delightfully prepared dinner, served by a number of charmingly dexterous girls, waited for a space. The habit of smoking had almost ceased from the face of the earth, but when he expressed a wish for that indulgence, enquiries were made and some excellent cigars were discovered in Florida, and sent to him by pneumatic despatch while the dinner was still in progress. Afterwards came the aeronauts, and a feast of ingenious wonders in the hands of a latter-day engineer. For the time, at any rate, the neat dexterity of counting and numbering machines, building machines, spinning engines, patent doorways, explosive motors, grain and water elevators, slaughterhouse machines and harvesting appliances, was more fascinating to Graham than any bayadère. 'We were savages,' was his refrain, 'we were savages. We were in the stone age – compared with this. . . . And what else have you?'

There came also practical psychologists with some very interesting developments in the art of hypnotism. The names of Milne Bramwell, Fechner, Liebault, William James, Myers and Gurney, he found, bore a value now that would have astonished their contemporaries. Several practical applications of psychology were now in general use; it had largely superseded drugs, antiseptics and anaesthetics in medicine; was employed by almost all who had any need of mental concentration. A real enlargement of human faculty seemed to have been effected in this direction. The feats of 'calculating boys', the wonders, as Graham had been wont to regard them, of mesmerizers, were now within the range of anyone who could afford the services of a skilled hypnotist. Long ago the old examination methods in education had been destroyed by these expedients. Instead of years of study, candidates had substituted a few weeks of trances, and during the trances expert coaches had simply to repeat all the points necessary for adequate answering, adding a suggestion of the post-hypnotic recollection of these points. In process mathematics particularly, this aid had been of singular service; and it was now invariably invoked by such players of chess and games of manual dexterity as were still to be found. In fact all operations conducted under finite rules, of a quasi-mechanical sort that is, were now systematically relieved from the wanderings of imagination and emotion, and brought to an unexampled pitch of accuracy. Little children of the labouring classes, so soon as they were of sufficient age to be hypnotized, were thus converted into beautifully punctual and trustworthy machine-minders, and released forthwith from the long, long thoughts of youth. Aeronautical pupils who gave way to giddiness could be relieved of their imaginary terrors. In every street were hypnotists ready to print permanent memories upon the mind. If anyone desired to remember a name, a series of numbers, a song, or a speech, it could be done by this method; and conversely memories could be effaced, habits removed, and desires eradicated – a sort of psychic surgery was, in fact, in general use. Indignities, humbling experiences, were thus forgotten; widows would obliterate their previous husbands, angry lovers release themselves from their slavery. To graft desires however was still impossible, and the facts of thought transference were yet unsystematized. The psychologists illustrated their expositions with some astounding experiments in mnemonics made through the agency of a troupe of pale-faced children in blue.

Graham, like most of the people of his former time, distrusted the hypnotist, or he might then and there have eased his mind of many painful preoccupations. But in spite of Lincoln's assurances he held to the old theory that to be hypnotized was in some way the surrender of his personality, the abdication of his will. At the banquet of wonderful experiences that was beginning, he wanted very keenly to remain absolutely himself.

The next day, and another day, and yet another day passed in such interests as these. Each morning Graham spent many hours in the glorious entertainment of flying. On the third, he soared across middle France, and within sight of the snow-clad Alps. These vigorous exercises gave him restful sleep; he recovered almost wholly from the spiritless anaemia of his first awakening. And whenever he was not in the air and awake, Lincoln was assiduous in the cause of his amusement; all that was novel and curious in contemporary invention was brought to him, until at last his appetite for novelty was well-nigh glutted. One might fill a dozen inconsecutive volumes with the strange things they exhibited. Each afternoon he held his court for an hour or so. He found his interest in his contemporaries becoming personal and intimate. At first he had been alert chiefly for unfamiliarity and peculiarity; any foppishness in their dress, any discordance with his preconceptions of nobility in their status and manners had jarred upon him, and it was remarkable to him how soon that strangeness and the faint hostility that arose from it, disappeared; how soon he came to appreciate the true perspective of his position, and see the old Victorian days remote and quaint. He was particularly amused by the red-haired daughter of the Manager of the European Piggeries. On the second evening after dinner he made the acquaintance of a latter-day dancing girl, and found her an astonishing artist. And after that, more hypnotic wonders. The third night Lincoln was moved to suggest that the Master should repair to a Pleasure City, but this Graham declined, nor would he accept the services of the hypnotists in his aeronautical experiments. The link of locality held him to London; he found a delight in topographical identifications that he would have missed abroad. 'Here – or a hundred feet below here,' he could say, 'I used to eat my midday cutlets during my London University days. Underneath here was Waterloo and the tiresome hunt for confusing trains. Often have I stood waiting down there, bag in hand, and stared up into the sky above the forest of signals, little thinking I should walk some day a hundred yards in the air. And now in that very sky that was once a grey smoke canopy, I circle in a monoplane.'

Graham was so occupied with these distractions that the vast political movements in progress outside his quarters had but a small share of his attention. Those about him told him little. Daily came Ostrog, the Boss, his Grand Vizier, his mayor of the palace, to report in vague terms the steady establishment of his rule; 'a little trouble' soon to be settled in this city, 'a slight disturbance' in that. The song of the social revolt came to him no more; he never learnt that it had been forbidden in the municipal limits; and all the great emotions of the crow's nest slumbered in his mind.

Presently he found himself, in spite of his interest in the daughter of the Pig Manager, or it may be by reason of the thoughts her conversation suggested, remembering the girl Helen Wotton who had spoken to him so oddly at the wind-vane keeper's gathering. The impression she had made was a deep one, albeit the incessant surprise of novel circumstances had kept him from brooding upon it for a space. But now her memory was coming to its own. He wondered what she had meant by those broken half-forgotten sentences; the picture of her eyes and the earnest passion of her face became more vivid as his mechanical interests faded.

18

Graham Remembers

She came upon him at last in a little gallery that ran from the wind-vane offices towards his state apartments. The gallery was long and narrow, with a series of recesses, each with an arched fenestration that looked upon a court of palms. He came upon her suddenly in one of these recesses. She was seated. She turned her head at the sound of his foot-steps and started at the sight of him. Every touch of colour vanished from her face. She rose instantly, made a step towards him as if to address him, and hesitated. He stopped and stood still, expectant. Then he perceived that a nervous tumult silenced her; perceived, too, that she must have sought speech with him to be waiting for him in this place.

'I have wanted to see you,' he said. 'A few days ago you wanted to tell me something – you wanted to tell me of the people. What was it you had to tell me?'

She looked at him with troubled eyes.

'You said the people were unhappy?'

For a moment she was silent still.

'It must have seemed strange to you,' she said abruptly.

'It did. And yet—'

'It was an impulse.'

'Well?'

'That is all.'

She looked at him with a face of hesitation. She spoke with an effort. 'You forget,' she said, drawing a deep breath.

'What?'

'The people—'

'Do you mean—?'

'You forget the people.'

He looked interrogative.

'Yes. I know you are surprised. For you do not understand what you are. You do not know the things that are happening.'

'Well?'

'You do not understand.'

'Not clearly, perhaps. But – tell me.'

She turned to him with sudden resolution. 'It is so hard to explain. I have meant to, I have wanted to. And now – I cannot. I am not ready with words. But about you – there is something. It is Wonder. Your sleep – your awakening. These things are miracles. To me at least – and to all the common people. You who lived and suffered and died, you who were a common citizen, wake again, live again, to find yourself Master almost of the earth.'

'Master of the Earth,' he said. 'So they tell me. But try and imagine how little I know of it.'

'Cities – Trusts – the Labour Department—'

'Principalities, powers, dominions – the power and the glory. Yes, I have heard them shout. I know. I am Master. King, if you wish. With Ostrog, the Boss—'

He paused.

She turned upon him and surveyed his face with a curious scrutiny. 'Well?'

He smiled. 'To take the responsibility.'

'That is what we have begun to fear.' For a moment she said no more. 'No,' she said slowly. '*You* will take the responsibility. You will take the responsibility. The people look to you.'

She spoke softly. 'Listen! For at least half the years of your sleep – in every generation – multitudes of people, in every generation greater multitudes of people, have prayed that you might awake – *prayed.*'

Graham moved to speak and did not.

She hesitated, and a faint colour crept back to her cheek. 'Do you know that you have been to myriads – King Arthur, Barbarossa – the King who would come in his own good time and put the world right for them?'

'I suppose the imagination of the people—'

'Have you not heard our proverb, "When the Sleeper wakes"? While you lay insensible and motionless there – thousands came. Thousands. Every first of the month you lay in state with a white robe upon you and the people filed by you. When I was a little girl I saw you like that, with your face white and calm.'

She turned her face from him and looked steadfastly at the painted wall before her. Her voice fell. 'When I was a little girl I used to look at your face . . . it seemed to me fixed and waiting, like the patience of God.

'That is what we thought of you,' she said. 'That is how you seemed to us.'

She turned shining eyes to him, her voice was clear and strong. 'In the city, in the earth, a myriad myriad men and women are waiting to see what you will do, full of strange expectations.'

'Yes?'

'Ostrog – no one – can take that responsibility.'

Graham looked at her in surprise, as her face lit with emotion. She seemed at first to have spoken with an effort, and to have fired herself by speaking.

'Do you think,' she said, 'that you who have lived that little life so far away in the past, you who have fallen into and risen out of this miracle of sleep – do you think that the wonder and reverence and hope of half the world has gathered about you only that you may live another little life? . . . That you may shift the responsibility to any other man?'

'I know how great this kingship of mine is,' he said haltingly. 'I know how great it seems. But is it real? It is incredible – dreamlike. Is it real, or is it only a great delusion?'

'It is real,' she said; 'if you dare.'

'After all, like all kingship, my kingship is Belief. It is an illusion in the minds of men.'

'If you dare!' she said.

'But—'

'Countless men,' she said, 'and while it is in their minds – they will obey.'

'But I know nothing. That is what I had in mind. I know nothing. And these others – the Councillors, Ostrog. They are wiser, cooler, they know so much, every detail. And, indeed, what are these miseries of which you speak? What am I to know? Do you mean—'

He stopped blankly.

'I am still hardly more than a girl,' she said. 'But to me the world seems full of wretchedness. The world has altered since your day, altered very strangely. I have prayed that I might see you and tell you these things. The world has changed. As if a canker had seized it – and robbed life of – everything worth having.'

She turned a flushed face upon him, moving suddenly. 'Your days were the days of freedom. Yes – I have thought. I have been made to think, for my life – has not been happy. Men are no longer free – no greater, no better than the men of your time. That is not all. This city – is a prison. Every city now is a prison. Mammon grips the key in his hand. Myriads, countless myriads, toil from the cradle to the grave. Is that right? Is that to be – for ever? Yes, far worse than in your time. All about us, beneath us, sorrow and pain. All the shallow delight of such life as you find about you, is separated by just a little from a life of wretchedness beyond any telling. Yes, the poor know it – they know they suffer. These countless multitudes who faced death for you two nights since–! You owe your life to them.'

'Yes,' said Graham, slowly. 'Yes. I owe my life to them.'

'You come,' she said, 'from the days when this new tyranny of the cities was scarcely beginning. It is a tyranny – a tyranny. In your days the feudal warlords had gone, and the new lordship of wealth had still to come. Half the men in the world still lived out upon the free countryside. The cities had still to devour them. I have heard the stories out of the old books – there was nobility! Common men led lives of love and faithfulness then – they did a thousand things. And you – you come from that time.'

'It was not – But never mind. How is it now—?'

'Gain and the Pleasure Cities! Or slavery – unthanked, unhonoured slavery.'

'Slavery!' he said.

'Slavery.'

'You don't mean to say that human beings are chattels.'

'Worse. That is what I want you to know, what I want you to see. I know you do not know. They will keep things from you, they will take you presently to a Pleasure City. But you have noticed men and women and children in pale-blue canvas, with thin yellow faces and dull eyes?'

'Everywhere.'

'Speaking a horrible dialect, coarse and weak.'

'I have heard it.'

'They are the slaves – your slaves. They are the slaves of the Labour Department you own.'

'The Labour Department! In some way – that is familiar. Ah! now I remember. I saw it when I was wandering about the city, after the lights returned, great fronts of buildings coloured pale blue. Do you really mean—?'

'Yes. How can I explain it to you? Of course the blue uniform struck you. Nearly a third of our people wear it – more assume it now every day. This Labour Department has grown imperceptibly.'

'What *is* this Labour Department?' asked Graham.

'In the old times, how did you manage with starving people?'

'There was the workhouse – which the parishes maintained.'

'Workhouse! Yes – there was something. In our history lessons. I remember now. The Labour Department ousted the workhouse. It grew – partly – out of something – you, perhaps, may remember it – an emotional religious organization called the Salvation Army – that became a business company. In the first place it was almost a charity. To save people from workhouse rigours. There had been a great agitation against the workhouse. Now I come to think of it, it was one of the earliest properties your Trustees acquired. They bought the Salvation Army and reconstructed it as this. The idea in the first place was to organize the labour of starving homeless people.'

'Yes.'

'Nowadays there are no workhouses, no refuges and charities, nothing but that Department. Its offices are everywhere. That blue is its colour. And any man, woman or child who comes to be hungry and weary and with neither home nor friend nor resort, must go to the Department in the end – or seek some way of death. The Euthanasy is beyond their means – for the poor there is no easy death. And at any hour in the day or night there is food, shelter and a blue uniform for all comers – that is the first condition of the Department's incorporation – and in return for a day's shelter the Department extracts a day's work, and then returns the visitor's proper clothing and sends him or her out again.'

'Yes?'

'Perhaps that does not seem so terrible to you. In your time men starved in your streets. That was bad. But they died – *men*. These people in blue – The proverb runs: "Blue canvas once and ever." The Department trades in their labour, and it has taken care to assure itself of the supply. People come to it starving and helpless – they eat and sleep for a night and day, they work for a day, and at the end of the day they go out again. If they have worked well they have a penny or so – enough for a theatre or a cheap dancing place, or a kinematograph story, or a dinner or a bet. They wander about after that is spent. Begging is prevented by the police of the ways. Besides, no one gives. They come back again the next day or the day after – brought back by the same incapacity that brought them first. At last their proper clothing wears out, or their rags get so shabby that they are ashamed. Then they must work for months to get fresh. If they want fresh. A great number of children are born under the Department's care. The mother owes them a month thereafter – the children they cherish and educate until they are fourteen, and they pay two years' service. You

545

may be sure these children are educated for the blue canvas. And so it is the Department works.'

'And none are destitute in the city?'

'None. They are either in blue canvas or in prison. We have abolished destitution. It is engraved upon the Department's checks.'

'If they will not work?'

'Most people will work at that pitch, and the Department has powers. There are stages of unpleasantness in the work – stoppage of food – and a man or woman who has refused to work once is known by a thumb-marking system in the Department's offices all over the world. Besides, who can leave the city poor? To go to Paris costs two lions. And for insubordination there are the prisons – dark and miserable – out of sight below. There are prisons now for many things.'

'And a third of the people wear this blue canvas?'

'More than a third. Toilers, living without pride or delight or hope, with the stories of Pleasure Cities ringing in their ears, mocking their shameful lives, their privations and hardships. Too poor even for the Euthanasy, the rich man's refuge from life. Dumb, crippled millions, countless millions, all the world about, ignorant of anything but limitations and unsatisfied desires. They are born, they are thwarted and they die. That is the state to which we have come.'

For a space Graham sat downcast.

'But there has been a revolution,' he said. 'All these things will be changed. Ostrog—'

'That is our hope. That is the hope of the world. But Ostrog will not do it. He is a politician. To him it seems things must be like this. He does not mind. He takes it for granted. All the rich, all the influential, all who are happy, come at last to take these miseries for granted. They use the people in their politics, they live in ease by their degradation. But you – you who come from a happier age – it is to you the people look. To you.'

He looked at her face. Her eyes were bright with unshed tears. He felt a rush of emotion. For a moment he forgot this city, he forgot the race, and all those vague remote voices, in the immediate humanity of her beauty.

'But what am I to do?' he said with his eyes upon her.

'Rule,' she answered, bending towards him and speaking in a low tone. 'Rule the world as it has never been ruled, for the good and happiness of men. For you might rule it – you could rule it.

'The people are stirring. All over the world the people are stirring. It wants but a word – but a word from you – to bring them all together. Even the middle sort of people are restless – unhappy.

'They are not telling you the things that are happening. The people will not go back to their drudgery – they refuse to be disarmed. Ostrog has awakened something greater than he dreamt of – he has awakened hopes.'

His heart was beating fast. He tried to seem judicial, to weigh considerations.

'They only want their leader,' she said.

'And then?'

'You could do what you would; – the world is yours.'

He sat, no longer regarding her. Presently he spoke. 'The old dreams, and the thing I have dreamt, liberty, happiness. Are they dreams? Could one man – *one man* –?' His voice sank and ceased.

'Not one man, but all men – give them only a leader to speak the desire of their hearts.'

He shook his head, and for a time there was silence.

He looked up suddenly, and their eyes met. 'I have not your faith,' he said, 'I have not your youth. I am here with power that mocks me. No – let me speak. I want to do – not right – I have not the strength for that – but something rather right than wrong. It will bring no millennium, but I am resolved now that I will rule. What you have said has awakened me. . . . You are right. Ostrog must know his place. And I will learn—. . . . One thing I promise you. This Labour slavery shall end.'

'And you will rule?'

'Yes. Provided – There is one thing.'

'Yes?'

'That you will help me.'

'*I* – a girl!'

'Yes. Does it not occur to you I am absolutely alone?'

She started and for an instant her eyes had pity. 'Need you ask whether I will help you?' she said.

'I am very helpless.'

'Father and Master,' she said. 'The world is yours.'

There came a tense silence, and then the beating of a clock striking the hour. Graham rose.

'Even now,' he said, 'Ostrog will be waiting.' He hesitated, facing her. 'When I have asked him certain questions – There is much I do not know. It may be, that I will go to see with my own eyes the things of which you have spoken. And when I return—?'

'I shall know of your going and coming. I will wait for you here again.'

They regarded one another steadfastly, questioningly, and then he turned from her towards the wind-vane office.

19

Ostrog's Point of View

Graham found Ostrog waiting to give a formal account of his day's stewardship. On previous occasions he had passed over this ceremony as speedily as possible, in order to resume his aerial experiences, but now he began to ask quick short questions. He was very anxious to take up his empire forthwith. Ostrog brought flattering reports of the development of affairs abroad. In Paris and Berlin, Graham perceived that he was saying, there had been trouble, not organized resistance indeed, but insubordinate proceedings. 'After all these years,' said Ostrog, when Graham pressed inquiries; 'the Commune has lifted its head again. That is the real nature of the struggle, to be explicit.' But order had been restored in those cities. Graham, the more deliberately judicial for the stirring emotions he felt, asked if there had been any fighting. 'A little,' said Ostrog. 'In one quarter only. But the Senegalese division of our African agricultural police – the Consolidated African Companies have a very well-drilled police – was ready, and so were the aeroplanes. We expected a little trouble in the continental cities, and in America. But things are very quiet in America. They are satisfied with the overthrow of the Council. For the time.'

'Why should you expect trouble?' asked Graham abruptly.

'There is a lot of discontent – social discontent.'

'The Labour Department?'

'You are learning,' said Ostrog with a touch of surprise. 'Yes. It is chiefly the discontent with the Labour Department. It was that discontent supplied the motive force of this overthrow – that and your awakening.'

'Yes?'

Ostrog smiled. He became explicit. 'We had to stir up their discontent, we had to revive the old ideals of universal happiness – all men equal – all men happy – no luxury that everyone may not share – ideas that have slumbered for two hundred years. You know that? We had to revive these ideals, impossible as they are – in order to overthrow the Council. And now—'

'Well?'

'Our revolution is accomplished, and the Council is overthrown, and people whom we have stirred up – remain surging. There was scarcely enough fighting. . . . We made promises, of course. It is extraordinary how violently and rapidly this vague out-of-date humanitarianism has revived and spread. We who sowed the seed even, have been astonished. In Paris, as I say – we have had to call in a little external help.'

'And here?'

'There is trouble. Multitudes will not go back to work. There is a general strike. Half the factories are empty and the people are swarming in the Ways. They are talking of a Commune. Men in silk and satin have been insulted in the streets. The blue canvas is expecting all sorts of things from you. . . . Of course there is no need for you to trouble. We are setting the Babble Machines to work with counter suggestions in the cause of law and order. We must keep the grip tight; that is all.'

Graham thought. He perceived a way of asserting himself. But he spoke with restraint.

'Even to the pitch of bringing a Negro police,' he said.

'They are useful,' said Ostrog. 'They are fine loyal brutes, with no wash of ideas in their heads – such as our rabble has. The Council should have had them as police of the Ways, and things might have been different. Of course, there is nothing to fear except rioting and wreckage. You can manage your own wings now, and you can soar away to Capri if there is any smoke or fuss. We have the pull of all the great things; the aeronauts are privileged and rich, the closest trades union in the world, and so are the engineers of the wind-vanes. We have the air, and the mastery of the air is the mastery of the earth. No one of any ability is organizing against us. They have no leaders – only the sectional leaders of the secret society we organized before your very opportune awakening. Mere busybodies and sentimentalists they are, and bitterly jealous of each other. None of them is man enough for a central figure. The only trouble will be a disorganized upheaval. To be frank – that may happen. But it won't interrupt your aeronautics. The days when the People could make revolutions are past.'

'I suppose they are,' said Graham. 'I suppose they are.' He mused.

'This world of yours has been full of surprises to me. In the old days we dreamt of a wonderful democratic life, of a time when all men would be equal and happy.'

Ostrog looked at him steadfastly. 'The day of democracy is past,' he said. 'Past for ever. That day began with the bowmen of Crécy, it ended when marching infantry, when common men in masses ceased to win the battles of the world, when costly cannon, great ironclads, and strategic railways became the means of power. Today is the day of wealth. Wealth now is power as it never was power before – it commands earth and sea and sky. All power is for those who can handle wealth. On your behalf. . . . You must accept facts, and these are facts. The world for the Crowd! The Crowd as Ruler! Even in your days that creed had been tried and condemned. Today it has only one believer – a multiplex, silly one – the man in the Crowd.'

Graham did not answer immediately. He stood lost in sombre preoccupations.

'No,' said Ostrog. The day of the common man is past. On the open countryside one man is as good as another, or nearly as good. The earlier aristocracy had a precarious tenure of strength and audacity. They were tempered – tempered. There were insurrections, duels, riots. The first real aristocracy, the first permanent aristocracy, came in with castles and armour, and vanished before the musket and bow. But this is the second aristocracy. The real one. Those days of gunpowder and democracy were only an eddy in the stream. The common man now is a helpless unit. In these days we have this great machine of the city, and an organization complex beyond his understanding.'

'Yet,' said Graham, 'there is something resists, something you are holding down – something that stirs and presses.'

'You will see,' said Ostrog, with a forced smile that would brush these difficult questions aside. 'I have not roused the force to destroy myself – trust me.'

'I wonder,' said Graham.

Ostrog stared.

'*Must* the world go this way?' said Graham with his emotions at the speaking point. 'Must it indeed go in this way? Have all our hopes been vain?'

'What do you mean?' said Ostrog. 'Hopes?'

'I come from a democratic age. And I find an aristocratic tyranny!'

'Well, – but you are the chief tyrant.'

Graham shook his head.

'Well,' said Ostrog, 'take the general question. It is the way that change has always travelled. Aristocracy, the prevalence of the best –

the suffering and extinction of the unfit, and so to better things.'

'But aristocracy! those people I met—'

'Oh! not *those*!' said Ostrog. 'But for the most part they go to their death. Vice and pleasure! They have no children. That sort of stuff will die out. If the world keeps to one road, that is, if there is no turning back. An easy road to excess, convenient Euthanasia for the pleasure-seekers singed in the flame, that is the way to improve the race!'

'Pleasant extinction,' said Graham. 'Yet —' He thought for an instant. 'There is that other thing – the Crowd, the great mass of poor men. Will that die out? That will not die out. And it suffers, its suffering is a force that even you—'

Ostrog moved impatiently, and when he spoke, he spoke rather less evenly than before.

'Don't trouble about these things,' he said. 'Everything will be settled in a few days now. The Crowd is a huge foolish beast. What if it does not die out? Even if it does not die, it can still be tamed and driven. I have no sympathy with servile men. You heard those people shouting and singing two nights ago. They were *taught* that song. If you had taken any man there in cold blood and asked why he shouted, he could not have told you. They think they are shouting for you, that they are loyal and devoted to you. Just then they were ready to slaughter the Council. Today – they are already murmuring against those who have overthrown the Council.'

'No, no,' said Graham. 'They shouted because their lives were dreary, without joy or pride, and because in me – in me – they hoped.'

'And what was their hope? What is their hope? What right have they to hope? They work ill and they want the reward of those who work well. The hope of mankind – what is it? That some day the Over-man may come, that some day the inferior, the weak and the bestial may be subdued or eliminated. Subdued if not eliminated. The world is no place for the bad, the stupid, the enervated. Their duty – it's a fine duty too! – is to die. The death of the failure! That is the path by which the beast rose to manhood, by which man goes on to higher things.'

Ostrog took a pace, seemed to think, and turned on Graham. 'I can imagine how this great world state of ours seems to a Victorian Englishman. You regret all the old forms of representative government – their spectres still haunt the world, the voting councils and parliaments and all that eighteenth-century tomfoolery. You feel moved against our Pleasure Cities. I might have thought of that, – had I not been busy. But you will learn better. The people are mad with envy – they would be in sympathy with you. Even in the streets now, they clamour to destroy the Pleasure Cities. But the Pleasure Cities are the excretory organs of the State, attractive places that year after year draw together all that is weak and vicious, all that is lascivious and lazy, all the easy roguery of the world, to a graceful destruction. They go there, they have their time, they die childless, all the pretty silly lascivious women die childless, and mankind is the better. If the people were sane they would not envy the rich their way of death. And you would emancipate the silly brainless workers that we have enslaved, and try to make their lives easy and pleasant again. Just as they have sunk to what they are fit for.' He smiled a smile that irritated Graham oddly. 'You will learn better. I know those ideas; in my boyhood I read your Shelley and dreamt of Liberty. There is no liberty save wisdom and self-control. Liberty is within – not without. It is each man's own affair. Suppose – which is impossible – that these swarming yelping fools in blue get the upper hand of us, what then? They will only fall to other masters. So long as there are sheep Nature will insist on beasts of prey. It would mean but a few hundred years' delay. The coming of the aristocrat is fatal and assured. The end will be the Over-man – for all the mad protests of humanity. Let them revolt, let them win and kill me and my like. Others will arise – other masters. The end will be the same.'

'I wonder,' said Graham doggedly.

For a moment he stood downcast.

'But I must see these things for myself,' he said, suddenly assuming a tone of confident mastery. 'Only by seeing can I understand. I must learn. That is what I want to tell you, Ostrog. I do not want to be King in a Pleasure City; that is not my pleasure. I have spent enough time with aeronautics – and those other things. I must learn how people live now, how the common life has developed. Then I shall understand these things better. I must learn how common people live – the labour people more especially – how they work, marry, bear children, die—'

'You get that from our realistic novelists,' suggested Ostrog, suddenly preoccupied.

'I want reality,' said Graham.

'There are difficulties,' said Ostrog, and thought. 'On the whole —

'I did not expect—

'I had thought – And yet perhaps – You say you want to go through the Ways of the city and see the common people.'

Suddenly he came to some conclusion. 'You would need to go disguised,' he said. 'The city is intensely excited, and the discovery of your presence among them might create a fearful tumult. Still this wish of yours to go into this city – this idea of yours – Yes, now I think the thing over, it seems to me not altogether – It can be contrived. If you would really find an interest in that! You are, of course, Master. You can go soon if you like. Asano will be able to manage a disguise. He would go with you. After all it is not a bad idea of yours.'

'You will not want to consult me in any matter?' asked Graham suddenly, struck by an odd suspicion.

'Oh, dear, no! No! I think you may trust affairs to me for a time, at any rate,' said Ostrog, smiling. 'Even if we differ—'

Graham glanced at him sharply.

'There is no fighting likely to happen soon?' he asked abruptly.

'Certainly not.'

'I have been thinking about those Negroes. I don't believe the people intend any hostility to me, and after all I am the Master. I do not want any Negroes brought to London. It is an archaic prejudice perhaps, but I have peculiar feelings about Europeans and the subject races. Even about Paris—'

Ostrog stood watching him from under his drooping brows. 'I am not bringing Negroes to London,' he said slowly. 'But if—'

'You are not to bring armed Negroes to London, whatever happens,' said Graham. 'In that matter I am quite decided.'

Ostrog bowed deferentially.

20

In the City Ways

And that night, unknown and unsuspected, Graham, dressed in the costume of an inferior wind-vane official keeping holiday and accompanied by Asano in Labour Department canvas, surveyed the city through which he had wandered when it was veiled in darkness. But now he saw it lit and waking, a whirlpool of life. In spite of the surging and swaying of the forces of revolution, in spite of the unusual discontent, the mutterings of the greater struggle of which the first revolt was but the prelude, the myriad streams of commerce still flowed wide and strong. He knew now something of the dimensions and quality of the new age, but he was not prepared for the infinite surprise of the detailed view, for the torrent of colour and vivid impressions that poured past him.

This was his first real contact with the people of these latter days. He realized that all that had gone before, saving his glimpses of the public theatres and markets, had had its element of seclusion, had been a movement within the comparatively narrow political quarter, that all his previous experiences had revolved immediately about the question of his own position. But here was the city at the busiest hours of night, the people to a large extent returned to their own immediate interests, the resumption of the real informal life, the common habits of the new time.

They emerged at first into a street whose opposite ways were crowded with the blue canvas liveries. This swarm Graham saw was a portion of a procession – it was odd to see a procession parading the city *seated.* They carried banners of coarse black stuff with red letters. 'No disarmament,' said the banners, for the most part in crudely daubed letters and with variant spelling, and 'Why should we disarm?' 'No disarming.' 'No disarming.' Banner after banner went by, a stream of banners flowing past, and at last at the end, the song of the revolt and a noisy band of strange instruments. 'They all ought to be at work,' said Asano. 'They have had no food these two days, or they have stolen it.'

Presently Asano made a detour to avoid the congested crowd that gaped upon the occasional passage of dead bodies from hospital to a mortuary, the gleanings after death's harvest of the first revolt.

That night few people were sleeping, everyone was abroad. A vast excitement, perpetual crowds perpetually changing, surrounded Graham; his mind was confused and darkened by an incessant tumult, by the cries and enigmatical fragments of the social struggle that was as yet only beginning. Everywhere festoons and banners of black and strange decorations, intensified the impression of his popularity. Everywhere he caught snatches of that crude thick dialect that served the illiterate class, the class, that is, beyond the reach of phonograph culture, in their commonplace intercourse. Everywhere this trouble of disarmament was in the air, with a quality of immediate stress of which he had had no inkling during his seclusion in the wind-vane quarter. He perceived that as soon as he returned he must discuss this with Ostrog, this and the greater issues of which it was the expression, in a far more conclusive way than he had so far done. Throughout that night, even in the earlier hours of their wanderings about the city, the spirit of unrest and revolt swamped his attention to the exclusion of countless strange things he might otherwise have observed.

This preoccupation made his impressions fragmentary. Yet amidst so much that was strange and vivid, no subject, however personal and insistent, could exert undivided sway. There were spaces when the revolutionary movement passed clean out of his mind, was drawn aside like a curtain from before some startling new aspect of the time. Helen had swayed his mind to this intense earnestness of inquiry, but there came times when she, even, receded beyond his conscious thoughts. At one moment, for example, he found they were traversing the religious quarter, for the easy transit about the city afforded by the moving ways rendered sporadic churches and chapels no longer necessary – and his attention was arrested by the façade of one of the Christian sects.

They were travelling seated on one of the swift upper ways, the place leapt upon them at a bend and advanced rapidly towards them. It was covered with inscriptions from top to base, in vivid white and blue, save where a coarse and glaring kinematograph transparency presented a realistic New Testament scene, and where a vast festoon of black to show that the popular religion followed the popular politics, hung across the lettering. Graham had already become familiar with the phonotype writing and these inscriptions arrested him, being to his sense for the most part almost incredible blasphemy. Among the less offensive were 'Salvation on the First Floor and turn to the Right.' 'Put your Money on your Maker.' 'The Sharpest Conversion in London, Expert Operators! Look Slippy!' 'What Christ would say to the Sleeper; – Join the Up-to-date Saints!' 'Be a Christian – without hindrance to your present Occupation.' 'All the Brightest Bishops on the Bench tonight and Prices as Usual.' 'Brisk Blessings for Busy Businessmen.'

'But this is appalling!' said Graham, as that deafening scream of mercantile piety towered above them.

'What is appalling?' asked his little officer, apparently seeking vainly for anything unusual in this shrieking enamel.

'*This*! Surely the essence of religion is reverence.'

'Oh *that*!' Asano looked at Graham. 'Does it shock you?' he said in the tone of one who makes a discovery. 'I suppose it would, of course. I had forgotten. Nowadays the competition for attention is so keen, and people simply haven't the leisure to attend to their souls, you know, as they used to do.' He smiled. 'In the old days you had quiet Sabbaths and the countryside. Though somewhere I've read of Sunday afternoons that—'

'But *that*,' said Graham, glancing back at the receding blue and white. 'That is surely not the only—'

'There are hundreds of different ways. But of course if a sect doesn't *tell* it doesn't pay. Worship has moved with the times. There are high-class sects with quieter ways – costly incense and personal attentions and all that. These people are extremely popular and prosperous. They pay several dozen lions for those apartments to the Council – to you, I should say.'

Graham still felt a difficulty with the coinage, and this mention of a dozen lions brought him abruptly to that matter. In a moment the screaming temples and their swarming touts were forgotten in this new interest. A turn of a phrase suggested, and an answer confirmed the idea that gold and silver were both demonetized, that stamped gold which had begun its reign amidst the merchants of Phoenicia was at last dethroned. The change had been graduated but swift, brought about by an extension of the system of cheques that had even in his previous life already practically superseded gold in all the larger business transactions. The common traffic of the city, the common currency indeed of all the world, was conducted by means of the little brown, green and pink council cheques for small amounts, printed with a blank payee. Asano had several with him, and at the first opportunity he supplied the gaps in his set. They were printed not on tearable paper but on a semi-transparent fabric of silken flexibility, interwoven with silk. Across them all sprawled a facsimile of Graham's signature, his first encounter with the curves and turns of that familiar autograph for two hundred and three years.

Some intermediary experiences made no impression sufficiently vivid to prevent the matter of the disarmament claiming his thoughts again; a blurred picture of a Theosophist temple that promised MIR-ACLES in enormous letters of unsteady fire was least submerged perhaps, but then came the view of the dining hall in Northumberland Avenue. That interested him very greatly.

By the energy and thought of Asano he was able to view this place from a little screened gallery reserved for the attendants of the tables. The building was pervaded by a distant muffled hooting, piping and bawling of which he did not at first understand the import, but which recalled a certain mysterious leathery voice he had heard after the resumption of the lights on the night of his solitary wandering.

He had grown accustomed to vastness and great numbers of people, nevertheless this spectacle held him for a long time. It was as he watched the table service more immediately beneath, and interspersed with many questions and answers concerning details, that the real-ization of the full significance of the feast of several thousand people came to him.

It was his constant surprise to find that points that one might have expected to strike vividly at the very outset never occurred to him until some trivial detail suddenly shaped as a riddle and pointed to the obvious thing he had overlooked. He discovered only now that this continuity of the city, this exclusion of weather, these vast halls and ways, involved the disappearance of the household; that the typical Victorian 'Home', the little brick cell containing kitchen and scullery, living rooms and bedrooms, had, save for the ruins that diversified the countryside, vanished as surely as the wattle hut. But now he saw what had indeed been manifest from the first, that London, regarded as a living place, was no longer an aggregation of houses but a prodigious hotel, an hotel with a thousand classes of accommodation, thousands of dining halls, chapels, theatres, markets and places of assembly, a synthesis of enterprises, of which he chiefly was the owner. People had their sleeping rooms, with, it might be, antechambers, rooms that were always sanitary at least whatever their degree of comfort and privacy, and for the rest they lived much as many people had lived in the new-made giant hotels of the Victorian days, eating, reading, thinking, playing, conversing, all in places of public resort, going to their work in the industrial quarters of the city or doing business in their offices in the trading section.

He perceived at once how necessarily this state of affairs had developed from the Victorian city. The fundamental reason for the modern city had ever been the economy of co-operation. The chief thing to prevent the merging of the separate households in his own generation was simply the still imperfect civilization of the people, the strong barbaric pride, passions and prejudices, the jealousies, rivalries and violence of the middle and lower classes, which had necessitated the entire separation of contiguous households. But the change, the taming of the people, had been in rapid progress even then. In his brief thirty years of previous life he had seen an enormous extension of the habit of consuming meals from home, the casually patronized horse-box coffee-house had given place to the open and crowded Aërated Bread Shop for instance, women's clubs had had their beginning, and an immense development of reading rooms, lounges and libraries had witnessed to the growth of social confidence. Those promises had by this time attained to their complete fulfilment. The locked and barred household had passed away.

These people below him belonged, he learnt, to the lower middle class, the class just above the blue labourers, a class so accustomed in the Victorian period to feed with every precaution of privacy that its members, when occasion confronted them with a public meal, would usually hide their embarrassment under horseplay or a markedly militant demeanour. But these gaily, if lightly dressed people below, albeit vivacious, hurried and uncommunicative, were dexterously mannered and certainly quite at their ease with regard to one another.

He noted a slight significant thing; the table, as far as he could see, was and remained delightfully neat, there was nothing to parallel the confusion, the broadcast crumbs, the splashes of viand and condiment, the overturned drink and displaced ornaments, which would have marked the stormy progress of the Victorian meal. The table furniture was very different. There were no ornaments, no flowers, and the table was without a cloth, being made, he learnt, of a solid substance having the texture and appearance of damask. He discerned that this damask substance was patterned with gracefully designed trade advertisements.

In a sort of recess before each diner was a complex apparatus of porcelain and metal. There was one plate of white porcelain, and by means of taps for hot and cold volatile fluids the diner washed this himself between the courses; he also washed his elegant white metal knife and fork and spoon as occasion required.

Soup and the chemical wine that was the common drink were delivered by similar taps, and the remaining covers travelled automatically in tastefully arranged dishes down the table along silver rails. The diner stopped these and helped himself at his discretion. They appeared at a little door at one end of the table, and vanished at the other. That democratic sentiment in decay, that ugly pride of menial souls which renders equals loth to wait on one another, was very strong he found among these people. He was so preoccupied with these details that it was only as he was leaving the place that he remarked the huge advertisement dioramas that marched majestically along the upper walls and proclaimed the most remarkable commodities.

Beyond this place they came into a crowded hall, and he discovered the cause of the noise that had perplexed him. They paused at a turnstile at which a payment was made.

Graham's attention was immediately arrested by a violent, loud hoot, followed by a vast leathery voice. 'The Master is sleeping peacefully,' it vociferated. 'He is in excellent health. He is going to devote the rest of his life to aeronautics. He says women are more beautiful than ever. Galloop! Wow! Our wonderful civilization astonishes him beyond measure. Beyond all measure. Galloop. He puts great trust in Boss Ostrog, absolute confidence in Boss Ostrog. Ostrog is to be his chief minister; is authorized to remove or reinstate public officers – all patronage will be in his hands. All patronage in the hands of Boss Ostrog! The Councillors have been sent back to their own prison above the Council House.'

Graham stopped at the first sentence, and, looking up, beheld a foolish trumpet face from which this was brayed. This was the General Intelligence Machine. For a space it seemed to be gathering breath, and a regular throbbing from its cylindrical body was audible. Then it trumpeted 'Galloop, Galloop,' and broke out again.

'Paris is now pacified. All resistance is over. Galloop! The black police hold every position of importance in the city. They fought with great bravery, singing songs written in praise of their ancestors by the poet Kipling. Once or twice they got out of hand, and tortured and mutilated wounded and captured insurgents, men and women. Moral – don't go rebelling. Haha! Galloop, Galloop! They are lively fellows. Lively brave fellows. Let this be a lesson to the disorderly banderlog of this city. Yah! Banderlog! Filth of the earth! Galloop, Galloop!'

The voice ceased. There was a confused murmur of disapproval among the crowd. 'Damned niggers.' A man began to harangue near them. 'Is this the Master's doing, brothers? Is this the Master's doing?'

'Black police!' said Graham. 'What is that? You don't mean—'

Asano touched his arm and gave him a warning look, and forthwith another of these mechanisms screamed deafeningly and gave tongue in a shrill voice. 'Yahaha, Yahah, Yap! Hear a live paper yelp! Live paper. Yaha! Shocking outrage in Paris. Yahahah! The Parisians exasperated by the black police to the pitch of assassination. Dreadful reprisals. Savage times come again. Blood! Blood! Yaha!' The nearer Babble Machine hooted stupendously, 'Galloop, Galloop,' drowned the end of the sentence, and proceeded in a rather flatter note than before with novel comments on the horrors of disorder. 'Law and order must be maintained,' said the nearer Babble Machine.

'But,' began Graham.

'Don't ask questions here,' said Asano, 'or you will be involved in an argument.'

'Then let us go on,' said Graham, 'for I want to know more of this.'

As he and his companion pushed their way through the excited crowd that swarmed beneath these voices, towards the exit, Graham conceived more clearly the proportion and features of this room. Altogether, great and small, there must have been nearly a thousand of these erections, piping, hooting, bawling, and gabbling in that great space, each with its crowd of excited listeners, the majority of them men dressed in blue canvas. There were all sizes of machines, from the little gossiping mechanisms that chuckled out mechanical sarcasm in odd corners, through a number of grades to such fifty-foot giants as that which had first hooted over Graham.

This place was unusually crowded because of the intense public interest in the course of affairs in Paris. Evidently the struggle had been much more savage than Ostrog had represented it. All the mechanisms were discoursing upon that topic, and the repetition of the people made the huge hive buzz with such phrases as 'Lynched policemen,' 'Women burnt alive,' 'Fuzzy Wuzzy.' 'But does the Master allow such things?' asked a man near him. 'Is *this* the beginning of the Master's rule?'

Is *this* the beginning of the Master's rule? For a long time after he had left the place, the hooting, whistling and braying of the machines pursued him; 'Galloop, Galloop,' 'Yahahah, Yaha, Yap! Yaha!' Is *this* the beginning of the Master's rule?

Directly they were out upon the ways he began to question Asano closely on the nature of the Parisian struggle. 'This disarmament! What was their trouble? What does it all mean?' Asano seemed chiefly anxious to reassure him that it was 'all right'. 'But these outrages!' 'You cannot have an omelette,' said Asano, 'without breaking eggs. It is only the rough people. Only in one part of the city. All the rest is all right. The Parisian labourers are the wildest in the world, except ours.'

'What! the Londoners?'

'No, the Japanese. They have to be kept in order.'

'But burning women alive!'

'A Commune!' said Asano. 'They would rob you of your property. They would do away with property and give the world over to mob rule. You are Master, the world is yours. But there will be no Commune here. There is no need for black police here.

'And every consideration has been shown. It is their own Negroes – French-speaking Negroes. Senegal regiments, and Niger and Timbuctoo.'

'Regiments?' said Graham, 'I thought there was only one—'

'No,' said Asano, and glanced at him. 'There is more than one.'

Graham felt unpleasantly helpless.

'I did not think,' he began and stopped abruptly. He went off at a tangent to ask for information about these Babble Machines. For the most part, the crowd present had been shabbily or even raggedly dressed, and Graham learnt that so far as the more prosperous classes were concerned, in all the more comfortable private apartments of the city were fixed Babble Machines that would speak directly a lever was pulled. The tenant of the apartment could connect this with the cables of any of the great News Syndicates that he preferred. When he learnt this presently, he demanded the reason of their absence from his own suite of apartments. Asano was embarrassed. 'I never thought,' he said. 'Ostrog must have had them removed.'

Graham stared. 'How was I to know?' he exclaimed.

'Perhaps he thought they would annoy you,' said Asano.

'They must be replaced directly I return,' said Graham after an interval.

He found a difficulty in understanding that this newsroom and the dining hall were not great central places, that such establishments were repeated almost beyond counting all over the city. But ever and again during the night's expedition his ears would pick out from the tumult of the ways the peculiar hooting of the organ of Boss Ostrog, 'Galloop, Galloop!' or the shrill 'Yahaha, Yaha Yap! – Hear a live paper yelp!' of its chief rival.

Repeated, too, everywhere, were such *crèches* as the one he now entered. It was reached by a lift, and by a glass bridge that flung across the dining hall and traversed the ways at a slight upward angle. To enter the first section of the place necessitated the use of his solvent signature under Asano's direction. They were immediately attended to by a man in a violet robe and gold clasp, the insignia of practising medical men. He perceived from this man's manner that his identity was known, and proceeded to ask questions on the strange arrangements of the place without reserve.

On either side of the passage, which was silent and padded, as if to deaden the footfall, were narrow little doors, their size and arrangement suggestive of the cells of a Victorian prison. But the upper portion of each door was of the same greenish transparent stuff that had enclosed him at his awakening, and within, dimly seen, lay in every case a very young baby in a little nest of wadding. Elaborate apparatus watched the atmosphere and rang a bell far away in the central office at the slightest departure from the optimum of temperature and moisture. A system of such *crèches* had almost entirely replaced the hazardous adventures of the old-world nursing. The attendant presently called Graham's attention to the wet nurses, a vista of mechanical figures, with arms, shoulders and breasts of astonishingly realistic modelling, articulation and texture, but mere brass tripods below, and having in the place of features a flat disc bearing advertisements likely to be of interest to mothers.

Of all the strange things that Graham came upon that night, none jarred more upon his habits of thought than this place. The spectacle of the little pink creatures, their feeble limbs swaying uncertainly in vague first movements, left alone, without embrace or endearment, was wholly repugnant to him. The attendant doctor was of a different opinion. His statistical evidence showed beyond dispute that in the Victorian times the most dangerous passage of life was the arms of the mother, that there human mortality had ever been most terrible. On the other hand this *crèche* company, the International Crèche Syndicate, lost not one-half per cent of the million babies or so that formed its peculiar care. But Graham's prejudice was too strong even for those figures.

Along one of the many passages of the place they presently came upon a young couple in the usual blue canvas peering through the transparency and laughing hysterically at the bald head of their first-born. Graham's face must have showed his estimate of them, for their merriment ceased and they looked abashed. But this little incident accentuated his sudden realization of the gulf between his habits of thought and the ways of the new age. He passed on to the crawling rooms and the Kindergarten, perplexed and distressed. He found the endless long playrooms were empty! the latter-day children at least still spent their nights in sleep. As they went through these, the little officer pointed out the nature of the toys, developments of those devised by that inspired sentimentalist Froebel. There were nurses here, but much was done by machines that sang and danced and dandled.

Graham was still not clear upon many points. 'But so many orphans,' he said perplexed, reverting to a first misconception, and learnt again that they were not orphans.

So soon as they had left the *crèche* he began to speak of the horror the babies in their incubating cases had caused him. 'Is motherhood gone?' he said. 'Was it a cant? Surely it was an instinct. This seems so unnatural – abominable almost.'

'Along here we shall come to the dancing place,' said Asano by way of reply. 'It is sure to be crowded. In spite of all the political unrest it will be crowded. The women take no great interest in politics – except a few here and there. You will see the mothers – most young women in London are mothers. In that class it is considered a creditable thing to have one child – a proof of animation. Few middle-class people have more than one. With the Labour Department it is different. As for motherhood! They still take an immense pride in the children. They come here to look at them quite often.'

'Then do you mean that the population of the world—?'

'Is falling? Yes. Except among the people under the Labour Department. In spite of scientific discipline they are reckless—'

The air was suddenly dancing with music, and down a way they approached obliquely, set with gorgeous pillars as it seemed of clear amethyst, flowed a concourse of gay people and a tumult of merry cries and laughter. He saw curled heads, wreathed brows, and a happy intricate flutter of gamboge pass triumphant across the picture.

'You will see,' said Asano with a faint smile. 'The world has changed. In a moment you will see the mothers of the new age. Come this way. We shall see those yonder again very soon.'

They ascended a certain height in a swift lift, and changed to a slower one. As they went on the music grew upon them, until it was near and full and splendid, and, moving with its glorious intricacies they could distinguish the beat of innumerable dancing feet. They made a payment at a turnstile and emerged upon the wide gallery that overlooked the dancing place, and upon the full enchantment of sound and sight.

'Here,' said Asano, 'are the fathers and mothers of the little ones you saw.'

The hall was not so richly decorated as that of the Atlas, but saving that, it was, for its size, the most splendid Graham had seen. The beautiful white-limbed figures that supported the galleries reminded him once more of the restored magnificence of sculpture; they seemed to writhe in engaging attitudes, their faces laughed. The source of the music that filled the place was hidden, and the whole vast shining floor was thick with dancing couples. 'Look at them,' said the little officer, 'see how much they show of motherhood.'

The gallery they stood upon ran along the upper edge of a huge screen that cut the dancing hall on one side from a sort of outer hall that showed through broad arches the incessant onward rush of the city ways. In this outer hall was a great crowd of less brilliantly dressed people, as numerous almost as those who danced within, the great majority wearing the blue uniform of the Labour Department that was now so familiar to Graham. Too poor to pass the turnstiles to the festival, they were yet unable to keep away from the sound of its seductions. Some of them even had cleared spaces, and were dancing also, fluttering their rags in the air. Some shouted as they danced, jests and odd allusions Graham did not understand. Once someone began whistling the refrain of the revolutionary song, but it seemed as though that beginning was promptly suppressed. The corner was dark and Graham could not see. He turned to the hall again. Above the caryatidae were marble busts of men whom that age esteemed great moral emancipators and pioneers; for the most part their names were strange to Graham, though he recognized Grant Allen, Le Gallienne, Nietzsche, Shelley and Godwin. Great black festoons and eloquent sentiments reinforced the huge inscription that partially defaced the upper end of the dancing place, and asserted that 'The Festival of the Awakening' was in progress.

'Myriads are taking holiday or staying from work because of that, quite apart from the labourers who refuse to go back,' said Asano. 'These people are always ready for holidays.'

Graham walked to the parapet and stood leaning over, looking down at the dancers. Save for two or three remote whispering couples, who had stolen apart, he and his guide had the gallery to themselves. A warm breath of scent and vitality came up to him. Both men and women below were lightly clad, bare-armed, open-necked, as the universal warmth of the city permitted. The hair of the men was often a mass of effeminate curls, their chins were always shaven, and many of them had flushed or coloured cheeks. Many of the women were very pretty, and all were dressed with elaborate coquetry. As they swept by beneath, he saw ecstatic faces with eyes half closed in pleasure.

'What sort of people are these?' he asked abruptly.

'Workers – prosperous workers. What you would have called the middle class. Independent tradesmen with little separate businesses have vanished long ago, but there are store servers, managers, engineers of a hundred sorts. Tonight is a holiday of course, and every dancing place in the city will be crowded, and every place of worship.'

'But – the women?'

'The same. There's a thousand forms of work for women now. But you had the beginning of the independent working-woman in your days. Most women are independent now. Most of these are married more or less – there are a number of methods of contract – and that gives them more money, and enables them to enjoy themselves.'

'I see,' said Graham, looking at the flushed faces, the flash and swirl of movement, and still thinking of that nightmare of pink helpless limbs. 'And these are – mothers.'

'Most of them.'

'The more I see of these things the more complex I find your problems. This, for instance, is a surprise. That news from Paris was a surprise.'

In a little while he spoke again:

'These are mothers. Presently, I suppose, I shall get into the modern way of seeing things. I have old habits of mind clinging about me – habits based, I suppose, on needs that are over and done with. Of course, in our time, a woman was supposed not only to bear children, but to cherish them, to devote herself to them, to educate them – all the essentials of moral and mental education a child owed its mother. Or went without. Quite a number, I admit, went without. Nowadays, clearly, there is no more need for such care than if they were butterflies. I see that! Only there was an ideal – that figure of a grave, patient woman, silently and serenely mistress of a home, mother and maker of men – to love her was a sort of worship—'

He stopped and repeated, 'A sort of worship.'

'Ideals change,' said the little man, 'as needs change.'

Graham awoke from an instant reverie and Asano repeated his words. Graham's mind returned to the thing at hand.

'Of course I see the perfect reasonableness of this. Restraint, soberness, the matured thought, the unselfish act, they are necessities of the barbarous state, the life of dangers. Dourness is man's tribute to unconquered nature. But man has conquered nature now for all practical purposes – his political affairs are managed by Bosses with a black police – and life is joyous.'

He looked at the dancers again. 'Joyous,' he said.

'There are weary moments,' said the little officer, reflectively.

565

'They all look young. Down there I should be visibly the oldest man. And in my own time I should have passed as middle-aged.'

'They are young. There are few old people in this class in the work cities.'

'How is that?'

'Old people's lives are not so pleasant as they used to be, unless they are rich to hire lovers and helpers. And we have an institution called Euthanasy.'

'Ah! that Euthanasy!' said Graham. 'The easy death?'

'The easy death. It is the last pleasure. The Euthanasy Company does it well. People will pay the sum – it is a costly thing – long beforehand, go off to some Pleasure City and return impoverished and weary, very weary.'

'There is a lot left for me to understand,' said Graham after a pause. 'Yet I see the logic of it all. Our array of angry virtues and sour restraints was the consequence of danger and insecurity. The Stoic, the Puritan, even in my time, were vanishing types. In the old days man was armed against Pain, now he is eager for Pleasure. There lies the difference. Civilization has driven pain and danger so far off – for well-to-do people. And only well-to-do people matter now. I have been asleep two hundred years.'

For a minute they leant on the balustrading, following the intricate evolution of the dance. Indeed the scene was very beautiful.

'Before God,' said Graham, suddenly, 'I would rather be a wounded sentinel freezing in the snow than one of these painted fools!'

'In the snow,' said Asano, 'one might think differently.'

'I am uncivilized,' said Graham, not heeding him. 'That is the trouble. I am primitive – Palaeolithic. *Their* fountain of rage and fear and anger is sealed and closed, the habits of a lifetime make them cheerful and easy and delightful. You must bear with my nineteenth-century shocks and disgusts. These people, you say, are skilled workers and so forth. And while these dance, men are fighting – men are dying in Paris to keep the world – that they may dance.'

Asano smiled faintly. 'For that matter, men are dying in London,' he said.

There was a moment's silence.

'Where do these sleep?' asked Graham.

'Above and below – an intricate warren.'

'And where do they work? This is – the domestic life.'

'You will see little work tonight. Half the workers are out or under arms. Half these people are keeping holiday. But we will go to the work places if you wish it.'

For a time Graham watched the dancers, then suddenly turned away. 'I want to see the workers. I have seen enough of these,' he said.

Asano led the way along the gallery across the dancing hall. Presently they came to a transverse passage that brought a breath of fresher, colder air.

Asano glanced at this passage as they went past, stopped, went back to it, and turned to Graham with a smile. 'Here, Sire,' he said, 'is something – will be familiar to you at least – and yet – But I will not tell you. Come!'

He led the way along a closed passage that presently became cold. The reverberation of their feet told that this passage was a bridge. They came into a circular gallery that was glazed in from the outer weather, and so reached a circular chamber which seemed familiar, though Graham could not recall distinctly when he had entered it before. In this was a ladder up which they went, and came into a high, dark, cold place in which was another almost vertical ladder. This they ascended, Graham still perplexed.

But at the top he understood, and recognized the metallic bars to which he clung. He was in the cage under the ball of St Paul's. The dome rose but a little way above the general contour of the city, into the still twilight, and sloped away, shining greasily under a few distant lights, into a circumambient ditch of darkness.

Out between the bars he looked upon the wind-clear northern sky and saw the starry constellations all unchanged. Capella hung in the west, Vega was rising, and the seven glittering points of the Great Bear swept overhead in their stately circle about the Pole.

He saw these stars in a clear gap of sky. To the east and south the great circular shapes of complaining wind-wheels blotted out the heavens, so that the glare about the Council House was hidden. To the south-west hung Orion, showing like a pallid ghost through a tracery of ironwork and interlacing shapes above a dazzling coruscation of lights. A bellowing and siren screaming that came from the flying stages warned the world that one of the aeroplanes was ready to start. He remained for a space gazing towards the glaring stage. Then his eyes went back to the northward constellations.

For a long time he was silent. 'This,' he said at last, smiling in the shadow, 'seems the strangest thing of all. To stand in the dome of St Paul's and look once more upon these familiar, silent stars!'

Thence Graham was taken by Asano along devious ways to the great gambling and business quarters where the bulk of the fortunes in the city were lost and made. It impressed him as a well-nigh interminable series of very high halls, surrounded by tiers upon tiers of galleries into which opened thousands of offices, and traversed by a complicated multitude of bridges, footways, aerial motor rails and trapeze and cable leaps. And here more than anywhere the note of vehement vitality, of uncontrollable, hasty activity, rose high. Everywhere was violent advertisement, until his brain swam at the tumult of light and colour. And Babble Machines of a peculiarly rancid tone were abundant and filled the air with strenuous squealing and an idiotic slang. 'Skin your eyes and slide,' 'Gewhoop, Bonanza,' 'Gollipers come and hark!'

The place seemed to him to be dense with people either profoundly agitated or swelling with obscure cunning, yet he learnt that it was comparatively empty, that the great political convulsion of the last few days had reduced transactions to an unprecedented minimum. In one hall were long avenues of roulette tables, each with a silent, watchful crowd about it; in another a yelping Babel of white-faced women and red-necked leathery-lunged men bought and sold the shares of an absolutely fictitious business undertaking which every five minutes paid a dividend of ten per cent and cancelled a certain proportion of its shares by means of a lottery wheel.

These business activities were prosecuted with an energy that readily passed into violence, and Graham approaching a dense crowd found at its centre a couple of prominent merchants in violent controversy with teeth and nails on some delicate point of business etiquette. Something still remained in life to be fought for. Further he had a shock at a vehement announcement in phonetic letters of scarlet flame, each twice the height of a man, that 'WE ASSURE THE PROPRAIET'R. WE ASSURE THE PROPRAIET'R.'

'Who's the proprietor?' he asked.

'You.'

'But what do they assure me?' he asked. 'What do they assure me?'

'Didn't you have assurance?'

Graham thought. 'Insurance?'

'Yes – Insurance. I remember that was the older word. They are insuring your life. Dozands of people are taking out policies, myriads of lions are being put on you. And further on other people are buying annuities. They do that on everybody who is at all prominent. Look there!'

A crowd of people surged and roared, and Graham saw a vast black screen suddenly illuminated in still larger letters of burning purple. 'Anuetes on the Propraiet'r – x 5 pr. G.' The people began to boo and shout at this, a number of hard-breathing, wild-eyed men came running past, clawing with hooked fingers at the air. There was a furious crush about a little doorway.

Asano did a brief, inaccurate calculation. 'Seventeen per cent per annum is their annuity on you. They would not pay so much per cent if they could see you now, Sire. But they do not know. Your own annuities used to be a very safe investment, but now you are sheer gambling, of course. This is probably a desperate bid. I doubt if people will get their money.'

The crowd of would-be annuitants grew so thick about them that for some time they could move neither forward nor backward. Graham noticed what appeared to him to be a high proportion of women among the speculators, and was reminded again of the economic independence of their sex. They seemed remarkably well able to take care of themselves in the crowd, using their elbows with particular skill, as he learnt to his cost. One curly-headed person caught in the pressure for a space, looked steadfastly at him several times, almost as if she recognized him, and then, edging deliberately towards him, touched his hand with her arm in a scarcely accidental manner, and made it plain by a look as ancient as Chaldea that he had found favour in her eyes. And then a lank, grey-bearded man, perspiring copiously in a noble passion of self-help, blind to all earthly things save that glaring bait, thrust between them in a cataclysmal rush towards that alluring 'x 5 pr. G.'

'I want to get out of this,' said Graham to Asano. 'This is not what I came to see. Show me the workers. I want to see the people in blue. These parasitic lunatics—'

He found himself wedged into a struggling mass of people.

21

The Underside

From the Business Quarter they presently passed by the running ways into a remote quarter of the city, where the bulk of the manufactures was done. On their way the platforms crossed the Thames twice, and passed in a broad viaduct across one of the great roads that entered the city from the north. In both cases his impression was swift and in both very vivid. The river was a broad wrinkled glitter of black sea water, overarched by buildings, and vanishing either way into a blackness starred with receding lights. A string of black barges passed seaward, manned by blue-clad men. The road was a long and very broad and high tunnel, along which big-wheeled machines drove noiselessly and swiftly. Here, too, the distinctive blue of the Labour Department was in abundance. The smoothness of the double tracks, the largeness and the lightness of the big pneumatic wheels in proportion to the vehicular body, struck Graham most vividly. One lank and very high carriage with longitudinal metallic rods hung with the dripping carcasses of many hundred sheep arrested his attention unduly. Abruptly the edge of the archway cut and blotted out the picture.

Presently they left the way and descended by a lift and traversed a passage that sloped downward, and so came to a descending lift again. The appearance of things changed. Even the pretence of architectural ornament disappeared, the lights diminished in number and size, the architecture became more and more massive in proportion to the spaces as the factory quarters were reached. And in the dusty biscuit-making place of the potters, among the feldspar mills, in the furnace rooms of the metal workers, among the incandescent lakes of crude Eadhamite, the blue canvas clothing was on man, woman and child.

Many of these great and dusty galleries were silent avenues of machinery, endless raked-out ashen furnaces testified to the revolutionary dislocation, but wherever there was work it was being done by slow-moving workers in blue canvas. The only people not in blue canvas were the overlookers of the workplaces and the orange-clad Labour Police. And fresh from the flushed faces of the dancing halls, the voluntary vigours of the Business Quarter, Graham could note the pinched faces, the feeble muscles, and weary eyes of many of the latter-day workers. Such as he saw at work were noticeably inferior in physique to the few gaily dressed managers and forewomen who were directing their labours. The burly labourer of the old Victorian times had followed the dray horse and all such living force producers, to extinction; the place of his costly muscles was taken by some dexterous machine. The latter-day labourer, male as well as female, was essentially a machine-minder and feeder, a servant and attendant, or an artist under direction.

The women, in comparison with those Graham remembered, were as a class distinctly plain and flat-chested. Two hundred years of emancipation from the moral restraints of Puritanical religion, two hundred years of city life, had done their work in eliminating the strain of feminine beauty and vigour from the blue canvas myriads. To be brilliant physically or mentally, to be in any way attractive or exceptional, had been and was still a certain way of emancipation to the drudge, a line of escape to the Pleasure City and its splendours and delights, and at last to the Euthanasy and peace. To be steadfast against such inducements was scarcely to be expected of meanly nourished souls. In the young cities of Graham's former life, the newly aggregated labouring mass had been a diverse multitude, still stirred by the tradition of personal honour and a high morality; now it was differentiating into an instinct class, with a moral and physical difference of its own – even with a dialect of its own.

They penetrated downward, ever downward, towards the working places. Presently they passed underneath one of the streets of the moving ways, and saw its platforms running on their rails far overhead, and chinks of white light between the transverse slits. The factories that were not working were sparsely lighted; to Graham they and their shrouded aisles of giant machines seemed plunged in gloom, and even where work was going on the illumination was far less brilliant than upon the public ways.

Beyond the blazing lakes of Eadhamite he came to the warren of the jewellers, and, with some difficulty and by using his signature, obtained admission to these galleries. They were high and dark, and rather cold. In the first a few men were making ornaments of gold filigree, each man at a little bench by himself, and with a little shaded light. The long vista of light patches, with the nimble fingers brightly lit and moving among the gleaming yellow coils, and the intent face like the face of a ghost, in each shadow, had the oddest effect.

The work was beautifully executed but without any strength of modelling or drawing, for the most part intricate grotesques or the ringing of the changes on a geometrical *motif*. These workers wore a peculiar white uniform without pockets or sleeves. They assumed this on coming to work, but at night they were stripped and examined before they left the premises of the Department. In spite of every precaution, the Labour policeman told them in a depressed tone, the Department was not infrequently robbed.

Beyond was a gallery of women busied in cutting and setting slabs of artificial ruby, and next to these were men and women working together upon the slabs of copper net that formed the basis of *cloisonné* tiles. Many of these workers had lips and nostrils a livid white, due to a disease caused by a peculiar purple enamel that chanced to be much in fashion. Asano apologized to Graham for this offensive sight, but excused himself on the score of the convenience of this route. 'This is what I wanted to see,' said Graham; 'this is what I wanted to see,' trying to avoid a start at a particularly striking disfigurement.

'She might have done better with herself than that,' said Asano.

Graham made some indignant comments.

'But, Sire, we simply could not stand that stuff without the purple,' said Asano. 'In your days people could stand such crudities, they were nearer the barbaric by two hundred years.'

They continued along one of the lower galleries of this *cloisonné* factory, and came to a little bridge that spanned a vault. Looking over the parapet, Graham saw that beneath was a wharf under yet more tremendous archings than any he had seen. Three barges, smothered in floury dust, were being unloaded of their cargoes of powdered felspar by a multitude of coughing men, each guiding a little truck; the dust filled the place with a choking mist, and turned the electric glare yellow. The vague shadows of these workers gesticulated about their feet, and rushed to and fro against a long stretch of whitewashed wall. Every now and then one would stop to cough.

A shadowy, huge mass of masonry rising out of the inky water, brought to Graham's mind the thought of the multitude of ways and galleries and lifts that rose floor above floor overhead between him and the sky. The men worked in silence under the supervision of two of the Labour Police; their feet made a hollow thunder on the planks along which they went to and fro. And as he looked at this scene, some hidden voice in the darkness began to sing.

'Stop that!' shouted one of the policemen, but the order was disobeyed, and first one and then all the white-stained men who were working there had taken up the beating refrain, singing it defiantly – the Song of the Revolt. The feet upon the planks thundered now to the rhythm of the song, tramp, tramp, tramp. The policeman who had shouted glanced at his fellow, and Graham saw him shrug his shoulders. He made no further effort to stop the singing.

And so they went through these factories and places of toil, seeing many painful and grim things. That walk left on Graham's mind a maze of memories, fluctuating pictures of swathed halls and crowded vaults seen through clouds of dust, of intricate machines, the racing threads of looms, the heavy beat of stamping machinery, the roar and rattle of belt and armature, of subterranean aisles of sleeping places, illimitable vistas of pinpoint lights. Here was the smell of tanning, and here the reek of a brewery, and here unprecedented reeks. Everywhere were pillars and cross archings of such a massiveness as Graham had never before seen, thick Titans of greasy, shining brickwork crushed beneath the vast weight of that complex city world, even as these anaemic millions were crushed by its complexity. And everywhere were pale features, lean limbs, disfigurement and degradation.

Once and again, and again a third time, Graham heard the Song of the Revolt during his long, unpleasant research in these places, and once he saw a confused struggle down a passage and learnt that a number of these serfs had seized their bread before their work was done. Graham was ascending towards the ways again when he saw a number of blue-clad children running down a transverse passage, and presently perceived the reason of their panic in a company of the Labour Police armed with clubs, trotting towards some unknown disturbance. And then came a remote disorder. But for the most part this remnant that worked, worked hopelessly. All the spirit that was left in fallen humanity was above in the streets that night, calling for the Master, and valiantly and noisily keeping its arms.

They emerged from these wanderings and stood blinking in the bright light of the middle passage of the platforms again. They became aware of the remote hooting and yelping of the machines of one of the General Intelligence Offices, and suddenly came men running, and along the platforms and about the ways everywhere was a shouting and crying. Then a woman with a face of mute white terror, and another who gasped and shrieked as she ran.

'What has happened now?' said Graham, puzzled, for he could not understand their thick speech. Then he heard it in English and perceived that the thing that everyone was shouting, that men yelled to one another, that women took up screaming, that was passing like the first breeze of a thunderstorm, chill and sudden through the city, was this: 'Ostrog has ordered the Black Police to London. The Black Police are coming from South Africa. . . . The Black Police. The Black Police.'

Asano's face was white and astonished; he hesitated, looked at Graham's face, and told him the thing he already knew. 'But how can they know?' asked Asano.

Graham heard someone shouting. 'Stop all work. Stop all work,' and a swarthy hunchback, ridiculously gay in green and gold, came leaping down the platforms towards him, bawling again and again in good English, 'This is Ostrog's doing, Ostrog the Knave! The Master is betrayed.' His voice was hoarse and a thin foam dropped from his ugly shouting mouth. He yelled an unspeakable horror that the Black Police had done in Paris, and so passed shrieking, 'Ostrog the Knave!'

For a moment Graham stood still, for it had come upon him again that these things were a dream. He looked up at the great cliff of buildings on either side, vanishing into blue haze at last above the lights, and down to the roaring tiers of platforms, and the shouting, running people who were gesticulating past. 'The Master is betrayed!' they cried. 'The Master is betrayed!'

Suddenly the situation shaped itself in his mind real and urgent. His heart began to beat fast and strong.

'It has come,' he said. 'I might have known. The hour has come.'

He thought swiftly. 'What am I to do?'

'Go back to the. Council House,' said Asano.

'Why should I not appeal—? The people are here.'

'You will lose time. They will doubt if it is you. But they will mass about the Council House. There you will find their leaders. Your strength is there – with them.'

'Suppose this is only a rumour?'

'It sounds true,' said Asano.

'Let us have the facts,' said Graham.

Asano shrugged his shoulders. 'We had better get towards the Council House,' he cried. 'That is where they will swarm. Even now the ruins may be impassable.'

Graham regarded him doubtfully and followed him.

They went up the stepped platforms to the swiftest one, and there Asano accosted a labourer. The answers to his questions were in the thick, vulgar speech.

'What did he say?' asked Graham.

'He knows little, but he told me that the Black Police would have arrived here before the people knew – had not someone in the wind-vane offices learnt. He said a girl.'

'A girl? Not—?'

'He said a girl – he did not know who she was. Who came out from the Council House crying aloud, and told the men at work among the ruins.'

And then another thing was shouted, something that turned an aimless tumult into determinate movements, it came like a wind along the street. 'To your Wards, to your Wards. Every man get arms. Every man to his Ward!'

22

The Struggle in the Council House

As Asano and Graham hurried along to the ruins about the Council House, they saw everywhere the excitement of the people rising. 'To your Wards! To your Wards!' Everywhere men and women in blue were hurrying from unknown subterranean employments, up the staircases of the middle path; at one place Graham saw an arsenal of the revolutionary committee besieged by a crowd of shouting men, at another a couple of men in the hated yellow uniform of the Labour Police, pursued by a gathering crowd, fled precipitately along the swift way that went in the opposite direction.

The cries of 'To your Wards!' became at last a continuous shouting as they drew near the government quarter. Many of the shouts were unintelligible. 'Ostrog has betrayed us,' one man bawled in a hoarse voice, again and again, dinning that refrain into Graham's ear until it haunted him. This person stayed close beside Graham and Asano on the swift way, shouting to the people who swarmed on the lower platforms as he rushed past them. His cry about Ostrog alternated with some incomprehensible orders. Presently he went leaping down and disappeared.

Graham's mind was filled with the din. His plans were vague and unformed. He had one picture of some commanding position from which he could address the multitudes, another of meeting Ostrog face to face. He was full of rage, of tense muscular excitement, his hands gripped, his lips were pressed together.

The way to the Council House across the ruins was impassable, but Asano met that difficulty and took Graham into the premises of the central post-office. The post-office was nominally at work, but the blue-clothed porters moved sluggishly or had stopped to stare through the arches of their galleries at the shouting men who were going by outside. 'Every man to his Ward! Every man to his Ward!' Here, by Asano's advice, Graham revealed his identity.

They crossed to the Council House by a cable cradle. Already in the brief interval since the capitulation of the Councillors a great change had been wrought in the appearance of the ruins. The spurting cascades of the ruptured sea-water mains had been captured and tamed, and huge temporary pipes ran overhead along a flimsy-looking fabric of girders. The sky was laced with restored cables and wires that served the Council House, and a mass of new fabric with cranes and other building machines going to and fro upon it projected to the left of the white pile.

The moving ways that ran across this area had been restored, albeit for once running under the open sky. These were the ways that Graham had seen from the little balcony in the hour of his awakening, not nine days since, and the hall of his trance had been on the further side, where now shapeless piles of smashed and shattered masonry were heaped together.

It was already high day and the sun was shining brightly. Out of their tall caverns of blue electric light came the swift ways crowded with multitudes of people, who poured off them and gathered ever denser over the wreckage and confusion of the ruins. The air was full of their shouting, and they were pressing and swaying towards the central building. For the most part that shouting mass consisted of shapeless swarms, but here and there Graham could see that a rude discipline struggled to establish itself. And every voice clamoured for order in the chaos. 'To your Wards! Every man to his Ward!'

The cable carried them into a hall which Graham recognized as the antechamber to the Hall of the Atlas, about the gallery of which he had walked days ago with Howard to show himself to the vanished Council, an hour from his awakening. Now the place was empty except for two cable attendants. These men seemed hugely astonished to recognize the Sleeper in the man who swung down from the cross seat.

'Where is Ostrog?' he demanded. 'I must see Ostrog forthwith. He has disobeyed me. I have come back to take things out of his hands.' Without waiting for Asano, he went straight across the place, ascended the steps at the further end, and, pulling the curtain aside, found himself facing the perpetually labouring Titan.

The Hall was empty. Its appearance had changed very greatly since his first sight of it. It had suffered serious injury in the violent struggle

577

of the first outbreak. On the right-hand side of the great figure the upper half of the wall had been torn away for nearly two hundred feet of its length, and a sheet of the same glassy film that had enclosed Graham at his awakening had been drawn across the gap. This deadened, but did not altogether exclude, the roar of the people outside. 'Wards! Wards! Wards!' they seemed to be saying. Through it there were visible the beams and supports of metal scaffoldings that rose and fell according to the requirements of a great crowd of workmen. An idle building machine, with lank arms of red painted metal, stretched gauntly across this green tinted picture. On it were still a number of workmen staring at the crowd below. For a moment he stood regarding these things, and Asano overtook him.

'Ostrog,' said Asano, 'will be in the small offices beyond there.' The little man looked livid now and his eyes searched Graham's face.

They had scarcely advanced ten paces from the curtain before a panel to the left of the Atlas rolled up, and Ostrog, accompanied by Lincoln and followed by two black- and yellow-clad Negroes, appeared crossing the remote corner of the hall, towards a second panel that was raised and open. 'Ostrog,' shouted Graham, and at the sound in his voice the little party turned astonished.

Ostrog said something to Lincoln and advanced alone.

Graham was the first to speak. His voice was loud and dictatorial. 'What is this I hear?' he asked. 'Are you bringing Negroes here – to keep the people down?'

'It is none too soon,' said Ostrog. 'They have been getting out of hand more and more, since the revolt. I under-estimated—'

'Do you mean that these infernal Negroes are on the way?'

'On the way. As it is, you have seen the people – outside?'

'No wonder! But – after what was said. You have taken too much on yourself, Ostrog.'

Ostrog said nothing, but drew nearer.

'These Negroes must not come to London,' said Graham. 'I am Master and they shall not come.'

Ostrog glanced at Lincoln, who at once came towards them with his two attendants close behind him. 'Why not?' asked Ostrog.

'White men must be mastered by white men. Besides—'

'The Negroes are only an instrument.'

'But that is not the question. I am the Master. I mean to be the Master. And I tell you these Negroes shall not come.'

'The people—'

'I believe in the people.'

'Because you are an anachronism. You are a man out of the Past –

an accident. You are Owner perhaps of the world. Nominally – legally. But you are not Master. You do not know enough to be Master.'

He glanced at Lincoln again. 'I know now what you think – I can guess something of what you mean to do. Even now it is not too late to warn you. You dream of human equality – of some sort of socialistic order – you have all those worn-out dreams of the nineteenth century fresh and vivid in your mind, and you would rule this age that you do not understand.'

'Listen!' said Graham. 'You can hear it – a sound like the sea. Not voices – but a voice. Do you altogether understand?'

'We taught them that,' said Ostrog.

'Perhaps. Can you teach them to forget it? But enough of this! These Negroes must not come.'

There was a pause and Ostrog looked him in the eyes.

'They will,' he said.

'I forbid it,' said Graham.

'They have started.'

'I will not have it.'

'No,' said Ostrog. 'Sorry as I am to follow the method of the Council – For your own good – you must not side with – Disorder. And now that you are here – It was kind of you to come here.'

Lincoln laid his hand on Graham's shoulder. Abruptly Graham realized the enormity of his blunder in coming to the Council House. He turned towards the curtains that separated the hall from the antechamber. The clutching hand of Asano intervened. In another moment Lincoln had grasped Graham's cloak.

He turned and struck at Lincoln's face, and incontinently a Negro had him by collar and arm. He wrenched himself away, his sleeve tore noisily, and he stumbled back, to be tripped by the other attendant. Then he struck the ground heavily and he was staring at the distant ceiling of the hall.

He shouted, rolled over, struggling fiercely, clutched an attendant's leg and threw him headlong, and struggled to his feet.

Lincoln appeared before him, went down again with a blow under the point of the jaw and lay still. Graham made two strides, stumbled. And then Ostrog's arm was round his neck, he was pulled over backward, fell, and his arms were pinned to the ground. After a few violent efforts he ceased to struggle and lay staring at Ostrog's heaving throat.

'You – are – a prisoner,' panted Ostrog, exulting. 'You – were rather a fool – to come back.'

Graham turned his head about and perceived through the irregular green window in the walls of the hall the men who had been working the building cranes gesticulating excitedly to the people below them. They had seen!

Ostrog followed his eyes and started. He shouted something to Lincoln, but Lincoln did not move. A bullet smashed among the mouldings above the Atlas. The two sheets of transparent matter that had been stretched across this gap were rent, the edges of the torn aperture darkened, curved, ran rapidly towards the framework, and in a moment the Council Chamber stood open to the air. A chilly gust blew in by the gap, bringing with it a war of voices from the ruinous spaces without, an elvish babblement, 'Save the Master!' 'What are they doing to the Master?' 'The Master is betrayed!'

And then he realized that Ostrog's attention was distracted, that Ostrog's grip had relaxed, and, wrenching his arms free, he struggled to his knees. In another moment he had thrust Ostrog back, and he was on one foot, his hand gripping Ostrog's throat, and Ostrog's hands clutching the silk about his neck.

But now men were coming towards them from the dais – men whose intentions he misunderstood. He had a glimpse of someone running in the distance towards the curtains of the antechamber, and then Ostrog had slipped from him and these newcomers were upon him. To his infinite astonishment, they seized him. They obeyed the shouts of Ostrog.

He was lugged a dozen yards before he realized that they were not friends – that they were dragging him towards the open panel. When he saw this he pulled back, he tried to fling himself down, he called for help with all his strength. And this time there were answering cries.

The grip upon his neck relaxed, and behold! in the lower corner of the rent upon the wall, first one and then a number of little black figures appeared hooting and waving arms. They came leaping down from the gap into the light gallery that had led to the Silent Rooms. They ran along it, so near were they that Graham could see the weapons in their hands. Then Ostrog was giving directions to the men who held him, and once more he was struggling with all his strength against their endeavours to thrust him towards the opening that yawned to receive him. 'They can't come down,' panted Ostrog. 'They daren't fire. It's all right. We'll save him from them yet.'

For long minutes as it seemed to Graham that inglorious struggle continued. His clothes were rent in a dozen places, he was covered in dust, one hand had been trodden upon. He could hear the shouts of his supporters, and once he heard shots. He could feel his strength giving way, feel his efforts wild and aimless. But no help came; and surely, irresistibly, that black, yawning opening came nearer.

The pressure upon him relaxed and he struggled up. He saw Ostrog's grey head receding and perceived that he was no longer held. He turned about and came full into a man in black. One of the green weapons cracked close to him, a drift of pungent smoke came into his face, and a steel blade flashed. The huge chamber span about him.

He saw a man in pale blue stabbing one of the black and yellow attendants not three yards from his face. Then hands were upon him again.

He was being pulled in two directions now. It seemed as though people were shouting to him. He wanted to understand and could not. Someone was clutching about his thighs, he was being hoisted in spite of his vigorous efforts. He understood suddenly, he ceased to struggle. He was lifted up on men's shoulders and carried away from that devouring panel. Ten thousand throats were cheering.

He saw men in blue and black hurrying after the retreating Ostrogites and firing. Lifted up, he saw now across the whole expanse of the hall beneath the Atlas image, saw that he was being carried towards the raised platform in the centre of the place. The far end of the hall was already full of people running towards him. They were looking at him and cheering.

He became aware that a bodyguard surrounded him. Active men about him gave vague orders. He saw close at hand the black-moustached man in yellow who had been among those who had greeted him in the public theatre, shouting directions. The hall was already densely packed with swaying people, the little metal gallery sagged with a howling load, the curtains at the end had been torn away, and the antechamber was revealed densely crowded. He could scarcely make the man near him hear for the tumult about them. 'Where has Ostrog gone?' he asked.

The man he questioned pointed over the heads towards the lower panels about the hall on the side opposite the gap. They stood open, and armed men, blue clad with black sashes, were running through them and vanishing into the chambers and passages beyond. It seemed to Graham that a sound of firing drifted through the riot. He was carried in a staggering curve across the great hall towards an opening beneath the gap.

He perceived men working with a sort of rude discipline to keep the crowd off him, to make a space clear about him. He passed out of the hall, and saw a crude, new wall rising blankly before him topped by blue sky. He was swung down to his feet; someone gripped his arm and guided him. He found the man in yellow close at hand. They were taking him up a narrow stairway of brick, and above rose the great red-painted masses, the cranes and levers and the still engines of the big building machine.

He was at the top of the steps. He was hurried across a narrow railed footway, and suddenly with a vast uproar the amphitheatre of ruins opened again before him. 'The Master is with us! The Master! The Master!' The cry swept athwart the lake of faces like a wave, broke against the distant cliff of ruins, and came back in a welter of sounds. 'The Master is on our side!'

Graham perceived that he was no longer encompassed by people, that he was standing upon a little temporary platform of white metal, part of a flimsy-seeming scaffolding that laced about the great mass of the Council House. Over all the huge expanse of the ruins swayed and eddied the people; and here and there the black banners of the revolutionary societies ducked and swayed and formed rare nuclei of organization in the chaos. Up the steep stairs of wall and scaffolding by which his rescuers had reached the opening in the Atlas Chamber clung a solid crowd, and little energetic black figures clinging to pillars and projections were strenuous to induce these congested masses to stir. Behind him, at a higher point on the scaffolding, a number of men struggled upwards with the flapping folds of a huge black standard. Through the yawning gap in the walls below him he could look down upon the packed attentive multitudes in the Hall of the Atlas. The distant flying stages to the south came out bright and vivid, brought nearer as it seemed by an unusual translucency of the air. A solitary monoplane beat up from the central stage as if to meet the coming aeroplanes.

'What has become of Ostrog?' asked Graham, and even as he spoke he saw that all eyes were turned from him towards the crest of the Council House building. He looked also in this direction of universal attention. For a moment he saw nothing but the jagged corner of a wall, hard and clear against the sky. Then in the shadow he perceived the interior of a room and recognized with a start the green and white decorations of his former prison. And coming quickly across this opened room and up to the very verge of the cliff of the ruins came a little white-clad figure followed by two other smaller-seeming figures in black and yellow. He heard the man beside him exclaim 'Ostrog,' and turned to ask a question. But he never did, because of the startled exclamation of another of those who were with him and a lank finger suddenly pointing. And behold! the monoplane that had been rising from the flying stage when last he had looked in that direction, was driving towards them. The swift steady flight was still novel enough to hold his attention.

Nearer it came, growing rapidly larger and larger, until it had swept over the further edge of the ruins and into view of the dense multitudes below. It drooped across the space and rose and passed overhead, rising to clear the mass of the Council House, a filmy translucent shape with the aeronaut peering down through its ribs. It vanished beyond the skyline of the ruins.

Graham transferred his attention to Ostrog. He was signalling with his hands, and his attendants were busy breaking down the wall beside him. In another moment the monoplane came into view again, a little thing far away, coming round in a wide curve and going slower.

Then suddenly the man in yellow shouted: 'What are they doing? What are the people doing? Why is Ostrog left there? Why is he not captured? They will lift him – the monoplane will lift him! Ah!'

The exclamation was echoed by a shout from the ruins. The rattling sound of the green weapons drifted across the intervening gulf to Graham, and, looking down, he saw a number of black and yellow uniforms running along one of the galleries that lay open to the air below the promontory upon which Ostrog stood. They fired as they ran at men unseen, and then emerged a number of pale-blue figures in pursuit. These minute fighting figures had the oddest effect; they seemed as they ran like little model soldiers in a toy. This queer appearance of a house cut open gave that struggle amidst furniture and passages a quality of unreality. It was perhaps two hundred yards away from him, and very nearly fifty above the heads in the ruins below. The black and yellow men ran into an open archway, and turned and fired a volley. One of the blue pursuers striding forward close to the edge, flung up his arms, staggered sideways, seemed to Graham's sense to hang over the edge for several seconds, and fell headlong down. Graham saw him strike a projecting corner, fly out, head over heels, head over heels, and vanish behind the red arm of the building machine.

And then a shadow came between Graham and the sun. He looked up and the sky was clear, but he knew the little monoplane had passed. Ostrog had vanished. The man in yellow thrust before him, zealous and perspiring, pointing and blatant.

'They are grounding!' cried the man in yellow. 'They are grounding. Tell the people to fire at him. Tell them to fire at him!'

Graham could not understand. He heard loud voices repeating these enigmatical orders.

Suddenly he saw the prow of the monoplane come gliding over the edge of the ruins and stop with a jerk. In a moment Graham understood that the thing had grounded in order that Ostrog might escape by it. He saw a blue haze climbing out of the gulf, perceived that the people below him were now firing up at the projecting stem.

A man beside him cheered hoarsely, and he saw that the blue rebels had gained the archway that had been contested by the men in black and yellow a moment before, and were running in a continual stream along the open passage.

And suddenly the monoplane slipped over the edge of the Council House and fell like a diving swallow. It dropped, tilting at an angle of forty-five degrees, so steeply that it seemed to Graham, it seemed perhaps to most of those below, that it could not possibly rise again.

It fell so closely past him that he could see Ostrog clutching the guides of the seat, with his grey hair streaming; see the white-faced aeronaut wrenching over the lever that turned the machine upward. He heard the apprehensive vague cry of innumerable men below.

Graham gripped the railing before him and gasped. The second seemed an age. The lower van of the monoplane passed within an ace of touching the people, who yelled and screamed and trampled one another below.

And then it rose.

For a moment it looked as if it could not possibly clear the opposite cliff, and then that it could not possibly clear the wind-wheel that rotated beyond.

And behold! it was clear and soaring, still heeling sideways, upward, upward into the wind-swept sky.

The suspense of the moment gave place to a fury of exasperation as the swarming people realized that Ostrog had escaped them. With belated activity they renewed their fire, until the rattling wove into a roar, until the whole area became dim and blue and the air pungent with the thin smoke of their weapons.

Too late! The flying machine dwindled smaller and smaller, and curved about and swept gracefully downward to the flying stage from which it had so lately risen. Ostrog had escaped.

For a while a confused babblement arose from the ruins, and then the universal attention came back to Graham, perched high among the scaffolding. He saw the faces of the people turned towards him, heard their shouts at his rescue. From the throat of the ways came the Song of the Revolt spreading like a breeze across that swaying sea of men.

The little group of men about him shouted congratulations on his escape. The man in yellow was close to him, with a set face and shining eyes. And the song was rising, louder and louder; tramp, tramp, tramp, tramp.

Slowly the realization came of the full meaning of these things to him, the perception of the swift change in his position. Ostrog, who had stood beside him whenever he had faced that shouting multitude before, was beyond there – the antagonist. There was no one to rule for him any longer. Even the people about him, the leaders and organizers of the multitude, looked to see what he would do, looked to him to act, awaited his orders. He was king indeed. His puppet reign was at an end.

He was very intent to do the thing that was expected of him. His nerves and muscles were quivering, his mind was perhaps a little confused, but he felt neither fear nor anger. His hand that had been trodden upon throbbed and was hot. He was a little nervous about his bearing. He knew he was not afraid, but he was anxious not to seem afraid. In his former life he had often been more excited in playing games of skill. He was desirous of immediate action, he knew he must not think too much in detail of the huge complexity of the struggle about him lest he should be paralysed by the sense of its intricacy.

Over there those square blue shapes, the flying stages, meant Ostrog; against Ostrog, who was so clear and definite and decisive, he who was so vague and undecided, was fighting for the whole future of the world.

23

Graham Speaks His Word

For a time the Master of the Earth was not even master of his own mind. Even his will seemed a will not his own, his own acts surprised him and were but a part of the confusion of strange experiences that poured across his being. Three things were definite, the Negroes were coming, Helen Wotton had warned the people of their coming, and he was Master of the Earth. Each of these facts seemed struggling for complete possession of his thoughts. They protruded from a background of swarming halls, elevated passages, rooms jammed with ward leaders in council, kinematograph and telephone rooms, and windows looking out on a seething sea of marching men. The men in yellow, and men who he fancied were called Ward Leaders, were either propelling him forward or following him obediently; it was hard to tell. Perhaps they were doing a little of both. Perhaps some power unseen and unsuspected propelled them all. He was aware that he was going to make a proclamation to the People of the Earth, aware of certain grandiose phrases floating in his mind as the thing he meant to say. He found himself with the man in yellow entering a little room where this proclamation of his was to be made.

This room was grotesquely latter-day in its appointments. In the centre was a bright oval lit by shaded electric lights from above. The rest was in shadow, and the double finely fitting doors through which he came from the swarming Hall of the Atlas made the place very still. The dead thud of these as they closed behind him, the sudden cessation of the tumult in which he had been living for hours, the quivering circle of light, the whispers and quick noiseless movements of vaguely visible attendants in the shadows, had a strange effect upon Graham.

The huge ears of a phonographic mechanism gaped in a battery for his words, the black eyes of great photographic cameras awaited his beginning, beyond metal rods and coils glittered dimly, and something whirled about with a droning hum. He walked into the centre of the light, and his shadow drew together black and sharp to a little blot at his feet.

The vague shape of the words he meant to say was already in his mind. But this silence, this isolation, this withdrawal from that contagious crowd, this audience of gaping, glaring machines, had not been in his anticipation. All his supports seemed taken away; he seemed to have dropped into this suddenly, suddenly to have discovered himself. In a moment he was changed. He found that he now feared to be inadequate, he feared to be theatrical, he feared the quality of his voice, the quality of his wit; astonished, he turned to the man in yellow with a propitiatory gesture. 'Just for a little while,' he said, 'I must wait. I did not think it would be like this. I must think again of what I have to say.'

While he was still hesitating there came an agitated messenger with news that the foremost aeroplanes were passing over Madrid.

'What news of the flying stages?' he asked.

'The people of the south-west wards are ready.'

'Ready!'

He turned impatiently to the blank circles of the lenses again.

'I suppose it must be a sort of speech. Would to God I knew certainly the thing that should be said! Aeroplanes at Madrid! They must have started before the main fleet.'

'Oh! what can it matter whether I speak well or ill?' he said, and felt the light grow brighter.

He had framed some vague sentence of democratic sentiment when suddenly doubts overwhelmed him. His belief in his heroic quality and calling he found had altogether lost its assured conviction. The picture of a little strutting futility in a windy waste of incomprehensible destinies replaced it. Abruptly it was perfectly clear to him that this revolt against Ostrog was premature, foredoomed to failure, the impulse of passionate inadequacy against inevitable things. He thought of that swift flight of aeroplanes like the swoop of Fate towards him. He was astonished that he could have seen things in any other light. In that final emergency he debated, thrust debate resolutely aside, determined at all costs to go through with the thing he had undertaken. And he could find no word to begin. Even as he stood, awkward, hesitating, with an indiscreet apology for his inability trembling on his lips, came the noise of many people crying out, the running to and fro of feet. 'Wait,' cried someone, and a door opened. Graham turned, and the watching lights waned.

Through the open doorway he saw a slight girlish figure approaching. His heart leapt. It was Helen Wotton. The man in yellow came out of the nearer shadows into the circle of light.

'This is the girl who told us what Ostrog had done,' he said.

She came in very quietly, and stood still, as if she did not want to interrupt Graham's eloquence. ... But his doubts and questionings fled before her presence. He remembered the things that he had meant to say. He faced the cameras again and the light about him grew brighter. He turned back to her.

'You have helped me,' he said lamely – 'helped me very much. ... This is very difficult.'

He paused. He addressed himself to the unseen multitudes who stared upon him through those grotesque black eyes. At first he spoke slowly.

'Men and women of the new age,' he said; 'you have arisen to do battle for the race! ... There is no easy victory before us.'

He stopped to gather words. He wished passionately for the gift of moving speech.

'This night is a beginning,' he said. 'This battle that is coming, this battle that rushes upon us tonight, is only a beginning. All your lives, it may be, you must fight. Take no thought though I am beaten, though I am utterly overthrown. I think I may be overthrown.'

He found the thing in his mind too vague for words. He paused momentarily, and broke into vague exhortations, and then a rush of speech came upon him. Much that he said was but the humanitarian commonplace of a vanished age, but the conviction of his voice touched it to vitality. He stated the case of the old days to the people of the new age, to the girl at his side. 'I come out of the past to you', he said, 'with the memory of an age that hoped. My age was an age of dreams – of beginnings, an age of noble hopes; throughout the world we had made an end of slavery; throughout the world we had spread the desire and anticipation that wars might cease, that all men and women might live nobly, in freedom and peace. ... So we hoped in the days that are past. And what of those hopes? How is it with man after two hundred years?

'Great cities, vast powers, a collective greatness beyond our dreams. For that we did not work, and that has come. But how is it with the little lives that make up this greater life? How is it with the common lives? As it has ever been – sorrow and labour, lives cramped and unfulfilled, lives tempted by power, tempted by wealth, and gone to

waste and folly. The old faiths have faded and changed, the new faith –
Is there a new faith?

'Charity and mercy,' he floundered; 'beauty and the love of beautiful
things – effort and devotion! Give yourselves as I would give myself –
as Christ gave Himself upon the Cross. It does not matter if you
understand. It does not matter if you seem to fail. You *know* – in the
core of your hearts you *know*. There is no promise, there is no security –
nothing to go upon but Faith. There is no faith but faith – faith which
is courage. ....'

Things that he had long wished to believe, he found that he believed.
He spoke gustily, in broken incomplete sentences, but with all his
heart and strength, of this new faith within him. He spoke of the
greatness of self-abnegation, of his belief in an immortal life of Humanity in which we live and move and have our being. His voice rose and
fell, and the recording appliances hummed as he spoke, dim attendants
watched him out of the shadow. ...

His sense of that silent spectator beside him sustained his sincerity.
For a few glorious moments he was carried away; he felt no doubt of
his heroic quality, no doubt of his heroic words, he had it all straight
and plain. His eloquence limped no longer. And at last he made an
end to speaking. 'Here and now,' he cried, 'I make my will. All that is
mine in the world I give to the people of the world. All that is mine
in the world I give to the people of the world. To all of you. I give it
to you, and myself I give to you. And as God wills tonight, I will live
for you, or I will die.'

He ended. He found the light of his present exaltation reflected in
the face of the girl. Their eyes met; her eyes were swimming with tears
of enthusiasm.

'I knew,' she whispered. 'Oh! Father of the World – *Sire!* I knew
you would say these things. ....'

'I have said what I could,' he answered lamely and for a moment
held her outstretched hands.

24

While the Aeroplanes Were Coming

The man in yellow was beside them. Neither had noted his coming. He was saying that the south-west wards were marching. 'I never expected it so soon,' he cried. 'They have done wonders. You must send them a word to help them on their way.'

Graham stared at him absent-mindedly. Then with a start he returned to his previous preoccupation about the flying stages.

'Yes,' he said. 'That is good, that is good.' He weighed a message. 'Tell them; – well done South West.'

He turned his eyes to Helen Wotton again. His face expressed his struggle between conflicting ideas. 'We must capture the flying stages,' he explained. 'Unless we can do that they will land Negroes. At all costs we must prevent that.'

He felt even as he spoke that this was not what had been in his mind before the interruption. He saw a touch of surprise in her eyes. She seemed about to speak and a shrill bell drowned her voice.

It occurred to Graham that she expected him to lead these marching people, that that was the thing he had to do. He made the offer abruptly. He addressed the man in yellow, but he spoke to her. He saw her face respond. 'Here I am doing nothing,' he said.

'It is impossible,' protested the man in yellow. 'It is a fight in a warren. Your place is here.'

He explained elaborately. He motioned towards the room where Graham must wait, he insisted no other course was possible. 'We must know where you are,' he said. 'At any moment a crisis may arise needing your presence and decision.'

A picture had drifted through his mind of such a vast dramatic struggle as the masses in the ruins had suggested. But here was no spectacular battlefield such as he imagined. Instead was seclusion – and suspense. It was only as the afternoon wore on that he pieced together a truer picture of the fight that was raging, inaudibly and invisibly, within four miles of him, beneath the Roehampton stage. A strange and unprecedented contest it was, a battle that was a hundred thousand little battles, a battle in a sponge of ways and channels, fought out of sight of sky or sun under the electric glare, fought out in a vast confusion by multitudes untrained in arms, led chiefly by acclamation, multitudes dulled by mindless labour and enervated by the tradition of two hundred years of servile security against multitudes demoralized by lives of venial privilege and sensual indulgence. They had no artillery, no differentiation into this force or that; the only weapon on either side was the little green metal carbine whose secret manufacture and sudden distribution in enormous quantities had been one of Ostrog's culminating moves against the Council. Few had had any experience with this weapon, many had never discharged one, many who carried it came unprovided with ammunition; never was wilder firing in the history of warfare. It was a battle of amateurs, a hideous experimental warfare, armed rioters fighting armed rioters, armed rioters swept forward by the words and fury of a song, by the tramping sympathy of their numbers, pouring in countless myriads towards the smaller ways, the disabled lifts, the galleries slippery with blood, the halls and passages choked with smoke beneath the flying stages, to learn there when retreat was hopeless the ancient mysteries of warfare. And overhead save for a few sharpshooters upon the roof spaces and for a few bands and threads of vapour that multiplied and darkened towards the evening, the day was a clear serenity. Ostrog it seems had no bombs at command and in all the earlier phases of the battle the flying machines played no part. Not the smallest cloud was there to break the empty brilliance of the sky. It was as though it held itself vacant until the aeroplanes should come.

Ever and again there was news of these, drawing nearer, from this Spanish town and then that, and presently from France. But of the new guns that Ostrog had made and which were known to be in the city came no news in spite of Graham's urgency, nor any report of successes from the dense felt of fighting strands about the flying stages. Section after section of the Labour Societies reported itself assembled, reported itself marching, and vanished from knowledge into the labyrinth of that warfare. What was happening there? Even the busy Ward Leaders did not know. In spite of the opening and closing of doors, the hasty messengers, the ringing of bells and the perpetual clitter-clack of recording implements, Graham felt isolated, strangely inactive, inoperative.

His isolation seemed at times the strangest, the most unexpected of all the things that had happened since his awakening. It had something of the quality of that inactivity that comes in dreams. A tumult, the stupendous realization of a world struggle between Ostrog and himself, and then this confined quiet little room with its mouthpieces and bells and broken mirror!

Now the door would be closed and Graham and Helen were alone together; they seemed sharply marked off then from all the unprecedented world storm that rushed together without, vividly aware of one another, only concerned with one another. Then the door would open again, messengers would enter, or a sharp bell would stab their privacy, and it was like a window in a brightly lit house flung open suddenly to a hurricane. The dark hurry and tumult, the stress and vehemence of the battle rushed in and overwhelmed them. They were no longer persons but mere spectators, mere impressions of a tremendous convulsion. They became unreal even to themselves, miniatures of personality, indescribably small, and the two antagonistic realities, the only realities in being were first the city, that throbbed and roared yonder in a belated frenzy of defence, and secondly the aeroplanes hurling inexorably towards them over the round shoulder of the world.

There came a sudden stir outside, a running to and fro, and cries. The girl stood up, speechless, incredulous.

Metallic voices were shouting 'Victory!' Yes it was 'Victory!'

Bursting through the curtains appeared the man in yellow, startled and dishevelled with excitement. 'Victory,' he cried, 'victory! The people are winning. Ostrog's people have collapsed.'

She rose. 'Victory?'

'What do you mean?' asked Graham. 'Tell me! *What?*'

'We have driven them out of the under galleries at Norwood, Streatham is afire and burning wildly, and Roehampton is ours. *Ours!* – and we have taken the monoplane that lay thereon.'

A shrill bell rang. An agitated grey-headed man appeared from the room of the Ward Leaders. 'It is all over,' he cried.

'What matters it now that we have Roehampton? The aeroplanes have been sighted at Boulogne!'

'The Channel!' said the man in yellow. He calculated swiftly. 'Half an hour.'

'They still have three of the flying stages,' said the old man.

'Those guns?' cried Graham.

'We cannot mount them – in half an hour.'

'Do you mean they are found?'

'Too late,' said the old man.

'If we could stop them another hour!' cried the man in yellow.

'Nothing can stop them now,' said the old man. 'They have near a hundred aeroplanes in the first fleet.'

'Another hour?' asked Graham.

'To be so near!' said the Ward Leader. 'Now that we have found those guns. To be so near – If once we could get them out upon the roof spaces.'

'How long would that take?' asked Graham suddenly. 'An hour – certainly.'

'Too late,' cried the Ward Leader, 'too late.'

'*Is* it too late?' said Graham. 'Even now – An hour!'

He had suddenly perceived a possibility. He tried to speak calmly, but his face was white. 'There is one chance. You said there was a monoplane—?'

'On the Roehampton stage, Sire.'

'Smashed?'

'No. It is lying crossways to the carrier. It might be got upon the guides – easily. But there is no aeronaut—'

Graham glanced at the two men and then at Helen. He spoke after a long pause. 'We have no aeronauts?'

'None.'

He turned suddenly to Helen. His decision was made. 'I must do it.'

'Do what?'

'Go to this flying stage – to this machine.'

'What do you mean?'

'I am an aeronaut. After all – Those days for which you reproached me were not altogether wasted.'

He turned to the old man in yellow. 'Tell them to put it upon the guides.'

The man in yellow hesitated.

'What do you mean to do?' cried Helen.

'This monoplane – it is a chance—'

'You don't mean—?'

'To fight – yes. To fight in the air. I have thought before – A big aeroplane is a clumsy thing. A resolute man—!'

'But – never since flying began —' cried the man in yellow.

'There has been no need. But now the time has come. Tell them now – send them my message – to put it upon the guides. I see now something to do. I see now why I am here!'

The old man dumbly interrogated the man in yellow, nodded, and hurried out.

Helen made a step towards Graham. Her face was white. 'But, Sire! – How can one fight? You will be killed.'

'Perhaps. Yet, not to do it – or to let someone else attempt it—'

'You will be killed,' she repeated.

'I've said my Word. Do you not see? It may save – London!'

He stopped, he could speak no more, he swept the alternative aside by a gesture, and they stood staring at one another.

There was no act of tenderness between them, no embrace, no parting word. The bare thought of personal love was swept aside by the tremendous necessities of his position. Her face expressed amazement and acceptance. A little movement of her hands gave him to his fate.

He turned towards the man in yellow. 'I am ready,' he said.

25

The Coming of the Aeroplanes

Two men in pale blue were lying in the irregular line that stretched along the edge of the captured Roehampton stage from end to end, grasping their carbines and peering into the shadows of the stage called Wimbledon Park. Now and then they spoke to one another. They spoke the mutilated English of their class and period. The fire of the Ostrogites had dwindled and ceased, and few of the enemy had been seen for some time. But the echoes of the fight that was going on now far below in the lower galleries of that stage, came every now and then between the staccato of shots from the popular side. One of these men was describing to the other how he had seen a man down below there dodge behind a girder, and had aimed at a guess and hit him cleanly as he dodged too far. 'He's down there still,' said the marksman. 'See that little patch. Yes. Between those bars.'

A few yards behind them lay a dead stranger, face upward to the sky, with the blue canvas of his jacket smouldering in a circle about the neat bullet hole on his chest. Close beside him a wounded man, with a leg swathed about, sat with an expressionless face and watched the progress of that burning. Behind them, athwart the carrier lay the captured monoplane.

'I can't see him *now*,' said the second man in a tone of provocation.

The marksman became foul-mouthed and high-voiced in his earnest endeavour to make things plain. And suddenly, interrupting him, came a noisy shouting from the substage.

'What's going on now?' he said, and raised himself on one arm to survey the stairheads in the central groove of the stage. A number of blue figures were coming up these, and swarming across the stage.

'We don't want all these fools,' said his friend. 'They only crowd up and spoil shots. What are they after?'

'Ssh! – they're shouting something.'

The two men listened. The newcomers had crowded densely about the machine. Three Ward Leaders, conspicuous by their black mantles and badges, clambered into the body and appeared above it. The rank and file flung themselves upon the vans, gripping hold of the edges, until the entire outline of the thing was manned, in some places three deep. One of the marksmen knelt up. 'They're putting it on the carrier – that's what they're after.'

He rose to his feet, his friend rose also. 'What's the good?' said his friend. 'We've got no aeronauts.'

'That's what they're doing anyhow.' He looked at his rifle, looked at the struggling crowd, and suddenly turned to the wounded man. 'Mind these, mate,' he said, handing his carbine and cartridge belt; and in a moment he was running towards the monoplane. For a quarter of an hour he was lugging, thrusting, shouting and heeding shouts, and then the thing was done, and he stood with a multitude of others cheering their own achievement. By this time he knew, what indeed everyone in the city knew, that the Master, raw learner though he was, intended to fly this machine himself, was coming even now to take control of it, would let no other man attempt it.

'He who takes the greatest danger, he who bears the heaviest burthen, that man is King,' so the Master was reported to have spoken. And even as this man cheered, and while the beads of sweat still chased one another from the disorder of his hair, he heard the thunder of a greater tumult, and in fitful snatches the beat and impulse of the revolutionary song. He saw through a gap in the people that a thick stream of heads still poured up the stairway. 'The Master is coming,' shouted voices, 'the Master is coming,' and the crowd about him grew denser and denser. He began to thrust himself towards the central groove. 'The Master is coming!' 'The Sleeper, the Master!' 'God and the Master!' roared the voices.

And suddenly quite close to him were the black uniforms of the revolutionary guard, and for the first and last time in his life he saw Graham, saw him quite nearly. A tall, dark man in a flowing black robe he was, with a white, resolute face and eyes fixed steadfastly before him; a man who for all the little things about him had neither ears nor eyes nor thoughts. . . .

For all his days that man remembered the passing of Graham's bloodless face. In a moment it had gone and he was fighting in the swaying crowd. A lad weeping with terror thrust against him, pressing

596

towards the stairways, yelling 'Clear for the start, you fools!' The bell
that cleared the flying stage became a loud unmelodious clanging.

With that clanging in his ears Graham drew near the monoplane,
marched into the shadow of its tilting wing. He became aware that a
number of people about him were offering to accompany him, and
waved their offers aside. He wanted to think how one started the
engine. The bell clanged faster and faster, and the feet of the retreating
people roared faster and louder. The man in yellow was assisting him
to mount through the ribs of the body. He clambered into the
aeronaut's place, fixing himself very carefully and deliberately. What
was it? The man in yellow was pointing to two small flying machines
driving upward in the southern sky. No doubt they were looking for
the coming aeroplanes. That – presently – the thing to do now was to
start. Things were being shouted at him, questions, warnings. They
bothered him. He wanted to think about the machine, to recall every
item of his previous experience. He waved the people from him, saw
the man in yellow dropping off through the ribs, saw the crowd cleft
down the line of the girders by his gesture.

For a moment he was motionless, staring at the levers, the wheel by
which the engine shifted, and all the delicate appliances of which he
knew so little. His eye caught a spirit level with the bubble towards him,
and he remembered something, spent a dozen seconds in swinging the
engine forward until the bubble floated in the centre of the tube. He
noted that the people were not shouting, knew they watched his
deliberation. A bullet smashed on the bar above his head. Who fired?
Was the line clear of people? He stood up to see and sat down again.

In another second the propeller was spinning and he was gliding
down the guides. He gripped the wheel and swung the engine back to
lift the stem. Then it was the people shouted. He was throbbing with
the quiver of the engine, and the shouts dwindled swiftly behind,
rushed down to silence. The wind whistled over the edges of the
screen, and the world sank away from him very swiftly.

Throb, throb, throb – throb, throb, throb; up he drove. He fancied
himself free of all excitement, felt cool and deliberate. He lifted the
stem still more, opened one valve on his left wing and swept round
and up. He looked down with a steady head, and up. One of the
Ostrogite monoplanes was driving across his course, so that he drove
obliquely towards it and would pass below it at a steep angle. Its little
aeronauts were peering down at him. What did they mean to do? His
mind became active. One, he saw, held a weapon pointing, seemed
prepared to fire. What did they think he meant to do? Instantly he
understood their tactics and his resolution was taken. His momentary

lethargy was past. He opened two more valves to his left, swung round, end on to this hostile machine, closed his valves, and shot straight at it, stem and windscreen shielding him from the shot. They tilted a little as if to clear him. He flung up his stem.

Throb, throb, throb – pause – throb, throb – he set his teeth, his face into an involuntary grimace, and crash! He struck it! He struck upward beneath the nearer wing.

Very slowly the wing of his antagonist seemed to broaden as the impetus of his blow turned it up. He saw the full breadth of it and then it slid downward out of his sight.

He felt his stem going down, his hands tightened on the levers, whirled and rammed the engine back. He felt the jerk of a clearance, the nose of the machine jerked upward steeply, and for a moment he seemed to be lying on his back. The machine was reeling and staggering, it seemed to be dancing on its screw. He made a huge effort, hung with all his weight on the levers, and slowly the engine came forward again. He was driving upward but no longer so steeply. He gasped for a moment and flung himself at the levers again. The wind whistled about him. One further effort and he was almost level. He could breathe. He turned his head for the first time to see what had become of his antagonists. Turned back to the levers and looked again. For a moment he could have believed they were annihilated. And then he saw between the two stages to the east was a chasm, and down this something, a slender edge, fell swiftly and vanished as a sixpence falls down a crack.

At first he did not understand, and then a wild joy possessed him. He shouted at the top of his voice, an inarticulate shout, and drove higher and higher up the sky. Throb, throb, throb, pause, throb, throb, throb. 'Where was the other?' he thought. 'They too —' As he looked round the empty heavens he had a momentary fear that this second machine had risen above him, and then he saw it alighting on the Norwood stage. They had meant shooting. To risk being rammed headlong two thousand feet in the air was beyond their latter-day courage. . . .

For a little while he circled, then swooped in a steep descent towards the westward stage. Throb throb throb, throb throb throb. The twilight was creeping on apace, the smoke from the Streatham stage that had been so dense and dark, was now a pillar of fire, and all the laced curves of the moving ways and the translucent roofs and domes and the chasms between the buildings were glowing softly now, lit by the tempered radiance of the electric light that the glare of the day overpowered. The three efficient stages that the Ostrogites held – for

Wimbledon Park was useless because of the fire from Roehampton, and Streatham was a furnace – were glowing with guide lights for the coming aeroplanes. As he swept over the Roehampton stage he saw the dark masses of the people thereon. He heard a clap of frantic cheering, heard a bullet from the Wimbledon Park stage tweet through the air, and went beating up above the Surrey wastes. He felt a breath of wind from the south-west, and lifted his westward wing as he had learnt to do, and so drove upward heeling into the rare swift upper air. Whirr, whirr, whirr.

Up he drove and up, to that pulsating rhythm, until the country beneath was blue and indistinct, and London spread like a little map traced in light, like the mere model of a city near the brim of the horizon. The south-west was a sky of sapphire over the shadowy rim of the world, and ever as he drove upward the multitude of stars increased.

And behold! In the southward, low down and glittering swiftly nearer, were two little patches of nebulous light. And then two more, and then a glow of swiftly driving shapes. Presently he could count them. There were four and twenty. The first fleet of aeroplanes had come! Beyond appeared a yet greater glow.

He swept round in a half circle, staring at this advancing fleet. It flew in a wedge-like shape, a triangular flight of gigantic phosphorescent shapes sweeping nearer through the lower air. He made a swift calculation of their pace, and spun the little wheel that brought the engine forward. He touched a lever and the throbbing effort of the engine ceased. He began to fall, fell swifter and swifter. He aimed at the apex of the wedge. He dropped like a stone through the whistling air. It seemed scarce a second from that soaring moment before he struck the foremost aeroplane.

No man of all that black multitude saw the coming of his fate, no man among them dreamt of the hawk that struck downward upon him out of the sky. Those who were not limp in the agonies of air sickness, were craning their black necks and staring to see the filmy city that was rising out of the haze, the rich and splendid city to which 'Massa Boss' had brought their obedient muscles. Bright teeth gleamed and the glossy faces shone. They had heard of Paris. They knew they were to have lordly times among the poor white trash.

Suddenly Graham hit them.

He had aimed at the body of the aeroplane, but at the very last instant a better idea had flashed into his mind. He twisted about and struck near the edge of the starboard wing with all his accumulated weight. He was jerked back as he struck. His prow went gliding across

599

its smooth expanse towards the rim. He felt the forward rush of the huge fabric sweeping him and his monoplane along with it, and for a moment that seemed an age he could not tell what was happening. He heard a thousand throats yelling, and perceived that his machine was balanced on the edge of the gigantic float, and driving down, down; glanced over his shoulder and saw the backbone of the aeroplane and the opposite float swaying up. He had a vision through the ribs of sliding chairs, staring faces, and hands clutching at the tilting guide bars. The fenestrations in the further float flashed open as the aeronaut tried to right her. Beyond, he saw a second aeroplane leaping steeply to escape the whirl of its heeling fellow. The broad area of swaying wings seemed to jerk upward. He felt he had dropped clear, that the monstrous fabric, clean overturned, hung like a sloping wall above him.

He did not clearly understand that he had struck the side float of the aeroplane and slipped off, but he perceived that he was flying free on the down glide and rapidly nearing earth. What had he done? His heart throbbed like a noisy engine in his throat and for a perilous instant he could not move his levers because of the paralysis of his hands. He wrenched the levers to throw his engine back, fought for two seconds against the weight of it, felt himself righting, driving horizontally, set the engine beating again.

He looked upward and saw two aeroplanes glide shouting far overhead, looked back, and saw the main body of the fleet opening out and rushing upward and outward; saw the one he had struck fall edgewise on and strike like a gigantic knife-blade along the windwheels below it.

He put down his stern and looked again. He drove up heedless of his direction as he watched. He saw the wind-vanes give, saw the huge fabric strike the earth, saw its downward vanes crumple with the weight of its descent, and then the whole mass turned over and smashed, upside down, upon the sloping wheels. Then from the heaving wreckage a thin tongue of white fire licked up towards the zenith. He was aware of a huge mass flying through the air towards him, and turned upwards just in time to escape the charge – if it was a charge – of a second aeroplane. It whirled by below, sucked him down a fathom, and nearly turned him over in the gust of its close passage.

He became aware of three others rushing towards him, aware of the urgent necessity of beating above them. Aeroplanes were all about him, circling wildly to avoid him, as it seemed. They drove past him, above, below, eastward and westward. Far away to the westward was the sound of a collision, and two falling flares. Far away to the southward a second squadron was coming. Steadily he beat upward. Presently all the aeroplanes were below him, but he doubted the height he had of them, and did not swoop again immediately. And then he came down upon a second victim and all its load of soldiers saw him coming. The big machine heeled and swayed as the fear-maddened men scrambled to the stern for their weapons. A score of bullets sang through the air, and there flashed a star in the thick glass windscreen that protected him. The aeroplane slowed and dropped to foil his stroke, and dropped too low. Just in time he saw the wind-wheels of Bromley hill rushing up towards him, and spun about and up as the aeroplane he had chased crashed among them. All its voices wove into a felt of yelling. The great fabric seemed to be standing on end for a second among the heeling and splintering vanes, and then it flew to pieces. Huge splinters came flying through the air, its engines burst like shells. A hot rush of flame shot overhead into the darkling sky.

' *Two!*' he cried, with a bomb from overhead bursting as it fell, and forthwith he was beating up again. A glorious exhilaration possessed him now, a giant activity. His troubles about humanity, about his inadequacy, were gone for ever. He was a man in battle rejoicing in his power. Aeroplanes seemed radiating from him in every direction, intent only upon avoiding him, the yelling of their packed passengers came in short gusts as they swept by. He chose his third quarry, struck hastily and did but turn it on edge. It escaped him, to smash against the tall cliff of London Wall. Flying from that impact he skimmed the darkling ground so nearly he could see a frightened rabbit bolting up a slope. He jerked up steeply, and found himself driving over south London with the air about him vacant. To the right of him a wild riot of signal rockets from the Ostrogites banged tumultuously in the sky. To the south the wreckage of half a dozen air ships flamed, and east and west and north they fled before him. They drove away to the east and north, and went about in the south, for they could not pause in the air. In their present confusion any attempt at evolution would have meant disastrous collisions.

He passed two hundred feet or so above the Roehampton stage. It was black with people and noisy with their frantic shouting. But why was the Wimbledon Park stage black and cheering, too? The smoke and flame of Streatham now hid the three further stages. He curved about and rose to see them and the northern quarters. First came the square masses of Shooter's Hill into sight, from behind the smoke, lit and orderly with the aeroplane that had landed and its disembarking Negroes. Then came Blackheath, and then under the corner of the reek the Norwood stage. On Blackheath no aeroplane had landed. Norwood was covered by a swarm of little figures running to and fro in a passionate confusion. Why? Abruptly he understood. The stubborn defence of the flying stages was over, the people were pouring into the under-ways of these last strongholds of Ostrog's usurpation. And then, from far away on the northern border of the city, full of glorious import to him, came a sound, a signal, a note of triumph, the leaden thud of a gun. His lips fell apart, his face was disturbed with emotion.

He drew an immense breath. 'They win,' he shouted to the empty air; 'the people win!' The sound of a second gun came like an answer. And then he saw the monoplane on Blackheath was running down its guides to launch. It lifted clean and rose. It shot up into the air, driving straight southward and away from him.

In an instant it came to him what this meant. It must needs be Ostrog in flight. He shouted and dropped towards it. He had the momentum of his elevation and fell slanting down the air and very swiftly. The other machine rose steeply at his approach. He allowed for its velocity and drove straight upon it.

It suddenly became a mere flat edge, and behold! he was past it, and driving headlong down with all the force of his futile blow.

He was furiously angry. He reeled the engine back along its shaft and went circling up. He saw Ostrog's machine beating up a spiral before him. He rose straight towards it, won above it by virtue of the impetus of his swoop and by the advantage and weight of a man. He dropped headlong – dropped and missed again! As he rushed past he saw the face of Ostrog's aeronaut confident and cool and in Ostrog's attitude a wincing resolution. Ostrog was looking steadfastly away from him – to the south. He realized with a gleam of wrath how bungling his flight must be. Below he saw the Croydon hills. He jerked upwards and once more he gained on his enemy.

He glanced over his shoulder and his attention was arrested. The eastward stage, the one on Shooter's Hill, appeared to lift; a flash changing to a tall grey shape, a cowled figure of smoke and dust, jerked into the air. For a moment this cowled figure stood motionless, dropping huge masses of metal from its shoulders, and then it began to uncoil a dense head of smoke. The people had blown it up, aeroplane and all! As suddenly a second flash and grey shape sprang up from the Norwood stage. And even as he stared at this came a dead report; and the air wave of the first explosion struck him. He was flung up and sideways.

For a moment his monoplane fell nearly edgewise with her nose down, and seemed to hesitate whether to overset altogether. He stood

602

on his windshield, wrenching the wheel that swayed up over his head. And then the shock of the second explosion took his machine sideways.

He found himself clinging to one of the ribs of his machine, and the air was blowing past him and *upwards*. He seemed to be hanging quite still in the air, with the wind blowing up past him. But the world below was rotating – more and more rapidly. It occurred to him that he was falling. Then he was sure that he was falling. He could not look down.

He found himself recapitulating with incredible swiftness all that had happened since his awakening, the days of doubt, the days of Empire, and at last the tumultuous discovery of Ostrog's calculated treachery.

The vision had a quality of utter unreality. Who was he? Why was he holding so tightly with his hands? Why could he not let go? In such a fall as this countless dreams have ended. But in a moment he would wake. . . .

His thoughts ran swifter and swifter. He wondered if he should see Helen again. It seemed so unreasonable that he should not see her again.

Although he could not look at it, he was suddenly aware that the whirling earth below him was very near.

Came a shock and a great crackling and popping of bars and stays.

THE WAR IN THE AIR

I

Of Progress and the Smallways Family

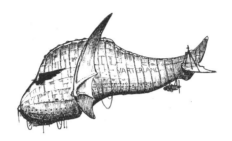

I

'This here Progress,' said Mr Tom Smallways, 'it keeps on.

'You'd hardly think it *could* keep on,' said Mr Tom Smallways.

It was long before the War in the Air began that Mr Smallways made this remark. He was sitting on the fence at the end of his garden and surveying the great Bun Hill gasworks with an eye that neither praised nor blamed. Above the clustering gasometers three unfamiliar shapes appeared, thin, wallowing bladders that flapped and rolled about, and grew bigger and bigger and rounder and rounder – balloons in course of inflation for the South of England Aero Club's Saturday-afternoon ascent.

'They goes up every Saturday,' said his neighbour, Mr Stringer, the milkman. 'It's only yestiday, so to speak, when all London turned out to see a balloon go over, and now every little place in the country has its weekly outings – uppings, rather. It's been the salvation of them gas companies.'

'Larst Satiday I got three barrer-loads of gravel off my petaters,' said Mr Tom Smallways. 'Three barrer-loads! What they dropped as ballase. Some of the plants was broke, and some was buried.'

'Ladies, they say, goes up!'

'I suppose we got to call 'em ladies,' said Mr Tom Smallways. 'Still, it ain't hardly my idea of a lady – flying about in the air, and throwing gravel at people. It ain't what I been accustomed to consider ladylike, whether or no.'

Mr Stringer nodded his head approvingly, and for a time they

609

continued to regard the swelling bulks with expressions that had changed from indifference to disapproval.

Mr Tom Smallways was a greengrocer by trade and a gardener by disposition; his little wife Jessica saw to the shop, and Heaven had planned him for a peaceful world. Unfortunately Heaven had not planned a peaceful world for him. He lived in a world of obstinate and incessant change, and in parts where its operations were unsparingly conspicuous. Vicissitude was in the very soil he tilled; even his garden was upon a yearly tenancy, and overshadowed by a huge board that proclaimed it not so much a garden as an eligible building-site. He was horticulture under notice to quit, the last patch of country in a district flooded by new and urban things. He did his best to console himself, to imagine matters near the turn of the tide.

'You'd hardly think it could keep on,' he said.

Mr Smallways' aged father could remember Bun Hill as an idyllic Kentish village. He had driven Sir Peter Bone until he was fifty, and then he took to drink a little and driving the station bus, which lasted him until he was seventy-eight. Then he retired. He sat by the fireside, a shrivelled, very, very old coachman, full charged with reminiscences and ready for any careless stranger. He could tell you of the vanished estate of Sir Peter Bone, long since cut up for building, and how that magnate ruled the countryside when it was countryside, of shooting and hunting and of coaches along the high road, of how 'where the gasworks is' was a cricket field, and of the coming of the Crystal Palace. The Crystal Palace was six miles away from Bun Hill, a great façade that glittered in the morning and was a clear blue outline against the sky in the afternoon, and at night a source of gratuitous fireworks for all the population of Bun Hill. And then had come the railway, and then villas and villas, and then the gasworks and the waterworks and a great ugly sea of workmen's houses, and then drainage, and the water vanished out of the Otterbourne and left it a dreadful ditch, and then a second railway station, Bun Hill South, and more houses and more, more shops, more competition, plate-glass shops, a board-school, rates, omnibuses, tramcars – going right away into London itself – bicycles, motor-cars, and then more motor-cars, a Carnegie library.

'You'd hardly think it could keep on,' said Mr Tom Smallways, growing up among these marvels.

But it kept on. Even from the first the greengrocer's shop which he had set up in one of the smallest of the old surviving village houses in the tail of the High Street had a submerged air, an air of hiding from something that was looking for it. When they had made up the

610

pavement of the High Street, they levelled it so that one had to go down three steps into the shop. Tom did his best to sell only his own excellent but limited range of produce; but Progress came shoving things into his window, French artichokes and aubergines, foreign apples – apples from the State of New York, apples from California, apples from Canada, apples from New Zealand, 'pretty-lookin' fruit, but not what I should call English apples,' said Tom – bananas, unfamiliar nuts, grapefruits, mangoes.

The motor-cars that went by northward and southward grew more and more powerful and efficient, whizzed faster and smelt worse; there appeared great clangorous petrol trolleys delivering coal and parcels in the place of vanishing horse-vans; motor-omnibuses ousted the horse-omnibuses, even the Kentish strawberries going Londonward in the night took to machinery and clattered instead of creaking, and became affected in flavour by progress and petrol.

And then young Bert Smallways got a motor-bicycle. . . .

2

Bert, it is necessary to explain, was a progressive Smallways.

Nothing speaks more eloquently of the pitiless insistence of progress and expansion in our time than that it should get into the Smallways blood. But there was something advanced and enterprising about young Smallways before he was out of short frocks. He was lost for a whole day when he was five, and nearly drowned in the reservoir of the new waterworks before he was seven. He had a real pistol taken away from him by a real policeman when he was ten. And he learnt to smoke, not with pipes and brown paper and cane as Tom had done, but with a penny packet of Boys of England American cigarettes. His language shocked his father before he was twelve, and by that age, what with touting for parcels at the station and selling the Bun Hill *Weekly Express*, he was making three shillings a week or more, and spending it on *Chips, Comic Cuts, Ally Sloper's Half-holiday*, cigarettes, and all the concomitants of a life of pleasure and enlightenment. All of this without hindrance to his literary studies, which carried him up to the seventh standard at an exceptionally early age. I mention these things so that you may have no doubt at all concerning the sort of stuff Bert had in him.

He was six years younger than Tom, and for a time there was an attempt to utilize him in the greengrocer's shop when Tom at twenty-one married Jessica – who was thirty and had saved a little money in service. But it was not Bert's *forte* to be utilized. He hated digging,

611

and when he was given a basket of stuff to deliver, a nomadic instinct arose irresistibly, it became his pack, and he did not seem to care how heavy it was nor where he took it, so long as he did not take it to its destination. Glamour filled the world, and he strayed after it, basket and all. So Tom took his goods out himself, and sought for Bert employers who did not know of this strain of poetry in his nature. Bert touched the fringe of a number of trades in succession – draper's porter, chemist's boy, doctor's page, junior assistant gas-fitter, envelope addresser, milk-cart assistant, golf-caddie, and at last helper in a bicycle shop. Here, apparently, he found the progressive quality his nature had craved. His employer was a pirate-souled young man named Grubb, with a black-smeared face by day and a music-hall side in the evening, who dreamt of a patent lever chain; and it seemed to Bert that he was the perfect model of a gentleman of spirit. He hired out quite the dirtiest and unsafest bicycles in the whole south of England, and conducted the subsequent discussions with astonishing verve. Bert and he settled down very well together. Bert lived in, became almost a trick rider – he could ride bicycles for miles that would have come to pieces instantly under you or me – took to washing his face after business and sometimes even his neck, and spent his surplus money upon remarkable ties and collars, cigarettes and shorthand classes at the Bun Hill Institute.

He would go round to Tom at times, and look and talk so brilliantly that Tom and Jessica, who both had a natural tendency to be respectful to anybody or anything, looked up to him immensely.

'He's a go-ahead chap, is Bert,' said Tom. 'He knows a thing or two.'

'Let's hope he don't know too much,' said Jessica, who had a fine sense of limitations.

'It's go-ahead Times,' said Tom. 'Noo petaters, and English at that; we'll be having 'em in March if things go on as they do go. I never see such Times. See his tie last night?'

'It wasn't suited to him, Tom. It was a gentleman's tie. He wasn't up to it – not the rest of him. It wasn't becoming.' . . .

Then presently Bert got a cyclist's suit, cap, badge and all; and to see him and Grubb going down to Brighton (and back) – heads down, handlebars down, backbones curved – was a revelation in the possibilities of the Smallways blood.

Go-ahead Times!

Old Smallways would sit over the fire mumbling of the greatness of other days, of old Sir Peter, who drove his coach to Brighton and back in eight-and-twenty hours, of old Sir Peter's white top-hats, of Lady

Bone, who never set foot to ground except to walk in the garden, of the great prize-fights at Crawley. He talked of pink and pigskin breeches, of foxes at Ring's Bottom, where now the County Council pauper lunatics were enclosed, of Lady Bone's chintzes and crinolines. Nobody heeded him. The world had thrown up a new type of gentleman altogether – a gentleman of most ungentlemanly energy, a gentleman in dusty oilskins and motor-goggles and a wonderful cap, a stink-making gentleman, a swift, high-class badger, who fled perpetually along high roads from the dust and stink he perpetually made. And his lady, as they were able to see her at Bun Hill, was a weather-bitten goddess as free from refinement as a gipsy – not so much dressed as packed for transit at a high velocity.

So Bert grew up, filled with ideals of speed and enterprise, and became, so far as he became anything, a kind of bicycle engineer of the let's-'ave-a-look-at-it and enamel-chipping variety. Even a road-racer, geared to a hundred and twenty, failed to satisfy him, and for a time he pined in vain at twenty miles an hour along roads that were continually more dusty and more crowded with mechanical traffic. But at last his savings accumulated, and his chance came. The hire-purchase system bridged a financial gap, and one bright and memorable Sunday morning he wheeled his new possession through the shop into the road, got on to it with the advice and assistance of Grubb, and teuf-teuffed off into the haze of the traffic-tortured high road, to add himself as one more voluntary public danger to the amenities of the south of England.

'Orf to Brighton!' said old Smallways, regarding his youngest son from the sitting-room window over the greengrocer's shop with something between pride and reprobation. 'When I was 'is age, I'd never bin to London, never bin south of Crawley – never bin anywhere on my own where I couldn't walk. And nobody didn't go. Not unless they was gentry. Now everybody's orf everywhere; the whole dratted country sims flying to pieces. Wonder they all get back. Orf to Brighton indeed! Anybody want to buy 'orses?'

'You can't say *I* bin to Brighton, father,' said Tom.

'Nor don't want to go,' said Jessica sharply; 'creering about and spendin' your money.'

3

For a time the possibilities of the motor-bicycle so occupied Bert's mind that he remained regardless of the new direction in which the striving soul of man was finding exercise and refreshment. He failed to observe that the type of motor-car, like the type of bicycle, was settling down and losing its adventurous quality. Indeed, it is as true as it is remarkable that Tom was the first to observe the new development. But his gardening made him attentive to the heavens, and the proximity of the Bun Hill gasworks and the Crystal Palace, from which ascents were continually being made, and presently the descent of ballast upon his potatoes conspired to bear in upon his unwilling mind the fact that the Goddess of Change was turning her disturbing attention to the sky. The first great boom in aeronautics was beginning.

Grubb and Bert heard of it in a music-hall, then it was driven home to their minds by the cinematograph, then Bert's imagination was stimulated by a sixpenny edition of that aeronautic classic, Mr George Griffith's *The Outlaws of the Air*, and so the thing really got hold of them.

At first the most obvious aspect was the multiplication of balloons. The sky of Bun Hill began to be infested by balloons! On Wednesday and Saturday afternoons particularly you could scarcely look skyward for a quarter of an hour without discovering a balloon somewhere. And then one bright day Bert, motoring towards Croydon, was arrested by the insurgence of a huge, bolster-shaped monster from the Crystal Palace grounds, and obliged to dismount and watch it. It was like a bolster with a broken nose, and below it, and comparatively small, was a stiff framework bearing a man and an engine with a screw that whizzed round in front and a sort of canvas rudder behind. The framework had an air of dragging the reluctant gas-cylinder after it like a brisk little terrier towing a shy, gas-distended elephant into society. The combined monster certainly travelled and steered. It went overhead perhaps a thousand feet up (Bert heard the engine), sailed away southward, vanished over the hills, reappeared a little blue outline far off in the east, going now very fast before a gentle south-west gale, returned above the Crystal Palace towers, circled round them, chose a position for descent, and sank down out of sight.

Bert sighed deeply, and turned to his motor-bicycle again.

And that was only the beginning of a succession of strange phenomena in the heavens – cylinders, cones, pear-shaped monsters, even at last a thing of aluminium that glittered wonderfully, and that Grubb, through some confusion of ideas about armour-plates, was inclined to consider a war machine.

There followed actual flight.

This, however, was not an affair that was visible from Bun Hill; it was something that occurred in private grounds or other enclosed places and under favourable conditions, and it was brought home to Grubb and Bert Smallways only by means of the magazine page of the halfpenny newspapers or by cinematograph records. But it was brought home very insistently, and in those days if ever one heard a man saying in a public place in a loud, reassuring confident tone, 'It's bound to come,' the chances were ten to one he was talking of flying. And Bert got a box lid and wrote out in correct window-ticket style, and Grubb put in the window this inscription: 'Aeroplanes made and repaired.' It quite upset Tom – it seemed taking one's shop so lightly; but most of the neighbours, and all the sporting ones, approved of it as being very good indeed.

Everybody talked of flying, everybody repeated over and over again, 'Bound to come,' and then you know it didn't come. There was a hitch. They flew – that was all right; they flew in machines heavier than air. But they smashed. Sometimes they smashed the engine, sometimes they smashed the aeronaut, usually they smashed both. Machines that made flights of three or four miles and came down safely, went up the next time to headlong disaster. There seemed no possible trusting to them. The breeze upset them, the eddies near the ground upset them, a passing thought in the mind of the aeronaut upset them. Also they upset – simply.

'It's this "stability" does 'em,' said Grubb, repeating his newspaper. 'They pitch and they pitch, till they pitch themselves to pieces.'

Experiments fell away after two expectant years of this sort of success, the public and then the newspapers tired of the expensive photographic reproductions, the optimistic reports, the perpetual sequence of triumph and disaster and silence. Flying slumped, even ballooning fell away to some extent, though it remained a fairly popular sport, and continued to lift gravel from the wharf of the Bun Hill gasworks and drop it upon deserving people's lawns and gardens. There were half a dozen reassuring years for Tom – at least so far as flying was concerned. But that was the great time of monorail development, and his anxiety was only diverted from the high heavens by the most urgent threats and symptoms of change in the lower sky.

There had been talk of monorails for several years. But the real mischief began when Brennan sprang his gyroscopic monorail car upon the Royal Society. It was the leading sensation of the 1907 soirées; that celebrated demonstration-room was all too small for its exhibition. Brave soldiers, leading Zionists, deserving novelists, noble ladies, congested the narrow passage, and thrust distinguished elbows into ribs the world would not willingly let break, deeming themselves fortunate if they could see 'just a little bit of the rail'. Inaudible but convincing, the great inventor expounded his discovery, and sent his obedient little model of the trains of the future up gradients, round curves and across a sagging wire. It ran along on its single rail, on its single wheels, simple and sufficient; it stopped, reversed, stood still, balancing perfectly. It maintained its astounding equilibrium amidst a thunder of applause. The audience dispersed at last, discussing how far they would enjoy crossing an abyss on a wire cable. 'Suppose the gyroscope stopped!' Few of them anticipated a tithe of what the Brennan monorail would do for their railway securities and the face of the world.

In a few years they realized better. In a little while no one thought anything of crossing an abyss on a wire, and the monorail was super-seding the tramlines, railways and indeed every form of track for mechanical locomotion. Where land was cheap the rail ran along the ground, where it was dear the rail lifted up on iron standards and passed overhead; its swift, convenient cars went everywhere and did everything that had once been done along made tracks upon the ground.

When old Smallways died, Tom could think of nothing more striking to say of him than, 'When he was a boy, there wasn't nothing higher than your chimbleys – there wasn't a wire nor a cable in the sky!'

Old Smallways went to his grave under an intricate network of wires and cables, for Bun Hill became not only a sort of minor centre of power distribution – the Home Counties Power Distribution Company set up transformers and a generating station close beside the old gasworks – but also a junction on the suburban monorail system. Moreover, every tradesman in the place, and indeed nearly every house, had its own telephone.

The monorail cable standards became a conspicuous fact in urban landscape, for the most part stout iron erections rather like tapering trestles, and painted a bright bluish green. One, it happened, bestrode Tom's house, which looked still more retiring and apologetic beneath its immensity; and another giant stood just inside the corner of his garden, which was still not built upon and unchanged except for a couple of advertisement boards, one recommending a two-and-six-penny watch, and one a nerve restorer. These, by-the-by, were placed almost horizontally to catch the eye of the passing monorail passengers above, and so served admirably to roof over a tool shed and a mush-room shed for Tom. All day and all night the fast cars from Brighton and Hastings went murmuring by overhead – long broad comfortable-looking cars, that were brightly lit after dusk. As they flew by at night, transient flares of light and a rumbling sound of passage, they kept up a perpetual summer lightning and thunderstorm in the street below.

Presently the English Channel was bridged – a series of great iron Eiffel Tower pillars carrying monorail cables at a height of a hundred and fifty feet above the water, except near the middle, where they rose higher to allow the passage of the London and Antwerp shipping and the Hamburg-America liners.

Then heavy motor-cars began to run about on only a couple of wheels, one behind the other, which for some reason upset Tom dreadfully and made him gloomy for days after the first one passed the shop. ...

All this gyroscopic and monorail development naturally absorbed a vast amount of public attention, and there was also a huge excitement consequent upon the amazing gold discoveries off the coast of Anglesey made by a submarine prospector, Miss Patricia Giddy. She had taken her degree in geology and mineralogy in the University of London, and while working upon the auriferous rocks of North Wales after a brief holiday spent in agitating for women's suffrage, she had been struck by the possibility of these reefs cropping up again under the water. She had set herself to verify this supposition by the use of the submarine crawler invented by Doctor Alberto Cassini. By a happy mingling of reasoning and intuition peculiar to her sex she found gold at her first descent, and emerged after three hours' submersion with about two hundredweight of ore containing gold in the unparalleled quantity of seventeen ounces to the ton. But the whole story of her submarine mining, intensely interesting as it is, must be told at some other time; suffice it now to remark simply that it was during the consequent great rise of prices, confidence and enterprise that the revival of interest in flying occurred.

4

It is curious how the final boom of flying began. It was like the coming of a breeze on a quiet day; nothing started it, it came. People began to talk of flying with an air of never having for one moment dropped the subject. Pictures of flying and flying machines returned to the newspapers; articles and allusions increased and multiplied in the serious magazines. People asked in monorail trains, 'When are we going to fly?' A new crop of inventors sprang up in a night or so like fungi. The Aero Club announced the project of a great Flying Exhibition in a large area of ground that the removal of slums in Whitechapel had rendered available.

The advancing wave soon produced a sympathetic ripple in the Bun Hill establishment. Grubb routed out his flying-machine model again, tried it in the yard behind the shop, got a kind of flight out of it, and broke seventeen panes of glass and nine flowerpots in the greenhouse that occupied the next yard but one.

And then, springing from nowhere, sustained one knew not how, came a persistent, disturbing rumour that the problem had been solved, that the secret was known. Bert met it one early-closing afternoon as he refreshed himself in an inn near Nutfield, whither his motor-bicycle had brought him. There smoked and meditated a person in khaki, an engineer, who presently took an interest in Bert's machine. It was a sturdy piece of apparatus, and it had acquired a kind of documentary value in these quick-changing times; it was now nearly eight years old. Its points discussed, the soldier broke into a new topic with, 'My next's going to be an aeroplane, so far as I can see. I've had enough of roads and ways.'

'They *tork*,' said Bert.

'They talk – and they do,' said the soldier. 'The thing's coming.'

'It keeps on coming,' said Bert; 'I shall believe when I see it.'

'That won't be long,' said the soldier.

The conversation seemed degenerating into an amiable wrangle of contradiction.

'I tell you they *are* flying,' the soldier insisted. 'I see it myself.'

'We've all seen it,' said Bert.

'I don't mean flap up and smash up; I mean real, safe, steady, controlled flying, against the wind, good and right.'

'You ain't seen that!'

'I 'ave! Aldershot. They try to keep it a secret. They got it right enough. You bet – our War Office isn't going to be caught napping this time.'

Bert's incredulity was shaken. He asked questions, and the soldier expanded.

'I tell you they got nearly a square mile fenced in – a sort of valley. Fences of barbed wire ten feet high, and inside that they do things. Chaps about the camp – now and then we get a peep. It isn't only us neither. There's the Japanese; you bet they got it too – and the Germans! And I never knowed anything of this sort yet that the Frenchies didn't get ahead with – after their manner! They started ironclads, they started submarines, they started navigables, and you bet they won't be far be'ind at this.'

The soldier stood with his legs very wide apart, and filled his pipe

618

thoughtfully. Bert sat on the low wall against which his motor-bicycle was leaning.

'Funny thing fighting'll be,' he said.

'Flying's going to break out,' said the soldier. 'When it *does* come, when the curtain does go up, I tell you you'll find everyone on the stage – busy. ... Such fighting, too! ... I suppose you don't read the papers about this sort of thing?'

'I read 'em a bit,' said Bert.

'Well, have you noticed what one might call the remarkable case of the disappearing inventor – the inventor who turns up in a blaze of publicity, fires off a few successful experiments, and vanishes?'

'Can't say I 'ave,' said Bert.

'Well, I 'ave, anyhow. You get anybody come along who does anything striking in this line, and, you bet, he vanishes. Just goes off quietly out of sight. After a bit, you don't hear anything more of 'em at all. See? They disappear. Gone – no address. First – oh! it's an old story now – there was those Wright Brothers out in America. They glided – they glided miles and miles. Finally they glided off stage. Why, it must be nineteen hundred and four, or five, *they* vanished! Then there was those people in Ireland – no, I forget their names. Everybody said they could fly. *They* went. They ain't dead that I've heard tell; but you can't say they're alive. Not a feather of 'em can you see. Then that chap who flew round Paris and upset in the Seine. De Booley, was it? I forget. That was a grand fly, in spite of the accident; but where's he got to? The accident didn't hurt him. Eh? '*E's* gone to cover.'

The soldier prepared to light his pipe.

'Looks like a secret society got hold of them,' said Bert.

'Secret society! *Naw!*'

The soldier lit his match, and drew. 'Secret society,' he repeated in response to these words, with his pipe between his teeth and the match flaring. 'War Departments; that's more like it.' He threw his match aside, and walked to his machine. 'I tell you, sir,' he said, 'there isn't a big Power in Europe, *or* Asia, *or* America, or Africa, that hasn't got at least one or two flying-machines hidden up its sleeve at the present time. Not one. Real, workable, flying-machines. And the spying! The spying and manoeuvring to find out what the others have got. I tell you, sir, a foreigner, or, for the matter of that, an unaccredited native, can't get within four miles of Lydd nowadays – not to mention our little circus at Aldershot, and the experimental camp in Galway. No!'

'Well,' said Bert, 'I'd like to see one of them, anyhow. Jest to help believing. I'll believe when I see, that I'll promise you.'

'You'll see 'em, fast enough,' said the soldier, and led his machine out into the road.

He left Bert on his wall, grave and pensive, with his cap on the back of his head, and a cigarette smouldering in the corner of his mouth.

'If what he says is true,' said Bert, 'me and Grubb, we been wasting our blessed old time. Besides incurring expense with thet green'ouse.'

5

It was while this mysterious talk with the soldier still stirred in Bert Smallways' imagination that the most astounding incident in the whole of that dramatic chapter of human history, the coming of flying, occurred. People talk glibly enough of epoch-making events; this *was* an epoch-making event. It was the unanticipated and entirely successful flight of Mr Alfred Butteridge from the Crystal Palace to Glasgow and back in a small businesslike-looking machine heavier than air – an entirely manageable and controllable machine that could fly as well as a pigeon.

It wasn't, one felt, a fresh step forward in the matter so much as a giant stride, a leap. Mr Butteridge remained in the air altogether for about nine hours, and during that time he flew with the ease and assurance of a bird. His machine was, however, neither bird-like nor butterfly-like, nor had it the wide, lateral expansion of the ordinary aeroplane. The effect upon the observer was rather something in the nature of a bee or wasp. Parts of the apparatus were spinning very rapidly, and gave one a hazy effect of transparent wings; but parts, including two peculiarly curved 'wing-cases' – if one may borrow a figure from the flying beetles – remained expanded stiffly. In the middle was a long rounded body like the body of a moth, and on this Mr Butteridge could be seen sitting astride, much as a man bestrides a horse. The wasp-like resemblance was increased by the fact that the apparatus flew with a deep booming hum, exactly the sound made by a wasp at a window-pane.

Mr Butteridge took the world by surprise. He was one of those gentlemen from nowhere Fate still succeeds in producing for the stimulation of mankind. He came, it was variously said, from Australia and America and the South of France. He was also described quite incorrectly as the son of a man who had amassed a comfortable fortune in the manufacture of gold nibs and the Butteridge fountain pens. But this was an entirely different strain of Butteridges. For some years, in spite of a loud voice, a large presence, an aggressive swagger, and an implacable manner, he had been an undistinguished member of most of the existing aeronautical associations. Then one day he wrote to all the London papers to announce that he had made arrangements for an ascent from the Crystal Palace of a machine that would demonstrate satisfactorily that the outstanding difficulties in the way of flying were finally solved. Few of the papers printed his letter, still fewer were the people who believed in his claim. No one was excited even when a fracas on the steps of a leading hotel in Piccadilly, in which he tried to horsewhip a prominent German musician upon some personal account, delayed his promised ascent. The quarrel was inadequately reported, and his name spelt variously Betteridge and Betridge. Until his flight indeed, he did not and could not contrive to exist in the public mind. There were scarcely thirty people on the lookout for him, in spite of all his clamour, when about six o'clock one summer morning the doors of the big shed in which he had been putting together his apparatus opened – it was near the big model of a megatherium in the Crystal Palace grounds – and his giant insect came droning out into a negligent and incredulous world.

But before he had made his second circuit of the Crystal Palace towers, Fame was lifting her trumpet, she drew a deep breath as the startled tramps who sleep on the seats of Trafalgar Square were roused by his buzz and awoke to discover him circling the Nelson column, and by the time he had got to Birmingham, which place he crossed about half past ten, her deafening blast was echoing throughout the country. The despaired-of thing was done. A man was flying securely and well.

Scotland was agape for his coming. Glasgow he reached by one o'clock, and it is related that scarcely a shipyard or factory in that busy hive of industry resumed work before half past two. The public mind was just sufficiently educated in the impossibility of flying to appreciate Mr Butteridge at his proper value. He circled the University buildings, and dropped to within shouting distance of the crowds in West End Park and on the slope of Gilmour Hill. The thing flew quite steadily at a pace of about three miles an hour, in a wide circle, making a deep hum that would have drowned his full, rich voice completely had he not provided himself with a megaphone. He avoided churches, buildings and monorail cables with consummate ease as he conversed.

'Me name's Butteridge,' he shouted; 'B-U-T-T-E-R-I-D-G-E. Got it? Me mother was Scotch.'

And having assured himself that he had been understood, he rose amidst cheers and shouting and patriotic cries, and then flew up very swiftly and easily into the south-eastern sky, rising and falling with long, easy undulations in an extraordinarily wasp-like manner.

His return to London – he visited and hovered over Manchester and Liverpool and Oxford on his way, and spelt his name out to each place – was an occasion of unparalleled excitement. Everyone was staring heavenward. More people were run over in the streets upon that one day than in the previous three months, and a County Council steamboat, the *Izaac Walton*, collided with a pier of Westminster Bridge, and narrowly escaped disaster by running ashore – it was low water – on the mud on the south side. He returned to the Crystal Palace grounds, that classic starting-point of aeronautical adventure, about sunset, re-entered his shed without disaster, and had the doors locked immediately upon the photographers and journalists who had been waiting his return.

'Look here, you chaps,' he said, as his assistant did so, 'I'm tired to death, and saddle sore. I can't give you a word of talk. I'm too – done. My name's Butteridge. B-U-T-T-E-R-I-D-G-E. Get that right. I'm an Imperial Englishman. I'll talk to you all tomorrow.'

Foggy snapshots still survive to record that incident. His assistant struggles in a sea of aggressive young men carrying notebooks or upholding cameras and wearing bowler hats and enterprising ties. He himself towers up in the doorway, a big figure with a mouth – an eloquent cavity beneath a vast black moustache – distorted by his shout to those relentless agents of publicity. He towers there, the most famous man in the country. Almost symbolically he holds and gesticulates with a megaphone in his left hand.

6

Tom and Bert Smallways both saw that return. They watched from the crest of Bun Hill, from which they had so often surveyed the pyrotechnics of the Crystal Palace. Bert was excited, Tom kept calm and lumpish, but neither of them realized how their own lives were to be invaded by the fruits of that beginning. 'P'raps old Grubb'll mind the shop a bit now,' he said, 'and put his blessed model in the fire. Not that that can save us, if we don't tide over with Steinhart's account.'

Bert knew enough of things and the problem of aeronautics to realize that this gigantic imitation of a bee would, to use his own idiom, 'give the newspapers fits'. The next day it was clear the fits had been given even as he said, their magazine pages were black with hasty photographs, their prose was convulsive, they foamed at the headline. The next day they were worse. Before the week was out they were not so much published as carried screaming into the street.

The dominant fact in the uproar was the exceptional personality of

Mr Butteridge, and the extraordinary terms he demanded for the secret of his machine.

For it was a secret, and he kept it secret in the most elaborate fashion. He built his apparatus himself, in the safe privacy of the great Crystal Palace sheds, with the assistance of inattentive workmen, and the day next following his flight he took it to pieces single-handed, packed certain portions, and then secured unintelligent assistance in packing and dispersing the rest. Sealed packing-cases went north and east and west to various pantechnicons, and the engines were boxed with peculiar care. It became evident these precautions were not inadvisable, in view of the violent demand for any sort of photograph or impressions of his machine. But Mr Butteridge, having once made his demonstration, intended to keep his secret safe from any further risk of leakage. He faced the British public now with the question whether they wanted his secret or not; he was, he said perpetually, an 'Imperial Englishman', and his first wish and his last was to see his invention the privilege and monopoly of the Empire. Only—

It was there the difficulty began.

Mr Butteridge, it became evident, was a man singularly free from any false modesty – indeed, from any modesty of any kind – singularly willing to see interviewers, answer questions upon any topic except aeronautics, volunteer opinions, criticisms and autobiography, supply portraits and photographs of himself, and generally spread his personality across the terrestrial sky. The published portraits insisted primarily upon an immense black moustache, and secondarily upon a fierceness behind the moustache. The general impression upon the public was that Butteridge was a small man. No one big, it was felt, could have so virulently aggressive an expression, though, as a matter of fact, Butteridge had a height of six feet two inches, and a weight altogether proportionate to that. Moreover, he had a love affair of large and unusual dimensions and irregular circumstances, and the still largely decorous British public learnt with reluctance and alarm that a sympathetic treatment of this story was inseparable from the exclusive acquisition by the British Empire of the priceless secret of aerial stability. The exact particulars of the irregularity never came to light, but apparently the lady had, in a fit of high-minded inadvertence, gone through the ceremony of marriage with – one quotes the unpublished discourse of Mr Butteridge – 'a white-livered skunk', and this zoological aberration did in some legal and vexatious manner mar her social happiness. Mr Butteridge wanted to talk about the business, to show the splendour of her nature in the light of its complications. It was really most embarrassing to a press that has always possessed a considerable turn for reticence, that wanted things personal indeed in the modern fashion, but not too personal. It was embarrassing, I say, to be inexorably confronted with Mr Butteridge's great heart, to see it laid open in relentless self-vivisection, and its pulsating dissepiments adorned with emphatic flag labels.

Confronted they were, and there was no getting away from it. He would make this appalling viscus beat and throb before the shrinking journalists – he was as insistent as an uncle with a big watch and a little baby; whatever evasion they attempted he set aside. He 'gloried in his love', he said, and compelled them to write it down.

'That's of course a private affair, Mr Butteridge,' they would object.

'The injustice, sorr, is public. I do not care whether I am up against institutions or individuals. I do not care if I am up against the Universal All. I am pleading the cause of a woman, a woman I lurve, sorr – a noble woman – misunderstood. I intend to vindicate her, sorr, to the four winds of heaven!

'I lurve England,' he used to say – 'I lurve England, but Puritanism, sorr, I abhor. It fills me with loathing. It raises my gorge. Take my own case. . . .'

He insisted relentlessly upon his heart, and upon seeing proofs of the interview. If they had not done justice to his erotic bellowings and gesticulations, he stuck in, in a large inky scrawl, all and more than they had omitted.

It was a strangely embarrassing thing for British journalism. Never was there a more obvious or uninteresting affair; never had the world heard the story of erratic affection with less appetite or sympathy. On the other hand, it was extremely curious about Mr Butteridge's invention. But when Mr Butteridge could be deflected for a moment from the cause of the lady he championed, then he talked chiefly, and usually with tears of tenderness in his voice, about his mother and his childhood – his mother who crowned a complete encyclopaedia of maternal virtue by being 'largely Scotch'. She was not quite neat, but nearly so. 'I owe everything in me to me mother,' he asserted – 'everything. Eh!' and – 'ask any man who's done anything. You'll hear the same story. All we have we owe to women. They are the species, sorr. Man is but a dream. He comes and goes. The woman's soul leadeth us upward and on!'

He was always going on like that.

What in particular he wanted from the Government for his secret did not appear, nor what beyond a money payment could be expected from a modern state in such an affair. The general effect upon judicious observers, indeed, was not that he was treating for anything, but that he was using an unexampled opportunity to bellow and show off to an attentive world. Rumours of his real identity spread abroad. It was said that he had been the landlord of an ambiguous hotel in Cape Town, and had there given shelter to and witnessed the experiments, and finally stolen the papers and plans of an extremely shy and friendless young inventor named Palliser, who had come to South Africa from England in an advanced stage of consumption, and died there. This, at any rate, was the allegation of the more outspoken American press. But the proof or disproof of that never reached the public.

Mr Butteridge also involved himself passionately in a tangle of disputes for the possession of a great number of valuable money prizes. Some of these had been offered so long ago as 1906 for successful mechanical flight. By the time of Mr Butteridge's success a really very considerable number of newspapers, tempted by the impunity of the pioneers in this direction, had pledged themselves to pay in some cases quite overwhelming sums to the first person to fly from Manchester to Glasgow, from London to Manchester, one hundred miles, two hundred miles in England and the like. Most had hedged a little with ambiguous conditions, and now offered resistance; one or two paid at once, and vehemently called attention to the fact; and Mr Butteridge plunged into litigation with the more recalcitrant, while at the same time sustaining a vigorous agitation and canvass to induce the Government to purchase his invention.

One fact, however, remained permanent throughout all the developments of this affair behind Butteridge's preposterous love interest, his politics and personality and all his shouting and boasting, and that was that so far as the mass of people knew he was in sole possession of the secret of the practicable aeroplane in which, for all one could tell to the contrary, the key of the future empire of the world resided. And presently, to the great consternation of innumerable people, including among others Mr Bert Smallways, it became apparent that whatever negotiations were in progress for the acquisition of this precious secret by the British Government were in danger of falling through. The London *Daily Requiem* first voiced the universal alarm, and published an interview under the terrific caption of 'Mr Butteridge Speaks his Mind'.

Therein the inventor – if he was an inventor – poured out his heart.

'I came from the end of the earth,' he said, which rather seemed to confirm the Cape Town story, 'bringing me Motherland the secret that would give her the empire of the world. And what do I get?' He paused. 'I am sniffed at by elderly mandarins! ... And the woman I love is treated like a leper!

'I am an Imperial Englishman,' he went on in a splendid outburst, subsequently written into the interview by his own hand; 'but there are limits to the human heart! There are younger nations – living nations! Nations that do not snore and gurgle helplessly in paroxysms of plethora upon beds of formality and red tape! There are nations that will not fling away the empire of earth in order to slight an unknown man and insult a noble woman whose boots they are not fitted to unlatch. There are nations not blinded to science, not given over hand and foot to effete snobocracies and Degenerate Decadents. In short, mark my words – *there are other nations!*' ...

This speech it was that particularly impressed Bert Smallways. 'If them Germans or them Americans get hold of this,' he said impressively to his brother, 'the British Empire's done. It's U.P. The Union Jack, so to speak, won't be worth the paper it's written on, Tom.'

'I suppose you couldn't lend us a hand this morning,' said Jessica, in his impressive pause. 'Everybody in Bun Hill seems wanting early potatoes at once. Tom can't carry half of them.'

'We're living on a volcano,' said Bert, disregarding the suggestion. 'At any moment war may come – such a war!'

He shook his head portentously.

'You'd better take this lot first, Tom,' said Jessica. She turned briskly on Bert. 'Can you spare us a morning?' she asked.

'I dessay I can,' said Bert. 'The shop's very quiet s'morning. Though all this danger to the Empire worries me something frightful.'

'Work'll take it off your mind,' said Jessica.

And presently he too was going out into a world of change and wonder, bowed beneath a load of potatoes and patriotic insecurity, that merged at last into a very definite irritation at the weight and want of style of the potatoes and a very clear conception of the entire detestableness of Jessica.

2

How Bert Smallways Got into Difficulties

I

It did not occur to either Tom or Bert Smallways that this remarkable aerial performance of Mr Butteridge was likely to affect either of their lives in any special manner, that it would in any way single them out from the millions about them; and when they had witnessed it from the crest of Bun Hill, and seen the fly-like mechanism, its rotating planes a golden haze in the sunset, sink humming to the harbour of its shed again, they turned back towards the sunken greengrocery beneath the great iron standard of the London to Brighton monorail, and their minds reverted to the discussion that had engaged them before Mr Butteridge's triumph had come in sight out of the London haze.

It was a difficult and unsuccessful discussion. They had to carry it on in shouts because of the moaning and roaring of the gyroscopic motor-cars that traversed the High Street, and in its nature it was contentious and private. The Grubb business was in difficulties, and Grubb in a moment of financial eloquence had given a half-share in it to Bert, whose relations with his employer had been for some time unsalaried and pallish and informal.

Bert was trying to impress Tom with the idea that the reconstructed Grubb and Smallways offered unprecedented and unparalleled opportunities to the judicious small investor. It was coming home to Bert, as though it were an altogether new fact, that Tom was entirely impervious to ideas. In the end he put the financial issues on one side, and, making the thing purely a matter of fraternal affection, succeeded in borrowing a sovereign on the security of his word of honour.

The firm of Grubb and Smallways, formerly Grubb, had indeed been persistently unlucky in the last year or so. For many years the business had struggled along with a flavour of romantic insecurity in a small, dissolute-looking shop in the High Street, adorned with brilliantly coloured advertisements of cycles, a display of bells, trouser clips, oilcans, pump clips, frame cases, wallets and other accessories, and the announcement of 'Bicycles on Hire', 'Repairs', 'Free Inflation', 'Petrol' and similar attractions. They were agents for several obscure makes of bicycle, two samples constituted the stock and occasionally they effected a sale, they also repaired punctures and did their best – though luck was not always on their side – with any other repairing that was brought to them. They handled a line of cheap gramophones, and did a little with musical boxes. The staple of their business was, however, the letting of bicycles on hire. It was a singular trade, obeying no known commercial or economic principles – indeed, no principles. There was a stock of ladies' and gentlemen's bicycles in a state of disrepair that passes description, the hiring stock, and these were let to unexacting and reckless people, inexpert in the things of this world, at a nominal rate of one shilling for the first hour and sixpence per hour afterwards. But really there were no fixed prices, and insistent boys could get bicycles and the thrill of danger for an hour for so low a sum as threepence, provided they could convince Grubb that that was all they had. The saddle and handlebar were then sketchily adjusted by Grubb, a deposit exacted, except in the case of familiar boys, the machine lubricated, and the adventurer started upon his career. Usually he or she came back, but at times, when the accident was serious, Bert or Grubb had to go out and fetch the machine home. Hire was always charged up to the hour of return to the shop and deducted from the deposit. It was rare that a bicycle started out from their hands in a state of pedantic efficiency. Romantic possibilities of accident lurked in the worn thread of the screw that adjusted the saddle, in the precarious pedals, in the loose-knit chain, in the handlebars, above all in the brakes and tyres. Tappings and clankings and strange rhythmic creakings awoke as the intrepid hirer pedalled out into the country. Then perhaps the bell would jam or a brake fail to act on a hill; or the seat pillar would get loose, and the saddle drop three or four inches with a disconcerting bump; or the loose and rattling chain would jump the cogs of the chain-wheel as the machine ran downhill, and so bring the mechanism to an abrupt and disastrous stop without at the same time arresting the forward momentum of the rider; or a tyre would bang, or sigh quietly, and give up the struggle and scrabble in the dust.

When the hirer returned, a heated pedestrian, Grubb would ignore all verbal complaints, and examine the machine gravely.

'This ain't 'ad fair usage,' he used to begin.

He became a mild embodiment of the spirit of reason. 'You can't expect a bicycle to take you up in its arms and carry you,' he used to say. 'You got to show intelligence. After all – it's machinery.'

Sometimes the process of liquidating the consequent claims bordered on violence. It was always a very rhetorical and often a trying affair, but in these progressive times you have to make a noise to get a living. It was often hard work, but nevertheless this hiring was a fairly steady source of profit, until one day all the panes in the window and door were broken and the stock on sale in the window greatly damaged and disordered by two overcritical hirers with no sense of rhetorical irrelevance. They were big, coarse stokers from Gravesend – one was annoyed because his left pedal had come off, and the other because his tyre had become deflated, small and indeed negligible accidents by Bun Hill standards, due entirely to the ungentle handling of the delicate machines entrusted to them, and they failed to see clearly how they put themselves in the wrong by this method of argument. It is a poor way of convincing a man that he has let you a defective machine to throw his foot-pump about his shop, and take his stock of gongs outside in order to return them through the window-panes. It carried no real conviction to the minds of either Grubb or Bert; it only irritated and vexed them. One quarrel makes many, and this unpleasantness led to a violent dispute between Grubb and the landlord upon the moral aspects of and legal responsibility for the consequent reglazing. Matters came to a climax upon the even of the Whitsuntide Holidays.

In the end Grubb and Smallways were put to the expense of a strategic nocturnal removal to another position.

It was a position they had long considered. It was a small, shed-like shop with a big window and one room behind, just at the sharp bend in the road at the bottom of Bun Hill, and here they struggled along bravely in spite of persistent annoyance from their former landlord, hoping for certain eventualities the peculiar situation of the shop seemed to promise. Here, too, they were doomed to disappointment.

The High Road from London to Brighton that ran through Bun Hill was like the British Empire or the British Constitution – a thing that had grown to its present importance. Unlike any other roads in Europe, the British high roads have never been subjected to any organized attempts to grade or straighten them out, and to that no doubt their peculiar picturesqueness is to be ascribed. The old Bun Hill High Street drops at its end for perhaps eighty or a hundred feet of descent at an angle of one in five, turns at right angles to the left, runs in a curve for about thirty yards to a brick bridge over the dry ditch that had once been the Otterbourne, and then bends sharply to the right again round a dense clump of trees and goes on, a simple, straightforward, peaceful high road. There had been one or two horse and van and bicycle accidents in the place before the shop Bert and Grubb took was built, and, to be frank, it was the probability of others that attracted them to it.

Its possibilities had come to them first with a humorous flavour.

'Here's one of the places where a chap might get a living by keeping hens,' said Grubb.

'You can't get a living by keeping hens,' said Bert.

'You'd keep the hen and have it spatchcocked,' said Grubb. 'The motor chaps would pay for it.'

When they really came to take the place they remembered this conversation. Hens, however, were out of the question; there was no place for a run unless they had it in the shop. It would have been obviously out of place there. The shop was much more modern than their former one, and had a plate-glass front. 'Sooner or later,' said Bert, 'we shall get a motor-car through this.'

'That's all right,' said Grubb. 'Compensation. I don't mind *when* that motor-car comes along. I don't mind even if it gives me a shock to the system.'

'And meanwhile,' said Bert, with great artfulness, '*I'm* going to buy myself a dog.'

He did. He bought three in succession. He surprised the people at the Dog's Home in Battersea by demanding a deaf retriever, and rejecting every candidate that pricked up its ears. 'I want a good, deaf, slow-moving dog,' he said. 'A dog that doesn't put himself out for things.'

They displayed inconvenient curiosity; they declared a great scarcity of deaf dogs.

'You see,' they said, 'dogs aren't deaf.'

'Mine's got to be,' said Bert. 'I've *had* dogs that aren't deaf. All I want. It's like this, you see – I sell gramophones. Naturally I got to make 'em talk and tootle a bit to show 'em orf. Well, a dog that isn't deaf doesn't like it – gets excited, smells round, barks, growls. That upsets the customer. See? Then a dog that has his hearing fancies things. Makes burglars out of passing tramps. Wants to fight every motor that makes a whizz. All very well if you want livening up, but our place is lively enough. I don't want a dog of that sort. I want a quiet dog.'

In the end he got three in succession, but none of them turned out well. The first strayed off into the infinite, heeding no appeals; the second was killed in the night by a fruit motor-wagon which fled before Grubb could get down; the third got itself entangled in the front wheel of a passing cyclist, who came through the plate glass, and proved to be an actor out of work and an undischarged bankrupt. He demanded compensation for some fancied injury, would hear nothing of the valuable dog he had killed or the window he had broken, obliged Grubb by sheer physical obduracy to straighten his buckled front wheel, and pestered the struggling firm with a series of inhumanly worded solicitor's letters. Grubb answered them – stingingly, and put himself, Bert thought, in the wrong.

Affairs got more and more exasperating and strained under these pressures. The window was boarded up, and an unpleasant altercation about their delay in repairing it with the new landlord, a Bun Hill butcher – and a loud, bellowing, unreasonable person at that – served to remind them of their unsettled troubles with the old. Things were at this pitch when Bert bethought himself of creating a sort of debenture capital in the business for the benefit of Tom. But as I have said, Tom had no enterprise in his composition. His idea of investment was the stocking; he bribed his brother not to keep the offer open.

And then ill-luck made its last lunge at their crumbling business and brought it to the ground.

2

It is a poor heart that never rejoices, and Whitsuntide had an air of coming as an agreeable break in the business complications of Grubb and Smallways. Encouraged by the practical outcome of Bert's nego-tiations with his brother, and by the fact that half the hiring stock was out from Saturday to Monday, they decided to ignore the residuum of hiring-trade on Sunday and devote that day to much-needed relaxation and refreshment – to have, in fact, an unstinted good time, a beano on Whit Sunday, and return invigorated to grapple with their diffi-culties and the Bank Holiday repairs on the Monday. No good thing was ever done by exhausted and dispirited men. It happened that they had made the acquaintance of two young ladies in employment in Clapham, Miss Flossie Bright and Miss Edna Bunthorne, and it was resolved therefore to make a cheerful little cyclist party of four into the heart of Kent, and to picnic and spend an indolent afternoon and evening among the trees and bracken between Ashford and Maidstone.

Miss Bright could ride a bicycle, and a machine was found for her, not among the hiring stock, but specially, in the sample held for sale. Miss Bunthorne, whom Bert particularly affected, could not ride, and so with some difficulty he hired a basketwork trailer from the big business of Wray's in the Clapham Road. To see our young men, brightly dressed and cigarettes alight, wheeling off to the rendezvous, Grubb guiding the lady's machine beside him with one skilful hand, and Bert teuf-teuffmg steadily, was to realize how pluck may triumph even over insolvency. Their landlord, the butcher, said 'Gurr!' as they passed, and shouted, 'Go it!' in a loud, savage tone to their receding backs.

Much they cared!

The weather was fine, and though they were on their way southward before nine o'clock, there was already a great multitude of holiday people abroad upon the roads. There were quantities of young men and women on bicycles and motor-bicycles, and a majority of gyroscopic motor-cars running bicycle-fashion on two wheels, mingled with old-fashioned four-wheeled traffic. Bank Holiday times always bring out old stored-away vehicles and odd people; one saw tricars and electric broughams and dilapidated old racing motors with huge pneumatic tyres. Once our holidaymakers saw a horse and cart, and once a youth riding a black horse amidst the badinage of the passers-by. And there were several navigable gas airships, not to mention balloons, in the sky. It was all immensely interesting and refreshing after the dark anxieties of the shop. Edna wore a brown straw hat with poppies that suited her admirably, and sat in the trailer like a queen, and the eight-year-old motor-bicycle ran like a thing of yesterday.

Little it seemed to matter to Mr Bert Smallways that a newspaper placard proclaimed:

GERMANY DENOUNCES THE MONROE
DOCTRINE.
AMBIGUOUS ATTITUDE OF JAPAN.
WHAT WILL BRITAIN DO?
IS IT WAR?

This sort of thing was always going on, and on holidays one disregarded it as a matter of course. Weekdays, in the slack time after the midday meal, then perhaps one might worry about the Empire and inter-national politics; but not on a sunny Sunday, with a pretty girl trailing behind one, and envious cyclists trying to race you. Nor did our young people attach any great importance to the flitting suggestions of military activity they glimpsed ever and again. Near Maidstone they came on a string of eleven motor-guns of peculiar construction halted by the roadside, with a number of businesslike engineers grouped about them watching through field-glasses some sort of entrenchment that was going on near the crest of the downs. It signified nothing to Bert.

'What's up?' said Edna.

'Oh! – manoeuvres,' said Bert.

'Oh! I thought they did them at Easter,' said Edna, and troubled no more.

The last great British war, the Boer War, was over and forgotten, and the public had lost the fashion of expert military criticism.

Our four young people picnicked cheerfully, and were happy in the manner of a happiness that was an ancient mode in Nineveh. Eyes were bright, Grubb was funny and almost witty, and Bert achieved epigrams; the hedges were full of honeysuckle and dog-roses; in the woods the distant toot-toot-toot of the traffic on the dust-hazy high road might have been no more than the horns of elf-land. They laughed and gossiped and picked flowers and made love and talked, and the girls smoked cigarettes. Also they scuffled playfully. Among other things they talked aeronautics, and how they would come for a picnic together in Bert's flying machine before ten years were out. The world seemed full of amusing possibilities that afternoon. They wondered what their great-grandparents would have thought of aeronautics. In the evening, about seven, the party turned homeward, expecting no disaster, and it was only on the crest of the downs, between Wrotham and Kingsdown, that disaster came.

They had come up the hill in the twilight, Bert was anxious to get as far as possible before he lit – or attempted to light, for the issue was a doubtful one – his lamps, and they had scorched past a number of cyclists, and by a four-wheeled motor-car of the old style lamed by a deflated tyre. Some dust had penetrated Bert's horn, and the result was a curious, amusing, wheezing sound had got into his 'honk, honk'. For the sake of merriment and glory he was making this sound as much as possible, and Edna was in fits of laughter in the trailer. They made a sort of rushing cheerfulness along the road that affected their fellow travellers variously, according to their temperaments. She did notice a good lot of bluish, evil-smelling smoke coming from about the bearings between his feet, but she thought this was one of the natural concomitants of motor-traction, and troubled no more about it, until abruptly it burst into a little yellow-tipped flame.

'Bert!' she screamed.

But Bert had put on the brakes with such suddenness that she found herself involved with his leg as he dismounted. She got to the side of the road and hastily readjusted her hat, which had suffered.

'Gaw!' said Bert.

He stood for some fatal seconds watching the petrol drip and catch; and the flame, which was now beginning to smell of enamel as well as oil, spread and grew. His chief idea was the sorrowful one that he had not sold the machine secondhand a year ago, and that he ought to have done so – a good idea in its way, but not immediately helpful. He turned upon Edna sharply. 'Get a lot of wet sand,' he said. Then he wheeled the machine a little towards the side of the roadway and laid it down and looked about for a supply of wet sand. The flames received this as a helpful attention, and made the most of it. They seemed to brighten and the twilight to deepen about them. The road was a flinty road in the chalk country, and ill-provided with sand.

Edna accosted a short, fat cyclist. 'We want wet sand,' she said, and added, 'our motor's on fire.' The short, fat cyclist stared blankly for a moment, then with a helpful cry began to scrabble in the road-grit. Whereupon Bert and Edna also scrabbled in the road-grit. Other cyclists arrived, dismounted and stood about, and their flame-lit faces expressed satisfaction, interest, curiosity. 'Wet sand,' said the short, fat man scrabbling terribly – 'wet sand.' One joined him. They threw hard-earned handfuls of road-grit upon the flames, which accepted them with enthusiasm.

Grubb arrived, riding hard. He was shouting something. He sprang off and threw his bicycle into the hedge. 'Don't throw water on it!' he said – 'don't throw water on it!' He displayed commanding presence of mind. He became captain of the occasion. Others were glad to repeat the things he said and imitate his actions. 'Don't throw water on it!' they cried. Also there was no water.

'Beat it out, you fools!' he said.

He seized a rug from the trailer (it was an Austrian blanket, and Bert's winter coverlet) and began to beat at the burning petrol. For a wonderful minute he seemed to succeed. But he scattered burning pools of petrol on the road, and others, fired by his enthusiasm, imitated his action. Bert caught up a trailer-cushion and began to beat; there was another cushion and a tablecloth, and these also were seized. A young hero pulled off his jacket and joined the beating. For a moment there was less talking than hard breathing, and a tremendous flapping. Flossie, arriving on the outskirts of the crowd, cried, 'Oh, my God!' and burst loudly into tears. 'Help!' she said, and 'Fire!'

The lame motor-car arrived, and stopped in consternation. A tall, goggled, grey-haired man who was driving inquired with an Oxford intonation and a clear, careful enunciation, 'Can *we* help at all?'

It became manifest that the rug, the tablecloth, the cushions, the jacket, were getting smeared with petrol and burning. The soul seemed to go out of the cushion Bert was swaying, and the air was full of feathers, like a snowstorm in the still twilight.

Bert had got very dusty and sweaty and strenuous. It seemed to him his weapon had been wrested from him at the moment of victory. The fire lay like a dying thing, close to the ground and wicked; it gave a leap of anguish at every whack of the beaters. But now Grubb had gone off to stamp out the burning blanket; the others were slacking just at the moment of victory. One was running to the motor-car. '*Ere!*' cried Bert; 'keep on!'

He flung the deflated burning rags of cushion aside, whipped off his jacket and sprang at the flames with a shout. He stamped into the ruin until flames ran up his boots. Edna saw him, a red-lit hero, and thought it was good to be a man.

A bystander was hit by a hot halfpenny flying out of the air. Then Bert thought of the papers in his pockets, and staggered back, trying to extinguish his burning jacket – checked, repulsed, dismayed.

Edna was struck by the benevolent appearance of an elderly spectator in a silk hat and Sabbatical garments. 'Oh!' she cried to him 'Help this young man! How can you stand and see it?'

A cry of 'The tarpaulin!' arose.

An earnest-looking man in a very light-grey cycling suit had suddenly appeared at the side of the lame motor-car and addressed the owner. 'Have you a tarpaulin?' he said.

'Yes,' said the gentlemanly man. 'Yes. We've got a tarpaulin.'

'That's it,' said the earnest-looking man, suddenly shouting. 'Let's have it, quick!'

The gentlemanly man, with feeble and deprecatory gestures, and in the manner of a hypnotized person, produced an excellent large tarpaulin.

'Here!' cried the earnest-looking man to Grubb. 'Ketch holt!'

Then everybody realized that a new method was to be tried. A number of willing hands seized upon the Oxford gentleman's tarpaulin. The others stood away with approving noises. The tarpaulin was held over the burning bicycle like a canopy, and then smothered down upon it.

'We ought to have done this before,' panted Grubb.

There was a moment of triumph. The flames vanished. Everyone who could contrive to do so touched the edge of the tarpaulin. Bert held down a corner with two hands and a foot. The tarpaulin, bulged up in the centre, seemed to be suppressing triumphant exultation. Then its self-approval became too much for it; it burst into a bright-red smile in the centre. It was exactly like the opening of a mouth. It laughed with a gust of flames. They were reflected redly in the observant goggles of the gentleman who owned the tarpaulin. Everybody recoiled.

'Save the trailer!' cried someone, and that was the last round in the battle. But the trailer could not be detached; its wickerwork had caught, and it was the last thing to burn. A sort of hush fell upon the gathering. The petrol burnt low, the wickerwork trailer banged and crackled. The crowd divided itself into an outer circle of critics, advisers and secondary characters, who had played undistinguished parts or no parts at all in the affair, and a central group of heated and distressed principals. A young man with an inquiring mind and a considerable knowledge of motor-bicycles fixed on to Grubb and wanted to argue that the thing could not have happened. Grubb was short and inattentive with him, and the young man withdrew to the back of the crowd, and there told the benevolent old gentleman in the silk hat that people who went out with machines they didn't understand had only themselves to blame if things went wrong.

The old gentleman let him talk for some time, and then remarked in a tone of rapturous enjoyment: 'Stone deaf,' and added, 'Nasty things.'

A rosy-faced man in a straw hat claimed attention. 'I *did* save the front wheel,' he said, 'you'd have had that tyre catch too, if I hadn't kept turning it round.' It became manifest that this was so. The front wheel had retained its tyre, was intact, was still rotating slowly among the blackened and twisted ruins of the rest of the machine. It had something of the air of conscious virtue, of unimpeachable respectability, that distinguishes a rent collector in a low neighbourhood. 'That wheel's worth a pound,' said the rosy-faced man, making a song of it. 'I kep' turning it round.'

Newcomers kept arriving from the south with the question, 'What's up?' until it got on Grubb's nerves. Londonward the crowd was constantly losing people; they would mount their various wheels with the satisfied manner of spectators who have had the best. Their voices would recede into the twilight; one would hear a laugh at the memory of this particularly salient incident or that.

'I'm afraid,' said the gentleman of the motor-car, 'my tarpaulin's a bit done for.'

Grubb admitted that the owner was the best judge of that.

'Nothing else I can do for you?' said the gentleman of the motor-car, it may be, with a suspicion of irony.

Bert was roused to action. 'Look here,' he said. 'There's my young lady. If she ain't 'ome by ten they lock her out. See? Well, all my money was in my jacket pocket, and it's all mixed up with the burnt stuff, and that's too 'ot to touch. *Is* Clapham out of your way?'

'All in the day's work,' said the gentleman with the motor-car, and turned to Edna. 'Very pleased indeed,' he said, 'if you'll come with us. We're late for dinner as it is, so it won't make much difference for us to go home by way of Clapham. We've got to get to Surbiton, anyhow. I'm afraid you'll find us a little slow.'

'But what's Bert going to do?' said Edna.

'I don't know that we can accommodate Bert,' said the motor-car gentleman, 'though we're tremendously anxious to oblige.'

'You couldn't take the whole lot?' said Bert, waving his hand at the deboshed and blackened ruins on the ground

'I'm awfully afraid I can't,' said the Oxford man. 'Awfully sorry, you know.'

'Then I'll have to stick 'ere for a bit,' said Bert. 'I got to see the thing through. You go on, Edna.'

'Don't like leavin' you, Bert.'

'You can't 'elp it, Edna.' ...

The last Edna saw of Bert was his figure, in charred and blackened shirt-sleeves, standing in the dusk. He was musing deeply by the mixed ironwork and ashes of his vanished motor-bicycle, a melancholy figure. His retinue of spectators had shrunk now to half a dozen figures. Flossie and Grubb were preparing to follow her desertion.

'Cheer up, old Bert,' cried Edna with artificial cheerfulness. 'So long.'

'So long, Edna,' said Bert.

'See you to-morrer.'

'See you to-morrer,' said Bert, though he was destined, as a matter of fact, to see much of the habitable globe before he saw her again.

Bert began to light matches from a borrowed boxful, and search for a half-crown that still eluded him among the charred remains. His face was grave and melancholy.

'I *wish* that 'adn't 'appened,' said Flossie, riding on with Grubb. ....

And at last Bert was left almost alone, a sad, blackened Promethean figure, cursed by the gift of fire. He had entertained vague ideas of hiring a cart, of achieving miraculous repairs, of still snatching some residual value from his one chief possession. Now, in the darkening night, he perceived the vanity of such intentions. Truth came to him bleakly, and laid her chill conviction upon him. He took hold of the handlebar, stood the thing up, tried to push it forward. The tyreless hind wheel was jammed hopelessly, even as he feared. For a minute or so he stood upholding his machine, a motionless despair. Then with a great effort he thrust the ruins from him into the ditch, kicked at it once, regarded it for a moment, and turned his face resolutely Londonward.

He did not once look back.

'That's the end of *that* game,' said Bert. 'No more teuf-teuf-teuf for Bert Smallways for a year or two. Good-bye, 'Olidays! . . . Oh! I ought to 'ave sold the blasted thing when I had a chance three years ago.'

3

The next morning found the firm of Grubb and Smallways in a state of profound despondency. It seemed a small matter to them that the newspaper and cigarette shop opposite displayed such placards as this:

REPORTED AMERICAN ULTIMATUM.
BRITAIN MUST FIGHT.
OUR INFATUATED WAR OFFICE STILL
REFUSES TO LISTEN TO MR BUTTERIDGE.
GREAT MONORAIL DISASTER AT
TIMBUCTOO.

or this:

WAR A QUESTION OF HOURS.
NEW YORK CALM.
EXCITEMENT IN BERLIN.

or again:

WASHINGTON STILL SILENT.
WHAT WILL PARIS DO?
THE PANIC ON THE BOURSE.
THE KING'S GARDEN-PARTY TO THE
MASKED TWAREGS.
MR BUTTERIDGE MAKES AN OFFER.
LATEST BETTING FROM TEHERAN.

or this:

WILL AMERICA FIGHT?
ANTI-GERMAN RIOT IN BAGDAD.
THE MUNICIPAL SCANDALS AT DAMASCUS.
MR BUTTERIDGE'S INVENTION FOR
AMERICA.

Bert stared at these over the card of pump clips in the pane in the door with unseeing eyes. He wore a blackened flannel shirt, and the jacketless ruins of the holiday suit of yesterday. The boarded-up shop was dark and depressing beyond words, the few scandalous hiring machines had never looked so hopelessly disreputable. He thought of their fellows who were 'out', and of the approaching disputations of the afternoon. He thought of their new landlord and of their old landlord, and of bills and claims. Life presented itself for the first time as a hopeless fight against fate. . . .

'Grubb, o' man,' he said, distilling the quintessence, 'I'm fair sick of this shop.'

'So'm I,' said Grubb.

'I'm out of conceit with it. I don't seem to care ever to speak to a customer again.'

'There's that trailer,' said Grubb, after a pause.

'Blow the trailer!' said Bert. 'Anyhow, I didn't leave a deposit on it. I didn't do that. Still—'

He turned round on his friend. 'Look 'ere,' he said, 'we aren't gettin' on here. We been losing money hand over fist. We got things tied up in fifty knots.'

'What can we do?' said Grubb.

'Clear out. Sell what we can for what it will fetch, and quit. See? It's no good 'anging on to a losing concern. No sort of good. Jest foolishness.'

'That's all right,' said Grubb – 'that's all right; but it ain't your capital been sunk in it.'

'No need for us to sink after our capital,' said Bert, ignoring the point.

'I'm not going to be held responsible for that trailer, anyhow. That ain't my affair.'

'Nobody arst you to make it your affair If you like to stick on here, well and good. I'm quitting. I'll see Bank Holiday through, and then I'm O.R.P.H. See?'

'Leavin' me?'

639

'Leavin' you. If you must be left.'

Grubb looked round the shop. It certainly had become distasteful. Once upon a time it had been bright with hope and new beginnings and stock and the prospect of credit. Now – now it was failure and dust. Very likely the landlord would be round presently to go on with the row about the window. . . . 'Where d'you think of going, Bert?' Grubb asked.

Bert turned round and regarded him. 'I thought it out as I was walking 'ome, and in bed. I couldn't sleep a wink.'

'What did you think out?'

'Plans.'

'What plans?'

'Oh! You're for sticking here.'

'Not if anything better was to offer.'

'It's only an ideer,' said Bert.

'Let's 'ear it.'

'You made the girls laugh yestiday, that song you sang.'

'Seems a long time ago now,' said Grubb.

'And old Edna nearly cried – over that bit of mine.'

'She got a fly in her eye,' said Grubb; 'I saw it. But what's this got to do with your plan?'

'No end,' said Bert.

''Ow?'

'Don't you see?'

'Not singing in the streets?'

'Streets! No fear! But 'ow about the Tour of the Waterin'-Places of England, Grubb? Singing! Young men of family doing it for a lark? You ain't got a bad voice, you know, and mine's all right. I never see a chap singing on the beach yet that I couldn't 'ave sung into a cocked hat. And we both know how to put on the toff a bit. Eh? Well, that's my ideer. Me and you, Grubb, with a refined song and a breakdown. Like we was doing for foolery yestiday. That was what put it into my 'ead. Easy make up a programme – easy. Six choice items, and one or two for encores and patter. I'm all right for the patter – anyhow.'

Grubb remained regarding his darkened and disheartening shop; he thought of his former landlord and his present landlord, and of the general disgustingness of business in an age which re-echoes to The Bitter Cry of the Middle Class; and then it seemed to him that afar off he heard the twankle, twankle of a banjo, and the voice of a stranded siren singing. He had a sense of hot sunshine upon sand, of the children of at least transiently opulent holidaymakers in a circle round about him, of the whisper, 'They are really gentlemen,' and then dollop, dollop came the coppers in the hat. Sometimes even silver. It was all income; no outgoings, no bills. 'I'm on, Bert,' he said.

'Right O!' said Bert, and, 'Now we shan't be long.'

'We needn't start without capital neither,' said Grubb. 'If we take the best of these machines up to the Bicycle Mart in Finsbury we'd raise six or seven pounds on 'em. We could easy do that tomorrow before anybody much was about. . . .'

'Nice to think of old Suet-and-Bones coming round to make his usual row with us, and finding a card up "Closed for Repairs".'

'We'll do that,' said Grubb with zest – 'we'll do that. And we'll put up another notice, and jest arst all inquirers to go round to 'im and inquire. See? Then they'll know all about us.'

Before the day was out the whole enterprise was planned. They decided at first that they would call themselves the Naval Mr O's, a plagiarism, and not perhaps a very good one, from the title of the well-known troupe of 'Scarlet Mr E's', and Bert rather clung to the idea of a uniform of bright blue serge, with a lot of gold lace and cord and ornamentation, rather like a naval officer's, but more so. But that had to be abandoned as impracticable, it would have taken too much time and money to prepare. They perceived they must wear some cheaper and more readily prepared costume, and Grubb fell back on white dominoes. They entertained the notion for a time of selecting the two worst machines from the hiring stock, painting them over with crimson enamel paint, replacing the bells by the loudest sort of motor-horn, and doing a ride about to begin and end the entertainment. They doubted the advisability of this step.

'There's people in the world,' said Bert, 'who wouldn't recognize us, who'd know them bicycles again like a shot, and we don't want to go on with no old stories. We want a fresh start.'

'*I* do,' said Grubb, 'badly.'

'We want to forget things – and cut all these rotten old worries. They ain't doin' us good.'

Nevertheless, they decided to take the risk of these bicycles, and they decided their costumes should be brown stockings and sandals, and cheap unbleached sheets with a hole cut in the middle, and wigs and beards of tow. The rest their normal selves! 'The Desert Dervishes', they would call themselves, and their chief songs would be those popular ditties, 'In my Trailer', and 'What Price Hairpins Now?'

They decided to begin with small seaside places, and gradually, as they gained confidence, attack larger centres. To begin with they selected Littlestone in Kent, chiefly because of its unassuming name.

641

So they planned, and it seemed a small and unimportant thing to them that as they chattered the governments of half the world and more were drifting into war. About midday they became aware of the first of the evening-paper placards shouting to them across the street:

THE WAR-CLOUD DARKENS.

Nothing else but that.

'Always rottin' about war now,' said Bert. 'They'll get it in the neck in real earnest one of these days, if they ain't precious careful.'

4

So you will understand the sudden apparition that surprised rather than delighted the quiet informality of Dymchurch sands. Dymchurch was one of the last places on the coast of England to be reached by the monorail, and so its spacious sands were still, at the time of this story, the secret and delight of a limited number of people. They went there to flee vulgarity and extravagance, and to bathe and sit and talk and play with their children in peace, and the Desert Dervishes did not please them at all.

The two white figures on scarlet wheels came upon them out of the infinite along the sands from Littlestone, grew nearer and larger and more audible, honk-honking and emitting weird cries, and generally threatening liveliness of the most aggressive type. 'Good heavens!' said Dymchurch, 'what's this?'

Then our young men, according to a preconcerted plan, wheeled round from file to line, dismounted and stood at attention. 'Ladies and gentlemen,' they said, 'we beg to present ourselves – the Desert Dervishes.' They bowed profoundly.

The few scattered groups upon the beach regarded them with horror for the most part, but some of the children and young people were interested and drew nearer. 'There ain't a bob on the beach,' said Grubb in an undertone, and the Desert Dervishes piled their bicycles with comic 'business', that got a laugh from one very unsophisticated little boy. Then they took a deep breath and struck into the cheerful strain of 'What Price Hairpins Now?' Grubb sang the song, Bert did his best to make the chorus a rousing one, and at the end of each verse they danced certain steps, skirts in hand, that they had carefully rehearsed.

> Ting-a-ling-a-ting-a-ling-a-ting-a-ling-a-tang.
> What Price Hairpins Now?

So they chanted and danced their steps in the sunshine on Dymchurch beach, and the children drew near these foolish young men, marvelling that they should behave in this way, and the older people looked cold and unfriendly.

All round the coasts of Europe that morning banjos were ringing, voices were bawling and singing, children were playing in the sun, pleasure-boats went to and fro; the common abundant life of the time, unsuspicious of the dangers that gathered darkly against it, flowed on its cheerful aimless way. In the cities men fussed about their businesses and engagements. The newspaper placards that had cried 'wolf!' so often, cried 'wolf!' now in vain.

5

Now as Bert and Grubb bawled their chorus for the third time, they became aware of a very big, golden-brown balloon low in the sky to the north-west, and coming rapidly towards them. 'Jest as we're gettin' hold of 'em,' muttered Grubb, 'up comes a counter-attraction. Go it, Bert!'

> Ting-a-ling-a-ting-aling-a-ting-a-ling-a-tang.
> What Price Hairpins Now?

The balloon rose and fell, went out of sight – 'landed, thank goodness,' said Grubb – reappeared with a leap. '*Eng!*' said Grubb. 'Step it, Bert, or they'll see it!'

They finished their dance, and then stood frankly staring.

'There's something wrong with that balloon,' said Bert.

Everybody now was looking at the balloon drawing rapidly nearer before a brisk north-westerly breeze. The song and dance were a 'dead frost'. Nobody thought any more about it. Even Bert and Grubb forgot it, and ignored the next item on their programme altogether. The balloon was bumping as though its occupants were trying to land; it would approach, sinking slowly, touch the ground and instantly jump fifty feet or so in the air and immediately begin to fall again. Its car touched a clump of trees, and the black figure that had been struggling in the ropes fell back, or jumped back, into the car. In another moment it was quite close. It seemed a huge affair, as big as a house, and it floated down swiftly towards the sands; a long rope trailed behind it,

643

and enormous shouts came from the man in the car. He seemed to be taking off his clothes, then his head came over the side of the car. 'Catch hold of the rope!' they heard, quite plain.

'Salvage, Bert!' cried Grubb, and started to head off the rope.

Bert followed him, and collided, without upsetting, with a fisherman bent upon a similar errand. A woman carrying a baby in her arms, two small boys with toy spades and a stout gentleman in flannels all got to the trailing rope at about the same time, and began to dance over it in their attempts to secure it. Bert came up to this wriggling, elusive serpent and got his foot on it, went down on all fours and achieved a grip. In half a dozen seconds the whole diffused population of the beach had, as it were, crystallized on the rope, and was pulling against the balloon under the vehement and stimulating directions of the man in the car. 'Pull, I tell you,' said the man in the car – 'Pull!'

For a second or so the balloon obeyed its momentum and the wind and tugged its human anchor seaward. It dropped, touched the water and made a flat, silvery splash, and recoiled as one's finger recoils when one touches anything hot. 'Pull her in,' said the man in the car. '*She's fainted!*'

He occupied himself with some unseen object while the people on the rope pulled him in Bert was nearest the balloon, and much excited and interested. He kept stumbling over the tail of the Dervish costume in his zeal. He had never imagined before what a big, light, wallowing thing a balloon was. The car was of brown coarse wickerwork, and comparatively small. The rope he tugged at was fastened to a stout-looking ring, four or five feet above the car. At each tug he drew in a yard or so of rope, and the waggling wickerwork was drawn so much nearer. Out of the car came wrathful bellowings: 'Fainted, she has!' and then: 'It's her heart – broken with all she's had to go through.'

The balloon ceased to struggle, and sank downward. Bert dropped the rope, and ran forward to catch it in a new place. In another moment he had his hand on the car. 'Lay hold of it,' said the man in the car, and his face appeared close to Bert's – a strangely familiar face, fierce eyebrows, a flattish nose, a huge black moustache. He had discarded coat and waistcoat – perhaps with some idea of presently having to swim for his life – and his black hair was extraordinarily disordered. 'Will all you people get hold round the car,' he said. 'There's a lady here fainted – or got failure of the heart. Heaven alone knows which! My name is Butteridge. Butteridge, my name is – in a balloon. Now please, all on to the edge. This is the last time I trust myself to one of these palaeolithic contrivances. The ripping-cord failed, and the valve wouldn't act. If ever I meet the scoundrel who ought to have seen—'

He stuck his head out between the ropes abruptly, and said, in a note of earnest expostulation: 'Get some brandy! – some neat brandy!' Someone went up the beach for it.

In the car, sprawling upon a sort of bed-bench, in an attitude of elaborate self-abandonment, was a large, blonde lady, wearing a fur coat and a big floriferous hat. Her head lolled back against the padded corner of the car, and her eyes were shut and her mouth open. 'Me dear!' said Mr Butteridge, in a common loud voice, 'we're safe!'

She gave no sign.

'Me dear!' said Mr Butteridge, in a greatly intensified loud voice, 'we're safe!'

She was still quite impassive.

Then Mr Butteridge showed the fiery core of his soul. 'If she is dead,' he said, slowly lifting a fist towards the balloon above him and speaking in an immense tremulous bellow, 'if she is dead, I will r-r-rend the heavens like a garment! I must get her out,' he cried, his nostrils dilated with emotion; 'I must get her out. I cannot have her die in a wickerwork basket nine feet square – she who was made for kings' palaces! Keep holt of this car! Is there a strong man among ye to take her if I hand her out?'

He swept the lady together by a powerful movement of his arms, and lifted her. 'Keep the car from jumping,' he said to those who clustered about him. 'Keep your weight on it. She is no light woman, and when she is out of it – it will be relieved.'

Bert leapt lightly into a sitting position on the edge of the car. The others took a firmer grip upon the ropes and ring.

'Are you ready?' said Mr Butteridge.

He stood upon the bed-bench and lifted the lady carefully. Then he sat down on the wicker edge opposite to Bert, and put one leg over to dangle outside. A rope or so seemed to incommode him. 'Will someone assist me?' he said. 'If they would take this lady?'

It was just at this moment, with Mr Butteridge and the lady balanced finely on the basket brim, that she came to. She came to suddenly and violently with a loud, heartrending cry of 'Alfred! Save me!' And she waved her arms searchingly, and then clasped Mr Butteridge about.

It seemed to Bert that the car swayed for a moment and then buck-jumped and kicked him. Also he saw the boots of the lady and the right leg of the gentleman describing arcs through the air, preparatory to vanishing over the side of the car. His impressions were complex, but they also comprehended the fact that he had lost his balance, and was going to stand on his head inside this creaking basket. He spread out clutching arms. He did stand on his head, more or less, his tow beard came off and got in his mouth, and his cheek slid along against padding. His nose buried itself in a bag of sand. The car gave a violent lurch, and became still.

'Confound it!' he said.

He had an impression he must be stunned, because of a surging in his ears, and because all the voices of the people about him had become small and remote. They were shouting like elves inside a hill.

He found it difficult to get on his feet. His limbs were mixed up with the garments Mr Butteridge had discarded when that gentleman had thought he must needs plunge into the sea. Bert bawled out, half angry, half rueful, 'You might have said you were going to tip the basket.' Then he stood up and clutched the ropes of the car convulsively.

Below him, far below him, shining blue, were the waters of the English Channel. Far off, minute in the sunshine, and rushing down as if someone was bending it hollow, was the beach and the irregular cluster of houses that constituted Dymchurch. He could see the little crowd of people he had so abruptly left. Grubb, in the white wrapper of a Desert Dervish, was running along the edge of the sea. Mr Butteridge was knee-deep in the water, bawling immensely. The lady was sitting up with her floriferous hat in her lap, shockingly neglected. The beach, east and west, was dotted with people – they seemed all heads and feet – looking up. And the balloon, released from the twenty-five stone or so of Mr Butteridge and his lady, was rushing up into the sky at the pace of a racing motor-car. 'My crikey!' said Bert; 'here's a go!'

He looked down with a pinched face at the receding beach, and reflected that he wasn't giddy; then he made a superficial survey of the cords and ropes about him with a vague idea of 'doing something'. 'I'm not going to mess about with the thing,' he said at last, and sat down upon the mattress. 'I'm not going to touch it. . . . I wonder what one ought to do?'

Soon he got up again and stared for a long time at the sinking world below, at white cliffs to the east and flattening marsh to the left, at a minute wide prospect of weald and downland, at dim towns and harbours, and rivers, and ribbon-like roads, at ships and ships, decks and foreshortened funnels upon the ever-widening sea, and at the great monorail bridge that straddled the Channel from Folkestone to Boulogne, until at length, first cobwebby wisps and then a veil of filmy cloud hid the prospect from his eyes. He wasn't at all giddy nor very much frightened, only in a state of enormous consternation.

3
The Balloon

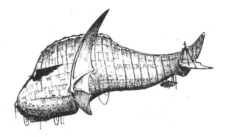

I

Bert Smallways was a vulgar little creature, the sort of pert, limited soul that the old civilization of the early twentieth century produced by the million in every country of the world. He had lived all his life in narrow streets, and between mean houses he could not look over, and in a narrow circle of ideas from which there was no escape. He thought the whole duty of man was to be smarter than his fellows, get his hands, as he put it, 'on the dibs', and have a good time. He was, in fact, the sort of man who had made England and America what they were. The luck had been against him so far, but that was by the way. He was a mere aggressive and acquisitive individual with no sense of the State, no habitual loyalty, no devotion, no code of honour, no code even of courage. Now by a curious accident he found himself lifted out of his marvellous modern world for a time, out of all the rush and confused appeals of it, and floating like a thing dead and disembodied between sea and sky. It was as if Heaven was experimenting with him, had picked him out as a sample from the English millions to look at him more nearly and to see what was happening to the soul of man. But what Heaven made of him in that case I cannot profess to imagine, for I have long since abandoned all theories about the ideals and satisfactions of Heaven.

To be alone in a balloon at a height of fourteen or fifteen thousand feet – and to that height Bert Smallways presently rose – is like nothing else in human experience. It is one of the supreme things possible to man. No flying machine can ever better it. It is to pass extraordinarily out of human things. It is to be still and alone to an unprecedented degree. It is solitude without the suggestion of intervention; it is calm without a single irrelevant murmur. It is to see the sky.

No sound reaches one of all the roar and jar of humanity, the air is clear and sweet beyond the thought of defilement. No bird, no insect comes so high. No wind blows ever in a balloon, no breeze rustles, for it moves with the wind and is itself a part of the atmosphere. Once started it does not rock nor sway; you cannot feel whether it rises or falls. Bert felt acutely cold, but he wasn't mountain-sick; he put on the coat and overcoat and gloves Butteridge had discarded – put them over the 'Desert Dervish' sheet that covered his cheap best suit – and sat very still for a long time, overawed by the new-found quiet of the world. Above him was the light, translucent, billowing globe of shining brown oiled silk and the blazing sunlight and the great deep-blue dome of the sky. Below, far below, was a torn floor of sunlit cloud, slashed by enormous rents, through which he saw the sea.

If you had been watching him from below you would have seen his head, a motionless little black knob, sticking out from the car first of all for a long time on one side, and then vanishing to reappear after a time at some other point.

He wasn't in the least degree uncomfortable nor afraid. He did think that as this uncontrollable thing had thus rushed up the sky with him it might presently rush down again, but this consideration did not trouble him very much. Essentially his state was wonder. There is no fear nor trouble in balloons – until they descend.

'Gollys!' he said at last, feeling a need for talking; 'it's better than a motor-bike.

'It's all right!

'I suppose they're telegraphing about, about me.' . . .

The second hour found him examining the equipment of the car with great particularity. Above him was the throat of the balloon, bunched and tied together, but with an open lumen through which Bert could peer up into a vast, empty, quiet interior, and out of which descended two fine cords of unknown import, one white, one crimson, to pockets below the ring. The netting about the balloon ended in cords attached to the ring, a big steel-bound hoop to which the car was slung by ropes. From it depended the trail-rope and grapnel, and over the sides of the car were a number of canvas bags that Bert decided must be ballast to 'chuck down' if the balloon fell. (Not much falling just yet,' said Bert.)

There were an aneroid and another box-shaped instrument hanging from the ring. The latter had an ivory plate bearing 'statoscope' and other words in French, and a little indicator quivered and waggled between *Montée* and *Descente*. 'That's all right,' said Bert. 'That tells if you're going up or down.' On the crimson padded seat of the balloon there lay a couple of rugs and a Kodak, and in opposite corners of the bottom of the car were an empty champagne bottle and a glass. 'Refreshments,' said Bert meditatively, tilting the empty bottle. Then he had a brilliant idea. The two padded bed-like seats, each with blankets and mattress, he perceived, were boxes, and within he found Mr Butteridge's conception of an adequate equipment for a balloon ascent: a hamper which included a game pie, a Roman pie, a cold fowl, tomatoes, lettuce, ham sandwiches, shrimp sandwiches, a large cake, knives and forks and paper plates, self-heating tins of coffee and cocoa, bread, butter and marmalade, several carefully packed bottles of champagne, bottles of Perrier water and a big jar of water for washing, a portfolio, maps and a compass, a rucksack containing a number of conveniences, including curling-tongs and hairpins, a cap with ear-flaps and so forth.

'A 'ome from 'ome,' said Bert, surveying this provision as he tied the ear-flaps under his chin.

He looked over the side of the car. Far below were the shining clouds. They had thickened so that the whole world was hidden. Southward they were piled in great snowy masses; he was half disposed to think them mountains; northward and eastward they were in wave-like levels, and blindingly sunlit.

'Wonder how long a balloon keeps up,' he said.

He imagined he was not moving, so insensibly did the monster drift with the air about it. 'No good coming down till we shift a bit,' he said.

He consulted the statoscope.

'Still Monty,' he said.

'Wonder what would happen if you pulled a cord?

'No,' he decided. 'I ain't going to mess it about.'

Afterwards he did pull both the ripping and the valve cords, but, as Mr Butteridge had already discovered, they had fouled a fold of silk in the throat. Nothing happened. But for that little hitch the ripping cord would have torn the balloon open as though it had been slashed by a sword, and hurled Mr Smallways to eternity at the rate of some thousand feet a second. 'No go!' he said, giving it a final tug. Then he lunched.

He opened a bottle of champagne, which, as soon as he cut the wire, blew its cork out with incredible violence, and for the most part followed it into space. Bert, however, got about a tumblerful.

'Atmospheric pressure,' said Bert, finding an application at last for the elementary physiography of his seventh-standard days. 'I'll have to be more careful next time. No good wastin' drink.'

Then he routed about for matches to utilize Mr Butteridge's cigars; but here again luck was on his side, and he couldn't find any wherewith to set light to the gas above him. Or else he would have dropped in a flare, a splendid but transitory pyrotechnic display. 'Eng old Grubb!' said Bert, slapping unproductive pockets. ''E didn't ought to 'ave kep' my box. 'E's always sneaking matches.'

He reposed for a time. Then he got up, paddled about, rearranged the ballast bags on the floor, watched the clouds for a time, and turned over the maps on the locker. Bert liked maps, and he spent some time in trying to find one of France or the Channel; but they were all British ordnance maps of English counties. That set him thinking about languages and trying to recall his seventh-standard French. 'Je suis Anglais. C'est une méprise. Je suis arrivé par accident ici,' he decided upon as convenient phrases. Then it occurred to him that he would entertain himself by reading Mr Butteridge's letters and examining his pocketbook, and in this manner he whiled away the afternoon.

2

He sat upon the padded locker wrapped about very carefully; for the air, though calm, was exhilaratingly cold and clear. He was wearing first a modest suit of blue serge and all the unpretending underwear of a suburban young man of fashion, with sandal-like cycling-shoes and brown stockings drawn over his trouser ends; then the perforated sheet proper to a Desert Dervish; then the coat and waistcoat and big fur-trimmed overcoat of Mr Butteridge; then a lady's large fur cloak, and round his knees a blanket. Over his head was a tow wig, surmounted by a large cap of Mr Butteridge's with the flaps down over his ears. And some fur sleeping-boots of Mr Butteridge's warmed his feet. The car of the balloon was small and neat, some bags of ballast the untidiest of its contents, and he had found a light folding table and put it at his elbow, and on that was a glass with champagne. And about him, above and below, was space – such a clear emptiness and silence of space as only the aeronaut can experience.

He did not know where he might be drifting, or what might happen next. He accepted this state of affairs with a serenity creditable to the Smallways' courage, which one might reasonably have expected to be of a more degenerate and contemptible quality altogether. His impression was that he was bound to come down somewhere, and that then, if he wasn't smashed, someone, some 'society' perhaps, would probably pack him and the balloon back to England. If not, he would ask very firmly for the British consul. 'Le consuelo Britannique,' he decided this would be. 'Apportez moi à le consuelo Britannique s'il vous plait,' he would say, for he was by no means ignorant of French. In the meanwhile he found the intimate aspects of Mr Butteridge an interesting study.

There were letters of an entirely private character addressed to Mr Butteridge, and among others several love letters of a devouring sort in a large feminine hand. These are no business of ours, and one remarks with regret that Bert read them.

When he had read them he remarked, 'Gollys!' in an awe-stricken tone, and then, after a long interval, 'I wonder if that was her?

'Lord!'

He mused for a time.

He resumed his exploration of the Butteridge interior. It included a number of press-cuttings of interviews and also several letters in German, then some in the same German handwriting, but in English. 'Hul-*lo!*' said Bert.

One of the latter, the first he took, began with an apology to Butteridge for not writing to him in English before, and for the inconvenience and delay that had been caused him by that, and went on to matter that Bert found exciting in the highest degree. 'We can understand entirely the difficulties of your position, and that you shall possibly be watched at the present juncture. But, sir, we do not believe that any serious obstacles will be put in your way if you wished to endeavour to leave the country and come to us with your plans by the customary routes – either via Dover, Ostend, Boulogne, or Dieppe. We find it difficult to think you are right in supposing yourself to be in danger of murder for your invaluable invention.'

'Funny!' said Bert, and meditated.

Then he went through the other letters.

'They seem to want him to come,' said Bert; 'but they don't seem hurting themselves to get 'im. Or else they're shamming don't care to get his prices down.

'They don't quite seem to be the gov'ment,' he reflected, after an interval. 'It's more like some firm's paper. All this printed stuff at the top. *Drachenflieger. Drachenballons. Ballonstoffe. Kugelballons.* Greek to me.

'But he was trying to sell his blessed secret abroad. That's all right. No Greek about that! Gollys! Here *is* the secret!'

He tumbled off the seat, opened the locker and had the portfolio

651

open before him on the folding table. It was full of drawings done in the peculiar flat style and conventional colours engineers adopt. And, in addition, there were some rather underexposed photographs, obviously done by an amateur at close quarters, of the actual machine Butteridge had made, in its shed near the Crystal Palace. Bert found he was trembling. 'Lord!' he said, 'here am I and the whole blessed secret of flying – lost up here on the roof of everywhere.'

'Let's see!' He fell studying the drawings and comparing them with the photographs. They puzzled him. Half of them seemed to be missing. He tried to imagine how they fitted together, and found the effort too great for his mind.

'It's tryin',' said Bert. 'I wish I'd been brought up to the engineering. If I could only make it out!'

He went to the side of the car and remained for a time staring with unseeing eyes at a huge cluster of great clouds – a cluster of slowly dissolving Monte Rosas, sunlit below. His attention was arrested by a strange black spot that moved over them. It alarmed him. It was a black spot moving slowly with him far below, following him down there, indefatigably over the cloud mountains. Why should such a thing follow him? What could it be? . . .

He had an inspiration. 'Ur course!' he said. It was the shadow of the balloon. But he still watched it dubiously for a time.

He returned to the plans on the table.

He spent a long afternoon between his struggles to understand them and fits of meditation. He evolved a remarkable new sentence in French. 'Voici Mossoo! – Je suis un inventeur Anglais. Mon nom est Butteridge. Beh. oo. teh. teh. eh. arr. e. deh. ghe. eh. J'avais ici pour vendre le secret de le *flying machine*. Comprenez? Vendre pour l'argent tout suite, l'argent en main. Comprenez? C'est le machine à jouer dans l'air. Comprenez? C'est le machine à faire l'oiseau. Comprenez? Balancer? Oui exactement! Battir l'oiseau, en fait, à son propre jeu. Je désire de vendre ceci à votre government national. Voulez vous me directer là?

'Bit rummy, I expect, from the point of view of grammar,' said Bert, 'but they ought to get the hang of it all right.

'But then, if they arst me to explain the blessed thing?'

He returned in a worried way to the plans. 'I don't believe it's all here!' he said. . . .

He got more and more perplexed up there among the clouds as to what he should do with this wonderful find of his. At any moment, so far as he could tell, he might descend amidst he knew not what foreign people.

'It's the chance of my life!' he said.

It became more and more manifest to him that it wasn't. 'Directly I come down they'll telegraph – put it in the papers. Butteridge'll know of it and come along – on my track.'

Butteridge would be a terrible person to be on anyone's track. Bert thought of the great black moustaches, the triangular nose, the searching bellow and the glare. His afternoon's dream of a marvellous seizure and sale of the great Butteridge secret crumpled up in his mind, dissolved and vanished. He awoke to sanity again.

'Wouldn't do. What's the good of thinking of it?' He proceeded slowly and reluctantly to replace the Butteridge papers in pockets and portfolio as he had found them. He became aware of a splendid golden light upon the balloon above him, and of a new warmth in the blue dome of the sky. He stood up and beheld the sun, a great ball of blinding gold, setting upon a tumbled sea of gold-edged crimson and purple clouds, strange and wonderful beyond imagining. Eastward cloudland stretched for ever, darkling blue, and it seemed to Bert the whole round hemisphere of the world was under his eyes.

Then far away over the blue he caught sight of three long, dark shapes like hurrying fish that drove one after the other, as porpoises follow one another in the water. They were very fishlike indeed – with tails. It was an unconvincing impression in that light. He blinked his eyes, stared again, and they had vanished. For a long time he scrutinized those remote blue levels and saw no more. . . .

'Wonder if I ever saw anything,' he said, and then: 'There ain't such things. . . .'

Down went the sun and down, not diving steeply but passing northward as it sank, and then suddenly daylight and the expansive warmth of daylight had gone altogether, and the index of the statoscope quivered over to *Descente*.

3

'*Now* what's going to 'appen?' said Bert.

He found the cold, grey cloud wilderness rising towards him with a wide, slow steadiness. As he sank down among them the clouds ceased to seem the snow-clad mountain slopes they had resembled heretofore, became unsubstantial, confessed an immense silent drift and eddy in their substance. For a moment, when he was nearly among their twilight masses, his descent was checked. Then abruptly the sky was hidden, the last vestiges of daylight gone, and he was falling rapidly in an evening twilight through a whirl of fine snowflakes that streamed past him towards the zenith, that drifted in upon the things about him and melted, that touched his face with ghostly fingers. He shivered. His breath came smoking from his lips, and everything was instantly bedewed and wet.

He had an impression of a snowstorm pouring with unexampled and increasing fury *upward;* then he realized that he was falling faster and faster.

Imperceptibly a sound grew upon his ears. The great silence of the world was at an end.

What was this confused sound?

He craned his head over the side, concerned, perplexed.

First he seemed to see, and then not to see. Then he saw clearly little edges of foam pursuing each other, and a wide waste of weltering waters below him. Far away was a pilot-boat with a big sail bearing dim black letters, and a little pinkish-yellow light, and it was rolling and pitching – rolling and pitching in a gale, while he could feel no wind at all. Soon the sound of waters was loud and near. He was dropping, dropping – into the sea!

He became convulsively active.

'Ballast!' he cried, and seized a little sack from the floor, and heaved it overboard. He did not wait for the effect of that, but sent another after it. He looked over in time to see a minute white splash in the dim waters below him, and then he was back in the snow and clouds again.

He sent out quite needlessly a third sack of ballast and a fourth, and presently had the immense satisfaction of soaring up out of the damp and chill into the clear, cold, upper air in which the day still lingered. 'Thang-God!' he said, with all his heart.

A few stars now had pierced the blue, and in the east there shone brightly a prolate moon.'

4

That first downward plunge filled Bert with a haunting sense of boundless waters below. It was a summer's night, but it seemed to him, nevertheless, extraordinarily long. He had a feeling of insecurity that he fancied quite irrationally the sunrise would dispel. Also he was hungry. He felt in the dark in the locker, put his fingers in the Roman pie, and got some sandwiches, and he also opened rather successfully a half-bottle of champagne. That warmed and restored him, he grumbled at Grubb about the matches, wrapped himself up warmly on the locker, and dozed for a time. He got up once or twice to make sure that he was still securely high above the sea. The first time the moonlit clouds were white and dense, and the shadow of the balloon ran athwart them like a dog that followed; afterwards they seemed thinner. As he lay still, staring up at the huge dark balloon above, he made a discovery. His – or rather Mr Butteridge's – waistcoat rustled as he breathed. It was lined with papers. But Bert could not see to get them out or examine them, much as he wished to do so. . . .

He was awakened by the crowing of cocks, the barking of dogs and a clamour of birds. He was driving slowly at a low level over a broad land lit golden by sunrise under a clear sky. He stared out upon hedgeless, well-cultivated fields intersected by roads, each lined with cable-bearing red poles. He had just passed over a compact, white-washed village with a straight church tower and steep red-tiled roofs. A number of peasants, men and women, in shiny blouses and lumpish footwear, stood regarding him, arrested on their way to work. He was so low that the end of his rope was trailing.

He stared out at these people. 'I wonder how you land,' he thought. 'S'pose I *ought* to land?'

He found himself drifting down towards a monorail line, and hastily flung out two or three handsful of ballast to clear it.

'Lemme see! One might say just "Prenez"! Wish I knew the French for take hold of the rope! . . . I suppose they are French?'

He surveyed the country again. 'Might be Holland. Or Lux-embourg. Or Lorraine's far as *I* know. Wonder what those big affairs over there are. Some sort of kiln? Prosperous-looking country. . . .'

The respectability of the country's appearance awakened answering chords in his nature.

'Make myself a bit shipshape first,' he said.

He resolved to rise a little and get rid of his wig (which now felt hot on his head) and so forth. He threw out a bag of ballast, and was astonished to find himself careering up through the air very rapidly.

'Blow!' said Mr Smallways. 'I've overdone the ballast trick. . . . Wonder when I shall get down again? . . . Brekfus' on board, anyhow.'

He removed his cap and wig, for the air was warm, and an improvi-dent impulse made him cast the latter object overboard. The statoscope responded with a vigorous swing to '*Montée*'.

'The blessed thing goes up if you only *look* overboard,' he remarked, and assailed the locker. He found among other items several tins of liquid cocoa containing explicit directions for opening that he followed with minute care. He pierced the bottom with the key provided in the holes indicated, and forthwith the can grew from cold to hotter and hotter, until at last he could scarcely touch it, and then he opened the can at the other end, and there was his cocoa smoking, without the use of match or flame of any sort. It was an old invention, but new to Bert. There was also ham and marmalade and bread, so that he had a really very tolerable breakfast indeed.

Then he took off his overcoat, for the sunshine was now inclined to be hot, and that reminded him of the rustling he had heard in the night. He took off the waistcoat and examined it. 'Old Butteridge won't like me unpicking this.' He hesitated, and finally proceeded to unpick it. He found the missing drawings of the lateral rotating planes, on which the whole stability of the flying machine depended.

An observant angel would have seen Bert sitting for a long time after this discovery in a state of intense meditation. Then at last he rose with an air of inspiration, took Mr Butteridge's ripped, demolished and ransacked waistcoat, and hurled it from the balloon – whence it fluttered down slowly and eddyingly until at last it came to rest with a contented flop upon the face of a German tourist sleeping peacefully beside the Hohenweg, near Wildbad. Also this sent the balloon higher, and so into a position still more convenient for observation by our imaginary angel, who would next have seen Mr Smallways tear open his own jacket and waistcoat, remove his collar, open his shirt, thrust his hand into his bosom, and tear his heart out – or at least, if not his heart, some large bright scarlet object. If the observer, overcoming a thrill of celestial horror, had scrutinized this scarlet object more narrowly, one of Bert's most cherished secrets, one of his essential weaknesses, would have been laid bare. It was a red-flannel chest-protector, one of those large quasi-hygienic objects that with pills and medicines take the place of beneficial relics and images among the Protestant peoples of Christendom. Always Bert wore this thing; it was his cherished delusion, based on the advice of a shilling fortune-teller at Margate, that he was weak in the lungs.

He now proceeded to unbutton his fetish, to attack it with a penknife, and to thrust the newfound plans between the two layers of imitation Saxony flannel of which it was made. Then with the help of Mr Butteridge's small shaving-mirror and his folding canvas basin he readjusted his costume with the gravity of a man who has taken an irrevocable step in life, buttoned up his jacket, cast the white sheet of the Desert Dervish on one side, washed temperately, shaved, resumed the big cap and the fur overcoat, and, much refreshed by these exercises, surveyed the country below him.

It was indeed a spectacle of incredible magnificence. If perhaps it was not so strange and magnificent as the sunlit cloudland of the previous day, it was at any rate infinitely more interesting. The air was at its utmost clearness, and, except to the south and south-west, there was not a cloud in the sky. The country was hilly, with occasional fir plantations and bleak upland spaces, but also with numerous farms, and the hills were deeply intersected by the gorges of several winding rivers interrupted at intervals by the banked-up ponds and weirs of electric generating wheels. It was dotted with bright-looking, steep-roofed villages, and each showed a distinctive and interesting church beside its wireless telegraph steeple; here and there were large châteaux and parks and white roads, and paths lined with red and white cable posts were extremely conspicuous in the landscape. There were walled enclosures like gardens, and rickyards, and great roofs of barns and many electric dairy centres. The uplands were populous with cattle. At places he would see the track of one of the old railroads (converted now to monorails) dodging through tunnels and crossing embankments, and a rushing hum would mark the passing of a train. Everything was extraordinarily clear as well as minute. Once or twice he saw guns and soldiers, and was reminded of the stir of military preparations he had witnessed on the Bank Holiday in England; but there was nothing to tell him that these military preparations were abnormal, or to explain an occasional faint irregular firing of guns that drifted up to him.

'Wish I knew how to get down,' said Bert, ten thousand feet or so above it all, and gave himself to much futile tugging at the red and white cords. Afterwards he made a sort of inventory of the provisions. Life in the high air was giving him an appalling appetite, and it seemed to him discreet at this stage to portion out his supply into rations. So far as he could see he might pass a week in the air.

At first all the vast panorama below had been as silent as a painted picture. But as the day wore on and the gas diffused slowly from the balloon, it sank earthward again, details increased, men became more visible, and he began to hear the whistle and moan of trains and cars, sounds of cattle, bugles and kettledrums, and presently even men's voices. And at last his guide-rope was trailing again, and he found it possible to attempt a landing. Once or twice, as the rope dragged over cables, he found his hair erect with electricity, and once he had a slight shock, and sparks snapped about the car. He took these things among the chances of the voyage. He had one idea now very clear in his mind, and that was to drop the iron grapnel that hung from the ring.

From the first this attempt was unfortunate, perhaps because the place for descent was ill-chosen. A balloon should come in an empty open space, and he chose a crowd. He made his decision suddenly, and without proper reflection. As he trailed, Bert saw ahead of him one of the most attractive little towns in the world – a cluster of steep gables surmounted by a high church-tower and diversified with trees, walled, and with a fine, large gateway opening out upon a tree-lined high road. All the wires and cables of the countryside converged upon it like guests to entertainment. It had a most homelike and comfortable quality, and it was made gayer by abundant flags. Along the road a quantity of peasant folk, in big pair-wheeled carts and afoot, were coming and going, beside an occasional monorail car; and at the car junction, under the trees outside the town, was a busy little fair of booths. It seemed a warm, human, well-rooted and altogether delightful place to Bert. He came low over the tree-tops, with his grapnel ready to throw, and so anchor him – a curious, interested and interesting guest, so his imagination figured it, in the very middle of it all.

He thought of himself performing feats with the sign language and chance linguistics amidst a circle of admiring rustics. . . .

And then the chapter of adverse accidents began.

The rope made itself unpopular long before the crowd had fully realized his advent over the trees. An elderly and apparently intoxicated peasant in a shiny black hat, and carrying a large crimson umbrella, caught sight of it first as it trailed past him, and was seized with a discreditable ambition to kill it. He pursued it briskly with unpleasant cries. It crossed the road obliquely, splashed into a pan of milk upon a stall and slapped its milky tail athwart a motor-car load of factory girls halted outside the town gates. They screamed loudly. People looked up and saw Bert making what he meant to be genial salutations, but what they considered, in view of the feminine outcry, to be insulting gestures. Then the car hit the roof of the gate-house smartly, snapped a flagstaff, played a tune upon some telegraph wires, and sent a broken wire like a whiplash to do its share in accumulating unpopularity. Bert, by clutching convulsively, just escaped being pitched headlong. Two young soldiers and several peasants shouted things up to him and shook fists at him, and began to run in pursuit as he disappeared over the wall into the town. Admiring rustics, indeed!

The balloon leapt at once, in the manner of balloons when part of their weight is released by touching down, with a sort of flippancy, and in another moment Bert was over a street crowded with peasants and soldiers, that opened into a busy market square. The wave of unfriendliness pursued him.

'Grapnel,' said Bert, and then with an afterthought shouted, ' *Têtes* there, you! I say! I say! *Têtes*. Eng it!'

The grapnel clattered down a steeply sloping roof, followed by an avalanche of broken tiles, jumped the street amidst shrieks and cries, and smashed into a plate-glass window with an immense and sickening impact. The balloon rolled nauseatingly, and the car pitched. But the grapnel had not held. It emerged at once bearing on one fluke, with a ridiculous air of fastidious selection, a small child's chair, and pursued by a maddened shopman. It lifted its catch, swung about with an appearance of painful indecision amidst a roar of wrath, and dropped it at last neatly, and as if by inspiration, over the head of a peasant woman in charge of an assortment of cabbages in the marketplace.

Everybody now was aware of the balloon. Everybody was either trying to dodge the grapnel or catch the trail-rope. With a pendulum-like swoop through the crowd that sent people flying right and left, the grapnel came to earth again, tried for and missed a stout gentleman in a blue suit and a straw hat, smacked away a trestle from under a stall of haberdashery, made a cyclist soldier in knickerbockers leap like a chamois, and secured itself uncertainly among the hind legs of a sheep – which made convulsive, ungracious efforts to free itself, and was dragged into a position of rest against a stone cross in the middle of the place. The balloon pulled up with a jerk. In another moment a score of willing hands were tugging it earthward. At the same instant Bert became aware for the first time of a fresh breeze blowing about him.

For some seconds he stood staggering in the car, which now swayed sickeningly, surveying the exasperated crowd below him and trying to collect his mind. He was extraordinarily astonished at this run of mishaps. Were these people really so annoyed? Everybody seemed angry with him No one seemed interested or amused by his arrival. A disproportionate amount of the outcry had the quality of impre-cation – had, indeed, a strong flavour of riot. Several greatly uniformed officials in cocked hats struggled in vain to control the crowd. Fists and sticks were shaken. And when Bert saw a man on the outskirts of the crowd run to a haycart and get a brightly pronged pitchfork, and a blue-clad soldier unbuckle his belt, his doubt whether this little town was after all such a good place for a landing became a certainty.

He had clung to the fancy that they would make something of a hero of him. Now he knew that he was mistaken.

He was perhaps ten feet above the people when he made his decision. His paralysis ceased. He leapt up on the seat, and, at imminent risk of falling headlong, disengaged the grapnel-rope from the toggle that held it, sprang on to the trail-rope and released that also. A hoarse shout of disgust greeted the descent of the grapnel-rope and the swift leap of the balloon, and something – he fancied afterwards it was a turnip – whizzed by his head. The trail-rope followed its fellow.

The crowd seemed to jump away from him. With an immense and horrifying rustle the balloon brushed against a telephone pole, and for a tense instant he anticipated either an electric explosion or a bursting of the oiled silk, or both. But fortune was with him.

In another second he was cowering in the bottom of the car, and, released from the weight of the grapnel and the two ropes, rushing up once more through the air. For a time he remained crouching, and when at last he looked out again, the little town was very small and travelling with the rest of lower Germany in a circular orbit round and round the car – or at least it appeared to be doing that.

When he got used to it he found this rotation of the balloon rather convenient; it saved moving about in the car.

5

Late in the afternoon of a pleasant summer day in the year 191—, if one may borrow a mode of phrasing that once found favour with the readers of the late G. P. R. James, a solitary balloonist – replacing the solitary horseman of the classic romances – might have been observed wending his way across Franconia in a north-easterly direction, at a height of about eleven thousand feet above the sea and still spinning slowly. His head was craned over the side of the car, and he surveyed the country below with an expression of profound perplexity; ever and again his lips shaped inaudible words. 'Shootin' at a chap,' for example, and 'I'll come down right enough soon as I find out 'ow.' Over the side of the basket the robe of the Desert Dervish was hanging, an appeal for consideration, an ineffectual white flag.

He was now very distinctly aware that the world below him, so far from being the naïve countryside of his earlier imaginings that day, sleepily unconscious of him and capable of being amazed and nearly reverential at his descent, was acutely irritated by his career, and extremely impatient with the course he was taking. But indeed it was not he who took that course, but his masters, the winds of heaven. Mysterious voices spoke to him in his ear, jerking the words up to him by means of megaphones, in a weird and startling manner, in a great variety of languages. Official-looking persons had signalled to him by means of flag-flapping and arm-waving. On the whole a guttural variant of English prevailed in the sentences that alighted upon the balloon; chiefly he was told to 'gome down or you will be shot'.

'All very well,' said Bert, 'but 'OW?'

Then they shot a little wide of the car. Latterly he had been shot at six or seven times, and once the bullet had gone by with a sound so persuasively like the tearing of silk that he had resigned himself to the prospect of a headlong fall. But either they were aiming near him or they had missed, and as yet nothing was torn but the air about him – and his anxious soul.

He was now enjoying a respite from these attentions, but he felt it was at best an interlude, and he was doing what he could to appreciate his position. Incidentally he was having some hot coffee and pie in an untidy inadvertent manner with an eye fluttering nervously over the side of the car. At first he had ascribed the growing interest in his career to his ill-conceived attempt to land in the bright little upland town, but now he was beginning to realize that the military rather than the civil arm was concerned about him.

He was quite involuntarily playing that weird mysterious part – the part of an International Spy. He was seeing secret things. He had, in fact, crossed the designs of no less a power than the German Empire, he had blundered into the hot focus of Welt-Politik, he was drifting helplessly towards the great Imperial secret, the immense aeronautic park that had been established at a headlong pace in Franconia to develop silently, swiftly and on a colossal scale the great discoveries of Hunstedt and Stossel, and so to give Germany before all other nations a fleet of airships, the air power and the Empire of the world.

Later, just before they shot him down altogether, Bert saw that great area of passionate work, warm lit in the evening light, a great area of upland on which the airships lay like a herd of grazing monsters at their feed. It was a vast busy space stretching away northward as far as he could see, methodically cut up into numbered sheds, gasometers, squad encampments, storage areas, interlaced with the omnipresent monorail lines, and altogether free from overhead wires or cables. Everywhere was the white, black and yellow of Imperial Germany, everywhere the black eagles spread their wings. Even without these indications, the large vigorous neatness of everything would have marked it German. Vast multitudes of men went to and fro, many in white and drab fatigue uniforms busy about the balloons, others drilling in sensible drab. Here and there a full uniform glittered.

The airships chiefly engaged his attention, and he knew at once it was three of these he had seen on the previous night, taking advantage of the cloud welkin to manoeuvre unobserved.

They were altogether fishlike. For the great airships with which Germany attacked New York in her last gigantic effort for world supremacy – before humanity realized that world supremacy was a dream – were the lineal descendants of the Zeppelin airship that flew over Lake Constance in 1906, and of the Lebaudy navigables that made their memorable excursions over Paris in 1907 and 1908.

These German airships were held together by riblike skeletons of steel and aluminium and a stout inelastic canvas outer skin, within which was an impervious rubber gas-bag, cut up by transverse dissepiments into from fifty to a hundred compartments. These were all absolutely gas tight and filled with hydrogen, and the entire aerostat was kept at any level by means of a long internal ballonette of oiled and toughened silk canvas, into which air could be forced and from which it could be pumped. So the airship could be made either heavier or lighter than air, and losses of weight through the consumption of fuel, the casting of bombs and so forth, could also be compensated by admitting air to sections of the general gas-bag. Ultimately that made a highly explosive mixture; but in all these matters risks must be taken and guarded against. There was a steel axis to the whole affair, a central backbone which terminated in the engine and propeller, and the men and magazines were forward in a series of cabins under the expanded beadlike fore part. The engine, which was of the extraordinarily powerful Pforzheim type, that supreme triumph of German invention, was worked by electric controls from this fore part, which was indeed the only really habitable part of the ship. If anything went wrong, the engineers went aft along a rope ladder beneath the frame or along a passage through the gas-chambers. The tendency of the whole affair to roll was partly corrected by a horizontal lateral fin on either side, and steering was chiefly effected by two vertical fins, which normally lay back like gill-flaps on either side of the head. It was indeed a most complete adaptation of the fish form to aerial conditions, the position of swimming bladder, eyes and brain being, however, below instead of above. A striking and unfishlike feature was the apparatus for wireless telegraphy that dangled from the forward cabin – that is to say, under the chin of the fish.

These monsters were capable of ninety miles an hour in a calm, so that they could face and make headway against nearly everything except the fiercest tornado. They varied in length from eight hundred to two thousand feet, and they had a carrying power of from seventy to two hundred tons. How many Germany possessed history does not record, but Bert counted nearly eighty great bulks receding in perspective during his brief inspection. Such were the instruments on which she relied to sustain her in her repudiation of the Monroe Doctrine and her bold bid for a share in the empire of the New World. But not altogether did she rely on these; she had also a one-man bomb-throwing *Drachenflieger* of unknown value among her resources.

But the *Drachenflieger* were away in the second great aeronautic park east of Hamburg, and Bert Smallways saw nothing of them in the bird's-eye view he took of the Franconian establishment before they shot him down. For they shot him down very neatly. They used the new bullets with steel trailers that Wolfe of Engelberg had invented for aerial warfare. The bullet tore past him and made a sort of pop as its trailer rent his balloon – a pop that was followed by a rustling sigh and a steady downward movement. And when in the confusion of the moment he dropped a bag of ballast, the Germans very politely but firmly overcame his scruples by shooting his balloon again twice.

4

The German Air-Fleet

I

Of all the productions of the human imagination that make the world in which Mr Bert Smallways lived confusingly wonderful, there was none quite so strange, so headlong and disturbing, so noisy and persuasive and dangerous, as the modernizations of patriotism produced by imperial and international politics. In the soul of all men is a liking for kind, a pride in one's own atmosphere, a tenderness for one's mother speech and one's familiar land. Before the coming of the Scientific Age this group of gentle and noble emotions had been a fine factor in the equipment of every worthy human being, a fine factor that had its less amiable aspect in a usually harmless hostility to strange people, and a usually harmless detraction of strange lands. But with the wild rush of change in the pace, scope, materials, scale and possibilities of human life that then occurred, the old boundaries, the old seclusions and separations were violently broken down. All the old settled mental habits and traditions of men found themselves not simply confronted by new conditions, but by constantly renewed and changing new conditions. They had no chance of adapting themselves. They were annihilated or perverted or inflamed beyond recognition.

Bert Smallways' grandfather, in the days when Bun Hill was a village under the sway of Sir Peter Bone's parent, had 'known his place' to the uttermost farthing, touched his hat to his betters, despised and condescended to his inferiors, and hadn't changed an idea from the cradle to the grave. He was Kentish and English, and that meant hops, beer, dog-roses, and the sort of sunshine that was best in the world. Newspapers and politics and visits to 'Lannon' weren't for the likes of him. Then came the change. These earlier chapters have given an idea of what happened to Bun Hill, and how the flood of novel things had poured over its devoted rusticity. Bert Smallways was only one of countless millions in Europe and America and Asia who, instead of being born rooted in the soil, were born struggling in a torrent they never clearly understood. All the faiths of their fathers had been taken by surprise, and startled into the strangest forms and reactions. Particularly did the fine old tradition of patriotism get perverted and distorted in the rush of the new times. Instead of the sturdy establishment in prejudice of Bert's grandfather, to whom the word 'Frenchified' was the ultimate term of contempt, there flowed through Bert's brain a squittering succession of thinly violent ideas about German competition, about the Yellow Peril, about the Black Menace, about the White Man's Burthen – that is to say Bert's preposterous right to muddle further the naturally very muddled politics of the entirely similar little cads to himself (except for a smear of brown) who smoked cigarettes and rode bicycles in Buluwayo, Kingston (Jamaica), or Bombay. These were Bert's 'Subject Races', and he was ready to die – by proxy in the person of anyone who cared to enlist – to maintain his hold upon that right. It kept him awake at nights to think that he might lose it.

The essential fact of the politics of the age in which Bert Smallways lived – the age that blundered at last into the catastrophe of the War in the Air – was a very simple one, if only people had had the intelligence to be simple about it. The development of Science had altered the scale of human affairs. By means of rapid mechanical traction it had brought men nearer together, so much nearer socially, economically, physically, that the old separations into nations and kingdoms were no longer possible, a newer, wider synthesis was not only needed but imperatively demanded. Just as the once independent dukedoms of France had to fuse into a nation, so now the nations had to adapt themselves to a wider coalescence, they had to keep what was precious and practicable, and concede what was obsolete and dangerous. A saner world would have perceived this patent need for a reasonable synthesis, would have discussed it temperately, achieved and gone on to organize the great civilization that was manifestly possible to mankind. The world of Bert Smallways did nothing of the sort. Its national governments, its national interests, would not hear of anything so obvious; they were too suspicious of each other, too wanting in generous imagination. They began to behave like ill-bred people in a crowded public car, to squeeze against one another, elbow, thrust, dispute and quarrel. Vain to point out to them that they had only to rearrange themselves to be comfortable. Everywhere, all over the world, the historian of the early twentieth century finds the same thing, the flow and rearrangement of human affairs inextricably entangled by the old areas, the old prejudices and a sort of heated irascible stupidity; and everywhere congested nations in inconvenient areas, slopping population and produce into each other, annoying each other with tariffs and every possible commercial vexation, and threatening each other with navies and armies that grew every year more portentous.

It is impossible now to estimate how much of the intellectual and physical energy of the world was wasted in military preparation and equipment, but it was an enormous proportion. Great Britain spent upon army and navy money and capacity that, directed into the channels of physical culture and education, would have made the British the aristocracy of the world. Her rulers could have kept the whole population learning and exercising up to the age of eighteen, and made a broad-chested and intelligent man of every Bert Smallways in the islands, had they given the resources they spent in war material to the making of men. Instead of which they waggled flags at him until he was fourteen, incited him to cheer, and then turned him out of school to begin that career of private enterprise we have compactly recorded. France achieved similar imbecilities; Germany was, if possible, worse; Russia under the waste and stresses of militarism festered towards bankruptcy and decay. All Europe was producing big guns and countless swarms of little Smallways. The Asiatic peoples had been forced in self-defence into a like diversion of the new powers science had brought them. On the eve of the outbreak of the war there were six great powers in the world and a cluster of smaller ones, each armed to the teeth and straining every nerve to get ahead of the others in deadliness of equipment and military efficiency. The great powers were first the United States, a nation addicted to commerce, but roused to military necessities by the efforts of Germany to expand into South America, and by the natural consequences of her own unwary annexations of land in the very teeth of Japan. She maintained two immense fleets east and west, and internally she was in violent conflict between Federal and state governments upon the question of universal service in a defensive militia. Next came the great alliance of Eastern Asia, a close-knit coalescence of China and Japan, advancing with rapid strides year by year to predominance in the world's affairs. Then the German alliance still struggled to achieve its dream of imperial expansion, and its imposition of the German language upon a forcibly united Europe. These were the three most spirited and aggressive powers in the world. Far more pacific was the British Empire, perilously scattered over the globe, and distracted now by insurrectionary movements in Ireland and among all its Subject Races. It had given these Subject Races cigarettes, boots, bowler hats, cricket, race meetings, cheap revolvers, petroleum, the factory system of industry, halfpenny newspapers in both English and the vernacular, inexpensive university degrees, motor-bicycles and electric trams; it had produced a considerable literature expressing contempt for the Subject Races and rendered it freely accessible to them, and it had been content to believe that nothing would result from these stimulants because somebody once wrote 'the immemorial east'; and also, in the inspired words of Kipling —

> East is east and west is west,
> And never the twain shall meet.

Instead of which, Egypt, India and the subject countries generally had produced new generations in a state of passionate indignation and the utmost energy, activity and modernity. The governing class in Great Britain was slowly adapting itself to a new conception of the Subject Races as waking peoples, and finding its efforts to keep the Empire together under these strains and changing ideas greatly impeded by the entirely sporting spirit with which Bert Smallways at home (by the million) cast his vote, and by the tendency of his more highly coloured equivalents to be disrespectful to irascible officials. Their impertinence was excessive; it was no mere stone-throwing and shouting. They would quote Burns at them and Mill and Darwin, and confute them in arguments.

Even more pacific than the British Empire were France and its allies, the Latin powers, heavily armed states indeed but reluctant warriors, and in many ways socially and politically leading western civilization. Russia was a pacific power perforce, divided within itself, torn between revolutionaries and reactionaries who were equally incapable of social reconstruction, and so sinking towards a tragic disorder of chronic political vendetta. Wedged in among these portentous larger bulks, swayed and threatened by them, the smaller states of the world maintained a precarious independence, each keeping itself armed as dangerously as its utmost ability could contrive.

So it came about that in every country a great and growing proportion of its energetic and inventive men was busied, either for offensive or defensive ends, in elaborating the apparatus of war, until the accumulating tensions should reach the breaking-point. Each power sought to keep its preparations secret, to hold new weapons in reserve, to anticipate and learn the preparations of its rivals. The feeling of danger from fresh discoveries affected the patriotic imagination of every people in the world. Now it was rumoured the British had an overwhelming gun, now the French an invincible rifle, now the Japanese a new explosive, now the Americans a submarine that would drive every ironclad from the seas. Each time there would be a war panic.

The strength and heart of the nations was given to the thought of war, and yet the mass of their citizens was a teeming democracy as heedless of and unfitted for fighting, mentally, morally, physically, as any population has ever been – or, one ventures to add, could ever be. That was the paradox of the time. It was a period altogether unique in the world's history. The apparatus of warfare, the art and method of fighting, changed absolutely every dozen years in a stupendous progress towards perfection, and people grew less and less warlike, and there was no war.

And then at last it came. It came as a surprise to all the world because its real causes were hidden. Relations were strained between Germany and the United States because of the intense exasperation of a tariff conflict and the ambiguous attitude of the former power towards the Monroe Doctrine, and they were strained between the United States and Japan because of the perennial citizenship question. But in both cases these were standing causes of offence. The real deciding cause, it is now known, was the perfecting of the Pforzheim engine by Germany and the consequent possibility of a rapid and entirely practicable airship. At that time Germany was by far the most efficient power in the world, better organized for swift and secret action, better equipped with the resources of modern science, and with her official and administrative classes at a higher level of education and training. These things she knew, and she exaggerated that knowledge to the pitch of contempt for the secret counsels of her neighbours. It may be that with the habit of self-confidence her spying upon them had grown less thorough. Moreover, she had a tradition of unsentimental and unscrupulous action that vitiated her international outlook profoundly. With the coming of these new weapons her collective intelligence thrilled with the sense that now her moment had come. Once again in the history of progress it seemed she held the decisive weapon. Now she might strike and conquer – before the others had anything but experiments in the air.

Particularly she must strike America swiftly, because there, if anywhere, lay the chance of an aerial rival. It was known that America possessed a flying machine of considerable practical value, developed out of the Wright model; but it was not supposed that the Washington War Office had made any wholesale attempts to create an aerial navy. It was necessary to strike before they could do so. France had a fleet of slow navigables, several dating from 1908, that could make no possible headway against the new type. They had been built solely for reconnoitring purposes on the eastern frontier, they were mostly too small to carry more than a couple of dozen men without arms or provisions, and not one could do forty miles an hour. Great Britain, it seemed, in an access of meanness, temporized and wrangled with the imperial-spirited Butteridge and his extraordinary invention. That also was not in play – and could not be for some months at the earliest. From Asia there came no sign. The Germans explained this by saying the yellow peoples were without invention. No other competitor was worth considering. 'Now or never,' said the Germans – 'now or never we may seize the air – as once the British seized the seas! While all the other powers are still experimenting.'

Swift and systematic and secret were their preparations, and their plan most excellent. So far as their knowledge went, America was the only dangerous possibility; America, which was also now the leading trade rival of Germany and one of the chief barriers to her Imperial expansion. So at once they would strike at America. They would fling a great force across the Atlantic heavens and bear America down unwarned and unprepared.

Altogether it was a well-imagined and most hopeful and spirited enterprise, having regard to the information in the possession of the German Government. The chances of it being a successful surprise were very great. The airship and the flying machine were very different things from ironclads, which take a couple of years to build. Given hands, given plant, they could be made innumerably in a few weeks. Once the needful parks and foundries were organized, airships and *Drachenflieger* could be poured into the sky. Indeed, when the time came, they did pour into the sky like, as a bitter French writer put it, flies roused from filth.

The attack upon America was to be the first move in this tremendous game. But no sooner had it started than instantly the aeronautic parks were to proceed to put together and inflate the second fleet which was to dominate Europe and manoeuvre significantly over London, Paris, Rome, St Petersburg, or wherever else its moral effect was required. A World Surprise it was to be –

no less, a World Conquest; and it is wonderful how near the calmly adventurous minds that planned it came to succeeding in their colossal design.

Von Sternberg was the Moltke of this War in the Air, but it was the curious hard romanticism of Prince Karl Albert that won over the hesitating Emperor to the scheme. Prince Karl Albert was indeed the central figure of the world drama. He was the darling of the Imperialist spirit in Germany, and the ideal of the new aristocratic feeling – the new Chivalry, as it was called – that followed the overthrow of Socialism through its internal divisions and lack of discipline, and the concentration of wealth in the hands of a few great families. He was compared by obsequious flatterers to the Black Prince, to Alcibiades, to the young Caesar. To many he seemed Nietzsche's Over-man revealed. He was big and blond and virile, and splendidly non-moral. The first great feat that startled Europe, and almost brought about a new Trojan war, was his abduction of the Princess Helena of Norway and his blank refusal to marry her. Then followed his marriage with Gretchen Krass, a Swiss girl of peerless beauty. Then came the gallant rescue, which almost cost him his life, of three drowning tailors whose boat had upset in the sea near Heligoland. For that and his victory over the American yacht *Defender*, C.C.I., the Emperor forgave him and placed him in control of the new aeronautic arm of the German forces. This he developed with marvellous energy and ability, being resolved, as he said, to give to Germany land and sea and sky. The national passion for aggression found in him its supreme exponent, and achieved through him its realization in this astounding war. But his fascination was more than national; all over the world his ruthless strength dominated minds as the Napoleonic legend had dominated minds. Englishmen turned in disgust from the slow, complex, civilized methods of their national politics to this uncompromising forceful figure. Frenchmen believed in him. Poems were written to him in American.

He made the war.

Quite equally with the rest of the world, the general German population was taken by surprise by the swift vigour of the Imperial government. A considerable literature of military forecasts beginning as early as 1906 with Rudolf Martin, the author not merely of a brilliant book of anticipations but of a proverb, 'The future of Germany lies in the air', had, however, partially prepared the German imagination for some such enterprise.

2

Of all these world forces and gigantic designs Bert Smallways knew nothing until he found himself in the very focus of it all and gaped down amazed on the spectacle of that giant herd of airships. Each one seemed as long as the Strand, and as big about as Trafalgar Square. Some must have been a third of a mile in length. He had never before seen anything so vast and disciplined as this tremendous park. For the first time in his life he really had an intimation of the extraordinary and quite important things of which a contemporary may go in ignorance. He had always clung to the illusion that Germans were fat, absurd men who smoked china pipes, and were addicted to knowledge and horseflesh and sauerkraut and indigestible things generally.

His bird's-eye view was quite transitory. He ducked at the first shot; and directly his balloon began to drop, his mind ran confusedly upon how he might explain himself, and whether he should pretend to be Butteridge or not. 'O, Lord!' he groaned, in an agony of indecision. Then his eye caught his sandals, and he felt a spasm of self-disgust. 'They'll think I'm a bloomin' idiot,' he said, and then it was he rose up desperately and threw over the sandbag and provoked the second and third shots.

It flashed into his head, as he cowered in the bottom of the car, that he might avoid all sorts of disagreeable and complicated explanations by pretending to be mad.

That was his last idea before the airships seemed to rush up about him as if to look at him, and his car hit the ground and bounded and pitched him out on his head. . . .

He awoke to find himself famous, and to hear a voice crying, 'Booteraidge! Ja! Ja! Herr Booteraidge! Selbst!'

He was lying on a little patch of grass beside one of the main avenues of the aeronautic park. The airships receded down a great vista, an immense perspective, and the blunt prow of each was adorned with a black eagle of a hundred feet or so spread. Down the other side of the avenue ran a series of gas generators, and big hosepipes trailed everywhere across the intervening space. Close at hand was his now nearly deflated balloon and the car on its side looking minutely small, a mere broken toy, a shrivelled bubble, in contrast with the gigantic bulk of the nearer airship. This he saw almost end-on, rising like a cliff and sloping forward towards its fellow on the other side so as to overshadow the alley between them. There was a crowd of excited people about him, mostly big men in tight uniforms. Everybody was talking, and several were shouting, in German; he knew that, because they splashed and aspirated sounds like startled kittens. Only one phrase, repeated again and again, could he recognize – the name of 'Herr Booteraidge'.

'Gollys!' said Bert. 'They've spotted it.'

'Besser,' said someone, and some rapid German followed.

He perceived that close at hand was a field-telephone, and that a tall officer in blue was talking threat about him. Another stood close beside him with the portfolio of drawings and photographs in his hand. They looked round at him.

'Do you spik Cherman, Herr Booteraidge?'

Bert decided that he had better be dazed. He did his best to seem thoroughly dazed. 'Where *am* I?' he asked.

Volubility prevailed. 'Der Prinz' was mentioned. A bugle sounded far away, and its call was taken up by one nearer, and then by one close at hand. This seemed to increase the excitement greatly. A monorail car bumbled past. The telephone bell rang passionately, and the tall officer seemed to engage in a heated altercation. Then he approached the group about Bert, calling out something about 'mitbringen'.

An earnest-faced, emaciated man with a white moustache appealed to Bert. 'Herr Booteraidge, sir, we are chust to start!'

'Where am I?' Bert repeated.

Someone shook him by the other shoulder. 'Are you Herr Booteraidge?' he asked.

'Herr Booteraidge, we are chust to start!' repeated the white moustache, and then helplessly, 'What is de goot? What can we do?'

The officer from the telephone repeated his sentence about 'Der Prinz' and 'mitbringen'. The man with the moustache stared for a moment, grasped an idea and became violently energetic, stood up and bawled directions at unseen people. Questions were asked, and the doctor at Bert's side answered, 'Ja! Ja!' several times, also something about 'Kopf'. With a certain urgency he got Bert rather unwillingly to his feet. Two huge soldiers in grey advanced upon Bert and seized hold of him. ''Ullo!' said Bert, startled. 'What's up?'

'It is all right,' the doctor explained; 'they are to carry you.'

'Where?' asked Bert, unanswered.

'Put your arms roundt their – *hals* – round them!'

'Yes! but where?'

'Hold tight!'

Before Bert could decide to say anything more he was whisked up by the two soldiers. They joined hands to seat him, and his arms were put about their necks. 'Vorwärts!' Someone ran before him with the portfolio, and he was borne rapidly along the broad avenue between the gas generators and the airships, rapidly and on the whole smoothly except that once or twice his bearers stumbled over hosepipes and nearly let him down.

He was wearing Mr Butteridge's Alpine cap, and his little shoulders were in Mr Butteridge's fur-lined overcoat, and he had responded to Mr Butteridge's name. The sandals dangled helplessly. Gaw! Everybody seemed in a devil of a hurry. Why? He was carried joggling and gaping through the twilight, marvelling beyond measure.

The systematic arrangement of wide convenient spaces, the quantities of businesslike soldiers everywhere, the occasional neat piles of material, the ubiquitous monorail lines, and the towering shiplike hulls about him, reminded him a little of impressions he had got as a boy on a visit to Woolwich Dockyard. The whole camp reflected the colossal power of modern science that had created it. A peculiar strangeness was produced by the lowness of the electric light, which lay upon the ground, casting all shadows upwards, and making a grotesque shadow figure of himself and his bearers on the airship sides, fusing all three of them into a monstrous animal with attenuated legs and an immense fan-like humped body. The lights were on the ground because as far as possible all poles and standards had been dispensed with to prevent complications when the airships rose.

It was deep twilight now, a tranquil blue-skyed evening; everything rose out from the splashes of light upon the ground into dim translucent tall masses; within the cavities of the airships small inspection lamps glowed like cloud-veiled stars, and made them seem marvellously unsubstantial. Each airship had its name in black letters on white on either flank, and forward the Imperial eagle sprawled, an overwhelming bird in the dimness. Bugles sounded, monorail cars of quiet soldiers slithered burbling by. The cabins under the heads of the airships were being lit up; doors opened in them, and revealed padded passages. Now and then a voice gave directions to workers indistinctly seen.

There was a matter of sentinels, gangways and a long narrow passage, a scramble over a disorder of baggage, and then Bert found himself lowered to the ground and standing in the doorway of a spacious cabin – it was perhaps ten feet square and eight high, furnished with crimson padding and aluminium. A tall, bird-like young man with a small head, a long nose and very pale hair, with his hands full of things like shaving-strops, boot-trees, hairbrushes and toilet tidies, was saying things about Gott and thunder and Dummer Booteraidge as Bert entered. He was apparently an evicted occupant. Then he vanished, and Bert was lying back on a locker in the corner with a pillow under his head and the door of the cabin shut upon him. He was alone. Everybody had hurried out again astonishingly.

'Gollys!' said Bert. 'What next?'

He stared about him at the room.

'Butteridge! Shall I try to keep it up, or shan't I?'

The room he was in puzzled him. ''Tisn't a prison and 'tisn't a norfis?' Then the old trouble came uppermost. 'I wish to 'eaven I 'adn't these silly sandals on,' he cried querulously to the universe. 'They give the whole blessed show away.'

3

His door was flung open, and a compact young man in uniform appeared, carrying Mr Butteridge's portfolio, rucksack and shaving-glass. 'I say!' he said, in faultless English, as he entered. He had a beaming face, and a sort of pinkish blond hair. 'Fancy you being Butteridge!'

He slapped Bert's meagre luggage down.

'We'd have started,' he said, 'in another half-hour! You didn't give yourself much time!'

He surveyed Bert curiously. His gaze rested for a fraction of a moment on the sandals. 'You ought to have come on your flying machine, Mr Butteridge.'

He didn't wait for an answer. 'The Prince says I've got to look after you. Naturally he can't see you now, but he thinks your coming's providential. Last grace of Heaven. Like a sign. Hullo!'

He stood still and listened.

Outside there was a going to and fro of feet, a sound of distant bugles suddenly taken up and echoed close at hand, men called out in loud tones short, sharp, seemingly vital things, and were answered distantly. A bell jangled, and feet went down the corridor. Then came a stillness more distracting than sound, and then a great gurgling and rushing and splashing of water. The young man's eyebrows lifted. He hesitated, and dashed out of the room. Presently came a stupendous bang to vary the noises without, then a distant cheering. The young-man reappeared.

'They're running the water out of the ballonette already.'

'What water?' asked Bert.

'The water that anchored us. Artful dodge. Eh?' Bert tried to take it in.

'Of course!' said the compact young man. 'You don't understand.'

A gentle quivering crept upon Bert's senses. 'That's the engine,' said the compact young man approvingly. 'Now we shan't be long.'

Another long listening interval.

The cabin swayed. 'By Jove! we're starting already,' he cried. 'We're starting!'

'Starting!' cried Bert, sitting up. 'Where?'

But the young man was out of the room again. There were noises of German in the passage, and other nerve-shaking sounds.

The swaying increased. The young man reappeared. 'We're off, right enough!'

'I say!' said Bert, 'where are we starting? I wish you'd explain. What's this place? I don't understand.'

'What!' cried the young man, 'you don't understand?'

'No. I'm all dazed-like from that crack on the nob I got. Where *are* we? *Where* are we starting?'

'Don't you know where you are – what this is?'

'Not a bit of it! What's all the swaying and the row?'

'What a lark!' cried the young man. 'I say! What a thundering lark! Don't you know? We're off to America, and you haven't realized. You've just caught us by a neck. You're on the blessed old flagship with the Prince. You won't miss anything. Whatever's on, you bet the *Vaterland* will be there.'

'Us! – off to America?'

'Ra-ther!'

'In an airship?'

'What do *you* think?'

'Me! going to America on an airship! After that balloon! 'Ere! I say – I don't want to go! I want to walk about on my legs. Let me get out! I didn't understand.'

He made a dive for the door.

The young man arrested Bert with a gesture, took hold of a strap, lifted up a panel in the padded wall, and a window appeared. 'Look!' he said. Side by side they looked out.

'Gaw!' said Bert. 'We're going up!'

'We are!' said the young man, cheerfully; 'fast!'

They were rising in the air smoothly and quietly, and moving slowly to the throb of the engine athwart the aeronautic park. Down below it stretched, dimly geometrical in the darkness, picked out at regular intervals by glow-worm spangles of light. One black gap in the long line of grey, round-backed airships marked the position from which the *Vaterland* had come. Beside it a second monster now rose softly, released from its bonds and cables, into the air. Then, taking a beautifully exact distance, a third ascended, and then a fourth.

'Too late, Mr Butteridge!' the young man remarked. 'We're off! I dare say it *is* a bit of a shock to you, but there you are! The Prince said you'd have to come.'

'Look 'ere,' said Bert. 'I really *am* dazed. What's this thing? Where are we going?'

'This, Mr Butteridge,' said the young man, taking pains to be explicit, 'is an airship. It's the flagship of Prince Karl Albert. This is the German air-fleet, and it is going over to America, to give that spirited people "what for". The only thing we were at all uneasy about was your invention. And here you are!'

'But! – you a German?' asked Bert.

'Lieutenant Kurt. Luft-lieutenant Kurt, at your service.'

'But you speak English!'

'Mother was English – went to school in England. Afterwards, Rhodes scholar. German none the less for that. Detailed for the present, Mr Butteridge, to look after you. You're shaken by your fall. It's all right, really. They're going to buy your machine and everything. You sit down, and take it quite calmly. You'll soon get the hang of the position.'

4

Bert sat down on the locker collecting his mind, and the young man talked to him about the airship.

He was really a very tactful young man indeed, in a natural sort of way. 'Dare say all this is new to you,' he said; 'not your sort of machine. These cabins aren't half bad.'

He got up and walked round the little apartment, showing its points.

'Here is the bed,' he said, whipping down a couch from the wall and throwing it back again with a click. 'Here are toilet things,' and he opened a neatly arranged cupboard. 'Not much washing. No water we've got; no water at all except for drinking. No baths or anything until we get to America and land. Rub over with loofah. One pint of hot for shaving. That's all. In the locker below you are rugs and blankets; you will need them presently. They say it gets cold. I don't know. Never been up before. Except a little work with gliders – which is mostly going down. Three-quarters of the chaps in the fleet haven't. Here's a folding chair and table behind the door. Compact, eh?'

He took the chair and balanced it on his little finger. 'Pretty light, eh? Aluminium and magnesium alloy and a vacuum inside. All these cushions stuffed with hydrogen. Foxy! The whole ship's like that. And not a man in the fleet, except the Prince and one or two others, over eleven stone. Couldn't sweat the Prince, you know. We'll go all over the thing tomorrow. I'm frightfully keen on it.'

He beamed at Bert. 'You *do* look young,' he remarked. 'I always thought you'd be an old man with a beard – a sort of philosopher. I don't know why one should expect clever people always to be old. I do.'

Bert parried that compliment a little awkwardly, and then the lieutenant was struck with the riddle why Herr Butteridge had not come in his own flying machine.

'It's a long story,' said Bert. 'Look here!' he said abruptly, 'I wish you'd lend me a pair of slippers, or something. I'm regular sick of these sandals. They're rotten things. I've been trying them for a friend.'

'Right O!'

The ex-Rhodes scholar whisked out of the room and reappeared with a considerable choice of footwear, pumps, cloth bath-slippers, and a purple pair adorned with golden sunflowers.

But these he repented of at the last moment. 'I don't even wear them myself,' he said. 'Only brought 'em in the zeal of the moment.' He laughed confidentially. 'Had 'em worked for me – in Oxford. By a friend. Take 'em everywhere.'

So Bert chose the pumps.

The lieutenant broke into a cheerful snigger. 'Here we are trying on slippers,' he said, 'and the world going by like a panorama below. Rather a lark, eh? Look!'

Bert peeped with him out of the window, looking from the bright pettiness of the red-and-silver cabin into a dark immensity. The land below, except for a lake, was black and featureless, and the other airships were hidden. 'See more outside,' said the lieutenant. 'Let's go! There's a sort of little gallery.'

He led the way into the long passage, which was lit by one small electric light, past some notices in German to an open balcony and a light ladder and gallery of metal lattice overhanging empty space. Bert followed his leader down to the gallery slowly and cautiously. From it he was able to watch the wonderful spectacle of the first air-fleet flying through the night. They flew in a wedge-shaped formation, the *Vaterland* highest and leading, the tail receding into the corners of the sky. They flew in long, regular undulations, great dark fish-like shapes, showing hardly any light at all, the engines making a throb-throb-throbbing sound that was very audible out on the gallery. They were going at a level of five or six thousand feet, and rising steadily. Below the country lay silent, a clear darkness dotted and lined out with clusters of furnaces, and the lit streets of a group of big towns. The world seemed to lie in a bowl; the overhanging bulk of the airship above hid all but the lowest levels of the sky.

They watched the landscape for a space.

'Jolly it must be to invent things,' said the lieutenant suddenly. 'How did you come to think of your machine first?'

'Worked it out,' said Bert, after a pause. 'Jest ground away at it.'

'Our people are frightfully keen on you. They thought the British had got you. Weren't the British keen?'

'In a way,' said Bert. 'Still – it's a long story.'

'I think it's an immense thing – to invent. I couldn't invent a thing to save my life.'

They both fell silent, watching the darkened world and following their thoughts until a bugle summoned them to a belated dinner. Bert was suddenly alarmed. 'Don't you 'ave to dress and things?' he said. 'I've always been too hard at Science and things to go into Society and all that.'

'No fear,' said Kurt. 'Nobody's got more than the clothes they wear. We're travelling light. You might perhaps take your overcoat off. They've an electric radiator each end of the room.'

And so presently Bert found himself sitting to eat in the presence of the 'German Alexander' – that great and puissant Prince, Prince Karl Albert, the War Lord, the hero of two hemispheres. He was a handsome blond man, with deep-set eyes, a snub nose, upturned moustache, and long white hands. He sat higher than the others, under a black eagle with widespread wings and the German Imperial flags; he was, as it were, enthroned, and it struck Bert greatly that as he ate he did not look at people, but over their heads like one who sees visions. Twenty officers of various ranks stood about the table – and Bert. They all seemed extremely curious to see the famous Butteridge, and their astonishment at his appearance was ill-controlled. The Prince gave him a dignified salutation, to which, by an inspiration, he bowed. Standing next the Prince was a brown-faced, wrinkled man with silver spectacles and fluffy, dingy-grey side-whiskers, who regarded Bert with a peculiar and disconcerting attention. The company sat after ceremonies Bert could not understand. At the other end of the table was the bird-faced officer Bert had dispossessed, still looking hostile and whispering about Bert to his neighbour. Two soldiers waited. The dinner was a plain one – a soup, some fresh mutton and cheese – and there was very little talk.

A curious solemnity indeed brooded over everyone. Partly this was reaction after the intense toil and restrained excitement of starting;

partly it was the overwhelming sense of strange new experiences, of portentous adventure. The Prince was lost in thought. He roused himself to drink to the Emperor in champagne, and the company cried 'Hoch!' like men repeating responses in church.

No smoking was permitted, but some of the officers went down to the little open gallery to chew tobacco. No lights whatever were safe amidst that bundle of inflammable things. Bert suddenly fell yawning and shivering. He was overwhelmed by a sense of his own insignificance amidst these great rushing monsters of the air. He felt life was too big for him – too much for him altogether.

He said something to Kurt about his head, went up the steep ladder from the swaying little gallery into the airship again, and so, as if it were a refuge, to bed.

5

Bert slept for a time, and then his sleep was broken by dreams. Mostly he was fleeing from formless terrors down an interminable passage in an airship – a passage paved at first with ravenous trapdoors, and then with openwork canvas of the most careless description.

'Gaw!' said Bert, turning over after his seventh fall through infinite space that night.

He sat up in the darkness and nursed his knees. The progress of the airship was not nearly so smooth as a balloon; he could feel a regular swaying up, up, up and then down, down, down, and the throbbing and tremulous quiver of the engines.

His mind began to teem with memories – more memories and more.

Through them, like a struggling swimmer in broken water, came the perplexing question, what am I to do tomorrow? Tomorrow, Kurt had told him, the Prince's secretary, the Graf von Winterfeld, would come to him and discuss his flying machine, and then he would see the Prince. He would have to stick it out now that he was Butteridge, and sell his invention. And then, if they found him out! He had a vision of infuriated Butteridges. . . . Suppose after all he owned up? Pretended it was their misunderstanding? He began to scheme devices for selling the secret and circumventing Butteridge.

What should he ask for the thing? Somehow twenty thousand pounds struck him as about the sum indicated.

He fell into that despondency that lies in wait in the small hours. He had got too big a job on – too big a job. . . .

Memories swamped his scheming.

'Where was I this time last night?'

He recapitulated his evenings tediously and lengthily. Last night he had been up above the clouds in Butteridge's balloon. He thought of the moment when he dropped through them and saw the cold twilight sea close below. He still remembered that disagreeable incident with a nightmare vividness. And the night before he and Grubb had been looking for cheap lodgings at Littlestone in Kent. How remote that seemed now. It might be years ago. For the first time he thought of his fellow Desert Dervish, left with the two red-painted bicycles on Dymchurch sands. ''E won't make much of a show of it, not without me. Any'ow 'e did 'ave the treasury – such as it was – in his pocket!' ... The night before that was Bank Holiday night, and they had sat discussing their minstrel enterprise, drawing up a programme and rehearsing steps. And the night before was Whit Sunday.

'Lord!' cried Bert, 'what a doing that motor-bicycle give me!' He recalled the empty flapping of the eviscerated cushion, the feeling of impotence as the flames rose again.

From among the confused memories of that tragic flare one little figure emerged very bright and poignantly sweet, Edna, crying back reluctantly from the departing motor-car, 'See you to-morrer, Bert?'

Other memories of Edna clustered round that impression. They led Bert's mind step by step to an agreeable state that found expression in, 'I'll marry 'er if she don't look out.' And then in a flash it followed in his mind that if he sold the Butteridge secret he could! Suppose after all he did get twenty thousand pounds; such sums have been paid! With that he could buy house and garden, buy new clothes beyond dreaming, buy a motor, travel, have every delight of the civilized life as he knew it, for himself and Edna. Of course, risks were involved. 'I'll 'ave old Butteridge on my track, I expect!'

He meditated upon that. He declined again to despondency. As yet he was only in the beginning of the adventure. He had still to deliver the goods and draw the cash. And before that – Just now he was by no means on his way home. He was flying off to America to fight there. 'Not much fighting,' he considered; 'all our own way.' Still, if a shell did happen to hit the *Vaterland* on the underside! ...

'S'pose I ought to make my will.'

He lay back for some time composing wills – chiefly in favour of Edna. He had settled now it was to be twenty thousand pounds. He left a number of minor legacies. The wills became more and more meandering and extravagant. ...

He woke from the eighth repetition of his nightmare fall through space. 'This flying gets on one's nerves,' he said.

He could feel the airship diving down, down, down, then slowly swinging to up, up, up. Throb, throb, throb, throb, quivered the engine.

He got up presently and wrapped himself about with Mr Butteridge's overcoat and all the blankets, for the air was very keen. Then he peeped out of the window to see a grey dawn breaking over clouds, then turned up his light and bolted his door, sat down to the table and produced his chest-protector.

He smoothed the crumpled plans with his hand, and contemplated them. Then he referred to the other drawings in the portfolio. Twenty thousand pounds. If he worked it right! It was worth trying, anyhow.

Presently he opened the drawer in which Kurt had put paper and writing materials.

Bert Smallways was by no means a stupid person, and up to a certain limit he had not been badly educated. His board-school had taught him to draw up to certain limits, taught him to calculate and understand a specification. If at that point his country had tired of its efforts, and handed him over unfinished to scramble for a living in an atmosphere of advertisements and individual enterprise, that was really not his fault. He was as his State had made him, and the reader must not imagine because he was a little Cockney cad, that he was absolutely incapable of grasping the idea of the Butteridge flying machine. But he found it stiff and perplexing. His motor-bicycle and Grubb's experiments and the 'mechanical drawing' he had done in standard seven all helped him out and, moreover, the maker of these drawings, whoever he was, had been anxious to make his intentions plain. Bert copied sketches, he made notes, he made a quite tolerable and intelligent copy of the essential drawings and sketches of the others. Then he fell into a meditation upon them.

At last he rose with a sigh, folded up the originals that had formerly been in his chest-protector and put them into the breast-pocket of his jacket, and then very carefully deposited the copies he had made in the place of the originals. He had no very clear plan in his mind in doing this, except that he hated the idea of altogether parting with the secret. For a long time he meditated profoundly – nodding. Then he turned out his light and went to bed again and schemed himself to sleep.

6

The hochgeborene Graf von Winterfeld was also a light sleeper that night, but then he was one of those people who sleep little and play chess problems in their heads to while away the time – and that night he had a particularly difficult problem to solve.

He came in upon Bert while he was still in bed in the glow of the sunlight reflected from the North Sea below, consuming the rolls and coffee a soldier had brought him. He had a portfolio under his arm, and in the clear, early morning light his dingy grey hair and heavy, silver-rimmed spectacles made him look almost benevolent. He spoke English fluently, but with a strong German flavour. He was particularly bad with his 'b's', and his 'th's' softened towards weak 'zd's'. He called Bert explosively, 'Pooterage'. He began with some indistinct civilities, bowed, took a folding table and chair from behind the door, put the former between himself and Bert, sat down on the latter, coughed drily and opened his portfolio. Then he put his elbows on the table, pinched his lower lip with his two forefingers and regarded Bert disconcertingly with magnified eyes. 'You came to us, Herr Pooterage, against your will,' he said at last.

''Ow d'you make that out?' asked Bert, after a pause of astonishment.

'I chuge by ze maps in your car. Zey were all English. And your provisions. Zey were all picnic. Also your cords were entangled. You haf been tugging – but no good. You could not manage ze balloon, and anuzzer power than yours prought you to us. Is it not so?'

Bert thought.

'Also – where is ze laty?'

''Ere! – what lady?'

'You started with a laty. That is evident. You shtarted for an afternoon excursion – a picnic. A man of your temperament – he would take a laty. She was not wiz you in your balloon when you came down at Dornhof. No! Only her chacket! It is your affair. Still I am curious.'

Bert reflected. ''Ow d'you know that?'

'I chuge by ze nature of your farious provisions. I cannot account, Mr Pooterage, for ze laty, what you haf done with her. Nor can I tell why you should wear nature-sandals, nor why you should wear such cheap plue clothes. Zese are outside my instructions. Trifles, perhaps. Officially they are to be ignored. Laties come and go – I am a man of ze worldt. I haf known wise men wear sandals and efen practise vegetarian habits. I haf known men – or at any rate I haf known chemists – who did not schmoke. You haf, no doubt, put ze laty down somewhere. Well. Let us get to business. A higher power' – his voice changed its emotional quality, his magnified eyes seemed to dilate – 'has prought you and your secret straight to us. So!' – he bowed his head – 'so pe it. It is ze Destiny of Chermany and my Prince. I can

682

undershtandt you always carry zat secret. You are afraidt of roppers and spies. So it comes wiz you – to us. Mr Pooterage, Chermany will puy it.'

'Will she?'

'She will,' said the secretary, looking hard at Bert's abandoned sandals in the corner of the locker. He roused himself, consulted a paper of notes for a moment, and Bert eyed his brown and wrinkled face with expectation and terror. 'Chermany, I am instructed to say,' said the secretary, with his eyes on the table and his notes spread out, 'has always been willing to puy your secret. We haf indeed peen eager to acquire it – fery eager; and it was only ze fear zat you might be, on patriotic groundts, acting in collusion with your Pritish War Office zat has made us discreet in offering for your marvellous invention through intermediaries. We haf no hesitation whatefer now, I am instructed, in agreeing to your proposal of a hundert tousand poundts.'

'Crikey!' said Bert, overwhelmed.

'I peg your pardon?'

'Jest a twinge,' said Bert, raising his hand to his bandaged head.

'Ah! Also I am instructed to say zat as for zat noble, unrightly accused laty you haf championed so brafely against Pritish hypocrisy and coldness, all ze chivalry of Chermany is on her site.'

'Lady?' said Bert faintly, and then recalled the great Butteridge love story. Had the old chap also read the letters? He must think him a scorcher if he had. 'Oh! that's aw-right,' he said, 'about 'er. I 'adn't any doubts about that. I—'

He stopped. The secretary certainly had a most appalling stare. It seemed ages before he looked down again. 'Well, ze laty as you please. She is your affair. I haf performt my instructions. And ze title of Paron, zat also can pe done. It can all pe done, Herr Pooterage.' He drummed on the table for a second or so, and resumed. 'I haf to tell you, sir, zat you come to us at a crisis in – Welt-Politik. Zere can be no harm now for me to tell our plans to you. Pefore you leafe this ship again zey will be manifest to all ze worldt. War is perhaps already declared. We go – to America. Our fleet will descend out of ze air upon ze United States – it is a country quite unprepared for war eferywhere – eferywhere. Zey have always relied on ze Atlantic. And zair navy. We have selected a certain point – it is at present ze secret of our commanders – which we shall seize, and zen we shall establish a depot – a sort of inland Gibraltar. It will be – what will it be? – an eagle's nest. Zere our airships will gazzer and repair, and zence zey will fly to and fro ofer ze United States, terrorizing cities, dominating Washington, levying what is necessary, until ze terms we dictate are accepted. You follow me?'

'Go on!' said Bert.

'We could haf done all zis wiz such *Luftschiffe* and *Drachenflieger* as we possess, but ze accession of your machine renders our project complete. It not only gifs us a better *Drachenflieger*, but it remofes our last uneasiness as to Great Pritain. Wizout you, sir, Great Pritain, ze land you lofed so well and zat has requited you so ill, zat land of Pharisees and reptiles, can do nozzing! nozzing! You see, I am perfectly frank wiz you. Well, I am instructed that Chermany recognizes all this. We want you to blace yourself at our disposal. We want you to become our Chief Head Flight Engineer. We want you to manufacture, we want to equib a swarm of hornets unter your direction. We want you to direct zis force. And it is at our depot in America we want you. So we offer you simply, and wizout haggling, ze full terms you demanded weeks ago – one hundert tousand poundts in cash, a salary of dree tousand poundts a year, a pension of one tousand poundts a year, and ze title of Paron as you desired. Zese are my instructions.'

He resumed his scrutiny of Bert's face.

'That's all right, of course,' said Bert, a little short of breath, but otherwise resolute and calm; and it seemed to him that now was the time to bring his nocturnal scheming to the issue.

The secretary contemplated Bert's collar with sustained attention. Only for one moment did his gaze move to the sandals and back.

'Jes' lemme think a bit,' said Bert, finding the stare debilitating. 'Look 'ere!' he said at last, with an air of great explicitness, 'I *got* the secret.'

'Yes.'

'But I don't want the name of Butteridge to appear – see? I been thinking that over.'

'A little delicacy?'

'Exactly. You buy the secret – leastways, I give it you – from Bearer – see?'

His voice failed him a little, and the stare continued. 'I want to do the thing Enonymously. See?'

Still staring. Bert drifted on like a swimmer caught by a current. 'Fact is, I'm going to edop' the name of Smallways. I don't want no title of Baron; I've altered my mind. And I want the money quiet-like. I want the hundred thousand pounds paid into benks – thirty thousand into the London and County Benk Branch at Bun Hill in Kent directly I 'and over the plans; twenty thousand into the Benk of England; 'arf the rest into a good French bank, the other 'arf the German National Bank, see? I want it put there, right away. I don't want it put in the name

684

of Butteridge. I want it put in the name of Albert Peter Smallways; that's the name I'm going to edop'. That's condition one.'

'Go on!' said the secretary.

'The nex' condition,' said Bert, 'is that you don't make any inquiries as to title. I mean what English gentlemen do when they sell or let you land. You don't arst 'ow I got it. See? 'Ere I am – I deliver you the goods; that's all right. Some people 'ave the cheek to say this isn't my invention, see? It is, you know – *that's* all right; but I don't want that gone into. I want a fair and square agreement saying that's all right See?'

His 'See?' faded into a profound silence.

The secretary sighed at last, leant back in his chair and produced a toothpick, and used it to assist his meditation on Bert's case. 'What was that name?' he asked at last, putting away the toothpick; 'I must write it down.'

'Albert Peter Smallways,' said Bert, in a mild tone.

The secretary wrote it down, after a little difficulty about the spelling because of the different names of the letters of the alphabet in the two languages.

'And now, Mr Schmallvays,' he said at last, leaning back and resuming the stare, 'tell me: how did you ket hold of Mister Pooterage's balloon?'

<h1 style="text-align:center">7</h1>

When at last the Graf von Winterfeld left Bert Smallways, he left him in an extremely deflated condition, with all his little story told.

He had, as people say, made a clean breast of it. He had been pursued into details. He had had to explain the blue suit, the sandals, the Desert Dervishes – everything. For a time scientific zeal consumed the secretary, and the question of the plans remained in suspense. He even went into speculation about the previous occupants of the balloon. 'I suppose,' he said, 'the laty *was* the laty. Bot that is not our affair.'

'It is fery curious and amusing, yes: but I am afraid the Prince may be annoyt. He acted wiz his usual decision – always he acts wiz wonterful decision. Like Napoleon. Directly he was tolt of your descent into ze camp at Dornhof, he said, "Pring him! – pring him! It is my schtar!" His schtar of Destiny! You see? He will be dthwarted. He directed you to come as Herr Pooterage, and you haf not done so. You haf triet, of course; but it has peen a poor try. His chugments of men are fery just and right, and it is better for men to act up to them – gompletely. Especially now. Barticularly now.'

He resumed that attitude of his, with his under lip pinched between his forefingers. He spoke almost confidentially. 'It will be awkward. I triet to suggest some doubt, but I was overruled. The Prince does not listen. He is impatient in the high air. Perhaps he will think his schtar has been making a fool of him. Perhaps he will think *I* haf been making a fool of him.' He wrinkled his forehead, and drew in the corners of his mouth.

'I got the plans,' said Bert.

'Yes. Zere is zat! Yes. But you see the Prince was interested in Herr Pooterage because of his romantic seit. Herr Pooterage was so much more – ah! – in the picture. I am afraid you are not equal to controlling ze flying-machine department of our aerial park as he wished you to do. He hadt promised himself zat. . . .

'And der was also ze prestige– ze worldt prestige of Pooterage wiz us. . . . Well, we must see what we can do.' He held out his hand. 'Gif me ze plans.'

A terrible chill ran through the being of Mr Smallways. To the end of his life he was never clear in his mind whether he wept or no, but certainly there was weeping in his voice. ''Ere I say!' he protested. 'Ain't I to 'ave – nothin' for 'em?'

The secretary regarded him with benevolent eyes. 'You do not deserve anyzing!' he said.

'I might 'ave tore 'em up.'

'Zey are not yours!'

'They weren't his, very likely.'

'No need to pay anyzing.'

Bert's being seemed to tighten towards desperate deeds. 'Gaw!' he said, clutching his coat, '*ain't* there?'

'Pe galm,' said the secretary. 'Listen! You shall haf five hundert poundts. You shall haf it on my promise. I will do zat for you, and zat is all I can do. Take it from me. Gif me ze name of zat bank. Write it down. So! I tell you ze Prince – is no choke. I do not think he approffed of your appearance last night. No! I can't answer for him. He wanted Pooterage, and you haf spoilt it. Ze Prince – I do not understandt quite, he is in a strange state. It is the excitement of the starting and this great soaring in the air. I cannot account for what he does. But if all goes well I will see to it – you shall haf five hundert poundts. Will that do? Then gif me the plans.'

'Old beggar!' said Bert, as the door clicked. 'Gaw! – what an ole beggar! – *Sharp!*'

He sat down in the folding chair, and whistled noiselessly for a time.

'Nice old swindle for 'im if I tore 'em up! I could 'ave.'

He rubbed the bridge of his nose thoughtfully. 'I gave the whole blessed show away. If I'd jes' kep' quiet about being Enonymous. . . . Gaw! . . . Too soon, Bert my boy – too soon and too rushy. I'd like to kick my silly self.

'I couldn't 'ave kep' it up.

'After all, it ain't so very bad,' he said.

'After all, five 'undred pounds. . . . It isn't *my* secret, anyhow. It's jes' a pick-up on the road. Five 'undred.

'Wonder what the fare is from America back 'ome?'

8

And later in the day an extremely shattered and disorganized Bert Smallways stood in the presence of the Prince Karl Albert.

The proceedings were in German. The Prince was in his own cabin, the end room of the airship, a charming apartment furnished in wickerwork with a long window across its entire breadth, looking forward. He was sitting at a folding table of green baize, with Von Winterfeld and two officers sitting beside him, and littered before them were American maps and Mr Butteridge's letters and his portfolio and a number of loose papers. Bert was not asked to sit down, and remained standing throughout the interview. Von Winterfeld told his story, and every now and then the words balloon and Pooterage struck on Bert's ears. The Prince's face remained stern and ominous, and the two officers watched it cautiously or glanced at Bert. There was something a little strange in their scrutiny of the Prince – a curiosity, an apprehension. Then presently he was struck by an idea, and they fell discussing the plans. The Prince asked Bert abruptly in English: 'Did you ever see this thing go op?'

Bert jumped. 'Saw it from Bun 'Ill, your Royal Highness.'

Von Winterfeld made some explanation.

'How fast did it go?'

'Couldn't say, your Royal Highness. The papers, leastways *The Daily Courier*, said eighty miles an hour.'

They talked German over that for a time.

'Couldt it standt still? Op in the air? That is what I want to know.'

'It could 'ovver, your Royal Highness, like a wasp,' said Bert.

'*Viel besser, nicht wahr?* said the Prince to Von Winterfeld, and then went on in German for a time.

Presently they came to an end, and the two officers looked at Bert. One rang a bell, and the portfolio was handed to an attendant, who took it away.

687

Then they reverted to the case of Bert, and it was evident the Prince was inclined to be hard with him. Von Winterfeld protested. Apparently theological considerations came in, for there were several mentions of 'Gott!' Some conclusions emerged, and it was apparent that Von Winterfeld was instructed to convey them to Bert.

'Mr Schmallvays, you haf obtained a footing in zis airship,' he said, 'by disgraceful and systematic lying.'

''Ardly systematic,' said Bert. 'I—'

The Prince silenced him by a gesture.

'And it is within ze power of his Highness to dispose of you as a spy.'

''Ere! – I came to sell—'

'Ssh!' said one of the officers.

'However, in consideration of ze happy chance zat mate you ze instrument unter Gott of zis Pooterage flying machine reaching his Highness's hand, you haf been spared. Yes – you were ze pearer of goot tidings. You will be allowed to remain on zis ship until it is convenient to dispose of you. Do you understandt?'

'We will bring him,' said the Prince, and added terribly with a terrible glare, '*als Ballast.*'

'You are to come wiz us,' said Winterfeld, 'as – pallast. Do you understandt?'

Bert opened his mouth to ask about the five hundred pounds, and then a saving gleam of wisdom silenced him. He met Von Winterfeld's eye, and it seemed to him the secretary nodded slightly. 'Go!' said the Prince, with a sweep of the great arm and hand towards the door. Bert went out like a leaf before a gale.

9

But in between the time when the Graf von Winterfeld had talked to him and this alarming conference with the Prince, Bert had explored the *Vaterland* from end to end. He had found it interesting in spite of grave preoccupations. Kurt, like the greater number of the men upon the German air-fleet, had known hardly anything of aeronautics before his appointment to the new flagship. But he was extremely keen upon this wonderful new weapon Germany had assumed so suddenly and dramatically. He showed things to Bert with a boyish eagerness and appreciation. It was as if he showed them over again to himself, like a child showing a new toy. 'Let's go all over the ship,' he said with zest. He pointed out particularly the lightness of everything, the use of exhausted aluminium tubing, of springy cushions inflated with compressed hydrogen; the partitions were hydrogen bags covered with light imitation leather, the very crockery was a light biscuit glazed in a vacuum, and weighed next to nothing. Where strength was needed there was the new Charlottenburg alloy, German steel as it was called, the toughest and most resistant metal in the world.

There was no lack of space. Space did not matter, so long as load did not grow. The habitable part of the ship was two hundred and fifty feet long, and the rooms in two tiers; above these one could go up into remarkable little white-metal turrets with big windows and air-tight double doors that enabled one to inspect the vast cavity of the gas-chambers. This inside view impressed Bert very much. He had never realized before that an airship was not one simple continuous gas-bag containing nothing but gas. Now he saw far above him the backbone of the apparatus and its big ribs, 'like the neural and haemal canals,' said Kurt, who had dabbled in biology.

'Rather!' said Bert appreciatively, though he had not the ghost of an idea what these phrases meant.

Little electric lights could be switched on up there if anything went wrong in the night. There were even ladders across the space. 'But you can't go into the gas,' protested Bert. 'You can't breve it.'

The lieutenant opened a cupboard door and displayed a diver's suit, only that it was made of oiled silk, and both its compressed-air knapsack and its helmet were of an alloy of aluminium and some light metal. 'We can go all over the inside netting and stick up bullet-holes or leaks,' he explained. 'There's netting inside and out. The whole outer case is rope ladder, so to speak.'

Aft of the habitable part of the airship was the magazine of explosives, coming near the middle of its length. They were all bombs of various types – mostly in glass – none of the German airships carried any guns at all except one small pom-pom (to use the old English nickname dating from the Boer War), which was forward in the gallery upon the shield at the heart of the eagle. From the magazine amidships a covered canvas gallery with aluminium treads on its floor and a hand-rope ran back underneath the gas-chamber to the engine-room at the tail; but along this Bert did not go, and from first to last he never saw the engines. But he went up a ladder against a gale of ventilation – a ladder that was encased in a kind of gas-tight fire-escape and ran right athwart the great forward air-chamber to the little lookout gallery with a telephone, that gallery that bore the light pom-pom of German steel and its locker of shells. This gallery was all of aluminium-magnesium alloy, the tight front of the airship swelled cliff-like above and below and the black eagle sprawled overwhelmingly gigantic, its extremities hidden by the bulge of the gas-bag.

And far down, under the soaring eagles, was England, four thousand feet below perhaps, and looking very small and defenceless indeed in the morning sunlight.

The realization that there was England gave Bert sudden and unexpected qualms of patriotic compunction. He was struck by a quite novel idea. After all, he might have torn up those plans and thrown them away. These people could not have done so very much to him. And even if they did, ought not an Englishman to die for his country? It was an idea that had hitherto been rather smothered up by the cares of a competitive civilization. He became violently depressed. He ought, he perceived, to have seen it in that light before. Why hadn't he seen it in that light before?

Indeed, wasn't he a sort of traitor? . . .

He wondered how the aerial fleet must look from down there. Tremendous, no doubt, and dwarfing all the buildings.

He was passing between Manchester and Liverpool, Kurt told him; a gleaming band across the prospect was the Ship Canal, and a weltering ditch of shipping far away ahead, the Mersey estuary. Bert was a southerner; he had never been north of the Midland counties, and the multitude of factories and chimneys – the latter for the most part obsolete and smokeless now, superseded by huge electric generating stations that consumed their own reek – old railway viaducts, monorail networks and goods yards, and the vast areas of dingy homes and narrow streets, spreading aimlessly, struck him as though Camberwell and Rotherhithe had run to seed. Here and there, as if caught in a net, were fields and agricultural fragments. It was a sprawl of undistinguished population. There were, no doubt, museums and town halls, and even cathedrals of a sort to mark theoretical centres of municipal and religious organization in this confusion; but Bert could not see them, they did not stand out at all in that wide disorderly vision of congested workers' houses and places to work, and shops and meanly conceived chapels and churches. And across this landscape of an industrial civilization swept the shadows of the German airships like a hurrying shoal of fishes. . . .

Kurt and he fell talking of aerial tactics, and presently went down to the under-gallery in order that Bert might see the *Drachenflieger* that the airships of the right wing had picked up overnight and were towing behind them; each airship towing three or four. They looked like big box-kites of an exaggerated form, soaring at the ends of invisible cords. They had long, square heads and flattened tails, with lateral propellers.

'Much skill is required for those! – much skill!'

'Rather!'

Pause.

'Your machine is different from that, Mr Butteridge?'

'Quite different,' said Bert. 'More like an insect, and less like a bird. And it buzzes, and don't drive about so. What can those things do?'

Kurt was not very clear upon that himself, and was still explaining when Bert was called to the conference we have recorded with the Prince. . . .

And after that was over, the last traces of Butteridge fell from Bert like a garment, and he became Smallways to all on board. The soldiers ceased to salute him, and the officers ceased to seem aware of his existence, except Lieutenant Kurt. He was turned out of his nice cabin, and packed in with his belongings to share that of Lieutenant Kurt, whose luck it was to be junior, and the bird-headed officer, still swearing slightly and carrying strops and aluminium boot-trees and weightless hairbrushes and hand-mirrors and pomade in his hands, resumed possession. Bert was put in with Kurt because in that close-packed vessel there was nowhere else for him to lay his bandaged head. He was to mess, he was told, with the men.

Kurt came and stood with his legs wide apart, and surveyed him for a moment as he sat despondent in his new quarters.

'What's your real name, then?' said Kurt, who was only imperfectly informed of the new state of affairs.

'Smallways.'

'I thought you were a bit of a fraud – even when I thought you were Butteridge. You're jolly lucky the Prince took it calmly. He's a pretty tidy blazer when he's roused. He wouldn't stick a moment at pitching a chap of your sort overboard if he thought fit. No! . . . They've shoved you on to me, but it's my cabin, you know.'

'I won't forget,' said Bert.

Kurt left him, and when he came to look about him the first thing he saw pasted on the padded wall was a reproduction of the great picture by Siegfried Schmalz of the War God, that terrible, trampling figure with the Viking helmet and the scarlet cloak, wading through destruction, sword in hand, which had so strong a resemblance to Karl Albert, the prince it was painted to please.

5

The Battle of the North Atlantic

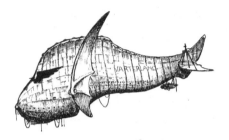

I

The Prince Karl Albert had made a profound impression upon Bert. He was quite the most terrifying person Bert had ever encountered. He filled the Smallways soul with passionate dread and antipathy. For a long time Bert sat alone in Kurt's cabin, doing nothing and not venturing even to open the door lest he should be by so much nearer that appalling presence.

So it came about that he was probably the last person on board to hear the news that wireless telegraphy was bringing to the airship in throbs and fragments of a great naval battle in progress in mid-Atlantic.

He learnt it at last from Kurt.

Kurt came in with a general air of ignoring Bert, but muttering to himself in English nevertheless. 'Stupendous!' Bert heard him say. 'Here!' he said, 'get off this locker.' And he proceeded to rout out two books and a case of maps. He spread them on the folding table, and stood regarding them. For a time his Germanic discipline struggled with his English informality and his natural kindliness and talk-ativeness, and at last lost.

'They're at it, Smallways,' he said.

'At what, sir?' said Bert, broken and respectful.

'Fighting! The American North Atlantic Squadron and pretty nearly the whole of our fleet. Our *Eiserne Kreuz* has had a gruelling and is sinking, and their *Miles Standish* – she's one of their biggest – has sunk with all hands. Torpedoes, I suppose. She was a bigger ship than the *Karl der Grosse*, but five or six years older. ... Gods! I wish we could

692

see it, Smallways; a square fight in blue water, guns or nothing, and all of 'em steaming ahead!'

He spread his maps, he had to talk, and so he delivered a lecture on the naval situation to Bert.

'Here it is,' he said, 'latitude 30° 50' N., longitude 30° 50' W. It's a good day off us anyhow, and they're all going south-west by south full pelt as hard as they can go. We shan't see a bit of it, worse luck! Not a sniff we shan't get!'

2

The naval situation in the North Atlantic at that time was a peculiar one. The United States was by far the stronger of the two powers upon the sea, but the bulk of the American fleet was still in the Pacific. It was in the direction of Asia that war had been most feared, for the situation between Asiatic and white had become unusually violent and dangerous, and the Japanese Government had shown itself quite unprecedentedly difficult. The German attack found half the American strength at Manila, and what was called the Second Fleet strung out across the Pacific in wireless contact between the Asiatic station and San Francisco. The North Atlantic Squadron was the sole American force on her eastern shore; it was returning from a friendly visit to France and Spain, and was pumping oil fuel from tenders in mid-Atlantic – for most of its ships were steamships – when the international situation became acute. It was made up of four battleships and five armoured cruisers, ranking almost with battleships, not one of which was of a later date than 1913. The Americans had indeed grown so accustomed to the idea that Great Britain could be trusted to keep the peace of the Atlantic that a naval attack on the eastern seaboard found them unprepared even in their imaginations. But long before the declaration of war – indeed, on Whit Monday – the whole German fleet of eighteen battleships, with a flotilla of fuel tenders and converted liners containing stores, to be used in support of the air-fleet, had passed through the Straits of Dover and headed boldly for New York. Not only did these German battleships outnumber the Americans two to one, but they were more heavily armed and more modern in construction – at least seven of them having high-explosive engines built of Charlottenburg steel, and all carrying Charlottenburg steel guns.

The fleets came into contact on Wednesday before any actual declaration of war. The Americans had strung out in the modern fashion at distances of thirty miles or so, and were steaming to keep themselves between the Germans and either the eastern states or Panama; because, vital as it was to defend the seaboard cities, and particularly New York, it was still more vital to save the canal from any attack that might prevent the return of the main fleet from the Pacific. No doubt, said Kurt, this was now making records across that ocean, 'unless the Japanese have had the same idea as the Germans'. It was obviously beyond human possibility that the American North Atlantic fleet could hope to meet and defeat the German; but, on the other hand, with luck it might fight a delaying action and inflict such damage as to weaken greatly the attack upon the coast defences. Its duty, indeed, was not victory but devotion, the severest task in the world. Meanwhile the submarine defences of New York, Panama, and the other more vital points could be put in some sort of order.

This was the naval situation, and until Wednesday in Whit week it was the only situation the American people had realized. It was then they heard for the first time of the real scale of the Dornhof aeronautic park, and the possibility of an attack coming upon them not only by sea, but by the air. But it is curious that so discredited were the newspapers of that period, that a large majority of New Yorkers, for example, did not believe the most copious and circumstantial accounts of the German air-fleet until it was actually in sight of New York.

Kurt's talk was half soliloquy. He stood with a map on Mercator's projection before him, swaying to the swaying of the ship and talking of guns and tonnage, of ships and their build and powers and speed, of strategic points and bases of operation. A certain shyness that reduced him to the status of a listener at the officers' table no longer silenced him.

Bert stood by, saying very little, but watching Kurt's finger on the map. 'They've been saying things like this in the papers for a long time,' he remarked. 'Fancy it coming real!'

Kurt had a detailed knowledge of the *Miles Standish*. 'She used to be a crack ship for gunnery – held the record. I wonder if we beat her shooting or how? I wish I was in it. I wonder which of our ships beat her. Maybe she got a shell in her engines. It's a running fight! I wonder what the *Barbarossa* is doing,' he went on. 'She's my old ship. Not a first-rater, but good stuff. I bet she's got a shot or two home by now if old Schneider's up to form. Just think of it! There they are whacking away at each other, great guns going, shells exploding, magazines bursting, ironwork flying about like straw in a gale, all we've been dreaming of for years! I suppose we shall fly right away to New York – just as though it wasn't anything at all. I suppose we shall reckon we aren't wanted down there. It's no more than a covering fight on our

694

side. All those tenders and storeships of ours are going on south-west by west to New York to make a floating depot for us. See?' He dabbed his forefinger on the map. 'Here we are. Our train of stores goes there, our battleships elbow the Americans out of our way there.' ...

When Bert went down to the men's mess-room to get his evening ration, hardly anyone took notice of him, except just to point him out for an instant. Everyone was talking of the battle, suggesting, contradicting – at times, until the petty officers hushed them, it rose to a great uproar. There was a new bulletin, but what it said he did not gather, except that it concerned the *Barbarossa*. Some of the men stared at him, and he heard the name of 'Booteraidge' several times; but no one molested him, and there was no difficulty about his soup and bread when his turn at the end of the queue came. He had feared there might be no ration for him, and if so he did not know what he would have done.

Afterwards he ventured out upon the little hanging gallery with the solitary sentinel. The weather was still fine, but the wind was rising and the rolling swing of the airship increasing. He clutched the rail tightly and felt rather giddy. They were now out of sight of land, and over blue water rising and falling in great masses. A dingy old brigantine under the British flag rose and plunged amid the broad blue waves – the only ship in sight.

3

In the evening it began to blow and the airship to roll like a porpoise as it swung through the air. Kurt said that several of the men were seasick, but the motion did not inconvenience Bert, whose luck it was to be of that mysterious gastric disposition which constitutes a good sailor. He slept well, but in the small hours the light awoke him, and he found Kurt staggering about in search of something. He found it at last in the locker, and held it in his hand unsteadily – a compass. Then he compared his map.

'We've changed our direction,' he said, 'and come into the wind. I can't make it out. We've turned away from New York to the south. Almost as if we were going to take a hand—'

He continued talking to himself for some time.

Day came, wet and windy. The window was bedewed externally, and they could see nothing through it. It was also very cold, and Bert decided to keep rolled up in his blankets on the locker until the bugle summoned him to his morning ration. That consumed, he went out on the little gallery; but he could see nothing but eddying clouds driving headlong by, and the dim outlines of the nearer airships. Only at rare intervals could he get a glimpse of grey sea through the pouring cloud-drift.

Later in the morning the *Vaterland* changed altitude, and soared up suddenly into a high, clear sky, going, Kurt said, to a height of nearly thirteen thousand feet.

Bert was in his cabin, and chanced to see the dew vanish from the window and caught the gleam of sunlight outside. He looked out, and saw once more that sunlit cloud floor he had seen first from the balloon, and the ships of the German air-fleet rising one by one from the white, as fish might rise and become visible from deep water. He stared for a moment and then ran out to the little gallery to see this wonder better. Below was cloudland and storm, a great drift of tumbled weather going hard away to the north-east, and the air about him was clear and cold and serene save for the faintest chill breeze and a rare drifting snowflake. Throb, throb, throb, throb went the engines in the stillness. That huge herd of airships rising one after another had an effect of strange, portentous monsters breaking into an altogether unfamiliar world. . . .

Either there was no news of the naval battle that morning, or the Prince kept to himself whatever came until past midday. Then the bulletins came with a rush, bulletins that made the lieutenant wild with excitement.

'*Barbarossa* disabled and sinking!' he cried. 'Gott im Himmel! Der alte *Barbarossa*! Aber welch ein braver Krieger!'

He walked about the swinging cabin, and for a time he was wholly German.

Then he became English again. 'Think of it, Smallways! The old ship we kept so clean and tidy! All smashed about, and the iron flying about in fragments, and the chaps one knew – Gott! – flying about too! Scalding water squirting, fire, and the smash, smash of the guns! They smash when you're near! Like everything bursting to pieces! Wool won't stop it – nothing! And me up here – so near and so far! Der alte *Barbarossa*!'

'Any other ships?' asked Smallways presently.

'Gott! Yes! We've lost the *Karl der Grosse*, our best and biggest. Run down in the night by a British liner that blundered into the fighting – in trying to blunder out. They're fighting in a gale. The liner's afloat with her nose broken, sagging about! There never was such a battle! – never before! Good ships and good men on both sides – and a storm and the night and the dawn and all in the open ocean full steam ahead! No stabbing! No submarines! Guns and shooting! Half our ships we don't hear of any more, because their masts are shot away. Latitude, 30° 38' N. – longitude, 40° 31' W. – where's that?'

He routed out his map again, and stared at it with eyes that did not see.

'Der alte *Barbarossa*! I can't get it out of my head – with shells in her engine-room, and the fires flying out of her furnaces, and the stokers and engineers scalded and dead. Men I've messed with, Smallways – men I've talked to close! And they've had their day at last! And it wasn't all luck for them!

'Disabled and sinking! I suppose everybody can't have all the luck in a battle. Poor old Schneider! I bet he gave 'em something back!'

So it was the news of the battle came filtering through to them all that afternoon. The Americans had lost a second ship, name unknown; the *Hermann* had been damaged in covering the *Barbarossa*. . . . Kurt fretted like an imprisoned animal about the airship, now going up to the forward gallery under the eagle, now down into the swinging gallery, now poring over his maps. He infected Smallways with a sense of the immediacy of this battle that was going on just over the curve of the earth. But when Bert went down to the gallery the world was empty and still, a clear inky-blue sky above and a rippled veil of still, thin sunlit cirrus below, through which one saw a racing drift of rain-cloud, and never a glimpse of sea. Throb, throb, throb, throb went the engines, and the long, undulating wedge of airships hurried after the flagship like a flight of swans after their leader. Save for the quiver of the engines it was as noiseless as a dream. And down there, somewhere in the wind and rain, guns roared, shells crashed home, and, after the old manner of warfare, men toiled and died.

4

As the afternoon wore on the lower weather abated, and the sea became intermittently visible again. The air-fleet dropped slowly to the middle air, and towards sunset they had a glimpse of the disabled *Barbarossa* far away to the east. Smallways heard men hurrying along the passage, and was drawn out to the gallery, where he found nearly a dozen officers collected and scrutinizing the helpless ruins of the battleship through field-glasses. Two other vessels stood by her, one an exhausted petrol tank, very high out of the water, and the other a converted liner. Kurt was at the end of the gallery, a little apart from the others.

'Gott!' he said at last, lowering his binocular, 'it is like seeing an old friend with his nose cut off – waiting to be finished. Der *Barbarossa*!'

With a sudden impulse he handed his glass to Bert, who had peered beneath his hands, ignored by everyone, seeing the three ships merely as three brown-black lines upon the sea.

Never had Bert seen the like of that magnified slightly hazy image before. It was not simply a battered ironclad that wallowed helpless, it was a mangled ironclad. It seemed wonderful she still floated. Her powerful engines had been her ruin. In the long chase of the night she had got out of line with her consorts, and nipped in between the *Susquehanna* and the *Kansas* City. They discovered her proximity, dropped back until she was nearly broadside on to the former battle-ship, and signalled up the *Theodore Roosevelt* and the little *Monitor*. As dawn broke she had found herself hostess of a circle. The fight had not lasted five minutes before the appearance of the *Hermann* to the east, and immediately after the *Fürst Bismarck* in the west, forced the Americans to leave her, but in that time they had smashed her iron to rags. They had vented the accumulated tensions of their hard day's retreat upon her. As Bert saw her, she seemed a mere metal-worker's fantasy of frozen metal writhings. He could not tell part from part of her, except by its position.

'Gott!' murmured Kurt, taking the glasses Bert restored to him – 'Gott! Da waren Albrecht – der gute Albrecht und der alte Zim-mermann – und von Rosen!' ...

Long after the *Barbarossa* had been swallowed up in the twilight and distance he remained on the gallery peering through his glasses, and when he came back into his cabin he was unusually silent and thoughtful.

'This is a rough game, Smallways,' he said at last – 'this war is a rough game. Somehow one sees it different after a thing like that. Many men there were worked to make that *Barbarossa*, and there were men in it – one does not meet the like of them every day. Albrecht – there was a man named Albrecht – played the zither and improvised; I keep on wondering what has happened to him. He and I – we were very close friends, after the German fashion.'

5

Smallways woke the next night to discover the cabin in darkness, a draught blowing through it, and Kurt talking to himself in German. He could see him dimly by the window, which he had unscrewed and opened, peering down. That cold, clear, attenuated light which is not so much light as a going of darkness, which casts inky shadows and so often heralds the dawn in the high air, was on his face.

'What's the row?' said Bert.

'Shut up!' said the lieutenant. 'Can't you hear?'

Into the stillness came the repeated heavy thud of guns, one, two, a pause, then three in quick succession.

'Gaw!' said Bert – 'guns!' and was instantly at the lieutenant's side. The airship was still very high and the sea below was masked by a thin veil of clouds. The wind had fallen, and Bert, following Kurt's pointing finger, saw dimly through the colourless veil first a red glow, then a quick red flash and then at a little distance from it another. They were, it seemed for a while, silent flashes, and seconds after, when one had ceased to expect them, came the belated thuds – thud, thud. Kurt spoke in German, very quickly.

A bugle call rang through the airship.

Kurt sprang to his feet, saying something in an excited tone, still using German, and went to the door.

'I say! What's up?' cried Bert. 'What's that?'

The lieutenant stopped for an instant in the doorway, dark against the light passage. 'You stay where you are, Smallways. You keep there and do nothing. We're going into action,' he explained, and vanished.

Bert's heart began to beat rapidly. He felt himself poised over the fighting vessels far below. In a moment, were they to drop like a hawk striking a bird? 'Gaw!' he whispered at last, in awestricken tones.

Thud! . . . thud! He discovered far away a second ruddy flare flashing back at the first. He perceived some difference on the *Vaterland* for which he could not account, and then he realized that the engines had slowed to an almost inaudible beat. He stuck his head out of the window and saw in the bleak air the other airships slowed down to a scarcely perceptible motion.

A second bugle sounded, was taken up faintly from ship to ship. Out went the lights; the fleet became dim, dark bulks against an intense blue sky that still retained an occasional star. For a long time they hung, for an interminable time it seemed to him, and then began the sound of air being pumped into the ballonette, and slowly, slowly the *Vaterland* sank down towards the clouds.

He craned his neck, but he could not see if the rest of the fleet was following them; the overhang of the gas-chambers intervened. There was something that stirred his imagination deeply in that stealthy, noiseless descent.

The obscurity deepened for a time, the last fading star on the horizon vanished, and he felt the cold presence of cloud. Then suddenly the glow beneath assumed distinct outlines, became flames, and the *Vaterland* ceased to descend and hung observant, and it would seem unobserved just beneath a drifting stratum of cloud a thousand feet, perhaps, over the battle below.

In the night the straggling naval battle and retreat had entered upon a new phase. The Americans had drawn together the ends of the flying line skilfully and dexterously, until at last it was a column and well to the south of the lax sweeping pursuit of the Germans. Then in the darkness before the dawn they had come about and steamed northward in close order with the idea of passing through the German battle line and falling upon the flotilla that was making for New York in support of the German air-fleet. Much had altered since the first contact of the fleets. By this time the American admiral, O'Connor, was fully informed of the existence of the airships, and he was no longer vitally concerned for Panama, since the submarine flotilla was reported arrived there from Key West, and the *Delaware* and *Abraham Lincoln*, two powerful and entirely modern ships, were already at Rio Grande, on the Pacific side of the canal. His manoeuvre was, however, delayed by a boiler explosion on board the *Susquehanna*, and dawn found this ship in sight of and indeed so close to the *Bremen* and *Weimar* that they instantly engaged. There was no alternative to her abandonment but a fleet engagement. O'Connor chose the latter course. It was by no means a hopeless fight. The Germans, though much more numerous and powerful than the Americans, were in a dispersed line measuring nearly forty-five miles from end to end, and there were many chances that before they could gather in for the fight the column of seven Americans would have ripped them from end to end.

The day broke dim and overcast, and neither the *Bremen* nor the *Weimar* realized they had to deal with more than the *Susquehanna* until the whole column drew out from behind her at a distance of a mile or less and bore down on them. This was the position of affairs when the *Vaterland* appeared in the sky. The red glow Bert had seen through the column of clouds came from the luckless *Susquehanna;* she lay almost immediately below, burning fore and aft, but still fighting two of her guns and steaming slowly southward. The *Bremen* and the *Weimar*, both hit in several places, were going west by south and away from her. The American fleet, headed by the *Theodore Roosevelt*, was crossing behind them, pounding them in succession, steaming in between them and the big modern *Fürst Bismarck*, which was coming up from the west. To Bert, however, the names of all these ships were unknown, and for a considerable time, indeed, misled by the direction in which the combatants were moving, he imagined the Germans to be Americans and the Americans Germans. He saw what appeared to him to be a column of six battleships pursuing three others, who were supported by a newcomer, until the fact that the *Bremen* and *Weimar* were firing into the *Susquehanna* upset his calculations. Then for a time he was hopelessly at a loss. The noise of the guns, too, confused him, they no longer seemed to boom; they went whack, whack, whack, whack, and each faint flash made his heart jump in anticipation of the instant impact. He saw these ironclads, too, not in profile, as he was accustomed to see ironclads in pictures, but in plan and curiously foreshortened. For the most part they presented empty decks, but here and there little knots of men sheltered behind steel bulwarks. The long agitated noses of their big guns jetting thin transparent flashes and the broadside activity of the quick-firers were the chief facts in this bird's-eye view. The Americans, being steam-turbine ships, had from two to four blast-funnels each; the Germans lay lower in the water, having explosive engines which now for some reason made an unwonted muttering roar. Because of their steam propulsion, the American ships were larger and with a more graceful outline. He saw all these foreshortened ships rolling considerably and fighting their guns over a sea of huge low waves and under the cold, explicit light of dawn. The whole spectacle waved slowly with the long rhythmic rising and beat of the airship.

At first only the *Vaterland* of all the flying fleet appeared upon the scene below. She hovered high over the *Theodore Roosevelt*, keeping pace with the full speed of that ship. From that ship she must have been intermittently visible through the drifting clouds. The rest of the German fleet remained above the cloud canopy at a height of six or seven thousand feet, communicating with the flagship by wireless telegraphy, but risking no exposure to the artillery below.

It is doubtful at what particular time the unlucky Americans realized the presence of this new factor in the fight. No account now survives of their experience. We have to imagine as well as we can what it must have been to a battle-strained sailor suddenly glancing upwards to discover that huge long silent shape overhead, vaster than any battle-ship, and trailing now from its hinder quarter a big German flag. Presently, as the sky cleared, more of such ships appeared in the blue through the dissolving clouds, and more, all disdainfully free of guns or armour, all flying fast to keep pace with the running fight below.

From first to last no gun whatever was fired at the *Vaterland*, and only a few rifle-shots. It was a mere adverse stroke of chance that she had a man killed aboard her. Nor did she take any direct share in the fight until the end. She flew above the doomed American fleet while the Prince by wireless telegraphy directed the movements of her consorts. Meanwhile the *Vogelstern* and *Preussen*, each with half a dozen

Drachenflieger in tow, went full speed ahead and then dropped through the clouds, perhaps five miles ahead of the Americans. The *Theodore Roosevelt* let fly at once with the big guns in her forward barbette, but the shells burst far below the *Vogelstern*, and forthwith a dozen single-man *Drachenflieger* were swooping down to make their attack.

Bert, craning his neck through the cabin porthole, saw the whole of that incident, that first encounter of aeroplane and ironclad. He saw the queer German *Drachenflieger*, with their wide flat wings and square box-shaped heads, their wheeled bodies and their single-man riders, soar down the air like a flight of birds. 'Gaw!' he said. One to the right pitched extravagantly, shot steeply up into the air, burst with a loud report, and flamed down into the sea; another plunged nose forward into the water and seemed to fly to pieces as it hit the waves. He saw little men on the deck of the *Theodore Roosevelt* below, men foreshortened in plan into mere heads and feet, running out preparing to shoot at the others. Then the foremost flying machine was rushing between Bert and the American's deck, and then bang! came the thunder of its bomb flung neatly at the forward barbette, and a thin little crackling of rifle-shots in reply. Whack, whack, whack went the quick-firing guns of the American's battery and smash came an answering shell from the *Fürst Bismarck*. Then a second and third flying machine passed between Bert and the American ironclad, dropping bombs also, and a fourth, its rider hit by a bullet, reeled down and dashed itself to pieces and exploded between the shot-torn funnels, blowing them apart. Bert had a momentary glimpse of a little black creature jumping from the crumpling frame of the flying machine, hitting the funnel, and falling limply, to be instantly caught and driven to nothingness by the blaze and rush of the explosion.

Smash! came a vast explosion in the forward part of the flagship, and a huge piece of metalwork seemed to lift out of her and dump itself into the sea, dropping men and leaving a gap into which a prompt *Drachenflieger* planted a flaring bomb. And then for an instant Bert perceived only too clearly in the growing, pitiless light a number of minute, convulsively active animalculae scorched and struggling in the *Theodore Roosevelt*'s foaming wake. What were they? Not men – surely not men? Those drowning, mangled little creatures tore with their clutching fingers at Bert's soul. 'Oh, Gord!' he cried, 'Oh, Gord!' almost whimpering. He looked again and they had gone, and the black stem of the *Andrew Jackson*, disfigured by the sinking *Bremen*'s last shot, was parting the water that had swallowed them into two neatly symmetrical waves. For some moments sheer blank horror blinded Bert to the destruction below.

Then with an immense rushing sound, bearing as it were a straggling volley of crashing minor explosions on its back, the *Susquehanna*, three miles and more now to the east, blew up and vanished abruptly in a boiling, steaming welter. For a moment nothing was to be seen but tumbled water, and then there came belching up from below, with immense gulping noises, eructations of steam and air and petrol and fragments of canvas and woodwork and men.

That made a distinct pause in the fight. It seemed a long pause to Bert. He found himself looking for the *Drachenflieger*. The flattened ruin of one was floating abeam of the *Monitor*, the rest had passed, dropping bombs down the American column; several were in the water and apparently uninjured, and three or four were still in the air and coming round now in a wide circle to return to their mother airships. The American ironclads were no longer in column formation; the *Theodore Roosevelt*, badly damaged, had turned to the south-east, and the *Andrew Jackson*, greatly battered but uninjured in any fighting part, was passing between her and the still fresh and vigorous *Fürst Bismarck* to intercept and meet the latter's fire. Away to the west the *Hermann* and the *Germanicus* had appeared and were coming into action.

In the pause after the *Susquehanna's* disaster Bert became aware of a trivial sound like the noise of an ill-greased, ill-hung door that falls ajar – the sound of the men in the *Fürst Bismarck* cheering.

And in that pause in the uproar, too, the sun rose, the dark waters became luminously blue and a torrent of golden light irradiated the world. It came like a sudden smile in a scene of hate and terror. The cloud veil had vanished as if by magic, and the whole immensity of the German air-fleet was revealed in the sky, the air-fleet stooping now upon its prey.

'Whack-bang, whack-bang,' the guns resumed, but ironclads were not built to fight the zenith, and the only hits the Americans scored were a few lucky chances in a generally ineffectual rifle-fire. Their column was now badly broken, the *Susquehanna* had gone, the *Theodore Roosevelt* had fallen astern out of the line, with her forward guns disabled, in a heap of wreckage, and the *Monitor* was in some grave trouble. These two had ceased fire altogether, and so had the *Bremen* and *Weimar*, all four ships lying within shot of each other in an involuntary truce and with their respective flags still displayed. Only four American ships now, with the *Andrew Jackson* leading, kept to the south-easterly course. And the *Fürst Bismarck*, the *Hermann* and the *Germanicus* steamed parallel to them and drew ahead of them, fighting heavily. The *Vaterland* rose slowly in the air in preparation for the concluding act of the drama.

Then falling into place one behind the other, a string of a dozen airships dropped with unhurrying swiftness down the air in pursuit of the American fleet. They kept at a height of two thousand feet or more until they were over and a little in advance of the rearmost ironclad, and then stooped swiftly down into a fountain of bullets, and going just a little faster than the ship below, pelted her thinly protected decks with bombs until they became sheets of detonating flame. So the airships passed one after the other along the American column as it sought to keep up its fight with the *Fürst Bismarck*, the *Hermann* and the *Germanicus*, and each airship added to the destruction and confusion its predecessor had made. The American gunfire ceased, except for a few heroic shots, but they still steamed on, obstinately unsubdued, bloody, battered and wrathfully resistant, spitting bullets at the airships and unmercifully pounded by the German ironclads. But now Bert had but intermittent glimpses of them between the nearer bulks of the airships that assailed them. ...

It struck Bert suddenly that the whole battle was receding and growing small and less thunderously noisy. The *Vaterland* was rising in the air, steadily and silently, until the impact of the guns no longer smote upon the heart but came to the ear dulled by distance, until the four silenced ships to the eastward were little distant things: but were there four? Bert now could see only three of those floating, blackened and smoking rafts of ruin against the sun. But the *Bremen* had two boats out; the *Theodore Roosevelt* was also dropping boats to where the drift of minute objects struggled, rising and falling on the big, broad Atlantic waves. ... The *Vaterland* was no longer following the fight. The whole of that hurrying tumult drove away to the south-eastward, growing smaller and less audible as it passed. One of the airships lay on the water burning, a remote monstrous fount of flames, and far in the south-west appeared first one and then three other German iron-clads hurrying in support of their consorts. ...

6

Steadily the *Vaterland* soared, and the air-fleet soared with her and came round to head for New York, and the battle became a little thing far away, an incident before breakfast. It dwindled to a string of dark shapes and one smoking yellow flare that presently became a more indistinct smear upon the vast horizon and the bright new day, that was at last altogether lost to sight. ...

So it was that Bert Smallways saw the first fight of the airship and the final fight of those strangest things in the whole history of war: the ironclad battleships, which began their career with the floating batteries of the Emperor Napoleon III in the Crimean war and lasted, with an enormous expenditure of human energy and resources, for seventy years. In that space of time the world produced over twelve thousand five hundred of these strange monsters, in schools, in types, in series, each larger and heavier and more deadly than its predecessors. Each in its turn was hailed as the last birth of time, most in their turn were sold for old iron. Only about five per cent of them ever fought in a battle. Some foundered, some went ashore and broke up, several rammed one another by accident and sank. The lives of countless men were spent in their service, the splendid genius and patience of thousands of engineers and inventors, wealth and material beyond estimating; to their account we must put stunted and starved lives on land, millions of children sent to toil unduly, innumerable opportunities of fine living undeveloped and lost. Money had to be found for them at any cost – that was the law of a nation's existence during that strange time. Surely they were the weirdest, most destructive and wasteful megatheria in the whole history of mechanical invention.

And then cheap things of gas and basketwork made an end of them altogether, smiting out of the sky! . . .

Never before had Bert Smallways seen pure destruction, never had he realized the mischief and waste of war. His startled mind rose to the conception, this also is in life. Out of all this fierce torrent of sensation one impression rose and became cardinal – the impression of the men of the *Theodore Roosevelt* who had struggled in the water after the explosion of the first bomb. 'Gaw!' he said at the memory; 'It might 'ave been me and Grubb! . . . I suppose you kick about, and get the water in your mouf. I don't suppose it lasts long.'

He became anxious to see how Kurt was affected by these things. Also he perceived he was hungry. He hesitated towards the door of the cabin and peeped out into the passage. Down forward, near the gangway to the men's mess, stood a little group of air-sailors looking at something that was hidden from him in a recess. One of them was in the light diver's costume Bert had already seen in the gas-chamber turret, and he was moved to walk along and look at this person more closely and examine the helmet he carried under his arm. But he forgot about the helmet when he got to the recess, because there he found lying on the floor the dead body of the boy who had been killed by a bullet from the *Theodore Roosevelt*.

Bert had not observed that any bullets at all had reached the

705

Vaterland or, indeed, imagined himself under fire. He could not understand for a time what had killed the lad and no one explained to him.

The boy lay just as he had fallen and died, with his jacket torn and scorched, his shoulder-blade smashed and burst away from his body and all the left side of his body ripped and rent. There was much blood. The sailors stood listening to the man with the helmet, who made explanations and pointed to the round bullet-hole in the floor and the smash in the panel of the passage upon which the still vicious missile had spent the residue of its energy. All the faces were grave and earnest; they were the faces of sober blond, blue-eyed men accustomed to obedience and an orderly life, to whom this waste, wet, painful thing that had been a comrade came almost as strangely as it did to Bert.

A peal of wild laughter sounded down the passage in the direction of the little gallery and something spoke – almost shouted – in German, in tones of exultation.

Other voices at a lower, more respectful pitch replied.

'*Der Prinz*,' said a voice, and all the men became stiffer and less natural. Down the passage appeared a group of figures, Lieutenant Kurt walking in front carrying a packet of papers.

He stopped pointblank when he saw the thing in the recess, and his ruddy face went white. 'So!' said he in surprise.

The Prince was following him, talking over his shoulder to Von Winterfeld and the Kapitän. 'Eh?' he said to Kurt, stopping in mid-sentence, and followed the gesture of Kurt's hand. He glared at the crumpled object in the recess and seemed to think for a moment.

He made a slight, careless gesture towards the boy's body and turned to the Kapitän.

'Dispose of that,' he said in German, and passed on, finishing his sentence to Von Winterfeld in the same cheerful tone in which it had begun.

7

The deep impression of helplessly drowning men that Bert had brought from the actual fight in the Atlantic mixed itself up inextricably with that of the lordly figure of Prince Karl Albert gesturing aside the dead body of the *Vaterland* sailor. Hitherto he had rather liked the idea of war as being a jolly, smashing, exciting affair, something like a Bank Holiday rag on a large scale, and on the whole agreeable and exhilarating. Now he knew it a little better.

The next day there was added to his growing disillusionment a third ugly impression, trivial indeed to describe, a mere necessary everyday incident of a state of war, but very distressing to his urbanized imagination. One writes 'urbanized' to express the distinctive gentleness of the period. It was quite peculiar to the crowded townsmen of that time, and different altogether from the normal experience of any preceding age, that they never saw anything killed, never encountered, save through the mitigating media of book or picture, the fact of lethal violence that underlies all life. Three times in his existence, and three times only, had Bert seen a dead human being, and he had never assisted at the killing of anything bigger than a new-born kitten.

The incident that gave him his third shock was the execution of one of the men on the *Adler* for carrying a box of matches. The case was a flagrant one. The man had forgotten he had it upon him when coming aboard. Ample notice had been given to everyone of the gravity of this offence, and notices appeared at numerous points all over the airships. The man's defence was that he had grown so used to the notices, and had been so preoccupied with his work, that he hadn't applied them to himself; he pleaded, in his defence, what is indeed in military affairs another serious crime, inadvertency. He was tried by his captain, and the sentence confirmed by wireless telegraphy by the Prince, and it was decided to make his death an example to the whole fleet. 'The Germans,' the Prince declared, 'hadn't crossed the Atlantic to go woolgathering.' And in order that this lesson in discipline and obedience might be visible to everyone, it was determined not to electrocute or drown, but hang the offender.

Accordingly the air-fleet came clustering round the flagship like carp in a pond at feeding-time. The *Adler* hung at the zenith immediately alongside the flagship. The whole crew of the *Vaterland* assembled upon the hanging gallery; the crews of the other airships manned the air-chambers, that is to say, clambered up the outer netting to the upper sides. The officers appeared upon the machine-gun platforms. Bert thought it an altogether stupendous sight, looking down, as he was, upon the entire fleet. Far off below two steamers on the rippled blue water, one British, and the other flying the American flag, seemed the minutest objects, and marked the scale. They were immensely distant. Bert stood on the gallery, curious to see the execution, but uncomfortable because that terrible blond Prince was within a dozen feet of him, glaring terribly, with his arms folded, and his heels together in military fashion.

They hung the man from the *Adler*. They gave him sixty feet of rope, so that he should hang and dangle in the sight of all evildoers who might be hiding matches or contemplating any kindred disobedience. Bert saw the man standing, a living, reluctant man, no doubt scared and rebellious enough in his heart, but outwardly erect and obedient, on the lower gallery of the *Adler* about a hundred yards away. Then they had thrust him overboard. ....

Down he fell, hands and feet extending, until with a jerk he was at the end of the rope. Then he ought to have died and swung edifyingly, but instead a more terrible thing happened; his head came right off, and down the body went spinning to the sea, feeble, grotesque, fantastic, with the head racing it in its fall.

'Ugh!' said Bert, clutching the rail before him, and a sympathetic grunt came from several of the men beside him.

'So!' said the Prince, stiffer and sterner, glared for some seconds, then turned to the gangway up into the airship.

For a long time Bert remained clinging to the railing of the gallery. He was almost physically sick with the horror of this trifling incident. He found it far more dreadful than the battle. He was indeed a very degenerate, latter-day, civilized person.

Late that afternoon Kurt came into the cabin and found him curled up on his locker, and looking very white and miserable. Kurt had also lost something of his pristine freshness.

'Seasick?' he asked.

'No!'

'We ought to reach New York this evening. There's a good breeze coming up under our tails. Then we shall see things.'

Bert did not answer.

Kurt opened out folding chair and table, and rustled for a time with his maps. Then he fell thinking darkly. He roused himself presently, and looked at his companion. 'What's the matter?' he said.

'Nothing!'

Kurt stared threateningly. 'What's the matter?' he repeated.

'I saw them kill that chap. I saw that flying-machine man hit the funnels of the big ironclad. I saw that dead chap in the passage. I seen too much smashing and killing today. That's the matter. I don't like it. I didn't know war was this sort of thing. I'm a civilian. I don't like it.'

'*I* don't like it,' said Kurt. 'By Jove, no!'

'I've read about war, and all that, but when you see it it's different. And I'm gettin' giddy. I'm gettin' giddy. I didn't mind a bit being up in that balloon at first, but all this looking down and floating over things and smashing up people, it's getting on my nerves. See?'

'It'll have to get off again. ....'

Kurt thought. 'You're not the only one. The men are all getting strung up. The flying – that's just flying. Naturally it makes one a little

708

swimmy in the head at first. As for the killing, we've got to be blooded; that's all. We're tame, civilized men. And we've got to get blooded. I suppose there's not a dozen men on the ship who've really seen bloodshed. Nice, quiet, law-abiding Germans they've been so far. . . . Here they are – in for it. They're a bit squeamy now, but you wait till they've got their hands in.'

He reflected. 'Everybody's getting a bit strung up,' he said.

He turned again to his maps. Bert sat crumpled up in the corner, apparently heedless of him. For some time both kept silence.

'Whadid the Prince want to go and 'ang that chap for?' asked Bert suddenly.

'That was all right,' said Kurt, 'that was all right. *Quite* right. Here were the orders, plain as the nose on your face, and here was that fool going about with matches—'

'Gaw! I shan't forget that bit in a 'urry,' said Bert irrelevantly.

Kurt did not answer him. He was measuring their distance from New York and speculating. 'Wonder what the American aeroplanes are like?' he said. 'Something like our *Drachenflieger.* . . . We shall know by this time tomorrow. . . . I wonder what we shall know? I wonder. Suppose, after all, they put up a fight. . . . Rum sort of fight!'

He whistled softly and mused. Presently he fretted out of the cabin, and later Bert found him in the twilight upon the swinging platform, staring ahead, and speculating about the things that might happen on the morrow. Clouds veiled the sea again, and the long straggling wedge of airships rising and falling as they flew seemed like a flock of strange new births in a Chaos that had neither earth nor water, but only mist and sky.

6

How War Came to New York

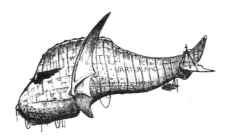

I

The City of New York was in the year of the German attack the largest, richest, in many respects the most splendid and in some the wickedest city the world had ever seen. She was the supreme type of the City of the Scientific Commercial Age; she displayed its greatness, its power, its ruthless anarchic enterprise, and its social disorganization most strikingly and completely. She had long ousted London from her pride of place as the modern Babylon, she was the centre of the world's finance, the world's trade and the world's pleasure; and men likened her to the apocalyptic cities of the ancient prophets. She sat drinking up the wealth of a continent, as Rome once drank the wealth of the Mediterranean, and Babylon the wealth of the east. In her streets one found the extremes of magnificence and misery, of civilization and disorder. In one quarter, palaces of marble, laced and crowned with light and flame and flowers, towered up into her marvellous twilights beautiful beyond description; in another, a black and sinister polyglot population sweltered in indescribable congestion in warrens and excavations beyond the power and knowledge of government. Her vice, her crime, her law alike were inspired by a fierce and terrible energy, and like the great cities of mediaeval Italy, her ways were dark and adventurous with private war.

It was the peculiar shape of Manhattan Island, pressed in by arms of the sea on either side, and incapable of comfortable expansion except along a narrow northward belt, that first gave the New York architects their bias for extreme vertical dimensions. Every need was lavishly supplied them – money, material, labour; only space was restricted. To begin with, therefore, they built high perforce. But to do so was to discover a whole new world of architectural beauty, of exquisite ascendant lines, and long after the central congestion had been relieved by tunnels under the sea, four colossal bridges over the East River, and a dozen monorail cables east and west, the upward growth went on. In many ways New York and her gorgeous plutocracy repeated Venice; in the magnificence of her architecture, painting, metalwork and sculpture, for example, in the grim intensity of her political method, in her maritime and commercial ascendancy. But she repeated no previous state at all in the lax disorder of her internal administration, a laxity that made vast sections of her area lawless beyond precedent, so that it was possible for whole districts to be impassable while civil war raged between street and street, and for Alsatias to exist in her midst in which the official police never set foot. She was an ethnic whirlpool. The flags of all nations flew in her harbour, and at the climax, the yearly coming and going overseas numbered together upwards of two million human beings. To Europe she was America, to America she was the gateway of the earth. But to tell the story of New York would be to write a social history of the world; saints and martyrs, dreamers and scoundrels, the traditions of a thousand races and a thousand religions, went to her making and throbbed and jostled in her streets. And over all that torrential con-fusion of men and purposes fluttered that strange flag, the stars and stripes, that meant at once the noblest thing in life and the least noble, that is to say Liberty on the one hand and on the other the base jealousy the individual self-seeker feels towards the common purpose of the State.

For many generations New York had taken no heed of war, save as a thing that happened far away, that affected prices and supplied the newspapers with exciting headlines and pictures. The New Yorkers felt perhaps even more certainly than the English had done that war in their own land was an impossible thing. In that they shared the delusion of all North America. They felt as secure as spectators at a bullfight; they risked their money perhaps on the result, but that was all. And such ideas of war as the common Americans possessed were derived from the limited, picturesque, adventurous war of the past. They saw war as they saw history, through an iridescent mist, deodor-ized, scented indeed, with all its essential cruelties tactfully hidden away. They were inclined to regret it as something ennobling, to sigh that it could no longer come into their own private experience. They read with interest, if not with avidity, of their new guns, of their immense and still more immense ironclads, of their incredible and still more incredible explosives, but just what these tremendous engines of destruction might mean for their personal lives never entered their heads. They did not, so far as one can judge from their contemporary literature, think that they meant anything to their personal lives at all. They thought America was safe amidst all this piling up of explosives. They cheered the flag by habit and tradition, they despised other nations, and whenever there was an international difficulty they were intensely patriotic, that is to say they were ardently against any native politician who did not threaten and do harsh and uncompromising things to the antagonist people. They were spirited to Asia, spirited to Germany, so spirited to Great Britain that the international attitude of the mother country to her great daughter was constantly compared in contemporary caricature to that between a henpecked husband and a vicious young wife. For the rest, they all went about their business and pleasure as if war had died out with the megatherium. . . .

And then suddenly, into a world peacefully busied for the most part upon armaments and the perfection of explosives, war came; came the shock of realizing that the guns were going off, that the masses of inflammable material all over the world were at last ablaze.

2

The immediate effect upon New York of the sudden onset of war was merely to intensify her normal vehemence.

The newspapers and magazines that fed the American mind – for books upon this impatient continent had become simply material for the energy of collectors – were instantly a coruscation of war pictures and of headlines that rose like rockets and burst like shells. To the normal high-strung energy of New York streets was added a touch of war-fever. Great crowds assembled, more especially in the dinner-hour, in Madison Square about the Farragut monument, to listen to and cheer patriotic speeches, and a veritable epidemic of little flags and buttons swept through these great torrents of swiftly moving young people, who poured into New York of a morning by car and monorail and subway and train, to toil and ebb home again between the hours of five and seven. It was dangerous not to wear a war button. The splendid music halls of the time sank every topic in patriotism and evolved scenes of wild enthusiasm, strong men wept at the sight of the national banner sustained by the whole strength of the ballet, and special searchlights and illuminations amazed the watching angels. The churches re-echoed the national enthusiasm in graver key and slower measure, and the aerial and naval preparations on the East River were greatly incommoded by the multitude of excursion steamers which thronged, helpfully cheering, about them. The trade in small arms was enormously stimulated, and many overwrought citizens found an immediate relief for their emotions in letting off fireworks of a more or less heroic, dangerous and national character in the public streets. Small children's air-balloons of the latest model attached to string became a serious check to the pedestrian in Central Park. And amidst scenes of indescribable emotion the Albany legislatures in permanent session, with a generous suspension of rules and precedents, passed through both Houses the long-disputed bill for universal military service in New York State.

Critics of the American character are disposed to consider that up to the actual impact of the German attack the people of New York dealt altogether too much with the war as if it was a political demonstration. Little or no damage, they urge, was done to either the German or Japanese forces by the wearing of buttons, the waving of small flags, the fireworks, or the songs. They forgot that under the conditions of warfare a century of science had brought about, the non-military section of the population could do no serious damage in any form to their enemies, and that there was no reason, therefore, why they should not do as they did. The balance of military efficiency was shifting back from the many to the few, from the common to the specialized. The days when the emotional infantryman decided battles had passed by for ever. War had become a matter of apparatus, of special training and skill of the most intricate kind. It had become undemocratic. And whatever the value of the popular excitement, there can be no denying that the small regular establishment of the United States Government, confronted by this totally unexpected emergency of an armed invasion from Europe, acted with vigour, science and imagination. They were taken by surprise so far as the diplomatic situation was concerned, and their equipment for building either navigables or aeroplanes was contemptible in comparison with the huge German parks. Still they set to work at once to prove to the world that the spirit that had created the *Monitor* and the Southern submarines of 1864 was not dead. The chief of the aeronautic establishment near West Point was Cabot Sinclair, and he allowed himself but one single moment of the posturing that was so universal in that democratic time. 'We have chosen our epitaphs,' he said to a reporter, 'and we are going to have, "They did all they could." Now run away!'

The curious thing is that they did do all they could; there is no exception known. Their only defect indeed was a defect of style.

One of the most striking facts historically about this war, and the one that makes the complete separation that had arisen between the methods of warfare and the necessity of democratic support, is the effectual secrecy of the Washington authorities about their airships. They did not bother to confide a single fact of their preparations to the public. They did not even condescend to talk to Congress. They burked and suppressed every inquiry. The war was fought by the President and the secretaries of state in an entirely autocratic manner. Such publicity as they sought was merely to anticipate and prevent inconvenient agitation to defend particular points. They realized that the chief danger in aerial warfare from an excitable and intelligent public would be a clamour for local airships and aeroplanes to defend local interests. This, with such resources as they possessed, might lead to a fatal division and distribution of the national forces. Particularly they feared that they might be forced into a premature action to defend New York. They realized with prophetic insight that this would be the particular advantage the Germans would seek. So they took great pains to direct the popular mind towards defensive artillery, and to divert it from any thought of aerial battle. Their real preparations they masked beneath ostensible ones. There was at Washington a large reserve of naval guns, and these were distributed rapidly, conspicuously, and with much press attention, among the Eastern cities. They were mounted for the most part upon hills and prominent crests round the threatened centres of population. They were mounted upon rough adaptations of the Doan swivel, which at that time gave the maximum vertical range to a heavy gun. Much of this artillery was still unmounted, and nearly all of it was unprotected when the German air-fleet reached New York. And down in the crowded streets when that occurred, the readers of the New York papers were regaling themselves with wonderful and wonderfully illustrated accounts of such matters as:

THE SECRET OF THE THUNDERBOLT.
AGED SCIENTIST PERFECTS ELECTRIC GUN
TO ELECTROCUTE AIRSHIP CREWS
BY UPWARD LIGHTNING.
WASHINGTON ORDERS FIVE HUNDRED.
WAR SECRETARY LODGE DELIGHTED.
SAYS THEY WILL SUIT THE GERMANS DOWN
TO THE GROUND.
PRESIDENT PUBLICLY APPLAUDS
THIS MERRY QUIP.

The German fleet reached New York in advance of the news of the American naval disaster. It reached New York in the late afternoon and was first seen by watchers at Ocean Grove and Long Branch coming swiftly out of the southward sea and going away to the north-west. The flagship passed almost vertically over the Sandy Hook observation station, rising rapidly as it did so, and in a few minutes all New York was vibrating to the Staten Island guns.

Several of these guns, and especially that at Giffords and the one on Beacon Hill above Matawan, were remarkably well handled. The former, at a distance of five miles, and with an elevation of six thousand feet, sent a shell to burst so close to the *Vaterland* that a pane of the Prince's forward window was smashed by a fragment. This sudden explosion made Bert tuck in his head with the celerity of a startled tortoise. The whole air-fleet immediately went up steeply to a height of about twelve thousand feet, and at that level passed unscathed over the ineffectual guns. The airships lined out as they moved forward into the form of a flattened V, with its apex towards the city, and with the flagship going highest at the apex. The two ends of the V passed over Plumfield and Jamaica Bay, respectively, and the Prince directed his course a little to the east of the Narrows, soared over the Upper Bay, and came to rest above Jersey City in a position that dominated lower New York. There the monsters hung, large and wonderful in the evening light, serenely regardless of the occasional rocket explosions and flashing shell-bursts in the lower air.

It was a pause of mutual inspection. For a time naïve humanity swamped the conventions of warfare altogether; the interest of the millions below and of the thousands above alike was spectacular. The evening was unexpectedly fine – only a few thin level bands of clouds at seven or eight thousand feet broke its luminous clarity. The wind had dropped; it was an evening infinitely peaceful and still. The heavy concussions of the distant guns and those incidental harmless pyrotechnics at the level of the clouds seemed to have as little to do with killing and force, terror and submission, as a salute at a naval review. Below, every point of vantage bristled with spectators, the roofs of the towering buildings, the public squares, the active ferry-boats, and every favourable street intersection had its crowds: all the river piers were dense with people, the Battery Park was solid black with East-Side population, and every position of advantage in Central Park and along Riverside Drive had its peculiar and characteristic assembly from the adjacent streets. The footways of the great bridges over the East River were also closely packed and blocked. Everywhere shopkeepers had left their shops, men their work, and women and children their homes, to come out and see the marvel.

'It beat,' they declared, 'the newspapers.'

And from above, many of the occupants of the airships stared with an equal curiosity. No city in the world was ever so finely placed as New York, so magnificently cut up by sea and bluff and river, so admirably disposed to display the tall effects of buildings, the complex immensities of bridges and monorail-ways and feats of engineering. London, Paris, Berlin were shapeless, low agglomerations beside it. Its port reached to its heart like Venice, and like Venice it was obvious, dramatic and proud. Seen from above it was alive with crawling trains and cars, and at a thousand points it was already breaking into quivering light. New York was altogether at its best that evening, its splendid best.

'Gaw! *What* a place!' said Bert.

It was so great, and in its collective effect so pacifically magnificent, that to make war upon it seemed incongruous beyond measure, like laying siege to the National Gallery or attacking respectable people in an hotel dining-room with battleaxe and mail. It was in its entirety so large, so complex, so delicately immense, that to bring it to the issue of warfare was like driving a crowbar into the mechanism of a clock. And the fishlike shoal of great airships hovering light and sunlit above, filling the sky, seemed equally remote from the ugly forcefulness of war. To Kurt, to Smallways, to I know not how many more of the people in the air-fleet came the distinctest apprehension of these incompatibilities. But in the head of the Prince Karl Albert were the vapours of romance: he was a conqueror, and this was the enemy's city. The greater the city, the greater the triumph. No doubt he had a time of tremendous exultation and sensed beyond all precedent the joys of power that night.

There came an end at last to that pause. Some wireless communications had failed of a satisfactory ending and fleet and city remembered they were hostile powers. 'Look!' cried the multitude. 'Look!'

'What are they doing?'

'What?' ... Down through the twilight sank five attacking airships, one to the Navy-Yard on East River, one to City Hall, two over the great business buildings of Wall Street and lower Broadway, one to the Brooklyn Bridge, dropping from among their fellows through the danger zone from the distant guns smoothly and rapidly to a safe proximity to the city masses. At that descent all the cars in the streets stopped with dramatic suddenness, and all the lights that had been coming on in the streets and houses went out again. For the City Hall had awakened and was conferring by telephone with the Federal command and taking measures for defence. The City Hall was asking for airships, refusing to surrender as Washington advised, and developing into a centre of intense emotion, of hectic activity. Everywhere and hastily the police began to clear the assembled crowds. 'Go to your homes,' they said; and the word was passed from mouth to mouth: 'There's going to be trouble.' A chill of apprehension ran through the city, and men hurrying in the unwonted darkness across City Hall Park and Union Square came upon the dim forms of soldiers and guns, and were challenged and sent back. In half an hour New York had passed from serene sunset and gaping admiration to a troubled and threatening twilight.

The first loss of life occurred in the panic rush from Brooklyn Bridge as the airship approached it.

With the cessation of the traffic an unusual stillness came upon New York, and the disturbing concussions of the futile defending guns on the hills about grew more and more audible. At last these ceased also. A pause of further negotiation followed. People sat in darkness, sought counsel from telephones that were dumb. Then into the expectant hush came a great crash and uproar, the breaking down of the Brooklyn Bridge, the rifle fire from the Navy-Yard, and the bursting of bombs in Wall Street and the City Hall. New York as a whole could do nothing, could understand nothing. New York in the darkness peered and listened to these distant sounds until presently they died away as suddenly as they had begun. 'What could be happening?' They asked it in vain.

A long vague period intervened, and people looking out of the windows of upper rooms discovered the dark hulls of German airships, gliding slowly and noiselessly, quite close at hand. Then quietly the electric lights came on again, and an uproar of nocturnal newsvendors began in the streets.

The units of that vast and varied population bought and learnt what had happened; there had been a fight and New York had hoisted the white flag. . . .

4

The lamentable incidents that followed the surrender of New York seem now in the retrospect to be but the necessary and inevitable consequence of the clash of modern appliances and social conditions produced by the scientific century on the one hand, and the tradition of a crude, romantic patriotism on the other. At first people received the fact with an irresponsible detachment, much as they would have received the slowing down of the train in which they were travelling or the erection of a public monument by the city to which they belonged.

'We have surrendered. Dear me! *have* we?' was rather the manner in which the first news was met. They took it in the same spectacular spirit they had displayed at the first apparition of the air-fleet. Only slowly was this realization of a capitulation suffused with the flush of patriotic passion, only with reflection did they make any personal application. '*We* have surrendered!' came later; 'in us America is defeated.' Then they began to burn and tingle.

The newspapers which were issued about one in the morning contained no particulars of the terms upon which New York had yielded – nor did they give any intimation of the quality of the brief conflict that had preceded the capitulation. The later issues remedied these deficiencies. There came the explicit statement of the agreement to victual the German airships, to supply the complement of explosives to replace those employed in the fight and in the destruction of the North Atlantic fleet, to pay the enormous ransom of forty million dollars, and to surrender the flotilla in the East River. There came, too, longer and longer descriptions of the smashing up of the City Hall and the Navy-Yard, and people began to realize faintly what those brief minutes of uproar had meant. They read the tale of men blown to bits, of futile soldiers in that localized battle fighting against hope amidst an indescribable wreckage, of flags hauled down by weeping men. And these strange nocturnal editions contained also the first brief cables from Europe of the fleet disaster, the North Atlantic fleet for which New York had always felt an especial pride and solicitude. Slowly, hour by hour, the collective consciousness woke up, the tide of patriotic astonishment and humiliation came flowing in. America had come upon disaster; suddenly New York discovered herself, with amazement giving place to wrath unspeakable, a conquered city under the hand of her conqueror.

As that fact shaped itself in the public mind, there sprang up, as flames spring up, an angry repudiation. 'No!' cried New York waking in the dawn. 'No! I am not defeated. This is a dream.'

Before day broke the swift American anger was running through all the city, through every soul in those contagious millions. Before it took action, before it took shape, the men in the airships could feel the gigantic insurgence of emotion, as cattle and natural creatures feel, it is said, the coming of an earthquake. The newspapers of the Knype group first gave the thing words and a formula. 'We do not agree,' they said simply. We have been betrayed!' Men took that up everywhere, it passed from mouth to mouth, at every street corner under the paling lights of dawn orators stood unchecked, calling upon the spirit of America to arise, making the shame a personal reality to everyone who heard. To Bert, listening five hundred feet above, it seemed that the city, which had at first produced only confused noises, was now humming like a hive of bees – of very angry bees.

After the smashing of the City Hall and Post Office, the white flag had been hoisted from a tower of the old Park Row Building, and thither had gone Mayor O'Hagen, urged thither indeed by the terror-stricken property-owners of lower New York, to negotiate the capitulation with Von Winterfeld. The *Vaterland* having dropped the secretary by a rope ladder, remained hovering, circling very slowly above the great buildings, old and new, that clustered round City Hall Park, while the *Helmholz*, which had done the fighting there, rose overhead to a height of perhaps two thousand feet. So Bert had a near view of all that occurred in that central place. The City Hall and Court-House, the Post Office, and a mass of buildings on the west side of Broadway, had been badly damaged, and the three former were a heap of blackened ruins. In the case of the first two the loss of life had not been considerable, but a great multitude of workers, including many girls and women, had been caught in the destruction of the Post Office, and a little army of volunteers with white badges entered behind the firemen, bringing out the often still living bodies, for the most part frightfully charred, and carrying them into the big Monson Building close at hand. Everywhere the busy firemen were directing their bright streams of water upon the smouldering masses: their hose lay about the square, and long cordons of police held back the gathering hordes of people, chiefly from the East Side.

In violent and extraordinary contrast with this scene of destruction, close at hand were the huge newspaper establishments of Park Row. They were all alight and working; they had not been abandoned even while the actual bomb-throwing was going on, and now staff and presses were vehemently active, getting out the story, the immense and dreadful story of the night, developing comment and, in most cases, spreading the idea of resistance under the very noses of the airships. For a long time Bert could not imagine what these callously active offices could be, then he detected the noise of the presses and emitted his 'Gaw!'

Beyond these newspaper buildings again, and partially hidden by the arches of the old Elevated Railway of New York (long since converted into a monorail), there was another cordon of police and a sort of encampment of ambulances and doctors, busy with the dead and wounded who had been killed earlier that night in the panic upon Brooklyn Bridge. All this he saw in the perspectives of a bird's-eye view, as things happening in a big, irregular-shaped pit below him, between cliffs of high buildings. Northward he looked along the steep canyon of Broadway, down whose length at intervals crowds were assembling about excited speakers; and when he lifted his eyes he saw the chimneys and cable-stacks and roof spaces of New York, and everywhere now over these the watching, debating people clustered, except where the fires raged and the jets of water flew. Everywhere, too, were flagstaffs devoid of flags; one white sheet drooped and flapped and drooped again over the Park Row buildings. And upon the lurid lights, the festering movement and intense shadows of this strange scene there was breaking now the cold, impartial dawn.

For Bert Smaliways all this was framed in the frame of the open porthole. It was a pale, dim world outside that dark and tangible rim. All night he had clutched at that rim, jumped and quivered at explosions, and watched phantom events. Now he had been high and now low; now almost beyond hearing, now flying close to crashings and shouts and outcries. He had seen airships flying low and swift over darkened and groaning streets; watched great buildings, suddenly red-lit amidst the shadows, crumple at the smashing impact of bombs; witnessed for the first time in his life the grotesque, swift onset of insatiable conflagrations. From it all he felt detached, disembodied. The *Vaterland* did not even fling a bomb; she watched and ruled. Then down they had come at last to hover over City Hall Park, and it had crept in upon his mind, chillingly, terrifyingly, that these illuminated black masses were great offices afire, and that the going to and fro of minute dim spectres of lantern-lit grey and white was a harvesting of the wounded and the dead. As the light grew clearer he began to understand more and more what these crumpled black things signified.
. . .

He had watched hour after hour since first New York had risen out of the blue indistinctness of the landfall. With the daylight he experienced an intolerable fatigue.

He lifted weary eyes to the pink flush in the sky, yawned immensely, and crawled back whispering to himself across the cabin to the locker. He did not so much lie down upon that as fall upon it and instantly become asleep.

There, hours after, sprawling undignified and sleeping profoundly,

Kurt found him, a very image of the democratic mind confronted with the problems of a time too complex for its apprehension. His face was pale and indifferent, his mouth wide open, and he snored. He snored disagreeably.

Kurt regarded him for a moment with a mild distaste. Then he kicked his ankle.

'Wake up!' he said to Smallways' stare, 'and lie down decent.'

Bert sat up and rubbed his eyes.

'Any more fightin' yet?' he asked.

'No,' said Kurt, and sat down, a tired man.

'Gott!' he cried presently, rubbing his hands over his face, 'but I'd like a cold bath! I've been looking for stray bullet-holes in the air-chambers all night until now.' He yawned. 'I must sleep. You'd better clear out, Smallways. I can't stand you here this morning. You're so infernally ugly and useless. Have you had your rations? No! Well, go in and get 'em, and don't come back. Stick in the gallery.' . . .

5

So Bert, slightly refreshed by coffee and sleep, resumed his helpless co-operation in the War in the Air. He went down into the little gallery as the lieutenant had directed, and clung to the rail at the extreme end beyond the lookout man, trying to seem as inconspicuous and harmless a fragment of life as possible.

A wind was rising rather strongly from the south-east. It obliged the *Vaterland* to come about in that direction, and made her roll a great deal as she went to and fro over Manhattan Island. Away in the north-west clouds gathered. The throb-throb of her slow screw working against the breeze was much more perceptible than when she was going full speed ahead; and the friction of the wind against the underside of the gas-chamber drove a series of shallow ripples along it and made a faint flapping sound like, but fainter than, the beating of ripples under the stem of a boat. She was stationed over the temporary City Hall in the Park Row building, and every now and then she would descend to resume communication with the mayor and with Washington. But the restlessness of the Prince would not suffer him to remain for long in any one place. Now he would circle over the Hudson and East Rivers; now he would go up high, as if to peer away into the blue distances; once he ascended so swiftly and so far that mountain-sickness overtook him and the crew and forced him down again; and Bert shared the dizziness and nausea.

The swaying view varied with these changes of altitude. Now they

724

would be low and close, and he would distinguish in that steep, unusual perspective, windows, doors, street and sky signs, people and the minutest details, and watch the enigmatical behaviour of crowds and clusters upon the roofs and in the streets; then as they soared the details would shrink, the sides of streets draw together, the view widen, the people cease to be significant. At the highest the effect was that of a concave relief map; Bert saw the dark and crowded land everywhere intersected by shining waters, saw the Hudson River like a spear of silver, and Long Island Sound like a shield. Even to Bert's unphilo-sophical mind the contrast of city below and fleet above pointed an opposition, the opposition of the adventurous American's tradition and character with German order and discipline. Below, the immense buildings, tremendous and fine as they were, seemed like the giant trees of a jungle fighting for life; their picturesque magnificence was as planless as the chances of crag and gorge, their casualness enhanced by the smoke and confusion of still unsubdued and spreading confla-grations. In the sky soared the German airships like beings in a different, entirely more orderly, world, all oriented to the same angle of the horizon, uniform in build and appearance, moving accurately with one purpose as a pack of wolves will move, distributed with the most precise and effectual co-operation.

It dawned upon Bert that hardly a third of the fleet was visible. The others had gone upon errands he could not imagine, beyond the compass of that great circle of earth and sky. He wondered, but there was no one to ask. As the day wore on, about a dozen reappeared in the east with their stores replenished from the flotilla and towing a number of *Drachenflieger*. Towards afternoon the weather thickened, driving clouds appeared in the south-west and ran together and seemed to engender more clouds, and the wind came round into that quarter and blew stronger. Towards the evening the wind became a gale into which the now tossing airships had to beat.

All that day the Prince was negotiating with Washington, while his detached scouts sought far and wide over the Eastern States for any-thing resembling an aeronautic park. A squadron of twenty airships detached overnight had dropped out of the air upon Niagara and was holding the town and power works.

Meanwhile the insurrectionary movement in the giant city grew uncontrollable. In spite of five great fires already involving many acres, and spreading steadily, New York was still not satisfied that she was beaten.

At first the rebellious spirit below found vent only in isolated shouts, street-crowd speeches, and newspaper suggestions; then it found much more definite expression in the appearance in the morning sunlight of American flags at point after point above the architectural cliffs of the city. It is quite possible that in many cases this spirited display of bunting by a city already surrendered was the outcome of the innocent informality of the American mind, but it is also undeniable that in many it was a deliberate indication that the people 'felt wicked'..

The German sense of correctitude was deeply shocked by this outbreak. The Graf von Winterfeld immediately communicated with the mayor, and pointed out the irregularity, and the fire lookout stations were instructed in the matter. The New York police was speedily hard at work, and a foolish contest in full swing between impassioned citizens resolved to keep the flag flying, and irritated and worried officers instructed to pull it down.

The trouble became acute at last in the streets above Columbia University. The captain of the airship watching this quarter seems to have stooped to lasso and drag from its staff a flag hoisted upon Morgan Hall. As he did so a volley of rifle and revolver shots was fired from the upper windows of the huge apartment building that stands between the university and Riverside Drive.

Most of these were ineffectual, but two or three perforated gas-chambers, and one smashed the hand and arm of a man upon the forward platform. The sentinel on the lower gallery immediately replied, and the machine-gun on the shield of the eagle let fly and promptly stopped any further shots. The airship rose and signalled the flagship and City Hall, police and militiamen were directed at once to the spot, and this particular incident closed.

But hard upon that came the desperate attempt of a party of young clubmen from New York who, inspired by patriotic and adventurous imaginations, slipped off in half a dozen motor-cars to Beacon Hill, and set to work with remarkable vigour to improvise a fort about the Doan swivel gun that had been placed there. They found it still in the hands of the disgusted gunners, who had been ordered to cease fire at the capitulation, and it was easy to infect these men with their own spirit. They declared their gun hadn't had half a chance, and were burning to show what it could do. Directed by the newcomers, they made a trench and bank about the mounting of the piece, and con-structed flimsy shelter-pits of corrugated iron.

They were actually loading the gun when they were observed by the airship *Preussen*, and the shell they succeeded in firing before the bombs of the latter smashed them and their crude defences to fragments, burst over the middle gas-chambers of the *Bingen*, and brought her to earth, disabled, upon Staten Island. She was badly deflated, and dropped among trees, over which her empty central gas-bags spread in canopies and festoons. Nothing, however, had caught fire, and her men were speedily at work upon her repair. They behaved with a confidence that verged upon indiscretion. While most of them commenced patching the tears of the membrane, half a dozen of them started off for the nearest road in search of a gas main, and presently found themselves prisoners in the hands of a hostile crowd. Close at hand were a number of villa residences, whose occupants speedily developed from an unfriendly curiosity to aggression. At that time the police control of the large polyglot population of Staten Island had become very lax, and scarcely a household but had its rifle or pistols and ammunition. These were presently produced, and after two or three misses one of the men at work was hit in the foot. Thereupon the Germans left their sewing and mending, took cover among the trees, and replied.

The crackling of shots speedily brought the *Preussen* and *Kiel* on the scene, and with a few hand grenades they made short work of every villa within a mile. A number of non-combatant American men, women and children were killed and the actual assailants driven off. For a time the repairs went on in peace under the immediate protection of these two airships. Then when they returned to their quarters an intermittent sniping and fighting round the stranded *Bingen* was resumed, and went on all the afternoon, and merged at last in the general combat of the evening. . . .

About eight the *Bingen* was rushed by an armed mob, and all its defenders killed after a fierce, disorderly struggle.

The difficulty of the Germans in both these cases came from the impossibility of landing any efficient force or, indeed, any force at all from the air-fleet. The airships were quite unequal to the transport of any adequate landing parties; their complement of men was just sufficient to manoeuvre and fight them in the air. From above they could inflict immense damage; they could reduce any organized government to a capitulation in the briefest space, but they could not disarm, much less could they occupy, the surrendered areas below. They had to trust to the pressure upon the authorities below of a threat to renew the bombardment. It was their sole resource. No doubt, with a highly organized and undamaged government and a homogeneous and well-disciplined people that would have sufficed to keep the peace. But this was not the American case. Not only was the New York government a weak one and insufficiently provided with police, but the destruction of the City Hall and Post Office and other central ganglia had hopelessly disorganized the co-operation of part with part. The streetcars and railways had ceased; the telephone service was out of gear and worked only intermittently. The Germans had struck at the head, and the head was conquered and stunned – only to release the body from its rule. New York had become a headless monster, no longer capable of collective submission. Everywhere it lifted itself rebelliously; everywhere authorities and officials, left to their own initiative, were joining in the arming and flag-hoisting and excitement of that afternoon.

6

The disintegrating truce gave place to a definite general breach with the assassination of the *Wetterhorn* – for that is the only possible word for the act – above Union Square, and not a mile away from the exemplary ruins of City Hall. This occurred late in the afternoon, between five and six. By that time the weather had changed very much for the worse, and the operations of the airships were embarrassed by the necessity they were under of keeping head on to the gusts. A series of squalls, with hail and thunder, followed one another from the south by south-east, and in order to avoid these as much as possible, the air-fleet came low over the houses, diminishing its range of observation and exposing itself to a rifle attack.

Overnight there had been a gun placed in Union Square. It had never been mounted, much less fired, and in the darkness after the surrender it was taken with its supplies and put out of the way under the arches of the great Dexter building. Here late in the morning it was remarked by a number of patriotic spirits. They set to work to hoist and mount it inside the upper floors of the place. They made, in fact, a masked battery behind the decorous office blinds, and there lay in wait as simply excited as children, until at last the stem of the luckless *Wetterhorn* appeared, beating and rolling at quarter speed over the recently reconstructed pinnacles of Tiffany's. Promptly that one-gun battery unmasked. The airship's lookout man must have seen the whole of the tenth storey of the Dexter building crumble out and smash in the street below, to discover the black muzzle looking out from the shadows behind. Then perhaps the shell hit him.

The gun fired two shells before the frame of the Dexter building collapsed, and each shell raked the *Wetterhorn* from stem to stern. They smashed her exhaustively. She crumpled up like a can that has been kicked by a heavy boot, her forepart came down in the square, and the rest of her length, with a great snapping and twisting of shafts and stays, descended, collapsing athwart Tammany Hall and the streets towards Second Avenue. Her gas escaped to mix with air, and the air of her rent ballonette poured into her deflating gas-chambers. Then with an immense impact she exploded. . . .

The *Vaterland* at that time was beating up to the south of City Hall from over the ruins of the Brooklyn Bridge, and the reports of the gun, followed by the first crashes of the collapsing Dexter building, brought Kurt and Smallways to the cabin porthole. They were in time to see the flash of the exploding gun, and then they were first flattened against the window and then rolled head over heels across the floor of the cabin by the airwave of the explosion. The *Vaterland* bounded like a football someone has kicked, and when they looked out again Union Square was small and remote and shattered, as though some cosmically vast giant had rolled over it. The buildings to the east of it were ablaze at a dozen points, under the flaming tatters and warping skeleton of the airship, and all the roofs and walls were ridiculously askew and crumbling as one looked. 'Gaw!' said Bert. 'What's happened? Look at the people!'

But before Kurt could produce an explanation, the shrill bells of the airship were ringing to quarters, and he had to go. Bert hesitated and stepped thoughtfully into the passage, looking back at the window as he did so. He was knocked off his feet at once by the Prince, who was rushing headlong from his cabin to the central magazine.

Bert had a momentary impression of the great figure of the Prince, white with rage, bristling with gigantic anger, his huge fist swinging. 'Blut und Eisen!' cried the Prince, as one who swears. 'Ach! Blut und Eisen!'

Someone fell over Bert – something in the manner of falling suggested Von Winterfeld – and someone else paused and kicked him spitefully and hard. Then he was sitting up in the passage, rubbing a freshly bruised cheek and readjusting the bandage he still wore on his head. 'Dem that Prince,' said Bert, indignant beyond measure. ''E 'asn't the menners of a 'og!'

He stood up, collected his wits for a minute, and then went slowly towards the gangway of the little gallery. As he did so he heard noises suggestive of the return of the Prince. The lot of them were coming back again. He shot into his cabin like a rabbit into its burrow, just in time to escape that shouting terror.

He shut the door, waited until the passage was still, then went across to the window and looked out. A drift of cloud made the prospect of the streets and squares hazy, and the rolling of the airship swung the picture up and down. A few people were running to and fro, but for the most part the aspect of the district was desertion. The streets seemed to broaden out, they became clearer, and the little dots that were people larger as the *Vaterland* came down again. Presently she was swaying along above the lower end of Broadway. The dots below, Bert saw, were not running now, but standing and looking up. Then suddenly they were all running again.

Something had dropped from the aeroplane, something that looked small and flimsy. It hit the pavement near a big archway just underneath Bert. A little man was sprinting along the sidewalk within half a dozen yards, and two or three others and one woman were bolting across the roadway. They were odd little figures, so very small were they about the heads, so very active about the elbows and legs. It was really funny to see their legs going. Foreshortened humanity has no dignity. The little man on the pavement jumped comically – no doubt with terror – as the bomb fell beside him.

Then blinding flames squirted out in all directions from the point of impact, and the little man who had jumped became, for an instant, a flash of fire and vanished – vanished absolutely. The people running out into the road took preposterous clumsy leaps, then flopped down and lay still, with their torn clothes smouldering into flame. Then pieces of the archway began to drop, and the lower masonry of the building to fall in with the rumbling sound of coals being shot into a cellar. A faint screaming reached Bert, and then a crowd of people ran out into the street, one man limping and gesticulating awkwardly. He halted, and went back towards the building. A falling mass of brickwork hit him and sent him sprawling to lie still and crumpled where he fell. Dust and black smoke came pouring into the street, and were presently shot with red flame. . . .

In this manner the massacre of New York began. She was the first of the great cities of the Scientific Age to suffer by the enormous powers and grotesque limitations of aerial warfare. She was wrecked as in the previous century endless barbaric cities had been bombarded, because she was at once too strong to be occupied, and too undisciplined and proud to surrender in order to escape destruction. Given the circumstances, the thing had to be done. It was impossible for the Prince to desist and own himself defeated, and it was impossible to subdue the city except by largely destroying it. The catastrophe was the logical outcome of the situation created by the application of science to warfare. It was unavoidable that great cities should be destroyed. In spite of his intense exasperation with his dilemma, the Prince sought to be moderate even in massacre. He tried to give a memorable lesson with the minimum waste of life and the minimum expenditure of explosives. For that night he proposed only the wrecking of Broadway. He directed the air-fleet to move in column over the route of this thoroughfare, dropping bombs, the *Vaterland* leading. And so our Bert Smallways became a participant in one of the most cold-blooded slaughters in the world's history, in which men who were neither excited nor, except for the remotest chance of a bullet, in any danger, poured death and destruction upon homes and crowds below.

He clung to the frame of the porthole as the airship tossed and swayed, and stared down through the light rain that now drove before the wind, into the twilit streets, watching people running out of the houses, watching buildings collapse and fires begin. As the airships sailed along they smashed up the city as a child will shatter its cities of brick and card. Below, they left ruins and blazing conflagrations and heaped and scattered dead; men, women and children mixed together as though they had been no more than Moors, or Zulus, or Chinese. Lower New York was soon a furnace of crimson flames, from which there was no escape. Cars, railways, ferries, all had ceased, and never a light led the way of the distracted fugitives in that dusky confusion but the light of burning. He had glimpses of what it must mean to be down there – glimpses. And it came to him suddenly as an incredible discovery, that such disasters were not only possible now in this strange, gigantic, foreign New York, but also in London – in Bun Hill! that the little island in the silver seas was at the end of its immunity, that nowhere in the world any more was there a place left where a Smallways might lift his head proudly and vote for war and a spirited foreign policy, and go secure from such horrible things.

7

The *Vaterland* Is Disabled

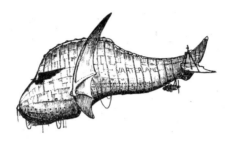

I

And then above the flames of Manhattan Island came a battle, the first battle in the air. The Americans had realized the price their waiting game must cost, and struck with all the strength they had, if haply they might still save New York from this mad Prince of Blood and Iron, and from fire and death.

They came down upon the Germans on the wings of a great gale in the twilight, amidst thunder and rain. They came from the yards of Washington and Philadelphia, full tilt in two squadrons, and but for one sentinel airship hard by Trenton, the surprise would have been complete.

The Germans, sick and weary with destruction, and half empty of ammunition, were facing up into the weather when the news of this onset reached them. New York they had left behind to the south-eastward, a darkened city with one hideous red scar of flames. All the airships rolled and staggered, bursts of hail-storm bore them down and forced them to fight their way up again; the air had become bitterly cold. The Prince was on the point of issuing orders to drop earthward and trail copper lightning-chains when the news of the aeroplane attack came to him. He faced his fleet in line abreast south, had the *Drachenflieger* manned and held ready to cast loose, and ordered a general ascent into the freezing clearness above the wet and darkness.

The news of what was imminent came slowly to Bert's perceptions. He was standing in the mess-room at the time, and the evening rations were being served out. He had resumed Butteridge's coat and gloves, and, in addition, he had wrapped his blanket about him He was dipping his bread into his soup and biting off big mouthfuls. His legs were wide apart, and he leant against the partition in order to steady himself amidst the pitching and oscillation of the airship. The men about him looked tired and depressed; a few talked, but most were sullen and thoughtful, and one or two were air-sick. They all seemed to share the peculiarly outcast feeling that had followed the murders of the evening, a sense of a land beneath them and an outraged humanity grown more hostile than the sea.

Then the news hit them. A red-faced sturdy man, a man with light eyelashes and a scar, appeared in the doorway and shouted something in German that manifestly startled everyone. Bert felt the shock of the altered tone though he could not understand a word that was said. The announcement was followed by a pause, and then a great outcry of questions and suggestions. Even the air-sick men flushed and spoke. For some minutes the mess-room was Bedlam, and then, as if it were a confirmation of the news, came the shrill bugles that called the men to their posts.

Bert, with pantomime suddenness, found himself alone.

'What's up?' he said, though he partly guessed.

He stayed only to gulp down the remainder of his soup and then ran along the swaying passage and, clutching tightly, down the ladder to the little gallery. The weather hit him like cold water squirted from a hose. The airship engaged in some new feat of atmospheric jiu-jitsu. He drew his blanket closer about him, clutching with one straining hand. He found himself tossing in a wet twilight, with nothing to be seen but mist pouring past him. Above him the airship was warm with lights and busy with the movements of men going to their quarters. Then abruptly the lights went out, and the *Vaterland* with bounds and twists and strange writhings was fighting her way up the air.

He had a glimpse, as the *Vaterland* rolled over, of some large buildings burning close below them, a quivering acanthus of flames, and then he saw indistinctly through the driving weather another airship wallowing along like a porpoise, and also working up. Presently the clouds swallowed her again for a time, and then she came back to sight as a dark and whalelike monster, amidst streaming weather. The air was full of flappings and pipings, of void, gusty shouts and noises; it buffeted him and confused him; ever and again his attention became rigid – a blind and deaf balancing and clutching.

'Wow!'

Something fell past him out of the vast darknesses above and vanished into the tumults below, going obliquely downward. It was a German *Drachenflieger.* The thing was going so fast he had but an instant apprehension of the dark figure of the aeronaut crouched together clutching at his wheel. It might be a manoeuvre, but it looked like a catastrophe.

'Gaw!' said Bert.

'Pup-pup-pup,' went a gun somewhere in the mirk ahead, and suddenly and quite horribly the *Vaterland* lurched, and Bert and the sentinel were clinging to the rail for dear life. 'Bang!' came a vast impact out of the zenith, followed by another huge roll, and all about him the tumbled clouds flashed red and lurid in response to flashes unseen, revealing immense gulfs. The rail went right overhead, and he was hanging loose in the air holding on to it.

For a time Bert's whole mind and being was given to clutching. 'I'm going into the cabin,' he said, as the airship righted again and brought back the gallery floor to his feet. He began to make his way cautiously towards the ladder. 'Whee-wow!' he cried as the whole gallery reared itself up forward and then plunged down like a desperate horse.

Crack! Bang! Bang! Bang! And then hard upon this little rattle of shots and bombs came, all about him, enveloping him, engulfing him, immense and overwhelming, a quivering white blaze of lightning and a thunderclap that was like the bursting of a world.

Just for the instant before that explosion, the universe seemed to be standing still in a shadowless glare.

It was then he saw the American aeroplane. He saw it in the light of the flash as a thing altogether motionless. Even its screw appeared still, and its men were rigid dolls. (For it was so near he could see the men upon it quite distinctly.) Its stern was tilting down and the whole machine was heeling over. It was of the Colt-Coburn-Langley pattern, with double uptilted wings and the screw ahead, and the men were in a boat-like body netted over. From this very light long body, magazine guns projected on either side. One thing that was strikingly odd and wonderful in that moment of revelation was that the left upper wing was burning *downward* with a reddish, smoky flame. But this was not the most wonderful thing about this apparition. The most wonderful thing was that it and a German airship five hundred yards below were threaded as it were on the lightning flash, which turned out of its path as if to take them, and that out from the corners and projecting points of its huge wings everywhere, little branching thorn trees of lightning were streaming.

Like a picture Bert saw these things, a picture a little blurred by a thin veil of wind-torn mist.

The crash of the thunderclap followed the flash and seemed a part of it, so that it is hard to say whether Bert was the rather deafened or blinded in that instant.

And then darkness, utter darkness, and a heavy report and a thin small sound of voices that went wailing downward into the abyss below.

2

There followed upon these things a long, deep swaying of the airship, and then Bert began a struggle to get back to his cabin. He was drenched and cold and terrified beyond measure, and now more than a little air-sick. It seemed to him that the strength had gone out of his knees and hands, and that his feet had become icily slippery over the metal they trod upon. But that was because a thin film of ice had frozen upon the gallery.

He never knew how long his ascent of the ladder back into the airship took him, but in his dreams afterwards, when he recalled it, that experience seemed to last for hours. Below, above, around him were gulfs, monstrous gulfs of howling wind and eddies of dark, whirling snowflakes, and he was protected from it all by a little metal grating and a rail, a grating and rail that seemed madly infuriated with him, passionately eager to wrench him off and toss him into the tumult of space.

Once he had a fancy that a bullet tore by his ear, and that the clouds and snowflakes were lit by a flash, but he never even turned his head to see what new assailant whirled past them in the void. He wanted to get into the passage! He wanted to get into the passage! He wanted to get into the passage! Would the arm by which he was clinging hold out, or would it give way and snap? A handful of hail smacked him in the face, so that for a time he was breathless and nearly insensible. Hold tight, Bert! He renewed his efforts.

He found himself, with an enormous sense of relief and warmth, in the passage. The passage was behaving like a dice-box, its disposition was evidently to rattle him about and then throw him out again. He hung on with the convulsive clutch of instinct until the passage lurched down ahead. Then he would make a short run cabinward, and clutch again as the fore end rose.

Behold! He was in the cabin!

He snapped to the door, and for a time he was not a human being, he was a case of air-sickness. He wanted to get somewhere that would fix him, that he needn't clutch. He opened the locker and got inside among the loose articles, and sprawled there helplessly, with his head sometimes bumping one side and sometimes the other. The lid shut upon him with a click. He did not care then what was happening any more. He did not care who fought who, or what bullets were fired or explosions occurred. He did not care if presently he was shot or smashed to pieces. He was full of feeble, inarticulate rage and despair. 'Foolery!' he said, his one exhaustive comment on human enterprise, adventure, war and the chapter of accidents that had entangled him. 'Foolery! Ugh!' He included the order of the universe in that comprehensive condemnation. He wished he was dead.

He saw nothing of the stars as presently the *Vaterland* cleared the rush and confusion of the lower weather, nor of the duel she fought with two circling aeroplanes, how they shot her rearmost chambers through, and how she fought them off with explosive bullets and turned to run as she did so.

The rush and swoop of these wonderful night-birds was all lost upon him; their heroic dash and self-sacrifice. The *Vaterland* was rammed, and for some moments she hung on the verge of destruction, and sinking swiftly, with the American aeroplane entangled with her smashed propeller, and the Americans trying to scramble aboard. It signified nothing to Bert. To him it conveyed itself simply as vehement swaying. Foolery! When the American airship dropped off at last, with most of its crew shot or fallen, Bert in his locker appreciated nothing but that the *Vaterland* had taken a hideous upward leap.

But then came infinite relief, incredibly blissful relief. The rolling, the pitching, the struggle ceased, ceased instantly and absolutely. The *Vaterland* was no longer fighting the gale; her smashed and exploded engines throbbed no more; she was disabled and driving before the wind as smoothly as a balloon, a huge, wind-spread, tattered cloud of aerial wreckage.

To Bert it was no more than the end of a series of disagreeable sensations. He was not curious to know what had happened to the airship, nor what had happened to the battle. For a long time he lay waiting apprehensively for the pitching and tossing and his qualms to return, and so lying, boxed up in the locker, he presently fell asleep.

3

He awoke tranquil but very stuffy, and at the same time very cold, and quite unable to recollect where he could be. His head ached, and he felt suffocated. He had been dreaming confusedly of Edna and Desert Dervishes, and of riding bicycles in an extremely perilous manner through the upper air amidst a pyrotechnic display of crackers and Bengal lights – to the great annoyance of a sort of composite person made up of the Prince and Mr Butteridge. Then for some reason Edna and he had begun to cry pitifully for each other, and he woke up with wet eyelashes into this ill-ventilated darkness of the locker. He would never see Edna any more, never see Edna any more.

He thought he must be back in the bedroom behind the cycle shop at the bottom of Bun Hill, and he was sure the vision he had had of the destruction of a magnificent city, a city quite incredibly great and splendid, by means of bombs, was no more than a particularly vivid dream.

'Grubb!' he called, anxious to tell him.

The answering silence, and the dull resonance of the locker to his voice, supplementing the stifling quality of the air, set going a new train of ideas. He lifted up his hands and feet, and met an inflexible resistance. He was in a coffin, he thought! He had been buried alive! He gave way at once to wild panic. ''Elp!' he screamed. ''Elp!' and drummed with his feet, and kicked and struggled. 'Let me out! Let me out!'

For some seconds he struggled with this intolerable horror, and then the side of his imagined coffin gave way, and he was flying out into daylight. Then he was rolling about on what seemed to be a padded floor with Kurt, and being punched and sworn at lustily.

He sat up. His head bandage had become loose and got over one eye, and he whipped the whole thing off. Kurt was also sitting up, a yard away from him, pink as ever, wrapped in blankets, and with an aluminium diver's helmet over his knee, staring at him with a severe expression, and rubbing his downy unshaven chin. They were both on a slanting floor of crimson padding, and above them was an opening like a long low cellar flap that Bert by an effort perceived to be the cabin door in a half-inverted condition. The whole cabin had in fact turned on its side.

'What the deuce do you mean by it, Smallways?' said Kurt, 'jumping out of that locker when I was certain you had gone overboard with the rest of them? Where have you been?'

'What's up?' asked Bert.

'This end of the airship is up. Most other things are down.'

'Was there a battle?'

'There was.'

'Who won?'

'I haven't seen the papers, Smallways. We left before the finish. We got disabled and unmanageable, and our colleagues – consorts,

I mean – were too busy most of them to trouble about us, and the wind blew us – Heaven knows where the wind is blowing us. It blew us right out of action at the rate of eighty miles an hour or so. Gott! what a wind that was! What a fight! And here we are!'

'Where?'

'In the air, Smallways – in the air! When we get down on the earth again we shan't know what to do with our legs.'

'But what's below us?'

'Canada, to the best of my knowledge – and a jolly bleak, empty, inhospitable country it looks.'

'But why ain't we right ways up?'

Kurt made no answer for a space.

'Last I remember was seeing a sort of flying machine in a lightning flash,' said Bert. 'Gaw! that was 'orrible. Guns going off! Things explodin'! Clouds and 'ail. Pitching and tossing. I got so scared and desperate – and sick. . . . You don't know how the fight came off?'

'Not a bit of it. I was up with my squad in those divers' dresses, inside the gas-chambers, with sheets of silk for caulking. We couldn't see a thing outside except the lightning flashes. I never saw one of those American aeroplanes. Just saw the shots flicker through the chambers and sent off men for the tears. We caught fire a bit – not much, you know. We were too wet, so the fires spluttered out before we banged. And then one of their infernal things dropped out of the air on us and rammed. Didn't you feel it?'

'I felt everything,' said Bert. 'I didn't notice any particular smash—'

'They must have been pretty desperate if they meant it. They slashed down on us like a knife; simply ripped the after gas-chambers like gutting herrings, crumpled up the engines and screw. Most of the engines dropped out as they fell off us, or we'd have grounded – but the rest is sort of dangling. We just turned up our nose to the heavens and stayed there. Eleven men rolled off us from various points, and poor old Winterfeld fell through the door of the Prince's cabin into the chart-room and broke his ankle. Also we got our electric gear shot or carried away – no one knows how. That's the position, Smallways. We're driving through the air like a common aerostat, at the mercy of the elements, almost due north – probably to the North Pole. We don't know what aeroplanes the Americans have, or anything at all about it. Very likely we have finished 'em up. One fouled us, one was struck by lightning, some of the men saw a third upset, apparently just for fun. They were going cheap anyhow. Also we've lost most of our *Drachenflieger*. They just skated off into the night. No stability in 'em. That's all. We don't know if we've won or lost. We don't know if

738

we're at war with the British Empire yet or at peace. Consequently we daren't get down. We don't know what we are up to or what we are going to do. Our Napoleon is alone, forward, and I suppose he's rearranging his plans. Whether New York was our Moscow or not remains to be seen. We've had a high old time and murdered no end of people! War! Noble war! I'm sick of it this morning. I like sitting in rooms right way up and not on slippery partitions. I'm a civilized man. I keep thinking of old Albrecht and the *Barbarossa*. . . . I feel I want a wash and kind words and a quiet home. When I look at you, I *know* I want a wash. Gott!' – he stifled a vehement yawn – 'What a Cockney tadpole of a ruffian you look!'

'Can we get any grub?' asked Bert.

'Heaven knows!' said Kurt.

He meditated upon Bert for a time. 'So far as I can judge, Smallways,' he said, 'the Prince will probably want to throw you overboard – next time he thinks of you. He certainly will if he sees you . . . After all, you know, you came *als Ballast*. . . . And we shall have to lighten ship extensively pretty soon. Unless I'm mistaken, the Prince will wake up presently and start doing things with tremendous vigour. . . . I've taken a fancy to you. It's the English strain in me. You're a rum little chap. I shan't like seeing you whizz down the air. . . . You'd better make yourself useful, Smallways. I think I shall requisition you for my squad. You'll have to work, you know, and be infernally intelligent, and all that. And you'll have to hang about upside down a bit. Still, it's the best chance you have. We shan't carry passengers much farther this trip, I fancy. Ballast goes overboard – if we don't want to ground precious soon and be taken prisoners of war. The Prince won't do that anyhow. He'll be game to the last.'

4

By means of a folding chair, which was still in its place behind the door, they got to the window and looked out in turn and contemplated a sparsely wooded country below, with no railways nor roads, and only occasional signs of habitation. Then a bugle sounded, and Kurt interpreted it as a summons to food. They got through the door and clambered with some difficulty up the nearly vertical passage, holding on desperately with toes and finger-tips to the ventilating perforations in its floor. The mess stewards had found their fireless heating arrangements intact, and there was hot cocoa for the officers and hot soup for the men.

Bert's sense of the queerness of this experience was so keen that it blotted out any fear he might have felt. Indeed, he was far more interested now than afraid. He seemed to have touched down to the bottom of fear and abandonment overnight. He was growing accustomed to the idea that he would probably be killed presently, that this strange voyage in the air was in all probability his death journey. No human being can keep permanently afraid: fear goes at last to the back of one's mind, accepted, and shelved, and done with. He consumed all his soup, sopping it up with his bread, and contemplated his comrades. They were all rather yellow and dirty with four-day beards, and they grouped themselves in the tired, unpremeditated manner of men on a wreck. They talked little. The situation perplexed them beyond any suggestion of ideas. Three had been hurt in the pitching up of the ship during the fight, and one had a bandaged bullet wound. It was incredible that this small band of men had committed murder and massacre on a scale beyond precedent. None of those who squatted on the sloping gas-padded partition, soup mug in hand, seemed really guilty of anything of the sort, seemed scarcely capable of hurting a dog wantonly. They were all so manifestly built for homely chalets on the solid earth and carefully tilled fields and blonde wives and cheery merrymaking. The red-faced sturdy man with light eyelashes who had brought the first news of the air battle to the men's mess had finished his soup, and with an expression of maternal solicitude was readjusting the bandages of a youngster whose arm had been sprained.

Bert was crumbling the last of his bread into the last of his soup, eking it out as long as possible, when suddenly he became aware that everyone was looking at a pair of feet that were dangling across the down-turned open doorway. Kurt appeared and adjusted himself across the hinge. In some mysterious way he had shaved his face and smoothed down his light golden hair. He looked extraordinarily cherubic. 'Der Prinz,' he said.

A second pair of boots followed, making wide and magnificent gestures in their attempts to feel the door frame. Kurt guided them to a foothold, and the Prince, shaved and brushed and beeswaxed and clean and big and terrible, slid down into position astride of the door. All the men and Bert also stood up and saluted.

The Prince surveyed them with the gesture of a man who sits a steed. The head of the Kapitän appeared beside him.

Then Bert had a terrible moment. The blue blaze of the Prince's eye fell upon him, the great finger pointed, a question was asked. Kurt intervened with explanations.

'So,' said the Prince, and Bert was disposed of.

Then the Prince addressed the men in short, heroic sentences, steadying himself on the hinge with one hand and waving the other in a fine variety of gesture. What he said Bert could not tell, but he perceived that their demeanour changed, their backs stiffened. They began to punctuate the Prince's discourse with cries of approval. At the end their leader burst into song and all the men with him. 'Ein feste Burg ist unser Gott,' they chanted in deep, strong tones, with an immense moral uplifting. It was glaringly inappropriate in a damaged, half-overturned and sinking airship, which had been disabled and blown out of action after inflicting the cruellest bombardment in the world's history; but it was immensely stirring nevertheless. Bert was deeply moved. He could not sing any of the words of Luther's great hymn, but he opened his mouth and emitted loud, deep and partially harmonious notes. . . .

Far below, this deep chanting struck on the ears of a little camp of Christianized half-breeds who were lumbering. They were breakfasting, but they rushed out cheerfully, quite prepared for the Second Advent. They stared at the shattered and twisted *Vaterland*, driving before the gale, amazed beyond words. In so many respects it was like their idea of the Second Advent, and then again in so many respects it wasn't. They stared at its passage, awestricken and perplexed. The hymn ceased. Then after a long interval a voice came out of heaven. 'Vat id diss blace here galled itself; vat?'

They made no answer. Indeed, they did not understand, though the question was repeated.

And at last the monster drove away northward over a crest of pine woods and was no more seen. They fell into a hot and long disputation. . . .

The hymn ended. The Prince's legs dangled up the passage again, and everyone was briskly prepared for heroic exertion and triumphant acts. 'Smallways!' cried Kurt, 'come here!'

5

Then Bert, under Kurt's direction, had his first experience of the work of an air-sailor.

The immediate task before the captain of the *Vaterland* was a very simple one. He had to keep afloat. The wind, though it had fallen from its earlier violence, was still blowing strongly enough to render the grounding of so clumsy a mass extremely dangerous, even if it had been desirable for the Prince to land in inhabited country, and so risk capture. It was necessary to keep the airship up until the wind fell and then, if possible, to descend in some lonely district of the Territory where there would be a chance of repair or rescue by some searching consort. In order to do this weight had to be dropped, and Kurt was detailed with a dozen men to climb down among the wreckage of the deflated air-chambers, and cut the stuff clear, portion by portion, as the airship sank. So Bert, armed with a sharp cutlass, found himself clambering about upon netting four thousand feet up in the air, trying to understand Kurt when he spoke in English and to divine him when he used German.

It was giddy work, but not nearly so giddy as a rather over-nourished reader sitting in a warm room might imagine. Bert found it quite possible to look down and contemplate the wild subarctic landscape below, now devoid of any sign of habitation, a land of rocky cliffs and cascades and broad swirling desolate rivers, and of trees and thickets that grew more stunted and scrubby as the day wore on. Here and there on the hills were patches and pockets of snow. And over all this he worked, hacking away at the tough and slippery oiled silk and clinging stoutly to the netting. Presently they cleared and dropped a tangle of bent steel rods and wires from the frame, and a big chunk of silk bladder. That was trying. The airship flew up at once as this loose hamper parted. It seemed almost as though they were dropping all Canada. The stuff spread out in the air and floated down and hit and twisted up in a nasty fashion on the lip of a gorge. Bert clung like a frozen monkey to his ropes, and did not move a muscle for five minutes.

But there was something very exhilarating, he found, in this dangerous work, and above everything else, there was the sense of fellowship. He was no longer an isolated and distrustful stranger among these others, he had now a common object with them, he worked with a friendly rivalry to get through with his share before them. And he developed a great respect and affection for Kurt, which had hitherto been only latent in him. Kurt with a job to direct was altogether admirable: he was resourceful, helpful, considerate, swift. He seemed to be everywhere. One forgot his pinkness, his light cheerfulness of manner. Directly one had trouble he was at hand with sound and confident advice. He was like an elder brother to his men.

Altogether they cleared three considerable chunks of wreckage, and then Bert was glad to clamber up into the cabins again and give place to a second squad. He and his companions were given hot coffee, and, indeed, even gloved as they were, the job had been a cold one. They sat drinking it and regarding each other with satisfaction. One man spoke to Bert amiably in German, and Bert nodded and smiled. Through Kurt, Bert, whose ankles were almost frozen, succeeded in getting a pair of top-boots from one of the disabled men.

In the afternoon the wind abated greatly, and small, infrequent snowflakes came drifting by. Snow also spread more abundantly below, and the only trees were clumps of pine and spruce in the lower valleys. Kurt went with three men into the still intact gas-chambers, let out a certain quantity of gas from them, and prepared a series of ripping panels for the descent. Also the residue of the bombs and explosives in the magazine were thrown overboard and fell, detonating loudly in the wilderness below. And about four o'clock in the afternoon, upon a wide and rocky plain within sight of snow-crested cliffs, the *Vaterland* ripped and grounded.

It was necessarily a difficult and violent affair, for the *Vaterland* had not been planned for the necessities of a balloon. The captain got one panel ripped too soon and the others not soon enough. She dropped heavily, bounced clumsily, and smashed the hanging gallery into the fore-part, mortally injuring Von Winterfeld, and then came down in a collapsing heap after dragging for some moments. The forward shield and its machine-gun tumbled in upon the things below. Two men were hurt badly – one got a broken leg and one was internally injured – by flying rods and wires, and Bert was pinned for a time under the side. When at last he got clear and could take a view of the situation, the great black eagle that had started so splendidly from Franconia six evenings ago, sprawled deflated over the cabins of the airship and the frost-bitten rocks of this desolate place and looked a most unfortunate bird – as though someone had caught it and wrung its neck and cast it aside. Several of the crew of the airship were standing about in silence, contemplating the wreckage and the empty wilderness into which they had fallen. Others were busy under the impromptu tent made by the empty gas-chambers. The Prince had gone a little way off and was scrutinizing the distant heights through his field-glass. They had the appearance of old sea-cliffs; here and there were small clumps of conifers, and in two places tall cascades. The nearer ground was strewn with glaciated boulders and supported nothing but a stunted Alpine vegetation of compact clustering stems and stalkless flowers. No river was visible, but the air was full of the rush and babble of a torrent close at hand. A bleak and biting wind was blowing. Ever and again a snowflake drifted past. The springless frozen earth under Bert's feet felt strangely dead and heavy after the buoyant airship.

6

So it came about that that great and powerful Prince Karl Albert was for a time thrust out of the stupendous conflict he chiefly had been instrumental in provoking. The chances of battle and the weather conspired to maroon him in Labrador, and there he raged for six long days, while war and wonder swept the world. Nation rose against nation and air-fleet grappled air-fleet, cities blazed and men died in multitudes; but in Labrador one might have dreamt that, except for a little noise of hammering, the world was at peace.

There the encampment lay; from a distance the cabins, covered over with the silk of the balloon part, looked like a gipsy's tent on a rather exceptional scale, and all the available hands were busy in building out of the steel of the framework a mast from which the *Vaterland*'s electricians might hang the long conductors of the apparatus for wireless telegraphy that was to link the Prince to the world again. There were times when it seemed they would never rig that mast. From the onset the party suffered hardship. They were not too abundantly provisioned, and they were put on short rations, and for all the thick garments they had, they were but ill-equipped against the piercing wind and inhospitable violence of this wilderness. The first night was spent in darkness and without fires. The engines that had supplied power were smashed and dropped far away to the south, and there was never a match among the company. It had been death to carry matches. All the explosives had been thrown out of the magazine, and it was only towards morning that the bird-faced man whose cabin Bert had taken in the beginning confessed to a brace of duelling-pistols and cartridges, with which a fire could be started. Afterwards the lockers of the machine-gun were found to contain a supply of unused ammunition.

The night was a distressing one and seemed almost interminable. Hardly anyone slept. There were seven wounded men aboard, and Von Winterfeld's head had been injured and he was shivering and in delirium, struggling with his attendant and shouting strange things about the burning of New York. The men crept together in the mess-room in the darkling, wrapped in what they could find, and drank cocoa from the fireless heaters and listened to his cries. In the morning the Prince made them a speech about Destiny, and the God of his Fathers, and the pleasure and glory of giving one's life for his dynasty, and a number of similar considerations that might otherwise have been neglected in that bleak wilderness. The men cheered without enthusiasm, and far away a wolf howled.

Then they set to work, and for a week they toiled to put up a mast of steel, and hang from it a gridiron of copper wires two hundred feet by twelve. The theme of all that time was work, work continually, straining and toilsome work, and all the rest was grim hardship and evil chances, save for a certain wild splendour in the sunset and sunrise, in the torrents and drifting weather, in the wilderness about them. They built and tended a ring of perpetual fires, gangs roamed for brushwood and met with wolves, and the wounded men and their beds were brought out from the airship cabins, and put in shelters about the fires. There old Von Winterfeld raved and became quiet and presently died, and three of the other wounded sickened for want of good food, while their fellows mended. These things happened, as it were, in the wings; the central facts before Bert's consciousness were always, firstly, the perpetual toil, the holding and lifting, and lugging at heavy and clumsy masses, the tedious filing and winding of wires; and secondly, the Prince, urgent and threatening whenever a man relaxed. He would stand over them and point over their heads, southward into the empty sky. 'The world there,' he said in German, 'is waiting for us! Fifty centuries come to their Consummation.' Bert did not understand the words, but he read the gesture. Several times the Prince grew angry; once with a man who was working slowly, once with a man who stole a comrade's ration. The first he scolded and set to a more tedious task; the second he struck in the face and ill-used. He did no work himself. There was a clear space near the fires, in which he would walk up and down, sometimes for hours together, with arms folded, muttering to himself of Patience and his destiny. At times these mutterings broke out into rhetoric, into shouts and gestures that would arrest the workers; they would stare at him until they perceived that his blue eyes glared and his waving hand addressed itself always to the southward hills. On Sunday the work ceased for half an hour, and the Prince preached on faith and God's friendship for David, and afterwards they all sang: 'Ein feste Burg ist unser Gott.'

In an improvised hovel lay Von Winterfeld, and all one morning he raved of the greatness of Germany. 'Blut und Eisen!' he shouted, and then, as if in derision, 'Welt-Politik – ha, ha!' Then he would explain complicated questions of polity to imaginary hearers, in low, wily tones. The other sick men kept still, listening to him. Bert's distracted attention would be recalled by Kurt. 'Smallways, take that end. So!'

Slowly, tediously, the great mast was rigged, and hoisted foot by foot into place. The electricians had contrived a catchment pool and a wheel in the torrent close at hand – for the little Mulhausen dynamo with its turbinal volute used by the telegraphists was quite adaptable

745

to water driving, and on the sixth day in the evening the apparatus was in working order and the Prince was calling – weakly, indeed, but calling – to his air-fleet across the empty spaces of the world. For a time he called unheeded.

The effect of that evening was to linger long in Bert's memory. A red fire spluttered and blazed close by the electricians at their work, and red gleams ran up the vertical steel mast and threads of copper wire towards the zenith. The Prince sat on a rock close by, with his chin on his hand, waiting. Beyond and to the northward was the cairn that covered Von Winterfeld, surmounted by a cross of steel, and from among the tumbled rocks in the distance the eyes of a wolf gleamed redly. On the other hand was the wreckage of the great airship and the men bivouacked about a second ruddy flare. They were all keeping very still, as if waiting to hear what news might presently be given them. Far away, across many hundreds of miles of desolation, other wireless masts would be clicking and snapping, and waking into responsive vibration. Perhaps they were not. Perhaps these throbs upon the ether wasted themselves upon a regardless world. When the men spoke, they spoke in low tones. Now and then a bird shrieked remotely, and once a wolf howled. All these things were set in the immense cold spaciousness of the wild.

7

Bert got the news last, and chiefly in broken English, from a linguist among his mates. It was only far on in the night that the weary telegraphist got an answer to his calls, but then the messages came clear and strong. And such news it was!

'I say,' said Bert at his breakfast, amidst a great clamour, 'tell us a bit.'

'All de vorlt is at vor!' said the linguist, waving his cocoa in an illustrative manner, 'all de vorlt is at vor!'

Bert stared southward into the dawn. It did not seem so.

'All de vorlt is at vor! They haf burn' Berlin; they haf burn' London; they haf burn' Hamburg and Paris. Chapan hass burn' San Francisco. We haf mate a camp at Niagara. Dat is whad they are telling us. China has cot *Drachenflieger* and *Luftschiffe* beyont counting. All de vorlt is at vor!'

'Gaw!' said Bert.

'Yess,' said the linguist, drinking his cocoa.

'Burnt up London, 'ave they? Like we did New York?'

'It wass a bombardment.'

'They don't say anything about a place called Clapham, or Bun Hill, do they?'

'I haf heard noding,' said the linguist.

That was all Bert could get for a time. But the excitement of the men about him was contagious, and presently he saw Kurt standing alone, hands behind him, and looking at one of the distant waterfalls very steadfastly. He went up and saluted, soldier-fashion. 'Beg pardon, lieutenant,' he said.

Kurt turned his face. It was unusually grave that morning. 'I was just thinking I would like to see that waterfall closer,' he said. 'It reminds me – what do you want?'

'I can't make 'ead or tail of what they're saying, sir. Would you mind telling me the news?'

'Damn the news,' said Kurt. 'You'll get news enough before the day's out. It's the end of the world. They're sending the *Graf Zeppelin* for us. She'll be here by the morning, and we ought to be at Niagara – or eternal smash – within eight-and-forty hours. . . . I want to look at that waterfall. You'd better come with me. Have you had your rations?'

'Yessir.'

'Very well. Come.'

And musing profoundly, Kurt led the way across the rocks towards the distant waterfall. For a time Bert walked behind him in the character of an escort; then as they passed out of the atmosphere of the encampment, Kurt lagged for him to come alongside.

'We shall be back in it all in two days' time,' he said. 'And it's a devil of a war to go back to. That's the news. The world's gone mad. Our fleet beat the Americans the night we got disabled, that's clear. We lost eleven – eleven airships certain, and all their aeroplanes got smashed. God knows how much we smashed or how many we killed. But that was only the beginning. Our start's been like firing a magazine. Every country was hiding flying machines. They're fighting in the air all over Europe – all over the world. The Japanese and Chinese have joined in. That's the great fact. That's the supreme fact. They've pounced into our little quarrels. . . . The Yellow Peril was a peril after all! They've got thousands of airships. They're all over the world. We bombarded London and Paris, and the French and English have smashed up Berlin. And now Asia is at us all, and on the top of us all. . . . It's mania. China on the top. And they don't know where to stop. It's limitless. It's the last confusion. They're bombarding capitals, smashing up dockyards and factories, mines and fleets.'

'Did they do much to London, sir?' asked Bert.

'Heaven knows. . . .'

He said no more for a time.

'This Labrador seems a quiet place,' he resumed at last. 'I'm half a mind to stay here. Can't do that. No! I've got to see it through. I've got to see it through. You've got to, too. Everyone. . . . But why? . . . I tell you – our world's gone to pieces. There's no way out of it, no way back. Here we are! We're like mice caught in a house on fire, we're like cattle overtaken by a flood. Presently we shall be picked up, and back we shall go into the fighting. We shall kill and smash again – perhaps. It's a Chino-Japanese air-fleet this time, and the odds are against us. Our turn will come. What will happen to you I don't know, but for myself, I know quite well; I shall be killed.'

'You'll be all right,' said Bert, after a queer pause.

'No!' said Kurt, 'I'm going to be killed. I didn't know it before, but this morning at dawn I knew it – as though I'd been told.'

''Ow?'

'I tell you I know.'

'But 'ow *could* you know?'

'I know.'

'Like being told?'

'Like being certain.

'I know,' he repeated, and for a time they walked in silence towards the waterfall.

Kurt, wrapped in his thoughts, walked heedlessly, and at last broke out again. 'I've always felt young before, Smallways, but this morning I feel old – old. So old! Nearer to death than old men feel. And I've always thought life was a lark. It isn't. . . . This sort of thing has always been happening, I suppose – these things, wars and earthquakes, that sweep across all the decency of life. It's just as though I had woke up to it all for the first time. Every night since we were at New York I've dreamt of it. . . . And it's always been so – it's the way of life. People are torn away from the people they care for; homes are smashed, creatures full of life and memories and little peculiar gifts are scalded and smashed and torn to pieces, and starved and spoilt. London! Berlin! San Francisco! Think of all the human histories we ended in New York! . . . And the others go on again as though such things weren't possible. As I went on! Like animals! Just like animals.'

He said nothing for a long time, and then he dropped out, 'The Prince is a lunatic!'

They came to a place where they had to climb, and then to a long peat level beside a rivulet. There a quantity of delicate little pink flowers caught Bert's eye. 'Gaw!' he said, and stooped to pick one. 'In a place like this.'

Kurt stopped and half turned. His face winced.

'I never see such a flower,' said Bert. 'It's so delicate.'

'Pick some more if you want to,' said Kurt.

Bert did so, while Kurt stood and watched him. 'Funny 'ow one always wants to pick flowers,' said Bert.

Kurt had nothing to add to that.

They went on again, without talking, for a long time.

At last they came to a rocky hummock, from which the view of the waterfall opened out. There Kurt stopped and seated himself on a rock. 'That's as much as I wanted to see,' he explained. 'It isn't very like, but it's like enough.'

'Like what?'

'Another waterfall I knew.'

He asked a question abruptly. 'Got a girl, Smallways?'

'Funny thing,' said Bert, 'those flowers, I suppose – I was jes' thinking of 'er.'

'So was I.'

' *What?* Edna?'

'No. I was thinking of *my* Edna. We've all got Ednas, I suppose, for our imaginations to play about. This was a girl. But all that's past for ever. It's hard to think I can't see her just for a minute – just let her know I'm thinking of her.'

'Very likely,' said Bert, 'you'll see 'er all right.'

'No,' said Kurt with decision, 'I *know.*

'I met her,' he went on, 'in a place like this – in the Alps – Engstlen Alp. There's a waterfall rather like this one – a broad waterfall down towards Innertkirchen. That's why I came here this morning. We slipped away and had half a day together beside it. And we picked flowers. Just such flowers as you picked. The same, for all I know. And gentian.'

'I know,' said Bert; 'me and Edna – we done things like that. Flowers. And all that. Seems years off now.'

'She was beautiful and daring and shy. Mein Gott! ... I can hardly hold myself for the desire to see her and hear her voice again before I die. Where is she? ... Look here, Smallways, I shall write a sort of letter– And there's her portrait.' He touched his breast pocket.

'You'll see 'er again all right,' said Bert.

'No! I shall never see her again. ... I don't understand why people should meet just to be torn apart. But I know she and I will never meet again. That I know as surely as that the sun will rise, and that cascade come shining over the rocks after I am dead and done. ... Oh! It's all foolishness and haste and violence and cruel folly, stupidity and blundering hate and selfish ambition – all the things that men have done – all the things they will ever do. Gott! Smallways, what a muddle and confusion life has always been – the battles and massacres and disasters, the hates and harsh acts, the murders and sweatings, the lynchings and cheatings. This morning I am tired of it all, as though I'd just found it out for the first time. I *have* found it out. When a man is tired of life I suppose it is time for him to die. I've lost heart, and death is over me. Death is close to me, and I know I have got to end. But think of all the hopes I had only a little time ago, the sense of fine beginnings! ... It was all a sham. There were no beginnings. ... We're just ants in anthill cities, in a world that doesn't matter; that goes on and rambles into nothingness. New York – New York doesn't even strike me as horrible. New York was nothing but an anthill kicked to pieces by a fool!

'Think of it, Smallways; there's war everywhere! They're smashing up their civilization before they have made it. The sort of thing the English did at Alexandria, the Japanese at Port Arthur, the French at Casablanca, is going on everywhere. Everywhere! Down in South America even they are fighting among themselves! No place is safe – no place is at peace. There is no place where a woman and her daughter can hide and be at peace. The war comes through the air, bombs drop in the night. Quiet people go out in the morning, and see air-fleets passing overhead – dripping death – dripping death!'

8

A World At War

I

It was only very slowly that Bert got hold of this idea that the whole world was at war, that he formed any image at all of the crowded countries south of these Arctic solitudes stricken with terror and dismay as these new-born aerial navies swept across their skies. He was used to thinking of the world not as a whole, but as a limitless hinterland of happenings beyond the range of his immediate vision. War in his imagination was something, a source of news and emotion, that happened in a restricted area called the Seat of War. But now the whole atmosphere was the Seat of War, and every land a cockpit. So closely had the nations raced along the path of research and invention, so secret and yet so parallel had been their plans and acquisitions, that it was within a few hours of the launching of the first fleet in Franconia that an Asiatic Armada beat its westward way across, high above, the marvelling millions in the plain of the Ganges. But the preparations of the Confederation of Eastern Asia had been on an altogether more colossal scale than the German. 'With this step,' said Tan Ting-siang, 'we overtake and pass the West. We recover the peace of the world that these barbarians have destroyed.'

Their secrecy and swiftness and inventions had far surpassed those of the Germans, and where the Germans had had a hundred men at work the Asiatics had ten thousand. There came to their great aero-nautic parks at Chinsi-fu and Tsingyen, by the monorails that now laced the whole surface of China, a limitless supply of skilled and able workmen, workmen far above the average European in industrial efficiency. The news of the German World Surprise simply quickened their efforts. At the time of the bombardment of New York it is doubtful if the Germans had three hundred airships altogether in the world; the score of Asiatic fleets flying east and west and south must have numbered several thousand. Moreover, the Asiatics had a real fighting flying machine, the *Niaio* as it was called, a light but quite efficient weapon, infinitely superior to the German *Drachenflieger.* Like that, it was a one-man machine; but it was built very lightly of steel and cane and chemical silk, with a transverse engine and a flapping side-wing. The aeronaut carried a gun firing explosive bullets loaded with oxygen, and in addition, and true to the best tradition of Japan, a sword. The riders were Japanese, and it is characteristic that from the first it was contemplated that the aeronaut should be a swordsman. The wings of these fliers had bat-like hooks forward, by which they were to cling to their antagonist's gas-chambers while boarding him. These light flying machines were carried with the fleets, and also sent overland or by sea to the front with the men. They were capable of flights of from two to five hundred miles, according to the wind.

So, hard upon the uprush of the first German air-fleet, these Asiatic swarms took to the atmosphere. Instantly every organized government in the world was frantically and vehemently building airships and whatever approach to a flying machine its inventors had discovered. There was no time for diplomacy. Warnings and ultimatums were telegraphed to and fro, and in a few hours all the panic-fierce world was openly at war, and at war in the most complicated way. For Britain and France and Italy had declared war upon Germany and outraged Swiss neutrality; India, at the sight of Asiatic airships, had broken into a Hindoo insurrection in Bengal and a Mahometan revolt hostile to this in the North-west Provinces – the latter spreading like wildfire from Gobi to the Gold Coast – and the Confederation of Eastern Asia had seized the oil wells of Burmah and was impartially attacking America and Germany. In a week they were building airships in Damascus and Cairo and Johannesburg; Australia and New Zealand were frantically equipping themselves. One unique and terrifying aspect of this development was the swiftness with which these monsters could be produced. To build an ironclad took from two to four years; an airship could be put together in as many weeks. Moreover, compared with even a torpedo boat the airship was remarkably simple to construct: given the air-chamber material, the engines, the gas plant and the design, it was really not more complicated and far easier than an ordinary wooden boat had been a hundred years before. And now from Cape Horn to Nova Zembla, and from Canton round to Canton again, there were factories and workshops and industrial resources.

And the German airships were barely in sight of the Atlantic waters, the first Asiatic fleet was scarcely reported from Upper Burmah, before the fantastic fabric of credit and finance that had held the world together economically for a hundred years strained and snapped. A tornado of realization swept through every stock exchange in the world; banks stopped payment, business shrank and ceased, factories ran on for a day or so by a sort of inertia, completing the orders of bankrupt and extinguished customers, then stopped. The New York Bert Smallways saw, for all its glare of light and traffic, was in the pit of an economic and financial collapse unparalleled in history. The flow of the food supply was already a little checked. And before the World War had lasted two weeks – by the time that mast was rigged in Labrador – there was not a city or town in the world outside China, however far from the actual centres of destruction, where police and government were not adopting special emergency methods to deal with a want of food and a glut of unemployed people.

The special peculiarities of aerial warfare were of such a nature as to trend, once it had begun, almost inevitably towards social disorganization. The first of these peculiarities was brought home to the Germans in their attack upon New York; the immense power of destruction an airship has over the thing below, and its relative inability to occupy or police or guard or garrison a surrendered position. Necessarily, in the face of urban populations in a state of economic disorganization and infuriated and starving, this led to violent and destructive collisions, and even where the air-fleet floated inactive above, there would be civil conflict and passionate disorder below. Nothing comparable to this state of affairs had been known in the previous history of warfare, unless we take such a case as that of a nineteenth-century warship attacking some large savage or barbaric settlement, or one of those naval bombardments that disfigure the history of Great Britain in the late eighteenth century. Then, indeed, there had been cruelties and destruction that faintly foreshadowed the horrors of the aerial war. Moreover, before the twentieth century the world had had but one experience, and that a comparatively light one, in the Communist insurrection of Paris, 1871, of the possibilities of a modern urban population under warlike stresses.

A second peculiarity of airship war as it first came to the world that also made for social collapse was the ineffectiveness of the early airships against each other. Upon anything below they could rain explosives in the most deadly fashion, forts and ships and cities lay at their mercy, but unless they were prepared for a suicidal grapple they could do remarkably little mischief to each other. The armament of the huge German airships, big as the biggest mammoth liners afloat, was one machine-gun that could easily have been packed up on a couple of mules. In addition, when it became evident that the air must be fought for, the air-sailors were provided with rifles with explosive bullets of oxygen or inflammable substance, but no airship at any time ever carried as much in the way of guns and armour as the smallest gunboat on the navy list had been accustomed to do. Consequently, when these monsters met in battle they manoeuvred for the upper place, or grappled and fought like junks, throwing grenades, fighting hand to hand in an entirely mediaeval fashion. The risks of a collapse and fall on either side came near to balancing in every case the chances of victory. As a consequence, and after their first experiences of battle, one finds a growing tendency on the part of the air-fleet admirals to evade joining battle and to seek rather the moral advantage of a destructive counter-attack.

And if the airships were too ineffective, the early *Drachenflieger* were either too unstable, like the German, or too light, like the Japanese, to produce immediately decisive results. Later, it is true, the Brazilians launched a flying machine of a type and scale that was capable of dealing with an airship, but they built only three or four, they operated only in South America and they vanished from history untraceably in the time when world bankruptcy put a stop to all further engineering production on any considerable scale.

The third peculiarity of aerial warfare was that it was at once enormously destructive and entirely indecisive. It had this unique feature, that both sides lay open to punitive attack. In all previous forms of war, both by land and sea, the losing side was speedily unable to raid its antagonist's territory and communications. One fought on a 'front', and behind that front the winner's supplies and resources, his towns and factories and capital, the peace of his country, were secure. If the war was a naval one, you destroyed your enemy's battle fleet and then blockaded his ports, secured his coaling stations, and hunted down any stray cruisers that threatened your ports of commerce. But to blockade and watch a coastline is one thing, to blockade and watch the whole surface of a country is another, and cruisers and privateers are things that take long to make, that cannot be packed up and hidden and carried unostentatiously from point to point. In aerial war the stronger side, *even* supposing it destroyed the main battle fleet of the weaker, had then either to patrol and watch or destroy every possible point at which he might produce another and perhaps novel and more deadly form of flier. It meant darkening his air with airships.

It meant building them by the thousand and making aeronauts by the hundred thousand. A small uninflated airship could be hidden in a railway shed, in a village street, in a wood; a flying machine is even less conspicuous.

And in the air are no streets, no channels, no point where one can say of an antagonist, 'If he wants to reach my capital he must come by here.' In the air all directions lead everywhere.

Consequently it was impossible to end a war by any of the established methods. A having outnumbered and overwhelmed B, hovers, a thousand airships strong, over his capital, threatening to bombard it unless B submits. B replies by wireless telegraphy that he is now in the act of bombarding the chief manufacturing city of A by means of three raider airships. A denounces B's raiders as pirates and so forth, bombards B's capital and sets off to hunt down B's airships, while B, in a state of passionate emotion and heroic unconquerableness, sets to work amidst his ruins, making fresh airships and explosives for the benefit of A. The war became perforce a universal guerilla war, a war inextricably involving civilians and homes and all the apparatus of social life.

These aspects of aerial fighting took the world by surprise. There had been no foresight to deduce these consequences. If there had been, the world would have arranged for a Universal Peace Conference in 1900. But mechanical invention had gone faster than intellectual and social organization, and the world, with its silly old flags, its silly unmeaning tradition of nationality, its cheap newspapers and cheaper passions and imperialisms, its base commercial motives and habitual insincerities and vulgarities, its race lies and conflicts, was taken by surprise. Once the war began there was no stopping it. The flimsy fabric of credit that had grown with no man foreseeing, and that had held those hundreds of millions in an economic interdependence that no man clearly understood, dissolved in panic. Everywhere went the airships dropping bombs, destroying any hope of a rally, and everywhere below were economic catastrophe, starving workless people, rioting, and social disorder. Whatever constructive guiding intelligence there had been among the nations vanished in the passionate stresses of the time. Such newspapers and documents and histories as survive from this period all tell one universal story of towns and cities with the food supply interrupted and their streets congested with starving unemployed; of crises in administration and states of siege, of provisional Governments and Councils of Defence, and in the cases of India and Egypt, insurrectionary committees taking charge, of the rearming of the population, of the making of batteries and gun-pits, of the vehement manufacture of airships and flying machines.

One sees these things in glimpses, in illuminated moments, as if through a driving reek of clouds, going on all over the world. It was the dissolution of an age; it was the collapse of the civilization that had trusted to machinery, and the instruments of its destruction were machines. But while the collapse of the previous great civilization, that of Rome, had been a matter of centuries, had been a thing of phase and phase like the ageing and dying of a man, this, like his killing by railway or motor-car, was one swift, conclusive smashing and an end.

2

The early battles of the aerial war were no doubt determined by attempts to realize the old naval maxim, to ascertain the position of the enemy's fleet and to destroy it. There was first the battle of the Bemese Oberland, in which the Italian and French navigables in their flank raid upon the Franconian Park were assailed by the Swiss experimental squadron, supported as the day wore on by German airships; and then the encounter of the British Winterhouse-Dunne aeroplanes with three unfortunate Germans.

Then came the battle of North India, in which the entire Anglo-Indian aeronautic settlement establishment fought for three days against overwhelming odds, and was dispersed and destroyed in detail.

And simultaneously with the beginning of that commenced the momentous struggle of the Germans and Asiatics that is usually known as the Battle of Niagara because of the objective of the Asiatic attack. But it passed gradually into a sporadic conflict over half a continent. Such German airships as escaped destruction in battle descended and surrendered to the Americans, and were remanned; and in the end it became a series of pitiless and heroic encounters between the Americans, savagely resolved to exterminate their enemies, and a continually reinforced army of invasion from Asia quartered upon the Pacific slope and supported by an immense fleet. From the first the war in America was fought with implacable bitterness; no quarter was asked, no prisoners were taken. With ferocious and magnificent energy the Americans constructed and launched ship after ship to battle and perish against the Asiatic multitudes. All other affairs were subordinate to this war, the whole population was presently living or dying for it. Presently, as I shall tell, the white men found in the Butteridge machine a weapon that could meet and fight the flying machines of the Asiatic swordsmen.

The Asiatic invasion of America completely effaced the German-

American conflict. It vanishes from history. At first it had seemed to promise quite sufficient tragedy in itself – beginning as it did in unforgettable massacre. After the destruction of central New York all America had risen like one man, resolved to die a thousand deaths rather than submit to Germany. The Germans grimly resolved upon beating the Americans into submission and, following out the plans developed by the Prince, had seized Niagara – in order to avail themselves of its enormous power works, expelled all its inhabitants and made a desert of its environs as far as Buffalo. They had also, directly Great Britain and France declared war, wrecked the country upon the Canadian side for nearly ten miles inland. They began to bring up men and material from the fleet off the east coast, stringing out to and fro like bees getting honey. It was then that the Asiatic forces appeared, and it was in their attack upon this German base at Niagara that the air-fleets of East and West first met and the greater issue became clear.

One conspicuous peculiarity of the early aerial fighting arose from the profound secrecy with which the airships had been prepared. Each power had had but the dimmest inkling of the schemes of its rivals, and even experiments with its own devices were limited by the needs of secrecy. None of the designers of airships and aeroplanes had known clearly what their inventions might have to fight; many had not imagined they would have to fight anything whatever in the air, and had planned them only for the dropping of explosives. Such had been the German idea. The only weapon for fighting another airship with which the Franconian fleet had been provided was the machine-gun forward. Only after the fight over New York were the men given short rifles with detonating bullets. Theoretically, the *Drachenflieger* were to have been the fighting weapon. They were declared to be aerial torpedo boats, and the aeronaut was supposed to swoop close to his antagonist and cast his bombs as he whirled past. But indeed these contrivances were hopelessly unstable; not one-third in any engagement succeeded in getting back to the mother airship. The rest were either smashed up or grounded.

The allied Chino-Japanese fleet made the same distinction as the Germans between airships and fighting machines heavier than air, but the type in both cases was entirely different from the Occidental models, and – it is eloquent of the vigour with which these great peoples took up and bettered the European methods of scientific research – in almost every particular the invention of Asiatic engineers. Chief among these, it is worth remarking, was Mohini K. Chatterjee, a political exile who had formerly served in the British-Indian aeronautic park at Lahore.

The German airship was fish-shaped, with a blunted head; the Asiatic airship was also fish-shaped, but not so much on the lines of a cod or goby as of a ray or sole. It had a wide flat underside, unbroken by windows or any opening except along the middle line. Its cabins occupied its axis, with a sort of bridge deck above, and the gas-chambers gave the whole affair the shape of a gipsy's hooped tent, except that it was much flatter. The German airship was essentially a navigable balloon very much lighter than air; the Asiatic airship was very little lighter than air and skimmed through it with much greater velocity if with considerably less stability. They carried fore and aft guns, the latter much the larger, throwing inflammatory shells, and in addition they had nests for riflemen on both the upper and the underside. Light as this armament was in comparison with the smallest gunboat that ever sailed, it was sufficient for them to outfight as well as outfly the German monster airships. In action they flew to get behind or over the Germans: they even dashed underneath, avoiding only passing immediately beneath the magazine, and then as soon as they had crossed let fly with their rear gun, and sent flares or oxygen shells into the antagonist's gas-chambers.

It was not in their airships but, as I have said, in their flying-machines proper that the strength of the Asiatics lay. Next only to the Butteridge machine these were certainly the most efficient heavier-than-air fliers that had ever appeared. They were the invention of a Japanese artist, and they differed in type extremely from the box-kite quality of the German *Drachenflieger*. They had curiously curved, flexible side wings, more like *bent* butterfly's wings than anything else, and made of a substance like celluloid and of brightly painted silk, and they had a long humming-bird tail. At the forward corner of the wings were hooks, rather like the claws of a bat, by which the machine could catch and hang and tear at the walls of an airship's gas-chamber. The solitary rider sat between the wings above a transverse explosive engine, an explosive engine that differed in no essential particular from those in use in the light motor-bicycles of the period. Below was a single large wheel. The rider sat astride a saddle, as in the Butteridge machine, and he carried a large double-edged two-handed sword, in addition to his explosive-bullet firing rifle.

3

One sets down these particulars and compares the points of the American and German pattern of aeroplane and navigable, but none of these facts were clearly known to any of those who fought in this monstrously confused battle above the American great lakes.

Each side went into action against it knew not what, under novel conditions and with apparatus that even without hostile attacks was capable of producing the most disconcerting surprises. Schemes of action, attempts at collective manoeuvring necessarily went to pieces directly the fight began, just as they did in almost all the early ironclad battles of the previous century. Each captain then had to fall back upon individual action and his own devices; one would see triumph in what another read as a cue for flight and despair. It is as true of the Battle of Niagara as of the Battle of Lissa that it was not a battle but a bundle of 'battlettes'!

To such a spectator as Bert it presented itself as a series of incidents, some immense, some trivial, but collectively incoherent. He never had a sense of any plain issue joined, of any point struggled for and won or lost. He saw tremendous things happen, and in the end his world darkened to disaster and ruin.

He saw the battle from the ground, from Prospect Park and from Goat Island, whither he fled.

But the manner in which he came to be on the ground needs explaining.

The Prince had resumed command of his fleet through wireless telegraphy long before the *Zeppelin* had located his encampment in Labrador. By his direction the German air-fleet, whose advance scouts had been in contact with the Japanese over the Rocky Mountains, had concentrated upon Niagara and awaited his arrival. He had rejoined his command early in the morning of the 12th, and Bert had his first prospect of the Gorge of Niagara while he was doing net drill outside the middle gas-chamber at sunrise. The *Zeppelin* was flying very high at the time, and far below he saw the water in the gorge marbled with froth, and then away to the west the great crescent of the Canadian Fall shining, flickering and foaming in the level sunlight, and sending up a deep, incessant thudding rumble to the sky. The air-fleet was keeping station in an enormous crescent, with its horns pointing south-westward, a long array of shining monsters with tails rotating slowly, and German ensigns now trailing from their bellies aft of their Marconi pendants.

Niagara city was still largely standing then, albeit its streets were empty of all life. Its bridges were intact, its hotels and restaurants still flying flags and inviting sky signs, its power stations running. But about it the country on both sides of the gorge might have been swept by a colossal broom. Everything that could possibly give cover to an attack upon the German position at Niagara had been levelled as ruthlessly as machinery and explosives could contrive; houses blown up and burnt, woods burnt, fences and crops destroyed. The monorails had been torn up, and the roads in particular cleared of all possibility of concealment or shelter. Seen from above the effect of this wreckage was grotesque. Young woods had been destroyed wholesale by dragging wires, and the spoilt saplings, smashed or uprooted, lay in swathes like corn after the sickle. Houses had an appearance of being flattened down by the pressure of a gigantic finger. Much burning was still going on, and large areas had been reduced to patches of smouldering and sometimes still glowing blackness. Here and there lay the débris of belated fugitives, carts and dead bodies of horses and men; and where houses had had water supplies there were pools of water and running springs from the ruptured pipes. In unscorched fields horses and cattle still fed peacefully. Beyond this desolated area the countryside was still standing, but almost all the people had fled. Buffalo was on fire to an enormous extent, and there were no signs of any efforts to grapple with the flames.

Niagara city itself was being rapidly converted to the needs of a military depot. A large number of skilled engineers had already been brought from the fleet, and were busily at work adapting the exterior industrial apparatus of the place to the purposes of an aeronautic park. They had made a gas recharging station at the corner of the American Fall above the funicular railway, and they were opening up a much larger area to the south for the same purpose. Over the power houses and hotels and suchlike prominent or important points, the German flag was flying.

The *Zeppelin* circled slowly over this scene twice while the Prince surveyed it from the swinging gallery; it then rose towards the centre of the crescent and transferred the Prince and his suit, Kurt included, to the *Hohenzollern*, which had been chosen as the flagship during the impending battle. They were swung up on a small cable from the forward gallery, and the men of the *Zeppelin* manned the outer netting as the Prince and his staff left them. The *Zeppelin* then came about, circled down and grounded in Prospect Park, in order to land the wounded and take aboard explosives; for she had come to Labrador with her magazines empty, it being uncertain what weight she might need to carry. She also replenished the hydrogen in one of her forward chambers which had leaked.

Bert was detailed as a bearer and helped carry the wounded one by one into the nearest of the large hotels that faced the Canadian shore. The hotel was quite empty except that there were two trained American

760

nurses and a Negro porter, and three or four Germans awaiting them. Bert went with the *Zeppelin's* doctor into the main street of the place, and they broke into a drug-shop and obtained various things of which they stood in need. As they returned they found an officer and two men making a rough inventory of the available material in the various stores. Except for them the wide, main street of the town was quite deserted, the people had been given three hours to clear out, and everybody, it seemed, had done so. At one corner a dead man lay against the wall – shot. Two or three dogs were visible up the empty vista, but towards its river end the passage of a string of monorail cars broke the stillness and the silence. They were loaded with hose, and were passing to the trainful of workers who were converting Prospect Park into an airship dock.

Bert pushed a case of medicine balanced on a bicycle taken from an adjacent shop, to the hotel, and then he was sent to load bombs into the *Zeppelin* magazine, a duty that called for elaborate care. From this job he was presently called off by the captain of the *Zeppelin*, who sent him with a note to the officer in charge of the Anglo-American Power Company, for the field telephone had still to be adjusted. Bert received his instructions in German, whose meaning he guessed, and saluted and took the note, not caring to betray his ignorance of the language. He started off with a bright air of knowing his way and turned a corner or so and was only beginning to suspect that he did not know where he was going when his attention was recalled to the sky by the report of a gun from the *Hohenzollern* and celestial cheering.

He looked up and found the view obstructed by the houses on either side of the street. He hesitated, and then curiosity took him back towards the bank of the river. Here his view was inconvenienced by trees, and it was with a start that he discovered the *Zeppelin*, which he knew had still a quarter of her magazines to fill, was rising over Goat Island. She had not waited for her complement of ammunition. It occurred to him that he was left behind. He ducked back among the trees and bushes until he felt secure from any afterthought on the part of the *Zeppelin's* captain. Then his curiosity to see what the German air-fleet faced overcame him, and drew him at last halfway across the bridge to Goat Island. From that point he had nearly a hemisphere of sky and got his first glimpse of the Asiatic airships low in the sky above the glittering tumults of the Upper Rapids.

They were far less impressive than the German ships. He could not judge the distance, and they flew edgeways to him, so as to conceal the broader aspect of their bulk.

Bert stood there in the middle of the bridge, in a place that most people who knew it remembered as a place populous with sightseers and excursionists, and he was the only human being in sight there. Above him, very high in the heavens, the contending air-fleets man-oeuvred; below him the river seethed like a sluice towards the American Fall. He was curiously dressed. His cheap blue serge trousers were thrust into German airship rubber boots, and on his head he wore an aeronaut's white cap that was a trifle too large for him. He thrust that back to reveal his staring little Cockney face, still scarred upon the brow. 'Gaw!' he whispered.

He stared. He gesticulated. Once or twice he shouted and applauded.

Then at a certain point terror seized him and he took to his heels in the direction of Goat Island.

4

For a time after they were in sight of each other, neither fleet attempted to engage. The Germans numbered sixty-seven great airships and they maintained the crescent formation at a height of nearly four thousand feet. They kept a distance of about one and a half lengths, so that the horns of the crescent were nearly thirty miles apart. Closely in tow of the airships of the extreme squadrons on either wing were about thirty *Drachenflieger* ready manned, but these were too small and distant for Bert to distinguish.

At first, only what was called the Southern fleet of the Asiatics was visible to him. It consisted of forty airships, carrying altogether nearly four hundred one-man flying machines upon their flanks, and for some time it flew slowly and at a minimum distance of perhaps a dozen miles from the Germans, eastward across their front. At first Bert could distinguish only the greater bulks, then he perceived the one-man machines as a multitude of very small objects drifting like motes in the sunshine about and beneath the larger shapes.

He saw nothing then of the second fleet of the Asiatics, though that was probably coming into sight of the Germans at the time, in the north-west.

The air was very still, the sky almost without a cloud, and the German fleet had risen to an immense height, so that the airships seemed no longer of any considerable size. Both ends of their crescent showed plainly. As they beat southward they passed slowly between Bert and the sunlight, and became black outlines of themselves. The

Drachenflieger appeared as little flecks of black on either wing of this aerial Armada.

The two fleets seemed in no hurry to engage. The Asiatics went far away into the east, quickening their pace and rising as they did so, and then tailed out into a long column and came flying back, rising towards the German left. The squadrons of the latter came about, facing this oblique advance, and suddenly little flickerings and a faint crepitating sound told that they had opened fire. For a time no effect was visible to the watcher on the bridge. Then, like a handful of snowflakes, the *Drachenflieger* swooped to the attack, and a multitude of red specks whirled up to meet them. It was to Bert's sense not only enormously remote but singularly inhuman. Not four hours since he had been on one of those very airships, and yet they seemed to him now not gas-bags carrying men, but strange sentient creatures that moved about and did things with a purpose of their own. The flight of the Asiatic and German flying machines joined and dropped earthward, became like a handful of white and red rose petals flung from a distant window, grew larger until Bert could see the overturned ones spinning through the air, and were hidden by great volumes of dark smoke that were rising in the direction of Buffalo. For a time they all were hidden; then two or three white and a number of red ones rose again into the sky like a swarm of big butterflies, and circled fighting and drove away out of sight again towards the east.

A heavy report recalled Bert's eyes to the zenith, and behold the great crescent had lost its dressing and burst into a disorderly long cloud of airships! One had dropped halfway down the sky. It was flaming fore and aft, and even as Bert looked it turned over and fell, spinning over and over itself, and vanished into the smoke of Buffalo.

Bert's mouth opened and shut, and he clutched tighter on the rail of the bridge. For some moments – they seemed long moments – the two fleets remained without any further change, flying obliquely towards each other, and making what came to Bert's ears as a midget uproar. Then suddenly from either side airships began dropping out of alignment, smitten by missiles he could neither see nor trace. The string of Asiatic ships swung round and either charged into or over (it was difficult to say from below) the shattered line of the Germans, who seemed to open out to give way to them. Some sort of man-oeuvring began, but Bert could not grasp its import. The left of the battle became a confused dance of airships. For some minutes up there the two crossing lines of ships looked so close it seemed like a hand-to-hand scuffle in the sky. Then they broke up into groups and duels. The descent of German airships towards the lower sky increased. One of them flared down and vanished far away in the north; two dropped with something twisted and crippled in their movements; then a group of antagonists came down from the zenith in an eddying conflict, two Asiatics against one German, and were presently joined by another, and drove away eastward all together with others dropping out of the German line to join them. One Asiatic either rammed or collided with a still more gigantic German, and the two went spinning to destruction together. The northern squadron of Asiatics came into the battle unnoted by Bert, except that the multitude of ships above seemed presently increased. In a little while the fight was utter confusion, drifting on the whole to the southwest against the wind. It became more and more a series of group encounters. Here a huge German airship flamed earthward with a dozen flat Asiatic craft about her, crushing her every attempt to recover. Here another hung with its crew fighting off the swordsmen from a swarm of flying machines. Here, again, an Asiatic aflame at either end swooped out of the battle. His attention went from incident to incident in the vast clearness overhead; these conspicuous cases of destruction caught and held his mind; it was only very slowly that any sort of scheme manifested itself between those nearer, more striking episodes.

The mass of the airships that eddied remotely above was, however, neither destroying nor destroyed. The majority of them seemed to be going at full speed and circling upward for position, exchanging ineffectual shots as they did so. Very little ramming was essayed after the first tragic downfall of rammer and rammed, and whatever attempts at boarding were made were invisible to Bert. There seemed, however, a steady endeavour to isolate antagonists, to cut them off from their fellows and bear them down, causing a perpetual sailing back and interlacing of these shoaling bulks. The greater numbers of the Asiatics and their swifter heeling movements gave them the effect of persistently attacking the Germans. Overhead, and evidently endeavouring to keep itself in touch with the works of Niagara, a body of German airships drew itself together into a compact phalanx, and the Asiatics became more and more intent upon breaking this up. He was grotesquely reminded of fish in a fish-pond struggling for crumbs. He could see puny puffs of smoke and the flash of bombs, but never a sound came down to him. . . .

A flapping shadow passed for a moment between Bert and the sun and was followed by another. A whirring of engines, click, clock, clitter clock, smote upon his ears. Instantly he forgot the zenith.

Perhaps a hundred yards above the water, out of the south, riding like Valkyries swiftly through the air on the strange steeds the engineering of Europe had begotten upon the artistic inspiration of Japan, came a long string of Asiatic swordsmen. The wings flapped jerkily, click, clock, clitter clock, and the machines drove up; they spread and ceased, and the apparatus came soaring through the air. So they rose and fell and rose again. They passed so closely overhead that Bert could hear their voices calling to one another. They swooped towards Niagara city and landed one after another in a long line in a clear space before the hotel. But he did not stay to watch them land. One yellow face had craned over and looked at him, and for one enigmatical instant met his eyes. . . .

It was then the idea came to Bert that he was altogether too conspicuous in the middle of the bridge, and that he took to his heels towards Goat Island. Thence, dodging about among the trees, with perhaps an excessive self-consciousness, he watched the rest of the struggle.

5

When Bert's sense of security was sufficiently restored for him to watch the battle again, he perceived that a brisk little fight was in progress between the Asiatic aeronauts and the German engineers for the possession of Niagara city. It was the first time in the whole course of the war that he had seen anything resembling fighting as he had studied it in the illustrated papers of his youth. It seemed to him almost as though things were coming right. He saw men carrying rifles and taking cover and running briskly from point to point in a loose attacking formation. The first batch of aeronauts had probably been under the impression that the city was deserted. They had grounded in the open near Prospect Park and approached the houses towards the power works before they were disillusioned by a sudden fire. They had scattered back to the cover of a bank near the water – it was too far for them to reach their machines again; they were lying and firing at the men in the hotels and frame-houses about the power works.

Then to their support came a second string of red flying-machines driving up from the east. They rose up out of the haze above the houses and came round in a long curve as if surveying the position below. The fire of the Germans rose to a roar, and one of those soaring shapes gave an abrupt jerk backwards and fell among the houses. The others swooped down exactly like great birds upon the roof of the powerhouse. They caught upon it, and from each sprang a nimble little figure and ran towards the parapet.

Other flapping bird-shapes came into this affair, but Bert had not seen their coming. A staccato of shots came over to him, reminding him of army manoeuvres, of newspaper descriptions of fights, of all that was entirely correct in his conception of warfare. He saw quite a number of Germans running from the outlying houses towards the powerhouse. Two fell. One lay still, but the other wriggled and made efforts for a time. The hotel that was used as a hospital, and to which he had helped carry the wounded men from the *Zeppelin* earlier in the day, suddenly ran up the Geneva flag. The town that had seemed so quiet had evidently been concealing a considerable number of Germans, and they were now concentrating to hold the central power- house. He wondered what ammunition they might have. More and more of the Asiatic flying machines came into the conflict. They had disposed of the unfortunate German *Drachenflieger* and were now aiming at the incipient aeronautic park, the electric gas generators and repair stations which formed the German base. Some landed, and their aeronauts took cover and became energetic infantry soldiers. Others hovered above the fight, their men ever and again firing shots down at some chance exposure below. The firing came in paroxysms; now there would be a watchful lull and now a rapid tattoo of shots, rising to a roar. Once or twice flying machines, as they circled warily, came right overhead, and for a time Bert gave himself body and soul to cowering.

Ever and again a larger thunder mingled with the rattle and reminded him of the grapple of airships far above, but the nearer fight held his attention.

Abruptly something dropped from the zenith; something like a barrel or a huge football.

CRASH! It smashed with an immense report. It had fallen among the grounded Asiatic aeroplanes that lay among the turf and flowerbeds near the river. They flew in scraps and fragments, turf, trees and gravel leapt and fell; the aeronauts still lying along the canal bank were thrown about like sacks, catspaws flew across the foaming water. All the windows of the hotel hospital that had been shiningly reflecting blue sky and airships the moment before became vast black stars. Bang! – a second followed. Bert looked up and was filled with a sense of a number of monstrous bodies swooping down, coming down on the whole affair like a flight of bellying blankets, like a string of vast dish-covers. The central tangle of the battle above was circling down as if to come into touch with the powerhouse fight. He got a new effect of airships altogether, as vast things coming down upon him, growing swiftly larger and larger and more overwhelming, until the houses over the way seemed small, the American rapids narrow, the bridge flimsy, the combatants infinitesimal. As they came down they became audible as a complex of shoutings and vast creakings and groanings and beatings and throbbings and shouts and shots. The foreshortened black eagles at the fore-ends of the Germans had an effect of actual combat of flying feathers.

Some of these fighting airships came within five hundred feet of the ground. Bert could see men on the lower galleries of the Germans firing rifles; could see Asiatics clinging to the ropes; saw one man in aluminium diver's gear fall flashing headlong into the waters above Goat Island. For the first time he saw the Asiatic airships closely. From this aspect they reminded him more than anything else of colossal snowshoes; they had a curious patterning in black and white, in forms that reminded him of the engine-turned cover of a watch. They had no hanging galleries, but from little openings on the middle line peeped out men and the muzzles of guns. So, driving in long descending and ascending curves, these monsters wrestled and fought. It was like clouds fighting, like puddings trying to assassinate each other. They whirled and circled about each other, and for a time threw Goat Island and Niagara into a smoky twilight, through which the sunlight smote in shafts and beams. They spread and closed and spread and grappled and drove round over the rapids, and two miles away or more into Canada, and back over the Falls again. A German caught fire, and the whole crowd broke away from her flare and rose about her dispersing, leaving her to drop towards Canada and blow up as she dropped. Then with renewed uproar the others closed again. Once from the men in Niagara city came a sound like an anthill cheering. Another German burnt, and one badly deflated by the prow of an antagonist, flopped out of action southward.

It became more and more evident that the Germans were getting the worst of the unequal fight. More and more obviously were they being persecuted. Less and less did they seem to fight with any object other than escape. The Asiatics swept by them and above them, ripped their bladders, set them alight, picked off their dimly seen men in diving clothes, who struggled against fire and tear with fire extinguishers and silk ribbons in the inner netting. They answered only with ineffectual shots. Thence the battle circled back over Niagara, and then suddenly the Germans, as if at a preconcerted signal, broke and dispersed, going east, west, north and south, in open and confused flight. The Asiatics, as they realized this, rose to fly above them and after them. Only one little knot of four German and perhaps a dozen Asiatics remained fighting about the *Hohenzollern* and the Prince as he circled in a last attempt to save Niagara.

Round they swooped once again over the Canadian Fall, over the waste of waters eastward, until they were distant and small, and then round and back, hurrying, bounding, swooping towards the one gaping spectator.

The whole struggling mass approached very swiftly, growing rapidly larger, and coming out black and featureless against the afternoon sun and above the blinding welter of the Upper Rapids. It grew like a storm cloud until once more it darkened the sky. The flat Asiatic airships kept high above the Germans and behind them, and fired unanswered bullets into their gas- chambers and upon their flanks; the one-man flying machines hovered and alighted like a swarm of attacking bees. Nearer they came and nearer, filling the lower heaven. Two of the Germans swooped and rose again, but the *Hohenzollern* had suffered too much for that. She lifted weakly, turned sharply as if to get out of the battle, burst into flames fore and aft, swept down to the water, splashed into it obliquely and rolled over and over and came downstream rolling and smashing and writhing like a thing alive, halting and then coming on again, with her torn and bent propeller still beating the air. The bursting flames spluttered out again in clouds of steam. It was a disaster gigantic in its dimensions. She lay across the rapids like an island, like tall cliffs, tall cliffs that came rolling, smoking, and crumpling and collapsing, advancing with a sort of fluctuating rapidity upon Bert. One Asiatic airship – it looked to Bert from below like three hundred yards of pavement – whirled back and circled two or three times over that great overthrow, and half a dozen crimson flying machines danced for a moment like great midges in the sunlight before they swept on after their fellows. The rest of the fight had already gone over the island, a wild crescendo of shots and yells and smashing uproar. It was hidden from Bert now by the trees of the island, and forgotten by him in the nearer spectacle of the huge advance of the defeated German airship. Something fell with a mighty smashing and splintering of boughs unheeded behind him.

It seemed for a time that the *Hohenzollern* must needs break her back upon the Parting of the Waters, and then for a time her propeller flopped and frothed in the river and thrust the mass of buckling, crumpled wreckage towards the American shore. Then the sweep of the torrent that foamed down to the American Fall caught her, and in another minute the immense mass of deflating wreckage, with flames spurting out in three new places, had crashed against the bridge that joined Goat Island and Niagara city, and forced a long arm, as it were, in a heaving tangle under the central span. Then the middle chambers blew up with a loud report, and in another moment the bridge had given way and the main bulk of the airship, like some grotesque cripple in rags, staggered, flapping and waving flambeaux, to the crest of the fall and hesitated there and vanished in a desperate suicidal leap.

Its detached fore-end remained jammed against that little island, Green Island it used to be called, which forms the stepping-stone between the mainland and Goat Island's patch of trees.

Bert followed this disaster from the Parting of the Waters to the bridgehead. Then, regardless of cover, regardless of the Asiatic airship hovering like a huge house roof without walls above the Suspension Bridge, he sprinted along towards the north and came out for the first time upon that rocky point by Luna Island that looks sheer down upon the American Fall. There he stood breathless amidst that eternal rush of sound, breathless and staring.

Far below, and travelling rapidly down the gorge, whirled something like a huge empty sack. For him it meant – what did it not mean? – the German air-fleet, Kurt, the Prince, Europe, all things stable and familiar, the forces that had brought him, the forces that had seemed indisputably victorious. And it went down the rapids like an empty sack and left the visible world to Asia, to yellow people beyond Christendom, to all that was terrible and strange!

Remote over Canada receded the rest of that conflict and vanished beyond the range of his vision. . . .

9

On Goat Island

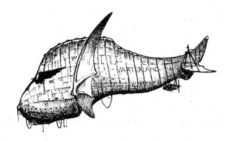

The whack of a bullet on the rocks beside him reminded him that he was a visible object and wearing at least portions of a German uniform. It drove him into the trees again, and for a time he dodged and dropped and sought cover like a chick hiding among reeds from imaginary hawks. 'Beaten,' he whispered. 'Beaten and done for. ... Chinese! Yellow chaps chasing 'em!'

At last he came to rest in a clump of bushes near a locked-up and deserted refreshment shed within view of the American side. They made a sort of hole and harbour for him; they met completely over-head. He looked across the rapids, but the firing had ceased now altogether and everything seemed quiet. The Asiatic aeroplane had moved from its former position above the Suspension Bridge, was motionless now above Niagara city, shadowing all that district about the powerhouse which had been the scene of the land fight. The monster had an air of quiet and assured predominance, and from its stern it trailed, serene and ornamental, a long streaming flag, the red, black and yellow of the great alliance, the Sunrise and the Dragon. Beyond to the east, and at a much higher level, hung a second; and Bert, presently gathering courage, wriggled out and craned his neck to find another still airship against the sunset in the south.

'Gaw!' he said. 'Beaten and chased! My Gawd!'

The fighting, it seemed at first, was quite over in Niagara city, though a German flag was still flying from one shattered house. A white sheet was hoisted above the powerhouse, and this remained flying all through the events that followed. But presently came a sound of shots and then German soldiers running. They disappeared among the houses, and then came two engineers in blue shirts and trousers hotly pursued by three Japanese swordsmen. The foremost of the two fugitives was a shapely man, and ran lightly and well; the second was a sturdy little man, and rather fat. He ran comically in leaps and bounds, with his plump arms bent up by his side and his head thrown back. The pursuers ran with uniforms and dark thin metal and leather headdresses. The little man stumbled, and Bert gasped, realizing a new horror in war.

The foremost swordsman won three strides on him and was near enough to slash at him and miss as he spurted.

A dozen yards they ran, and then the swordsman slashed again, and Bert could hear across the waters a faint sound like the moo of an elfin cow as the fat little man fell forward. Slash went the swordsman and slash at something on the ground that tried to save itself with ineffectual hands. 'Oh I carn't!' cried Bert, near blubbering and staring with starting eyes.

The swordsman slashed a fourth time and went on as his fellows came up after the better runner. The hindmost swordsman stopped and turned back. He had perceived some movement perhaps; but at any rate he stood, and ever and again slashed at the fallen body.

'Oo-oo!' groaned Bert at every slash, and shrank closer into the bushes and became very still. Presently came a sound of shots from the town, and then everything was quiet, everything, even the hospital.

He saw presently little figures sheathing swords come out from the houses and walk to the debris of the flying machines the bomb had destroyed. Others appeared wheeling undamaged aeroplanes upon their wheels as men might wheel bicycles, and sprang into the saddles and flapped into the air. A string of three airships appeared far away in the east and flew towards the zenith. The one that hung low above Niagara city came still lower and dropped a rope ladder to pick up men from the powerhouse.

For a long time he watched the further happenings in Niagara city as a rabbit might watch a meet. He saw men going from building to building to set fire to them, as he presently realized, and he heard a series of dull detonations from the wheel-pit of the powerhouse. Some similar business went on among the works on the Canadian side. Meanwhile more and more airships appeared, and many more flying machines, until at last it seemed to him nearly a third of the Asiatic fleet had reassembled. He watched them from his bush, cramped but immovable, watched them gather and range themselves and signal and pick up men, until at last they sailed away towards the glowing sunset, going to the great Asiatic rendezvous above the oil wells of Cleveland. They dwindled and passed away, leaving him alone, so far as he could tell, the only living man in a world of ruin and strange loneliness almost beyond describing. He watched them recede and vanish. He stood gaping after them.

'Gaw!' he said at last, like one who rouses himself from a trance.

It was far more than any personal desolation and extremity that flooded his soul. It seemed to him indeed that this must be the sunset of his race.

2

He did not at first envisage his own plight in any definite and comprehensible terms. Things had happened to him so much of late, his own efforts had counted for so little, that he had become passive and planless. His last scheme had been to go round the coast of England as a Desert Dervish giving refined entertainment to his fellow creatures. Fate had quashed that. Fate had seen fit to direct him to other destinies, had hurried him from point to point, and dropped him at last upon this little wedge of rock between the cataracts. It did not instantly occur to him that now it was his turn to play. He had a singular feeling that all must end as a dream ends, that presently surely he would be back in the world of Grubb and Edna and Bun Hill, that this roar, this glittering presence of incessant water, would be drawn aside as a curtain is drawn aside after a holiday lantern-show, and old, familiar, customary things reassume their sway. It would be interesting to tell people how he had seen Niagara. And then Kurt's words came into his head: 'People torn away from the people they care for; homes smashed, creatures full of life and memories and peculiar little gifts – torn to pieces, starved and spoilt.' ...

He wondered, half incredulous, if that was indeed true. It was so hard to realize it. Out beyond there was it possible that Tom and Jessica were also in some dire extremity? That the little greengrocer's shop was no longer standing open, with Jessica serving respectfully, warming Tom's ear in sharp asides, or punctually sending out the goods?

He tried to think what day of the week it was, and found he had lost his reckoning. Perhaps it was Sunday. If so were they going to church – or were they hiding perhaps in bushes? What had happened to the landlord, the butcher, and to Butteridge and all those people on Dymchurch beach? Something, he knew, had happened to London –

a bombardment. But who had bombarded? Were Tom and Jessica too being chased by strange brown men with long bare swords and evil eyes? He thought of various possible aspects of affliction, but presently one phase ousted all the others. Were they getting much to eat? The question haunted him, obsessed him.

If one was very hungry would one eat rats?

It dawned upon him that a peculiar misery that oppressed him was not so much anxiety and patriotic sorrow as hunger. Of course he was hungry!

He reflected and turned his steps towards the refreshment shed that stood near the end of the ruined bridge. 'Ought to be somethin'—'

He strolled round it once or twice, and then attacked the shutters with his pocket-knife, reinforced presently by a wooden stake he found conveniently near. At last he got a shutter to give, and tore it back and stuck in his head.

'Grub,' he remarked, 'anyhow. Leastways—'

He got at the inside fastening of the shutter and had presently this establishment open for his exploration. He found several sealed bottles of sterilized milk, much mineral water, two tins of biscuits and a crock of very stale cakes, cigarettes in great quantities but very dry, some rather dry oranges, nuts, some tins of canned meat and fruit, and plates and knives and forks and glasses sufficient for several score of people. There was also a zinc locker, but he was unable to negotiate the padlock of this.

'Shan't starve,' said Bert, 'for a bit, anyhow.' He sat on the vendor's seat and regaled himself with biscuits and milk, and felt for a moment quite contented.

'Quite restful,' he muttered, munching and glancing about him restlessly, 'after what I been through.

'Crikey! *Wot* a day! Oh! *Wot* a day!'

Wonder took possession of him. 'Gaw!' he cried: 'What a fight it's been! Smashing up the poor fellers! 'Eadlong! The airships – the fliers and all. I wonder what happened to the *Zeppelin?* ... And that chap Kurt – I wonder what happened to 'im? 'E was a good sort of chap was Kurt.'

Some phantom of imperial solicitude floated through his mind. 'Injia,' he said. ...

A more practical interest arose.

'I wonder if there's anything to open one of these tins of corned beef?'

After he had feasted, Bert lit a cigarette and sat meditative for a time. 'Wonder where Grubb is,' he said. 'I do wonder that! Wonder if any of 'em wonder about me?'

He reverted to his own circumstances. 'Dessay I shall 'ave to stop on this island for some time.'

He tried to feel at his ease and secure, but presently the indefinable restlessness of the social animal in solitude distressed him. He began to want to look over his shoulder, and, as a corrective, roused himself to explore the rest of the island.

It was only very slowly that he began to realize the peculiarities of his position, to perceive that the breaking down of the arch between Green Island and the mainland had cut him off completely from the world. Indeed it was only when he came back to where the fore-end of the *Hohenzollern* lay like a stranded ship, and was contemplating the shattered bridge, that this dawned upon him. Even then it came with no sort of shock to his mind, a fact among a number of other extraordinary and unmanageable facts. He stared at the shattered cabins of the *Hohenzollern* and its widow's garment of dishevelled silk for a time, but without any idea of its containing any living thing; it was all so twisted and smashed and entirely upside down. Then for a while he gazed at the evening sky. A cloud haze was now appearing and not an airship was in sight. A swallow flew by and snapped some invisible victim. 'Like a dream,' he repeated.

Then for a time the rapids held his mind. 'Roaring. It keeps on roaring and splashin' always and always. Keeps on. . . .'

At last his interests became personal. 'Wonder what I ought to do now?'

He reflected. 'Not an idee,' he said.

He was chiefly conscious that a fortnight ago he had been in Bun Hill with no idea of travel in his mind, and that now he was between the Falls of Niagara amidst the devastation and ruins of the greatest air fight in the world, and that in the interval he had been across France, Belgium, Germany, England, Ireland and a number of other countries. It was an interesting thought and suitable for conversation, but of no great practical utility. 'Wonder 'ow I can get orf this?' he said. 'Wonder if there is a way out? If not . . . rummy!'

Further reflection decided, 'I believe I got myself in a bit of a 'ole coming over that bridge. . . .

'Any'ow – got me out of the way of them Japanesy chaps. Wouldn't 'ave taken 'em long to cut my froat. No. Still—'

He resolved to return to the point of Luna Island. For a long time he stood without stirring, scrutinizing the Canadian shore and the wreckage of hotels and houses and the fallen trees of the Victoria Park, pink now in the light of sundown. Not a human being was perceptible in that scene of headlong destruction. Then he came back to the American side of the island, crossed close to the crumpled aluminium wreckage of the *Hohenzollern* to Green Island, and scrutinized the hopeless breach in the further bridge and the water that boiled beneath it. Towards Buffalo there was still much smoke, and near the position of the Niagara railway station the houses were burning vigorously. Everything was deserted now, everything was still. One little abandoned thing lay on a transverse path between town and road, a crumpled heap of clothes with sprawling limbs. . . .

''Ave a look round,' said Bert, and taking a path that ran through the middle of the island he presently discovered the wreckage of the two Asiatic aeroplanes that had fallen out of the struggle that ended the *Hohenzollern.*

With the first he found the wreckage of an aeronaut, too.

The machine had evidently dropped vertically and was badly knocked about amidst a lot of smashed branches in a clump of trees. Its bent and broken wings and shattered stays sprawled amidst new splintered wood, and its forepeak stuck into the ground. The aeronaut dangled weirdly head downward among the leaves and branches some yards away, and Bert only discovered him as he turned from the aeroplane. In the dusky evening light and stillness – for the sun had gone now and the wind had altogether fallen – this inverted yellow face was anything but a tranquillizing object to discover suddenly a couple of yards away. A broken branch had run clean through the man's thorax, and he hung, so stabbed, looking limp and absurd. In his hand he still clutched, with the grip of death, a short light rifle.

For some time Bert stood very still, inspecting this thing.

Then he began to walk away from it, looking constantly back at it. Presently in an open glade he came to a stop.

'Gaw!' he whispered, 'I don't like dead bodies some'ow! I'd almost rather that chap was alive.'

He would not go along the path athwart which the Chinaman hung. He felt he would rather not have trees round him any more, and that it would be more comfortable to be quite close to the sociable splash and uproar of the rapids.

He came upon the second aeroplane in a clear grassy space by the side of the streaming water, and it seemed scarcely damaged at all. It looked as though it had floated down into a position of rest. It lay on its side with one wing in the air. There was no aeronaut near it, dead or alive. There it lay abandoned, with the water lapping about its long tail.

Bert remained a little aloof from it for a long time, looking into the gathering shadows among the trees, in the expectation of another Chinaman alive or dead. Then very cautiously he approached the machine and stood regarding its widespread vans, its big steering wheel and empty saddle. He did not venture to touch it.

'I wish that other chap wasn't there,' he said. 'I do wish 'e wasn't there!'

He saw, a few yards away, something bobbing about in an eddy that spun within a projecting head of rock. As it went round it seemed to draw him unwillingly towards it. . . .

What could it be?

'Blow!' said Bert. 'It's another of 'em.'

It held him. He told himself that it was the other aeronaut that had been shot in the fight and fallen out of the saddle as he strove to land. He tried to go away, and then it occurred to him that he might get a branch or something and push this rotating object out into the stream. That would leave him with only one dead body to worry about. Perhaps he might get along with one. He hesitated, and then with a certain emotion forced himself to do this. He went towards the bushes and cut himself a wand and returned to the rocks and clambered out to a corner between the eddy and the stream. By that time the sunset was over and the bats were abroad, and he was wet with perspiration.

He prodded the floating blue-clad thing with his wand, failed, tried again successfully as it came round, and as it went out into the stream it turned over, the light gleamed on golden hair, and – it was Kurt!

It was Kurt, white and dead and very calm. There was no mistaking him. There was still plenty of light for that. The stream took him and he seemed to compose himself in its swift grip as one who stretches himself to rest. Whitefaced he was now, and all the colour gone out of him.

A feeling of infinite distress swept over Bert as the body swept out of sight towards the fall. 'Kurt!' he cried. 'Kurt! I didn't mean to! Kurt! don' leave me 'ere! Don' leave me!'

Loneliness and desolation overwhelmed him. He gave way. He stood on the rock in the evening light, weeping and wailing passionately like a child. It was as though some link that had held him to all these things had broken and gone. He was afraid like a child in a lonely room, shamelessly afraid.

The twilight was closing about him. The trees were full now of strange shadows. All the things about him became strange and unfamiliar with that subtle queerness one feels oftenest in dreams. 'O God! I carn't stand this,' he said, and crept back from the rocks to the grass and crouched down, and suddenly wild sorrow for the death of Kurt, Kurt the brave, Kurt the kindly, came to his help, and he broke from whimpering to weeping. He ceased to crouch; he sprawled upon the grass and clenched an impotent fist.

'This war,' he cried, 'this blarsted foolery of a war.

'O Kurt! Lieutenant Kurt!

'I done,' he said: 'I done. I've 'ad all I want, and more than I want. The world's all rot, and there ain't no sense in it. The night's coming. ... If 'E comes after me— 'E can't come after me— 'E can't! ...

'If 'E comes after me, I'll fro' myself into the water.' ...

Presently he was talking again in a low undertone.

'There ain't nothing to be afraid of reely. It's jest imagination. Poor old Kurt – he thought it would happen. Prevision like. 'E never gave me that letter or tole me who the lady was. It's like what 'e said – people tore away from everything they belonged to – everywhere. Exactly like what 'e said. ... 'Ere I am cast away – thousand of miles from Edna or Grubb or any of my lot – like a plant tore up by the roots. ... And every war's been like this, only I 'adn't the sense to understand it. Always. All sorts of 'oles and corners chaps 'ave died in. And people 'adn't the sense to understand, 'adn't the sense to feel it and stop it. Thought war was fine. My Gawd! ...

'Dear old Edna. She was a fair bit of all right – she was. That time we 'ad a boat at Kingston. ...

'I bet – I'll see 'er again yet. Won't be my fault if I don't.' ...

4

Suddenly, on the very verge of this heroic resolution, Bert became rigid with terror. Something was creeping towards him through the grass. Something was creeping and halting and creeping again towards him through the dim, dark grass. The night was electrical with horror. For a time everything was still. Bert ceased to breathe. It could not be. No, it was too small!

It advanced suddenly upon him with a rush, with a little meawling cry and tail erect. It rubbed its head against him and purred. It was a tiny, skinny little kitten.

'Gaw, pussy! 'ow you frightened me!' said Bert, with drops of perspiration on his brow.

5

He sat with his back to a tree stump all that night, holding the kitten in his arms. His mind was tired, and he talked or thought coherently no longer. Towards dawn he dozed.

When he awoke he was stiff but in better heart, and the kitten slept warmly and reassuringly inside his jacket. And fear, he found, had gone from amidst the trees.

He stroked the kitten, and the little creature woke up to excessive fondness and purring. 'You want some milk,' said Bert. 'That's what you want. And I could do with a bit of brekker too.'

He yawned and stood up, with the kitten on his shoulder, and started about him, recalling the circumstances of the previous day, the grey, immense happenings.

'Mus' do something,' he said.

He turned towards the trees, and was presently contemplating the dead aeronaut again. The kitten he held companionably against his neck. The body was horrible, but not nearly so horrible as it had been at twilight, and now the limbs were limper and the gun had slipped to the ground and lay half hidden in the grass.

'I suppose we ought to bury 'im, Kitty,' said Bert, and looked helplessly at the rocky soil about him. 'We got to stay on the island with 'im.'

It was some time before he could turn away and go on towards that provision shed. 'Brekker first,' he said, 'anyhow,' stroking the kitten on his shoulder. She rubbed his cheek affectionately with her furry little face and presently nibbled at his ear. 'Wan' some milk, eh?' he said, and turned his back on the dead man as though he mattered nothing.

He was puzzled to find the door of the shed open, though he had closed and latched it very carefully overnight, and he found also some dirty plates he had not noticed before on the bench. He discovered that the hinges of the tin locker were unscrewed and that it could be opened. He had not observed this overnight.

'Silly of me!' said Bert. ''Ere I was puzzlin' and whackin' away at the padlock, never noticing.' It had been used apparently as an ice-chest, but it contained nothing now but the remains of half a dozen boiled chickens, some ambiguous substance that might once have been butter, and a singularly unappetizing smell. He closed the lid again carefully.

He gave the kitten some milk in a dirty plate and sat watching its busy little tongue for a time. Then he was moved to make an inventory of the provisions. There were six bottles of milk unopened and one opened, sixty bottles of mineral water and a large stock of syrups, about two thousand cigarettes and upward of a hundred cigars, nine oranges, two unopened tins of corned beef and one opened, two tins of biscuits and eleven hard cakes, a hatful of nuts and five large tins of Californian peaches. He jotted it down on a piece of paper. "Ain't much solid food,' he said. 'Still— A fortnight, say!

'Anything might happen in a fortnight.'

He gave the kitten a small second helping and a scrap of beef and then went down with the little creature running after him, tail erect and in high spirits, to look at the remains of the *Hohenzollern*. It had shifted in the night and seemed on the whole more firmly grounded on Green Island than before. From it his eye went to the shattered bridge and then across to the still desolation of Niagara city. Nothing moved over there but a number of crows. They were busy with the engineer he had seen cut down on the previous day. He saw no dogs, but he heard one howling.

'We got to get out of this some'ow, Kitty,' he said. 'That milk won't last for ever – not at the rate you lap it.'

He regarded the sluice-like flood before him. 'Plenty of water,' he said. 'Won't be drink we shall want.'

He decided to make a careful exploration of the island. Presently he came to a locked gate labelled 'Biddle Stairs', and clambered over to discover a steep old wooden staircase leading down the face of the cliff amidst a vast and increasing uproar of waters. He left the kitten above and descended these, and discovered with a thrill of hope a path leading among the rocks at the foot of the roaring downrush of the centre fall. Perhaps this was a sort of way!

It led him only to the choking and deafening experience of the Cave of the Winds, and after he had spent a quarter of an hour in a partially stupefied condition flattened between solid rock and nearly as solid waterfall, he decided that this was after all no practicable route to Canada, and retraced his steps. As he reascended the Biddle Stairs, he heard what he decided at last must be a sort of echo, a sound of someone walking about on the gravel paths above. When he got to the top the place was as solitary as before.

Thence he made his way, with the kitten skirmishing along beside him in the grass, to a staircase that led to a lump of projecting rock that enfiladed the huge green majesty of the Horseshoe Fall. He stood there for some time in silence.

'You wouldn't think,' he said at last, 'there was so much water. . . . This roarin' and splashin', it gets on your nerves. . . . Sounds like people

779

talking. .... Sounds like people going about. .... Sounds like anything you fancy.'

He retired up the staircase again. 'I s'pose I shall keep on goin' round this blessed island,' he said drearily. 'Round and round and round.'

He found himself presently beside the less damaged Asiatic aeroplane again. He stared at it and the kitten smelt it. 'Broke!' he said.

He looked up with a convulsive start.

Advancing slowly towards him out from among the trees were two tall, gaunt figures. They were blackened and tattered and bandaged; the hindmost one limped and had his head swathed in white, but the foremost one still carried himself as a Prince should do, for all that his left arm was in a sling and one side of his face scalded a livid crimson. He was the Prince Karl Albert, the War Lord, the 'German Alexander', and the man behind him was the bird-faced man whose cabin had once been taken from him and given to Bert.

6

With that apparition began a new phase of Goat Island in Bert's experience. He ceased to be a solitary representative of humanity in a vast and violent and incomprehensible universe, and became once more a social creature, a man in a world of other men. For an instant these two were terrible, then they seemed sweet and desirable as brothers. They too were in this scrape with him, marooned and puzzled. He wanted extremely to hear exactly what had happened to them. What mattered it, if one was a Prince and both were foreign soldiers, if neither perhaps had adequate English? His native Cockney freedom flowed too generously for him to think of that, and surely the Asiatic fleets had purged all such trivial differences. "Ul-*lo!*' he said; "ow did you get 'ere?'

'It is the Englishman who brought us the Butteridge machine,' said the bird-faced officer in German, and then in a tone of horror as Bert advanced, 'Salute!' and again louder, '*Salute!*'

'Gaw!' said Bert, and stopped with a second comment under his breath. He started and saluted awkwardly and became at once a masked defensive thing with whom co-operation was impossible.

For a time these two perfected modern aristocrats stood regarding the difficult problem of the Anglo-Saxon citizen, that ambiguous citizen who, obeying some mysterious law in his blood, would neither drill nor be a democrat. Bert was by no means a beautiful object, but in some inexplicable way he looked resistant. He wore his cheap suit of serge, now showing many signs of wear, and its loose fit made him seem sturdier than he was; above his disengaging face was a white German cap that was altogether too big for him, and his trousers were crumpled up his legs and their ends tucked into the rubber highlows of a deceased German aeronaut. He looked an inferior, though by no means an easy inferior, and instinctively they hated him.

The Prince pointed to the flying-machine and said something in broken English that Bert took for German and failed to understand. He intimated as much.

'Dummer Kerl! said the bird-faced officer from among his bandages.

The Prince pointed again with his undamaged hand. 'You understan' dis *Drachenflieger?*'

Bert began to comprehend the situation. He regarded the Asiatic machine. The habits of Bun Hill returned to him. 'It's a foreign make,' he said ambiguously.

The two Germans consulted. 'You are – an expert?' said the Prince.

'We reckon to repair,' said Bert, in the exact manner of Grubb.

The Prince sought in his vocabulary. 'Is dat,' he said, 'goot to fly?'

Bert reflected, and scratched his chin slowly. 'I got to look at it,' he replied. . . . 'It's 'ad rough usage!'

He made a sound with his teeth he had also acquired from Grubb, put his hands in his trouser pockets and strolled back to the machine. Typically Grubb chewed something, but Bert could chew only imaginatively. 'Three days' work in this,' he said, teething. For the first time it dawned on him that there were possibilities in this machine. It was evident that the wing that lay on the ground was disabled. The three stays that held it rigid had snapped across a ridge of rock, and there was also a strong possibility of the engine being badly damaged. The wing hook on that side was also askew, but probably that would not affect the flight. Beyond that there probably wasn't much the matter. Bert scratched his cheek again, and contemplated the broad sunlit waste of the Upper Rapids. 'We might make a job of this. . . . You leave it to me.'

He surveyed it intently again, and the Prince and his officer watched him. In Bun Hill Bert and Grubb had developed to a very high pitch among the hiring stock a method of repair by substitution; they substituted bits of other machines. A machine that was too utterly and obviously done for even to proffer for hire had nevertheless still capital value. It became a sort of quarry for nuts and screws and wheels, bars and spokes, chain-links and the like; a mine of ill-fitting 'parts' to replace the defects of machines still current. And back among the trees was a second Asiatic aeroplane.

The kitten caressed Bert's airship boots unheeded.

'Mend dat *Drachenflieger*,' said the Prince.

'If I do mend it,' said Bert, struck by a new thought, 'none of us ain't to be trusted to fly it.'

'*I* vill fly it,' said the Prince.

'Very likely break your neck,' said Bert, after a pause.

The Prince did not understand him and disregarded what he said. He pointed his gloved finger to the machine and turned to the bird-faced officer with some remark in German. The officer answered and the Prince responded with a sweeping gesture towards the sky. Then he spoke – it seemed eloquently. Bert watched him and guessed his meaning. 'Much more likely to break your neck,' he said: ''Owever. 'Ere goes.'

He began to pry about the saddle and engine of the *Drachenflieger* in a search for tools. Also he wanted some black oily stuff for his hands and face. For the first rule in the art of repairing as it was known to the firm of Grubb and Smallways was to get your hands and face thoroughly and conclusively blackened. Also he took off his jacket and waistcoat and put his cap carefully to the back of his head in order to facilitate scratching.

The Prince and the officer seemed disposed to watch him, but he succeeded in making it clear to them that this would inconvenience him and that he had to 'puzzle out a bit' before he could get to work. They thought him over, but his shop experience had given him something of the authoritative way of the expert with common men. And at last they went away. Thereupon he went straight to the second aeroplane, got the aeronaut's gun and ammunition and hid them in a clump of nettles close at hand. 'That's all right,' said Bert, and then proceeded to a careful inspection of the debris of the wings in the trees. Then he went back to the first aeroplane to compare the two. The Bun Hill method was quite possibly practicable if there was nothing hopeless or incomprehensible in the engine.

The Germans returned presently to find him already generously smutty and touching and testing knobs and screws and levers with an expression of profound sagacity. When the bird-faced officer addressed a remark to him he waved him aside with, 'Nong comprong. Shut it! It's no good.'

Then he had an idea. 'Dead chap back there wants burying,' he said, jerking a thumb over his shoulder.

7

With the appearance of these two men Bert's whole universe had changed again. A curtain fell before the immense and terrible desolation that had overwhelmed him. He was in a world of three people, a minute human world that nevertheless filled his brain with eager speculations and schemes and cunning ideas. What were they thinking of? What did they think of him? What did they mean to do? A hundred busy threads interlaced in his mind as he pottered studiously over the Asiatic aeroplane. New ideas came up like bubbles in soda water.

'Gaw!' he said suddenly. He had just appreciated as a special aspect of this irrational injustice of fate that these two men were alive and that Kurt was dead. All the crew of the *Hohenzollern* were shot or burnt or smashed or drowned, and these two lurking in the padded forward cabin had escaped.

'I suppose 'e thinks it's 'is bloomin' Star,' he muttered, and found himself uncontrollably exasperated.

He stood up, facing round to the two men. They were standing side by side regarding him. 'It's no good,' he said, 'starin' at me. You only put me out.' And then seeing they did not understand, he advanced towards them, wrench in hand. It occurred to him as he did so that the Prince was really a very big and powerful and serene-looking person. But he said, nevertheless, pointing through the trees, 'Dead man!'

The bird-faced man intervened with a reply in German.

'Dead man!' said Bert to him. 'There.'

He had great difficulty in inducing them to inspect the dead Chinaman, and at last led them to him. Then they made it evident that they proposed that he, as a common person below the rank of officer, should have the sole and undivided privilege of disposing of the body by dragging it to the water's edge. There was some heated gesticulation, and at last the bird-faced officer abased himself to help. Together they dragged the limp and now swollen Asiatic through the trees, and after a rest or so – for he trailed very heavily – dumped him into the westward rapid. Bert returned to his expert investigation of the flying machine at last with aching arms and in a state of gloomy rebellion. 'Brasted cheek!' he said. 'One'd think I was one of 'is beastly German slaves!

'Prancing beggar!'

And then he fell speculating what would happen when the flying machine was repaired – if it could be repaired.

The two Germans went away again, and after some reflection Bert removed several nuts, resumed his jacket and vest, pocketed those nuts and his tools and hid the set of tools from the second aeroplane in the fork of a tree. 'Right O,' he said, as he jumped down after the last of these precautions. The Prince and his companion reappeared as he returned to the machine by the water's edge. The Prince surveyed his progress for a time, and then went towards the Parting of the Waters and stood with folded arms gazing upstream in profound thought. The bird-faced officer came up to Bert, heavy with a sentence in English.

'Go,' he said with a helping gesture, 'und eat.'

When Bert got to the refreshment shed he found all the food had vanished except one measured ration of corned beef and three biscuits. He regarded this with open eyes and mouth. The kitten appeared from under the vendor's seat with an ingratiating purr. 'Of course!' said Bert. 'Why! Where's your milk?'

He accumulated wrath for a moment or so, then seized the plate in one hand, and the biscuits in another, and went in search of the Prince, breathing vile words anent 'grub' and his intimate interior. He approached without saluting.

''Ere!' he said fiercely. 'Whad the devil's this?'

An entirely unsatisfactory altercation followed. Bert expounded the Bun Hill theory of the relations of grub to efficiency in English, the bird-faced man replied with points about nations and discipline in German. The Prince, having made an estimate of Bert's quality and physique, suddenly hectored. He gripped Bert by the shoulder and shook him, making his pockets rattle, shouted something to him, and flung him struggling back. He hit him as though he was a German private. Bert went back, white and scared, but resolved by all his Cockney standards upon one thing. He was bound in honour to 'go for' the Prince. 'Gaw!' he gasped, buttoning his coat.

'Now,' cried the Prince, 'vill you go!' and then, catching the heroic gleam in Bert's eyes, drew his sword.

The bird-faced officer intervened, saying something in German and pointing skyward.

Far away in the south-west appeared a Japanese airship coming fast towards them. Their conflict ended at that. The Prince was first to grasp the situation and lead the retreat. All three scuttled like rabbits for the trees, and ran to and fro for cover until they found a hollow in which the grass grew rank. There they all squatted within six yards of one another. They sat in this place for a long time, up to their necks in the grass and watching through the branches for the airship. Bert had dropped some of his corned beef, but he found the biscuits in his hand and ate them quietly. The monster came nearly overhead and then went away to Niagara and dropped beyond the power works. When it was near they all kept silence, and then presently they fell into an argument that was robbed perhaps of immediate explosive effect only by their failure to understand one another.

It was Bert began the talking, and he talked on, regardless of what they understood or failed to understand. But his voice must have conveyed his cantankerous intentions.

'You want that machine done,' he said first, 'you better keep your 'ands off me!'

They disregarded that and he repeated it.

Then he expanded his idea, and the spirit of speech took hold of him. 'You think you got 'old of a chap you can kick and 'it like you do your private soldiers – you're jolly well mistaken. See? I've 'ad about enough of you and your antics. I been thinking you over, you and your war and your Empire, and all the rot of it. Rot it is. It's you Germans made all the trouble in Europe first and last. And all for nothin'. Jest silly prancing! Jest because you've got the uniforms and flags! 'Ere I was – didn't want to 'ave anything to do with you. I jest didn't care a 'eng at all about you. Then you get 'old of me – steal me practically – and 'ere I am, thousands of miles away from 'ome and everything, and all your silly fleet smashed up to rags. And you want to go on prancin' *now!* Not if I know it!

'Look at the mischief you done. Look at the way you smashed up New York – the people you killed, the stuff you wasted. Can't you learn?'

'Dummer Kerl!' said the bird-faced man suddenly, in a tone of concentrated malignity, glaring under his bandages. 'Esel!'

'That's German for silly ass! I know. But who's the silly ass – 'im or me? When I was a kid I used to read penny dreadfuls about 'aving adventures and being a great c'mander and all that rot. I stowed it. But what's 'e got in 'is 'ead? Rot about Napoleon, rot about Alexander, rot about 'is blessed family and 'im and Gawd and David and all that. Anyone who wasn't a dressed-up silly fool of a Prince could 'ave told all this was goin' to 'appen. There was us in Europe all at sixes and sevens with our silly flags and our silly newspapers raggin' us up against each other and keepin' us apart, and there was China as solid as a cheese, with millions and millions of men only wantin' a bit of science, and a bit of enterprise, to be as good as all of us. You thought they couldn't get at you. And then they got flying machines. And bif! –'ere we are. Why, when they didn't go on making guns and armies in China we went and poked 'em up until they did. They *'ad* to give us this lickin' they've give us. We wouldn't be 'appy till they did. And, as I say, 'ere we are!'

The bird-faced officer shouted to him to be quiet, and then began a conversation with the Prince.

'British citizen,' said Bert. 'You ain't obliged to listen, but I ain't obliged to shut up.' And for some time he continued his dissertation upon Imperialism, militarism and international politics. But their talking put him out, and for a time he was merely repeating abusive terms, 'prancin' nincompoops' and the like, old terms and new.

Then suddenly he remembered his essential grievance. "Owever, look 'ere – 'ere! – the thing I started this talk about is where's that food there was in that shed? That's what I want to know. Where you put it?'

He paused. They went on talking in German. He repeated his question. They disregarded him. He asked a third time in a manner insupportably aggressive.

There fell a tense silence. For some seconds the three regarded one another. The Prince eyed Bert steadfastly, and Bert quailed under his eye. Slowly the Prince rose to his feet and the bird-faced officer jerked up beside him Bert remained squatting.

'Be quaiat,' said the Prince.

Bert perceived this was no moment for eloquence.

The two Germans regarded him as he crouched there. Death for a moment seemed near.

Then the Prince turned away and the two of them went towards the flying machine.

'Gaw!' whispered Bert, and then uttered under his breath one single word of abuse. He sat crouched together for perhaps three minutes, then he sprang to his feet and went off towards the Chinese aeronaut's gun hidden among the weeds.

8

There was no pretence after that moment that Bert was under the orders of the Prince or that he was going on with the repairing of the flying machine. The two Germans took possession of that and set to work upon it. Bert, with his new weapon, went off to the neigh- bourhood of Terrapin Rock, and there sat down to examine it. It was a short rifle with a big cartridge and a nearly full magazine. He took out the cartridges carefully and then tried the trigger and fittings until he felt sure he had the use of it. He reloaded carefully. Then he remembered he was hungry and went off, gun under his arm, to hunt in and about the refreshment shed. He had the sense to perceive that he must not show himself with the gun to the Prince and his companion. So long as they thought him unarmed they would leave him alone, but there was no knowing what the Napoleonic person might do if he saw Bert's weapon. Also he did not go near them because he knew that within himself boiled a reservoir of rage and fear, that he wanted to shoot these two men. He wanted to shoot them, and he thought that to shoot them would be a quite horrible thing to do. The two sides of his inconsistent civilization warred within him.

Near the shed the kitten turned up again, obviously keen for milk. This greatly enhanced his own angry sense of hunger. He began to talk as he hunted about, and presently stood still shouting insults. He talked of war and pride and Imperialism. 'Any other Prince but you would have died with his men and his ship!' he cried.

The two Germans at the machine heard his voice going ever and again amidst the clamour of the waters. Their eyes met and they smiled slightly.

He was disposed for a time to sit in the refreshment shed waiting for them, but then it occurred to him that so he might get them both at close quarters. He strolled off presently to the point of Luna Island to think the situation out.

It had seemed a comparatively simple one at first, but as he turned it over in his mind its possibilities increased and multiplied. Both these men had swords – had either a revolver?

Also if he shot them both he might never find the food!

So far he had been going about with his gun under his arm and a sense of lordly security in his mind, but what if they saw the gun and decided to ambush him? Goat Island is nearly all cover, trees, rocks, thickets and irregularities.

Why not go and murder them both now?

'I carn't,' said Bert, dismissing that. 'I got to be worked up.'

But it was a mistake to get right away from them. That suddenly became clear. He ought to keep them under observation, ought to 'scout' them. Then he would be able to see what they were doing, whether either of them had a revolver, where they had hidden the food. He would be better able to determine what they meant to do to him. If he didn't 'scout' them, presently they would begin to 'scout' him. This seemed so eminently reasonable that he acted upon it forthwith. He thought over his costume and threw his collar and the telltale aeronaut's white cap into the water far below. He turned his coat collar up to hide any gleam of his dirty shirt. The tools and nuts in his pockets were disposed to clank, but he rearranged them and wrapped some letters and his pocket-handkerchief about them He started off circumspectly and noiselessly, listening and peering at every step. As he drew near his antagonists, much grunting and creaking served to locate them. He discovered them engaged in what looked like a wrestling match with the Asiatic flying machine. Their coats were off, their swords laid aside, they were working magnificently. Apparently they were turning it round and were having a good deal of difficulty with the long tail among the trees. He dropped flat at the sight of them and wriggled into a little hollow, and so lay watching their exertions. Ever and again, to pass the time, he would cover one or other of them with his gun.

He found them quite interesting to watch, so interesting that at times he came near shouting advice to them. He perceived that when they had the machine turned round they would then be in immediate want of the nuts and tools he carried. Then they would come after him. They would certainly conclude he had them or had hidden them. Should he hide his gun and do a deal for food with these tools? He felt he would not be able to part with the gun again now he had once felt its reassuring company. The kitten turned up and made a great fuss with him and licked and bit his ear.

The sun clambered to midday, and once that morning he saw, though the Germans did not, an Asiatic airship very far to the south, going swiftly eastward.

At last the flying machine was turned and stood poised on its wheels, with its hooks pointing up the rapids. The two Germans wiped their faces, resumed jackets and swords, spoke and bore themselves like men who congratulated themselves on a good laborious morning. Then they went off briskly towards the refreshment shed, the Prince leading. Bert became active in pursuit; but he found it impossible to stalk them quickly enough and silently enough to discover the hiding-place of the food. He found them, when he came into sight of them again, seated with their backs against the shed, plates on knee, and a tin of corned beef and a plateful of biscuits between them. They seemed in fairly good spirits, and once the Prince laughed. At this vision of eating Bert's plans gave way. Fierce hunger carried him. He appeared before them suddenly at a distance of perhaps twenty yards gun in hand. "Ands up!' he said in a hard, ferocious voice.

The Prince hesitated, and then up went two pairs of hands. The gun had surprised them both completely.

'Stand up,' said Bert. . . . 'Drop that fork!'

They obeyed again.

'What nex'?' said Bert to himself. ''Orf stage I suppose. That way,' he said. 'Go!'

The Prince obeyed with remarkable alacrity. When he reached the head of the clearing he said something quickly to the bird-faced man and they both, with an entire lack of dignity, *ran*!

Bert was struck with an exasperating afterthought.

'Gord!' he cried with infinite vexation. 'Why! I ought to 'ave took their swords! 'Ere!'

But the Germans were already out of sight, and no doubt taking cover among the trees. Bert fell back upon imprecations, then he went up to the shed, cursorily examined the possibility of a flank attack, put his gun handy and set to work, with a convulsive listening pause before each mouthful, on the Prince's plate of corned beef. He had finished that up and handed its gleanings to the kitten and he was falling-to on the second plateful, when the plate broke in his hand! He stared, with the fact slowly creeping upon him that an instant before he had heard a crack among the thickets. Then he sprang to his feet, snatched up his gun in one hand and the tin of corned beef in the other, and fled round the shed to the other side of the clearing. As he did so came a second crack from the thickets, and something went *phwit!* by his ear.

He didn't stop running until he was in what seemed to him a strongly defensible position near Luna Island. Then he took cover, panting, and crouched expectant.

'They got a revolver after all!' he panted. .... 'Wonder if they got two? If they 'ave – Gord! – I'm done!'

'Where's the kitten? Finishin' up that corned beef, I suppose. Little beggar!'

9

So it was that war began upon Goat Island. It lasted a day and a night, the longest day and the longest night in Bert's life. He had to lie close and listen and watch. Also he had to scheme what he should do. It was clear now that he had to kill these two men if he could, and that if they could they would kill him. The prize was first food and then the flying machine, and the doubtful privilege of trying to ride it. If one failed one would certainly be killed, if one succeeded one would get away somewhere over there. For a time Bert tried to imagine what it was like over there. His mind ran over possibilities, deserts, angry Americans, Japanese, Chinese – perhaps Red Indians! (Were there still Red Indians?)

'Got to take what comes,' said Bert. 'No way out of it that I can see!'

Was that voices? He realized that his attention was wandering. For a time all his senses were alert. The uproar of the falls was very confusing, and it mixed in all sorts of sounds, like feet walking, like voices talking, like shouts and cries.

'Silly great catarac',' said Bert. 'There ain't no sense in it, fallin' and fallin'.'

Never mind that now! What were the Germans doing?

Would they go back to the flying machine? They couldn't do anything with it, because he had those nuts and screws and the wrench and other tools. But suppose they found the second set of tools he had hidden in a tree! He had hidden the things well, of course, but they *might* find them. One wasn't sure, of course – one wasn't sure. He tried to remember just exactly how he had hidden those tools. He tried to persuade himself they were certainly and surely hidden, but his memory began to play antics. Had he really left the handle of the wrench sticking out, shining out at the fork of the branch?

Ssh! What was that? Someone stirring in those bushes? Up went an expectant muzzle. No! Where was the kitten? No! It was just imagination, not even the kitten.

The Germans would certainly miss and hunt about for the tools and nuts and screws he carried in his pockets; that was clear. Then they would decide he had them and come for him. He had only to remain still under cover, therefore, and he would get them. Was there any flaw in that? Would they take off more removable parts of the flying machine and then lie up for him? No, they wouldn't do that, because they were two to one; they would have no apprehension of his getting off in the flying machine, and no sound reason for supposing he would approach it, and so they would do nothing to damage or disable it. That, he decided, was clear. But suppose they lay up for him by the food. Well, that they wouldn't do, because they would know he had this corned beef; there was enough in this can to last, with moderation, several days. Of course they might try to tire him out instead of attacking him—

He roused himself with a start. He had just grasped the real weakness of his position. He might go to sleep!

It needed but ten minutes under the suggestion of that idea before he realized that he was going to sleep!

He rubbed his eyes and handled his gun. He had never before realized the intensely soporific effect of the American sun, of the American air, the drowsy, sleep-compelling uproar of Niagara.

Hitherto these things had on the whole seemed stimulating. . . .

If he had not eaten so much and eaten it so fast, he would not be so heavy. Are vegetarians always bright? . . .

He roused himself with a jerk again.

If he didn't do something he would fall asleep, and if he fell asleep it was ten to one they would find him snoring, and finish him forthwith. If he sat motionless and noiseless he would inevitably sleep. It was better, he told himself, to take even the risks of attacking than that. This sleep trouble, he felt, was going to beat him, must beat him in the end. They were all right; one could sleep and the other could watch. That, come to think of it, was what they would always do; one would do anything they wanted done, the other would lie under cover near at hand, ready to shoot. They might even trap him like that. One might act as a decoy.

That set him thinking of decoys. What a fool he had been to throw his cap away. It would have been invaluable on a stick – especially at, night.

He found himself wishing for a drink. He settled that for a time by putting a pebble in his mouth. And then the sleep craving returned.

It became clear to him he must attack.

Like many great generals before him, he found his baggage, that is to say his tin of corned beef, a serious impediment to mobility. At last he decided to put the beef loose in his pocket and abandon the tin. It was not perhaps an ideal arrangement, but one must make sacrifices when one is campaigning. He crawled perhaps ten yards, and then for a time the possibilities of the situation paralysed him.

The afternoon was still. The roar of the cataract simply threw up that immense stillness in relief. He was doing his best to contrive the deaths of two better men than himself. Also they were doing their best to contrive his. What, behind this silence, were they doing?

Suppose he came upon them suddenly and fired and missed?

10

He crawled, and halted listening, and crawled again until nightfall, and no doubt the German Alexander and his lieutenant did the same. A large-scale map of Goat Island marked with red and blue lines to show these strategic movements would no doubt have displayed much interlacing, but as a matter of fact neither side saw anything of the other throughout that age-long day of tedious alertness. Bert never knew how near he got to them nor how far he kept from them. Night found him no longer sleepy, but athirst, and near the American Fall.

He was inspired by the idea that his antagonists might be in the wreckage of the *Hohenzollern* cabins that was jammed against Green Island. He became enterprising, broke from any attempt to conceal himself, and went across the little bridge at the double. He found nobody. It was his first visit to these huge fragments of airship, and for a time he explored them curiously in the dim light. He discovered the forward cabin was nearly intact, with its door slanting downward and a corner under water. He crept in, drank, and then was struck by the brilliant idea of shutting the door and sleeping on it.

But now he could not sleep at all.

He nodded towards morning and woke up to find it fully day. He breakfasted on corned beef and water, and sat for a long time appreciative of the security of his position. At last he became enterprising and bold. He would, he decided, settle this business forthwith, one way or the other. He was tired of all this crawling. He set out in the morning sunshine, gun in hand, scarcely troubling to walk softly. He went round the refreshment shed without finding anyone, and then through the trees towards the flying machine. He came upon the bird-faced man sitting on the ground with his back against a tree, bent up over his folded arms, sleeping, his bandage very much over one eye.

Bert stopped abruptly and stood perhaps fifteen yards away, gun in hand ready. Where was the Prince? Then, sticking out at the side of the tree beyond, he saw a shoulder. Bert took five deliberate paces to the left. The great man became visible, leaning up against the trunk, pistol in one hand and sword in the other, and yawning – yawning. You can't shoot a yawning man, Bert found. He advanced upon his antagonist with his gun levelled, some foolish fancy of 'hands up!' in his mind. The Prince became aware of him, the yawning mouth shut like a trap, and he stood stiffly up. Bert stopped, silent. For a moment the two regarded one another.

Had the Prince been a wise man he would, I suppose, have dodged behind the tree. Instead, he gave vent to a shout, and raised pistol and sword. At that, like an automaton, Bert pulled his trigger.

It was his first experience of an oxygen-containing bullet. A great flame spurted from the middle of the Prince, a blinding flare, and there came a thud like the firing of a gun. Something hot and wet struck Bert's face. Then through a whirl of blinding smoke and steam he saw limbs and a collapsing, burst body fling themselves to earth.

Bert was so astonished that he stood agape, and the bird-faced officer might have cut him to the earth without a struggle. But instead the bird-faced officer was running away through the undergrowth, dodging as he went. Bert roused himself to a brief ineffectual pursuit, but he had no stomach for further killing. He returned to the mangled, scattered thing that had so recently been the great Prince Karl Albert. He surveyed the scorched and splashed vegetation about it. He made some speculative identifications. He advanced gingerly and picked up the hot revolver, to find all its chambers strained and burst. He became aware of a cheerful and friendly presence. He was greatly shocked that one so young should see so frightful a scene.

"Ere, Kitty,' he said, 'this ain't no place for you.'

He made three strides across the devastated area, captured the kitten neatly, and went his way towards the shed, with her purring loudly on his shoulder.

'*You* don't seem to mind,' he said.

For a time he fussed about the shed, and at last discovered the rest of the provisions hidden in the roof. 'Seems 'ard,' he said, as he administered a saucerful of milk, 'when you get three men in a 'ole like this, they can't work together. But 'im and 'is princing was jest a bit too thick!

'Gaw!' he reflected, sitting on the counter and eating, 'what a thing life is! 'Ere am I; I seen 'is picture, 'eard 'is name since I was a kid in frocks. Prince Karl Albert! And if anyone 'ad tole me I was going to blow 'im to smithereens – there! I shouldn't 'ave believed it, Kitty.

'That chap at Margit ought to 'ave tole me about it. All 'e tole me was that I got a weak chess.

'That other chap, 'e ain't going to do much. Wonder what I ought to do about 'im?'

He surveyed the trees with a keen blue eye and fingered the gun on his knee. 'I don't like this killing, Kitty,' he said. 'It's like Kurt said about being blooded. Seems to me you got to be blooded young. . . . If that Prince 'ad come up to me and said: "Shake 'ands!" I'd 'ave shook 'ands. . . . Now 'ere's that other chap, dodging about! 'E's got 'is 'ead 'urt already, and there's something wrong with his leg. And burns. Golly! it isn't three weeks ago I first set eyes on 'im, and then 'e was smart and set up – 'ands full of 'airbrushes and things, and swearin' at me. A regular gentleman! Now 'e's 'arf-way to a wild man. What am I to do with 'im? What the 'ell am I to do with 'im? I can't let 'im 'ave that flying machine; that's a bit *too* good, and if I don't kill 'im 'e'll jest hang about this island and starve. . . .

"E's got a sword, of course.' . . .

He resumed his philosophizing after he had lit a cigarette.

'War's a silly gaim, Kitty. It's a silly gaim! We common people – we were fools. We thought those big people knew what they were up to – and they didn't. Look at that chap! 'E 'ad all Germany be'ind 'im, and what 'as 'e made of it? Smeshin' and blunderin' and destroyin', and there 'e 'is! Jest a mess of blood and boots and things! Jest an 'orrid splash! Prince Karl Albert! And all the men 'e led and the ships 'e 'ad, the airships and the dragonfliers – all scattered like a paperchase between this 'ole and Germany. And fightin' going on and burnin' and killin' that 'e started, war without end all over the world!

'I suppose I shall 'ave to kill that other chap. I suppose I must. But it ain't at all the sort of job I fancy, Kitty!'

For a time he hunted about the island amidst the uproar of the waterfall looking for the wounded officer, and at last he started him out of some bushes near the head of Biddle Stairs. But as he saw the bent and bandaged figure in limping flight before him, he found his Cockney softness too much for him again; he could neither shoot nor pursue. 'I carn't,' he said, 'that's flat. I 'aven't the guts for it! 'E'll 'ave to go.'

He turned his steps towards the flying machine. . . .

He never saw the bird-faced officer again, nor any further evidence of his presence. Towards evening he grew fearful of ambushes and hunted vigorously for an hour or so but in vain. He slept in a good defensible position at the extremity of the rocky point that runs out to the Canadian Fall, and in the night he woke in panic terror and fired his gun. But it was nothing. He slept no more that night. In the morning he became curiously concerned for the vanished man, and hunted for him as one might for an erring brother. 'If I knew some German,' he said, 'I'd 'oller. It's jest not knowing German does it. You can't explain.'

He discovered, later, traces of an attempt to cross the gap in the broken bridge. A rope with a bolt attached had been flung across and had caught in a fenestration of a projecting fragment of railing. The end of the rope trailed in the seething water towards the fall.

But the bird-faced officer was already rubbing shoulders with certain inert matter that had once been Lieutenant Kurt and the Chinese aeronaut and a dead cow, and much other uncongenial company, in the huge circle of the Whirlpool two and a quarter miles away. Never had that great gathering-place, that incessant, aimless, unprogressive hurry of waste and battered things, been so crowded with strange and melancholy derelicts. Round they went and round, and every day brought its new contributions, luckless brutes, shattered fragments of boat and flying machine, endless citizens from the cities upon the shores of the great lakes above. Much came from Cleveland. It all gathered here, and whirled about indefinitely, and over it all gathered daily a greater abundance of birds.

10

The World under the War

I

Bert spent two more days upon Goat Island, and finished all his provisions except the cigarettes and mineral water, before he brought himself to try the Asiatic flying machine.

Even at last he did not so much go off upon it as get carried off. It had taken only an hour or so to substitute wing stays from the second flying machine and to replace the nuts he had himself removed. The engine was in working order, and differed only very simply and obviously from that of a contemporary motor-bicycle. The rest of the time was taken up by a vast musing and delaying and hesitation. Chiefly he saw himself splashing into the rapids and whirling down them to the fall, clutching and drowning, but also he had a vision of being hopelessly in the air, going fast and unable to ground. His mind was too concentrated upon the business of flying for him to think very much of what might happen to an indefinite-spirited Cockney without credentials who arrived on an Asiatic flying machine amidst the war-infuriated population beyond.

He still had a lingering solicitude for the bird-faced officer. He had a haunting fancy he might be lying disabled or badly smashed in some nook or cranny of the island; and it was only after a most exhaustive search that he abandoned that distressing idea. 'If I found 'im,' he reasoned the while, 'what could I do wiv 'im? You can't blow a chap's brains out when 'e's down. And I don' see 'ow else I can 'elp 'im.'

Then the kitten bothered his highly developed sense of social responsibility. 'If I leave 'er she'll starve. ... Ought to catch mice for 'erself. . . . *Are* there mice? . . . Birds? . . . She's too young. . . . She's like me; she's a bit too civilized.'

Finally he stuck her in his side pocket, and she became greatly interested in the memories of corned beef she found there.

With her in his pocket, he seated himself in the saddle of the flying machine. Big, clumsy thing it was – and not a bit like a bicycle. Still the working of it was fairly plain. You set the engine going – *so*; kicked yourself up until the wheel was vertical, *so*; engaged the gyroscope, *so*, and then – then – you just pulled up this lever.

Rather stiff it was, but suddenly it came over—

The big curved wings on either side flapped disconcertingly, flapped again, click, clock, click, clock, clitter-clock!

Stop! The thing was heading for the water; its wheel was in the water. Bert groaned from his heart and struggled to restore the lever to its first position. Click, clock, clitter-clock, he was rising! The machine was lifting its dripping wheel out of the eddies, and he was going up! There was no stopping now, no good in stopping now. In another moment Bert, clutching and convulsive and rigid, with staring eyes and a face pale as death, was flapping up above the rapids, jerking to every jerk of the wings, and rising, rising.

There was no comparison in dignity and comfort between a flying machine and a balloon. Except in its moments of descent, the balloon was a vehicle of faultless urbanity; this was a buck-jumping mule, a mule that jumped up and never came down again. Click, clock, click, clock; with each beat of the strangely shaped wings it jumped Bert upward and caught him neatly again half a second later on the saddle. And while in ballooning there is no wind, since the balloon is a part of the wind, flying is a wild perpetual creation of, and plunging into, wind. It was a wind that above all things sought to blind him, to force him to close his eyes. It occurred to him presently to twist his knees and legs inward and grip with them, or surely he would have been bumped into two clumsy halves. And he was going up, a hundred yards high, two hundred, three hundred, over the streaming, frothing wilderness of water below – up, up, up. That was all right, but how presently would one go horizontally? He tried to think if these things did go horizontally. No! They flapped up and then they soared down. For a time he would keep on flapping up. Tears streamed from his eyes. He wiped them with one temerariously disengaged hand.

Was it better to risk a fall over land or over water – such water?

He was flapping up above the upper rapids towards Buffalo. It was at any rate a comfort that the falls and the wild swirl of waters below them were behind him. He was flying up straight. That he could see. How did one turn?

He was presently almost cool, and his eyes got more used to the rush of air, but he was getting very high, very high. He tilted his head forwards and surveyed the country, blinking. He could see all over Buffalo, a place with three great blackened scars of ruin, and hills and stretches beyond. He wondered if he was half a mile high, or more. There were some people among some houses near a railway station between Niagara and Buffalo, and then more people. They went like ants busily in and out of the houses. He saw two motor-cars gliding along the road towards Niagara city. Then far away in the south he saw a great Asiatic airship going eastward. 'Oh, Gord!' he said, and became earnest in his ineffectual attempts to alter his direction. But that airship took no notice of him, and he continued to ascend convulsively. The world got more and more extensive and map-like. Click, clock, clitter-clock. Above him and very near to him now was a hazy stratum of cloud.

He determined to disengage the wing clutch. He did so. The lever resisted his strength for a time, then over it came, and instantly the tail of the machine cocked up and the wings became rigidly spread. Instantly everything was swift and smooth and silent. He was gliding rapidly down the air against a wild gale of wind, his eyes three-quarters shut. . . .

A little lever that had hitherto been obdurate now confessed itself mobile. He turned it over gently to the right, and whiroo! – the left wing had in some mysterious way given at its edge, and he was sweeping round and downward in an immense right-handed spiral. For some moments he experienced all the helpless sensations of catastrophe. He restored the lever to its middle position with some difficulty, and the wings were equalized again.

He turned it to the left and had a sensation of being spun round backwards. 'Too much!' he gasped.

He discovered that he was rushing down at a headlong pace towards a railway line and some factory buildings. They appeared to be tearing up to him to devour him. He must have dropped all that height. For a moment he had the ineffectual sensations of one whose bicycle bolts downhill. The ground had almost taken him by surprise. "Ere!' he cried; and then with a violent effort of all his being he got the beating engine at work again and set the wings flapping. He swooped down and up and resumed his quivering and pulsating ascent of the air.

He went high again, until he had a wide view of the pleasant upland country of western New York State, and then made a long coast down, and so up again, and then a coast. Then as he came swooping a quarter of a mile above a village he saw people running about, running away – evidently in relation to his hawk-like passage. He got an idea that he had been shot at.

'Up!' he said, and attacked that lever again. It came over with remarkable docility, and suddenly the wings seemed to give way in the middle. But the engine was still! It had stopped. He flung the lever back rather by instinct than design. What to do?

Much happened in a few seconds, but also his mind was quick, he thought very quickly. He couldn't get up again, he was gliding down the air; he would have to hit something.

He was travelling at the rate of perhaps thirty miles an hour, down, down.

That plantation of larches looked the softest thing – mossy almost!

Could he get it? He gave himself to the steering. Round to the right – left!

Swirroo! Crackle! He was gliding over the tops of the trees, ploughing through them, tumbling into a cloud of green sharp leaves and black twigs. There was a sudden snapping, and he fell off the saddle forward, a thud and a crashing of branches. Some twigs hit him smartly in the face. . . .

He was between a tree stem and the saddle, with his leg over the steering lever and, so far as he could realize, not hurt. He tried to alter his position and free his leg, and found himself slipping and dropping through branches with everything giving way beneath him. He clutched, and found himself in the lower branches of a tree beneath the flying machine. The air was full of a pleasant resinous smell. He stared for a moment motionless, and then very carefully clambered down branch by branch to the soft needle-covered ground below.

'Good business,' he said, looking up at the bent and tilted kite-wings above.

'I dropped soft!'

He rubbed his chin with his hand and meditated. 'Blowed if I don't think I'm a rather lucky fellow!' he said, surveying the pleasant, sun-bespattered ground under the trees. Then he became aware of a violent tumult at his side. 'Lord!' he said, 'you must be 'arf smothered,' and extracted the kitten from his pocket-handkerchief and pocket. She was twisted and crumpled and extremely glad to see the light again. Her little tongue peeped between her teeth. He put her down, and she ran a dozen paces and shook herself and stretched and sat up and began to wash.

'Nex'?' he said, looking about him, and then with a gesture of vexation, 'Desh it! I ought to 'ave brought that gun!'

He had rested it against a tree when he had seated himself in the flying-machine saddle.

He was puzzled for a time by the immense peacefulness in the quality of the world, and then he perceived that the roar of the cataract was no longer in his ears.

2

He had no very clear idea of what sort of people he might come upon in this country. It was, he knew, America. Americans he had always understood were the citizens of a great and powerful nation, dry and humorous in their manner, addicted to the use of the bowie-knife and revolver, and in the habit of talking through the nose like Norfolk, and saying 'allow' and 'reckon' and 'calculate', after the manner of the people who live on the New Forest side of Hampshire. Also they were very rich, had rocking-chairs, and put their feet at unusual altitudes, and they chewed tobacco, gum and other substances with untiring industry. Commingled with them were cowboys, Red Indians and comic, respectful niggers. This he had learnt from the fiction in his public library. Beyond that he had learnt very little. He was not surprised therefore when he met armed men.

He decided to abandon the shattered flying machine. He wandered through the trees for some time, and then struck a road that seemed to his urban English eyes to be remarkably wide but not properly 'made'. Neither hedge nor ditch nor kerbed distinctive footpath separated it from the woods, and it went in that long easy curve which distinguishes the tracks of an open continent. Ahead he saw a man carrying a gun under his arm, a man in a soft black hat, a blue blouse and black trousers, and with a broad round fat face quite innocent of goatee. This person regarded him askance and heard him speak with a start.

'Can you tell me whereabouts I am at all?' asked Bert.

The man regarded him, and more particularly his rubber boots, with sinister suspicion. Then he replied in a strange outlandish tongue that was, as a matter of fact, Czech. He ended suddenly at the sight of Bert's blank face with 'Don't spik English.'

'Oh!' said Bert. He reflected gravely for a moment, and then went his way.

'Thanks,' he said as an afterthought. The man regarded his back for a moment, was struck with an idea, began an abortive gesture, sighed, gave it up and went on also with a depressed countenance.

Presently Bert came to a big wooden house standing casually among the trees. It looked a bleak, bare box of a house to him, no creeper grew on it, no hedge nor wall nor fence parted it off from the woods about it. He stopped before the steps that led up to the door, perhaps thirty yards away. The place seemed deserted. He would have gone up to the door and rapped, but suddenly a big black dog appeared at the side and regarded him. It was a huge heavy-jawed dog of some unfamiliar breed, and it wore a spike-studded collar. It did not bark nor approach him, it just bristled quietly and emitted a single sound like a short, deep cough.

Bert hesitated and went on.

He stopped thirty paces away and stood peering about him among the trees. 'If I 'aven't been and lef' that kitten,' he said.

Acute sorrow wrenched him for a time. The black dog came through the trees to get a better look at him and coughed that well-bred cough again. Bert resumed the road.

'She'll do all right,' he said. ... 'She'll catch things. ...

'She'll do all right,' he said presently, without conviction. But if it had not been for the black dog he would have gone back.

When he was out of sight of the house and the black dog, he went into the woods on the other side of the way and emerged after an interval trimming a very tolerable cudgel with his pocket-knife. Presently he saw an attractive-looking rock by the track and picked it up and put it in his pocket. Then he came to three or four houses, wooden like the last, each with an ill-painted white veranda (that was his name for it) and all standing in the same casual way upon the ground. Behind, through the woods, he saw pigsties and a rooting black sow leading a brisk, adventurous family. A wild-looking woman with sloe-black eyes and dishevelled black hair sat upon the steps of one of the houses nursing a baby, but at the sight of Bert she got up and went inside, and he heard her bolting the door. Then a boy appeared among the pigsties, but he would not understand Bert's hail.

'I suppose it is America!' said Bert.

The houses became more frequent down the road, and he passed two other extremely wild and dirty-looking men without addressing them. One carried a gun and the other a hatchet, and they scrutinized him and his cudgel scornfully. Then he struck a crossroad with a monorail at its side, and there was a noticeboard at the corner with 'Wait here for the cars'. 'That's all right any'ow,' said Bert. 'Wonder 'ow long I should 'ave to wait?' It occurred to him that in the present disturbed state of the country the service might be interrupted, and as there seemed more houses to the right than the left he turned to the right. He passed an old Negro. "Ullo!" said Bert. 'Goo' morning!'

'Good day, sah!' said the old Negro in a voice of almost incredible richness.

'What's the name of this place?' asked Bert.

'Tanooda, sah!' said the Negro.

Thenks; said Bert.

'Thank *you*, sah!' said the Negro overwhelmingly.

Bert came to houses of the same detached, unwalled, wooden type, but adorned now with enamelled advertisements partly in English and partly in Esperanto. Then he came to what he concluded was a grocer's shop. It was the first house that professed the hospitality of an open door, and from within came a strangely familiar sound. 'Gaw!' he said, searching in his pockets. 'Why! I 'aven't wanted money for free weeks! I wonder if I– Grubb 'ad most of it. Ah!' He produced a handful of coins and regarded it; three pennies, sixpence and a shilling. 'That's all right,' he said, forgetting a very obvious consideration.

He approached the door, and as he did so a compactly built, grey-faced man in shirt-sleeves appeared in it and scrutinized him and his cudgel. 'Mornin',' said Bert. 'Can I get anything to eat 'r drink in this shop?'

The man in the door replied, thank Heaven, in clear, good American. 'This, sir, is not A shop, it is A store.'

'Oh!' said Bert, and then, 'Well, can I get anything to eat?'

'You can,' said the American in a tone of confident encouragement, and led the way inside.

The shop seemed to him by his Bun Hill standards extremely roomy, well lit and unencumbered. There was a long counter to the left of him, with drawers and miscellaneous commodities ranged behind it, a number of chairs, several tables and two spittoons to the right, various barrels, cheeses and bacon up the vista, and beyond, a large archway leading to more space. A little group of men was assembled round one of the tables, and a woman of perhaps five-and-thirty leant with her elbows on the counter. All the men were armed with rifles, and the barrel of a gun peeped above the counter. They were all listening idly, inattentively, to a cheap, metallic-toned gramophone that occupied a table near at hand. From its brazen throat came words that gave Bert a qualm of homesickness, that brought back in his memory a sunlit beach, a group of children, red-painted bicycles, Grubb and an approaching balloon:

Ting-a-ling-a-ting-a-ling-a-ting-a-ling-a-tang
What price hairpins now?

A heavy-necked man in a straw hat, who was chewing something, stopped the machine with a touch, and they all turned their eyes on Bert. And all their eyes were tired eyes.

'Can we give this gentleman anything to eat, mother, or can we not?' said the proprietor.

'He kin have what he likes,' said the woman at the counter, without moving, 'right up from a cracker to a square meal.' She struggled with a yawn, after the manner of one who has been up all night.

'I want a meal,' said Bert, 'but I 'aven't very much money. I don't want to give mor'n a shillin'.'

'Moern a *what*?' said the proprietor sharply.

'Mor'n a shillin',' said Bert, with a sudden disagreeable realization coming into his mind.

'Yes,' said the proprietor, startled for a moment from his courtly bearing, 'but what in hell *is* a shilling?'

'He means a quarter,' said a wise-looking, lank young man in riding gaiters.

Bert, trying to conceal his consternation, produced a coin. 'That's a shilling,' he said.

'He calls A store A shop,' said the proprietor, 'and he wants A meal for A shilling. May I ask you, sir, what part of America you hail from?'

Bert replaced the shilling in his pocket as he spoke. 'Niagara,' he said.

'And when did you leave Niagara?'

'Bout an hour ago.'

'Well,' said the proprietor, and turned with a puzzled smile to the others. 'Well!'

They asked various questions simultaneously.

Bert selected one or two for reply. 'You see,' he said, 'I been with the German air-fleet. I got caught up by them, sort of by accident, and brought over here.'

'From England?'

'Yes – from England. Way of Germany. I was in a great battle with them Asiatics, and I got lef' on a little island between the falls.'

'Goat Island?'

'I don't know what it was called. But any'ow I found a flying machine and made a sort of fly with it and got here.'

Two men stood up with incredulous eyes on him. 'Where's the flying machine?' they asked; 'outside?'

'It's back in the woods here – 'bout 'arf a mile away.'

'Is it good?' said a thick-lipped man with a scar.

'I come down rather a smash—'

Everybody got up and stood about him and talked confusingly. They wanted him to take them to the flying machine at once.

'Look 'ere,' said Bert, 'I'll show you – only I 'aven't 'ad anything to eat since yestiday – except mineral water.'

A gaunt, soldierly looking young man with long lean legs in riding gaiters and a bandolier, who had hitherto not spoken, intervened now on his behalf in a note of confident authority. 'That's aw right,' he said. 'Give him a feed, Mr Logan – from me. I want to hear more of that story of his. We'll see his machine afterwards. If you ask me, I should say it's a remarkably interesting accident had dropped this gentleman here. I guess we requisition that flying machine – if we find it – for local defence.'

3

So Bert fell on his feet again, and sat eating cold meat and good bread and mustard and drinking very good beer, and telling in the roughest outline and with the omissions and inaccuracies of statement natural to his type of mind, the simple story of his adventures. He told how he and a 'gentleman friend' had been visiting the seaside for their health, how a 'chep' came along in a balloon and fell out as he fell in, how he had drifted to Franconia, how the Germans had seemed to mistake him for someone and had 'took him prisoner' and brought him to New York, how he had been to Labrador and back, how he had got to Goat Island and found himself there alone. He omitted the matter of the Prince and the Butteridge aspect of the affair, not out of any deep deceitfulness, but because he felt the inadequacy of his narrative powers. He wanted everything to seem easy and natural and correct, to present himself as a trustworthy and understandable Englishman in a sound mediocre position, to whom refreshment and accommodation might be given with freedom and confidence.

When his fragmentary story came to New York and the battle of Niagara they suddenly produced newspapers which had been lying about on the table, and began to check him and question him by these vehement accounts. It became evident to him that his descent had revived and roused to flames again a discussion, a topic, that had been burning continuously, that had smouldered only through sheer exhaustion of material during the temporary diversion of the gramophone, a discussion that had drawn these men together, rifle in hand, the one supreme topic of the whole world, the War and the methods of War. He found any question of his personality and his personal adventures falling into the background, found himself taken for granted, and no more than a source of information. The ordinary affairs of life, the buying and selling of everyday necessities, the cultivation of the ground, the tending of beasts, was going on as it were by force of routine, as the common duties of life go on in a house whose master lies under the knife of some supreme operation. The overruling interest was furnished by those great Asiatic airships that went upon incalculable missions across the sky, the crimson-clad swordsmen who might come fluttering down demanding petrol, or food, or news. These men were asking, all the continent was asking, 'What are we to do? What can we try? How can we get at them?' Bert fell into his place as an item, ceased even in his own thoughts to be a central and independent thing.

After he had eaten and drunken his fill and sighed and stretched and told them how good the food seemed to him, he lit a cigarette they gave him and led the way, with some doubts and trouble, to the flying machine amidst the larches. It became manifest that the gaunt young man, whose name, it seemed, was Laurier, was a leader both by position and natural aptitude. He knew the names and characters and capabilities of all the men who were with him, and he set them to work at once with vigour and effect to secure this precious instrument of war. They got the thing down to the ground deliberately and carefully, felling a couple of trees in the process, and they built a wide flat roof of timbers and tree boughs to guard their precious find against its chance discovery by any passing Asiatics. Long before evening they had an engineer from the next township at work upon it, and they were casting lots among the seventeen picked men who wanted to take it for its first flight. And Bert found his kitten and carried it back to Logan's store and handed it with earnest admonition to Mrs Logan. And it was reassuringly clear to him that in Mrs Logan both he and the kitten had found a congenial soul.

Laurier was not only a masterful person and a wealthy property-owner and employer – he was president, Bert learnt with awe, of the Tanooda Canning Corporation – but he was popular and skilful in the arts of popularity. In the evening quite a crowd of men gathered in the store and talked of the flying machine and of the war that was tearing the world to pieces. And presently came a man on a bicycle with an ill-printed newspaper of a single sheet which acted like fuel in a blazing furnace of talk. It was nearly all American news; the old-fashioned cables had fallen into disuse for some years, and the Marconi stations across the ocean and along the Atlantic coastline seemed to have furnished particularly tempting points of attack.

But such news it was.

Bert sat in the background – for by this time they had gauged his personal quality pretty completely – listening. Before his staggering mind passed strange vast images as they talked, of great issues at a crisis, of nations in tumultuous march, of continents overthrown, of famine and destruction beyond measure. Ever and again, in spite of his efforts to suppress them, certain personal impressions would scamper across the weltering confusion, the horrible mess of the exploded Prince, the Chinese aeronaut upside down, the limping and bandaged bird-faced officer blundering along in miserable and hopeless flight.

They spoke of fire and massacre, of cruelties and counter-cruelties, of things that had been done to harmless Asiatics by race-mad men, of the wholesale burning and smashing up of towns, railway junctions, bridges, of whole populations in hiding and exodus. 'Every ship they've got is in the Pacific,' he heard one man exclaim. 'Since the fighting began they can't have landed on the Pacific slope less than a million men. They've come to stay in these States, and they will – living or dead.'

Slowly, broadly, invincibly, there grew upon Bert's mind realization of the immense tragedy of humanity into which his life was flowing; the appalling and universal nature of the epoch that had arrived; the conception of an end to security and order and habit. The whole world was at war and it could not get back to peace; it might never recover peace.

He had thought the things he had seen had been exceptional, conclusive things, that the besieging of New York and the battle of the Atlantic were epoch-making events between long years of security. And they had been but the first warning impacts of universal cataclysm. Each day destruction and hate and disaster grew, the fissures widened between man and man, new regions of the fabric of civilization crumbled and gave way. Below, the armies grew and the people perished; above, the airships and aeroplanes fought and fled, raining destruction.

It is difficult perhaps for the broad-minded and long-perspectived reader to understand how incredible the breaking down of the scientific civilization seemed to those who actually lived at this time, who in their own persons went down in that débâcle. Progress had marched as it seemed invincible about the earth, never now to rest again. For three hundred years and more the long, steadily accelerated diastole of Europeanized civilization had been in progress: towns had been multiplying, populations increasing, values rising, new countries

805

developing; thought, literature, knowledge unfolding and spreading. It seemed but a part of the process that every year the instruments of war were vaster and more powerful, and that armies and explosives outgrew all other growing things. . . .

Three hundred years of diastole, and then came the swift and unexpected systole, like the closing of a fist. They could not understand it was a systole. They could not think of it as anything but a jolt, a hitch, a mere oscillatory indication of the swiftness of their progress. Collapse, though it happened all about them, remained incredible. Presently some falling mass smote them down, or the ground opened beneath their feet. They died incredulous. . . .

These men in the store made a minute, remote group under this immense canopy of disaster. They turned from one little aspect to another. What chiefly concerned them was defence against Asiatic raiders swooping for petrol or to destroy weapons or communications. Everywhere levies were being formed at that time to defend the plant of the railroads day and night in the hope that communication would speedily be restored. The land war was still far away. A man with a flat voice distinguished himself by a display of knowledge and cunning. He told them all with confidence just what had been wrong with the German *Drachenflieger* and the American aeroplanes, just what advantage the Japanese fliers possessed. He launched out into a romantic description of the Butteridge machine and riveted Bert's attention. 'I *see* that,' said Bert, and was smitten silent by a thought. The man with the flat voice talked on, without heeding him, of the strange irony of Butteridge's death. At that Bert had a little twinge of relief – he would never meet Butteridge again. It appeared Butteridge had died suddenly, very suddenly.

'And his secret, sir, perished with him! When they came to look for the parts – none could find them. He had hidden them all too well.'

'But couldn't he tell?' asked the man in the straw hat. 'Did he die so suddenly as that?'

'Struck down, sir. Rage and apoplexy. At a place called Dymchurch in England.'

'That's right,' said Laurier. 'I remember a page about it in the Sunday *American*. At the time they said it was a German spy had stolen his balloon.'

'Well, sir,' said the flat-voiced man, 'that fit of apoplexy at Dymchurch was the worst thing – ab-so-lutely the worst thing that ever happened to the world. For if it had not been for the death of Mr Butteridge—'

'No one knows his secret?'

'Not a soul. It's gone. His balloon, it appears, was lost at sea, with all the plans. Down it went, and they went with it.'

Pause.

'With machines such as he made we could fight these Asiatic fliers on more than equal terms. We could outfly and beat down those scarlet humming-birds wherever they appeared. But it's gone, it's gone, and there's no time to reinvent it now. We got to fight with what we got – and the odds are against us. *That* won't stop us fightin'. No! but just think of it!'

Bert was trembling violently. He cleared his throat hoarsely.

'I say,' he said, 'look here, I—'

Nobody regarded him. The man with the flat voice was opening a new branch of the subject. 'I allow —' he began.

Bert became violently excited. He stood up. He made clawing motions with his hands. 'I say!' he exclaimed, 'Mr Laurier. Look 'ere – I want – about that Butteridge machine—'

Mr Laurier, sitting on an adjacent table, with a magnificent gesture arrested the discourse of the flat-voiced man. 'What's *he* saying?' said he.

Then the whole company realized that something was happening to Bert; either he was suffocating or going mad. He was spluttering, 'Look 'ere! I say!' 'Old on a bit!' and trembling and eagerly unbuttoning himself.

He tore open his collar and opened vest and shirt. He plunged into his interior and for an instant it seemed he was plucking forth his liver. Then as he struggled with buttons on his shoulder they perceived this flattened horror was in fact a terribly dirty flannel chest-protector. In another moment Bert, in a state of irregular décolletage, was standing over the table displaying a sheaf of papers.

'These!' he gasped. 'These are the plans! ... You know! Mr Butteridge – his machine! What died! I was the chap that went off in that balloon!'

For some seconds everyone was silent. They stared from these papers to Bert's white face and blazing eyes, and back to the papers on the table. Nobody moved. Then the man with the flat voice spoke.

'Irony!' he said, with a note of satisfaction. 'Real right-down Irony! *When it's too late to think of making 'em any more!*'

4

They would all no doubt have been eager to hear Bert's story over again, but it was at this point that Laurier showed his quality. 'No, *sir*,' he said, and slid from off his table.

He impounded the dispersing Butteridge plans with one comprehensive sweep of his arms, rescuing them even from the expository fingermarks of the man with the flat voice, and handed them to Bert. 'Put those back,' he said, 'where you had 'em. We have a journey before us.'

Bert took them.

'Whar?' said the man in the straw hat.

'Why, sir, we are going to find the President of these States and give these plans over to him. I decline to believe, sir, we are too late.'

'Where is the President?' asked Bert weakly in the pause that followed.

'Logan,' said Laurier, disregarding that feeble inquiry, 'you must help us in this.'

It seemed only a matter of a few minutes before Bert and Laurier and the storekeeper were examining a number of bicycles that were stowed in the hinder room of the store. Bert didn't like any of them very much. They had wood rims, and an experience of wood rims in the English climate had taught him to hate them. That, however, and one or two other objections to an immediate start were overruled by Laurier. 'But where *is* the President?' Bert repeated as they stood behind Logan while he pumped up a deflated tyre.

Laurier looked down on him. 'He is reported in the neighbourhood of Albany – out towards the Berkshire Hills. He is moving from place to place and, as far as he can, organizing the defence by telegraph and telephone. The Asiatic air-fleet is trying to locate him. When they think they have located the seat of government they throw bombs. This inconveniences him, but so far they have not come within ten miles of him. The Asiatic air-fleet is at present scattered all over the Eastern States, seeking out and destroying gasworks and whatever seems conducive to the building of airships or the transport of troops. Our retaliatory measures are slight in the extreme. But with these machines– Sir, this ride of ours will count among the historical rides of the world!'

He came near to striking an attitude.

'We shan't get to him tonight?' asked Bert.

'No, sir!' said Laurier. We shall have to ride some days, sure!'

'I suppose we can't get a lift on a train – or anything?'

'No, sir! There's been no transit by Tanooda for three days. It is no good waiting. We shall have to get on as well as we can.'

'Startin' now?'

'Starting now!'

'But 'ow about– We shan't be able to do much tonight.'

'May as well ride till we're fagged and sleep then. So much clear gain. Our road is eastward.'

'Of course—' began Bert, with memories of the dawn upon Goat Island, and left his sentence unfinished.

He gave his attention to the more scientific packing of the chest-protector, for several of the plans flapped beyond his vest.

5

For a week Bert led a life of mixed sensations. Amidst these fatigue in the legs predominated. Mostly he rode, rode with Laurier's back inexorably ahead, through a land like a larger England, with bigger hills and wider valleys, larger fields, wider roads, fewer hedges and wooden houses with commodious piazzas. He rode. Laurier made inquiries, Laurier chose the turnings, Laurier doubted, Laurier decided. Now it seemed they were in telephonic touch with the President; now something had happened and he was lost again. But always they had to go on, and always Bert rode. A tyre was deflated. Still he rode. He grew saddle sore. Laurier declared that unimportant. Asiatic flying-ships passed overhead, the two cyclists made a dash for cover until the sky was clear. Once a red Asiatic flying machine came fluttering after them, so low they could distinguish the aeronaut's head. He followed them for a mile. Now they came to regions of panic, now to regions of destruction, here people were fighting for food, here they seemed hardly stirred from the countryside routine. They spent a day in a deserted and damaged Albany. The Asiatics had descended and cut every wire and made a cinder-heap of the Junction, and our travellers pushed on eastward. They passed a hundred half-heeded incidents, and always Bert was toiling after Laurier's indefatigable back. . . .

Things struck upon Bert's attention and perplexed him, and then he passed on with unanswered questionings fading from his mind.

He saw a large house on fire on a hillside to the right, and no man heeding it. . . .

They came to a narrow railroad bridge and presently to a monorail train standing in the track on its safety feet. It was a remarkably sumptuous train, the Last Word Trans-Continental Express, and the passengers were all playing cards or sleeping or preparing a picnic meal on a grassy slope near at hand. They had been there six days. . . .

At one point ten dark-complexioned men were hanging in a string from the trees along the roadside. Bert wondered why. . . .

At one peaceful-looking village where they stopped off to get Bert's

809

tyre mended and found beer and biscuits, they were approached by an extremely dirty little boy without boots, who spoke as follows:

'Deyse been hanging a Chink in dose woods!'

'Hanging a Chinaman?' said Laurier.

'Sure. Der sleuths got him rubberin' der railroad sheds!'

'Oh!'

'Dose guys done wase cartridges. Deyse hung him and dey pulled his legs. Deyse doin' all der Chinks dey can fine dat weh! Dey ain't takin' no risks. All der Chinks dey can fine.'

Neither Bert nor Laurier made any reply, and presently, after a little skilful expectoration, the young gentleman was attracted by the appearance of two of his friends down the road, and shuffled off, whooping weirdly. . . .

That afternoon they almost ran over a man shot through the body and partly decomposed, lying near the middle of the road, just outside Albany. He must have been lying there for some days. . . .

Beyond Albany they came upon a motor-car with a tyre burst and a young woman sitting absolutely passive beside the driver's seat. An old man was under the car trying to effect some impossible repairs. Beyond, sitting with a rifle across his knees, with his back to the car, and staring into the woods, was a young man. The old man crawled out at their approach and still on all fours accosted Bert and Laurier. The car had broken down overnight. The old man said he could not understand what was wrong, but he was trying to puzzle it out. Neither he nor his son-in-law had any mechanical aptitude. They had been assured this was a foolproof car. It was dangerous to have to stop in this place. His party had been attacked by tramps and had had to fight. It was known they had provisions. He mentioned a great name in the world of finance. Would Laurier and Bert stop and help him? He proposed it first hopefully, then urgently, at last in tears and terror.

'No!' said Laurier inexorably. 'We must go on! We have something more than a woman to save. We have to save America!'

The girl never stirred. . . .

Once they passed a madman singing . . .

At last they found the President hiding in a small saloon upon the outskirts of a place called Pinkerville on the Hudson, and gave the plans of the Butteridge machine into his hands.

II

The Great Collapse

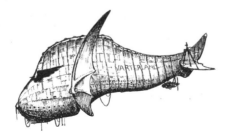

I

And now the whole fabric of civilization was bending and giving, and dropping to pieces and melting in the furnace of the war.

The stages of the swift and universal collapse of the financial and scientific civilization with which the twentieth century opened followed each other very swiftly, so swiftly that upon the foreshortened page of history they seem altogether to overlap. To begin with, one sees the world nearly at a maximum of wealth and prosperity. To its inhabitants indeed it seemed also at a maximum of security. When now in retrospect the thoughtful observer surveys the intellectual history of this time, when one reads its surviving fragments of literature, its scraps of political oratory, the few small voices that chance has selected out of a thousand million utterances to speak to later days, the most striking thing of all this web of wisdom and error is surely that hallucination of security. To men living in our present world state, orderly, scientific and secured, nothing seems so precarious, so giddily dangerous, as the fabric of the social order with which the men of the opening of the twentieth century were content. To us it seems that every institution and relationship was the fruit of haphazard and tradition and the manifest sport of chance, their laws each made for some separate occasion and having no relation to any future needs, their customs illogical, their education aimless and wasteful. Their method of economic exploitation indeed impresses a trained and informed mind as the most frantic and destructive scramble it is possible to conceive; their credit and monetary system resting on an unsubstantial tradition of the worthiness of gold, seems a thing almost fantastically unstable. And they lived in planless cities, for the most part dangerously congested, their rails and roads and population were distributed over the earth in the wanton confusion ten thousand irrelevant considerations had made. Yet they thought confidently that this was a secure and permanent progressive system, and on the strength of some three hundred years of chance and irregular improvement answered the doubter with, 'Things always *have* gone well. We'll worry through!'

But when we contrast the state of man in the opening of the twentieth century with the condition of any previous period in his history, then perhaps we may begin to understand something of that blind confidence. It was not so much a reasoned confidence as the inevitable consequence of sustained good fortune. By such standards as they possessed, things *had* gone amazingly well for them It is scarcely an exaggeration to say that for the first time in history whole populations found themselves regularly supplied with more than enough to eat, and the vital statistics of the time witness to an amelioration of hygienic conditions rapid beyond all precedent, and to a vast development of intelligence and ability in all the arts that make life wholesome. The level and quality of the average education had risen tremendously; and at the dawn of the twentieth century comparatively few people in Western Europe or America were unable to read or write. Never before had there been such reading masses. There was wide social security. A common man might travel safely over three-quarters of the habitable globe, could go round the earth at a cost of less than the annual earnings of a skilled artisan. Compared with the liberality and comfort of the ordinary life of the time, the order of the Roman Empire under the Antonines was local and limited. And every year, every month, came some new increment to human achievement, a new country opened up, new mines, new scientific discoveries, a new machine!

For those three hundred years the movement of the world seemed wholly beneficial to mankind. Men said, indeed, that moral organization was not keeping pace with physical progress, but few attached any meaning to these phrases, the understanding of which lies at the basis of our present safety. Sustaining and constructive forces did indeed for a time more than balance the malign drift of chance and the natural ignorance, prejudice, blind passion and wasteful self-seeking of mankind.

The accidental balance on the side of Progress was far slighter and infinitely more complex and delicate in its adjustments than the people of that time suspected; but that did not alter the fact that it was an effective balance. They did not realize that this age of relative good fortune was an age of immense but temporary opportunity for their kind. They complacently assumed a necessary progress towards which they had no moral responsibility. They did not realize that this security of progress was a thing still to be won or lost, and that the time to win it was a time that passed. They went about their affairs energetically enough, and yet with a curious idleness towards those threatening things. No one troubled over the real dangers of mankind. They saw their armies and navies grow larger and more portentous; some of their ironclads at the last cost as much as their whole annual expenditure upon advanced education; they accumulated explosives and the machinery of destruction; they allowed their national traditions and jealousies to accumulate; they contemplated without concern or understanding a steady enhancement of race hostility as the races drew closer, and they permitted the growth in their midst of an evil-spirited press, mercenary and unscrupulous, incapable of good and powerful for evil. Their State had practically no control over the press at all. Quite heedlessly they allowed this touchpaper to lie at the door of their war magazine for any spark to fire. The precedents of history were all one tale of the collapse of civilizations, the dangers of the time were manifest. One is incredulous now to believe they could not see.

Could mankind have prevented this disaster of the War in the Air? An idle question that, as idle as to ask could mankind have prevented the decay that turned Assyria and Babylon to empty deserts or the slow decline and fall, the gradual social disorganization, phase by phase, that closed the chapter of the Empire of the West. They could not, because they did not, they had not the will to arrest it. What mankind could achieve with a different will is a speculation as idle as it is magnificent. And this was no slow decadence that came to the Europeanized world; those other civilizations rotted and crumbled down, the Europeanized civilization was, as it were, blown up. Within the space of five years it was altogether disintegrated and destroyed. Up to the very eve of the War in the Air one sees a spacious spectacle of incessant advance, a worldwide security, enormous areas with highly organized industry and settled populations, gigantic cities spreading gigantically, the seas and oceans dotted with shipping, the land netted with rails and open ways. Then suddenly the German air-fleets sweep across the scene, and we are in the beginning of the end.

This story has already told of the swift rush upon New York of the first German air-fleet and of the wild, inevitable orgy of inconclusive destruction that ensued. Behind it a second air-fleet was already swelling at its gasometers when England and France and Spain and Italy showed their hands. None of these countries had prepared for aeronautic warfare on the magnificent scale of the Germans, but each guarded secrets, each in a measure was making ready, and a common dread of German vigour and that aggressive spirit Prince Karl Albert embodied had long been drawing these powers together in secret anticipation of some such attack. This rendered their prompt co-operation possible, and they certainly co-operated promptly. The second aerial power in Europe at this time was France; the British, nervous for their Asiatic empire, and sensible of the immense moral effect of the airship upon half-educated populations, had placed their aeronautic parks in North India, and were able to play but a subordinate part in the European conflict. Still, even in England they had nine or ten big navigables, twenty or thirty smaller ones and a variety of experimental aeroplanes. Before the fleet of Prince Karl Albert had crossed England, while Bert was still surveying Manchester in bird's-eye view, the diplomatic exchanges were going on that led to an attack upon Germany. A heterogeneous collection of navigable balloons of all sizes and types gathered over the Bernese Oberland, crushed and burnt in the battle of the Alps the twenty-five Swiss airships that unexpectedly resisted this concentration, and then, leaving the Alpine glaciers and valleys strewn with strange wreckage, divided into two fleets and set itself to terrorize Berlin and destroy the Franconian Park, seeking to do this before the second air-fleet could be inflated.

Both over Berlin and Franconia the assailants with their modern explosives effected great damage before they were driven off. In Franconia twelve fully distended and five partially filled and manned giants were able to make head against, and at last, with the help of a squadron of *Drachenflieger* from Hamburg, defeat and pursue the attack and to relieve Berlin, and the Germans were straining every nerve to get an overwhelming fleet in the air, and were already raiding London and Paris when the advance fleets from the Asiatic air-parks, the first intimation of a new factor in the conflict, were reported from Burmah and Armenia.

Already, when that occurred, the whole financial fabric of the world was staggering. With the destruction of the American fleet in the North Atlantic, and the smashing conflict that ended the naval existence of

Germany in the North Sea, with the burning and wrecking of billions of pounds' worth of property in the four cardinal cities of the world, the fact of the hopeless costliness of war came home for the first time, came like a blow in the face, to the consciousness of mankind. Credit went down in a wild whirl of selling. Everywhere appeared a phenomenon that had already in a mild degree manifested itself in preceding periods of panic; a desire to *secure and hoard gold* before prices reached bottom. But now it spread like wildfire, it became universal. Above was visible conflict and destruction; below something was happening far more deadly and incurable to the flimsy fabric of finance and commercialism in which men had so blindly put their trust. As the airships fought above, the visible gold supply of the world vanished below. An epidemic of private cornering and universal distrust swept the world. In a few weeks, money, except for depreciated paper, vanished into vaults, into holes, into the walls of houses, into ten million hiding-places. Money vanished, and at its disappearance trade and industry came to an end. The economic world staggered and fell dead. It was like the stroke of some disease; it was like the water vanishing out of the blood of a living creature; it was a sudden, universal coagulation of intercourse. . . .

And as the credit system, that had been the living fortress of the scientific civilization, reeled and fell upon the millions it had held together in economic relationship, as these people, perplexed and helpless, faced this marvel of credit utterly destroyed, the airships of Asia, countless and relentless, poured across the heavens, swooped eastward to America and westward to Europe. The page of history becomes a long crescendo of battle. The main body of the British-Indian air-fleet perished upon a pyre of blazing antagonists in Burma; the Germans were scattered in the great battle of the Carpathians; the vast peninsula of India burst into insurrection and civil war from end to end, and from Gobi to Morocco rose the standards of the 'Jehad'. For some weeks of warfare and destruction it seemed as though the Confederation of Eastern Asia must needs conquer the world, and then the jerry-built 'modern' civilization of China too gave way under the strain. The teeming and peaceful population of China had been 'westernized' during the opening years of the twentieth century with the deepest resentment and reluctance; they had been dragooned and disciplined under Japanese and European influence into an acquiescence with sanitary methods, police controls, military service and a wholesale process of exploitation against which their whole tradition rebelled. Under the stresses of the war their endurance reached the breaking point. China rose in incoherent revolt, and the practical destruction of the central government at Peking by a handful of British and German airships that had escaped from the main battles rendered that revolt invincible. Japan followed suit. In Yokohama appeared barricades, the black flag and the social revolution. With that the whole world became a welter of conflict.

So that a universal social collapse followed, as it were a logical consequence, upon worldwide war. Wherever there were great populations, great masses of people found themselves without work, without money and unable to get food. Famine was in every working-class quarter in the world within three weeks of the beginning of the war. Within a month there was not a city anywhere in which the ordinary law and social procedure had not been replaced by some form of emergency control, in which firearms and military executions were not being used to keep order and prevent violence. And still in the poorer quarters, and in the populous districts, and even here and there already among those who had been wealthy, famine spread.

3

So what historians have come to call the Phase of the Emergency Committees sprang from the opening phase and from the phase of social collapse. Then followed a period of vehement and passionate conflict against disintegration; everywhere the struggle to keep order and to keep fighting went on. And at the same time the character of the war altered through the replacement of the huge gas-filled airships by flying-machines as the instruments of war. So soon as the big fleet engagements were over, the Asiatics endeavoured to establish in close proximity to the more vulnerable points of the countries against which they were acting, fortified centres from which flying-machine raids could be made. For a time they had everything their own way in this, and then, as this story has told, the lost secret of the Butteridge machine came to light, and the conflict became equalized and less conclusive than ever. For these small flying machines, ineffectual for any large expedition or conclusive attack, were horribly convenient for guerilla warfare, rapidly and cheaply made, easily used, easily hidden. The design of them was hastily copied and printed in Pinkerville, and scattered broadcast over the United States, and copies were sent to Europe, and there reproduced. Every man, every town, every parish that could, was exhorted to make and use them In a little while they were being constructed not only by governments and local authorities, but by robber bands, by insurgent committees, by every type of private person. The peculiar social destructiveness of the Butteridge machine lay in its complete simplicity. It was nearly as simple as a motor-bicycle. The broad outlines of the earlier stages of the war disappeared under its influence, the spacious antagonism of nations and empires and races vanished in a seething mass of detailed conflict. The world passed at a stride from a unity and simplicity broader than that of the Roman Empire at its best, to a social fragmentation as complete as the robber-baron period of the Middle Ages. But this time, for a long descent down gradual slopes of disintegration, comes a fall like a fall over a cliff. Everywhere were men and women perceiving this, and struggling desperately to keep, as it were, a hold upon the edge of the cliff.

A fourth phase follows. Through the struggle against Chaos, in the wake of the Famine, came now another old enemy of humanity – the Pestilence, the Purple Death. But the war does not pause. The flags still fly. Fresh air-fleets rise, new forms of airship, and beneath their swooping struggles the world darkens – scarcely heeded by history.

It is not within the design of this book to tell that further story, to tell how the War in the Air kept on through the sheer inability of any authorities to meet and agree and end it, until every organized government in the world was as shattered and broken as a heap of china beaten with a stick. With every week of those terrible years history becomes more detailed and confused, more crowded and uncertain. Not without great and heroic resistance was civilization borne down. Out of the bitter social conflict below rose patriotic associations, brotherhoods of order, city mayors, princes, provisional committees, trying to establish an order below and to keep the sky above. The double effort destroyed them. And as the exhaustion of the mechanical resources of civilization clears the heavens of airships at last altogether, Anarchy, Famine and Pestilence are discovered triumphant below. The great nations and empires have become but names in the mouths of men. Everywhere there are ruins and unburied dead, and shrunken, yellow-faced survivors, in a mortal apathy. Here there are robbers, here vigilance committees, and here guerilla bands ruling patches of exhausted territory, strange federations and brotherhoods form and dissolve, and religious fanaticisms begotten of despair gleam in famine-bright eyes. It is a universal dissolution. The fine order and welfare of the earth have crumpled like an exploded bladder. In five short years the world and the scope of human life have undergone a retrogressive change as great as that between the age of the Antonines and the Europe of the ninth century. . . .

Across this sombre spectacle of disaster goes a minute and insignificant person for whom perhaps the readers of this story have now some slight solicitude. Of him there remains to be told just one single miraculous thing. Through a world darkened and lost, through a civilization in its death-agony, our little Cockney errant went and found his Edna! He found his Edna!

He got back across the Atlantic partly by means of an order from the President and partly through his own good luck. He contrived to get himself aboard a British brig in the timber trade that put out from Boston without cargo, chiefly, it would seem, because its captain had a vague idea of 'getting home' to South Shields. Bert was able to ship himself upon her mainly because of the seamanlike appearance of his rubber boots. They had a long, eventful voyage, they were chased, or imagined themselves to be chased, for some hours by an Asiatic ironclad, which was presently engaged by a British cruiser. The two ships fought for three hours, circling and driving southward as they fought, until the twilight and the cloud-drift of a rising gale swallowed them up. A few days later Bert's ship lost her rudder and mainmast in a gale. The crew ran out of food and subsisted on fish. They saw strange airships going eastward near the Azores, and landed to get provisions and repair the rudder at Tenerife. There they found the town destroyed, and two big liners, with dead still aboard, sunken in the harbour. From these they got canned food and material for repairs, but their operations were greatly impeded by the hostility of a band of men amidst the ruins of the town, who sniped them and tried to drive them away.

At Mogador they stayed and sent a boat ashore for water, and were nearly captured by an Arab ruse. Here, too, they got the Purple Death aboard, and sailed with it incubating in their blood. The cook sickened first, and then the mate, and presently everyone was down and three in the forecastle were dead. It chanced to be calm weather, and they drifted helplessly and indeed careless of their fate backwards towards the Equator. The captain doctored them all with rum. Nine died altogether, and of the four survivors none understood navigation; when at last they took heart again and could handle a sail they made a course by the stars roughly northward, and were already short of food once more when they fell in with a petrol-driven ship from Rio to Cardiff, short-handed by reason of the Purple Death and glad to take them aboard. So at last after a year of wandering Bert reached England. He landed in bright June weather, and found the Purple Death was there just beginning its ravages.

The people were in a state of panic in Cardiff and many had fled to the hills, and directly the steamer came to the harbour she was boarded and her residue of food impounded by some unauthenticated Provisional Committee. Bert tramped through a country disorganized by pestilence, foodless, and shaken to the very base of its immemorial order. He came near death and starvation many times, and once he was drawn into scenes of violence that might have ended his career. But the Bert Smallways who tramped from Cardiff to London vaguely 'going home', vaguely seeking something of his own that had no tangible form but Edna, was a very different person from the Desert Dervish who was swept out of England in Mr Butteridge's balloon a year before. He was brown and lean and enduring, steady-eyed and pestilence-salted, and his mouth, which had once hung open, shut now like a steel trap. Across his brow ran a white scar that he had got in a fight on the brig. In Cardiff he had felt the need of new clothes and a weapon, and had, by means that would have shocked him a year ago, secured a flannel shirt, a corduroy suit and a revolver and fifty cartridges from an abandoned pawnbroker's. He also got some soap and had his first real wash for thirteen months in a stream outside the town. The Vigilance bands that had at first shot plunderers very freely were now either entirely dispersed by the plague, or busy between town and cemetery in a vain attempt to keep pace with it. He prowled on the outskirts of the town for three or four days, starving, and then went back to join the Hospital Corps for a week, and so fortified himself with a few square meals before he started eastward.

The Welsh and English countryside at that time presented the strangest mingling of the assurance and wealth of the opening twentieth century with a sort of Düreresque mediaevalism. All the gear, the houses and monorails, the farm hedges and power cables, the roads and pavements, the signposts and advertisements of the former order were still for the most part intact. Bankruptcy, social collapse, famine and pestilence had done nothing to damage these; it was only to the great capitals and ganglionic centres, as it were, of the State that positive destruction had come. Anyone dropped suddenly into the country would have noticed very little difference. He would have remarked first, perhaps, that all the hedges needed clipping, that the roadside grass grew rank, that the road tracks were unusually rainworn, and that the cottages by the wayside seemed in many cases shut up, that a telephone wire had dropped here, and that a cart stood abandoned by the wayside. But he would still find his hunger whetted by the bright

821

assurance that Wilder's Canned Peaches were excellent, or that there was nothing so good for the breakfast table as Gobble's Sausages. And then suddenly would come the Düreresque element; the skeleton of a horse, or some crumpled mass of rags in the ditch, with gaunt extended feet and a yellow, purple-blotched skin and face, or what had been a face, gaunt and glaring and devastated. Then here would be a field that had been ploughed and not sown, and here a field of corn carelessly trampled by beasts, and here a hoarding torn down across the road to make a fire.

Then presently he would meet a man or a woman, yellow-faced and probably negligently dressed and armed – prowling for food. These people would have the complexions and eyes and expressions of tramps or criminals, and often the clothing of prosperous middle-class or upper-class people. Many of these would be eager for news, and willing to give help and even scraps of queer meat, or crusts of grey and doughy bread in return for it. They would listen to Bert's story with avidity, and attempt to keep him with them for a day or so. The virtual cessation of postal distribution and the collapse of all newspaper enterprise had left an immense and aching gap in the mental life of this time. Men had suddenly lost sight of the ends of the earth and had still to recover the rumour-spreading habits of the Middle Ages. In their eyes, in their bearing, in their talk, was the quality of lost and deoriented souls.

As Bert travelled from parish to parish and from district to district, avoiding as far as possible those festering centres of violence and despair, the larger towns, he found the condition of affairs varying widely. In one parish he would find the large house burnt, the vicarage wrecked, evidently in violent conflict for some suspected and perhaps imaginary store of food, unburied dead everywhere, and the whole mechanism of the community at a standstill. In another he would find organizing forces stoutly at work, newly painted noticeboards warning off vagrants, the roads and still cultivated fields policed by armed men, the pestilence under control, even nursing going on, a store of food husbanded, the cattle and sheep well guarded, and a group of two or three justices, the village doctor or a farmer, dominating the whole place; a reversion, in fact, to the autonomous community of the fifteenth century. But at any time such a village would be liable to a raid of Asiatics or Africans or suchlike air-pirates, demanding petrol and alcohol or provisions. The price of its order was an almost intolerable watchfulness and tension Then the approach to the confused problems of some larger centre of population and the presence of a more intricate conflict would be marked by roughly smeared notices of

'Quarantine' or 'Strangers Shot', or by a string of decaying plunderers dangling from the telephone poles at the roadside. About Oxford big boards were put on the roofs warning all air wanderers off with the single word, 'Guns'.

Taking their risks amidst these things, cyclists still kept abroad, and once or twice during Bert's long tramp powerful motor-cars containing masked and goggled figures went tearing past him. There were few police in evidence, but ever and again squads of gaunt and tattered soldier-cyclists would come drifting along, and such encounters became more frequent as he got out of Wales into England. Amidst all this wreckage they were still campaigning. He had had some idea of resorting to the workhouses for the night if hunger pressed him too closely, but some of these were closed and others converted into temporary hospitals, and one he came up to at twilight near a village in Gloucestershire stood with all its doors and windows open, silent as the grave, and, as he found to his horror by stumbling along evil-smelling corridors, full of unburied dead.

From Gloucestershire Bert went northward to the British aeronautic park outside Birmingham, in the hope that he might be taken on and given food, for there the Government, or at any rate the War Office, still existed as an energetic fact, concentrated amidst collapse and social disaster upon the effort to keep the British flag still flying in the air, and trying to brisk up mayor and mayor and magistrate and magistrate in a new effort of organization. They had brought together all the best of the surviving artisans from that region, they had provisioned the park for a siege, and they were urgently building a larger type of Butteridge machine. Bert could get no footing at this work: he was not sufficiently skilled, and he had drifted to Oxford when the great fight occurred in which these works were finally wrecked. He saw something, but not very much, of the battle from a place called Boar's Hill. He saw the Asiatic squadron coming up across the hills to the south-west, and he saw one of their airships circling southward again chased by two aeroplanes, the one that was ultimately overtaken, wrecked and burnt at Edge Hill. But he never learnt the issue of the combat as a whole.

He crossed the Thames from Eton to Windsor and made his way round the south of London to Bun Hill; and there he found his brother Tom, looking like some dark, defensive animal in the old shop, just recovering from the Purple Death, and Jessica upstairs delirious, and, as it seemed to him, dying grimly. She raved of sending out orders to customers, and scolded Tom perpetually lest he should be late with Mrs Thompson's potatoes and Mrs Hopkins' cauliflower, though all business had long since ceased and Tom had developed a quite uncanny skill in the snaring of rats and sparrows and the concealment of certain stores of cereals and biscuits from plundered grocers' shops. Tom received his brother with a sort of guarded warmth.

'Lor!' he said, 'it's Bert. I thought you'd be coming back some day, and I'm glad to see you. But I carn't arst you to eat anything, because I 'aven't got anything to eat. . . . Where you been, Bert, all this time?'

Bert reassured his brother by a glimpse of a partly eaten swede, and was still telling his story in fragments and parentheses, when he discovered behind the counter a yellow and forgotten note addressed to himself, 'What's this?' he said, and found it was a year-old note from Edna. 'She came 'ere,' said Tom, like one who recalls a trivial thing, 'arstin' for you and arstin' us to take 'er in. That was after the battle and settin' Clapham Rise afire. I was for takin' 'er in, but Jessica wouldn't 'ave it – and so she borrowed five shillings of me quiet like and went on. I dessay she's tole you—'

She had, Bert found. She had gone on, she said in her note, to an aunt and uncle who had a brickfield near Horsham. And there at last, after another fortnight of adventurous journeying, Bert found her.

5

When Bert and Edna set eyes on one another they stared and laughed foolishly, so changed they were, and so ragged and surprised. And then they both fell weeping.

'Oh! Bertie, boy!' she cried. 'You've come – you've come!' and put out her arms and staggered. 'I told 'im. He said he'd kill me if I didn't marry him.'

But Edna was not married, and when presently Bert could get talk from her she explained the task before him. That little patch of lonely agricultural country had fallen under the power of a band of bullies led by a chief called Bill Gore, who had begun life as a butcher boy and developed into a prize-fighter and a professional 'sport'. They had been organized by a local nobleman of former eminence upon the turf, but after a time he had disappeared, no one quite knew how, and Bill had succeeded to the leadership of the countryside, and had developed his teacher's methods with considerable vigour. There had been a strain of advanced philosophy about the local nobleman, and his mind ran to 'improving the race' and producing the Over-Man, which in practice took the form of himself especially and his little band in moderation marrying with some frequency. Bill followed up this idea with an enthusiasm that even trenched upon his popularity with his followers.

One day he had happened upon Edna tending her pigs, and had at once fallen a-wooing with great urgency among the troughs of slush. Edna had made a gallant resistance, but he was still vigorously about and extraordinarily impatient. He might, she said, come at any time; and she looked Bert in the eyes. They were back already in the barbaric stage when a man must fight for his love.

And here one deplores the conflicts of truth with the chivalrous tradition. One would like to tell of Bert sallying forth to challenge his rival, of a ring formed and a spirited encounter, and Bert by some miracle of pluck and love and good fortune winning. But indeed nothing of the sort occurred. Instead, he reloaded his revolver very carefully, and then sat in the best room of the cottage by the derelict brickfield, looking anxious and perplexed, and listening to talk about Bill and his ways, and thinking, thinking. Then suddenly Edna's aunt, with a thrill in her voice, announced the appearance of that individual. He was coming with two others of his gang through the garden gate. Bert got up, put the women aside and looked out. They presented remarkable figures. They wore a sort of uniform of red golfing jackets and white sweaters, football singlets and stockings and boots, and each had let his fancy play about his headdress. Bill had a woman's hat full of cocks' feathers, and all had wild, slouching cowboy brims.

Bert sighed and stood up, deeply thoughtful, and Edna watched him, marvelling. The women stood quite still. He left the window, and went out into the passage rather slowly, and with the careworn expression of a man who gives his mind to a complex and uncertain business. 'Edna!' he called, and when she came he opened the front door.

He asked very simply, and pointing to the foremost of the three, 'That 'im? ... Sure?' ... and being told that it was, shot his rival instantly and very accurately through the chest. He then shot Bill's best man much less tidily in the head, and then shot at and winged the third man as he fled. The third gentleman yelped, and continued running with a comical end-on twist.

Then Bert stood still meditating with the pistol in his hand, and quite regardless of the women behind him.

So far things had gone well.

It became evident to him that if he did not go into politics at once he would be hanged as an assassin, and accordingly, and without a word to the women, he went down to the village public-house he had passed an hour before on his way to Edna, entered it from the rear, and confronted the little band of ambiguous roughs, who were drinking in the taproom and discussing matrimony and Bill's affections in a facetious but envious manner, with a casually held but carefully reloaded revolver, and an invitation to join what he called, I regret to say, a 'Vigilance Committee' under his direction. 'It's wanted about 'ere, and some of us are gettin' it up.' He presented himself as one having friends outside, though indeed he had no friends at all in the world but Edna and her aunt and two female cousins.

There was a quick but entirely respectful discussion of the situation. They thought him a lunatic who had tramped into this neighbourhood ignorant of Bill. They desired to temporize until their leader came. Bill would settle him Someone spoke of Bill.

'Bill's dead,' said Bert. 'I jest shot 'im. We don't need reckon with '*im*. 'E's shot, and a red-'aired chap with a squint, '*e's* shot. We've settled up all that. There ain't going to be no more Bill, ever. 'E'd got wrong ideas about marriage and things. It's 'is sort of chap we're after.'

That carried the meeting.

Bill was perfunctorily buried, and Bert's Vigilance Committee (for so it continued to be called) reigned in his stead.

That is the end of this story so far as Bert Smallways is concerned. We leave him with his Edna to become squatters among the clay and oak thickets of the Weald, far away from the stream of events. From that time forth life became a succession of peasant's encounters, an affair of pigs and hens and small needs and little economies and children, until Clapham and Bun Hill and all the life of the Scientific Age became to Bert no more than the fading memory of a dream. He never knew how the War in the Air went on, nor whether it still went on. There were rumours of airships going and coming, and of happenings Londonward. Once or twice their shadows fell on him as he worked, but whence they came or whither they went he could not tell. Even his desire to tell died out for want of food. At times came robbers and thieves, at times came diseases among the beasts and shortness of food, once the country was worried by a pack of boar-hounds he helped to kill; he went through many inconsecutive, irrelevant adventures. He survived them all.

Accident and death came near them both ever and again, and passed them by; and they loved and suffered and were happy, and she bore him many children – eleven children – one after the other, of whom only four succumbed to the necessary hardships of their simple life. They lived and did well, as well was understood in those days. They went the way of all flesh, year by year.

THE EPILOGUE

It happened that one bright summer's morning exactly thirty years after the launching of the first German air-fleet, an old man took a small boy to look for a missing hen through the ruins of Bun Hill and out towards the splintered pinnacles of the Crystal Palace. He was not a very old man; he was, as a matter of fact, still within a few weeks of sixty-three, but constant stooping over spades and forks and the carrying of roots and manure, and exposure to the damps of life in the open air without a change of clothing, had bent him into the form of a sickle. Moreover, he had lost most of his teeth, and that had affected his digestion and through that his skin and temper. In face and expression he was curiously like that old Thomas Smallways who had once been coachman to Sir Peter Bone, and this was just as it should be, for he was Tom Smallways the son, who formerly kept the little greengrocer's shop under the straddle of the monorail viaduct in the High Street of Bun Hill. But now there were no greengrocers' shops, and Tom was living in one of the derelict villas hard by that unoccupied building site that had been and was still the scene of his daily horticulture. He and his wife lived upstairs, and in the drawing and dining rooms, which had each French windows opening on the lawn, and all about the ground floor generally, Jessica, who was now a lean and lined and baldish but still very efficient and energetic old woman, kept her three cows and a multitude of gawky hens.

These two were part of a little community of stragglers and returned fugitives, perhaps a hundred and fifty souls of them altogether, that had settled down to the new condition of things after the Panic and Famine and Pestilence that followed in the wake of the War. They had come back from strange refuges and hiding-places and had squatted down among the familiar houses and begun that hard struggle against nature for food which was now the chief interest of their lives. They were by sheer preoccupation with that a peaceful people, more particularly after Wilkes, the house agent, driven by some obsolete dream of acquisition, had been drowned in the pool by the ruined gasworks for making inquiries into title and displaying a litigious turn of mind. (He had not been murdered, you understand, but the people had carried an exemplary ducking ten minutes or so beyond its healthy limits.)

This little community had returned from its original habits of suburban parasitism to what no doubt had been the normal life of humanity for nearly immemorial years, a life of homely economies in the most intimate contact with cows and hens and patches of ground, a life that breathes and exhales the scent of cows and finds the need for stimulants satisfied by the activity of the bacteria and vermin it engenders. Such had been the life of the European peasant from the dawn of history to the beginning of the Scientific Era, so it was the large majority of the people of Asia and Africa had always been wont to live. For a time it had seemed that by virtue of machines and scientific civilization, Europe was to be lifted out of this perpetual round of animal drudgery, and that America was to evade it very largely from the outset. And with the smash of the high and dangerous and splendid edifice of mechanical civilization that had arisen so marvellously, back to the land came the common man, back to the manure.

The little communities, still haunted by ten thousand memories of a greater state, gathered and developed almost tacitly a customary law and fell under the guidance of a medicine-man or a priest. The world rediscovered religion and the need of something to hold its communities together. At Bun Hill this function was entrusted to an old Baptist minister. He taught a simple but adequate faith. In his teaching a good principle called the Word fought perpetually against a diabolical female influence called the Scarlet Woman and an evil being called Alcohol. This alcohol had long since become a purely spiritualized conception deprived of any element of material application; it had no relation to the occasional finds of whisky and wine in Londoners' cellars that gave Bun Hill its only holidays. He taught this doctrine on Sundays, and on weekdays he was an amiable and kindly old man, distinguished by his quaint disposition to wash his hands, and if possible his face, daily, and with a wonderful genius for cutting up pigs. He held his Sunday services in the old church in the Beckenham Road, and then the countryside came out in a curious reminiscence of the urban dress of Edwardian times. All the men without exception wore frock coats, top hats and white shirts, though many had no boots. Tom was particularly distinguished on these occasions because he wore a top hat with gold lace about it and a green coat and trousers that he had found upon a skeleton in the basement of the Urban and District Bank. The women, even Jessica, came in jackets and immense hats extravagantly trimmed with artificial flowers and exotic birds' feathers – of which there were abundant supplies in the shops to the north – and the children (there were not many children, because a large proportion of the babies born in Bun Hill died in a few days' time of inexplicable maladies) had similar clothes cut down to accommodate them; even Stringer's little grandson of four wore a large top hat.

That was the Sunday costume of the Bun Hill district, a curious and interesting survival of the genteel traditions of the Scientific Age. On a weekday the folk were dingily and curiously hung about with dirty rags of housecloth and scarlet flannel, sacking, curtain serge and patches of old carpet, and went either barefooted or on rude wooden sandals. These people, the reader must understand, were an urban population sunken back to the state of a barbaric peasantry, and so without any of the simple arts a barbaric peasantry would possess. In many ways they were curiously degenerate and incompetent. They had lost any idea of making textiles, they could hardly make up clothes when they had material, and they were forced to plunder the continually dwindling supplies of the ruins about them for cover. All the simple arts they had ever known they had lost, and with the breakdown of modern drainage, modern water supply, shopping and the like, their civilized methods were useless. Their cooking was worse than primitive. It was a feeble muddling with food over wood fires in rusty drawing-room fireplaces; for the kitcheners burnt too much fuel. Among them all no sense of baking or brewing or metal-working was to be found.

Their employment of sacking and suchlike coarse material for work-aday clothing, and their habit of tying it on with string and of thrusting wadding and straw inside it for warmth, gave these people an odd, 'packed' appearance, and as it was a weekday when Tom took his little nephew for the hen-seeking excursion, so it was they were attired.

'So you've really got to Bun Hill at last, Teddy,' said old Tom, beginning to talk and slackening his pace so soon as they were out of range of old Jessica. 'You're the last of Bert's boys for me to see. Wat

I've seen, young Bert I've seen, Sissie and Matt, Tom what's called after me, and Peter. The traveller people brought you along all right, eh?'

'I managed,' said Teddy, who was a dry little boy.

'Didn't want to eat you on the way?'

'They was all right,' said Teddy. 'And on the way near Leatherhead we saw a man riding on a bicycle.'

'My word!' said Tom, 'there ain't many of those about nowadays. Where was he going?'

'Said he was going to Dorking if the High Road was good enough. But I doubt if he got there. All about Burford it was flooded. We came over the hill, uncle – what they call the Roman Road. That's high and safe.'

'Don't know it,' said old Tom. 'But a bicycle! You're sure it was a bicycle? Had two wheels?'

'It was a bicycle right enough.'

'Why! I remember a time, Teddy, when there was bicycles no end, when you could stand just here – the road was as smooth as a board then – and see twenty or thirty coming and going at the same time, bicycles and moty bicycles, moty cars, all sorts of whirly things.'

'No!' said Teddy.

'I do. They'd keep on going by all day – 'undreds and 'undreds.'

'But where was they all going?' asked Teddy.

'Tearin' off to Brighton – you never seen Brighton, I expect – it's down by the sea, used to be a moce 'mazing place – and coming and going from London.'

'Why?'

'They did.'

'But why?'

'Lord knows why, Teddy. They did. Then you see that great thing there like a great big rusty nail sticking up higher than all the houses, and that one yonder, and that, and how something's fell in between 'em among the houses. They was parts of the monorail. They went down to Brighton too, and all day and night there was people going, great cars as big as 'ouses full of people.'

The little boy regarded the rusty evidences across the narrow muddy ditch of cow-droppings that had once been a High Street. He was clearly disposed to be sceptical, and yet there the ruins were! He grappled with ideas beyond the strength of his imagination.

'What did they go for?' he asked; 'all of 'em?'

'They 'ad to. Everything was on the go those days – everything.'

'Yes, but where did they come from?'

'All round 'ere, Teddy, there was people living in those 'ouses, and

830

up the road more 'ouses and more people. You'd hardly believe me, Teddy, but it's Bible truth. You can go on that way for ever and ever, and keep on coming on 'ouses, more 'ouses, and more. There's no end to 'em. No end. They get bigger and bigger.' His voice dropped as though he named strange names. 'It's *London*,' he said.

'And it's all empty now and left alone. All day it's left alone. You don't find 'ardly a man, you won't find nothing but dogs and cats after the rats until you get round by Bromley and Beckenham, and there you find the Kentish men herding swine. (Nice rough lot they are too!) I tell you that so long as the sun is up it's as still as the grave. I been about by day – orfen and orfen.' He paused.

'And all those 'ouses and streets and ways used to be full of people before the War in the Air and the Famine and the Purple Death. They used to be full of people, Teddy, and then came a time when they was full of corpses, when you couldn't go a mile that way before the stink of 'em drove you back. It was the Purple Death 'ad killed 'em every one. The cats and dogs and 'ens and vermin caught it. Everything and everyone 'ad it. Jest a few of us 'appened to live. I pulled through and your aunt, though it made 'er lose 'er 'air. Why, you find the skeletons in the 'ouses now. This way we been into all the 'ouses and took what we wanted and buried moce of the people, but up that way, Norwood way, there's 'ouses with the glass in the windows still, and the furniture not touched – all dusty and falling to pieces – and the bones of the people lying, some in bed, some about the 'ouse, jest as the Purple Death left 'em five-and-twenty years ago. I went into one – me and old Higgins las' year – and there was a room with books, Teddy – you know what I mean by books, Teddy?'

'I seen 'em. I seen 'em with pictures.'

'Well, books all round, Teddy, 'undreds of books, beyond rhyme or reason, as the saying goes, green-mouldy and dry. I was for leavin' 'em alone – I was never much for reading – but ole Higgins he must touch 'em. "I believe I could read one of 'em *now*," 'e says.

'"Not it," I says.

'"I could," 'e says, laughing, and takes one out and opens it.

'I looked, and there, Teddy, was a cullud picture, oh, so lovely! It was a picture of women and serpents in a garden. I never see anything like it.

'"This suits me," said old Higgins, "to rights."

'And then kind of friendly he gave the book a pat—'

Old Tom Smallways paused impressively.

'And then?' said Teddy.

'It all fell to dus'. White dus'!' ... He became still more impressive.

'We didn't touch no more of them books that day. Not after that.'

For a long time both were silent. Then Tom, playing with a subject that attracted him with a fatal fascination, repeated. 'All day long they lie – still as the grave.'

Teddy took the point at last. 'Don't they lie o' nights?' he asked.

Old Tom shook his head. 'Nobody knows, boy, nobody knows.'

'But what could they do?'

'Nobody knows. Nobody ain't seen to tell – not nobody.'

'Nobody?'

'They tell tales,' said old Tom. 'They tell tales, but there ain't no believing 'em. I gets 'ome about sundown, and keeps indoors, so I can't say nothing, can I? But there's them that thinks some things and them as thinks others. I've 'eard it's unlucky to take clo'es off of 'em unless they got white bones. There's stories—'

The boy watched his uncle sharply. '*Wot* stories?' he said.

'Stories of moonlight nights and things walking about. But I take no stock in 'em. I keeps in bed. If you listen to stories – Lord! You'll get afraid of yourself in a field at midday.'

The little boy looked round and ceased his questions for a space.

'They say there's a 'og man in Beck'n'am what was lost in London three days and three nights. 'E went up after whisky to Cheapside, and lorst 'is way among the ruins and wandered. Three days and three nights 'e wandered about and the streets kep' changing so's 'e couldn't get 'ome. If 'e 'adn't remembered some words out of the Bible 'e might 'ave been there now. All day 'e went and all night – and all day long it was still. It was as still as death all day long, until the sunset came and the twilight thickened, and then it began to rustle and whisper and go pit-a-pat with a sound like 'urrying feet.'

He paused.

'Yes,' said the little boy breathlessly. 'Go on. What then?'

'A sound of carts and 'orses there was, and a sound of cabs and omnibuses, and then a lot of whistling, shrill whistles, whistles that froze 'is marrer. And directly the whistles began things begun to show, people in the streets 'urrying, people in the 'ouses and shops busying themselves, moty cars in the streets, a sort of moonlight in all the lamps and winders. People, I say, Teddy, but they wasn't people. They was the ghosts of them that was overtook, the ghosts of them that used to crowd those streets. And they went past 'im and through 'im and never 'eeded 'im, went by like fogs and vapours, Teddy. And sometimes they was cheerful and sometimes they was 'orrible, 'orrible beyond words. And once 'e come to a place called Piccadilly, Teddy, and there was lights blazing like daylight and ladies and gentlemen in splendid clo'es crowding the pavement, and taxicabs follering along the road. And as 'e looked, they all went evil – evil in the face, Teddy. And it seemed to 'im suddenly *they saw'im*, and the women began to look at 'im and say things to 'im – 'orrible – wicked things. One come very near 'im, Teddy, right up to 'im, and looked into 'is face – close. And she 'adn't got a face to look with, only a painted skull, and then 'e see they was all painted skulls. And one after another they crowded on 'im saying 'orrible things, and catchin' at 'im and threatenin' and coaxing 'im, so that 'is 'eart near left 'is body for fear.' . . .

'Yes,' gasped Teddy in an unendurable pause.

'Then it was he remembered the words of Scripture and saved himself alive. "The Lord is my 'Elper," 'e says, "therefore I will fear nothing," and straightaway there came a cock-crowing and the street was empty from end to end. And after that the Lord was good to 'im and guided 'im 'ome.'

Teddy stared and caught at another question. 'But who was the people,' he asked, 'who lived in all these 'ouses? What was they?'

'Gent'men in business, people with money – leastways we thought it was money till everything smashed up, and then seemingly it was jes' paper – all sorts. Why, there was 'undreds of thousands of them. There was millions. I've seen that 'I Street there regular so's you couldn't walk along the pavements, shoppin' time, with women and people shoppin'.'

'But where'd they get their food and things?'

''Bort 'em in shops like I used to 'ave. I'll show you the place, Teddy, 's we go back. People nowadays 'aven't no idee of a shop – no idee. Plate-glass winders – it's all Greek to them. Why, I've 'ad as much as a ton and a 'arf of petaties to 'andle all at one time. You'd open your eyes till they dropped out to see jest what I used to 'ave in my shop. Baskets of pears 'eaped up, marrers, apples and pears, d'licious great nuts.' His voice became luscious – 'Benanas, oranges.'

'What's Benanas?' asked the boy, 'and Oranges?'

'Fruits they was. Sweet, juicy, d'licious fruits. Foreign fruits. They brought 'em from Spain and N' York and places. In ships and things. They brought 'em to me from all over the world, and I sold 'em in my shop. *I* sold 'em, Teddy! Me what goes about now with you, dressed up in old sacks and looking for lost 'ens. People used to come into my shop, great beautiful ladies like you'd 'ardly dream of now, dressed up to the nines, and say, "Well, Mr Smallways, what you got 'smorning?" and I'd say, "Well, I got some very nice C'nadian apples," or p'raps I got custed marrers. See? And they'd buy 'em. Right off they'd say, "Send me some up." Lord! what a life that was. The business of it, the bussel, the smart things you saw, moty cars going by, kerridges, people, organ-grinders, German bands. Always something going past – always. If it wasn't for those empty 'ouses I'd think it all a dream.'

'But what killed all the people, uncle?' asked Teddy.

'It was a smash-up,' said old Tom. 'Everything was going right until they started that War. Everything was going like clockwork. Everybody was busy and everybody was 'appy and everybody got a good square meal every day.' He met incredulous eyes. 'Everybody,' he said firmly. 'If you couldn't get it anywhere else, you could get it in the workhuss, a nice 'ot bowl of soup called skilly, and bread better'n anyone knows 'ow to make now, reg'lar *white* bread, gov'ment bread.'

Teddy marvelled, but said nothing. It made him feel deep longings that he found it wisest to fight down.

For a time the old man resigned himself to the pleasures of gustatory reminiscence. His lips moved. 'Pickled Sammin!' he whispered, 'an' vinegar. . . . Dutch cheese, *Beer*! A pipe of terbakker.'

'But *'ow* did the people get killed?' asked Teddy presently.

'There was the War. The War was the beginning of it. The War banged and flummocked about, but it didn't really *kill* many people. But it upset things. They came and set fire to London and burnt and sank all the ships there used to be in the Thames – we could see the smoke and steam for weeks – and they threw a bomb into the Crystal Palace and made a bust-up, and broke down the rail lines and things like that. But as for killin' people, it was just accidental if they did. They killed each other more. There was a great fight all hereabout one day, Teddy – up in the air. Great things bigger than fifty 'ouses, bigger than the Crystal Palace – bigger, bigger than anything, flying about up in the air and whacking at each other and dead men fallin' off 'em. T'riffic! But it wasn't so much the people they killed as the business they stopped. There wasn't any business doin', Teddy, there wasn't any money about, and nothin' to buy if you 'ad it.'

'But 'ow did the people get *killed*?' said the little boy in the pause.

'I'm tellin' you, Teddy,' said the old man. 'It was the stoppin' of business come nex'. Sudden, some'ow, there didn't seem to be any money. There was cheques – they was a bit of paper written on, and they was jes' as good as money – jes' as good if they come from customers you knew. Then all of a sudden they wasn't. I was lef' with three of 'em and two I'd given change. Then it got about that five-pun' notes were no good, and then the silver sort of went off. Gold you couldn't get for love or – anything. The banks in London 'ad got it, and the banks was all smashed up. Everybody went bankrup'. Everybody was thrown out of work. Everybody!'

He paused, and scrutinized his hearer. The small boy's intelligent face expressed hopeless perplexity.

'That's 'ow it 'appened,' said old Tom. He sought for some means of expression. 'It was like stoppin' a clock,' he said. 'Things were quiet for a bit, deadly quiet, except for the airships fighting about in the sky, and then people begun to get excited. I remember my lars' customer, the very lars' customer that ever I 'ad. He was a Mr Moses Gluckstein, a city gent and very pleasant and fond of sparrowgrass and chokes, and 'e cut in – there 'adn't been no customers for days – and began to talk very fast, offerin' me for anything I 'ad, anything, petaties or anything, its weight in gold. 'E said it was a little speculation 'e wanted to try. 'E said it was a sort of bet reely, and very likely 'e'd lose; but never mind that, 'e wanted to try. 'E always 'ad been a gambler, 'e said. 'E said I'd only got to weigh it out and 'e'd give me 'is cheque right away. Well, that led to a bit of a argument, perfectly respectful it was, but a argument about whether a cheque was still good, and while 'e was explaining there come by a lot of these here unemployed with a great banner they 'ad for everyone to read – everyone could read those days – "We want Food." Three or four of 'em suddenly turns and comes into my shop.

'"Got any food?" says one.

'"No," I says, "not to sell. I wish I 'ad. But if I 'ad I'm afraid I couldn't let you have it. This gent, 'e's been offerin' me—"

'Mr Gluckstein 'e tried to stop me, but it was too late.

'"What's 'e been offerin' you?" says a great big chap with a 'atchet; "what's 'e been offerin' you?" I 'ad to tell.

'"Boys," 'e said, "'ere's another feenancier!" and they took 'im out there and then, and 'ung 'im on a lam'pose down the street. 'E never lifted a finger to resist. After I tole on 'im 'e never said a word. . . .'

Tom meditated for a space. 'First chap I ever sin 'ung!' he said.

''Ow old was you?' asked Teddy.

''Bout thirty,' said old Tom.

'Why! I saw free pig-stealers 'ung before I was six,' said Teddy. 'Father took me because of my birfday being near. Said I ought to be blooded. . . .'

'Well, you never saw no one killed by a moty car, any'ow,' said old Tom after a moment of chagrin. 'And you never saw no dead men carried into a chemis' shop.'

Teddy's momentary triumph faded. 'No,' he said, 'I 'aven't.'

'Nor won't. Nor won't. You'll never see the things I've seen, never. Not if you live to be a 'undred. . . . Well, as I was saying, that's how the Famine and Riotin' began. Then there was strikes and Socialism, things I never did 'old with, worse and worse. There was fightin' and shootin' down, and burnin' and plunderin'. They broke up the banks up in London and got the gold. But they couldn't make food out of gold. 'Ow did *we* get on? Well, we kep' quiet. We didn't interfere with no one and no one didn't interfere with us. We 'ad some old 'tatoes about, but mocely we lived on rats. Ours was a old 'ouse, full of rats, and the famine never seemed to bother 'em. Orfen we got a rat. Orfen. But mose of the people who lived hereabouts was too tender stummicked for rats. Didn't seem to fancy 'em. They'd been used to all sorts of fallals, and they didn't take to 'onest feeding, not till it was too late. Died rather.

'It was the famine began to kill people. Even before the Purple Death come along they was dying like flies at the end of the summer. 'Ow I remember it all! I was one of the first to 'ave it. I was out seein' if I mightn't get 'old of a cat or somethin', and then I went round to my bit of ground to see whether I couldn't get up some young turnips I'd forgot, and I was took something awful. You've no idee the pain, Teddy – it doubled me up pretty near. I jes' lay down by that there corner, and your aunt come along to look for me and dragged me 'ome like a sack.

'I'd never 'ave got better if it 'adn't been for your aunt. "Tom," she says to me, "you got to get well," and I *'ad* to. Then *she* sickened. She sickened, but there ain't much dyin' about your aunt. "Lor!" she says, "as if I'd leave you to go muddlin' along alone!" That's what she says. She's got a tongue 'as your aunt. But it took 'er 'air off – and arst though I might, she's never cared for the wig I got 'er – orf the old lady what was in the vicarage garden.

'Well, this 'ere Purple Death – it jes' wiped people out, Teddy. You couldn't bury 'em. And it took the dogs and the cats too, and the rats and 'orses. At last every 'ouse and garden was full of dead bodies. London way you couldn't go for the smell of them, and we 'ad to move out of the 'I Street into that villa we got. And all the water run short that way. The drains and underground tunnels took it. Gor' knows where the Purple Death come from; some say one thing and some another. Some said it come from eatin' rats and some from eatin' nothin'. Some say the Asiatics brought it from some 'I place, Thibet, I think, where it never did nobody much 'arm. All I know is it come after the Famine. And the Famine come after the Penic, and the Penic come after the War.'

Teddy thought. 'What made the Purple Death?' he asked.

''Aven't I tole you!'

'But why did they 'ave a penic?'

'They 'ad it.'

'But why did they start the War?'

'They couldn't stop theirselves. 'Aving them airships made 'em.'

'And 'ow did the War end?'

'Lord knows if it's ended, boy,' said old Tom. 'Lord knows if it's ended. There's been travellers through 'ere – there was a chap only two summers ago – say it's goin' on still. They say there's bands of people up north who keep on with it, and people in Germany and China and 'Merica and places. 'E said they still got flying machines and gas and things. But we 'aven't seen nothin' in the air now for seven years, and nobody 'asn't come nigh of us. Last we saw was a crumpled sort of airship going away – over there. It was a littleish-sized thing and lopsided, as though it 'ad something the matter with it.'

He pointed, and came to a stop at a gap in the fence, the vestiges of the old fence from which, in the company of his neighbour, Mr Stringer the milkman, he had once watched the South of England Aero Club's Saturday-afternoon ascents. Dim memories, it may be, of that particular afternoon returned to him.

'There, down there, where all that rus' looks so red and bright, that's the gasworks.'

'What's gas?' asked the little boy.

'Oh a hairy sort of nothin' what you put in balloons to make 'em go up. And you used to burn it till the 'lectricity come.'

The little boy tried vainly to imagine gas on the basis of these particulars. Then his thoughts reverted to a previous topic.

'But why didn't they stop the War?'

'Obstinacy. Everybody was getting 'urt, but everybody was 'urtin' and everybody was 'igh-spirited and patriotic, and so they smeshed up things instead. They jes' went on smeshin'. And afterwards they jes' got desp'rite and savige.'

'It ought to 'ave ended,' said the little boy.

'It didn't ought to 'ave begun,' said old Tom. 'But people was proud. People was la-dy-da-ish and uppish and proud. Too much meat and drink they 'ad. Give in – not them! And after a bit nobody arst 'em to give in. Nobody arst 'em. . . .'

He sucked his old gums thoughtfully, and his gaze strayed away across the valley to where the shattered glass of the Crystal Palace glittered in the sun. A dim large sense of waste and irrevocable lost opportunities pervaded his mind. He repeated his ultimate judgement upon all these things, obstinately, slowly and conclusively, his final saying upon the matter.

'You can say what you like,' he said: 'It didn't ought ever to 'ave begun.'

He said it simply – somebody somewhere ought to have stopped something, but who or how or why were all beyond his ken.

Wells' Prefaces to the 1941 Penguin Edition

When *The War in the* Air was reprinted by Collins in 1921, Wells added a preface to introduce it to a new generation of readers who had grown up during the First World War. A similar but much briefer explanation forms the first paragraph of his preface to Volume 20 of the Atlantic edition of his works in 1926. The 1941 Penguin edition of the novel, the last to be produced during his lifetime, reprints the 1921 preface together with a new preface containing his much-discussed 'epitaph'.

Preface to the 1921 Edition

A short preface to *The War in the Air* has become necessary if the reader is to do justice to that book. It is one of a series of stories I have written at different times; *The World Set Free* is another, and *When the Sleeper Wakes* a third; which are usually spoken of as 'scientific romances' or 'futurist romances', but which it would be far better to call 'fantasias of possibility'. They take some developing possibility in human affairs and work it out so as to develop the broad consequences of that possibility. This *War in the* Air was written, the reader should note, in 1907, and it began to appear as a serial story in the *Pall Mall Magazine* in January, 1908. This was before the days of the flying machine; Blériot did not cross the Channel until July, 1909; and the Zeppelin airship was still in its infancy. The reader will find it amusing now to compare the guesses and notions of the author with the achieved realities of today.

But the book, I venture to think, has not been altogether superseded. The main idea is not that men will fly, or to show how they will fly; the main idea is a thesis that the experiences of the intervening years strengthen rather than supersede. The thesis is this: that with the flying machine war alters in its character; it ceases to be an affair of 'fronts' and becomes an affair of 'areas'; neither side, victor or loser, remains immune from the gravest injuries, and while there is a vast increase in the destructiveness of war, there is also an increased indecisiveness. Consequently 'War in the Air' means social destruction instead of victory as the end of war. It not only alters the methods of war but the consequences of war. After all that has happened since this fantasia of possibility was written, I do not think that there is much wrong with that thesis. And after a recent journey to Russia, of which I have given an account in *Russia in the Shadows*, I am inclined to think very well of myself as I reread the entirely imaginary account of the collapse of civilization under the strain of modern war which forms the Epilogue of this story. In 1907 this chapter was read with hearty laughter as the production of an 'imaginative novelist's' distempered brain. Is it quite so wildly funny today?

And I ask the reader to remember that date of 1907 also when he reads of Prince Karl Albert and the Graf von Winterfeld. Seven years before the Great War, its shadow stood out upon our sunny world as plainly as all that, for the 'imaginative novelist' – or anyone else with ordinary common sense – to see. The great catastrophe marched upon us in the daylight. But everybody thought that somebody else would stop it before it really arrived. Behind that great catastrophe march others today. The steady deterioration of currency, the shrinkage of production, the ebb of educational energy in Europe, work out to consequences that are obvious to every clear-headed man. National and imperialist rivalries march whole nations at the quickstep towards social collapse. The process goes on as plainly as the militarist process was going on in the years when *The War in the Air* was written.

Do we still trust to somebody else?

H. G. WELLS

EASTON GLEBE, 1921

Preface to the 1941 Edition

Here in 1941 *The War in the Air* is being reprinted once again. It was written in 1907 and first published in 1908. It was reprinted in 1921, and then I wrote a preface which also I am reprinting. Again I ask the reader to note the warnings I gave in that year, twenty years ago. Is there anything to add to that preface now? Nothing except my epitaph. That, when the time comes, will manifestly have to be: 'I told you so. You *damned* fools.' (The italics are mine.)

H. G. Wells